King Breaker

First published 2013 by Solaris
an imprint of Rebellion Publishing Ltd,
Riverside House, Osney Mead,
Oxford, OX2 0ES, UK

www.solarisbooks.com

ISBN: 978 1 78108 150 1

Maps by Rowena Cory Daniells and Luke Preece

10 9 8 7 6 5 4 3 2 1

A CIP catalogue record for this book is available from the British Library.

Designed & typeset by Rebellion Publishing
Printed in the US

ROWENA CORY DANIELLS

King Breaker

THE STUNNING CONCLUSION TO
THE CHRONICLES OF KING ROLEN'S KIN

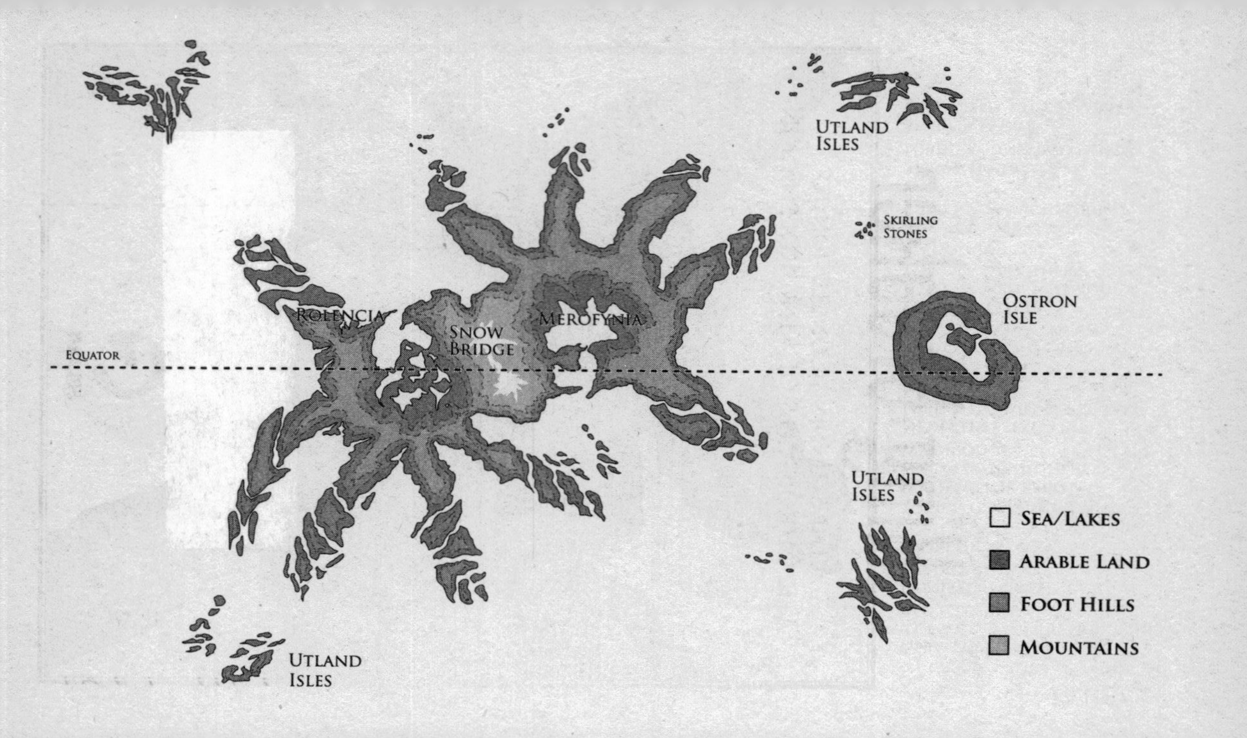
Utland Isles
Skirling Stones
Rolencia
Snow Bridge
Merofynia
Ostron Isle
Equator
Utland Isles
Utland Isles
Sea/Lakes
Arable Land
Foot Hills
Mountains

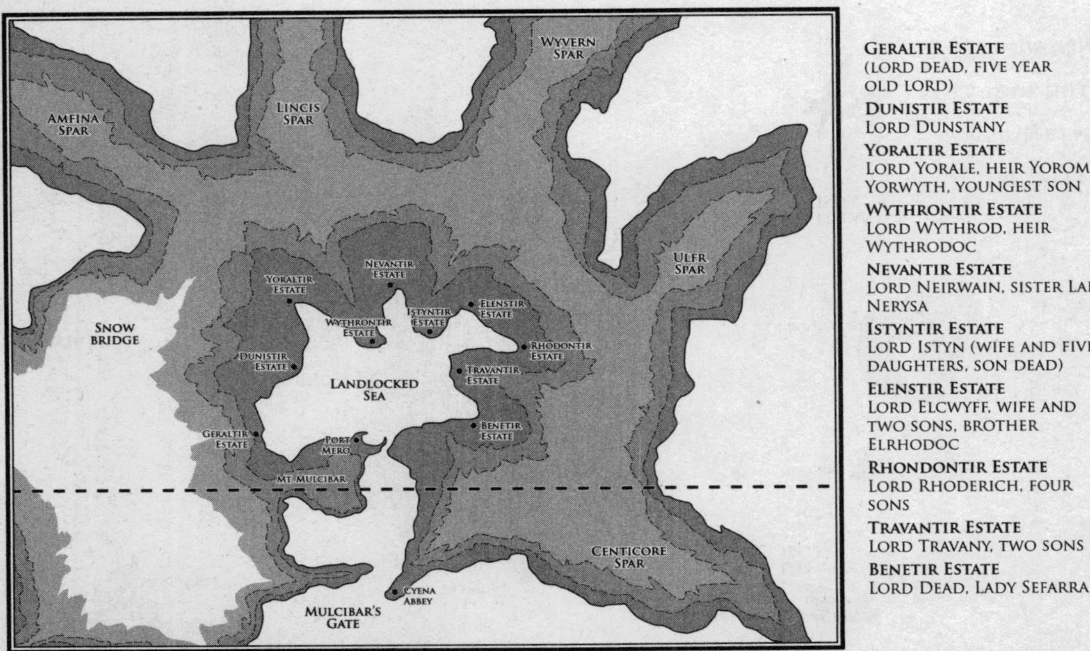
Wyvern Spar
Amfina Spar
Lincis Spar
Ulfr Spar
Snow Bridge
Yoraltir Estate
Nevantir Estate
Wythrontir Estate
Istyntir Estate
Elenstir Estate
Rhodontir Estate
Dunistir Estate
Travantir Estate
Landlocked Sea
Benetir Estate
Geraltir Estate
Port Mero
Mt. Mulcibar
Centicore Spar
Cyena Abbey
Mulcibar's Gate
Geraltir Estate
(Lord dead, five year old lord)
Dunistir Estate
Lord Dunstany
Yoraltir Estate
Lord Yorale, heir Yoromer, Yorwyth, youngest son
Wythrontir Estate
Lord Wythrod, heir Wythrodoc
Nevantir Estate
Lord Neirwain, sister Lady Nerysa
Istyntir Estate
Lord Istyn (wife and five daughters, son dead)
Elenstir Estate
Lord Elcwyff, wife and two sons, brother Elrhodoc
Rhondontir Estate
Lord Rhoderich, four sons
Travantir Estate
Lord Travany, two sons
Benetir Estate
Lord dead, Lady Sefarra

Chapter One

BYREN CLIMBED THE steps to the ship's reardeck.

'Just as well you shaved.' Orrade greeted him with a grin. 'You were beginning to look like an Utland raider.'

Byren rubbed his jaw. For the first three days of the voyage home, he'd been feverish, and Orrade hadn't left his side. Now, with the morning sun on his face, he felt more like himself, although his knees were still a bit weak. 'Hate being sick. Hate feeling helpless.'

'You'd been beaten and starved, and were awaiting execution, yet you still found the strength to swing a sword when we freed you. You're lucky you had nothing worse than a fever.' Orrade glanced to the helmsman, then leant closer. 'You might have recovered sooner, if you'd had an ulfr pack for company.'

Byren shook his head. Smarter and bigger than ordinary wolves, ulfrs were god-touched Affinity beasts. His father had always hated Affinity, and Byren had grown up seeing those afflicted with Affinity sent to the abbeys, or banished. When his youngest brother, Fyn, had been sent to Halcyon Abbey, it had broken his mother's heart. Since King Rolen's death, Byren had learnt that Affinity was a tool and, like any tool, could be a weapon in the wrong hands. He grimaced. 'I don't have Affinity.'

'No, but you have something. Those ulfrs—'

'First time it happened,' Byren found himself trying to explain, 'I was hiding in an Affinity seep.' Normally he would have avoided the hollow, where untamed power rose from the earth's heart, but he'd been injured and desperate to escape the Merofynian invaders. 'I was hoping the power would deter my pursuers. Instead it attracted the ulfr pack. I thought I was dead for sure. But they'd come to bathe in the wild power. Like horses taking a dust bath.' He shivered.

'They should have ripped your throat out.'

'I know, but I was wrapped in my ulfr fur and the Affinity seemed to befuddle their senses. Then one of the females whelped a cub right next to me and...' He shrugged. Somehow, he'd formed a bond with the pack.

'I'll admit that first time was pure luck.' Orrade held his eyes. 'But the second time you were also injured. Both scars looked days old overnight.'

Byren shook his head. If he wanted to reclaim his father's throne, there could be no taint attached to his name; he had enough problems without adding to them. When the Merofynians attacked Rolencia, his cousin, Cobalt, had colluded with Palatyne, handing Byren over to be executed. But Byren had killed Palatyne and claimed the young Merofynian queen for his betrothed, and now he was racing home to Rolencia, before the news could reach Cobalt.

'You need strength to lead an army.' Orrade sent Byren a teasing look. 'Perhaps we should've moored off a wyvern eyrie, or is it only land-based Affinity beasts that—'

'No one in their right mind goes near saltwater wyverns.' Or so he'd been told, yet his betrothed had a wyvern for a pet. Byren frowned. Much of what he'd been taught about Affinity had been wrong.

'Look, there's no point hiding from it. You have an affinity for Affinity.' Orrade's mouth lifted in a wry grin.

Byren felt an answering smile tug at his lips. 'You can talk. It took you ages to admit—'

Before he could broach the subject of Orrade's visions, the cabin boy interrupted. 'Cap'n Talltrees invites you to his table for dinner, King Byren.'

Byren met Orrade's eyes. As the younger twin, Byren had been spared the attentions of men eager to curry favour with the king's heir, but now that Lence was dead... He shut down the thought. This was not the time to mourn his twin.

Dropping into a crouch, Byren faced the little cabin boy. To think, Fyn had been this small when their father sent him away. Byren's large hand settled on the six-year-old's shoulder. 'Just call me kingsheir for now. I won't be the king until I sit on my father's throne and Cobalt the Usurper is dead.'

'Does that mean you won't dine at the captain's table?'

Byren ruffled the lad's hair and came to his feet. 'I'd be honoured to dine with him.'

Beaming, the cabin boy ran back towards the steps to middeck. A large wyvern swooped down, wing tips brushing the sails. It caught the lad by the shoulder.

Even before the boy screamed, Byren was running. He leapt onto the wyvern's back, his hunting knife drawn, and drove it down to the deck. The boy tumbled free, rolled across the planks and lay unmoving.

The wyvern screeched and writhed in fury. Byren knew as soon as the beast rolled onto its back, it would bring its powerful lower legs up and slit his belly wide open. In desperation, he drove his knife into the side of the wyvern's neck and tore out the front of its throat.

The beast gurgled and thrashed; aware the death throes could just as easily kill him, Byren threw himself aside. Orrade braved the flashing claws to drag him to safety.

'Where's the boy? Is he—'

'Safe. The boatswain's got him. Trust you to tackle a full-grown wyvern with nothing but a hunting knife.'

'Didn't think.' If he'd had time to think, he would never have tried it.

Orrade helped him to his feet. Byren's legs seemed to belong to someone else. The big beast lay dead, beautiful scales glinting in the sun like jewels.

Sailors poured up from below decks, calling to each other in amazement and congratulating Byren. The boatswain came over with the cabin boy in his arms and tried to thank him, but Byren couldn't hear for the rushing of blood in his ears. Any moment now, he'd pass out and make a fool of himself. 'Get me to the cabin, before I puke.'

Orrade didn't hesitate, leading him through the sailors gathered around the wyvern now discussing their good luck. The beast's skin was worth a small fortune. Someone would have to settle the wyvern's Affinity, but that wasn't Byren's problem.

As his sailors rejoiced, the merchant captain sent Byren a cryptic look that he couldn't interpret. Relief had turned into a pounding headache. Sparks floated in his vision. It was all he could do to negotiate the steps to middeck.

'You're feverish again,' Orrade said as they entered the passage to the cabins.

Byren felt his knees give way and darkness closed in.

When his vision cleared, he found himself stretched out on his bedroll by the cabin's brazier. A shiver took him. Orrade pulled the blanket more closely around him.

'You're too good for me, Orrie. I don't deserve—'

'Yes, I know. You only ever had eyes for my sister.'

Once.

But when the fever left him, Byren had not thought of Elina, his dead first love, or Isolt, the prim betrothed he'd inherited when his older twin died. He'd thought of Florin, the mountain girl who'd helped him escape the Merofynians. She'd defied him and irritated him, yet she'd somehow slipped under his guard. But, as far as Florin was concerned, he was her king, nothing more.

And he could never be anything more. Byren knew his duty—marry Isolt to unite Merofynia and Rolencia, and put an end to the warring. Frustration churned in him. He'd never wanted to be king. Certainly, he had never wanted the throne at the price of his father's and twin's lives...

Orrade's cool hand settled on his forehead, soothing away his frown and easing his racing mind. 'Sleep.'

Byren nodded. Lence and his parents might be dead but his brother and sister were safe. Fyn was in Merofynia protecting Queen Isolt until Byren could claim her, and Piro was sailing for Ostron Isle under Mage Tsulamyth's protection.

Exhausted, Byren let his breath out in a long sigh and felt sleep take him.

FLORIN PAUSED TO gaze up at the Rolencian banner strung over the castle gate. The deep red foenix, picked out in gold, gleamed in the morning sun, bright against the banner's black background. She was surprised Cobalt hadn't replaced it with his own banner. But then, he didn't want to remind people that he was a usurper. He wanted to reinforce his claim to the throne, even if this meant reminding them his father had been King Byren the Fourth's bastard.

As she strode up the steep switch-back road, her heart missed a beat. She told herself she had nothing to lose. As far as her father and brother knew, she'd been killed in the aftermath of battle.

If things went to plan, she would not leave alive.

But to implement her plan, Florin had to be employed by the castle-keep, and she had no illusions. She was taller than most men and not even her father, fond as he was, had ever called her pretty. Somehow she had to get inside the castle and get close to Cobalt. In an ideal world, she would have been a renowned Ostronite assassin; but she was simply a mountain girl with a grudge. That would have to be enough to get her past the guards, to cut Cobalt's throat.

Only then would Byren be avenged.

She didn't know how it had all gone so horribly wrong in the Battle of Narrowneck, only that Byren had saved her life and sent her to safety, before going in search of Orrade.

That very night she'd returned looking for Byren, but she was too late. By the time she'd heard of his capture and reached the castle, Cobalt had packed him off to port. By the time she'd reached the docks, Byren was on a ship bound for Merofynia, where he was to be executed. She hadn't been able to afford a berth—not when all the ships were packed with Merofynian lords heading home with their war booty, not when she had no sailing skills or beauty to barter.

So here she was, back in Rolenhold, trying to win a castle servant's position so she could have her revenge on Cobalt.

But revenge wouldn't bring Byren back.

Her stomach cramped with pain. She'd had no idea love could hurt this much. Hadn't even known she'd loved Byren, until she'd lost him.

Focus! If there was one thing mountain people were good at, it was holding a grudge. Illien, Lord of Cobalt, had sent Byren to his death. This meant he had to die.

She knew as soon as she killed Cobalt, his honour guard would kill her. So be it.

After going through the long gate tunnel, she came out into daylight. The cold made her shiver. It was not long until summer's cusp, but this year Sylion, cruel god of winter, hadn't released his hold on the twin isles. The farmers said a late summer meant a poor harvest and a lean winter to follow.

It was hiring day. There was no shortage of pretty young things and eager lads, desperate to provide for their families. More than ever, after the Merofynians had stripped Rolencia of its wealth.

Florin was surprised Cobalt hadn't crowned himself king yet. If she had her way, he would never get the chance. But first she had to be hired, and that did not look hopeful. If she'd been slight and pretty like the two girls behind her...

Instead, she squared her shoulders and hoped she appeared reliable. The castle-keep walked along the line, her iron-grey hair pulled back in a severe bun, her black eyes sharp despite her age. Rumour had it she'd served Cobalt since he was a lad. Rumour had it she was as unflinchingly loyal as she was hard to please.

The castle-keep walked right past and Florin felt a wave of relief. Her vision faded, then returned on a surge of self-contempt.

She could hear the castle-keep, pausing to speak with likely looking lads and lasses in the line behind her.

'What can you do?'

'I was a scullery maid and my sister was a chambermaid. We worked at the Sleeping Sylion,' a girl said. Although Florin was the daughter of a tradepost keeper, she couldn't place the inn.

Florin cast a glance over her shoulder. Sure enough, the castle-keep had paused to speak with the two pretty girls. The younger of the two reminded Florin of Byren's sister, Piro. Everyone believed Piro dead but, according to the family's old nurse, Piro had been taken to Merofynia disguised as a slave. Byren had meant to save her.

He'd meant to do so many things. Florin's eyes burned and her chest ached. She hardened her heart and thought of revenge.

'A couple of pretty lasses like you will do well as long as you don't think being pretty means you don't have to pull your weight,' the castle-keep told them. Clearly charm would not move her. Just as well, Florin was no flatterer. 'Mark my words, keep your legs closed. I won't have my serving maids sent home big with child or running off with the first rich man who gives her a bauble!'

'Yes, my lady.'

'Don't *my lady* me. I was born on a farm and worked my way up to castle-keep. Everything I have, I worked for.'

'Yes, m...' The first girl floundered.

'Just go.' The castle-keep waved them off and the two girls hurried past Florin, all long black hair, swaying hips and sweet curves.

'What can you do?' the castle-keep asked the next lad.

'Chop wood,' a youth answered, voice not yet broken. 'Repair fences—'

'Can you mend saddles?'

'I could learn.'

'Good. You can report to the stable-master. He's been complaining all the men are cack-handed, thanks to the Merofynians.'

It was true. When the reward for news of Byren hadn't produced results, the Merofynians had searched the countryside. If a man didn't provide useful information, they'd chopped off his right hand—hard to join Byren's rebellion and wield a weapon without it.

A tall skinny lad, all awkward knees and elbows, hurried past Florin, heading for the next courtyard.

'That's enough. Be off with you.' The castle-keep dismissed the rest of the hopefuls.

Desperate, Florin spoke up. 'Baubles can't buy me.'

The castle-keep had to lift her chin to hold Florin's gaze. Her eyes widened, then narrowed. 'Go on?'

'I need work. My home burned down.' It was true enough. Everything on Narrowneck had burned the day the Merofynian god's breath blew across Byren's warriors. The very air had burned. They'd only escaped by jumping off the cliff into Lake Sapphire. Unable to swim, Florin still had nightmares.

The castle-keep lifted her chin to hold Florin's eyes. 'Give me one good reason why I should take you on.'

'I know my figures. I can do sums and read—'

'Read? A rough mountain girl like you?'

'I can read a little,' Florin conceded. 'But I tell you this, I can work harder than any man!'

'Hmph. Something to prove...' She studied Florin. 'Why are you dressed like a man?'

'I've always worn breeches. Shoulda been born a boy.'

Florin held her breath as the castle-keep considered her. The woman still had all her teeth, but Florin guessed she'd never been pretty. Perhaps it was this that decided her.

'Your name, girl?'

'Leif.' Florin had only met Cobalt once and doubted if he would remember her face, let alone her name, but it was best to be sure.

'A boy's name?'

'Da wanted a boy.'

'Well, Leif, my assistant charmed her way into a merchant's bed and rode off with him two days ago. Fancied herself his lady markiza, but she'll end up with child and nowhere to go, mark my words. You can take her place. Slack off and you'll be out on your arse. Serve me well and I'll see you're fed and you learn how to read more than "a little." At least I won't have to worry about you charming your way into a wealthy man's bed. Come along.'

Cheeks burning, Florin followed the woman into the castle. All she needed was a couple of days to learn Cobalt's routine, then Byren would be avenged.

After that, nothing mattered.

Chapter Two

BYREN WOKE FEELING disoriented. His bed was hard. That's right... being too tall for the bunk, he'd been sleeping on the cabin floor. He rolled over to find Orrade perched on the bed under the window, reading.

'Feeling better?' Orrade asked. He'd always been a great one for reading, when Byren would've rather been out wandering the castle courtyards, teasing his father's master-at-arms.

Byren grinned. 'Remember that time we asked Captain Temor to teach us sword work and he sent for my mother's dancing master?'

'You were furious.' Orrade marked the page in his book and put it aside with a smile. 'But Captain Temor was right. We needed to be light on our feet.'

'Lence never did get...' Byren couldn't go on. With the death of his twin, he felt like he'd lost a limb. But Lence had turned against him. Lence should never have believed Cobalt's treacherous lies.

'It's all right to mourn him,' Orrade said.

Byren met his friend's gaze. 'I used to think I lost him when Cobalt returned and father formally recognised him as our cousin, but Lence and I had already started to grow apart. For some reason Lence resented me.' His own words surprised him. 'Why—'

'Because he knew you'd make a better king.'

Byren shook his head. 'I'm as flawed as the next man.'

'But you can admit it. That's a rare trait in a man, and especially rare in king.'

Someone knocked on the door, and Byren told them to come in.

The cabin boy entered with a bottle of uncorked wine and two fine glasses. 'Compliments of the cap'n.'

The lad went to leave, but Byren stopped him. 'Let me see your shoulder.'

The cabin boy shrugged off his oversized jerkin, revealing unmarked skin. 'The wyvern's claws hooked through me seal-skin instead of me. It's in shreds.'

Byren shook his head in amazement. He had been afraid the child would die; wyvern wounds were inclined to fester. 'Halcyon must smile on you. You're one lucky lad!'

'Uncle reckons you're favoured by the goddess. He's never seen a man take down a full-grown wyvern with a hunting knife before. No one has!'

'Eh, I doubt that.' Byren ruffled the boy's hair. 'Off you go.'

After he left, Orrade examined the wine bottle. 'Dovecote vineyard...' His voice broke. 'I wish—'

'We did everything we could. Your father was already dead when we got there.'

'And now he and I will never be reconciled.'

Byren said nothing. Knowing the Old Dove, he would never have forgiven Orrade for being a lover of men. Like many back home in Rolencia, Lord Dovecote couldn't separate the legendary warrior Palos, lover of men, from the Servants of Palos. These traitors had tried to put King Byren the Fourth's bastard on the throne, thirty years earlier.

It was unfair.

It was also a complication Byren could have done without. Orrade's declaration of love had been an unwelcome surprise. His friend had only revealed the truth because he believed they were about to die; but they'd survived and Byren had, on more than one occasion, wished the words unsaid.

Still... you couldn't help who you loved. Byren knew that now. It would be best for them all if he never saw his mountain girl again. 'Pour two glasses. We'll drink to the Old Dove.' *And to doing our duty, not matter what our hearts want.*

'No wine for you. You're getting over a fever.'

'You sound like Seela. Hope she's safe.' Seela was Byren's old nurse. 'Have a glass for me.'

'I don't drink alone.'

Byren frowned. 'Why didn't your Affinity warn us of the wyvern attack, Orrie?'

'Visions don't come to order. I've had a recurring dream about a wyvern, but the wyvern is on a rock and I'm the one fighting for my life.' He shrugged. 'Useless.'

'Surely it means something?'

'Byren...' Orrade shook his head. 'Every night, I dream of what could go wrong when you try to reclaim Rolencia. They can't all be prophetic. Besides, my dreams have always been filled with vivid visions.'

'Comes of being too smart.'

Orrade snorted. 'Something you don't have to worry about.'

Byren grinned.

'Be serious.' Orrade leant across the table. 'All going well, we'll be in port tomorrow evening. While you were negotiating with the Merofynian nobles, I had a chance to speak with Agent Tyro. He said the mage could possibly organise Ostronite mercenaries—'

'I won't use mercenaries to reclaim Rolencia.'

'Cobalt used them.'

'Exactly,' Byren said. He was happy to accept gold from the Merofynian treasury, because so much of it had been stolen from Rolencia. Not that he blamed his betrothed. He shook his head. 'Isolt wanted to send me home on one of her ships with a Merofynian escort.'

'She meant well. An escort would add to your importance.'

'Not a Merofynian one.' Byren grimaced. 'I'd rather call on the spar warlords, but I can't expect them to honour their oaths, not after the debacle at Narrowneck.'

'You couldn't have anticipated that the abbey mystics master would be taken over by a renegade Power-worker and open the gate.'

Byren exhaled in frustration. 'Doesn't change the fact that I lost the Battle of Narrowneck and now I need to prove myself to the spar warlords. I won't use Ostronite mercenaries.'

'Not even if Mage Tsulamyth vouches for them?'

Byren shook his head.

'You'll need more than your honour guard to retake Rolencia.'

'Aye.' Talk of the mage reminded him of Piro and, as much as he adored his little sister... 'It's time Piro grew up. She's old enough to be betrothed. I don't want to force her into anything—'

'But you need an ally who will loan you an army,' Orrade said. 'But it gains you nothing to promise her to one of the spar warlords. They lost the majority of their warriors when Narrowneck fell. One of the Ostronite ruling families would be useful, or...' Orrade looked up. 'Didn't King Rolen's spies report that one of the Snow Bridge city states had conquered the others? Do you remember who led them?'

Byren shook his head. 'I should have paid more attention to foreign affairs, but...' This time last year, his father had been secure on the throne, Rolencia had known thirty years of peace, his parents had been planning their jubilee and he'd been searching for a gift to outdo his twin. He'd found it in some rare lincurium stones, which he'd had set on matching rings for his parents. There'd been a pendant, too. Whatever had happened to them?

'If I learnt one thing from Agent Tyro and Lord Dunstany, it's this,' Orrade said. 'To win back your father's kingdom, you have to win the people as well as the crown. Cobalt has ruined your reputation. He claimed your mother had Affinity, which annulled her marriage to your father. He claimed you ran off when you heard about the invasion—'

'Father sent me to fetch the warrior monks.'

'The men who heard King Rolen give that order are all dead. Cobalt has Rolencia convinced you left your parents and sister to die. Then, when you lost the Battle of Narrowneck, he branded you incompetent as well as a coward.'

Byren flushed. 'That—'

'That is what I overheard in the taverns and on the street corners. So you see, you have to win the people to win the throne.' Orrade shrugged. 'I'd slip into the castle and kill Cobalt m'self, but it would only confirm what he's said about you.'

Byren sprang to his feet and paced the cabin. 'I need to convince men to flock to my banner.'

'Exactly.' Orrade frowned then shrugged and rubbed his temples. 'Sorry, can't think for this confounded headache.'

'You're not...'

Orrade rolled his eyes then winced. 'Not every headache is the precursor of a vision.'

'More's the pity.' Byren slumped in a chair. 'I could do with some direction right now.'

'All in good time. Four days ago you escaped execution, crushed Palatyne and claimed the Merofynian throne.'

'Do you think Cobalt's heard the good news?' Byren relished the thought of his cousin's dismay.

'Can't have. He has no pica birds.'

'What I'd give to—'

'Not all messages get through. The birds can be eaten by predators or lost in storms.'

Byren shrugged. 'They're still a great advantage. No wonder the ruling Ostronite families kill to protect breeding pairs.'

Orrade went very still, then grinned.

'What?'

'I just recalled that Cobalt has a small personal guard of Ostronite mercenaries but the majority of his men-at-arms are Merofynians, on loan.' Orrade smiled. 'When they hear you've claimed Merofynia, they're sure to abandon him and sail home.'

Byren grinned. With Orrade at his side, Piro safely on her way back to Ostron Isle and Fyn looking after his interests in Merofynia, he didn't need to worry.

PIRO BRACED HER feet, adjusting for the rise and fall of the deck. She loved the way the sleek sea-hound ship, built to hunt down Utland raiders, cut through the waves.

'Don't try to match a man's strength,' Bantam told her. A faded scar made one side of the wiry sea-hound's mouth lift in a perpetual grin, but real laughter lit his eyes as he gestured to the big boatswain. 'If Jaku gets into a fight, he can throw his weight around. But we're small, so we have to use our wits.'

'I can't always talk my way out of trouble,' Piro objected.

'Watch and learn.' Bantam's black eyes crinkled at the corners. 'I'm you, and Jaku is some big lad who fancies lifting my skirts.'

'Here, girlie. I've got something for you.' Jakulos leered, lunging for the older sea-hound, caught Bantam's wrist and pulled him closer, making elaborate kissing noises. Piro would never have guessed the big man had a yen for the stage.

The cabin boy giggled. He perched on a water barrel lashed to the mainmast, swinging his skinny legs. Runt was all of ten and, for him, this was as good as a summer fair.

'You'll never beat Jaku,' Bantam said. 'So go with him. Make him underestimate you. Like this.' The quartermaster sagged against the bigger man's chest, put on a falsetto voice and cringed. 'Please don't hurt me, sor.'

Little Runt gave a hoot of delight.

Bantam ignored him and stayed in character. 'I'm a good girl. Please don't...' But even as he said this, he reached down, grabbed the other man's balls and twisted.

Jakulos doubled over, cursing fluently in Merofynian. Runt gasped with horror, then collapsed laughing. Piro winced.

Bantam grinned as he stood over his moaning friend. 'What're you complaining about? That was just a love pat.'

'I shoulda known not to trust you,' Jakulos ground out. 'Next time I'll play the girl.'

'There won't be a next time,' Piro said. 'I won't forget.'

'She's a real mulcy,' Jakulos muttered.

'Mulcy?' Piro asked.

Bantam gestured to the boatswain. 'Jaku grew up on the streets of Port Mero. It's slang for a girl who fights back.'

'Mulcy... Mulcibar,' Piro muttered. 'After the Merofynian god of war.'

'Told you she was smart.' Bantam winked at the big boatswain. Then he turned to Piro. 'Make sure you really do hurt him. Don't just anger him. That'll make him mean. The moment he lets you go, run. Get outta there fast, because if he catches you, he'll make you pay. Understood?'

She nodded. Back home, Captain Temor had said it was her brothers' job to protect her, but she'd had to save herself when the castle fell. Of all her brothers, only Fyn had taught her how to escape unwanted attention, and his techniques had been more... polite. If Fyn had a fault, it was that he was too honourable. She, on the other hand, was determined to survive at any price.

Grumbling under his breath, Jakulos came to his feet. Runt caught her eye and grinned.

'What if I can't break free?' Piro asked Bantam.

'Then you take that little knife you keep hidden here, like a real mulcy.' The sea-hound's hand slipped into the waistband of her breeches and deftly freed her paring knife; she was sure he'd grown up picking pockets. 'And you cut him here.' He indicated the top of her thigh, deep in the groin. 'Or here.' He indicated her throat. 'A man'll bleed out fast in those two spots. Or you go for here, up under the rib, straight for the heart—'

'Bantam!' Captain Nefysto's voice cracked like a whip.

Piro glanced over her shoulder to find that the captain and the mage's agent had come out of the reardeck cabin. She should have picked a better time for the lesson, but they would reach Ostron Isle tomorrow. Bantam glanced to Piro. She'd let him assume the lessons had been authorised by the captain.

Nefysto strode over, knee-length coat flying open to reveal boots and hard-muscled thighs encased in tight breeches. 'What are you doing with the kingsdaughter?'

'Nothing, cap'n.' The quartermaster returned Piro's paring knife. 'Nothing that she didn't ask for.'

Piro tucked the knife away. 'It's true.'

'Knife fighting is hardly suitable for—'

'I might have been born a kingsdaughter, but that didn't protect me when the Merofynians invaded,' Piro told Nefysto. She had no time for soft words and blandishments. 'I saw my father murdered under a flag of truce and my mother cut down in our own hall. I only survived because I escaped as Lord Dunstany's slave. And I never want to feel helpless again!'

The captain's eyes widened. She'd finally made him see past her looks. Good, because if she had to listen to one more of his poems she'd jump overboard.

The sea-hound captain gave Piro a bow, his long black curls falling forward. 'You're right, kingsdaughter. Ultimately, we must take responsibility for our own lives.'

Pleased, she looked to Agent Tyro. He'd counselled her to put up with the Nefysto's gallantry, to be polite and patient like Isolt, but that wasn't her nature. Never would be. And now she wanted Tyro to acknowledge she'd been right not to reshape herself to suit others.

Instead the agent's dark eyes held a strange intensity.

Disconcerted, she blinked.

'Piro's right,' Agent Tyro agreed, expression avuncular now. 'She only escaped because she swapped her velvet gown for a dead servant's pinafore and the poor maid was identified as Pirola Rolen Kingsdaughter in her place.'

'And because Lord Dunstany hid my clean toes.' Piro added, incorrigibly honest. Dunstany had known who she was right from the start. He'd helped her get out of the castle, and he'd endangered himself to protect her from Palatyne. She'd grown to trust him, love him even.

But all along, Dunstany had been Agent Tyro in disguise, and she didn't know if she could ever forgive him. Putting her back to Tyro, she turned to Bantam and Jakulos. 'Show me more.'

Chapter Three

FYN CLIMBED THE mainmast. Reaching the crow's nest, he shaded his eyes to study the eastern shore of the Landlocked Sea. Today there was no wind, and the sea reflected the foothills of Merofynia's majestic Dividing Mountains. He felt he should bring Isolt up here but, despite the dangers they'd shared, he didn't know if she had a head for heights.

The oars of the royal barge cut the still water in rhythmic strokes, leaving twin ribbons of lace-edged eddies in the vessel's wake.

With no wind, the royal yacht would have been becalmed; it was just as well they'd taken the barge. But that wasn't why Dunstany had advised them against the yacht. For over two hundred years, Merofynian kings had used the royal barge to visit their nobles, and fifteen-year-old Queen Isolt needed to invoke her proud heritage.

Fyn sighed. He should join Isolt and her court and resume his role as lord protector. Strange, in some ways, he'd been happier as a sea-hound captive. But that was before he'd met Isolt, and he wouldn't go back. Not for anything.

From above, he watched her dark head as she made for the prow with Abbess Celunyd. The abbess was always at Isolt's side, always whispering. Everyone was eager to win the young queen's favour. Just as well Isolt had grown up watching the same sycophantic dance around her father.

Barefoot and nimble, Fyn climbed down.

'...the lord-monk. He never leaves her side,' Neiron complained.

Fyn froze and looked down to see Captain Neiron and his best friend at the base of the mainmast.

Lord-monk... Fyn grimaced as he rubbed his head, feeling the bristles. Eventually, his hair would grow back and hide the abbey tattoos, but he had a feeling the nickname would stick.

Neiron was captain of the queen's guard; the second sons of noble families, they strutted about the city in dashing uniforms, filling their days with one part weapons practice and two parts drinking and gambling.

'Lord-monk's only one man,' Elrhodoc told Neiron. 'One man can't change the fate of a kingdom.'

'Palatyne nearly did.'

'That upstart spar warlord? Look what happened to him.'

Neiron nodded. 'But I don't see why we should accept a Rolencian king for our queen's consort.'

'A deposed Rolencian king at that!'

Righteous anger made Fyn's heart race. The Merofynian nobles had been grateful enough when Byren defeated Palatyne.

Elrhodoc slid his arm around Neiron's shoulder. 'Queen Isolt's a pretty little thing and sweet-tempered. No sign of her father in her. She should take a Merofynian lord for her husband and forget this betrothal made by dead men. Your brother's ship has not returned. It's time to declare him dead, may he feast in Mulcibar's halls forever. You're next in line for the title—'

'I'm sworn to serve the queen.'

'Just think how much better you'd serve her in bed!'

They both laughed.

Fyn bristled. As the grandson of King Merofyn the Fifth, Byren was more entitled to the throne than Isolt *or* her father, who had taken the crown by assassinating his cousin, Byren's uncle, King Sefon. Isolt was only queen because her father had been an ambitious bully who did not scruple to kill his own blood. Not that Fyn blamed Isolt; like him, she'd been a child at the time.

He waited until Neiron and Elrhodoc moved off, then made his way to join Isolt, thinking he must not fail his brother. Somehow he had to ensure Merofynia remained loyal to Byren.

IT WAS FORTUNATE that Florin had helped her father run Narrowneck Tradepost these last seven winters. During the busy season it had been much like what she had been through today in Rolenhold Castle. Run, run, run...

During the tradepost's busy season, she'd be at her wit's end, juggling beds as new travellers arrived and demanded precedence over those already there. It wasn't much different in the castle. Except Rolenhold was many times bigger and there was an army of servants.

First, the castle-keep had insisted she bathe then dress in upper-servant clothes. It was only as she followed the woman around that Florin realised she'd been given a male servant's attire: a knitted under-shirt, breeches, thigh-length tabard, boots and skull-cap. If it was meant to deter male attention, the castle-keep needn't have bothered. Nothing was further from Florin's mind.

Now it was mid-afternoon and Florin returned from running a message to find the castle-keep with a grey-haired man. Judging by his calloused hands, he was a tradesman.

'Before we bother his lordship, I'll just take a look at this body,' the castle-keep said and strode off, adding over her shoulder, 'I hope you have a strong stomach, girl.'

As Florin followed, her mind raced. Surely if the Merofynians had sent Byren's body back to Rolencia to be displayed on the castle gate, they'd send him with men-at-arms, not a tradesman. The thought of what she might be about to see made Florin feel sick. She vowed to remain strong.

The castle-keep marched out the door to the courtyard, then down the stairs, stopping on the third to last step. From here it was easy to see into the back of the stone-mason's cart. Amid the tools of his trade lay a canvas-covered body.

A surprising number of stable hands had found their way into the courtyard, and Florin saw several maids watching from various windows.

The castle-keep gestured. 'Go on, uncover it.'

The stone-mason flicked the canvas back to reveal a body. It was too small to be Byren's Relief made Florin dizzy.

'Fyn Rolen Kingson,' the stone-mason announced.

Fyn had survived the fall of the abbey to join his brother, Byren. The last time Florin had seen Fyn alive was at the Battle of Narrowneck, and since this body had been burned badly enough to make identification difficult, it could be...

'Fyn Rolen Kingson?' The castle-keep sounded dubious. 'What makes you think this is him?'

In answer the old man held up a pendant on a chain. It had been badly damaged by fire, but it was still identifiable.

'The royal foenix!' a woman cried. Others gasped.

'It's half-melted,' the castle-keep objected.

'That's because I found it with the body. I was in charge of rebuilding the burned chamber at the abbey.'

Fyn had escaped the abbey alive. The body could not be his.

'What's this I hear about the missing kingson?' a man with an Ostronite accent asked. He wore the thigh-length tabard of a castle servant, richly embroidered on the chest and shoulders. 'Why wasn't I sent for? His lordship needs to be informed.'

The castle-keep cast the stone-mason a look, then lowered her voice. 'How do we know it is the missing kingson, Amil? The royal foenix is so badly damaged, it could be a fake. The reward for finding the kingson's body is substantial...'

They both glanced to the body on the cart.

'I found him,' the stone-mason said. 'I want the reward.'

'I'm sure you do.' The castle-keep sniffed. 'But this—'

'If Fyn Rolen Kingson lived, he would have come to reclaim his father's throne by now,' Amil said. 'He must be dead.'

This was what Florin had heard whispered in the taverns in town. With Byren sent to Merofynia to be executed, the people thought King Rolen's kin were all dead, except for the bastard's son—Cobalt.

'Send for Lord Cobalt,' Amil ordered. 'He'll want to verify this.'

The castle-keep signalled a servant, then strode off.

Later, when word came that Lord Cobalt wanted to lay his cousin to rest that very afternoon, she muttered under her breath. 'Just what I need, another ceremony to organise. Lucky for us the new abbot happens to be visiting the castle. He can say words, but we can't have the burial place being turned into a shrine. The body will have to be burned.'

Florin held her tongue as she helped the castle-keep arrange the funeral of the false kingson. If Cobalt suspected he had been fleeced by the stone-mason, he did not reveal it. And why should he, when it suited him to declare all of King Rolen's kin dead?

* * *

PIRO LOOKED UP as someone tapped on her cabin door. She sat on the bunk, hugging her knees and nursing her sense of injustice. When she'd come aboard the *Wyvern's Whelp*, the captain had tried to give her his cabin. She'd argued that wasn't the kingsdaughter anymore, and she didn't want to be treated like one. She wanted Tyro to go away and Dunstany to come back, but the Lord Dunstany she'd known had never been real. Tyro had disguised himself as Dunstany so that he could advise the Merofynian king, and even that had not saved Rolencia.

The tapping came again.

'Oh, come in.'

Tyro opened the door but did not enter. 'Kingsdaughter—'

'I'm not giving up my lessons.' Piro hated it when the agent resorted to formality. 'You promised you'd teach me how to control my Affinity and you haven't.'

'The ship is hardly the place for—'

'I know you went back to the palace after we came on board.' Grievances left festering since they'd set sail from Merofynia bubbled up. 'What did you say about me?'

'Not everything is about you, child. Dunstany held a war table discussion about how best to hold the kingdom.' He tilted his head to study her. 'Why? What did you think—'

'I don't know what to think. I don't even know your real name!'

'Piro...' He slipped into the cabin, closing the door. 'I know you are impatient.'

That wasn't the half of it. Her Affinity was driving her crazy. 'The power... it has to be used!'

'I know.' He reached into his pocket, pulling out a stone on a silver chain. 'This is for you.'

Piro slipped off the bunk and crossed the cabin in three steps. As much as she hated the restrictions of being female, she loved pretty things, and the pendant was... 'Lovely, but how is it going to help me with—'

'This is not a piece of jewellery. This is the same stone as the orb on the tip of Dunstany's staff.'

'But that one's almost clear. This is blue.'

'The stone comes in many colours. Remember how Dunstany focused power—'

'Lightning struck the tip of his staff.'

'Power attracts power. Lightning had gathered in the clouds looking for a path to earth.' He frowned as she went to interrupt. 'Are you going to let me finish?'

She nodded, and he smiled despite himself. At that moment she quite liked him.

'The first step is to learn to focus your power, Piro, then control it. Watch me.'

She felt him gather his Affinity. The blue stone stirred, warming with an inner radiance she found entrancing.

'Now you try.'

Piro concentrated. She had no trouble calling on her power, but she couldn't focus it in the stone. Instead, it focused in her hands, as it would if she was about to pet one of the Affinity beasts in her grandfather's menagerie. Only her foenix was not here to absorb the power. It coiled within her until frustration made her spin on her heel and fling herself on her bunk.

'Really, Piro!'

She glowered at the agent. He was part of the problem, although she didn't understand why.

As he dropped the pendant into her palm, she felt the buzz of his power in the stone, and that annoyed her too. She should have been able to do this.

'Practise, Piro. Your control must match your ability. When you can make the stone glow, come to me for your next lesson.'

He sounded like Dunstany, and she felt her eyes burn with tears of loss. 'I'm sorry. I don't know what's wrong with me. Thank you, Tyro.'

He paused with his hand on the door. 'My name's Siordun.' Then he left.

'Siordun...'

He was Dunstany's bastard grandson, which was how he was able to pass for him. This explained the 'dun' part of his name. His mother had probably been called Siorra. He'd told her his mother had sold him to the mage when he was five. But he'd also said the mage had discovered his strong Affinity and claimed him.

Since his other grandfather was Mage Tsulamyth, it wasn't surprising that he had strong Affinity.

Tyro—*Siordun* thought he was so smart.

He had everyone fooled. Byren and Orrade didn't even know that Lord Dunstany was really him. Isolt and Fyn knew, but they didn't know about his other disguise.

No one but Piro knew that Tyro was also Mage Tsulamyth.

Back on Ostron Isle, she'd discovered him masquerading as the mage and had wormed the truth from him. For nearly two hundred years, fear of Mage Tsulamyth's wrath had kept rogue Power-workers in line. When twin Utland Power-workers had ambushed the mage and fatally wounded him, he had died in Siordun's arms.

Rather than see all Mage Tsulamyth's good work destroyed, Siordun had stepped into his master's shoes. It had always been intended that he would assume the mantle of Mage Tsulamyth, just as his master had done, ever since the real mage had died and his own apprentice had taken on the name. But Siordun hadn't finished his training; all that kept him safe from rogue Power-workers was the mage's reputation and bluff.

Now he was training her, and she had to prove herself worthy.

Piro attempted to focus her power in the stone, but no matter how hard she tried, her Affinity would not behave. It felt like the stone refused to accept her power.

Instead, power settled in her hands again. The sensation reminded of her of her pet foenix, Resolute. She missed him terribly. Ever since her Affinity had manifested, she'd been letting Resolute absorb excess power from her skin.

Now it was time for her to take control.

As Piro stared at the beautiful blue pendant, determination solidified within her. She was not leaving the cabin until she could make the stone glow.

She'd show Siordun!

Chapter Four

SEEING ISOLT HAPPY made Fyn happy. The royal barge boasted every possible luxury, but the young queen spent all her time with her pet Affinity beast. She tossed sea-fruit into the air for the wyvern to catch. 'Here, Loyalty!'

Lithe and powerful, the beast leapt to catch the pungent treat. As Loyalty's sharp teeth snapped shut, five of the queen's guards cheered. Truly, Isolt had earned her name: Isolt Wyvern Queen.

Loyalty preened, enjoying the attention while she watched Isolt for more treats.

'The beast is clever,' the abbot of Mulcibar Abbey observed, joining Fyn. 'According to my sources, Affinity beasts are as smart as five-year-olds.'

'You can't compare them to children. They're beasts, with a craving for power. They don't think like people.'

The abbot cast Fyn a thoughtful look. 'Then you'll forgive me if I speak plainly. It won't be long before the wyvern matures. When that happens, she'll feel the call of her kind, and if our queen hasn't bonded with her—'

'They'll bond.'

'Perhaps, but...' Abbot Murheg broke off and his lips twitched as he removed a stray wyvern scale from the cuff of his red velvet robe. 'Best to be wary, Lord Protector Merofyn.'

Fyn had never expected to become lord protector, just as he had never expected to be advised by an abbot. Murheg was forty years younger than the abbot of Halcyon Abbey; to have risen so quickly, he had to be both clever and ruthless, despite his affectations.

Piro's pet foenix, Resolute, gave voice, his mournful cry cutting through the shouts of the queen's guards. Perched on the barge's figurehead, the foenix was the symbol of Rolencia. When Byren reclaimed the throne, he would take Resolute home, but it wasn't Byren who'd reared the Affinity bird from a hatchling. Resolute clearly missed Piro.

The abbot made an offhand gesture. 'Which branch of Halcyon Abbey did you say you belonged to?'

'I didn't.' Fyn met the abbot's eyes. Murheg was his height. At seventeen, Fyn was still growing, but he would never be as big as his brothers—his brother. He found it hard to believe Lence was dead. *No time to mourn. Concentrate*. If the abbot knew he had been accepted by the mystics, he would assume Fyn had strong Affinity and be on his guard. But Fyn's Affinity was only slight. It had been thanks to Piro's interference that he'd found the pendant known as Halcyon's Fate and seen the vision that had secured him a place with the mystics. And it had been thanks to the Merofynian invasion that the abbey had fallen before he could begin his studies. 'I had only just finished my acolyte training.'

The dark-haired abbot nodded. 'Halcyon's monks spend longer as acolytes than we do.'

And Mulcibar's monks despised their counterparts. A fierce rivalry raged between the abbeys of Rolencia and Merofynia; just as fierce as the rivalry between the gods of winter and summer. This was why Merofynia's abbot and abbess had both insisted on accompanying the young queen on the royal barge.

Luckily, Isolt was no fool.

Fyn could not hear what the white-robed abbess had just whispered in Isolt's ear. The young queen cast Fyn a quick look. If the abbess was trying to destroy Isolt's trust in him, she'd fail. Isolt knew he was loyal, loyal to her and loyal to Byren...

More's the pity.

But he mustn't think like that. Aware of the abbot's sharp eyes, Fyn looked away. No one must suspect.

The wyvern uttered a cry that would normally have sent men running for cover. She flexed her wings, exhibiting shimmering arcs of silky leather. Not to be outdone, Resolute flew down from the figurehead and landed near Loyalty. Puffing up his feathers, he extended his head-crest.

Although neither beast was fully grown yet, the intent was clear—proud display that could quickly turn to aggression.

The wyvern's tail coiled and uncoiled, and she nudged Isolt. Resolute edged closer to the queen. Isolt clicked her tongue and both beasts presented their throats for petting.

As the queen stroked them, a rumbling sound of pleasure came from deep within the Affinity beasts' chests. Isolt laughed and glanced over her shoulder to Fyn. Sunlight sparkled on the Landlocked Sea, making Isolt's blue-black hair gleam. Joy illuminated her black eyes.

She stole his breath. But she was promised to his brother Byren, to cement the peace between their two kingdoms. Fyn was just her servant, her lord protector.

Hers to command.

'Fyn?' Isolt sent him a quizzical look.

He gestured to the Affinity beasts. 'They love you.' Isolt smiled. While King Merofyn still lived, she had been on edge, watching everything she said and did. Back then it had been a matter of survival. Now, she was learning to laugh again and, every time she did, it made Fyn's heart rise. If anything or anyone threatened her, he'd cut them down in a heartbeat. She may not be his, but there was no shame in looking as she leant forward to hug the wyvern and the foenix, revealing the sweet curve of her waist and hips.

'It's good to see the foenix and wyvern getting on,' Abbot Murheg said.

'Good to see Rolencia and Merofynia at peace,' Fyn agreed. As if he needed another reminder why Isolt could never be his.

'The wyvern's horns could rip a man's belly open,' the barge captain warned as he joined them. He ducked his head. 'Beggin' your pardon, Lord Protector Merofyn, but seein' the beastie so near our queen makes me uncomfortable.'

'Loyalty adores Isolt,' Fyn said.

'Maybe... but it's not natural, keepin' a saltwater wyvern for a pet. Even the smaller freshwater variety are too dangerous. All the captains of the Landlocked Sea avoid the wyvern eyries.'

Frustration welled up in Fyn. He'd been taught to fear Power-workers, taught that Affinity was only safe when under the guardianship of the abbeys, but after serving Mage Tsulamyth he knew that it was all a lie. He refused to kill two innocent Affinity beasts.

'That's all for now,' Isolt told the foenix and wyvern. They looked downcast. She laughed and glanced to Fyn. 'I swear they understand every word I say.'

A servant approached with warm, scented water for Isolt to wash her hands, and another offered scented oil to keep her skin soft. Even so, when Isolt joined Fyn, he sensed the residual power on her skin. Unlike him, Isolt had no natural Affinity. The beasts' wild power clung to her skin like an exotic perfume, alluring, intoxicating and...

Oh, he had it bad.

'We'll arrive at Lord Benvenute's estate in time for the evenin' meal, my queen,' the barge captain said. 'The Benetir people will stage entertainments and...'

Fyn filtered out the captain's voice. Before Byren and Orrade set sail, they'd held a war table discussion. Queen Isolt was new to her throne, young and untried. It was decided she should make a royal tour to visit each of the ten lords around the Landlocked Sea and accept their oaths of loyalty.

Benetir Estate was the first to the east. The lord's wife was Isolt's aunt—more correctly her father's aunt—and they were sure of the estate's loyalty. After each visit, the lord would follow the queen on his pleasure yacht. Eventually, all the lords and their families would complete the circuit of the Landlocked Sea and return to the palace for a grand celebration.

The warlords of the five spars also had to give their loyalty oaths, but Isolt would not go to them. They would come over the Dividing Mountains for the midsummer celebrations. So many Merofynian customs were the same as in Rolencia that Fyn had to keep reminding himself this was not his home.

Then something unfamiliar would happen and he would remember Merofynia was the ancestral enemy of his father's kingdom. But it was also his mother's homeland, and he'd sat at her knee as a small child listening to her tales.

Servants approached, offering white wine and little savoury pastries. The abbot and abbess helped themselves. Murheg was in his mid-thirties, while Celunyd was around fifteen years older. The abbess had been a bitter enemy of the previous abbot, and she was wary of Murheg.

A servant presented Isolt with a tray of pastries. She smiled and turned him away. 'If I keep eating at this rate, I'll be the size of a house.' She offered Fyn her arm. 'Take a walk with me.'

They strolled towards the ship's figurehead in full view

of everyone, and there, Isolt turned to Fyn. It was the Merofynian fashion to pluck the eyebrows and elongate the eyes with kohl. The first time he'd seen her in a vision triggered by Halcyon's Fate, he'd thought her lack of eyebrows odd. Now he thought her perfect.

'I know what they're saying.' Isolt glanced to the abbot and the others. 'If Loyalty doesn't bond with me, she could become violent and hurt someone. But I can't send her away. She's too gentle to live amongst wild wyvern. She trusts you. If the worst happens, promise me you'll kill her. Promise?'

Fyn stared into Isolt's beautiful black eyes. He could refuse her nothing. 'Of course. But you don't have to worry. Loyalty loves you.'

'For now,' Isolt conceded. 'But I'm not like you and Piro. I don't have Affinity. What if she rejects me?'

They both turned to watch the wyvern stretch, supple scales gleaming like jewels.

'I don't think you need Affinity,' Fyn said. 'You just need patience and love.' But he was only guessing. Maybe there was a book on Affinity beasts that would reveal more. 'I'll check the palace library.'

'Look up foenixes, too,' Isolt urged, as Resolute extended one wing to preen his brilliant red feathers.

She was right. Everyone had just assumed that the foenix would bond with Piro. Only his sister wasn't here, and the Affinity beast was maturing fast. If Resolute went rogue and had to be killed, Piro would be heartbroken.

In the wild, wyverns and foenixes were enemies. Fyn's stomach clenched. What if these two turned on each other?

Agent Tyro had taught Fyn the power of popular opinion. If the wyvern and foenix fought in a public place, the populace would think it foretold war between the two kingdoms. 'Perhaps we should separate—'

'Is that the Benetir pleasure yacht?' Isolt shaded her eyes. 'According to Lord Benvenute, the *Flying Sarre* is faster than all the other nobles' yachts.'

'Without wind, the royal barge is faster than her today,'

Fyn said. He squinted against the glare of the sun-kissed sea. 'She's dead in the water.'

'It is the *Flying Sarre*!' Isolt said. 'Come on.'

As the royal barge drew nearer, however, it became clear that this was no welcome party. People waved urgently from the overcrowded deck.

The barge captain cupped his hands. 'What news?'

'Spar raid,' several voices yelled.

'But the accord,' Isolt protested, turning horrified eyes to Fyn. 'The spars have not raided for two hundred years!

The Merofynians muttered. Their shock quickly turned to outrage as they helped the wheezing gaffers, walking wounded and frightened children aboard. Isolt had been trained as a healer and she assessed the injured, while Fyn pieced together events.

'They came in the night,' an old man said.

'With no warning,' a woman added, shivering. 'They attacked us as we prepared for the queen's visit.'

'Spar warriors?' Captain Neiron spat. 'No better than Utlanders!'

The barge captain cursed. 'May Mulcibar burn their homes and families!'

That reminded Fyn of the flaming balls flung by catapult during the battle of Narrowneck. Supposedly Mulcibar himself blessed the balls with his fiery breath, ensuring they incinerated everything they touched. Fyn turned to the abbot. 'Can we call on Mulcibar's mystics to save Benetir Estate?'

'Unfortunately, the balls of flame are—'

'Hard to control.' The abbess's eyes gleamed with malicious joy. 'They resulted in a tragic loss of life at the Battle of Narrowneck. The nobles—'

'Fire does not distinguish between enemy and friend,' Murheg spoke over her. 'I warned the previous abbot some weapons should be used only as a last resort.'

Intrigued, Fyn asked, 'Which branch of the abbey did you serve?'

'I was the history master.'

Fyn had always loved reading about the past. 'In Rolencia, we have a saying. "Those who do not learn from history are doomed to repeat it."'

The abbot met his eyes. 'We have the same saying.'

With a flick of her long robe, the abbess moved off to help Isolt. Disturbed by the new arrivals and the smell of blood, the Affinity beasts sought comfort from the queen.

'Lady Gennalla!' The queen darted through the crowd to reach a middle-aged woman who had climbed aboard with a small child. Isolt took the little boy and settled him on her hip. 'What happened, Aunt Genni? Where's Rhyderic? Where's—'

'They're dead.' The woman shuddered. 'They're all dead—my husband, my son and his...' She gestured to the child in Isolt's arms. 'Little Benowyth and I only just escaped!'

'Don't worry,' Fyn said. 'We'll send for the warlord and demand that he hand over these renegades—'

'They weren't renegades!' Lady Gennalla's voice shook with outrage. 'The warlord himself led the attack.'

'What's the world coming to?' the abbess cried.

'The spar warlord was behind this?' The abbot sent Fyn a warning look. 'This breaks with two hundred years of—'

'My queen, you can't allow this outrage to go unpunished,' Captain Neiron insisted. 'The warlord must be dragged through the city in chains and hung from the linden tree.'

Others echoed him and Isolt was swamped with advice.

Lady Gennalla swayed.

'My lady...' An old servant offered her his arm even though his white hair was caked with blood and he was himself supported by a young lad. The old man sought Fyn's eyes. 'We've been awake since yesterday. The Lady Gennalla is exhausted. She should rest.'

'I can't,' Gennalla protested. 'Not until we save Sefarra.' With a sob, she dropped to her knees, clutching Isolt's free hand. 'You must save Sefarra, my queen. She's only fourteen.'

'Sefarra?' Fyn looked to Isolt.

'Her daughter. My cousin,' Isolt said slowly, eyes wide with shock.

Fyn knew exactly what would happen to Sefarra. Had already happened to her.

'She's a dreamer, always has her head in a book. This will shatter her.' Lady Gennalla bit back a sob. 'You must save her!'

Fyn frowned as he helped Lady Gennalla to her feet. 'How many men did Warlord...?'

'Cortigern.' Isolt's eyes narrowed. 'Cortigern the Oath-breaker. I was there when he renewed his fealty oath last midsummer.'

'Looks like his fealty died with your father,' Fyn said.

Lady Gennalla turned to the queen. 'You must save my Seffi.'

'Yes, of course, Aunt.' Isolt gestured to the abbess. 'Take Lady Gennalla and her grandson into my cabin, and see to their needs.'

As the abbess led them away, Fyn turned to the old servant. 'How many warriors did Warlord Cortigern have?'

'At a guess, nearly two hundred.'

Fyn cursed. 'So many...'

The old man nodded, his voice choked with anger. 'It's an outrage. It's—'

'It's Palatyne,' Fyn told Isolt. 'He united the spars, then declared himself overlord. He grew powerful enough to sit at King Merofyn's table, trusted enough to lead the king's army into Rolencia and cunning enough to defeat my father. When he returned to Merofynia, he became a duke and aspired to wed the king's only daughter. After seeing what Palatyne achieved, Cortigern wanted—'

'Merofynia?' Isolt whispered. 'He can't—'

'He's taken Benetir Estate and Lady Sefarra...' The old man swayed.

Isolt gestured to the lad. 'Help him inside. I'll be there in a moment.' She faced Fyn. 'We must save Sefarra, but—'

'We only brought twenty queen's guards on the barge.'

'We're sworn to protect the queen.' Captain Neiron had caught the gist of their conversation. 'I won't send my men on a pointless attempt to rescue a girl who's already ruined.'

Isolt gasped and Fyn went to protest.

'The captain's right,' the abbot said. Seeing their shocked expressions, he picked his words with care. 'There's no point saving the Benetir girl now, my queen. The damage has been done. These spar warriors...' He shook his head. 'When King Merofyn welcomed Palatyne to his table, I said no good would—'

'Father had to recognise Palatyne,' Isolt insisted. 'Once he'd united the spars, he was too powerful to ignore.'

'We cannot leave Sefarra in their hands,' Fyn said.

Neiron and the abbot exchanged looks.

'I don't know how it is in Rolencia,' the captain said. 'But in Merofynia, if a highborn girl is raped, she's ruined. No respectable man will have her.'

Abbot Murheg nodded. 'The best she can hope for is to dedicate herself to the goddess of winter and live out her days in the Cyena Abbey.'

'If she doesn't take the honourable way out,' Captain Neiron added. 'If it was my sister, I'd—'

'You'd what?' Isolt rounded on him. 'Kill her yourself?'

'No, I... I'd kill the bastard who ruined her.'

'You keep talking about her like she's a piece of rotting fruit.' Isolt dismissed him with an impatient gesture. 'She's a girl who deserves better.'

The abbot took Isolt's hand in a fatherly way. 'You're young and idealistic, my queen. You do not know the ways of men. What if Cortigern realises how vulnerable we are? You're not safe, my queen.'

Isolt brushed off his hand, but she could not brush off his words. She turned worried eyes to Fyn.

He beckoned the barge captain. 'How soon can we return to Port Mero?'

'No wind.' The man grimaced. 'We'll have to row. Be there around midnight.'

'Do it,' Isolt ordered.

The captain hurried off.

'The warrior monks of Mulcibar are at your service, my queen.' Abbot Murheg gave a bow. 'But our ranks were decimated in the Rolenciån invasion. Every Merofynian is in the same position.'

'Except the spar warlords,' Fyn muttered. 'The nobles refused to fight alongside spar warriors.'

Isolt wrung her hands.

Fyn hated to see the line of worry between her plucked eyebrows. He wanted to take her in his arms and promise that everything would be all right. Even more, he wanted the right to do this. At the very least, he wanted to be rid of this nosy abbot. 'Comfort the survivors, Murheg.'

The abbot went with good grace and Fyn turned to Isolt, ready to offer solace.

But she lifted dark, determined eyes. 'We need to call on the lords to gather their men. The sooner we crush Warlord Cortigern, the less chance the other warlords will get the same idea.' Her eyes widened. 'What if all five spar warlords attacked Merofynia? Fyn, we must send for Lord Dunstany.'

'Dunstany...' He frowned. They'd been stunned to learn her father's trusted advisor was really Mage Tsulamyth's agent, Tyro, in disguise. 'He's sailing for Ostron Isle. As soon as we return to port, I'll go to Dunstany's townhouse. His servant keeps a pair of pica birds.'

'I'd forgotten,' Isolt admitted. 'It's odd, I know Lord Dunstany is really the mage's agent, but I still miss him. Dunstany, I mean.'

Fyn glanced to Isolt. She'd grown up turning to

Dunstany for advice and support, and he suspected she would rather not have learned he'd died and been replaced by the mage's agent.

Isolt frowned. 'Even if Tyro sets sail the moment he gets the message, it'll take at least five days for him to reach Merofynia. We must save Sefarra before then. When I think of her... ' She gave an odd little shiver. 'At least Palatyne never laid a hand on me.'

It made Fyn wonder if Isolt had come close to suffering the same fate as Sefarra. He took her by the shoulders. 'Palatyne's dead and gone. Loyalty saw to that.'

'I know, and I'm grateful. But Sefarra has no one to protect her.' Isolt raised determined eyes to Fyn. 'No one but us. Promise me you'll save her?'

'If it is at all possible, I'll save her.'

Chapter Five

Florin hadn't been outside except to view the body in the cart. Now, as she climbed the stairs, she caught a glimpse of distant Mount Halcyon painted gold by the setting sun, and realised the day was almost over. No wonder she was tired. There had been so much to learn... all the servants' names, their responsibilities, the castle's customs... and still it went on.

'Now we must see his lordship to approve the seating arrangements,' the castle-keep said. 'He'll be changing for the feast. Even as a boy, Illien was fastidious. And private. He won't have anyone but his manservant in his bedchamber.'

Florin nodded, growing nervous. Soon she would see Cobalt in his private chambers. Maybe she'd have the chance to kill him tonight and get it over with.

They left the stairs and entered a corridor.

'I've put the female servants in here.' The castle-keep gestured to a door on their right. 'No shenanigans on my watch. Not that Old Mirona would be up to it.' As they went down the passage, the castle-keep's boots clicked on the polished wooden floor. She walked so fast Florin was glad of her long legs. 'Tonight we had planned a feast to celebrate the investiture of Abbot Firefox. Now the feast will be a solemn affair in honour of Fyn Rolen Kingson's passing.' She patted the pocket of her over-smock. 'I have the guest list here. Mark my words. Who gets precedence is important...'

She trailed off as they rounded the corner and saw a female servant weighed down by two buckets.

'Here, you.' The castle-keep snapped her fingers. 'Why are you fetching his lordship's bathing water? There's manservants for that. And where's Old Mirona?'

The servant gave a jump of fright and put the buckets down. It was the pretty chambermaid who'd been hired that morning. She bobbed her head respectfully. 'Mirona took bad, my la... ma'am. I didn't know about the manservants. Back home—'

'I don't care how you did things back home. This is the royal castle. Do not speak unless spoken to and repeat nothing that you hear in his lordship's chamber. If I catch you gossiping, I'll tear strips off your hide.'

The girl blanched.

'And call for a manservant to carry those.'

'The bath's nearly full.'

'Have it your way.' The castle-keep strode past her.

Florin went to take one of the buckets.

'What are you doing?' The castle-keep rounded on her. 'You're my assistant, not hers. Come along.'

Florin gave the girl an apologetic look and hurried after the castle-keep, remaining one step behind her as she'd been taught. The stiff brocade of Florin's servant tabard brushed her thighs. With her hair pulled back in a braid and a male servant's cap fitting snugly on her head, she didn't look like the bedraggled messenger who skated night and day to deliver news of the Merofynian invasion. Not that she needed to worry, Cobalt had only ever seen her the once.

The castle-keep knocked on the door, waited for a muffled answer, then strode in.

They entered in time to catch a man in the act of pulling his shirt over his head and tossing it aside. He was illuminated by a flickering candle. Turned side-on to them, with his long black hair and broad shoulders, he reminded Florin of Byren.

Then he faced them and she saw that although he was tall and well-proportioned like Byren, his features were more classically handsome. She wouldn't trade perfection for Byren's crooked grin. And she would never mistake Cobalt for Byren, not when Cobalt was missing his right arm.

Florin was used to seeing maimed men, survivors of the war against Merofynia thirty years ago. But they were old men and Cobalt was beautifully formed, in the prime of life, which made his shoulder stump more shocking. She'd heard Byren's mother had tried to kill him and only the ministrations of the Merofynian healer had saved him.

Seeing the castle-keep, Cobalt smiled. 'Yegora.' With his white teeth and flashing black eyes, he was the most handsome man Florin had ever seen. But it was his affection for the castle-keep that made him appealing. 'I was wondering when you'd get here. Show me the list.'

The castle-keep joined him at the desk, leaving Florin by the door.

Cobalt gestured to Florin. 'I see you've replaced your assistant. Did the girl run off?'

'The less said about her, the better. She had ideas above her station, that one.' The castle-keep sniffed primly. 'Come here, Leif.'

Florin went over, telling herself that Cobalt couldn't possibly recognise her after all this time.

The usurper cast Florin an assessing look.

'Surely you mean Leiflyr, Yegora?' Cobalt's smiled. 'That male attire fooled me at first, but I swear she's too pretty to be a boy.'

His charm had no effect on Florin. She could not accept false coin. 'Just Leif, sor.'

'Mark my words, Leif.' Cobalt winked at the castle-keep. 'This place would fall apart without Yegora's steady hand on the reins.'

The castle-keep blushed. 'Stop your blandishments.'

'She rescued me from a pig sty,' Cobalt said. 'The state the Merofynians left this place in... I don't know what I would have done without her.'

Cheeks very pink, Yegora spread out the guest list. 'Everyone accepted your invitation, except for the abbess. I still haven't heard from her.'

'I could send some men down to the castle oratory and haul the highest-ranking nun up here,' Cobalt muttered. 'But who knows what the stupid women would do? Sylion's nuns are as unyielding as the frosts of winter.'

'Don't worry, you'll win the abbess over,' the castle-keep said. She tapped the list. 'I would put the Merofynian captains at this table with the old Rolencian nobility, but the lords might take offence. I could put the Merofynians with the merchant markizes and their markizas.'

While she'd been speaking, the new chambermaid had arrived and begun emptying the buckets into the tub.

Cobalt nodded. 'I need them all to recognise my claim to the throne. They know I've confiscated estates from Byren's loyal lords. As long as I hold those titles and estates in reserve—'

'King Byren the Fourth was your grandfather. That should be enough for them!'

'Ah, Yegora...' Cobalt shook his head. 'The nobles will never let me forget my father was a bas—' He broke off, staring intently at the chambermaid.

The castle-keep frowned. 'Illien?'

'You.' Cobalt snapped his fingers at the chambermaid. 'Come here.'

The girl hugged the empty buckets to her chest and trotted over, eyes lowered, cheeks flushed. 'I'm sorry, sor.

I didn't mean to spill the water. I'll mop it up.'

'Quiet.' He lifted her chin. 'Bring the candle closer, Leif.'

Florin did as she was bid.

Cobalt turned the girl's face this way and that, studying her features. 'Halcyon's Blessing, she's the spitting image of Piro. Wouldn't you say so, Yegora?'

'I wouldn't know. I never saw the kingsdaughter but at a distance.'

'Exactly. Most people only ever saw Piro Kingsdaughter from a distance. She was dainty and pretty, just like this lass. Why haven't I seen her before?'

'She just arrived today.'

'That's lucky.' He addressed the bemused girl. 'Who have you spoken with today?'

She glanced at those present. 'Apart from you, only my sister and old Mirona, your lordship.'

'Excellent. How old are you?'

'Just turned fourteen, sor.'

Cobalt smiled. 'Turns out, I won't have to rely on my dinner guests to legitimise my claim to the throne. Today Rolencia wept for Fyn Rolen Kingson. Tonight, Rolencia will rejoice when they hear how I rescued Piro Rolen Kingsdaughter from the Merofynians and kept her hidden in my chambers all this time. Tonight I will stake my claim on the throne by becoming betrothed to Piro Rolen Kingsdaughter.'

The castle-keep stood open-mouthed. 'But... But won't the dinner guests know this is not the kingsdaughter?'

'Not this lot. The lords who were closest to the old king fell at the Battle of Narrowneck. Queen Myrella...' His voice faltered. 'The queen kept Piro out of the public eye because the girl could not be relied upon to behave herself. The new abbot is eager to please me, and those merchant markizes with the royal seal still fresh on their titles would cheer if I called a goose-girl the kingsdaughter.'

'What of the castle servants?' Florin asked, before she could censor her tongue.

'Good point.' Cobalt turned to the castle-keep. 'What of the servants, Yegora? Will they denounce this Piro?'

The castle-keep frowned. 'When I arrived, there were hardly any of the original servants left. Most had run off and the rest had been enslaved and taken back to Merofynia. There might be an old servant here and there but, unless they served the kingsdaughter, they wouldn't know her face.'

'And they'll keep quiet if they know what's good for them,' Cobalt said. 'I'll speak to Amil. He'll send Old Mirona and the sister home with a bag of coins to ensure their silence.'

'But...' the girl began.

'But nothing, Piro.' He lifted her chin with the tip of his finger. 'You are my sweet little half-cousin, grateful to me for saving your life. Do as you're told, and you won't regret it. How would you like to wear a crown, fine jewels and velvets?'

Two bright spots of colour burned in the girl's cheeks.

'Well?' Cobalt pressed.

The girl bobbed her head, too tongue-tied to speak.

Florin seethed.

'Excellent, much better behaved than the real Piro. She was a spiteful little wyvern.' Cobalt turned away from the girl to the castle-keep. 'See that she is bathed and dressed as befits a kingsdaughter. For tonight, she can keep her mouth shut, but tomorrow I want you to train her to act the part. No more calling me *sor*.'

The castle-keep's mouth dropped open in dismay.

'On second thoughts, you have more than enough to do.' Cobalt called over his shoulder. 'Amil, come in here.'

'My lord?' The Ostronite manservant entered so promptly, Florin guessed he had been listening at the door.

'I can manage, milord,' the castle-keep insisted.

'No, Yegora. I shouldn't have asked.' Cobalt took her worn hand in his, planting a kiss on her cheek. 'I know how hard you work for me. Amil's been complaining that he doesn't have enough to do.' Cobalt stepped back, beckoning the manservant. 'Can you turn this chambermaid into Piro Rolen Kingsdaughter?'

'But of course, my lord.' The Ostronite manservant was a little shorter than Florin, and solidly built for all that his hands fluttered like delicate butterflies. Amil caught her studying him and looked her up and down. He gestured dismissively. 'Why, I could even teach this great lump of a girl to pass for a noble.'

Cobalt looked startled then gave a short bark of laughter. He cast Florin a thoughtful look. 'I think you'd be surprised.' And before Florin could grasp that she'd been complimented—not that she cared—he'd moved on. 'Yegora, go through Piro's clothes and find something suitable for her to wear tonight. Let someone see you and let slip that I'll be making a great announcement tonight. Lay the groundwork, so that the castle servants spread rumours of Piro's return to the nobles.'

Clever. Florin was impressed.

Cobalt gestured to her. 'Help my betrothed bathe, Leif. My sweet cousin needs a bath scented with rose petals. She'll wear the finest of velvets and jewels, as befits a kingsdaughter. Meanwhile, Amil will help me change in the other chamber.'

They went off, leaving Florin alone with the girl, who trembled as Florin took the buckets from her hands. Did she realise she'd be killed the moment she was no longer useful? In fact, now that Florin was a party to this deception, her life was also in danger.

Not that it mattered.

Florin went to fill the buckets one last time and returned, to find Amil waiting in the hall door. He took her arm, his grip surprisingly strong. 'The master wants you to keep watch over the new Piro Kingsdaughter. Let me know if she is unhappy. You understand?'

Florin nodded. She understood all right. Cobalt was trying to turn her against the chambermaid, just as he had turned the castle-keep against Amil, ensuring that both strove to win his affection and each would betray the other for a smile from him.

'Good. The master is generous,' Amil told Florin, 'but he is also sharp. Don't ever cross him.'

Then he opened the door for her, going across the chamber to Cobalt's private room to help his master dress for dinner.

Frustrated, Florin poured the water into the tub then stepped back. 'Your bath is ready, kingsdaughter.'

No sound came from behind the screen.

'Kingsdaughter?'

Florin peered over the screen. No sign of the girl or her clothes. With a curse, Florin darted into the hall. If the chambermaid had panicked and fled, she would need her things.

Florin ran to the female servants' chamber, throwing the door open. A cheap, painted statuette of Goddess Halcyon sat on a stool by one of the pallet beds, where an old woman lay. A votive candle burned, illuminating the statuette, the old woman and, in the far corner, the girl. Seeing Florin, she gave a squeak of fright and clutched her bundle to her chest.

'Are you mad?' Florin whispered, furious. 'Leave your things and come with me.'

The girl did not release the bundle. In fact, she glanced over Florin's shoulder as if contemplating flight.

Florin strode over. 'Here, give me that.' She took the bundle, dropping it onto the bed.

'Leave her be,' Old Mirona croaked.

'She ran from her post,' Florin said, sending the girl a warning look. 'The castle-keep will be ever so angry.'

'Eh, you can't do that, Varuska.' Old Mirona shook her head. 'Back to work with you. You'll be lucky to escape with only a tongue lashing.'

'But—'

'But nothing,' Florin said quickly. 'Varuska, that's your name?

The girl nodded. 'Ruska for short. But—'

'Come on.' Florin drew Varuska out into the hall, where she confronted her. 'You're lucky I was the one who came after you. What were you thinking?'

'His lordship scares me. I want to go home. I don't want—'

'It doesn't matter what you want. Cobalt's got it into his head that you'll do for Piro and that's it.'

'Ask Anatoley to play Piro. She'd like to be a kingsdaughter. It was her idea to come to the castle.'

'Anatoley's your sister?'

Varuska nodded.

Florin considered this. 'She's the right size and age, but she doesn't look enough like Piro. Not like you do.' The resemblance was uncanny. Right down to mannerisms.

'Can't I just go home?' Varuska tugged on Florin's arm, trying to slip from her grip. 'I won't tell anyone, I promise. I don't want to marry Lord Cobalt. He smiles, but when he touches me I feel cold inside. Please let me go. I won't tell anyone.'

'If you ran, I'd be in trouble.'

'We could both run.'

'Not yet.' Florin smiled as Varuska's eyes widened. The girl was quick. 'I'll get you out of the castle, I promise, but there's something I must do first.'

'You'll get me out? What about Anatoley?'

'Cobalt's sending your sister home tonight,' Florin reminded her. 'Play along for now. Come on. We need to go back before they realise you tried to run.' And she drew the girl along the corridor.

'You're right.' Varuska had to take two steps for each of Florin's. 'If they think I'm going to run, they'll set a guard on me.'

'Exactly. You're smart.'

'No one's ever called me smart before.' Varuska paused to look up at Florin. 'Only pretty.'

'It doesn't pay to let them know you're smart. So

pretend to be eager for pretty dresses and jewels. Make sure they underestimate you.'

Varuska's eyes widened. 'You're clever.'

Maybe, but was she clever enough to outwit Cobalt, kill him and ensure Varuska escaped alive? Florin licked dry lips. 'Come on.'

They slipped into the chamber. To Florin's relief it was empty. 'Quick, off with your things and into the tub. You should be almost finished by now.'

Varuska tore off her servant's cap and gown. Like all girls of her class, she wore no knickers. Useless things.

The sound of the castle-keep's footsteps reached them.

'Into the tub.' Florin guided her in then poured a bucket of water over the girl's hair. She grabbed some scented soap and began massaging it into Varuska's scalp. By the time the castle-keep walked in the door, Florin had worked up a good lather.

'What, not finished yet?' The castle-keep's lips pursed in disapproval. 'This will never do. Rinse her hair.' She draped a vivid blue gown over a chair. 'There's a gown, jewels and beaded slippers. Bathe her, then dry her hair by the fire. Use this head-dress.' She indicated a little cap inlaid with silver chains and gleaming stones that might have been diamonds. 'I can't stay. I have work to do.' With a sniff, she was gone.

As Florin helped Varuska out of the tub, the girl caught her hand. 'Will you take a message to my sister? She'll be worried if they send her home without me.'

Florin hesitated.

'Please?'

'It will have to be later tonight. Now let's get you dry.'

Florin helped Varuska dress in Piro's gown. There seemed to be an inordinate amount of under garments—lacy pantaloons that came down to her knees, a chemise, two petticoats—and then the blue gown that did up under her breasts.

When it was laced, Florin sat Varuska by the fire to

comb her long dark hair. It was almost dry by the time Cobalt returned with Amil.

The lord's empty sleeve had been pinned up. He wore a coat the same shade of blue as Varuska's gown, which Florin now realised was the Cobalt Estate's colour. His coat was tapered at the waist. Knee-high boots, tight trews that moulded to his strong thighs and a hand's span of lace at this throat and cuffs completed his outfit. When he turned his head, the long curls glinted; his hair had been threaded with jewels.

'Let me see you, Piro.' Cobalt spoke sweetly, but it was still a command.

Varuska turned around, looking back over her shoulder. The stance was coquettish, but her expression was earnest.

'Good. The dress is a perfect fit. Amil, do her hair,' Cobalt said. 'Take note, Leif. This will be your task.'

The Ostronite manservant used a heated metal tong to create long ringlets. 'A few more pins.' He completed his work with the girl's hair. 'Now the zircon cap.'

He pinned the cap, letting the chains and zircons fall to Varuska's shoulders. Florin could not see the difference between diamonds and zircons.

'Lovely.' But Cobalt's eyes did not light up with the hunger of desire. 'Show her how to respond to the dinner guests, Amil.'

'These guests,' the manservant said, acting the part of a proud noble, 'they are beneath you. You are a kingsdaughter. You tilt your head so and smile just a little. You keep your hand on your lord's arm and answer everyone with no more than a nod.'

The girl listened earnestly. Varuska was lucky, Florin decided. Few people would look past her pretty face.

'Very well. Until we polish the rough edge off your tongue, you'll keep your mouth shut.' Cobalt offered his arm.

Varuska took it as she had been instructed.

'Very good.' The lord turned her to face Florin. 'This is Lord Leif, greet him as you've been taught.'

'Lord Leif,' Varuska murmured, inclining her head.

'Excellent, cousin, we will deal well together.' Cobalt kissed her hand. Florin saw Varuska shudder. His lordship must have put it down to excitement, because he squeezed her fingers. 'Good girl. Come.'

Varuska hesitated.

'Do not fear. I will be at your side and Amil and Leif will be right behind us. For all that Amil knows how to dress hair, he is a corax of House Nictocorax. Ahh, from your expression you have heard of Ostron Isle's assassins. So you see, you need fear nothing while he is with us.'

A trained assassin? Florin would never have guessed. She expected an Ostronite assassin to be sinister. Although, now that she thought about it, an assassin stood a better chance of getting near their prey if they appeared harmless, and she had certainly underestimated Amil.

So, Florin was there when Cobalt introduced the false Piro and everyone applauded her miraculous escape. She was there when he announced they were to be married on midsummer's day.

And not one person denounced the imposter.

Chapter Six

Garzik looked through the pages until he found a picture of a ship, then he wrote the Utland word for *ship* and a sentence about it. 'Try this.'

'Ship,' Rusan read then frowned as he sounded out the words. 'Captain Rusan sails his ship upon the Stormy Sea.'

Garzik nodded. 'Very good.'

The Utland captain pointed to the book's original text. 'Why can't I read these words?'

'I thought you wanted to learn to read and write in your own language.'

'What's the point when there are no books?'

'You could write the stories of your people.'

'Who would read them?' Rusan countered. 'Why do you think I made you promise to tell no one? Reading and writing are hot-land skills.'

And Utlanders despised the hot-landers, as they called Garzik's people.

Yet the captain wanted to learn to read and write. Everything Garzik had been taught about Utlanders had proven to be inaccurate. Yes, they were savage, but only because they had to survive in the savage Utland Isles.

'You hesitate?' Rusan bristled. 'Do you think because I'm an Utlander I won't be able to—'

'I was wondering which language to teach you.' Garzik indicated the page. 'I chose this book because it was made for the children of nobles and rich merchants to teach them the three languages of the hot-lands. This is the Rolencian word for ship, then the Merofynian word and finally the Ostronite. Which language do you want to learn?'

Rusan frowned. 'Which is most useful?'

Garzik thought about it. 'Ostronite is the trading tongue.'

'Then I'll learn it.'

'While learning to read and write in your own tongue as well?'

The Utland captain shrugged. 'Why not?'

Garzik grinned. Rusan was smart; maybe as smart as Garzik's brother, Orrade. Thinking of his old life made Garzik's stomach tighten with frustration. He should be helping Byren win back Rolencia, yet here he was, tutor to an Utland captain. But he hadn't started out here.

He'd been a prisoner of war, a seven-year slave, sent to Merofynia to serve Lord Travany. He'd come a long way since the Utlanders captured Travany's ship with its Rolencian war booty and made him their slave, but he was still no closer to going home.

'Captain?' Young Luvrenc tapped on the cabin door.

Rusan slipped off the window seat, lifted the lid and hid the book along with Garzik's ink and nib. There was no desk. The cabin had been stripped right back to lighten the captured merchant ship.

'What is it?' Rusan called.

'Lookout spotted sails.'

'It better be a lone ship,' Rusan muttered as he made for the door.

Since leaving their settlement, the Utlanders hadn't made a capture. They'd seen plenty of ships returning from

Rolencia laden with stolen riches, but they hadn't dared attack, not when the merchant vessels were protected by sleek sea-hound ships, full of fierce fighting men.

Luvrenc fell into step with Garzik, hand on his sword hilt, witchy Utland eyes shining with excitement. 'With any luck it'll be a merchant ship travelling alone!'

As the newest crew member, he had yet to prove himself. Thirteen to Garzik's fifteen, Luvrenc seemed even younger.

Luvrenc followed Garzik onto the high reardeck but he didn't approach the captain and his half-brother.

Garzik did. He'd won his freedom and the brothers' trust, helping to defend their settlement the night Captain Vultar and his renegades attacked.

Olbin handed Rusan the farseer. 'I can't spot the sails.'

Rusan braced his legs and lifted the farseer to his eyes as the stolen merchant ship plunged through the waves on a southern heading, timbers creaking, ropes singing. The wind stirred the captain's long black hair and beard, rattling the wyvern teeth plaited through it.

The first time Garzik had seen a wyvern-cloaked Utland captain, he'd thought the man a barbarian. But after Rusan had single-handedly killed a wyvern to confirm his leadership of the captured ship, Garzik had understood what the Affinity beast trophies signified.

For all that Rusan was a captain and led nearly thirty men, he was younger than Byren. Troubled, Garzik fingered the hilt of his Utland short sword. Here he was, sworn to serve the Utland captain when he was already sworn to Byren.

His vow to Byren was of an earlier making; as soon as the opportunity arose, Garzik was going to betray Rusan and Olbin and go over to their enemy, the hot-landers.

'See anything?' Olbin asked.

'Nothing.' Rusan lowered the farseer with a grimace of frustration. Vultar and his renegades had stolen the settlement's prized twin oracles and much-needed supplies. For the moment, Rusan could do nothing about the loss of the oracles, but he was desperate to replace their supplies. 'The lookout's imagining things.'

Olbin shook his head. 'The men are getting restless.'

'Would they rather I led them in a pointless attack and got them all killed?'

'They'd rather you led them in a glorious attack and rewarded their bravery with riches. They don't much care how you do it.' Olbin grinned, then nudged Rusan. 'Look at Wynn here, so eager to win a name for himself he can't keep his hands off his blade!'

Garzik flushed. He was a fraud. He hadn't even given them his real name. He'd been Wynn, short for Wyvern, ever since he'd woken and found himself captured by Merofynians. At first he hadn't remembered his name; then, he'd been overcome with the shame of failing Byren.

The night the Merofynians had invaded, Byren had told him to light the warning beacon, but he'd been knocked out and captured. For a while he'd hoped to make up for his failure by spying, with the help of his fellow captive, Mitrovan. But the scribe had been sent to serve Lord Travany, while Garzik had remained on the ship to serve the surgeon. Then the ship had been captured and Rusan had claimed it for his own, taking him even further from Byren and his duty.

The man in the crow's nest yelled again.

'Not sails,' Rusan said. 'Sarres.'

Although Garzik had been quick to pick up the Utland tongue, this word was new to him and he looked to Olbin. The big Utlander slung an arm across his shoulders, guiding him to the starboard rail.

'Sarres.' He pointed behind the ship to a school of sleek silver fish. They skimmed the surface of the water, leaping into the air, wing-fins extended. 'Affinity-blessed flying fish.'

Garzik gasped. 'I'd heard tales, but never... They really do fly.'

'They have wings.' Rusan joined them. 'But they're not flying. They glide through the air, then drop back into the sea, build up speed and glide some more.'

Now that the sarres were closer, Garzik could see Rusan was right. He could also see... 'They're huge.'

'Good eating, too.' Olbin winked. 'If you can catch them.'

The Utlanders didn't settle Affinity beasts' power before consuming their flesh. Garzik suspected this was the reason for their strange eyes, which contained a pale ring inside the iris. Other than this, they were the same as him and not a baser race, as he'd been taught.

Rusan's crew cheered the Affinity fish.

'They could easily overtake the ship. Why do they stay alongside us?' Garzik asked. 'Why do they leap out of the water? Surely it takes more effort than swimming?'

Olbin shrugged and glanced to Rusan.

'They're curious,' the captain said, accepting his pipes from Luvrenc. 'They like to play.'

Rusan began a high, fluting tune that seemed to follow the movements of the elegant, leaping sarres.

Garzik watched, entranced. Then he frowned. 'Are they...'

'Keeping time with the music?' Olbin nodded.

'Amazing.' Garzik knew Affinity beasts were smarter than their mundane counterparts, but he had never thought of fish as being intelligent. Orrie would find this fascinating.

Yet again, Garzik was reminded that he lived a lie. And he did not even know if his brother and sister had survived the Merofynian invasion.

Luvrenc clutched Garzik's arm. 'Look!'

Several large creatures sped through the water towards the ship. Coming in at an angle, it looked like the predators would trap the sarres against the side of the vessel.

Rusan blew one shrill note and the sarres reacted. Garzik had thought them fast before; now they took off, easily outstripping the ship.

But not fast enough, as their pursuers put on a burst of speed. Garzik's heart leapt as a sleek, rainbow skinned predator shot out of the water, taking one of the sarres in mid-flight, disappearing with it below the surface. 'Was that—'

'A scytalis? Yes.' Rusan fingered his pipes. 'They hunt like a pack of wolves.'

'Sea serpents...' Garzik had heard sailor's tales of the Affinity beasts, with coats of iridescent scales. The scytalises were bigger than the biggest of the flying fish. And fast. Both hunter and prey had left the ship behind, but he could still see flashes of silver as the fish glided through the air. Only the old and slow would get eaten, leaving the fastest to survive and breed. 'The sarres developed the ability to leap and glide to escape their predators.'

Olbin laughed. 'Always watching, always thinking.'

But Rusan gave Garzik a thoughtful look, as he handed Luvrenc his pipes. 'Back to work, Wynn.'

Garzik went down to the middeck, where the Utlanders returned to their tasks.

'Get over here,' Jost snarled, as if Garzik was still a slave. He had made Garzik's life miserable since the day the ship had been captured. On that day he'd sliced off Garzik's ear to match his own missing ear.

Behind Jost, Trafyn watched with a malicious gleam in his eye. Lord Travany's son, he'd been serving as Lord Neirn's squire. He and Garzik had been enslaved together and suffered indignities Garzik would rather not remember. Driven by hunger, they had eaten unclean Affinity-tainted meat like Utlanders. But Trafyn was still a slave, having made no attempt to learn their captors' language or earn their respect. The squire did as little work as possible, certain his father would ransom him.

'Yes, you.' Jost beckoned Garzik, then gestured to the ropes. 'See that these are mended by the time I come back.'

He aimed a blow at Garzik, who ducked just enough to lessen the force of impact, but this didn't satisfy Jost.

He gestured to Garzik's Utlander jacket. Thigh-length and belted at the hips, it was made of goat's wool, dyed red, with elaborate embroidery around the hem, sleeves and neck. It had been given to him the night the settlement accepted him. 'Rusan might have declared you one of us, but he won't be captain forever. So move when I tell you.'

As Garzik turned away, Jost shoved him so hard he collided with Trafyn.

The squire smirked. 'Looks like being the captain's joy-boy has some drawbacks.'

'Looks like being a prick comes naturally to you,' Garzik muttered, but he watched Jost's retreating back. Was Rusan's leadership in danger?

The one-eared Utlander said something to his companions, and they all glanced to Garzik and laughed.

Trafyn snorted. 'Looks like you'll be a joy-boy long after I'm—'

Garzik spun around, caught the front of Trafyn's jerkin and pulled him close. 'I was there the night we were captured. I know what went on. What still goes on.'

Shame and anger made Trafyn flush, and his eyes gleamed with unshed tears. Up this close, Garzik noticed the tell-tale pale circles around his pupils. The Utland marking in Trafyn's eyes wasn't visible from a distance, but the effect of eating Affinity contaminated meat had begun.

Garzik was so shocked he let Trafyn go.

Were his own eyes undergoing the same change? Would he be marked forever?

The squire straightened his ragged Merofynian jerkin, voice shaking. 'At least I didn't side with savages.'

'And I didn't kill a twelve-year-old boy.'

'He was a renegade. They would have killed him anyway.'

Garzik frowned. Vultar had escaped on one of his ships, but the other had burned to the waterline, stranding some of his renegades. Rusan's people had cut their throats.

'You know I'm right. They're savages!'

'Shut up. Just... shut up.' Garzik stalked across to the coiled ropes and knelt.

His fingers flew as he spliced the hemp fibres. Maybe he wasn't as smart as Orrade, but he wasn't slow, and he'd been quick to learn the ways of the sea. And maybe he had changed sides the night the renegades attacked, but he'd fought to protect the settlement's women and children, and he hadn't killed an unconscious boy to prove he was a man.

'Why is it so cold?' The squire hunched low to keep out of the wind. 'It shouldn't be this cold, this close to summer.'

Garzik said nothing.

'These crazy Utlanders don't seem to feel the cold.'

It was true. Enduring without complaint was a matter of pride with them. Scorning hot-land luxuries, the Utlanders slept on deck, wrapped in furs. In some ways, Garzik had more in common with Rusan and Olbin than with Trafyn.

'We're sailing south. Every day we draw closer to home.' The squire lowered his voice. 'You should tell them about my father. You know enough of their language now. Tell them he'll pay well for my return.'

Garzik said nothing.

'Tell them and I promise you'll be rewarded. My father's a powerful man. He'll—'

'Shut up about your father. Shut up and work.'

'I'm not taking orders from you. At least I *have* a father.'

'Shut up.'

'Soon I'll be home free, but you'll be a savage sucking cock for the rest of your life,' Trafyn sneered. 'Utland lover!'

Garzik leapt for his throat, driving him backwards onto the deck. As they struggled, the Utlanders gathered around, shouting encouragement. Garzik had grown up wrestling with his older brother and Byren, and both of them had outclassed him in weight and strength.

By the time Olbin pulled him off Trafyn, Garzik was pleased to see that the squire was bruised and bleeding. Maybe Trafyn was right, and he was turning into a savage.

He didn't care.

Olbin thumped Trafyn to silence his whining, then turned to Garzik. 'What did Lazy-Legs do now?'

Garzik shook his head.

Olbin shrugged and thrust Trafyn towards the ropes. 'Back to work, *belongs-to-no-one*.'

It was the Utland word for *slave*. It meant there was no one to avenge his death.

The squire staggered, then recovered his balance. He straightened his jerkin. They were not far from home, which seemed to embolden him. He lifted his chin, addressing the big Utlander as if he were a servant.

'I'm Trafyn of Travantir Estate.' He gestured to Garzik. 'I'm tired of waiting. Tell them my father is Lord Travany, and he'll give them gold for my release.'

Garzik was about to refuse, when he realised he might be able to escape during the exchange, so he struggled to convey the concept of ransom in the Utlanders' tongue.

'Trafyn of Travantir Estate?' Olbin mocked the squire, speaking Merofynian parrot fashion. He glanced around, inviting the others to laugh. Nearly twenty raiders had gathered, eager for entertainment.

'My word's as good as gold,' Trafyn insisted.

'He is worth gold,' Garzik translated.

'I see no gold. I see a lazy hot-lander who thinks he's better than us.' And with that, Olbin grabbed Trafyn. Despite his size, the big Utlander was fast. 'I see a belongs-to-no-one who needs to learn his place.'

Olbin hauled him to the side of the ship, Trafyn protesting indignantly, then desperately. Up near the foredeck cabins, Olbin tied a rope around the squire's chest and dangled him over the side. Each time the ship cut into the wave Trafyn got a drenching, and each time the prow rose he screamed louder. Garzik didn't blame him. He'd seen what those scytalises could do.

As the Utlanders laughed at the squire's desperate cries, Garzik hardened his heart. Trafyn had brought this on himself.

Finally, Olbin hauled the squire up and dropped him onto the deck, where he huddled shivering and sobbing with fury.

'Sail over the port bow!' the lookout called.

Olbin ran up the steps to the reardeck to join the captain. Everyone waited, hoping.

A moment later, Olbin returned to the rail bellowing orders to raise more sail. Garzik felt the ship respond as she changed course. The Utlanders cheered, checked their weapons and boasted of their prowess in battle.

Garzik peered at the other ship's silhouette, feeling sorry for the crew. When the Utlanders had captured Garzik's ship, they'd put everyone but him, Trafyn and another squire to the sword.

Trafyn stumbled over, teeth chattering so badly he could hardly speak. 'Y-you were n-no help.'

He looked so miserable, Garzik took pity on him. 'Strip and find some dry clothes before you catch your death. I'll finish the ropes.'

But Trafyn didn't get a chance. Jost sent Vesnibor to grab the squire. Vesnibor was only a couple of years older than them, but those years had been spent raiding, as his scars and twice-broken nose attested. He dragged Trafyn to the mainmast and tied him up, jerking on the ropes with unnecessary force.

Garzik watched; the last time the crew had attacked a ship he'd been a slave, and they'd tied him to the mast along with Trafyn.

Vesnibor strode over to Garzik. They were the same

height, yet somehow the raider still managed to loom. 'If I had my way, you'd be tied up, too. Once a hot-lander, always a hot-lander.'

Vesnibor swaggered off to join Jost and his two half-brothers. The one-eared Utlander met Garzik's eyes and spat.

Shame filled Garzik. If he escaped, it would confirm their opinion of him and undermine Rusan's leadership.

But he had a duty to Byren. If Byren still lived.

The ship plunged through the waves, timbers groaning in protest. This was a flat-bellied merchant vessel, designed to carry cargo, not travel at great speed.

'Fly the hot-landers' flag,' Rusan yelled from the reardeck. 'When we get close, everyone out of sight. I'll take the wheel.' He adjusted the fit of his fancy Merofynian coat and everyone laughed.

Luvrenc raised the Merofynian flag, and Garzik's heart sank. The other ship's captain wouldn't realise he was being attacked until it was too late. In fact, he would probably welcome another merchant ship. Safety in numbers.

But there was still a chance the merchant sailors might fight off the Utland raiders. Garzik fingered the hilt of his short sword, wondering if he should help the sailors. To be brutally pragmatic, there was no point helping them unless it looked like they would survive and he could escape with them.

'Don't tell me you're going to kill your own people to win favour with a bunch of savages?' Trafyn sneered. 'Traitor.'

Garzik considered the squire. Lord Travany would be grateful to have his son back, especially if he didn't need to pay a huge ransom. Mitrovan would be Lord Travany's slave by now, and the scribe might have useful information for Garzik to pass along to Byren.

He edged closer to Trafyn. 'This might be a good chance to escape. I'll loosen the ropes. If the Rolencians look like they're fighting off the attack, wriggle free and—'

'I'm not going to risk my life. Not when I'm going to be ransomed.'

'Wouldn't your father prefer you to save yourself?' Garzik glanced around to be sure no one was watching, and adjusted the ropes so that they would part easily. 'Wouldn't you like to save him the cost of your ransom?'

Trafyn's eyes lit up at the thought, then his shoulders slumped. 'What if Utlanders take the ship and kill everyone?'

'There's a chance they might, but the other ship could fight them off and, if they do, we can escape. So be ready.'

Trafyn looked torn.

Garzik didn't know if he would come through. Just as he didn't know what he would find when he got home. Last he'd heard, Rolenhold Castle had fallen, the king and queen were dead, Lence Kingsheir was dead, and Piro...

He mustn't think of her.

Last he'd heard, Byren had fled and Cobalt the Usurper sat on the throne.

But Garzik refused to despair. All he had to do was escape, return Lord Travany's son and see if Mitrovan had learnt anything that would help Byren, then return to Rolencia and find Byren.

All Garzik had to do was betray Rusan and Olbin.

To be forsworn was a terrible thing.

Chapter Seven

PIRO LOOKED UP as Runt backed into the cabin with her evening meal. She had refused to join the captain and Siordun for dinner. After spending all afternoon trying to make the pendant glow, she was beyond frustrated.

'The lookout spotted sails,' Runt reported.

'Utland raiders?'

'A merchant ship.'

'If it had been Utlanders, would Nefysto attack?'

'Probably not with you and Agent Tyro on board,' Runt admitted and left.

Music started in the captain's cabin. Siordun played the dolcimela while the captain spouted poetry. She was glad she'd chosen to eat in her cabin. When she finished, she tried the pendant again.

But nothing worked.

'Stupid stone.' She glared at it. The music from the captain's cabin continued. 'Stupid music.'

That was odd. The ship's rhythm felt different, somehow. She placed her bare feet on the boards, the better to feel the movement.

The *Wyvern's Whelp* had changed course.

The music stopped. Jakulos' deep voice bellowed orders.

Piro found the sea-hounds on the high reardeck, staring at the other ship as their paths converged. The Rolencian vessel was headed west, back to the twin isles, while the *Wyvern's Whelp* was going east to Ostron Isle.

It was dusk, but there was enough light for Piro to make out the faces of the gathered sea-hounds. The reclusive ship's surgeon had come up from below with his apprentice; even the cook and his slow-top helper were there. Intrigued, her first instinct was to go to Dunstany for an explanation, but Dunstany had never existed. He had always been Siordun. So she went to Bantam instead. 'What's wrong with the other ship?'

'No one on deck. Lookout thinks they've lashed the wheel to maintain their heading.'

'What if the wind changes suddenly?'

'Exactly.'

'Why would they lash the wheel?'

'Perhaps everyone on board has come down with a terrible sickness,' the surgeon said. There was some muttering at this. 'But that isn't likely. We're only one day's sail from Ostron Isle. There wouldn't be time for the whole crew to take sick.'

'Mebbe they all jumped overboard,' a leathery old sea-hound muttered. 'When I was a cabin boy—'

'A hundred years ago,' some wit inserted, and several sailors chuckled.

The old sea-hound ignored them. 'We came across a ship like this, only the sails were in shreds. She'd been abandoned, y'see. There were several half-eaten'—he glanced to Piro—'...goats in the hold. Why would the crew abandon a perfectly good ship?'

'What did your captain do?' Nefysto asked.

'Bad Affinity, he said, so he—'

'There's no such thing as bad Affinity,' Siordun corrected. 'The evil is in the one who wields it.'

'Be that as it may. The cap'n wasn't taking no chances. He set fire to the ship. But the funny thing was... y'know how yer see rats abandon a sinking ship? Not one rat fled that ship.' The old sea-hound held Nefysto's eyes. 'If I was cap'n, I'd sail on by.'

'I'd be a fool not to claim a deserted ship, with a full hold,' Nefysto said. 'You heard Old Dalf. They explored the ship. Nothing attacked them. None of them took sick and nothing left the ship while it was burning. Whatever had killed or driven off the crew had moved on. Is it safe to board, Agent Tyro?'

Siordun turned to the old sailor. 'When they boarded the ship, did they spot any scales, feathers or droppings?'

'I dunno,' the old salt admitted. 'I was a lad of six summers. I kept me head down and did as I was told.'

Siordun shrugged. 'Then there's no way of knowing what drove the crew off. The bigger sea-dwelling Affinity beasts will kill and devour a man if they get the chance. The biggest of wyverns can carry off a man, but this was a whole ship and the crew would have banded together to fight off—'

'What of shade-rays?' a scarred sea-hound whispered. 'A seaman once told me they house the souls of dead Utlanders who long to go home. They say shade-rays can change into men, but can't walk on dry land. I figure Utlanders hate us, and a deck isn't dry land, so...'

Siordun shook his head.

'Nennirs?' Old Dalf suggested. 'Sea-horses can change form, too.'

'Despite the stories, very few things change form. And if they do, it is part of their life-cycle. Nennirs only drown sailors once they fall into the sea. I suppose a flock of Affinity birds could have landed on the ship. If they got down below...' Siordun fell silent as they drew alongside the abandoned vessel.

'No bodies or blood on the deck, and no sign of any damage to the sails or rigging,' Captain Nefysto reported. 'Bring her 'round. Prepare for boarding.'

The sea-hounds scattered, and Piro found herself alone with Siordun. 'Is it wise to board the ship?'

'Piro?' He frowned. 'Go to your cabin and stay there.'

She went, but only as far as the passage to the cabin and only until Siordun was distracted.

FYN STOOD IN the prow of the royal barge. He couldn't tell if the smudge on the horizon was Port Mero or a low cloud. The sun had set, and it was that time of day when the sky is brighter than the earth. The royal barge, for all the effort the rowers put in, seemed to barely move, yet they had left the becalmed yacht far behind.

He smelled wyvern and sensed Affinity. Hoping it was Isolt with Loyalty, he turned.

The wyvern was alone and she whined like a dog seeking comfort. Beast she might be, but she knew something was wrong.

'Come here, Loyalty.' He didn't offer a taste of power to entice her; unlike Piro, he didn't have Affinity to spare. Just sympathy. 'Isolt is looking after her people. She'll be sewing up wounds and giving medicines.'

The foenix flew down from the empty mainsail spar and landed near him. Fyn lifted his hand to stroke Resolute. The bird's long neck and legs looked too skinny, but his chest was developing scales to protect him in mating fights, and those spurs on his feet would one day contain deadly poison.

A lad of thirteen approached hesitantly.

'Time to feed them, Rhalwyn?'

The lad nodded and led the Affinity beasts away

A moment later a hand touched Fyn's back. He spun, arm rising in defence.

'Fyn?' Isolt stepped back, alarmed.

'I'm sorry.' He steadied her. 'Didn't hear you come up behind me.'

'Sometimes I forget you're a warrior monk.'

He released her and stepped away. 'You've seen to the wounded?'

'I've used all the supplies we have on board. But the children...' Her breath caught in a sob.

Unable to do otherwise, he pulled her into his arms, tucking her head under his chin. Her body shook as she wept, the heat of her damp tears seeping through his shirt. He felt himself harden and turned his hips away from her.

What was wrong with him?

He hated seeing her cry and wanted nothing more than to protect her. Every instinct told him to offer solace. To kiss her until she could think only of him.

Gently but firmly, he went to pull away.

She responded instantly, drawing back, wiping her cheeks and summoning a smile. It hurt him to see her like this. She'd had to be brave all her life before he came along.

'I've read of battles,' she said, her voice a little hoarse. 'I thought I knew what to expect. But you don't think of children getting hurt.'

'There is no glory in war.' He'd never believed there was. Well, maybe back when he was very young. But he'd been training under the abbey's weapons master since he was six. He'd seen the way the old monk looked at the boys sometimes, as if he was already mourning them.

The sound of a crying child reached them.

Isolt sighed. 'I should go back. Even the children who weren't injured are suffering from nightmares. I don't know what to do for them. I feel so useless.'

He caught her hand. 'You're not useless. Just seeing you helps them.'

'Maybe, but it's not enough.' And she left him.

It was not enough, these stolen moments. He wanted...

'The queen is nothing like her father,' Murheg said.

Fyn wondered how long the abbot had been watching from the shadows and set out to divert him. 'Back in Halcyon Abbey, I was trained in strategy and tactics by the weapons master. I memorised all the noble houses of Rolencia and their alliances, but I did not study Merofynia in the same detail. You know the noble houses. I'd appreciate your advice.'

'I'm honoured.' Murheg inclined his head. 'The spar attack will shock the nobles. Be prepared to have them descend on the palace. Quite a few are in Port Mero, and as for the rest... News travels fast across the Landlocked Sea.'

The words were meant to be reassuring, but they sent a stab of fear through Fyn.

The warlord of Centicore Spar was on their doorstep, flushed with success. What if Cortigern's true goal was Port Mero and the palace? If he marched his men along the shore, he would have to battle prosperous towns and farms, and he would still have to cross the Grand Canal to reach the palace. He'd be better off making the journey by sea. That meant stealing ships, but once he did, Port Mero would be at his mercy. The city-watch were trained to keep the peace and catch footpads, not fight off spar warriors. The docks were not defensible, and the palace was built for beauty.

As lord protector, Fyn had his work cut out for him.

Byren blinked when Orrade lit the lamp. Through the windows across the rear of the cabin, he could see the after-glow of the sun's setting rays.

'Feeling better?' Orrade asked.

Byren lifted his head off the table. Last he remembered they'd been talking...

'You fell asleep again.'

'Sorry.'

'You'll be right by tomorrow. You always did have the constitution of an ox.'

'Speaking of...' Byren's stomach rumbled. 'Is it dinner time yet?'

Orrade laughed.

Right on cue, the cabin boy knocked and opened the door. 'Cap'n Talltrees sent me to fetch you for dinner. They've set up a table on the reardeck.'

'About time.' Byren grinned and caught Orrade's eye. They came to their feet. As he went through the door into the passage, Byren had to duck. Nothing was built for a man his size. 'What's for dinner?'

'Beef an' red-wine stew,' the cabin boy supplied.

'Sounds good.'

'Probably wants to congratulate you on killing that wyvern,' Orrade said, following Byren down the passage towards the middeck door. 'Probably wants to make a long speech before we eat.'

Byren groaned.

'That or they've sighted Utland raiders.'

The cabin boy gave a squeak of fright.

'Don't say that, Orrie,' Byren chided. 'Not even in jest.'

'I wasn't jesting. I overheard the sailors. With all the war booty making its way back to Merofynia, the Utlanders have grown bold. Why, only...'

As Byren stepped out onto the middeck, a cloak swung over his head and he was dragged to one side.

Byren bellowed, driving himself backwards. He was rewarded with a grunt as his attackers collided with the cabin wall. But more men tackled him, bundling him up in the cloak. He struggled to free his arms, heard shouting, and realised they'd captured Orrade. He was not as big as Byren, but he was fast and, from the sound of the cursing, they were having trouble pinning him down.

Byren felt for his knife, only to discover someone had taken it. He tried to throw off his attackers and failed.

'I thought you said they'd be drugged?' the first mate shouted.

'I sent the wine,' Captain Talltrees snarled. 'Did you deliver it, brat?'

'I did, cap'n. But why would you drug—' The cabin boy yelped in pain.

Byren managed to get the cloak off and backed up, trying to work out what was going on.

The cabin boy wept in the boatswain's arms. Of the two dozen sailors, half had attacked and half hung back, looking surprised and uncertain.

Four sailors had hauled Orrade off his feet. They held him by his arms and legs as he struggled.

'Grab him,' Captain Talltrees ordered. Three of his sailors advanced on Byren.

'You'd betray me?' Byren demanded, noting how the boatswain and his men ducked their heads in shame. 'When I'm king—'

'King of nothing,' Captain Talltrees snarled. 'Cobalt'll pay a king's ransom for Byren the Usurper.'

'Usurper?' Byren repeated, almost speechless with fury. 'I'm no bastard!'

'According to Cobalt, your mother had Affinity. That makes you a bastard! A cowardly bastard who deserted his family because he wanted to claim the throne for himself and his lover.' The captain gestured. 'Throw the usurper's Servant of Palos overboard.'

'No!' Byren charged.

Orrade kicked and writhed as his captors carried him to the ship's side. Byren roared, trying to force his way through. The boatswain and his companions attacked the captain's supporters. It was a free for all, but they weren't going to make it in time. Byren saw them throw Orrade over the side, into the cold cruel sea.

Filled with a desperate fury, he fought his captors, cracking skulls and thumping ribs. He had to get free, had to save Orrie.

A roaring filled his head.

No. The roaring came from a horde of savage

Utlanders, pouring onto the deck. Byren grabbed a fallen weapon as the sailors united against the Utlanders.

But first Byren made sure the captain wouldn't betray him again. Before he could throw Orrade a rope, the Utlanders attacked him.

Garzik crouched below the ship's side as they approached their prey. He risked a look at the other vessel. The merchant sailors had gathered on deck for some kind of ceremony, or maybe a whipping. Around him, the Utlanders mocked the other ship's lookouts for not sounding the alarm. But why should they fear a fellow merchant ship, even a Merofynian ship? On the open sea, all hot-land merchant sailors united against their common enemies.

Another quick look told him the attack was imminent.

Olbin caught Garzik's eye and grinned, then leaped to his feet and gave the raiders' ferocious war cry. The Utlanders took up the cry. With a shudder their ship's timbers ground up against the merchant ship and the Utlanders swarmed the deck.

Garzik was in the rear, along with Luvrenc. The jostling for position had been fierce. Before he even set foot on the other ship he could hear screams, punctuated by the ring of metal striking metal.

He leaped onto the ship's gunwale, caught hold of a rope and searched the deck. If it was clear the merchant sailors were losing, he'd hang back. To his relief, it looked like the other ship's crew had united behind a real warrior.

Garzik jumped down and plunged into the fray, dodging struggling men. He was so intent on what was happening up ahead, he didn't notice someone staggering his way; he collapsed under an injured sailor. Hot sticky blood covered his face and throat. He shoved the man aside, rolling to his feet.

Weighing up the odds, Garzik turned the flat of his sword against the defenders. At one point Olbin's unprotected back was right in front of him, but he could not bring himself to strike the big Utlander. The battle for the ship swirled and eddied like a river, flowing from one side of the deck to the other.

Somehow, Garzik found himself in the thick of battle. The defenders' leader was a huge warrior who swung his sword like...

Byren? Garzik couldn't believe his eyes. Surely it couldn't be? In the fading light, he wasn't sure. This man looked thinner and older. And he'd never seen Byren's face twisted in such a ferocious grimace.

An Utlander screamed and went down beside Garzik, who found himself facing Byren, too stunned to move. Without a glimmer of recognition, Byren brought his sword around in a powerful arc to decapitate Garzik. Olbin stepped in and took the force of the blow, shoving Garzik aside.

Rusan sounded the Utland horn, signalling retreat. The raiders turned and ran, helping injured companions.

Garzik tripped over a body. He sprawled on the deck, pretending to be stunned, hoping he'd be left behind.

Olbin hauled Garzik to his feet, swung him over his shoulder and ran for their ship. A dark, sea-filled gap had opened up between the two vessels.

Olbin jumped.

The impact of the landing drove the air from Garzik's chest with a grunt. Gasping for breath, he looked back. Already, the other ship had fallen away behind them, its sails silhouetted against the first of the evening stars.

Garzik was shocked. Byren had nearly struck his head from his shoulders. Surely he had not changed that much?

Olbin lowered him to the deck. 'You all right?' His big hands ran over Garzik, looking for injuries. Finding nothing, he grinned. 'A blow to the head stunned you? Just as well you've got a thick skull.'

'Look at this!' Jost pointed to Trafyn, who was hardly restrained at all. Half the ropes had fallen to his feet.

'I didn't...' Trafyn protested. 'It wasn't...'

The big Utlander nudged Garzik. 'Set him free, then take your turn in the crow's nest. Watch for wyverns. Blood attracts them, so wash first.'

Garzik scrambled to obey him. As he released Trafyn, he warned, 'Say nothing of our plans.'

'As if I would,' Trafyn sneered.

Then Garzik doused himself in seawater and scrambled up to the lookout.

While the Utlanders dealt with their dead and injured on the deck below, he scanned the horizon. Night had fallen. The sky was awash with a froth of stars and the other ship was a dark silhouette in the distance. No doubt they were counting themselves lucky.

What was Byren doing on a ship headed for Rolencia? Had he been to Ostron Isle? He couldn't have been to Merofynia, not when they were at war.

It was frustrating to have come so close, only to miss his chance. At least he knew Byren still lived.

THE MOMENT THE Utlanders began to retreat, Byren ran to the ship's side. He could see nothing in the dark sea other than the ship's wake glowing on the wave crests behind them. Cupping his mouth, he shouted for all he was worth. 'Orrie! Orrie, hold on. I'm coming for you.'

No answer. The waves were so deep a man could be lost a stone's throw away.

Byren swung around, grabbing the boatswain.

'I didn't know the cap'n meant to sell you to Cobalt,' the old sailor protested.

'You're captain now.' Byren had no time for this. He'd been lucky that the Utlanders had struck when they did. 'Turn back. Find my friend.'

The newly appointed captain's expression told Byren

he did not to hold out much hope, but he ordered the ship to change tack.

Byren rolled Talltrees's body over and retrieved the farseer. He ran up the steps to the high foredeck, to search the sea.

Sylion's Luck. It was too dark. He raked the sea, searching... searching. Behind him he heard the new captain yell orders. The dead Utlanders were to be thrown overboard. The crew's dead were sewn into shrouds and buried at sea.

All this was done, and still Byren searched without success.

He lowered the farseer and beckoned the captain. 'We've gone past the point where my friend was thrown overboard, haven't we?'

He nodded.

'Which way would the current carry him?'

The old sailor glanced to one side.

'Then that's the way we go. We'll quarter the sea until we find him.'

The captain didn't talk about the cold, or the sea's predators. His expression was far more eloquent.

Byren cursed. Why hadn't he moved faster? Why hadn't he suspected Talltrees of treachery? Come to think of it, why hadn't the captain gotten rid of Orrade earlier?

Because they'd needed him to nurse Byren back to health. Cobalt needed Byren alive so he could hold a trial and destroy his reputation before executing him. And he only needed to do this if there were Rolencians who still believed in Byren.

But that was cold comfort right now.

No time for doubts. He would save Orrie.

He would never give up.

Chapter Eight

JUDGING THE MOMENT right, Piro slipped out of the passage onto the middeck. Keeping close to the wall, she remained out of sight of those on the reardeck. A quick glance told her they were preoccupied.

It had taken time to turn the vessel. Now they were only a bowshot behind the abandoned merchant ship and gaining rapidly.

Jakulos waited with several sailors, all carrying grappling hooks and ropes. A thrill ran through Piro. This was how the sea-hounds tackled Utland ships.

'I'll go first,' Siordun said, coming down the steps. 'Board on my signal.'

Piro held her breath, but he hadn't seen her. The rest of the sea-hounds clustered along the side of the ship as they approached the merchant vessel.

'A light!' Runt cried, pointing.

Piro darted over. She was in time to see a boy of about ten come out of the merchant ship's cabins with a lantern. He was followed by a white-whiskered man swinging a cleaver and a lad of about fourteen with a large wooden carpenter's mallet. All three had bandages wrapped around their heads, and they searched the deck as if they were after small but dangerous creatures.

So preoccupied were the merchant ship's crew, they didn't notice the *Wyvern's Whelp*.

The youth pointed and all three charged across the deck towards the mainmast.

At the same moment, four grown men climbed out of the hold. Like the others, their heads were bandaged. One carried a lantern, the second a net, the third a shovel and the fourth a wooden bucket with a lid.

'Stop!' the shovel-wielder yelled at the first three, who appeared to have something cornered between the mainmast and the water barrel.

Either the white-whiskered man didn't hear him or he chose to ignore him as he raised the cleaver. The cabin boy yelped and jumped back, dropping the lantern. It smashed, spilling burning oil across the deck.

Instead of stamping out the fire, the sailors concentrated their efforts on the trapped creature. Piro didn't understand. What could be more terrifying than fire on a ship?

Siordun cupped his hands and shouted across to the other ship. 'Leave it alone. You'll only make it defend itself.'

The fourteen-year-old screamed. Falling to the deck, he hugged his leg and rolled about. 'Me foot! Me foot! Quick, cut it off!'

Siordun turned to Jakulos. 'I need to board that ship.'

The boatswain flung the grappling hook, which connected with a satisfying *thunk*. Others followed. As the vessels drew closer, the lad kept begging them to cut off his foot.

'Don't do it!' Siordun shouted. 'I'm coming over. I can help.'

The lad had passed out. Just as well. Two of the men held his leg straight, while another raised the cleaver. Meanwhile, the remaining crew stamped out the flames.

Piro assumed the creature had escaped in the confusion.

The vessels shuddered as their sides touched and the sea-hounds lashed them together. Startled, the other crew looked up, some reaching for weapons.

'Captain Nefysto of the *Wyvern's Whelp*, come to your aid,' the captain yelled and gestured to Siordun. 'We have a Power-worker and a ship's surgeon.'

The white-whiskered man sprang to his feet, pulled the bandage off his head and took something out of both ears. 'What?'

Nefysto repeated himself, adding, 'Looks like you're having trouble with an Affinity beast.'

'Aye. Thanks to the spice merchant. A Power-worker, ye say? Come aboard.'

'Don't amputate the lad's leg. Not yet, anyway.' Siordun jumped onto the other deck. 'Bring everyone up on deck. If you see the creatures, back off and let me know.' He looked over his shoulder to the surgeon. 'Wasilade?'

'Coming.' The surgeon pushed past Piro. 'Where is that stupid boy? He should be back by now.' He grabbed Runt's arm. 'Find my apprentice. I sent him below for my bag.'

Piro caught up with Runt at the hatch to the hold. 'I'll get him.'

Eager to stay and watch, Runt did not argue.

She headed for the surgeon's workroom, where she found the apprentice holding a bag in one hand and a rolled-up leather apron in the other.

Seeing her, he jumped with fear and guilt.

'The surgeon wants you,' Piro told him. 'They're about to cut off the lad's foot. Hurry or you'll miss it.'

Etore went even paler, dumped the things on the work table, covered his mouth and ran out of the cabin. She heard him throwing up in the passage.

Piro smiled, grabbed the bag and the apron, and went up on deck. No one tried to stop her as she climbed onto the merchant ship's deck.

The belligerent shovel-wielder and the white-whiskered man had gone, but the rest of the crew stood around watching the surgeon, who knelt by the side of the unconscious youth, listening to his chest.

'This is for Surgeon Wasilade.' Piro handed the bag and apron to one of the men, then went around behind the group, trying to find a good vantage point.

'He's stopped breathing,' the net-man told the surgeon. 'Yer too late.'

'Not if the Power-worker is right. A few drops of this under his tongue should...' Wasilade opened a jar. 'Hold the boy's mouth open.'

Several men shook their heads. The net-man muttered, 'I'm not touchin'—'

Piro shoved past them and did as instructed. The surgeon was focused on his patient and didn't acknowledge her. She saw him dribble some of the liquid into the lad's mouth.

'Hold him.'

None of the men moved.

'Hold him!'

The youth's body arched and his heels drummed on the deck. The merchant sailors fought to hold his arms and legs down and Piro almost lost her grip on his head.

No one spoke until the seizures stopped.

Pale and still, the lad lay there with blood-flecked spittle dribbling from the side of his mouth. The sailors waited in silence as the surgeon tried to wake the youth. There was no reaction.

'I told yer...' the net-man muttered.

'His heart beats,' Wasilade said. 'If you believe in a god or goddess, now is the time to pray.'

Piro went to find Siordun. She heard angry shouting, interspersed with Siordun's measured tones, and slipped into the passage where she found the cabin boy listening at a partially open door. Piro joined him and they peeped into the captain's cabin. The white-whiskered man sat behind the desk and the belligerent man still held his shovel, which he shook to emphasise what he was saying. '...and I'm telling you, this is all legal and above board. Lord Cobalt relaxed the laws on importing Affinity beasts and products, and Merchant Yarraskem brought the cargo on Ostron Isle. I have the papers to prove it. It's none of your business what my master imports.'

'Don't tell me what's legal, Nikoforus,' Siordun said. 'I'm talking about what's *right*. And it'll be everyone's business if your master brings dangerous Affinity creatures into Rolencia.'

'Niko told me they were safe,' the white-whiskered captain said.

'Affinity beasts are never "safe,"' Siordun said, turning to the merchant's agent. 'They can never be truly tamed.'

He was wrong. Piro knew her foenix loved her.

'Affinity beasts are safe if they haven't hatched,' Nikoforus argued. 'What's safer than an egg? And if yon silly cabin boy hadn't opened the box to take a look—'

'But they *had* hatched. Miron heard them crying,' the captain countered. 'You told me they wouldn't hatch until after we made port. You told me they were to be sold as pets for rich men's wives and children. You told me they were pretty little winged creatures, which sang sweet songs. You—'

'And so they are, if they're looked after proper. But your crazy cook took to them with a cleaver. No wonder they're frightened.'

'My cook and boatswain are both dead. These—'

'What kind of Affinity beasts are they?' Siordun asked the merchant's agent.

'You won't have heard of them,' Nikoforus told him. 'They're a new crossbreed, kresatrices. Kressies for short. Bred to be pets.'

'Next you'll be telling me you got them for a good price,' Siordun said. 'Keeping Affinity beast as pets has gone out of fashion on Ostron Isle. I bet the breeder was glad to be rid of them. How big did you say they were?'

'Big as a half-grown cat.'

'And how big are they supposed to grow?'

'He said knee high...' But now Nikoforus sounded uneasy.

'If the hatchlings' bites can kill a man, what do you think they'll do when they are mature?'

Piro suspected the men were going to argue all night. Meanwhile the Affinity creatures roamed the ship. She turned to the boy. 'You're Miron?'

He nodded. 'I didn't know they'd turn nasty. They looked so sweet and frightened, but when I tried to give them a bowl of milk and honey they swarmed all over me.'

Piro nodded. 'Kresatrices...' She supposed they were a mix between a cockatrice and a kresillum. A full grown male cockatrice stood taller than a man, with razor sharp leg spurs, wings and a serpent's tail. It could spit deadly poison, accurate up to two body-lengths. The feathers of a cockatrice were fine as fur and highly prized, but the beasts were not something you'd keep as a pet. The kresillum, on the other hand, was the size of a cat. Its hard shell protected it from predators, and if that failed it would sing so sweetly that the predator forgot everything. They weren't poisonous, but if someone had been cross-breeding the two, who knew what the result would be?

The spice merchant's agent was right about one thing—the creatures had been defending themselves. If she left it up to the captain, he'd catch them and kill them. If she left it up to the merchant, he'd sell them. She would have to catch the frightened hatchlings herself.

Florin and Varuska left the betrothal celebrations early. Florin felt weary as she helped the false-Piro strip off her finery. So much had happened since they'd both entered the castle this morning.

'This is your chance,' Varuska whispered. She stood by the fire, wearing one of Piro's nightgowns. Stray wisps of her long hair rose in the hot drafts coming from the flames. 'Go find my sister now.'

'As soon as you're in bed.'

Varuska climbed in and pulled up the covers. 'Give her my bundle. Anatoley can wear my things.'

Florin nodded.

'Tell her I'm safe. Don't tell her about...' Varuska gestured to the chamber, her pretty face pinched with fear. 'Granna mustn't worry.'

Florin nodded.

Here she was, running messages for Piro's imposter when she should have been assassinating Cobalt. But it was thanks to Varuska's masquerade that Florin knew Cobalt's manservant was really an Ostronite assassin. She would have to take Amil into consideration when she killed Cobalt.

Whatever happened, she was not going to put Varuska's life in danger.

Florin closed the door to Piro's chamber and backed into a man-at-arms. Fool, she should have anticipated Cobalt would set a guard.

'Here, where are you off to?' He steadied her. A gleam lit up his eyes. 'Breeches, eh?'

Florin sent him a cold look. 'I need my bundle.'

Just then two men came down the corridor carrying a blanket-wrapped body between them. In a castle this size, with its many servants and visitors, someone was always sick and dying.

After they'd gone, the man-at-arms was no longer interested in her breeches. 'Fetch your bundle. An' be quick about it.'

Florin nodded, heading off down the passage. With every step she took, a feeling of foreboding grew. From Byren's description, Cobalt was not the benevolent kind. Now that she thought about it, Old Mirona and Anatoley would be better off leaving tonight before Cobalt could reconsider and give Amil different orders.

As Florin rounded the bend, she nearly bumped into a candle-trimmer. They both jumped. He was half her size and nervous as a mouse. She would have apologised, but he hurried away with his step-stool and candle snuffer.

Florin entered the female servants' chamber to find it in darkness. Only a glimmer of light came through the high window. She collected Varuska's bundle and felt her way towards the old woman's pallet. 'Mirona?'

No answer.

Of course, it had been her body the men had been carrying. Poor old thing...

Florin's boot crunched on something underfoot. She tucked the bundle under her arm, knelt and felt for the object. Her fingers found the shattered goddess.

Old Mirona had not died of natural causes.

Florin had to find Anatoley before Cobalt's thugs did. Sick with horror, she fled.

Piro turned to the cabin boy. 'Show me where you were keeping the kresatrices.'

'We had them in the galley.' Miron scurried along the hall and out onto the middeck, where the crew were still gathered around the injured youth. They crossed the deck unnoticed and climbed down the ladder.

The huge cast-iron stove, with its many warming plates and two ovens, stood amidst the chaos of copper pots, pans and food. Half-covered in debris, a large grey-haired man sprawled dead on the galley floor.

'That's Cookie. Staz is his apprentice.' Miron saw she didn't understand. Tears filled his eyes. 'Staz got bitten. I shoulda—'

'Couldn't be helped.' Piro squeezed his shoulder. It made sense to keep the Affinity beast eggs in the galley, where it was warm. 'Bet Cookie didn't like having Affinity cargo in his kitchen.'

'How did you know?'

She knew cooks and she knew Affinity beasts. If she was lucky, she'd find the kresatrices curled up asleep in their nest. 'Where were they kept?'

'This way.' Miron picked a path through the pots and pans, giving the dead cook a wide berth.

'It must have been a terrible fight,' Piro observed.

'When they swarmed me, Cookie roared like a wyvern and swung his cleaver. He saved my life.'

'How many kressies were there?'

'Nine.'

'All of them hatched?'

Miron nodded.

'Did Cookie kill any?'

'Just the one.' Miron pointed to a large over-turned baking dish on the floor. 'There.'

Piro lifted the dish gingerly. She needn't have worried. The kresatrice was well and truly dead, its body hacked to bits.

Miron sniffed and hunkered down. 'Poor kressie.'

Piro turned the little thing over. It had the hard plates of a kresillum, but with its lizard's tail, legs and neck, it was most like a cockatrice. The small, feathered wings wouldn't have been strong enough to lift it off the ground. The face was curiously sweet. Now dull in death, in life the large eyes would have been jewel-like, but that small snout contained...

'Fangs.' Piro pointed. 'That'll be how it injects poison. Wish I knew what the surgeon used to revive—'

'He saved Staz?'

'Too soon to be sure,' Piro told him. 'Are the kressies all this pretty?'

'I only got a quick look, but some were prettier.' Miron crawled over to the stove. 'This is where we kept them.' The great cast iron stove sat in a tiled sand-box to prevent the heat from the stove scorching the deck. The cabin boy pointed to a chest with a distinctive symbol on the side. 'It was filled with straw to stop the eggs from breaking.'

Now it was filled with eggshells.

'It's very deep. Are there more eggs underneath?' Piro went to dig her hands down into the straw, then thought better of it. Taking a knife, she carefully parted the broken eggshells and straw. 'There's a rock.'

She put the knife aside and removed the rock. There were veins of something pretty running through it, and when she touched these, she sensed...

'Affinity?' It all made sense. 'The mother would have kept the eggs warm, but they needed both heat and Affinity or the babies wouldn't mature and hatch.'

Piro placed the Affinity stone on the table and dusted off her hands. Siordun would want to see this. 'We should take the body up. I'll need a big pot with a lid.' She spotted just the thing.

Behind her, Miron whimpered.

Piro slowly turned. Three kresatrices had climbed over the cook's body. They perched on the cook's broad chest, their tiny mouths stained with blood. Serpentine tongues tasted the air.

Two of them had red chests with iridescent blue markings on the neck and legs. The third was emerald green with red markings. Three sets of jewel-bright eyes fixed on Piro.

'They're so colourful,' she whispered. 'They should have been easy to find.'

Miron dug into his pockets. 'Where did I put me...'

The kresatrices began to whine. Piro found the sound annoying, but Miron swayed in time to it, sinking to his knees. She caught his arm. 'What are you...'

He gave her a dreamy smile.

The kresatrices made a soft noise, and she looked up. They were now less than a body-length away, eyes bright with malice.

No time to call for help. Piro knew her Affinity was good for only one thing. She concentrated on gathering her power, felt it slide down her arm until her fingers throbbed with each beat of her heart.

On sensing her Affinity, the kresatrices' whine became higher-pitched and eager.

'Come here, kressies,' Piro crooned, edging to one side so that the empty roasting pot was between her and the creatures. 'Come taste what I have for you.'

They came, scattering food and pans. She held one hand over the roasting pot, reaching for the lid with the other. The kresatrices reached the edge of the pot. Intent on the treat, two climbed into it while the third struggled to climb in.

The first two reached Piro's hand. Their tongues flickered out, tickling her skin. They stopped whining and Miron gasped as if waking.

'Don't move,' Piro whispered. The third kresatrice tumbled into the pot and she slammed the lid down fast.

'You did it!' Miron marvelled. 'But how did you do it?'

'I offered them my Affinity,' Piro said. She might not be able to make Siordun's stupid stone glow, but surely this proved she was worth training. 'I'm the Power-worker's apprentice.'

'What are you doing down here?' Siordun barked from the doorway. Behind him were Nikoforus and the ship's captain.

'Catching kresatrices,' Piro said, coming to her feet with the big roasting pot in her arms. 'There's three in here. With the dead one, that leaves five still to catch.'

'We have three dead ones laid out on deck,' the captain said.

'There goes my commission,' Nikoforus muttered.

Piro ignored him. 'That leaves two for us to find.'

'You lured them with Affinity?' Siordun asked.

She nodded.

'I don't need your help, Power-worker,' Nikoforus said. 'I have it under control.'

'Like you did when you left an Affinity stone in the same chest as the eggs?' Piro asked, pointing to the chest.

Siordun went over and inspected the stone. 'Look at the size of it. It's no wonder the creatures hatched early.'

'The breeder assured me they needed it.' Nikoforus sent Piro a look of loathing. He beckoned the cabin boy. 'There's a chest in my cabin with the same symbol as that one. Go fetch it.'

Miron ran off, and Nikoforus swept everything off the galley table onto the floor. The loud clatter of pots and pans made the kresatrices panic. Piro heard their little claws scrabbling around inside the metal pot. The lid rose slightly. She put the roasting pot on a chair and sat on it, which gave her a good view of the table when Miron returned with the second chest.

Nikoforus opened it and felt around in the packing straw. 'These are talismans. When a child is given a pet kresatrice, they're also given a talisman to tame it.'

He pulled out an object the size of his fist, tied up in cloth. The captain and the cabin boy watched, fascinated, as he untied the cloth to reveal two stones, one much larger than the other. The large one had been worked so that the small one slotted into it neatly. He displayed the two stones. 'The large one is to chastise and the smaller is to reward.'

'A pair of sorbt stones?' Piro guessed.

'Sorbt stones,' Siordun agreed.

Piro frowned. 'I don't see—'

'The larger one absorbs power. It would sting a kresatrice,' Siordun said. 'The smaller one is a sealer stone. As long as the two stones are in contact, the small one stops the larger one from absorbing power.'

'Then why would the small one reward the kressies?' Piro asked.

'Because, over time, the small stone absorbs the power stored in the big stone. Think how good a fire-warmed stone feels on a cold winter's night when you crawl into bed. That's how it would feel to an Affinity creature.'

Piro held out her hand. 'Can I see?'

With reluctance, the merchant's agent gave her the joined stones. She hissed, dropping them.

'Stupid girl,' Nikoforus snarled. 'You'll break the talisman.'

'It burned my skin.' Piro licked her palm and blew on it.

'That's not right. Show me.' Siordun held out his hand.

'Careful,' Piro warned.

Siordun tucked his sleeve over his palm, then tested the talisman on his bare skin. He grimaced. 'You've been had twice over, Nikoforus.'

'The absorber stone works. I saw you flinch.'

'That's true. But the sealer stone doesn't.' Siordun put the stones on the table. 'Turn up the lamp. I'll need the sharpest knife you can find.'

Miron adjusted the lamp.

'Here.' The captain handed over his dagger. 'Best steel there is, and I sharpen it every day.'

'The absorber stone is obsidiate,' Siordun said. 'It's rare, but not as rare as jadian, the sealer stone. Jadian is harder even than steel. If I can scratch this piece...' He removed the smaller stone from its niche and scraped the tip of the knife over the surface.

The blade left a mark. Siordun expelled his breath. 'Just as I thought. Soapstone.'

'Stone made of soap?' Miron muttered.

'No, a stone that looks like jadian but is softer and easy to carve. Unscrupulous gem merchants will sell it as—'

Nikoforus bristled. 'One poor quality stone does not mean the rest—'

'Then give me another to test.'

'Pick one yourself.'

'I'm not putting my hands in there. I could be burnt.'

'Miron.' Piro nodded to the cabin boy, who dug around in the straw for another talisman. 'Now take the jadian out of the absorber stone.'

While he was tipping the jadian out, Siordun asked for a hair. Intrigued, Piro supplied one. He tied the hair tightly around the sealer stone, then lit a taper.

'If this stone is pure jadian, it will absorb the heat and the hair won't burn. Come closer.'

They all obeyed.

The hair burned.

Siordun blew out the taper. 'You were cheated, Nikoforus. The breeder was glad to get rid of the kresatrices, and the talismans are cheap fakes.'

The merchant's agent dropped into a chair, head in his hands. 'What will Master Yarraskem say?'

'Tell him he's lucky the creatures hatched early,' Piro suggested. 'Imagine what would have happened if they'd hatched after you'd sold them. The talismans would have made the kressies really angry, and the rich merchants and nobles would have—'

'Tell Yarraskem he shouldn't be dealing in Affinity if he doesn't know enough about it. Tell him that Agent Tyro confiscated the kresatrices and the useless talismans.' Siordun gestured to the chests. 'When I get back to Ostron Isle, I'll be having a word with my master. Mage Tsulamyth doesn't condone the breeding of dangerous Affinity beasts, *or* the sale of fraudulent Affinity talismans.'

At the mention of the mage, the captain sucked in his breath and the merchant's agent went pale.

'Please assure the mage that Merchant Yarraskem doesn't want any trouble,' Nikoforus said quickly.

Piro glanced to Siordun. So much rested on him. It was just as well no one knew Siordun was really the mage. She realised she was proud of him.

Siordun wiped his hands. 'Now we must catch the surviving kresatrices.'

Piro handed the roasting pot to the captain. 'I'll help. The kressies will come to me.'

Chapter Nine

FLORIN TUCKED THE bundle under her arm and ran off to find Varuska's sister. Fortunately, she knew just where to look for Anatoley.

To discourage licentious behaviour, the castle-keep separated male and female servants. Scullery maids and the like bunked down in the castle laundry.

Heart pounding, Florin paused at the laundry door to catch her breath. She could hear the women singing a sentimental song, and glanced inside to see them mending clothes by candlelight. The aroma of starch and lye hung on the air, reminding Florin of washdays back home at the tradepost. That was one thing she did not miss.

Two dozen pallet beds fanned out from the great copper where the castle's laundry was boiled. As the most recently hired servant, Anatoley would be most distant from the warmth of the copper's brazier.

One bed was empty. She was too late.

Stunned, Florin pulled back, closing the door after her. Why hadn't she been suspicious when Cobalt told Amil to send Old Mirona and Anatoley home with a bag of coins? How could the castle-keep be so blind? Or was the woman willing to overlook anything her darling Illien did?

A noise made Florin turn. Varuska's sister came around the corner. The poor girl was almost asleep on her feet.

Florin ran to meet her.

Frightened, Anatoley backed up into a doorway. 'I wasn't slacking off. I only just finished scrubbing the floor.' She held up her reddened hands as evidence. 'See.'

'...have some fun with the juicy young bird,' a rough voice said.

The thugs had gotten rid of Old Mirona's body and now they were coming for Varuska's sister. Desperate, Florin pushed the girl into a doorway.

Anatoley went to protest.

'Quiet.' Florin felt for the door catch. Locked. Where could they hide?

Too late; the men were upon them.

More than once today, Florin had been mistaken for a manservant from behind, thanks to her broad shoulders. Desperate, she cupped the girl's chin and kissed her. Anatoley gasped.

Florin made sure her larger body hid the girl's as the thugs offered her some crude advice before carrying on past them. Dimly, she heard the men asking at the laundry for Anatoley.

Varuska's sister froze.

A woman told the thugs that the girl they sought was scrubbing the kitchen floor. As the men went the other way, Florin kept up the pretence, shielding Anatoley.

The moment the thugs rounded the corner, Florin broke the kiss, grabbed Anatoley's hand and ran. The dark corridors quickly swallowed them.

After only one false turn, she found the door to the stable courtyard. A froth of stars filled the sky, and the night was bright enough to cast sharp shadows. Florin drew Varuska's sister onto the landing.

'Why were they looking for me?' Anatoley gasped. 'Did the castle-keep send you?'

'Varuska sent me. Here, take this.' She thrust the bundle into the girl's arms.

Anatoley eyed it suspiciously. 'This is my sister's. What's happened to her?'

'She's all right, but you...' Florin had no practice at lying. 'Your sister is doing a special job for Lord Cobalt. She told me to send you away.'

Anatoley hesitated. 'Those men—'

'Were sent to kill you. They've already killed Old Mirona. Anyone who knows Varuska's true identity has to die. Cobalt wants her to impersonate the kingsdaughter. She looks a lot like Piro.'

'Does she?' Anatoley asked, then gave a little crow of laughter. 'Of course she does. I must tell Granna. How she'll laugh.'

'Why?'

The girl rolled her eyes. 'Granna is King Byren the Fourth's bastard. Cobalt's father was not King Byren's only by-blow.'

Florin felt her jaw drop.

'When he was seventeen and still only the king's heir, Byren the Fourth killed an Affinity beast that had been preying on our village. The elders gave him the prettiest girl. She wasn't supposed to fall pregnant, but she did. The village elders married her off to the blacksmith's son and Granna was born. She is King Rolen's half-sister, it's no wonder Varuska looks like King Rolen's daughter,' Anatoley announced triumphantly.

She looked so pleased that Florin shook her by the shoulders. 'You can't tell *anyone*. If word gets out, Cobalt will have Varuska killed.' It occurred to Florin that once the girl had provided him with an heir, he would have her killed anyway. But she wasn't going to let it get that far.

'Leave tonight,' Florin told Anatoley. 'Run away. Don't go home. Sail for Ostron isle. You'll be safe there.'

'But Granna and Varuska are all I have.'

'If you want to protect them, go away.'

Anatoley stared at her. 'I'll be all alone.'

'You'll be alive.'

'And my silly sister will be queen. It's not fair!'

'Look, we don't have time for this. Go to the stables. Hide in one of the carts that goes down to Rolenton tomorrow. Work your passage on a ship. I promised Varuska I'd help you escape. Now it's up to you. Promise me you'll go?'

The girl looked more aggrieved than frightened, but she nodded.

'Good.' Florin gave her a shove. 'Keep out of sight. Those men, or others like them, will be looking for you.'

With that, she shut the door on Anatoley and made her way back to Piro's chambers, where the man-at-arms waited.

He glanced to her empty hands. 'What took you so long, and where's your bundle?'

'Someone nicked it.' The lie sprang from desperation. 'I spent ages looking.'

'Well, what d'you expect? Besides, you're serving the kingsdaughter. You'll want for nothing.' He opened the door for her.

Florin thanked him and ducked into the chamber. It was dim, lit only by the fire.

Varuska sat up. 'Is—'

'Just me,' Florin said. Was the guard listening at the door? She shivered. 'I c-couldn't find my bundle, someone had taken it.'

Varuska looked confused, but didn't say anything.

Florin bent down to unstrap her boots. Then, without invitation, she climbed into bed with Varuska. Under the covers, she whispered, 'Don't worry, your sister's safe.'

'Why wouldn't she be?'

Hearing the edge of panic in Varuska's voice, Florin decided not to reveal Old Mirona's fate. 'I gave Anatoley your bundle. She's going to leave tomorrow.'

'Thank you.'

Florin swung her legs out of bed. The floor was cold.

'Where are you going?'

'You're a kingsdaughter. I'm a mountain girl who's masquerading as your servant. I sleep on the floor.'

Florin curled up on the rug in front of the fire and dreamed of Byren, who laughed as large as life. She woke with tears on her cheeks.

PIRO ENJOYED WORKING alongside Siordun. They captured the kresatrices and returned to the *Wyvern's Whelp*, where the creatures were placed in a cage in the hold.

Piro sat with Siordun, watching the five kresatrices explore their temporary home. She was ready to soothe them with Affinity if they needed it, but they curled up together on the blanket.

'They're falling asleep.' Piro hugged her knees and sighed with satisfaction. It was nice down here, away from everyone else. Her Affinity no longer troubled her. This reminded her... 'You're wrong, you know.'

'No. But I'm sure you're about to tell me why.'

She grinned. 'You said Affinity beasts could never be tamed, only contained. But Resolute loves me.'

'That's because you shared your Affinity with him.'

'What about Isolt? Loyalty loves her even though Isolt has no Affinity. Why did you tell us to take Loyalty with us if she couldn't be tamed?'

'The wyvern is the symbol of Merofynian royalty. I thought she might be useful.' Siordun cast Piro a quick look. 'You might recall I also told you to bring the sea-fruits to keep the wyvern quiet.'

But Piro had already thought of something else. 'Back on Ostron Isle, when the Utland Power-worker's men abducted Isolt, Loyalty tried to save her. The wyvern would have died, if you hadn't healed her. Why heal her if...' Piro's eyes widened. 'You lied to Nikoforus and the captain!'

'I said what I did to prevent them importing Affinity beasts.' Siordun shrugged. 'Who knows if Affinity beasts are ever truly tamed? Is a cat truly tamed, or does it just put up with us?'

Piro laughed. 'That's something Lord Dunstany would say.'

'I am Dunstany.'

And the mage, but that made her uncomfortable. She cast about for another topic. 'I miss Resolute and Loyalty. I miss Isolt. Can I visit her? Will she have a big celebration for her fifteenth birthday?'

'Isolt's already fifteen. She'll be sixteen midsummer.'

'Oh. I'm sure Seela said Isolt wasn't much older than—'

'How old was your nurse? Sixty? Two years would be nothing to her.'

Piro looked down. She should have paid more attention to her mother and Seela, but they were always reprimanding her for not behaving like a respectable kingsdaughter.

No, this was the life for her. She liked being useful and being valued for what she could do. One of the kresatrices twitched in its sleep, making her smile. 'Will the kressies need more Affinity?'

'You gave them more than enough. Too much power can be bad for Affinity beasts. There's a theory they can become addicted to it. There's another theory that it spurs unnaturally rapid growth.'

'Theories... doesn't anyone know for sure?'

'Power-workers guard their knowledge.'

'Why not share it? Then everyone would be safer. If Affinity wasn't shrouded in so much secrecy, Nikoforus wouldn't have been fooled.'

'True.'

'Just as well I was there.' Piro wanted one word of praise. She wanted Siordun to admit he'd needed her help.

But he seemed distracted.

Disappointed, Piro stood up. 'I'm tired. I guess I'll...'

Without warning, Siordun sprang to his feet and grabbed her shoulders. 'I told you to go back to your cabin. Why—'

'You're hurting me. Why are you so angry?'

He let her go. 'Why did you board the merchant ship?'

'To help you.'

'I didn't need your help.'

Tears stung her eyes. 'I saved lives.'

'You put yourself in danger.'

'And you didn't?'

'That's different.'

'How is it different?' She pushed his chest. 'How?'

He lifted his hands, as if he'd like to grab her. 'You... you're impossible!'

For some reason, this pleased her. 'You needed me. Even if you won't admit it.'

With a toss of her head, she walked off.

AFTER A RAID, the Utlanders usually had a drunken celebration. But after the disastrous attack, there was nothing to celebrate. Instead they treated their wounded and sat around in small groups, muttering darkly. From what Garzik overhead, they believed their people had been cursed since Vultar's renegades had kidnapped the settlement's oracles. Born fused, back-to-back, one could see past and the other the future, earning them the names Yesterday and Tomorrow. In the Utlands, those born with afflictions tended to be blessed by Affinity, and the twins had been famous throughout the Northern Dawn Isles. Now the settlement was without their Affinity-touched to intervene with the gods.

Too exhausted to stay awake, Garzik curled up in his furs. After a while, he felt Trafyn creep in next to him and did not object. As a slave, the squire didn't have furs of his own.

Sometime later the squire's shivering woke him. Trafyn

tossed and turned, muttering under his breath about wyverns and raiders. Garzik shoved him. 'Quiet.'

The squire whimpered and called for his Da, sounding more like a lad of five than fifteen. Garzik felt Trafyn's forehead. He was burning him up with fever.

As much as Garzik disliked the squire, he could not ignore him. Trafyn wasn't hardy like the Utlanders. If he slept exposed on deck, it would be the end of him. He needed herbs to bring the fever down.

With a sigh, Garzik rolled to his feet and looked around. Strange, the sleeping furs were empty except for the badly wounded. Where had... Voices carried to him and he realised the majority of the Utlanders were on the high reardeck, where they appeared to be holding a meeting.

Garzik rolled the squire onto the furs and dragged him into the merchant captain's cabin. There, he tucked the fur around the sick lad and lit a lamp. Olbin might have something to bring down the fever.

As he straightened up with the lamp, Garzik glimpsed himself reflected in the window glass. No wonder Byren hadn't recognised him. His long hair was loose, covering the ugly crater where his ear had been. Along with the scar across his cheek, it made him look like a true Utlander. His face was leaner and harder, and he was a head taller than he had been the last time Byren had seen him.

Garzik took a step closer to peer into the imperfect mirror of the window. Witchy Utlander eyes stared back at him, a pale circle in each iris. Would they return to normal when he went home and ate properly prepared food?

One thing was certain, the longer he stayed with the Utlanders, the more his eyes would change, until he was marked forever. Then, even if he did make his way back home, he would never be truly accepted.

He had to escape, and the sooner the better.

Stepping out onto the middeck, he heard angry raised voices from the high reardeck. As he climbed the steps, he saw that Jost and his two half-brothers were going up against Rusan and Olbin, posturing and shouting insults while the crew looked on.

Jost had gathered the disgruntled crew members to his cause. Instead of rich pickings, they'd lost two men, and three more had been injured in the evening's attack. Seeing Garzik, Vesnibor smirked.

'We've gone days without a prize!' Jost barked. 'A blind nennir could do better.'

The Utlanders waited for their captain to respond.

Garzik glanced to Rusan. Captaincy of an Utland ship was much like being a spar warlord. The spar warriors chose the strongest leader from amongst the old warlord's extended family, then swore to follow him—or, more rarely, her. If the warlord did not lead them well, they elected another.

'You've had your chance.' Jost thumped his chest. 'I—'

'Wait.' The last thing Garzik wanted was Jost and his supporters taking over the ship. Rusan needed a success. 'There's still gold to be had.'

The raiders stared at him.

'Trafyn's father is a rich noble. He'll pay well for his son's safe return. If Trafyn lives long enough to reach Merofynia, you'll have all the gold you want.'

Jost spat. 'We can't eat gold.'

'Then take your payment in supplies.'

'That's all very well,' Rusan said. 'But we can't drop anchor in Port Mero and ask for a meeting with the brat's father. A thousand hot-land warriors would swarm our ship while we waited to negotiate.'

The raiders laughed.

Garzik hadn't thought it through. While the Utlanders could sail the captured Merofynian ship into port unchallenged, the moment they identified themselves they'd be surrounded and executed. What's more, Port Mero would be packed with the sea-hound ships that had escorted merchant vessels laden with Rolencian war booty—

Of course.

'If you went in quick, and struck hard and fast, you could claim some of the riches stolen from Rolencia—red wine for you, grains and smoked meat to fill your children's bellies, warm wool and velvets for your women. This is a merchant ship. You could dress like Merofynian sailors, shave off your beards and plait your hair. By the time the enemy was close enough to see the Utland cast to your eyes, it would be too late. You would be in and out before they knew what hit them—'

'I'm no fool. The hot-lander is trying to lead us to our deaths,' Jost said, and his supporters muttered in agreement. 'We'd be surrounded and attacked.'

'Not if you go in flying the Merofynian flag, wait until dark, then board a ship and deal with the crew quietly. Last time I was there, the wharves were so packed, ships were transferring stores at anchor. No one would be suspicious.' Garzik looked around, trying to gauge the reaction of the crew. 'You might even be able to capture another ship.' *And get rid of Jost and his troublemakers.*

Even better, they'd strike a blow against Merofynia; and, in some small way, Garzik would be helping Byren.

'Imagine sailing right into Port Mero and tweaking the hot-landers' noses!' Olbin grinned, a wicked light in his eyes.

The thought appealed to them, and every one had something to say. Eventually, Rusan held up his hands for silence. 'We disguise ourselves and slip into port, wait for dark, sidle up to a ship and transfer the stores. Then anyone who wants to leave can sail with Jost.'

'On a ship you've already plundered? Why should I take your leavings?' Jost objected. He gestured to the captain and his half-brother. 'How can you follow them into Port Mero after they lost the oracles? They're cursed.'

'You were off hunting manticores when Vultar kidnapped the oracles. We fought off the renegades and burned one of Vultar's ships. But we'll do more. I'll swear a blood-oath!' Rusan drew his knife and cut his hand, turning in a circle. 'I swear before all of you here tonight, we will restore the oracles and exact vengeance on Vultar.'

The crew cheered.

Jost stepped forward, furious. 'We wouldn't have to save the oracles if you hadn't lost them in the first place.'

Rusan's hands curled into fists. 'What's your problem, Jost?'

Everyone fell silent. Jost glanced around the group, weighed the odds, then looked down.

Rusan turned away.

'I know what you do in the cabin with Wynn, hot-land lover,' Jost muttered. 'You—'

Rusan spun around, punching Jost so hard the one-eared warrior was lifted from his feet and stretched his length on the deck.

For a heartbeat there was utter silence; then the crew laughed and jeered. They were going to Port Mero, into the very jaws of death. The Utlands would sing of their daring for years to come!

Now that it was decided, Garzik hoped he was right and they could pass for Merofynians. Because if he wasn't...

If he wasn't, he wouldn't be around long to find out.

As soon as the Utlanders were distracted, he was going over the side. The water would be cold, but he was a strong swimmer and he spoke Merofynian like a noble, thanks to Byren's mother. He was going to deliver Trafyn to Lord Travany, where the scribe would have news of the Merofynians' plans. That way, Garzik wouldn't go back to Byren empty-handed. But for his plan to work, Trafyn had to recover.

Garzik sought out Olbin and led him into the captain's cabin. The squire had thrown off his covers and was muttering under his breath.

'He's sick,' Garzik said. 'Really sick.'

Olbin touched Trafyn's forehead. 'Weak hot-landers.' He left without another word.

Garzik sat hugging his knees beside Trafyn, not sure if the big Utlander was coming back. After a while, Olbin returned with a vile-smelling liquid, which he forced down the squire's throat.

'It'll help?' Garzik asked.

'That, or kill him.' Olbin grinned. 'Come on.'

'I must look after him.'

'Why? He hates you.'

Garzik shrugged. 'I must help him because he needs it.'

Olbin shook his head. 'Are all hot-landers like you, brave but foolish?'

Garzik didn't know what to say.

The big Utlander laughed and left him.

Garzik built up the brazier and put out the lamp. He placed a sack of watered wine beside Trafyn and prepared to sit up with him. After a while, the Utland drink sent the squire into a deep, troubled sleep.

In three, maybe four days, they'd both be free—as long as the Utlanders stuck to the plan.

But Jost and his brothers resented Rusan and Olbin. Back at the settlement, they'd been rivals over the beautiful singer, Sarijana.

Leaving Trafyn asleep, Garzik slipped out of the cabin. He found Olbin on the prow, watching the star-silvered sea.

Garzik glanced around to be sure they could not be overheard. 'I thought Jost would jump at the chance for a ship of his own, but he hates you and Rusan because you two stole Sarijana.'

Olbin snorted. 'She would never have settled for him and his brothers. She'd more than half promised to have us. One more successful voyage, and we could've...'

The brothers could have built a cottage for themselves and taken the beautiful singer for their wife. At first Garzik had found the Utlanders' marriage customs strange, but after living with them, he understood how hard their lives were. They couldn't feed many children, and the men often died young. If two or three brothers married a girl, all the children were considered theirs. If one brother died, the survivors reared the children.

The night Vultar attacked, all that had changed. They'd fought off the renegades, but not in time to prevent...

Garzik asked the question that had been troubling him. 'Sarijana has joined the beardless.' These women swore off men and vowed to die to protect the settlement. 'What happens if she's pregnant? What happens if the renegades planted...'—he didn't know the Utland word for bastards—'babies in the bellies of the women they raped?'

'The babies will be born.' Olbin shrugged. 'Can't stop that.'

'But who will provide for them?'

'The beardless,' Olbin said, as if this was obvious. 'Babies born of rape are always raised by the beardless.' He hesitated. 'I wasn't there to save Sari—'

'You did everything you could,' Garzik told him. Just as he'd done everything he could to light the warning beacon for Byren.

'Yet we lost the oracles.'

'You'll get them back. I know you will.' But Garzik wouldn't be around to help them do it, and that troubled him.

Chapter Ten

BYREN BLEW ON his numb hands and raised the farseer to search the sea again. Even dressed and dry, he was chilled to the bone. He didn't see how Orrade could have survived immersed in the cold, cold water.

Even so, he searched the star-silvered sea, unable to give up hope.

A man came up behind Byren and cleared his throat.

Byren lowered the farseer, feeling his heart sink with it.

'Kingsheir, no man could survive so long in the open sea.'

'This isn't winter.'

'Even if it was midsummer.'

Byren knew he was right, but he couldn't accept it. 'We'll search till dawn.'

For a heartbeat it seemed the captain would refuse, but he nodded and left Byren alone with his guilt.

If only he'd been quicker.

* * *

Fyn helped Isolt escort the weary Benetir Estate survivors from the royal barge. The starlit terraces stretched up before them to the palace. Young Rhalwyn had run on ahead, and already servants hurried down the wide steps, bringing lanterns and blankets. Despite her weariness, Isolt was in her element, organising everyone.

They were half a body-length apart when Fyn caught her eye. He was going to Lord Dunstany's townhouse to send the message.

Isolt sent him a swift nod. No words were needed.

In that moment, he felt his world shift and he knew they were meant for each other. The *knowing* bypassed all reason. The depth and power of it stole his breath.

She tilted her head. 'What's wrong?'

Fyn shook his head and backed away.

Deep in thought, he went to the stables, where the stable-master found him saddling a horse. The poor man was so distraught to think he had failed in his duty that Fyn had to stand back and let stable-master finish cinching the saddle girth himself.

If King Merofyn the Despot had this effect on a grown man, how had Isolt survived his bullying? Fyn had only seen the king when he was frail in mind and body.

With a word of thanks, Fyn led the horse out into the yard, mounted up and set off. Being a sensible creature, the horse was not happy about being taken out of a warm stall and moved at a reluctant trot.

With his mount's hooves clattering on the paving, Fyn threaded through the palace grounds, past manicured gardens, fountains and follies. He reached the main entrance and passed under the linden tree where Byren had once hung in a cage, awaiting execution.

Fyn could not betray his brother, yet the thought of Isolt married to Byren... There was no doubt his brother would treat her well. Byren knew his duty, but he didn't love Isolt and she deserved to be loved.

She deserved to be loved the way Fyn loved her.

With a nod to the palace guards, Fyn passed through the gate and crossed the market square. It was a little after midnight. The taverns were closing and soon the bakers would start work.

Nearly two hundred years ago, King Sefon the Fourth, Fyn's several-times great grandfather, had laid out the streets in a circular pattern, with Mulcibar's Abbey atop Mount Mero at the centre. According to the histories, he'd based the design on a spider's web. Wide avenues led down to the bay on the south side of the slope; on the north, the avenues led to the Landlocked Sea, and to the east, they led to the Grand Canal which King Sefon had built to connect the sea to Port Mero.

With a start, Fyn realised that he'd reached Lord Dunstany's townhouse. Ignoring the formal entrance, he went around to the tradesman's entrance, where the sweet scent of lemon blossom filled the small courtyard. No light burned in the kitchen. Of course, with their master away, the servants would be abed.

When he'd stayed here before, one servant had been privy to Fyn's comings and goings, supplying costumes and props for his disguises. Only Gwalt knew Lord Dunstany was really Tyro.

Fyn dismounted, tied his horse's reins to the lemon tree and collected several pebbles to throw at Gwalt's window. The stones made soft plinking noises as they hit the glass.

The servant opened the window and leaned out. 'Who disturbs an honest man's...' His deceptively mild face sharpened. 'Fyn? I'll be right down.'

A moment later, candlelight glowed in the kitchen and the door swung open. Fyn slipped inside. 'Spar raiders have taken Benetir Estate. The queen needs Lord Dunstany's advice. You must send a message to the mage.'

'It will be done.'

'How long before the pica bird reaches him?'

'Best flight time is half a day. Better allow a day.'

'What about predators and storms?'

'I'll send two birds. One will get through.'

'How do you reconcile serving Tyro in the guise of Lord Dunstany when, by rights, Dunstany's true heir should inherit the title?' Fyn flushed. 'I'm sorry, I—'

'It's a fair question. I'm loyal, like my father before me,' Gwalt said. 'Lord Dunstany despised his heir. Duncaer is a drunkard and a gambler. If he got his hands on the estate, it would be lost to the Dunistir line. When Dunstany's last son died, my lord planned to acknowledge his bastard grandson. Dunstany had my father sign forged papers that would have legitimised Siordun. But the mage tested the lad and discovered he had Affinity. So, you see, I serve the true lord of Dunistir Estate.' He shrugged. 'Dunstany shared the mage's dream of peace for the three islands. Siordun carries on his work.'

Fyn nodded. He did see. Loyalty was a strange thing. It legitimised Tyro's... *Siordun's* deception and made something noble of it. 'I should go.'

It was still some time until dawn, but the first of the morning workers already stirred. Laden carts trundled past in pools of lantern light, delivering goods before the carriage-ways became crowded. Fyn heard cackling chickens headed for market.

He was tired. The journey across the Landlocked Sea had been filled with talk of which lords and merchants they could call on to help retake the estate. Names he did not know, alliances hinted at. Faces and phrases echoed in his mind as he let the horse make its way home.

Fyn guided his mount around two carters, arguing over right of way. A familiar tailor's sign told him he was four blocks over from the market square and the palace gates.

As Lord Dunstany, Siordun was acquainted with every Merofynian lord. He knew their complicated alliances and whether they could be trusted. Lord Dunstany was well respected, feared even, by his fellow nobles. Truly, if Siordun's deception was revealed, the lords would be furious. They'd lynch him like a common thief.

Fyn shivered. He did not know how Siordun kept his nerve.

Angry voices made Fyn look up to see another altercation. A wine carter had collided with a cart of farm produce. Wine barrels and smashed pumpkins blocked the road.

Fyn back-tracked and took the nearest lane. Halfway down the lane, a scurrying cat made Fyn's horse shy, and he leant down to reassure his mount.

Something whistled past his head. A crossbow bolt struck the nearest stone wall, metal tip showering sparks.

Shocked, Fyn dug his heels into the horse's flanks.

Sensing his fear, the beast took off for the patch of light at the end of the lane. Fyn stayed low in the saddle, cursing his bad luck.

Two figures stepped into the lane just ahead of him.

He glanced over his shoulder. Two more thugs closed off the far end of the lane. The carters' altercation was no accident. He'd been ambushed.

Out of time and out of options, he charged the nearest men. As one of Halcyon's warrior monks, he'd been trained to bring down a mounted man. These footpads didn't have his training, and they'd expected him to be injured.

As he rode towards them, their eyes widened with fear.

Fyn aimed his mount for the man on the right, who leapt aside at the last moment.

The other man grabbed Fyn's leg as he passed. The force of Fyn's charge pulled his attacker off his feet, but the horse staggered.

Fyn drew his ceremonial dagger and slashed at the man's arm.

'Don't let the lord-monk get away,' someone yelled.

Another crossbow bolt hissed past. Fyn stabbed for the man's eye. The blade skittered across his attacker's skull, and hot blood soaked through Fyn's breeches.

Terrified, the horse reared, breaking the footpad's hold, and Fyn gave his mount its head. He sped up the rise towards the markets, his horse's hooves clattering on the cobbles.

At the end of the next block, he slowed his mount. Maintaining a steady pace, he wove through stall-holders and their carts, trusting his pursuers would not get a clear shot.

Heart pounding, he approached the palace gates. The guards eyed him, but did not rush to his aid. He was the son of the Rolencian king, an interloper.

Had they sent a message when they saw him ride out?

His horse shivered, dancing sideways. Fyn cursed and concentrated on keeping his seat.

By the time he reached the stables, he had the horse and himself under control. Of course the stable-master was waiting, along with several lads. When they saw the blood they set up a racket, and Fyn wished he'd stopped to wash his leg in a palace fountain.

As a lad led the horse away, Fyn tried to make light of it. 'Just my luck to come across thieves. They spooked the horse. No harm done.'

'But the blood...' The stable-master gestured to his leg and then to his shoulder.

Surprised, Fyn glanced at his shoulder. A rip revealed his undershirt, stained with blood. A bolt had skimmed him. Any lower and it would have gone through his shoulder, yet he hadn't felt a thing. He laughed. 'It's nothing.'

He needed to get to his chamber, strip off his bloodied clothes and make sense of what had just happened. Fyn opened the door to his chamber to find Kyral waiting to serve him. 'What are you doing here?'

'Kingson...' The middle-aged man flinched.

Fyn tempered his tone. 'I was raised in an abbey. I don't need a servant, and I certainly don't want you to wait up for me. Go back to your bed. I'll send for you if I need you.'

The manservant backed out and Fyn wondered if he had been too harsh. But he did not know if Kyral reported on his comings and goings.

Besides, he didn't need a servant. This wasn't Rolencia, where they drew hot water from the spigot at the end of the hall. In Merofynia, the best bedchambers held marble bathing rooms, complete with sunken tubs and hot and cold running water.

Fyn lit a single lamp and took it into the bathing chamber. He shed his clothes as he went. His undershirt stuck to his skin, stinging when he peeled it away from the gash on his shoulder. The shallow cut started bleeding again.

Wearing only his breeches and boots, he knelt by the sunken tub to run the water. As the water poured in, he pulled off his boots. A pool of golden light illuminated the steam-filled air. He stood, unbuckled the belt that held his ceremonial dagger, and hung it over the chair, then began unlacing his breeches. One leg was drenched in his attacker's blood.

The door flew open.

He spun, reaching for the dagger.

'Fyn?' Eyes wide, face pale, Isolt took in his bloodied, half-naked state. 'They told me you were hurt. What happened?'

'Footpads,' he said, wishing she'd come closer.

'Footpads?'

'An opportunistic attack,' he lied. They'd called him *lord-monk*.

'I'll double the city-watch.' Isolt frowned. 'You're bleeding.' She went to approach then hesitated.

'A graze. I've had worse in training.' He wanted her sweet hands to wash the blood from his shoulder and apply a salve. She was trained in the healing arts. He had only to ask.

No, he couldn't. He wanted it too much.

She clasped her hands in front of her. 'I'll send up the healer.'

'No need.'

'It could fester.'

'It could.' *But, if I can't have you, I don't want anyone to tend me. Fool that I am.* 'Very well, send up the healer.'

She nodded, yet she did not leave.

The tub was full. Fyn glanced from it to her.

She turned and ran.

He let out a breath he hadn't realised he was holding.

When he went to unlace his breeches, his hands shook so badly he had to stop. *Concentrate.*

The men had been sent to kill him. Upon his death, Isolt would need a new lord protector, and there would be many eager to serve her.

Captain Neiron, for one.

Fyn bristled. None of them valued Isolt for who she was. They saw only her position and pretty face.

He admired her strength. Lesser men would have been crippled, growing up with a father like hers. But she'd remained true to herself and good-hearted despite everything.

None of them deserved her.

Not even Byren.

Chapter Eleven

BYREN PACED.

The captain waited for him to call off the search.

Dawn had given him no reason to hold onto hope. What was the use of Orrade's Affinity visions if they did not warn him of the attack? He... Byren spun to face the captain. 'There's a wyvern eyrie nearby, right?'

The old sailor looked surprised.

'I knew it! Take us there.'

'It's not worth our lives. Would you send another dozen men to their deaths?'

This was true. Yet... 'You stood back and did nothing. You knew what Captain Talltrees intended—'

'*Not me*,' the cabin boy protested. 'I didn't know.'

Byren hadn't noticed him there; he tempered his tone. 'Aye, you were duped, lad, as were we.' He met the eyes of the man who had been the boatswain and followed a hunch. 'But you knew and you didn't warn us.'

'He was my captain.'

'He was a man who put gold above honour. All it takes

for evil to flourish is for a good man to stand by and do nothing.' It was something Byren's old nurse used to say. Now he understood what she meant. 'You owe Orrie this much. Take us near enough for me to search the eyrie.'

The old sailor looked grim, but gave the orders. Ponderously, the ship veered due east. Byren strode to the rail.

He waited, watching, fingering the farseer.

The captain joined him. 'You should be able to spot the outlying rocks by the time the sun is two fingers above the horizon. We have to watch out for dangerous shoals just below the sea's surface. There's rocks that can rip a ship's belly wide open. The wyverns lie in wait, ready to pluck sailors off the sinking ships.'

Byren grimaced but remained determined.

If he had seen Orrade die of a wound, his blood seeping into the earth as the light left his eyes, it would be different. 'I have to be sure.'

The captain nodded his understanding, then pointed. 'There, that's what we have to look out for. See the way water's peeling back off that rock? The tide is rising, and soon it'll be impossible to spot the shoals.'

Byren lifted the farseer.

But he wasn't looking at the nearby rock. He'd seen another one in the middle distance, silhouetted against the rising sun. He trained the farseer on it. The rock was smooth, like a tilted table. Waves slid up the low side, then rolled back. There was something on the rock, just above the waterline.

Byren looked away and rubbed his eyes. He'd been up all night. 'Eh, lad.' He beckoned the cabin boy. 'Take a look.'

Byren showed him how to hold the farseer, then lifted the lad up so he could sight along his arm. 'What do you see?'

'A rock.'

'What else?' Byren tried to keep the hope from his voice as he imagined Orrade clambering onto the rock at low tide. 'Is there something on it?'

'Yes. A sleeping wyvern.'

Retrieving the farseer, Byren took a look for himself. Sure enough, now that the sun was a little higher, the wyvern was no longer in silhouette.

Byren felt sick with disappointment. He searched the sea again, noting other spots where waves boiled around rocks.

'The wyverns'll be waking for the day soon, heading off to hunt. Best go below, lad,' the captain told the cabin boy, who ran off. The old sailor faced Byren. 'We must turn back.'

Byren swept the sea one last time.

A wave rolled up the low side of the flat rock. It stirred the wyvern, rolling the creature.

'That wyvern's dead.' Byren pointed. They were still a good two bow shots away.

'Mating battles,' the captain said. 'They fight for females this time of year. Like horses, one male protects a group of females. Mayhap he was too old and lost his herd.'

Byren nodded and scanned the sea again. Nothing.

He checked the flat rock one last time, just as another wave stirred the wyvern's body, revealing something white and pale under it.

'A leg...' A dismembered, naked human leg. Byren cursed. Orrade's dream had been a true vision. He'd had to battle a wyvern for a patch of rock.

Bile rose in Byren's throat.

He thrust the farseer into the captain's hands, leaned over the side and retched. There was nothing in his stomach to bring up.

Tears burned his eyes. Hardly able to see, he went to the water barrel, rinsed his mouth and washed his face. Shattered, he rubbed his face.

When he had command of himself, Byren returned to the ship's rail.

The captain lowered the farseer, frowned then lifted it again.

'What?' Byren didn't want to look.

Silently, the captain passed him the farseer.

Byren saw a wave stir the dead wyvern yet again, and this time it was clear the leg was attached to a body, trapped under the Affinity beast's carcass.

'Your friend... He killed the wyvern, but died of his wounds.'

'No.' Byren knew what Orrade had done. Hope made his heart race. 'He's smart. He killed the beast, slit its belly open and climbed inside to keep warm. He's not under it, he's inside it.' *And about to be washed into the sea by the rising tide.* 'We have to get him off that rock.'

The captain shook his head, pointing to nearby patches of white water, evidence of dangerous shoals. 'We can't go any closer. We'd be driven onto the rocks.'

'Give me a row boat.'

'You'd never get it onto the rock in these swells. Every sixth or seventh wave is bigger than the rest.'

'Then tie a rope to me.' If what the captain said was true, the next big wave would sweep Orrade into the sea. 'I have to bring him back.'

Until he held Orrade's cold dead body in his arms, Byren would cling to hope. He snapped the farseer shut. 'Tie a rope to me. I'll swim out to him. When I signal, pull us both back.'

The captain studied his face as if debating with himself, then nodded.

In a mad rush, Byren went down to the middeck where he stripped off everything but his breeches. The captain made a harness from rope and leather and tied it securely around his chest and shoulders.

Byren kept glancing back to the rock. A great wave rolled up the low side, but to Byren's relief, the wyvern's heavy body was not sucked back into the sea.

'Listen.' The captain forcibly turned Byren around. 'The sea will be cold. Get in and get over there fast. Secure him to your chest with these straps here. When you raise your arm, we'll bring you in. Got that?'

'Got it.'

'You know you're stark raving mad?'

'He'd do the same for me.'

'Would he?'

Byren nodded without hesitation.

Without another word, he climbed onto the ship's rail. Early morning sunlight danced on the waves. Back home, he'd fallen in the lake early one spring. By the time they'd pulled him out, he'd been blue.

He knew what cold was.

Byren took several deep, quick breaths, slapped his shoulders and face until he felt the blood sing, then dived out, driving himself as far as he could.

He hit the sea, felt the impact like a blow as he plunged deep.

The cold grabbed him, punching him in the chest. He fought to reach the surface. As soon as his head broke free, a wave hit his face.

He spat salt water out, coughing, then struck out for the rock. Each time the waves lifted him, he glimpsed Orrade's pale limbs protruding from the wyvern's torso, and he worried that the next time he looked the rock would be bare.

Arms burning, Byren felt the sea lift him again. He looked up. A body-length to go and Orrade was still there.

Byren rode the next wave as it surged up the low side of the rock, lifting the body of the wyvern. Byren tried to grab Orrade, but before he could, the wave retreated, sucking them all into the sea.

Byren could have saved himself.

Instead, he held onto Orrade's arm and went under as the weight of the dead beast dragged them down. Byren fought to free his friend, pulling him from the beast's body like he would pull a foal from a mare. The wyvern fell away into the cold depths as Byren kicked for the surface, hugging Orrade to him.

Chest burning, Byren gasped for air.

A wave drove him and Orrade, up onto the sloping rock again, leaving them there as it retreated.

'Orrie? Orrie, can you hear me?'

No answer.

Byren turned Orrade's face to him. Blue lips, cold limp body. The wyvern had raked his friend's chest and bitten his shoulder. There was no bleeding.

Was there a heartbeat? Byren's hands were too numb to tell but he could sense the taint of the dead wyvern's power coming from Orrade's skin. The predator's Affinity had settled in Orrade. In the past when they'd killed an Affinity beast, the castle's Affinity warder had always settled the creature's power. Now... now there was no time to worry.

Seeing another wave headed towards them, Byren scrambled further up the rock, pulling Orrade with him. He could go no higher. Behind him was a sheer drop into the sea. He tried to strap Orrade to his chest, but his chilled hands fumbled with the catch on the makeshift harness.

The waved rolled up the rock, barely reaching his knees.

'You could help, instead of just lying there like a lump,' he grumbled.

No answer.

Finally, he slipped the strap through the buckle and tightened it, making sure Orrade was secure. Not a moment too soon; the next wave was bigger than the last. As it came towards him he saw the crest gleaming in the sun, almost level with his eyes.

Desperate, he raised both arms, signalling the ship. 'This is it, Orrie.' Cold seawater surged up around Byren's neck, lifting his body and pouring over the far side of the rock, but he held firm. Then the wave rolled down off the rock, taking him and Orrade with it.

He felt the pull on the harness, felt himself turn around so that he was dragged on his back through the sea, with Orrade's back strapped to his chest.

A wave engulfed them both. Spluttering, he concentrated on keeping their heads above water.

The trip back seemed interminable. Then his shoulder collided with the ship's hull. He was so cold he was barely aware of his back scraping across the barnacles as the sailors hauled them both out of the water up the ship's side.

Arms reached for him, dragging them onto the deck.

His legs shook so much he barely could stand. The sailors cheered and the captain unbuckled the harness. All he could do was grin like a fool. The moment the sailors took Orrade's weight, his knees gave out.

Byren sank to the deck, and the captain reached for Byren's harness.

'See to Orrie. I'm all right.' It's what he'd *meant* to say, but his teeth were chattering so much, he was unintelligible.

Somehow the captain understood. Byren fumbled free of the rope and harness, then crawled across the deck to his friend. They'd already wrapped Orrade in a blanket, and now they tried to force warmed wine down his throat.

One of the sailors pressed his ear to Orrade's chest, listening for a heartbeat.

'Is—' Byren didn't want to ask, but he had to know. 'Can you hear his heart?'

The man lifted his head. 'It barely beats.'

'Will he live?' the cabin boy asked.

'If his heart beats, he'll live,' Byren insisted.

'It was a brave thing you did, going after him like that,' the captain said. He put a hand on Byren's shoulder. 'But I've seen men like this before. It looks like they're going to come good, but then they die.'

'He's going to live.'

'He might, if we take it slow.' The captain nodded. 'Try not to warm him too fast.'

Byren nodded his understanding, then slid his arms under Orrade's body and drove himself to his feet. He staggered, and one of the sailors steadied him. 'I need to patch up his chest. I need warm food and more blankets.'

'All prepared in your cabin,' the captain said.

Byren sent him a nod of thanks, turned and headed for the reardeck cabins. Orrade's cold body felt like a dead weight in his arms.

'Your back and shoulders...' The captain called after him. 'You were cut to shreds on the ship's barnacles.'

Byren ignored him.

Two shadows passed over the deck, followed by another, and Byren heard the cry of a hunting wyvern. A whirring clatter came from the crow's nest as the lookout tried to drive off the Affinity beasts. Sailors clasped their amulets, calling on their gods for protection, and the captain bellowed orders to set a new heading.

Byren entered the cabin to find the brazier burning fiercely. He assumed the air was warm, but he was too cold to tell.

His knee joints popped as he knelt to place Orrade on the bedroll in front of the brazier. First, he peeled off his own wet breeches then he set to work on Orrade.

Stitch his wounds. Do what needed to be done. No room for doubts.

Warm water steamed on the brazier's hotplate. Byren added wine to it and cleaned Orrade's wounds. There were two sets of long cuts in his chest where the wyvern had raked him, and there were teeth marks in his shoulder. Byren had served in the mountain patrols since he was fifteen and knew how to deal with Affinity beast wounds. Clean the injury, stitch it, bind it, and hope it didn't fester.

'Lucky for you, you're out cold,' he told Orrade, as he stitched the long wounds across his friend's chest. 'These scars'll impress the girls.' Realising what he had just said, Byren shook his head. 'I just don't get it. All those times we shared the lasses, you never...' He glanced to Orrade's pale face, frustration driving him on. 'You certainly looked like you were enjoying yourself.' He tied off the last stitch. 'All those times the girl slipped away and we woke up sleeping naked in the furs...' There'd been times when they were younger, before the girls... 'But that was just playing around. Showing off.'

Byren cleaned Orrade's shoulder, finding a broken tooth in the deepest wound. 'Eh, lucky you're out cold.' He dug the tooth out and dropped it in the bowl.

When he bound the wounds, lifting Orrade's chest to pass the bandages under him, his friend did not react, remaining chill and limp.

'Don't do this, Orrie. Don't you dare leave me!' Byren wanted to shake him. Slap him. Anything to get some reaction. Anything to give him reason to hope.

Instead, he stretched out and pulled Orrade's back against his chest, so that they both faced the brazier. 'Don't give up.' Furious, he tugged the furs over them. 'Don't you dare give up!'

But there was no response, just the residual hum of the wyvern's Affinity. This reassured Byren. If Orrade died, the power would leave his body.

Byren's shivers returned as the cold from Orrade's body seeped deep into his bones. The last time he'd been this cold...

Was the night he'd escaped the brigands. The ulfr pack had led him to a seep before curling up around him, enveloping him in warmth and predator Affinity.

The feel of their great bodies nestled around him and the deep, purring sound that came from their chests as they breathed in unison returned to him. He found himself breathing like that now—a soft, deep growl on each exhalation, vibrating in his chest.

He would not let Orrade die.

GARZIK WOKE TO find himself stretched out next to Trafyn. The squire had kicked the covers off, and his faded jerkin was damp with sweat. Unaware of Garzik,

Trafyn twitched and shifted as though he couldn't get comfortable, pleading for water.

Garzik picked up the sack of watered wine. It was almost empty. He offered the squire a drink. Trafyn's skin was still too hot.

The squire gulped greedily, then hiccupped and groaned. His gaze cleared for a heartbeat. 'Where've you been? I called out for you, but you didn't come. You're the worst servant I've ever had. Wait till I tell Father. He'll...'

'Trafyn?'

But there was no light of reason in the squire's face.

Garzik considered asking for more of the Utland medicine, but Olbin had made it clear Trafyn was on his own now.

Leaving the squire on the bunk, feverish and fretful, Garzik went below deck to refill the sack of watered wine and get something to eat. When he returned to the cabin, he found the squire lucid for the moment.

Trafyn's frowned. 'I'm sick, and it's all your fault.'

Garzik almost preferred him delirious. He helped him lift his head. 'Here, sip this.'

Trafyn swallowed then frowned. 'This is watered wine. I need dreamless-sleep. My old nurse used to give me dreamless-sleep in honeyed milk when I was sick.'

'You were lucky to get the herbal drink the Utlanders gave you last night. Slaves are usually ignored and left to live or die.'

Trafyn gulped another mouthful then sank back. 'Everything aches.'

'Get better. We're sailing for Port Mero. When we're close to shore, we're going to slip overboard and swim for it.'

'But my father will pay—'

'The Utlanders don't want your father's gold. Besides, they wouldn't live long enough to collect it. No, our best bet is to go over the side. So you need to get well.' He picked up the plate of beans. 'Are you hungry?'

No answer. Trafyn had fallen asleep.

Chapter Twelve

FLORIN ACCEPTED THE breakfast tray and returned to Varuska. There was enough food—berries and cream, fresh bread and mushrooms cooked in butter—for both of them, even if the mushrooms were a little cold by the time the tray reached their chamber.

They sat on the window seat to eat.

'Whipped cream, strawberries and blueberries,' Varuska marvelled. 'I like this part of being a kingsdaughter.' She frowned. 'How did they get the berries to ripen? It isn't even summer's cusp yet.'

'Gardens under glass, warmed by Halcyon's bounty.' Byren had told her how the water was piped up from the hot spring far below the castle. Such luxury. 'Even with all of this, I wouldn't swap my life for that of a kingsdaughter.'

'Oh, I didn't mean—'

'I know.'

'I was just saying.' Varuska clearly felt she had to justify herself. 'Many's the time we went hungry waiting for the first crops to ripen.'

'I know. My mother was a mountain girl.' That's what Byren had called her: Mountain Girl. Now he would never tease her again. Anger and sorrow made it impossible for her to eat. 'I'll put the tray out in the hall. Time to get dressed.'

It was a process fraught with frustration and giggles as neither of them was used to grand clothes. There were embroidered breeches, a chemise and two underskirts before the gown went over the top.

'Why would anyone wear breeches under a skirt?' Varuska marvelled.

Florin shrugged. All the while, she listened for shouts in the courtyard below, or running steps in the corridor outside. If Anatoley was discovered and Florin's role in her escape revealed, Cobalt would not hesitate to order her execution. Not by so much as a blink did she betray the fear churning in her stomach. Instead, she dropped the second petticoat over Varuska's head and tugged on the drawstring to tighten it. The girl pulled her waist-length hair out of the way. A shout from the courtyard made Florin tense.

'What is it?' Varuska whispered.

Florin went to the window. A carter making a delivery had spilled his load, blocking the courtyard entrance. She let out her breath. 'It's nothing.' Florin returned her attention to Varuska. The girl looked flushed and pretty, but her hair was a mess. 'We have to do something about your hair.'

Varuska fiddled with the drawstring on her borrowed chemise a moment, then looked up. 'Do you think if I promised to tell no one, Lord Cobalt would let me go?'

'Varuska!' Florin took her by the shoulders. In some ways, this girl seemed younger than Piro. The kingsdaughter had been raised in court and knew that power could bring out the worst in people. Florin held Varuska's eyes. 'Whatever you do, don't mention this again, and keep your voice down.'

'Why? Why are you so scared? What aren't you telling me?' She gestured to the chamber door. 'Do you really think someone is listening?'

Florin shrugged. 'There's a man-at-arms standing just on the other side of that door. He's as much your guard as your protector. These are not good people, Var—*Piro*. I must call you that all the time now, or I'll slip up when it matters.'

Varuska's eyes widened and Florin felt a shiver of fear run through her body. Florin hugged the younger girl, whispering in her ear. 'We must bide our time and go along with this charade for the time being. Then, when they drop their guard—'

'We escape!'

Then she killed Cobalt. The plan had never been to escape, but now... Florin frowned. Varuska looked to her with such trust, yet Florin was only five years older and almost as new to castle politics.

Florin reached for the over-gown, the same one Varuska had worn last night. She hesitated. Would a kingsdaughter wear this gown now? Perhaps it was only suitable for evening feasts?

Someone rapped on the door.

Varuska jumped.

Florin signalled for her to sit and handed her a hair brush. 'Do your hair. Never show fear.'

Varuska nodded and Florin went to the door.

Cobalt's manservant, Amil, swept in, carrying a grand gown and a small lacquered box. He draped the gown over a chair and opened the box on the bed to reveal jewellery, scent bottles, powders and face paints—all things alien to Florin's life. What made them think she would be a good lady's maid?

'His lordship is taking his betrothed for a carriage ride through Rolenhold today,' Amil announced, then frowned. 'Don't brush your hair like that, girl, you'll flatten the curl. Ah, I see I'll have to curl it again.' He took the brush from her and snapped his fingers at Florin. 'Come here.'

She stepped up behind him, thinking a knife through the ribs would shut him up. He might be one of Ostron Isle's renowned assassins, but he wasn't on his guard right now. 'It's Leif.'

'Leif? A barbaric name...' Amil looked her up and down. 'Still, my lord thinks you can be trained, so watch.' He separated Varuska's hair into long sections, wound them around a hot iron, then counted to ten. 'You unravel the hair gently so the curl doesn't come out while the hair is still warm.' He finished a third ringlet. 'Think you can do this?'

Florin nodded.

'Take over.' He pulled Varuska to her feet and eased the new gown over her head, giving it a tug to settle it into place. This one was a deep plum red, trimmed with seed-pearls.

As Florin curled Varuska's hair, Amil pulled the lacings tight under her breasts.

'You will be seated in an open carriage,' he told Varuska. 'You will smile and wave.'

Varuska nodded.

'Good.' He sat her down, pushed Florin aside and began pinning up Varuska's hair. 'Here and here, see. Now the cap with the pearl netting. It sits just so. A maiden's cap.' He darted around to the front and selected a bottle of Ostronite myrrh. 'One dab here, between the breasts.' His hands were business-like. 'Another behind each ear. More is vulgar, you understand?'

They both nodded.

'Now the features. Such a pretty face.' But his eyes held only consideration. 'A little kohl on the lids... What?'

Florin had been about to say that Piro never bothered to paint her face, but Florin should not have known this, so she asked, 'How do you avoid smudges?'

'A steady hand and an artist's eye.' He mixed oil with

the kohl and began to apply it with a small brush. As Florin watched him elongate Varuska's tilted black eyes, she had to admit he had a flair for it. 'Now the lip paint, deep red to match the gown.' He handed the girl a small pot. 'You need to take this with you. If his lordship kisses you, you'll have to re-apply it.'

Varuska looked like a trapped, frightened bird.

'I should go with her,' Florin offered, fearing the girl might panic.

Amil considered then sighed. 'Wait here.' He darted out.

Varuska peered at herself in a polished glass. 'I look odd.' She wrinkled her nose. 'My lips feel funny, like I can't talk without worrying about smudging them. How do women do this?'

Florin had no idea. 'You smile. You look pretty and vulnerable, and you never give them reason to look past your face. Men always underestimate pretty girls.' And they ignored plain ones, which suited her.

Varuska nodded. 'Anatoley would have been better at this.'

'Maybe.' Florin conceded. 'But you're the one who looks most like Piro.' In fact, now that she thought about it, Varuska was more classically beautiful than Piro. The real kingsdaughter had a sharper chin, and her mouth was larger. But only someone who saw the two side by side would notice.

'Wear this, Leif.' Amil returned carrying a man-servant's thigh-length tabard, decorated with gold brocade. 'If we are to accompany his lordship in public, we must add to his magnificence.'

Varuska covered her mouth to suppress a giggle.

Amil ignored her. He wore the same style of tabard but Florin noticed, as he leant forward, that there was a knife strapped to his upper thigh.

She turned her back, removed her simple tabard and dropped the fancy new one over her head. Then she tugged her plait free and settled the male servant's skullcap in place. 'Ready.'

Amil looked her up and down. 'As you'll ever be.' Florin ignored the jibe.

The Ostronite assassin offered Varuska his arm. 'Come, kingsdaughter.'

Varuska went to take it as a country girl would, then remembered and placed her arm along his.

'Good girl.' His voice held approval, but Florin knew he would slit her throat without hesitation on Cobalt's orders. 'We'll make a kingsdaughter of you yet.'

They found the lord at the top of the stairs, deep in conversation with the castle-keep. She was accompanied by a youth, who Florin assumed was her new assistant. He looked overwhelmed. She had probably worn the same expression yesterday herself. When his gaze fell on the false Piro, he gave a little start of surprise.

Had he known the real Piro? Florin tensed, expecting him to denounce Varuska, but he stared at her as if he couldn't believe his eyes.

Florin took another look. With the seed pearls gleaming in her dark hair, the red gown contrasting with her pale skin, her eyes enhanced by the kohl and her painted lips, Varuska was enough to turn any man's head.

The castle-keep looked Florin up and down. 'A day ago you were begging for work. Now look at you in your fine feathers. Mark my words, Leif, fail his lordship and you'll be out on the street just as quickly.'

Fail his lordship and she'd be dead. But Florin bowed and said, 'I live to serve.'

Yegora sniffed and bustled off, with the youth in tow. Meanwhile, Cobalt turned and held out his arm to Varuska.

'Little Piro, how lovely you look.' He leant down to place a chaste kiss on each cheek. 'Cold, my dear?' Lifting her hand to his mouth, he breathed warm air over her fingers and pressed her palm to his chest. 'Do not fear. The people will be delighted to see you've escaped the

Merofynian invasion. My servants tell me commoners have been gathering in the square since dawn, in the hope of catching a glimpse of you.'

With that, they descended the stairs. Servants clustered at every balcony and in every doorway, whispering, pointing and marvelling. One youth was bold enough to cheer, setting them all off. Excited cheering followed the royal party out into the courtyard, where the stable hands waited to catch a glimpse of the kingsdaughter. Florin spotted the tall, skinny boy who'd been hired at the same time as Varuska and her sister. Her stomach clenched with fear, but he gazed on the false Piro with the same adoration as the rest of the stable lads.

And in that moment, Florin understood the power of Cobalt's ploy. After the delivery of Fyn Rolen Kingson's body, the people *wanted* to believe that Piro had survived. They wanted the legitimacy that betrothal to King Rolen's daughter brought to Cobalt's claim.

More prosaically, they wanted life to settle down, so they could plant their crops, bake their bread and sit around the dinner table with their families without fear of war.

'Up here.'

'What?' Florin turned to Amil.

He gestured to the back of the carriage. 'We ride up here, behind Lord Cobalt and the kingsdaughter.'

When they rolled out of the castle and onto the steep switchback road, Florin looked out across the kingdom. It was a crystal clear day. In the distance she could just discern Mount Halcyon. Between the mountain and the castle were patches of farmland and forest, interspersed with lakes reflecting the perfect spring sky.

Directly below, Lake Sapphire lived up to its name, gleaming like a jewel. The township of Rolenton nestled on the lake's banks and the wharfs were full of ships. Even from up here, Florin could see the town square was packed.

'Is that music?' Varuska asked, tilting her head. Now

that she mentioned it, Florin could just pick out the faint thread of music on the air.

'Castle musicians are entertaining the crowd until our arrival,' Cobalt explained. 'This will be every bit as grand as last night, cousin Piro.'

He was right.

As they trundled under the town's defensive gates, word of their arrival spread and a hush fell over the street leading to the square. People watched from first floor balconies, shop fronts and even roof tops.

'Smile and wave, Piro,' Cobalt ordered softly, smiling benignly. Florin caught his expression when he turned to wave, and it made her shiver.

Varuska lifted her hand and the crowd cried Piro's name. The cheering rolled ahead of them, so that by the time they arrived in the square the music had been drowned out. People ran alongside the carriage, some threw early blooming flowers. Many waved scarves and shawls in every shade of red and burgundy.

The roar of the crowd made Florin's head ache. The carriage completed a circuit of the square, before pulling up in front of the merchants' guildhall. The castle musicians had set up on the top steps. Above them, the tower stretched into the clear blue sky.

Cobalt stood and drew Varuska to her feet. The people hushed.

'I give you my betrothed, Pirola Rolen Kingsdaughter.'

Maybe he had intended to give a speech as well, but the crowd's roar was so loud, he could not go on. He smiled and bent to kiss Varuska's cheek. Meanwhile, the musicians resumed playing, battling valiantly to be heard.

Florin gripped the back seat of the carriage. In the crowd she saw apprentices hugging and laughing, fathers with small children on their shoulders, old women wiping tears from their cheeks and couples dancing.

One face, however, wasn't smiling. Anatoley glared up

at her sister. Florin glanced sideways to Varuska, but she hadn't noticed Anatoley in the crush.

An overdressed, middle-aged man came down to the carriage and tugged on Amil's arm. The Ostronite assassin crouched to hear what he had to say.

Cobalt glanced over his shoulder. 'What is it?'

'The merchants have organised a grand feast in the hall,' Amil reported. 'They wish to wine and dine the betrothed couple.'

'Excellent.'

Florin searched the crowd, but Anatoley had disappeared. She hoped the girl had the sense to leave Rolencia.

'Come, cousin Piro.' Cobalt climbed down and offered his hand. The overdressed merchant waited on the steps, eager to welcome them.

Florin followed Cobalt and Varuska up the steps into the merchant guildhall, where a dozen self-important merchants waited, eager to celebrate the usurper's betrothal to King Rolen's only surviving heir.

Cobalt took pride of place at the guildhall table with the false Piro at his side. Everything was going according to his plan.

But it wouldn't be for long. Tears of fury burned Florin's eyes. Cobalt sat in Byren's chair, and soon he would regret it.

GARZIK SMILED AS he imagined Byren and Orrade's surprise when he returned. All his life, he'd been the little brother running after them, trying to earn a place at their sides. Soon he'd return having led a raid against the enemy, bearing useful information on the Merofynians.

'Wynn?' Olbin's hand landed on his shoulder, making him jump. 'Dreamer...'

The big Utlander drew him towards the captain's cabin. They passed Vesnibor, who watched Garzik with narrowed eyes. Then they passed Trafyn, who lay in the passage lost in his fever. Had the squire babbled something about their plans?

Garzik's stomach clenched with fear, but he told himself the Utlanders would have confronted him with Trafyn present.

In the captain's cabin, Garzik found Rusan waiting with seven of his strongest and most respected crew. Hard men, dangerous men. Garzik caught Jost's calculating look. Had the one-eared Utlander sabotaged his plans somehow?

'I've been going through the Merofynian captain's charts, but I can't find one for Mero Bay. Only this.' Rusan pointed to a map spread out on the floor. It showed Merofynia and the spars.

A wave of relief swept Garzik. 'The Merofynian captain wouldn't need a detailed map of his home port.'

'You know Port Mero,' Rusan said. 'What can you tell us?'

Garzik had only been to Port Mero once. Now he racked his brains to recall every snippet of information. He dropped to his knees and pretended to study the map, to buy time.

Merofynia's fertile shores overlooked one large sea, linked to Mero Bay by a canal. The bay was roughly the same size as the Landlocked Sea and was dotted with small fishing villages. Back when he'd sailed into port on Lord Travany's ship, he could remember avoiding sandbars, but...

Rusan crouched next to him. 'I can take my ship just about anywhere by feeling my way, but I can't do that in Port Mero. It would destroy our ruse.'

Garzik pointed to one of the headlands protecting the entrance to Mero Bay and infused his voice with confidence. 'That's Mulcibar's Gate. At its tip is a slow-moving river of lava that makes the sea boil and steam. Once we're beyond that we make north for the port, where we'll drop anchor as if we're waiting for a berth.'

Rusan and Garzik rose and everyone moved to stand each side of the map, revealing their loyalties. Jost was joined by his two half-brothers and another two supporters, leaving Rusan with Olbin, Garzik and the identical twins who had fathered the oracles. They were so alike that when Garzik had first come aboard, he hadn't realised there were two of them. Even now, he could only tell them apart by their scars.

'We'll we need someone who speaks Merofynian like a native,' Crisdun said, and his twin nodded.

'That's where Wynn comes in.' Rusan gestured to Garzik. 'He'll do the talking.'

'Why should we trust him?' Jost looked Garzik up and down. 'He's a slave.'

'Former slave.' Olbin bristled. 'He earned his freedom.'

'Once a slave always a slave, and you're a fool if you think otherwise,' Jost said. 'Why should he betray his own people? For all we know, he's leading us into a trap.'

The twins edged away from Garzik, eyeing him with suspicion. One wrong word now and there would be no trip to Port Mero. Jost would be captain and Garzik's life would be short and horrible.

'I *could* be leading you into a trap,' he admitted, heart racing. 'But these aren't my people. They're Merofynians.' Garzik thought of his father, hanging from their great hall's front doors with a spear through his chest, and his voice grew thick with fury and loss. 'They invaded Rolencia, murdered my father, burned my home and enslaved me. For all I know my sister and brother are dead. I hate them. Death to hot-landers!'

'Death to hot-landers!' Rusan shouted.

All of them echoed him and Olbin opened a crate of wine. Uncorking several bottles, he passed them around, giving one to Garzik, who accepted it, dizzy with relief.

Rusan lifted his bottle. 'We sail into the hot-landers' jaws. Our children's children will sing of this!'

The others cheered and drank.

Olbin slung an arm around Garzik's shoulders and held Jost's eyes in blatant challenge. 'To Wynn!'

The raiders repeated the toast.

Garzik drained his wine, his cheeks hot with shame. He was digging himself deeper and deeper, and taking Rusan and Olbin with him.

The day after tomorrow they'd be in Port Mero. He'd stay on the ship long enough to set up the attack, then escape. Hopefully, the success of the raid would shore up Rusan's leadership.

Why was he worrying? These Utlanders had enslaved and abused him. His duty was to Byren.

Olbin caught Garzik's eye, winked and lifted his bottle in a silent toast.

Chapter Thirteen

FYN WOKE TO the soft *snick* of the door latch as someone entered his chamber. Heart racing, he remained perfectly still. After last night's attack, he had not been able to rest easy in his bed; he'd crept into a dark corner and curled up in the shadows.

Now only a glimmer of morning light entered through the thick curtains, and Fyn could just distinguish the intruder's outline. It couldn't be his manservant. Kyral was short and stocky, and this person was tall and thin.

Had his attackers sent someone to finish the job?

The intruder crept towards his bed. It was a grand oak four-poster embossed with the Merofynian coat of arms. Fyn had pulled the bed-curtains closed to disguise his absence. He drew his knife and rose into a crouch.

The person pulled back the bed curtain, whispering urgently, 'Lord Protector Merofyn, you need to get up.'

Feeling shaky with relief, Fyn came out of hiding. 'Why do I need to get up, and who are you?'

The servant gave a gasp but recovered quickly. 'Queen

Isolt is at the war-table with the captain of the city-watch, and every merchant and noble—'

Fyn cursed, put his knife aside and thrust back the curtains. The light made him wince. It was mid-morning and his head felt stale from lack of sleep.

'How long have they been there?' Fyn asked as he pulled on his breeches then laced his boots.

No answer.

He looked up. The chamber was empty. With a shrug, he finished dressing and left his bedchamber.

The hubbub from the war room echoed down the corridor. The chamber was filled with angry, indignant men, the majority of them nobles and merchants he did not know. Fyn had intended to use the royal tour to meet the lords and take their measure but the only thing he'd learned was how Merofynians really felt about King Rolen's sons.

The long chamber stretched before him. On his right, three tall windows faced north across the Landlocked Sea.

Fyn's first instinct was to find Isolt, but he needed to understand the forces at work here. While he had never joined his father's war-table discussions, he had experienced first-hand the power machinations of Halcyon Abbey. For now, the wisest course was to remain in the shadows and observe, find out who was driving the discussion and, if possible, learn their agenda. He slipped into the chamber unnoticed and stood in the shadows.

Just like back home, the war-table itself was a model of the known world. At the eastern end, closest to where he stood, was Ostron Isle, surrounded by the Ring Isle with its narrow entrance. Down the other end were the twin isles, sitting together like discarded horseshoes.

Merofynia's harbour opened to the south. The kingdom was hemmed in by the Dividing Mountains on three sides. From the Divide stretched the spars, like the spokes of a broken wheel.

West of Merofynia lay Rolencia, its mirror image. The two kingdoms were linked by the Snow Bridge, a broad plateau of ridges and deep valleys.

Nobles and merchants crowded around the war-table. Fyn identified the lords and their companions by their flamboyant dress. Forbidden to wear ermine, sable and silk by sumptuary laws, the merchant margraves were clothed more austerely.

Captain Neiron and Elrhodoc strutted about like peacocks in their fashionable uniforms. By contrast, the captain of the city-watch wore plain fabric, sensibly cut. Nobles did not serve on the city-watch; grey-haired Captain Aeran must have earned his position through merit.

Fyn gathered Isolt had ordered Aeran to take his men and set sail for Benetir Estate. But the merchants protested that this would leave their warehouses and storefronts unprotected, citing the civil unrest and looting that had taken place after King Merofyn died.

'If the city-watch went to the aid of Benetir Estate, my queen, how could we protect the city?' Captain Aeran chose his words with care. Fyn could only catch a glimpse of Isolt between the men, who towered over her.

'Then the nobles must sail for Benetir Estate. They've sworn to aid each other.'

'And so we would, my queen,' Lord Yorale agreed readily. His lands rivalled Lord Dunstany's in size and, like Dunstany, he had been one of the old king's advisors. In his mid-fifties, he wore his grey hair elegantly styled. His accent was refined, yet he still reminded Fyn of King Rolen's trusted master-at-arms. 'We would happily aid a fellow lord, but we lost many men-at-arms in the Rolencian invasion. We can't leave our estates vulnerable.'

Yorale gestured to Benetir Estate. 'If Warlord Cortigern has the gall to lead an attack over the Divide, what's to stop Lincis Spar breaking the accord and laying waste to my estate?'

The other nobles echoed him.

'What of the bay lord?' Isolt asked. 'His lands don't back onto a spar.'

'Cadmor?' Neiron's mouth twitched. 'That inbred sea-hound. Why, he's little better than a spar warlord himself.'

'He did not go to war with Rolencia,' Isolt said. 'He must have fresh men-at-arms.'

'He did not ride to war with us because he was not invited,' Neiron said.

'I must avenge my daughter.' Skin grey with grief, an old lord shook his head. 'Who would have thought marrying her to Benvenute's son would lead to her death?'

'At least she's safely dead, Wytharon,' Lord Yorale told him. 'Not like the poor Benetir girl.'

The bereaved man turned to a middle-aged lord with heavy jowls. 'Travany, your estate lies alongside Ben—'

'I'll do my part, as much as I can without leaving my people unguarded. The Rolencian invasion cost me dearly, my...' Travany's voice faltered. 'My youngest son, Trafyn, was on the same ship as Istyn's heir and Neiron's brother.'

Several nobles offered their condolences; others complained that the invasion had cost more than it was worth.

Fyn had no sympathy.

'Abbot Murheg, what say you?' Lord Yorale asked. 'Will you declare Lord Neirn dead, so that young Neiron can inherit? Nevantir Estate needs to be defended.'

The abbot adjusted the fall of his velvet robe. 'The paperwork—'

'Yes, prepare the paperwork, abbot,' Isolt said. 'It is the royal prerogative to formalise inheritance. Come here, Captain Neiron.'

Fyn had to change position and even then all he could see was the back of Neiron's head as he knelt before Isolt.

'You have served me well, captain of the queen's guard. I name you Lord Neiron of Nevantir Estate. But there is one last task before you resign your commission. You must name your successor as captain of my guard.'

It came as no surprise when Neiron named his best friend, Elrhodoc, captain of the queen's guards.

While Elrhodoc gave his oath, Fyn watched those who stood near the centre of power. Yorale was on the queen's right. Abbot Murheg stood on her left with the abbess.

Everyone drank to the health of the new lord and captain.

'The invasion of Rolencia has cost us dearly,' Travany complained. 'And what have we gained?'

'Shiploads of red wine,' one wit replied.

There was some laughter.

'Our granaries are full, we've more silver plate and seven-year slaves than we know what to do with,' Travany conceded. 'But do we have Rolencia?'

'No,' they grumbled.

'And what's more, the market is glutted,' a merchant protested. 'There's no profit to be made on my wool.'

'Travany's right.' Yorale was not going to let the men of commerce divert the conversation. 'We don't have Rolencia. Yet we left five companies of our finest men to help Cobalt hold the kingdom. We need to recall them.' He shook his head. 'The spar warlord's attack on Benetir Estate is an outrage, but until we recall our men—'

'What of the seven-year slaves?' the wool merchant asked.

'Those churls?' Travany sneered. 'They'd cut your throat first chance they got, you know Rolencians.'

The gathering laughed and Fyn's face flamed. It did not surprise him that the only two lords willing to bestir themselves to help Benetir Estate were the two with a vested interest—Wytharon and Travany.

'We can't wait for our men from Rolencia. We need to act now. What of the queen's guards?' Lord Wytharon asked.

They all turned to Neiron, who gestured to the new captain of the queen's guard.

'Naturally we despise the spar barbarians, but we swore to protect the queen,' Elrhodoc said. 'Our place is with her.'

'I'm glad to hear that,' Isolt said, 'because I'm going to save Lady Sefarra.'

This caused an outcry. They were quick to advise her against it, and the discussion soon deteriorated, voices escalating as tempers rose.

Old King Merofyn should never have invaded Rolencia; no, the invasion was Palatyne's idea; King Merofyn should never have acknowledged Palatyne as overlord of the spars; Merofyn should have crushed the upstart warlord.

Sefarra's fate was the last thing on their minds.

Anger ignited Fyn and he was just about to call for quiet when he spotted Isolt making her way around behind the arguing men. She nodded to the door.

They slipped out of the war-table chamber, going along the corridor to a window seat. Neither of them sat down. From here Fyn could see the terraced gardens stepping down to the Landlocked Sea. It was too hazy to make out the distant shore. Graceful white cyena birds glided on the sparkling shallows.

Fyn turned to Isolt. 'Why did you start the war-table discussion without me?'

'I didn't call a council. I was studying the war-table, trying to think of a way to save Sefarra, when everyone just arrived.' Fury made her eyes glitter and she shook with anger. 'They don't care about her. One of them told me since we can't save her purity, there's no point saving her!'

Isolt prowled back and forth, before dropping into the window seat. She rubbed her temples. 'I swear my head hurts from all their shouting.'

Mid-morning sun warmed her pale skin. She looked fragile; Fyn wanted to take her in his arms.

Instead, he sat beside her. 'Travany and Wytharon have volunteered their support. They both have something at stake.'

'But Wytharon's estate lies across the Landlocked Sea, and even Travany will take several days to gather his men, arm them and prepare for battle,' Isolt said, as organised in war as she was when staging a feast. 'That's why I wanted Captain Neiron—I mean Elrhodoc—to assist Captain Aeran. Both guards are armed and ready. Even if the other lords agreed to help, they would have to sail home to gather their men.'

Fyn nodded. 'I suspect some would delay in the hope we'd sail without them. More than Benetir Estate could be lost before the nobles honoured their vows. They're greedy, short-sighted fools, thinking only of their own gain.' Frustration welled up in him. 'Why can't they see that Merofynia needs them? *Sefarra* needs—' He shook his head, unable to go on.

Isolt covered his hand with hers. 'You're a good person.'

He felt the heat race up his cheeks and shook his head. 'I don't—'

'You see the best in people. Me, I've seen the worst.' She squeezed his hand and let him go. 'Of all my father's advisors, Dunstany and Yorale were the most loyal, and Dunstany was my favourite. But we can't wait for him. Every day we delay is a day Sefarra suffers in the warlord's hands.'

'Every day we delay makes you look weak.'

'You're right. And they already think me weak because of my sex. If only we could organise an attack. We could be there within half a day.' Isolt's eyes widened. 'Why, Cortigern could attack the city this very night!' She sprang to her feet. 'We must warn the others.'

Fyn wasn't convinced Cortigern intended to attack Port Mero, and if he did, he'd have to steal boats to cross the Landlocked Sea. If Fyn knew spar warriors, Cortigern's men would be celebrating the capture of Benetir Estate by drinking themselves insensible.

'Fyn?'

He came to his feet. 'A threat to Port Mero will

motivate the merchants and nobles. We might be able to pull together enough men to sail this evening.'

'Good. The sooner we get there, the sooner we save—'

'You're not coming. You sent for me, let me—'

'I didn't send for you.'

'Then who—'

'Fyn, if I stay in the palace, the nobles won't respect me. They already think that I'm fit only for bearing the next heir. If I am to be queen, I must be seen to lead.' Isolt held his eyes. 'I must do this.'

'Isolt...' There she stood, so determined yet so vulnerable. He couldn't bear it if anything happened to her. Yet, as much as he hated to admit it, she was right.

Seeing his expression, she smiled. 'Don't worry. I won't insist on fighting. I'm no warrior.'

'You're Isolt Wyvern Queen.' Fyn offered his arm. He was ready to confront the Merofynian nobles. He didn't do this for Byren, he did it for Isolt; and he must not let her down.

When they reached the door, Fyn gestured for Isolt to go first. She swept into the chamber, with him one step behind.

'My people.' Isolt waited for them to fall silent. 'Warlord Cortigern is less than a day's sail from us, and the city has no defensive walls. There's nothing to stop him striking into the heart of Port Mero.'

'All the more reason to keep the city-watch close,' a merchant insisted, voice rising in panic.

'All the more reason to strike swiftly,' Fyn said. 'We don't want fighting in the streets. Townhouses will burn and shops will be looted.' He paused to let that sink in. 'I promised Lady Gennalla I'd save Benetir Estate. If we set sail by dusk, we'll be there by midnight. If Cortigern's warriors are anything like the spar warriors in Rolencia, they'll be drinking, boasting and bedding...' Thinking of poor Sefarra's fate he hurried on. 'They'll be so drunk they won't know what's hit them!'

That lit a fire under them.

To Fyn's relief, no one asked him why the port was in imminent danger if Cortigern's warriors were rolling drunk.

Eager to protect their investments, the merchants offered their support. The captain of the city-watch had no choice but to volunteer his men, and the queen's guards were in the same position. All that remained was for Wytharon and Travany to gather what men they could from their household staff and honour guards.

Everyone trooped out, leaving Fyn and Isolt with Lord Yorale.

'It is unfortunate this uprising has happened so early in your reign,' Yorale told Isolt. 'But you've acted decisively to quell it. I promised your father, if anything happened to him, I would watch over you. I wish I could offer more practical support, but one of my best captains is still in Rolencia and my two surviving sons are inexperienced lads of seventeen and ten.' He put his hand on Isolt's shoulder. 'If you'll forgive an old family friend, your father would be proud of you, my queen.'

Isolt's eyes gleamed with unshed tears. 'Thank you.'

'And you...' Yorale turned to Fyn. 'You handled yourself well. It can't be easy, being King Rolen's son and serving your brother's interests in Merofynia.' He studied Fyn. 'You remind me of your Uncle Sefon.'

Fyn had never met his mother's brother. 'What was he like?'

'A thinker, a scholar. But I suspect you have more backbone than him. Well done, lad.'

Fyn flushed. 'I do my best. Now I must oversee the preparations.'

Much later, as Fyn headed to his chamber to grab his weapons, he realised there was someone following him. Heart hammering, he stepped into a dim alcove and waited. Furtive footsteps approached.

Timing his attack, Fyn sprang out, caught the person and slammed them up against the alcove wall with his knife at their throat. It was the tall, skinny servant who had woken him, but Fyn did not lower the knife. 'Who sent you?'

The servant swallowed audibly, Adam's apple bobbing

against the knife. 'He never admitted it, but I think he was Lord Dovecote's youngest son. I'm supposed to collect information to help Byren's cause.'

Fyn licked his lips. Crazy, impossible hope filled him. If Garzik still lived... 'Did he have a small gap between his two front teeth?'

'Yes.'

The world swung; Fyn had to lean forward until his vision cleared. He must let Byren and Orrade know. Steadying himself against the wall, Fyn lifted his head. 'What's your name?'

'Mitrovan. I scribe for Lord Travany, who serves Lord Yorale's interests. If I learn anything useful, I'm supposed to send a message back to Byren. Wynn...' Mitrovan shrugged. 'That's the name he went by, and that's how I think of him. He was going to take news to Byren, but we were separated, and...' His chin trembled.

'And?' Fyn's mouth went dry.

'He was sent on another voyage. Lord Travany's ship did not return, and Travany lost his youngest son. He was heartbroken.'

For the second time in as many moments, Fyn bent double. He fought nausea. To have such hope, then to have it dashed away... His throat felt tight with grief.

'I'm sorry I don't have better news,' the scribe said. 'I promised Wynn I'd spy for Byren.'

Fyn nodded, unable to speak. It was good to know Garzik's legacy lived on in Mitrovan.

'To prove myself, I told you about the war-table meeting,' Mitrovan explained. 'The nobles wanted to hold the council without you.'

'Thank you for warning me.'

'Lord Protector Merofyn, what would you have me do?'

'Call me Fyn. And if you hear anything that might help Byren, let me know.'

Chapter Fourteen

Byren woke to low voices. For a moment, he didn't know where he was. He was ravenously hungry, but had the feeling something terrible had happened.

'Why does it smell so bad in here?' the cabin boy whispered.

'It's the ulfr furs,' the captain replied. 'In the heat, it stinks like an Affinity beast's den.'

'Should I open a window?'

'No. They need to keep warm.'

And it all came back to Byren... Orrade cold and still, as good as dead, him crawling under the furs to keep his friend warm.

'Will Lord Dovecote be all right?' the boy whispered.

The old sailor's silence was answer enough.

Byren was aware of someone coming closer.

The boy inspected Orrade. 'He's breathing now.'

'If he wasn't breathing before, he'd be dead now.'

'But—'

'Don't get your hopes up, lad.' The captain sounded grim. 'I've seen men start to warm up, but their hands and feet will still be cold, so we'll try to warm them. Then, for no reason, their hearts just give out. Come along, now.'

There was a sound of shuffling feet and the door closed.

Byren opened his eyes. A finger of golden, late-afternoon light came through the window. He'd slept the better part of the day away.

He sat up to check on Orrade. The fine ulfr fur near Orrie's mouth stirred with each breath. Byren slid his hand under the covers, felt Orrade's shoulder and back. Warm, but his extremities were still icy cold.

Byren's first instinct was to chafe Orrade's hands and feet to get the blood circulating but, if this was what the sailors had done for their companions, it hadn't helped. In fact, it might have contributed to their deaths. Imagine all that chilled blood flowing back into Orrade's chest, shocking his heart...

Byren might yet lose him.

Resisting the impulse to hasten the warming, he freshened up, ate something.

If he'd still believed in Goddess Halcyon, he would have prayed to her; but so much had happened since the Merofynian invasion that he no longer had faith in the bringer of summer. As for Sylion, the cold-hearted god of winter, he felt sure the cruelty in the world could all be laid at the feet of bad luck and heartless men, rather than dark gods.

Affinity was real enough. He'd seen the evidence with his own eyes. He was reminded of something Orrade had once said, something to the effect that the gods were man's explanation for Affinity.

All their lives, Orrade had been one step ahead of him. He didn't know what he would do without Orrie. Panic threatened to overwhelm him, but Byren refused to give in.

Orrade was going to live.

He glanced to his friend, who slept on oblivious. At least he hoped it was sleep. It would be too cruel if

Orrade lost his wits. That would be worse than death. Orrie would not want to live a halfwit. Byren would have to kill him. It was the least he could do for his friend.

Tears stung Byren's eyes.

He lay down and pulled Orrade against his chest. This time he deliberately sought the ulfr breathing pattern. The deep rumble in his chest sounded like the purring of a great cat. Byren smiled. If only the captain could hear him now.

PIRO TRIED TO be patient.

She sat on a brocade window seat in House Cinnamome's palace. A balmy breeze brought the exotic scents of Ostron Isle—citrus flowers from the courtyard below and, underneath that, the sweet tang of honey-cinnamon tea. The rise and fall of voices continued behind her, their words disguised by a servant plucking a dolcimela's strings. Siordun was deep in conversation with the old comtissa of House Cinnamome.

Piro had nearly asked after the middle-aged comtissa, but the last time she'd been on Ostron Isle she'd been disguised as Isolt's servant. Back then she'd been excluded from conversations, and this time was no better.

Waiting drove Piro to distraction.

A spike of impatience made her stomach knot—no excess Affinity. She needed to channel it, but she couldn't focus power on the stone Siordun had given her.

Frustrated, she looked over the courtyard. Beyond the red-tiled roofs, she could see Mage Isle with its famous white tower, the tallest tower in the world.

Why couldn't they have gone straight there?

She glanced to Siordun and the old woman. What could be so important here? The fighting over the role of elector had ceased, and Ostron Isle had a new elector in Comtissa Cera of House Cerastus. Unless she died in office, there would be peace for another five years.

The mournful cry of a wyvern carried on the breeze. Piro sat up and glanced quickly to Siordun and the comtissa. They kept talking.

The cry had come from beyond the three-storey building on the other side of the courtyard. Piro's skin prickled as she detected a hint of Affinity. Of course... this was why she'd been feeling impatient. She'd sensed the wyvern's power and hers had responded.

Piro had grown accustomed to being around Isolt's pet wyvern. She missed Loyalty and her own pet foenix terribly. If she was honest, she resented having to leave Resolute behind.

The strange wyvern gave voice again.

Piro stood and stretched.

Siordun and the comtissa turned to her. She'd thought they'd been intent on their discussion.

Assuming her most innocent face, she asked, 'Is it all right if I go for a walk? I've been cooped up on the ship so long.'

'Of course, dear,' the old comtissa said.

Siordun gave her a sharp look, but the comtissa distracted him before he could question her.

Piro slipped out of the chamber, down the stairs and into the courtyard. She continued straight across the white flagstones, past a fountain and between two rows of topiary citrus trees, heading for the building on the far side.

It was shaded by a deep verandah, and beyond that was a dark ground floor chamber, filled with heavy furniture, rugs and urns. She hardly noticed, as she made for the far doors, the next courtyard and the wyvern.

As soon as she stepped into the courtyard, her heart lifted and her Affinity stirred. The wyvern was nearby and, by the sound of it, the beast was growing impatient.

Rows of vegetables stretched out before her. From the buildings that bounded the courtyard on three sides she heard laughter and singing. She smelled baking bread and boiling starch, reminding her of laundry days back home. Beyond the vegetable garden was a lower terrace, where lines of washing hung in the afternoon sun, stirring in the light breeze. The minstrels sang of how it was always summer in Ostron Isle. This afternoon, she almost believed them.

An aviary stood against the courtyard wall on her left, and this was where she found the wyvern. Caged.

Back at Rolenhold, one courtyard had housed her grandfather's menagerie. Most of the beasts had died of old age by the time she was born, but she'd made friends with the unistag and her brothers had brought back the foenix egg that she'd cared for and hatched. Back then, she hadn't realised how cruel it was to keep Affinity beasts caged. Now she knew better, and she bristled on the wyvern's behalf.

Her steps slowed as she approached the cage. The wyvern's intelligent eyes tracked Piro. A tingle of excitement ran through her as she felt her Affinity surge. The wyvern was much larger than Isolt's pet; the beast's wings brushed the top of the cage.

A surge of anger warmed Piro. 'Why, there's not enough room for you to stretch your wings. You poor boy.'

The wyvern was male, very definitely.

She checked to see if she could open the cage, but it was padlocked.

The build-up of her Affinity reached a peak. She felt it concentrate in her hand until the skin throbbed and itched.

'Handsome boy,' she crooned, extending her hand through the bars of the cage. The wyvern nuzzled her fingers.

'Here, what're you doing, girlie?' Rough hands pulled her away from the cage.

The wyvern hissed, barred his teeth and roared. Piro covered her ears, staggering back.

'Are you all right?' the old man asked, his voice softening. 'You mustn't go near the beastie, girl, it—'

'I was fine until you came along. You startled the poor thing.'

'That poor thing near killed the young master.'

'No.'

'Yes.'

She studied the wyvern. The force of his rage and anger could not be contained by the cage. Already she could see the bolts holding the cage to the wall were working loose.

'The beast failed to bond with the young master. Now...' The old retainer eyed the caged wyvern.

'He'll be turned loose?' Piro asked. It shamed her to realise she'd never thought to ask what happened to Affinity pets that didn't bond.

The old retainer sent her a guarded look.

'They'll turn the wyvern loose, won't they?' Piro insisted.

'The beastie doesn't know how to hunt, or how to live with its own kind. Be cruel to turn it out to die.'

'So they'll kill him?' Piro could not hide her horror. 'Is that what happens to all the pets that don't bond with their owners?'

'Pet wyverns are no longer fashionable. Too many injuries.'

'You mean none of them bonded?' She had to warn Isolt.

He would not meet her eyes.

She studied the wyvern. 'I think you should set him free. And I'm going to tell the comtissa!'

'Piro?' Siordun sounded annoyed. He was beckoning from the far end of the courtyard.

She hurried over to him, full of righteous indignation. 'Have you heard about the pet wyverns?'

'No.' He walked off and she had to hurry to keep up with him as he led her through the building, towards the formal courtyard. 'I've been busy trying to avert a war, if you hadn't noticed.'

'If they don't bond with their owners, they're killed!'

'I'm not surprised.' He strode between the citrus trees. 'I told them making pets of wyverns was not a good idea.

Certainly they are intelligent and beautiful, and the pups are very winsome, but they aren't like abeilles or pica birds. The more intelligent, the more dangerous—'

'We have to do something.'

'The fashion's changed, Piro. The Ostronites are constructing observatories to study the stars. They believe the stars can foretell—'

'But what about the wyverns? I can't just stand back and let them kill Affinity beasts.'

'Affinity beasts get killed all the time.' His sharp black eyes studied her. 'As I recall, your brothers were renowned for their hunting skills. Byren the Leogryf Slayer?'

She flushed. 'Only in defence of villagers.'

'You killed a manticore.'

'It was trying to kill me!' He was deliberately misunderstanding her. She wanted to shake him, but they had entered the building. Their voices echoed up to the vaulted ceiling far above. 'I know better now. We have to stop this. We have to free the pet wyverns.'

'So their own kind can kill them? I'm sorry Piro, but wyverns are social animals, much like horses or manticores. Is the wyvern male or—'

'Male.'

'Then the other males would kill it.'

'I want to speak with the comtissa. Which reminds me, where's the younger comtissa anyway? The one who was there the night the elector—'

'Lower your voice!' He glanced around quickly. 'She died when the great houses fought over the new elector. Besides, you weren't there the night the last elector died. That was Isolt and her maid, not—'

'I know. I'm not stupid.'

'Listen, Piro. You are to stay here, with the comtissa. She will—'

'No...' Piro took a step back. 'You said you'd take me to Mage Isle. You said you'd teach me.'

'Yes, I know. But the voyage gave me time to think, and

you must see that's impossible. You're a kingsdaughter. While I'm—'

'I know exactly who you are, and I preferred Lord Dunstany to you any day!' She'd loved the old lord and missed him fiercely. Tears burned her eyes. She found it hard to reconcile Siordun with his other identities. The voyage home was the longest time she'd spent with him in his true form. 'Lord Dunstany was kind to me. You're always snapping at me. Everything I do is wrong. You're as bad as my mother.'

His mouth tightened and a flush crept up his cheeks.

'I miss her,' Piro admitted. 'I never thought I would, but...'

'I'm sorry, Piro, so sorry.' Siordun sighed. 'I cannot take you to Mage Isle. It was foolish of me to even suggest it. You're almost of marriageable age—'

She laughed. 'I'm never going to marry. I told you I don't want to be just another game piece.'

'That's not what I meant.' He appeared embarrassed for her. 'It would be unseemly to stay alone with me in the tower.'

'But you're so old.' She rolled her eyes. He had to be at least twenty-five. 'Besides, we wouldn't be alone. The mage will be there.'

He frowned in warning.

She smiled sweetly, assuming the innocent look that used to fool her father's guards. 'No one would think it improper if I stayed with Mage Tsulamyth.'

'You don't want to stay with a crotchety old mage,' the comtissa said, making her slow, painful way down the stairs towards them.

A youth of about Fyn's age aided her with his good arm; the other arm was bound and strapped in a sling. Although a trifle pale, he looked determined. He was dressed in the Ostronite fashion. His coat was tapered at the waist, and there was lace at his throat and wrists. Like the sea-hound captain, he wore his long black curls loose on his shoulders. In fact, now that she looked more closely, he bore a strong resemblance to Nefysto, except his cheeks were soft. And he was as beautiful as a girl, while the sea-hound captain was strong-jawed and handsome. She revised the lad's age down from seventeen to fifteen—Garzik's age, had he survived the invasion.

Garzik's death hit her all over again.

Garzik and Elina were lost, Lence, too. Her father no longer sat on the throne with her mother to advise him. Rolencia was no longer her home, and now Siordun was trying to get rid of her. Panic pierced Piro. She gulped in a breath and fought to slow her racing heart.

The comtissa negotiated the last step and gestured grandly. 'I offer you the protection of House Cinnamome, Pirola Rolen Kingsdaughter. This is my grandson, Kaspian, the new Comtes Cinnamome. Kaspian can escort you to balls and concerts. You'll have pretty dresses and flirt with the handsomest youths of Ostron Isle's five families. By midsummer you'll have broken a dozen hearts!'

Piro turned to Siordun in horror. 'Please, don't leave me here.'

'Piro.' He sent the comtissa an apologetic look and as he took Piro's hands in both of his, speaking kindly, he reminded her of Lord Dunstany. 'You'll have a wonderful time. I'll come to visit every day and give you lessons. Soon you'll be sick of the sight of me.'

Piro shook her head. Even before her family and friends had been murdered, she'd never enjoyed parties. Now that they were all dead...

She could not contain her tears. Sobs shattered her. Siordun went to take her in his arms, then hesitated.

'Poor dear.' The comtissa waved him off. 'After what the child's been through...'

Before Piro knew what was happening, the comtissa had swept her into a gardenia-scented embrace. Soon Piro found herself in luxurious private chambers where the comtissa tried to divert her with talk of dresses and parties.

Piro had never been more miserable in her life.

Chapter Fifteen

FYN SURVEYED THE hotchpotch flotilla that followed the royal barge across the Landlocked Sea. The sun set behind them, painting the sails a brilliant orange. The city-watch crowded onto the royal barge with the queen's guards. There were several small fishing boats, two broad-bellied merchant boats packed with hired swords and sturdy workmen, and the three pleasure yachts, belonging to Lords Wytharon, Travany and Benvenute.

Self-interest was a great motivator.

The captain of the city-watch joined Fyn and Isolt at the prow. Captain Elrhodoc stiffened at his approach.

'The barge captain tells me we're making good time,' Aeran said. 'Hopefully, we'll surprise the greedy warlord before his men remember where they left their weapons.'

'You bring us luck, my queen.' Elrhodoc gave Isolt a graceful half-bow.

The contrast between the handsome nobleman and the grizzled captain of the city-watch was never more evident, but Fyn knew which man he would trust at his back.

One of the city-watchmen gave a yelp as Isolt's wyvern snapped at him. Three of the queen's guards laughed and urged the wyvern on.

'I trust your men won't let us down.' Elrhodoc turned to Aeran. 'They're used to dealing with pickpockets masquerading as jugglers and raddled whores, not hardened spar warriors.'

'I hope your parade-ground warriors don't let us down.' The light of battle gleamed in Aeran's eyes. 'From what I hear, they are most comfortable dealing cards and juggling whores.'

Elrhodoc flushed. 'At least my men aren't the sons of whores.'

Aeran bristled.

There was a shout of laughter. Two more of the city-watch had joined the first, bringing the foenix with them. The watchmen threatened to turn the foenix on the wyvern.

'Stop!' Fyn and Isolt yelled at once.

'Loyalty, Resolute, to me!' Isolt called. Both Affinity beasts came at her call. 'See to your men, Aeran.'

Furious, the captain bowed and left them.

'Is it any wonder my men refuse to fight alongside such trash?' Elrhodoc asked.

Isolt sent Fyn a worried look.

'Do not fear, my queen. I'll leave half a dozen men on the barge to keep you safe. We'll...' Elrhodoc broke off; the altercation had escalated. He excused himself and went over to deal with it.

Frustration filled Fyn. How could he defeat the spar warlord, when his own men were at each other's throats? He turned to Isolt. 'You shouldn't have come.'

She stroked the two Affinity beasts. 'Loyalty and Resolute won't leave my side. If anyone tried to hurt me, they'd tear them to shreds.'

* * *

Piro went down to dinner, determined to catch Kaspian alone and confront him about the way he was treating his wyvern. As she watched her escort's broad back, she wondered if she was a prisoner.

Never mind, she'd slipped past her father's honour guards many a time. Men tended to see a dainty young woman with a pretty face and not much more.

Not Siordun. That was why it was so frustrating being cooped up here.

'Kingsdaughter.' The servant opened the door.

The chamber was filled with scented candles, their myriad flickering flames reflected in many gilt-edged mirrors. The sweet sound of a dolcimela greeted her as she stepped across the threshold.

Perhaps there was a chance Siordun had come to dinner. At least she wouldn't be bored.

But when she looked over, it was Kaspian who played the stringed instrument. He'd slipped his bandaged arm free of the sling and frowned in concentration as he exercised his injured limb. The old comtissa sat by the fire watching him fondly.

Seeing Piro, she patted a footstool at her side. 'There you are, sweetling. Feeling better? You look better. My, but that colour suits you, and the fit is excellent. Turn around. Let me look at you.'

Piro obeyed, not fooled for a moment by the old woman's prattle. The comtissa was sharp as a blade.

The taffeta skirt swirled out. It was a red so deep it was almost burgundy. This was her family's colour, which, she now realised, was also House Cinnamome's colour.

'I must thank you for the gown,' she said. 'It's very pretty.'

The comtissa made a dismissive gesture. 'A ready-made dress, but it is from Ostron Isle's greatest fashionista. She will design originals just for you. Now, sit by my side and listen to Kaspian.'

It was warm by the fire, and Piro felt a little light-headed. She took the proffered seat and the comtissa took her hand. Despite the heat, the old woman's fingers were cool and dry.

The moment she took the comtissa's hand, Piro's vision slipped from the seen to the unseen world and her Affinity surged. Under the comtissa's powdered, painted cheeks, she saw a skull. Piro's heart faltered, then raced so fast she found it hard to catch her breath.

The last time that Piro had seen a skull behind someone's face, the person had been dead before the night was out. Did this mean...

'Just look at him.' The comtissa gestured to her grandson. With his long curled hair and soft cheeks, he had an androgynous beauty. 'Surely a grandmother could not wish for a more handsome heir?'

'But he's so young,' Piro blurted. How could he lead House Cinnamome?

'Kaspian's nearly sixteen. He's been sitting beside me while I run House Cinnamome's interests, since the last elector died. He's trained in merchant law, speaks three languages and knows the history of the three islands. You could do worse, Pirola.' Those sharp black eyes fixed on her. 'Forgive an old woman for speaking plainly but, when you get to my age, you don't have time for prevarication. You are a kingsdaughter, yet both kings of the twin isles are your brothers. Who will you marry? A brash spar warlord? An Utland barbarian? Better to ally yourself with House Cinnamome, richest of the five great merchant families of Ostron Isle.'

Piro did not know what to say. Apart from the fact that she had no intention of *ever* marrying, the comtissa seemed to think Fyn was king of Merofynia. 'My brother is minding Merofynia until Byren can defeat our cousin, reclaim Rolencia and then marry Queen Isolt.'

'What a man has, he holds. It is instinctive.'

'Fyn's not like that. He's honourable.'

The comtissa squeezed her hand. 'Think on what I've said. If young Kaspian is not to your liking, another of my boys is coming to dinner, my niece's son Natteo. The gossips of Ostron Isle will tell you Nat is a dilettante, renowned only for his poetry and many lovers, but he is so much more.'

'But I don't want a husband,' Piro protested.

'What girl does not want a husband?'

Piro shook her head. 'I just want...' What did she want?

First she wanted to study Affinity, but then what?

Back in Rolencia those with Affinity served the abbeys, or faced banishment. She didn't want to be shut up in an abbey, but she didn't want power or wealth for its own sake. That left studying under Siordun, serving Mage Tsulamyth's great plan to maintain the balance of power between the three kingdoms.

As a kingsdaughter, she'd been groomed to serve. Her mother had taught her to read and write in three languages. She knew Rolencian law, how to balance the castle accounts and how to run a castle. All good preparation for marrying into a royal family, but a queen's reach was limited by her husband's intelligence and the boundaries of custom.

As one of Tsulamyth's agents, she could cross borders and change her identity at will. She could stand one step behind the rulers and influence their decisions.

She could make a real difference!

Kaspian put the dolcimela aside and joined them. He placed a fond kiss on the comtissa's papery cheek. 'How are you feeling tonight, grandmother?'

Piro felt a pang of jealousy. She hadn't known either of her grandmothers.

'Piro was just telling me how much she admired your playing,' the comtissa lied, straight-faced. 'You must teach her.'

'If you wish.' The youth gave Piro a graceful bow. She would have liked him better if he'd hadn't been so formal.

As he took his seat in a chair upholstered in the house colours, with the crest on the high back, Piro was reminded of a throne. For all that Ostron Isle was led by an elector—she was still playing at Duelling Kingdoms.

'Did I hear Nat's name?' Kaspian asked eagerly. 'Will my cousin be coming to dinner?'

The comtissa beamed. 'Most assuredly.'

Kaspian cast Piro a sharp glance. She got the impression he resented her presence. Before she could pursue this, the door opened and Captain Nefysto walked in.

Piro had to look twice to be sure it was really him. What had been a tendency to flamboyant dress on the *Wyvern's Whelp* had become a parody on Ostron Isle. Instead of velvet, he wore a pale satin coat with ridiculously padded shoulders. His face was powdered and painted, and even his walk was different, a mince in place of the swagger of a sea-hound. From his perfumed hair to his jewelled high-heels, he was everything her brothers despised about Ostron Isle.

She glanced to Kaspian. Surely, if he was being trained to lead House Cinnamome, he knew Nefysto's true calling.

'Natteo.' The comtissa beckoned Nefysto to her side, then made the formal introductions. 'Meet Pirola Rolen Kingsdaughter.'

Nefysto's painted black eyes laughed as he kissed her hand with an elaborate flourish.

'Viscomtes,' she addressed him, grateful for her mother's lessons in protocol. 'Natteo, how nice to finally meet you.'

'Give an old woman time to speak with her favourite grand-nephew,' the comtissa said. 'Kaspian, show our guest the miniatures.'

This was Piro's chance to ask him about his pet wyvern. He led her to the far end of the chamber, past paintings of comtes and comtissas, past silver statuettes of Affinity beasts and urns of fresh flowers.

'House Cinnamome's collection is the envy of the five houses.' He gestured to a glass-fronted cabinet which contained intricately-jewelled miniatures of Affinity beasts. 'Would you like to hold one?'

'Do you want to save your wyvern?'

His beautiful lips parted in surprise.

'Do you want to save him? They're going to kill him, you know. Or don't you care?'

'Of course I care.' He bristled. 'Don't presume to judge me. I raised him from a pup. I love Val.' He lifted his bandaged arm. 'I was trying to bond with him when this happened.'

Piro decided she liked Kaspian after all. 'Good. Then we can save... what did you call him? Val?'

'Valiant.'

It was such a typical name for a boy to choose that she smiled.

Kaspian frowned. 'What?'

'I can help you.' She'd always been good with animals and since her Affinity had manifested she'd become even better. 'Meet me on the balcony after supper.'

Chapter Sixteen

FLORIN LEANED ON the back of Varuska's chair. The evening seemed interminable. She'd already counted the forest of columns holding up the great hall's ceiling, compared the painted gilt-edged carvings and worked out how many repetitions there were per column. She glanced to Amil, who was standing behind Cobalt's chair. How did he fend off boredom?

Would that minstrel never stop singing?

She didn't understand why Cobalt wanted to hold another feast. After all, how many feasts did it take to legitimise his rule?

Cobalt had recognised the new lord of Steadford Estate, and awarded another markiz title, ensuring the merchant's loyalty. The new markiz had hired a minstrel to compose a song of praise in Cobalt's honour. If the minstrel was to be believed, Cobalt had saved the kingdom singlehandedly, from a cruel dictator and his arrogant sons.

The rewriting of King Rolen's reign infuriated Florin.

She clenched her jaw and stared straight ahead. By chance, her gaze settled on a vicomtissa from one of the great merchant houses of Ostron Isle.

The Merofynian invasion had impoverished Rolencian nobles and merchants alike, but they would be rich again. The vicomtissa was deep in negotiations, arranging loans so that the nobles and merchants could restock. Florin found it fascinating to watch a woman who looked like someone's elderly aunt drive hard men to their knees as she bargained. She had never seen lords and markizes defer to a woman before.

She'd been moving in the wrong circles.

Meanwhile, Cobalt was deep in conversation with the new markiz and the abbot, leaving Varuska to her own devices.

The girl tugged on Florin's arm. 'Can I go now?'

Florin glanced around. No one appeared to be listening to the minstrel. The feasters chattered on, their tongues loosened by rich red wine. There was so much smoke from the many scented candles that Florin doubted if the people at the far end could even *see* the rest of the royal table. Would anyone notice if they left?

She tapped Amil's shoulder. 'Piro is tired. I'll escort her up to bed.'

He leaned forward to whisper to Cobalt, who bid Varuska a fond good night. Turning back to his companions, he made a comment about her sleeping now because she wouldn't get much once they were married. This roused the kind of vile male laughter that made Florin want to punch someone.

Varuska glanced to Florin. Clearly, the thought of marrying Cobalt terrified her.

Florin helped the girl to her feet. 'Hide your true feelings.'

Varuska nodded. Florin had seen that pinched expression on other women's faces. For every woman who single-handedly ran a castle or merchant house, there were a dozen men ready to teach her her place. Florin grimaced. Back when she served alongside Byren's honour guard, she'd had trouble with Winterfall. On more than one occasion, he'd tried to slide his hands into places they didn't belong, and when she'd made it clear she wasn't interested, he'd turned nasty.

While the guests chattered on oblivious, Florin led Varuska down to the end of the table.

They'd just reached the steps of the royal dais, when Varuska hesitated. 'I can't do this, Leif. The thought of his hands on me—'

'Piro Rolen Kingsdaughter,' an old woman called as she hobbled towards them. Her white hair was bound up in a bun and she wore a widow's gown.

Florin felt Varuska tremble with fear.

'Just as I thought.' The old woman looked Varuska up and down, her top lip curling with contempt. 'This girl is not Piro.' She gestured to the guests on the royal dais, inviting them to look. 'Are you all blind?'

The closest guests had fallen silent, but others further back chattered on.

'I held Piro when she was born.' The aged voice cracked with emotion. 'I saw her take her first step. I loved her as my own...'

'Seela?' Florin hadn't seen Byren's old nurse since she'd left the hidden mountain camp. Seela had aged so much that Florin barely recognised her.

'Who?' Varuska breathed.

'Piro's old nurse,' Florin whispered. 'She came from Merofynia with Queen Myrella.'

Varuska tried to take a step back, but Florin stopped her.

'Are you blind?' Seela repeated, voice carrying.

The musicians missed the beat and the singer faltered before falling silent. Everyone turned to look at Varuska and Florin, and the frail old woman who confronted them.

'What is this?' Cobalt asked, rising to his feet.

'If you admit the truth, we're both dead,' Florin whispered in Varuska's ear. 'Go hug Seela. Claim her sight is going. She's gotten so frail and thin, perhaps it has. You—'

'What's going on?' Cobalt demanded.

Florin glanced over her shoulder. Amil was already moving. She prodded Varuska.

'S-Seela? Is that you?' The girl's hesitation sounded natural, although Florin knew it sprang from terror. 'You've grown so thin, I hardly knew you.'

The old woman blinked, shocked.

'Run to her,' Florin urged. 'Piro is impetuous.'

Lifting her skirts, Varuska ran down the three steps and across the floor, to throw her arms around Piro's old nurse.

By the time Florin reached them, Seela had pulled out of the embrace. She drew breath to speak, then recognised Florin and a flash of understanding passed over the old nurse's face. Her manner changed instantly.

She caught Varuska's face in her hands. 'Is it really you?' Seela searched the imposter's face. 'It *is* you. My dear, sweet Piro.' The nurse pulled her into another hug. 'They told you me you were dead, but I never believed it. Never!'

Varuska wept with relief.

'Ah, Seela,' Cobalt said, striding over to join them. 'I did not recognise you at first.' He gave her a hard look, his black eyes glittering as his hand settled possessively on Varuska's shoulder. 'See how our little Piro has grown. We are to be wed—' He broke off, then smiled, although it never reached his eyes. 'You are all the family she has left. Now that you are here, why wait for midsummer? We will marry on the first day of summer.'

Florin saw Varuska's mouth open in dismay.

'How exciting!' Seela said quickly. 'Everyone loves a wedding, especially a royal wedding. But it's customary for girls to wait until they are fifteen to marry.'

'Customary, but not obligatory,' Cobalt said smoothly. 'And we need to unite Rolencia. I've already spoken with Abbot Firefox. He'll give us special dispensation. He understands that our marriage will heal the kingdom and herald a new age of peace and prosperity.'

'In that case...' Seela slid her arm around Varuska's shoulders, drawing her away from Cobalt. 'Come, child, let's go find your mother's wedding gown. We must see if it needs altering.' She gave Cobalt the quick obeisance of an old retainer. 'With your permission.'

'Yes, go.' But first he planted an affectionate kiss on Varuska's cheek.

The girl went white at his touch and Seela swept her off.

As Florin went to follow, Cobalt caught her arm. 'Watch the old woman. She may just want her cosy life back, but I don't trust her. Report to Amil.'

Florin nodded. Contempt filled her. She would never sell out her friends for the favour of a powerful man. She caught up with Varuska and Seela, who maintained a stream of inconsequential chatter as they headed up the steps to Piro's chambers, where the guard nodded and opened the door for them.

Once inside, Seela lifted a finger to her lips, still rattling on. 'Now, let me hear you play your dolcimela, Piro. Have you been keeping up your lessons?' She removed the stringed instrument from a chest and, after checking that it was in tune, began to play a child's nursery song.

Under cover of the music, she beckoned Varuska and Florin to the window seat.

'Well, Florin?' Seela's face might be seamed with age, but her mind was sharp as ever. Her fingers did not miss a note.

'Florin?' Varuska repeated. She glanced from Florin to the old nurse. 'How does a mountain girl know the royal nurse? How did you know that Piro was impetuous? What lies have you told me, *Leif*?'

Florin marshalled her thoughts and began to explain.

Telling how she came to be serving the false Piro meant revealing her plan to assassinate Cobalt. She would have to somehow assure Varuska that she would not be harmed.

'You're going to kill Cobalt?' Varuska asked, torn between hope and terror.

'I knew you were up to something.' Seela nodded. 'You'll need my help.'

Florin felt a surge of relief. The old nurse was familiar with every twist and turn of the castle, and she'd had a lifetime's observation of royal politics.

'I'm not a willing imposter,' Varuska told Seela, even though Florin had already made this clear. She plucked at the fancy gown. 'I never wanted this. I tried to run, but—'

'I found her and brought her back,' Florin confirmed. 'She wouldn't have gotten out of the castle alive. As it was, I nearly didn't save her sister.'

'What?' Varuska jumped to her feet. 'What happened to Anatoley?'

'Nothing. Your sister's safe, she escaped the castle. But I wasn't quick enough to save old Mirona. Cobalt's men got to her first. Death is the best way to ensure silence. That's why you must tread carefully, Varuska. Our lives depend on you.'

The girl lifted her fingers to her mouth. 'I can't do this. I feel sick all the time.'

'It will be over soon.' Seela stopped playing the dolcimela long enough to give the girl's trembling hands a squeeze. 'We'll work out a plan.'

'I'm not marrying him,' Varuska told Florin. 'I'm not marrying him just so you can get close enough to kill him.'

'Would you marry him if he never made it to your bed?' Seela asked. 'The wedding night would be the perfect opportunity to kill him. What man doesn't let down his guard and take wine on his wedding day?'

'I won't put Varuska's life at risk,' Florin said.

'Knowing Cobalt, he'll want to surround his marriage with pomp and pageantry,' Seela said, eyes bright. 'We could suggest the wedding take place in the town square, like King Rolen and Myrella's. If it is held outside the castle, it'll be easier to escape.'

Florin felt hopeful. 'You'll have to get cosy with the castle-keep, Seela. Yegora rules this place, and she thinks Cobalt can do no wrong.'

'I can deal with her.'

'Oh, and another thing,' Florin said. 'Cobalt's manservant, Amil, is a corax.'

'An assassin?' Varuska gasped. 'But... but he wears perfume and curls his hair.'

Florin laughed. She couldn't help it.

Seela stopped playing and nudged Varuska. 'Laugh. Laugh loudly. This is a happy day. We want the guard to tell Cobalt his betrothed laughed with joy while planning her wedding.'

Somehow Varuska summoned a laugh, and Florin laughed along with her. Soon Varuska's laughter turned to sobs. Seela sent Florin to tell the guard to fetch hot water for a bath.

When Florin came back, the old nurse's worried eyes sought her. So much rested on Varuska. If she faltered...

The girl caught them. 'I won't let you down.' She wiped her flushed cheeks. 'But I do wish I'd never come to the castle looking for work.'

'Well, you did, so we have to make the best of it,' Seela told her. 'Count yourself lucky, for if we hadn't come along, Cobalt would probably have gotten rid of you after you delivered him an heir. Many's the woman who's conveniently died of child-bed fever. For now, all you have to do is to play along until the wedding day.'

'He has such sharp eyes. What if he suspects?' Varuska objected. 'I'm not a fair-ground player.'

'You're a pretty girl. Smile and act simple,' Seela

said. 'Most men don't look beyond a pretty girl's face. Meanwhile, Florin and I will go unnoticed.'

Florin's cheeks burned.

So what if men looked right through her? There had only ever been one man she'd hoped would notice her, and he'd never seen her as anything other than a useful source of information about the mountain passes.

ORRADE STIRRED. 'THIRSTY.'

Byren was so relieved he was ready to weep.

Orrade grimaced. He eyes flickered open and he winced, even though the room was only lit by one candle. 'M'throat feels like it's been scraped raw.'

Not trusting himself to speak, Byren reached for the watered wine and lifted Orrade's head so he could take a sip.

His friend gulped greedily, then groaned as he lay back.

'Not so fast,' Byren told him, putting the watered wine aside. 'Your chest and shoulder are all torn up. Trust you to take on a wyvern with only a hunting knife. You had to try and match me.' He grinned, then pulled back the furs and unwrapped the bandages.

Orrie winced. 'Could you be any rougher?'

Byren laughed.

Orrade caught his hand. 'You came back for me.'

'Of course I did.' Byren couldn't meet Orrade's eyes, and instead studied the wounds. There'd been no bleeding while he sewed Orrade up, but there'd been bleeding since, which he took to be a good sign. 'Need to get you cleaned up and freshly bandaged. Wyvern wounds can turn bad in the blink of an eye.'

Orrade watched as he stood to fetch warm water. 'Your back's been cut to shreds.'

'Barnacles on the side of the ship.' Byren shrugged, feeling the skin pull. He added alcohol to the warm water, then returned to kneel at his friend's side. 'This'll sting.'

Orrade rolled his eyes.

As Byren sponged the crusted blood from Orrade's chest wounds, his friend stared up at the ceiling, frowning in concentration. 'Last I remember is gutting the wyvern and crawling inside him. I didn't expect to live. Didn't expect anyone to come after me. Last I saw of you, the captain had you pinned under half a dozen men. I should have known they couldn't keep you down. What happened?'

Byren told him, voice faltering as the crusted blood peeled away to reveal scars that looked ten days old even though only a single day had passed.

'What?' Orrade asked. 'Is it festering?'

Byren shook his head.

Orrade lifted his head. 'Days old. Byren, what did you do?'

He shrugged, not sure how to put it into words.

'Not that I'm complaining,' Orrade assured him. 'I'm not about to denounce you for having healing Affinity.'

'I'm not an Affinity-healer. All I did was try to repeat what happened when I was in the seep with the ulfrs. You're the one with Affinity. In fact...' He leant closer and concentrated. 'The wyvern's power has gone.' He saw Orrade was confused. 'You killed the beast but didn't settle its—'

'Affinity. I'm guessing you tapped into that power to hasten my healing. Well, I'm grateful. Here, lend a hand.'

Byren helped him sit up.

'I ache all over,' Orrade muttered. 'Feels like I've been in the battle to end all battles.' He sucked in a shaky breath. 'Guess I have. Back there in the water, I was shivering so bad it's a wonder I didn't chip a tooth.'

'Speaking of teeth.' Byren showed him the wyvern's tooth. It was almost as long as his little finger. 'I dug this out of your shoulder. You should get it set on a chain. Wear it with honour.'

'You didn't bring the body back? I fancy a wyvern coat.'

Byren shuddered, remembering the wyvern falling into the dark, cold sea. 'Not possible.'

Orrade reached for him. 'I'm alive, thanks to you.'

Byren met his eyes. Last night, thinking Orrade would die, was the worst night of his life. Going on without him had seemed pointless. Somehow, he summoned a grin. 'Shoulda known you were too tough to kill.'

'If this was my after-life in Halcyon's Sacred Heart, I wouldn't be in so much pain and I wouldn't have to pee.'

'I'll bring a chamber pot.'

'I might feel like a grandfather, but I'm not going to act like one. Help me up.'

Byren helped him to his feet.

Orrade cursed fluently and staggered, falling against Byren's chest; that was when Byren realised they were both naked.

They'd grown up together, swimming in the lake, sharing a bed-roll during hunting parties and spar raids, but it was different now. Byren stepped back as soon as Orrade was steady on his feet.

'Can you—'

'I can manage.'

He watched Orrade make his careful way across the cabin. Of course he could manage; Orrie was proud and fiercely determined. But he was only flesh and blood, and he'd been as good as dead.

Byren's knees shook. He stumbled to the bunk, sitting abruptly. Tears of relief burned his eyes.

After a moment, Byren wiped his face, pulled on a pair of breeches and began heating the food that had been delivered earlier. He broke the crusty bread rolls apart and sat them on the edge of the brazier to warm up.

Orrade came back into the cabin and joined him by the brazier, standing too close to the metal. 'Felt like I'd never be warm again.' He inhaled. 'Smells good. Beef and red wine stew.'

'You're shaking.' Byren gestured to the bed. 'Lie down. I'll bring it to you.'

'Hate feeling weak.' Orrade crept back to the furs and lowered himself with care.

'You'll be better in a day or two.'

He nodded. 'Hungry now.'

'Be ready soon. Keep warm.'

Orrade pulled up the furs.

By the time the food was hot, he was fast asleep. Byren nudged him awake.

He took a few mouthfuls, then shook his head.

'More wine?' Byren didn't wait for an answer. He stood, put the bowl back on the brazier and reached for the watered-wine.

'I'm sorry I've been such a burden on you,' Orrade whispered.

'You never—'

'S'true. Because of me, you lost both your father and your twin's trust. You shoulda sent me away when I offered to go.' Exhausted, Orrade slurred his words like a drunkard. 'Don't know why you put up with me. Jus' wanted ta say I'm grateful.'

'It's not...' Byren spooned stew into his bowl. He owed Orrie this much honesty. 'When I thought you were dead, I didn't see how I'd go on without you. So don't talk of...'

Orrade was fast asleep.

Chapter Seventeen

Piro tried dismissing the maid, but the woman wouldn't leave. So she undressed herself and climbed into bed; satisfied, the maid left her alone.

Piro promptly climbed out of bed.

Dinner had been interminable. She'd had to listen to Nefysto recite—apparently 'Natteo' was a renowned poet—and then she'd had to sit through Kaspian's latest composition for the dolcimela. To escape her turn, she'd pleaded ignorance of music, which only made the comtissa promise her lessons, since 'a kingsdaughter should not be without a musical instrument.' Her poor mother would have been mortified.

Piro had been on edge all night, afraid the old comtissa would drop dead between one course and next. She longed to tell Siordun about her vision, but he'd sent his apologies, claiming 'the mage needed him'.

Very well, if he had more important things to do, then so had she. By the time he arrived tomorrow, if all went according to plan, the wyvern and Kaspian would be bonded.

Opening the tall glass doors, Piro slipped out onto her balcony and looked for Kaspian on his. There was no sign of him. Had he fallen asleep while waiting for her?

She judged the distance to Kaspian's balcony. It was not too far.

Wearing her sea-hound breeches, which she'd rescued from the overzealous maid, Piro climbed over the balustrade and crept along the ledge and onto the next balcony. She went to open his doors.

Locked. She could not believe it! Furious, she tapped on the glass.

After a several moments, Kaspian opened the door, looking ghostly in his nightshirt. He'd taken off his sling; a pale bandage was wound around his forearm. 'Piro, you shouldn't—'

She pushed past him, entering the dim chamber. 'Why aren't you ready? I waited for you. You want to bond with Valiant, don't you?'

'Of course I do, but...'

'Well, come on. Pull on a pair of breeches.'

He stared at her.

She returned his stare.

He let his breath out in a huff of annoyance. 'Turn around.'

She put her back to him and folded her arms, waiting impatiently while he dressed.

'You shouldn't come to my chamber,' he told her. 'We're not betrothed. You're not a married woman. Even if you were, I'd go to you. As an unmarried girl, you must be circumspect—'

'Are you done yet?' She turned. He was still bare-chested, and lacing up his breeches. His face might be as pretty as a girl's but the rest of him was all male. 'Do you have the key to the wyvern's cage?'

'I do, but—'

'Then come on.'

He didn't budge. 'You're not going to let Val out, are you? Because I don't think that's a good idea.'

'No. I'm not going to let him out.'

'Then why do we need the key?'

'In case.' She said no more and headed for the balcony.

'You're going to climb down?' He caught her arm. 'Are you serious?'

She slipped free of his grasp. 'There's a servant at my door, a big fellow who moves like a fighter. He's been told to watch me. Fera-something.'

'Feratore.' His lips twitched. 'Not much gets past you.'

'I'm not stupid.' Piro nodded to his bandage. 'Is your arm too sore to climb?'

'No. It's almost healed.'

'Then follow me.' She darted through the balcony doors and peered over the balustrade. The climb had not looked hard when she'd inspected it that afternoon. By starlight, the ledges and carvings were not easy to make out.

Kaspian joined her. 'Reconsidering?'

'Never.' She swung her leg over the balustrade and climbed onto the ledge. 'Come on.'

Piro scrambled down the wall, then jumped the last stretch to the ground. She waited only long enough for him to land beside her, before making her way through the courtyard's ornamental fruit trees.

As she headed for the building on the far side, he caught her arm. 'If we don't want to be seen, we need to go through the kitchen herb garden.'

The wooden gate to the walled-garden swung on well-oiled hinges. Here, warmth lingered on the still air, radiating from the stone walls. Piro smelled oregano and sage. It made her homesick for her mother's herb garden.

Kaspian caught her arm at the far door. 'Since they locked him up, I've been sneaking out to see Valiant before I go to bed and sometimes the cook sips wine with the gardener.'

She liked him better for this confession.

Kaspian opened the door ever so slightly to peer through. He let out his breath. 'No one's there tonight. Come on.'

They slipped into the servant's courtyard. Piro could smell the freshly turned soil and sensed the wyvern. Her Affinity surged with each beat of her heart and slid down her arms into her hands until it felt as if she wore gloves of power.

'I'm later than usual,' Kaspian whispered. 'I wonder if Val's awake.'

'Oh, he's awake alright.'

'Your Affinity tells you this? That must be why the mage wants Agent Tyro to train you. My grandmother says you're wasted on the mage. She says you'd be a valuable asset to house Cinnamome. She says I'm to charm you, but—'

'Don't worry. No one can charm me.' Eyes fixed on the cage against the far wall, Piro almost tripped over a raised garden bed.

As Kaspian steadied her, she felt a sharp sting just before his hand closed around her bare arm.

Kaspian gasped. 'What was that?'

'A little warning slap of power,' Piro guessed. 'You have Affinity?'

'Some.'

'Good. That will help.' She'd reached the cage. 'Now give me the key.'

'I don't think that's—'

The wyvern gave voice.

'Quickly,' Piro urged. 'Before someone comes.'

'I'm not opening it. Val's very strong and doesn't like strangers. I...' Kaspian broke off.

Piro had reached through the cage bars to stroke the wyvern's throat. A deep rumble came from the Affinity beast.

'He likes you.' Kaspian sounded as if he was torn between amazement and resentment.

'All animals like me.'

'You must take after Mad King Byren the Fourth.'

'Mad?' She'd never heard her grandfather described this way before.

'My apologies. A slip of the tongue.'

'Why mad? What's he supposed to have done?'

He hesitated.

'Kaspian...'

He sighed. 'They say King Byren liked animals better than people.'

Piro laughed. 'That's because he kept a menagerie of Affinity beasts.' The wyvern butted the cage, clearly impatient. 'Open the door.'

But still the youth hesitated. It wasn't until Piro had the wyvern on his knees, with his vulnerable neck exposed, that Kaspian unlocked the cage.

Piro slipped inside, drawing Kaspian after her. The moment her hand touched Kaspian's, she felt his Affinity trying to connect with the wyvern's primal power.

Kaspian's Affinity was weak in comparison, and would have remained contained by his earnest personality and self discipline, if she hadn't been able to link them. She became a channel for power. For her, it was the most natural thing in the world.

'There.' She opened her eyes. 'You complement each other. Valiant needs guidance. You need to unleash your true potential.'

But Kaspian wasn't listening. He dropped to his knees to hug Valiant, pressing his cheek to the wyvern's throat, where the beast's Affinity-rich blood pulsed just under the skin.

'It's done,' Piro said. 'We should be getting back.'

Too deeply immersed in their bond, neither beast nor boy acknowledged her. She should have seen this coming.

Well, Kaspian could just stay here tonight. With the wyvern for company, he wouldn't feel the cold. She left the cage door ajar.

It had been easy to facilitate the bond between Kaspian and his Affinity beast. She didn't see what all the fuss was about. Next time she was in Merofynia, she'd help Isolt bond with her wyvern, and then Loyalty would be safe.

Feeling the satisfaction of a job well done, Piro returned to her chamber, climbed into bed and fell asleep as soon as her head touched the pillow.

As Fyn followed the lad from Benetir Estate, his stomach cramped with an odd combination of fear and excitement, and his mind raced. Tonight, he had to prove himself worthy of Byren's faith as well as proving himself to the Merofynian nobles. Most importantly, he had to prove himself to Isolt. He'd tried to anticipate every eventuality, but so much could go wrong his head ached.

'This way.' Young Garyth led Fyn up the wharf.

The lad's grandfather had lived long enough to see Lady Gennalla to safety before his heart gave out. Now the boy was all alone in the world, and eager to prove himself. After the things he'd seen during the spar attack, Fyn had expected the lad to balk but if he was afraid, he hid it well.

Fyn hoped he hid his own fear. He knew what they were up against. Spar warriors were a tough breed, and the warlord had to be even tougher to keep his men in line.

'When they attacked, we fought to hold them off so everyone could board the yacht,' Garyth whispered. 'Fought to hold them off while we scuttled the fishing fleet.'

He gestured to the masts protruding drunkenly from the water. Unfortunately for Fyn's plans, it was a cloudless night and the stars were bright enough to cast shadows. He had to trust to Garyth's ability to get them close to the estate's great house unseen, just as he had to trust to his knowledge of spar warriors and hope Cortigern's men would still be in a drunken stupor.

In another day or so the warlord would rouse his warriors and do one of two things. They would attack the next village along the shore of the Landlocked Sea, where they would find enough boats to attack Port Mero, or they would pack up and go home.

At least Isolt was safe on the royal barge.

When she'd bid them good luck, she'd been dry-eyed... hard-eyed. If she feared for Fyn, she did not show it. If she loved him, even a fraction as much as he loved her, she had never shown it. Fyn told himself he was grateful for that.

'Over here.' Garyth led Fyn across to a low retaining wall.

Benetir Estate's great house stood on a rise. Fyn glanced up the long straight road, cut into a succession of terraces. The road was bordered on each side by tall thin trees, dark against the stars.

Fyn checked behind him. Captain Aeran led the city-watch and the merchants' men. They poured off the wharf and ran to join Fyn, crouching in the shadow of the retaining wall. The nobles ran the other way, to the far side of the road, and crouched behind the opposite wall.

Fyn had done the best he could with his divided men. Elrhodoc and the queen's guards were happy to fight alongside Wytharon and Travany. While Garyth led Fyn and the city-watch around the back to the kitchen entrance, the nobles would wait at the front of the great house. Then Garyth would slip through to open the doors and let them in. If Fyn's guess was correct, Cortigern's warriors would be sleeping on the floor of the great hall. Both of Fyn's forces would attack before the spar warriors found their weapons or their breeches. His men disarmed, Cortigern should be ready to listen to reason.

Fyn and Garyth made their way up the terraces, climbing the shallow steps.

They waited in the shadow of the very last wall for Captain Aeran and his men to catch up. Fyn could see the nobles moving into position on the other side of the road.

Peering over the lip of the last retaining wall, Fyn spotted a raised dais before the great house. Starlight revealed shattered statues of once-proud Affinity beasts. Some had been decapitated, while others had suffered broken wings and missing tails.

'Barbarians!' Fyn shook his head in disgust.

'What, the statues? That's the old lord's folly.' Garyth grinned, teeth flashing white. He saw Fyn didn't understand. 'His lordship tried to buy statues from Ruin Isle, but King Rolen wouldn't sell, so he smuggled out drawings and had a stone-mason recreate them, complete with missing horns an' wings.' The lad shook his head. 'Everyone thought he was mad. But then he held his son's wedding in the ruins and it became all the rage.'

'Everyone's in position,' Captain Aeran reported.

Fyn nodded to Garyth and the lad took off.

Back when the Merofynians had attacked at Narrowneck, there had been no time for Fyn to prepare. It had been a mad scramble. This time he was leading the attack, but he still felt unready as he followed Garyth along the side of the great house, past a verandah with many glass-panelled doors. This place was not built for defence.

They passed through the herb garden and climbed the kitchen steps. Inside, they found a lad of about ten scrubbing a big table by the light of a single lamp. He looked up, startled.

Garyth lifted his finger to his lips. 'Where's Cortigern, Lynos?'

'In his lordship's chamber. He took the Lady Sefarra and locked her in there last night. The screams...' The boy shuddered.

Fyn put a hand on his shoulder. 'It's all right. We're here now. Where are the other spar warriors?'

'Sleepin' off their wine in the great hall.'

Fyn hid his relief. 'Lynos, can you lead my men to the great hall, then open the doors without waking Cortigern's men?'

The boy nodded.

Fyn felt a moment's compunction. If Lynos misjudged, he would be killed. But Fyn needed to get to Cortigern before the alarm was given. If the warlord felt vindictive, he'd put Sefarra to the sword. He turned to Captain Aeran. 'I'm going—'

'—after the girl. May Mulcibar guide your blade.'

Fyn nodded. It still seemed strange to associate the god of summer with war. His heart raced as Garyth led him up the servant's stairs and into the corridor that led to the family's bedchambers. If fighting started before he could reach Cortigern...

'Here.' Garyth stopped near a pair of tall doors.

'No need to be heroes. We'll try to get her out without waking Cortigern,' Fyn whispered. 'Then I want you to take her back to the wharf and signal the ship. The queen will send a boat for you. If you can't get her down to the wharf, the pair of you are to hide somewhere safe. Understood?'

The lad nodded, but fingered a borrowed hunting knife. Fyn hoped Garyth wouldn't have cause to use it.

Fyn drew his sword, then peered into the chamber.

It was lit by a single, smoking lamp. The girl was blocked from view beneath Cortigern's massive shoulders and back.

Fyn slipped into the room. Cortigern's weapons lay on a bedside chest, almost within reach. Creeping up behind the grunting warlord, he struck the back of his head with the hilt of his sword.

Cortigern collapsed, pinning the girl beneath him. Sefarra blinked and tried to scramble out from under him, but Cortigern was too heavy. Fyn went to help her.

'Step back,' someone warned, in thickly-accented Merofynian.

Fyn turned to find a second warrior had stepped naked from the bathing chamber. He held Garyth by the throat.

Garzik woke to find Olbin crouched over him. The Utlander's eager expression made Garzik's heart sink. Now that he was a free man, he thought he'd be safe from this kind of unwanted attention.

Resentment burned in Garzik as Olbin pulled him to his feet and led him past sleeping Utlanders. Some lay in each other's arms, ship-lovers, yet on land they had wives or girlfriends. Ship-lovers... Was this what the big Utlander offered? How could he say no, when he needed Olbin's protection from Jost?

When the Utlander led him towards the reardeck stairs, Garzik was so relieved his knees shook. The helmsman grinned as if they shared a secret. Curious, Garzik joined Olbin at the stern rail. It was a calm night, and there was hardly a wave to disturb the star-silvered sea.

Olbin slung an arm around Garzik's shoulder and pointed to a luminescent patch behind the ship. 'There. See it?'

'I do,' Garzik whispered. 'But what is it?'

'You haven't read of this in your books?' Olbin teased with just a hint of resentment. 'It's a shade-ray. A big one.'

'You mean a manta ray.'

Olbin shook his head. 'Shade-rays house the souls of Utland warriors who die in battle at sea. They come to see us on still nights like this, drawn back to their people but never able to set foot on land again.'

Rusan joined them with his pipes. He played a sweetly haunting tune, bringing tears to Garzik's eyes. Olbin wept unashamedly.

Garzik marvelled as the Affinity beast drew closer. 'It's huge. Why, it must be wider than the ship is long.'

Olbin nodded.

Garzik grasped the ship's rail and the creature came closer still. It swam just under the surface, keeping pace with the vessel. He could just make its undulating wings. Along the edge of each wing were luminescent patterns like delicate lace, and more patterns ran down the centre of the creature's back.

Rusan lowered the pipes, whispering a name Garzik didn't catch. The captain gestured to the shade-ray. 'We know the shade-rays by their markings. This is the founder of our settlement. He's come to wish us luck.'

Garzik was not so sure, but he respected their beliefs. 'He honours you.'

Olbin nodded, wiping tears from his cheeks. 'We knew you'd want to see this.'

Chapter Eighteen

PIRO WALKED THROUGH a Rolencian festival surrounded by music and laughter. Banners fluttered in the sunshine. Carts trundled past laden with food and singing workers. To each side of her there were tents, and in front of the tents stood men-at-arms wearing their best ceremonial armour. They joked as they shared wine skins. She was home at last and everyone was happy.

Yet she felt an underlying dread.

At the top of the rise, two grand tents faced each other. A Rolencian banner hung before the tent on her right, the red foenix's feathers picked out in gold thread. On her left was another Rolencian banner. Sun glinted on gold thread, blurring her vision. When it cleared, the banner had changed colour, turning blue...

An Affinity vision.

Was this the day Byren would marry his Merofynian bride?

Or was she seeing her mother's wedding to her father? But that had taken place in the town square.

The blue banner stirred in the breeze, revealing leaping

dalfino and an inverted crown that denoted a royal bastard—Cobalt's banner.

Fear solidified inside her as Cobalt stepped out of the tent on the left. He adjusted the empty sleeve of his fine satin coat.

A drummer and two pipers emerged from the other tent, escorting a dozen pretty girls, ranging in age from five to seventeen. The girls all wore dresses in their family colours. Ribbons and flowers were threaded through their hair.

Cobalt offered his left arm to one of the girls. As she glanced up at him, Piro recognised herself.

She was the girl about to marry Cobalt?

Piro fought a surge of panic. She would never agree to marry Cobalt. Never!

Not even if he held both her brothers' lives to ransom.

The musicians struck up a happy air, the girls sang and the bridal party walked down the long red carpet. The Rolencian people lined up, waving banners of red and blue.

Piro tried to run, but the smallest movement took incredible effort. Frustration filled her. The crowd cheered.

Roaring, Byren thrust through the gathering. He swung his sword at Cobalt, who ducked and ran. The girls shrieked and scattered. People fled. Red banners came fluttering down around Piro.

No, they were flames.

People screamed and fled as the fire took hold.

Byren searched the crowd, calling for Piro. Cobalt appeared behind him and swung his sword.

Piro sucked in a breath to warn her brother...

... and woke with his name on her lips.

She sat bolt upright in bed. After-images more real than the dimly lit Ostronite bedroom filled her head, and her heart raced as if she'd been running.

Last time she'd had an Affinity vision, she'd dreamed of wyverns chasing her through the castle. Seela had tried to convince her they were only nightmares and had dosed her on dreamless-sleep.

But the dreams had foretold the fall of her father's castle. According to Siordun, her Affinity allowed her to sense moments of great change, when the future could take different paths. And he'd made her promise to tell him if she had another vision.

She must see him first thing tomorrow.

FYN FROZE.

'Step away from the bed,' the spar warrior ordered. 'I swear I'll wring the boy's neck.'

Despite his terror, Garyth's eyes held a calculating gleam. With a tiny shake of his head, Fyn tried to warn the lad not to do anything rash.

At that moment, Sefarra did something behind Fyn that distracted the spar warrior. Garyth drove his elbow into the warrior's groin and ran.

The man crumpled.

Garyth made a strangled sound in his throat and pointed to the bed.

Fyn turned to discover the girl had used Cortigern's own dagger to cut off his cock and balls.

Nausea swept through Fyn. Garyth dropped to his knees, retching.

No chance of a negotiating a peace with Cortigern now. Fyn cursed.

The spar warrior staggered to his feet, pale and sweating. Fyn charged, before he could reach his weapons.

The spar warrior snatched a vase from a side-table and brought it down on Fyn's head. It shattered, shards flying everywhere.

Momentarily stunned, Fyn swung his sword and felt the flat of the blade connect. When his vision cleared, he found the warrior laid out at his feet, unconscious.

'Why didn't you kill him?' Garyth asked, his voice raw from retching.

'Halcyon's monks value life.' Fyn cut the curtain cords.

He made the first loop of a sailor's knot, grateful for his time on the *Wyvern's Whelp*.

Garyth gasped and reached for Fyn, pointing to the bed again.

Naked and bloodied, her long dark hair dripping, Sefarra crouched over the warlord. She was trying to cut through his thick neck, but her knife had wedged in the man's spine.

With a curse, Fyn finished tying up the unconscious spar warrior.

'Sefarra!' Fyn caught her arm.

She bared her teeth at him.

'Sefarra...'

Abandoning the knife, she sprang at him, trying to claw out his eyes. He caught her wrists and tried to calm her, but nothing seemed to reach her.

She was as tall as him, and in this state she was surprisingly strong. In desperation, he shoved her away. She tripped and her head caught a glancing blow on the bed post. He winced in sympathy.

Naked, bruised and bleeding, she lay there like a broken doll.

'Garyth, when the Lady Sefarra wakes, help clean her up.'

No answer.

'Garyth?'

The boy couldn't take his eyes off the mutilated body of Warlord Cortigern.

From the front end of the house Fyn heard a great roaring. Surely, if the spar warriors had been drunk, the fighting would be over by now. 'Garyth. I have to go.'

The lad blinked and focused on Fyn.

'Watch over Sefarra. I'll be back as soon as I can.'

This time the boy nodded. They both glanced to the girl, who'd come round and was watching them from behind ragged black hair.

Fyn shook his head. What was Isolt going to say when he brought back this half-crazed creature?

As he ran out of the chamber and down the hall, the tone of battle struck him as wrong.

He came to an abrupt stop on the balcony. Broad stairs stretched down to the great hall, where fires had broken out amidst overturned tables and broken crockery. Cortigern's warriors had surrendered and been herded into small groups, but the slaughter had not stopped there.

He watched, appalled, as the Merofynians put the spar warriors to the sword, one by one.

Knowing their fate, the raiders fought like wild beasts, roaring and cursing as they died.

Each time one of them died, the Merofynians howled in triumph. Their raw bestiality made Fyn's stomach turn. He'd never seen anything like it. '*Stop!*'

They ignored him. They probably didn't hear him.

The methodical slaughter went on. A man did terrible things in battle, but this...

Fyn ran down the grand staircase, across to a cluster of Lord Wytharon's men. 'I want prisoners. Leave them alive.'

Only one man turned to him, and there was no humanity in his face.

Fyn took a step back. 'Where's Lord Wytharon?'

'Dead.' The man gestured. 'Killed by these bastards.'

This just got worse and worse.

Another victorious howl greeted another spar warrior's death.

In desperation, Fyn glanced around and spotted the captain of the city-watch. Leaping across a body, he dodged an overturned chair and grabbed Aeran from behind. 'Captain, control your men.'

The grizzled veteran turned, weapon raised. Fyn diverted the blade with a practised sweep.

Aeran blinked. And the blood lust faded from his eyes.

'Get the men under control. This is murder.'

Aeran shrugged. 'That's easier said than done. Wytharon's dead, and his men want revenge. Lord

Travany and that pup Elrhodoc won't take orders from me. As for the men... They've seen spar barbarians come over the divide for the first time in two hundred years, and they're out for blood.'

Fyn glanced around in time to see one of the queen's guards pull a lad from under a table where he'd been hiding. For a heartbeat, Fyn thought it was Lynos, but then he saw the lad's leather vest was embossed with the horned head of a centicore.

The lad twisted and writhed as his captor handed him to Elrhodoc, who held him off the floor.

The commoners and lords' men alike watched unmoved while Elrhodoc raised his knife.

'Stop right there!' Fyn marched towards them. 'He's only a boy, for pity's sake.'

'Spar brats grow into spar barbarians.' Elrhodoc's voice was thick with contempt.

'Is that any reason for Merofynians to behave like barbarians? Is that what the queen's guard has come to?'

Elrhodoc's gaze faltered. A few of his men looked down, but others glared and muttered.

Fyn drew breath with no idea what he would say next. The abbey weapons-master had once told him that some men only obeyed if the order was backed up by violence. Did he have to kill someone to make his point?

A high, eerie laugh echoed through the hall.

Everyone turned to look up at the grand staircase.

Naked, covered in blood, Sefarra stood with one arm raised, holding something bloody. In her other hand she swung Cortigern's head by his hair.

The men in the hall below went absolutely still.

She gave a shriek of triumph and threw both objects down the stairs. The head rolled over and over, bouncing in time to her laughter.

'Mulcibar's Fiery Breath!' Elrhodoc's voice shook.

Taking advantage of their shock, Fyn grabbed the spar lad and crossed the hall. He thrust the lad into Captain

Aeran's arms, then ran halfway up the steps and turned to face the hall.

'Captain Elrhodoc, have your men put out the fires. Captain Aeran, restrain the prisoners. Lord Travany, see that Lord Wytharon's body is carried back to his yacht. See to the wounded and bury the dead. Have your men clean this hall. Lady Gennalla doesn't want to return to a charnel house!'

He did not wait to see if he would be obeyed, but pivoted on his heel and bounded up the steps. Sefarra had fallen to her knees, tears streaming down her face. Young Garyth crouched behind her, trying ineffectually to console her.

Fyn crouched so that he was level with the girl. 'Your mother sent me to get you.'

She blinked, but did not quite focus on him.

Fyn swept off his cloak, wrapped it around her shoulders and helped her to her feet. She stumbled a little as he led her down the passage.

Garyth trotted along beside them. 'I tried to stop her. I really did.'

'Don't worry,' Fyn told him, speaking for Sefarra's benefit. 'Everything's going to be all right now.'

As he passed the bedchamber, the hog-tied warrior lifted his head and glared at them. Fyn shielded the captive from Sefarra. He wasn't sure if she would weep or try to cut his throat.

'Bring a candle, Garyth.' Fyn entered the opposite bedroom and passed into the bathing chamber. 'Run a bath.'

The lad lit the burner, then ran water in the sunken tub.

'You'll feel better after a bath,' Fyn told Sefarra. It was what his old nurse used to say. But the girl just stood there.

'Garyth, go find a woman to help her.'

Alone with Sefarra, Fyn had no idea what to say. Everything he thought of seemed woefully inadequate.

After a moment, she drew a shaky breath. 'I'm all right.'

He didn't believe her.

'I promised myself I'd kill him, and I did. He can't hurt anyone ever again.' She met Fyn's eyes, her expression calm and contained. 'You can go now.'

Fyn shook his head and waited until Garyth returned with three women, all older than the girl. One carried a change of clothes. They clucked over Sefarra and shooed him out.

It was time to deal with the surviving spar warriors.

In the other bedchamber he pulled the hog-tied warrior onto his knees and stood over him. 'Who are you?'

The man spat.

'Threaten to cut him,' Garyth suggested.

Fyn hadn't realised the lad had followed him. 'You can leave now.'

'But—'

'*Go.*'

The boy muttered as he went.

Fyn saw the warrior look past him to the bed where Cortigern's mutilated corpse lay. From this angle only his foot was visible, but they both knew what had happened to him.

'Your warlord's dead, and your fellow warriors are now captives,' Fyn told him. 'Cortigern broke two hundred years of peace—'

'...in here with you.' Captain Aeran's voice carried as he thrust the spar lad Fyn had saved into the chamber ahead of him.

The captive warrior stiffened and Fyn noted their similar features.

The boy's horrified eyes went straight to the mutilated body on the blood-soaked bed. Fyn cursed. Crossing the chamber, he drew the bed curtains, hiding the grisly scene.

By chance, Fyn happened to glance at the boy the moment the lad noticed the captive. The boy's mouth opened in dismay, then closed firmly. Clearly, the lad expected the worst, which was not surprising after what he'd seen.

Captain Aeran made his report. The estate was secure, the fires were out and the prisoners all safely locked in the ice-lined cold cellar. 'That should take the fire out of their bellies!'

'Well done.' Fyn wanted to ask what Travany and Elrhodoc were up to, but did not want to reveal his distrust of the Merofynian nobility before their common enemy.

Aeran gestured to the captive warrior. 'Who's that?'

'The boy's father,' Fyn said, guessing. Both boy and man gave a tiny jump of surprise. 'And Cortigern's second in command.'

Fyn drew his knife and walked towards the captive. The man stiffened, giving the lad the smallest shake of his head. *Be brave, be strong. Don't shame me by crying out when I die.* Fyn didn't need to hear words to know what passed between them.

Without a word, Fyn went around behind Cortigern's second in command and cut the rope that bound his hands and ankles. The captive fell forward.

'Get up.'

The man struggled to stand on numb limbs. Fyn glanced around the chamber and spotted a pair of breeches. He tossed the pants to the boy. 'Help your father.'

The man looked up, surprised by this courtesy.

Fyn moved so he could watch the warrior and his son, while speaking with Aeran. 'Have your men remove Cortigern's body. Then meet me in the next room.'

Aeran eyed the man and boy. 'If it's all the same to you, I'll leave a couple of men with you.'

So Fyn and two city-watchmen escorted the captives to the next chamber. Fyn gestured to a chest at the end of the bed. 'Sit, both of you.'

The two watchmen waited at the door, while Fyn built up a fire. It was the cold time of night before dawn.

He turned to face his captives. 'I'm King Byren's brother, Lord Protector Merofyn. It is within my rights to have you and all your men taken to Port Mero and executed.'

'Why don't you?' the man asked.

Because it went against everything Fyn believed in. He glanced to the fire. 'The deaths of the warlord and his best warriors will leave a power vacuum on Centicore Spar. You don't want another spar's warlord marching in and capturing your women and land. Am I right?'

The man gave one short nod.

Fyn studied the man. 'Your name?'

'Cortovar, half-brother to Cortigern.'

'And the lad?'

'My son, Cortomir.'

'If you give your word there will be no more attacks from Centicore Spar, you can return home with your men.'

Cortovar nodded once. 'You have it.'

'You will need to swear your spar's oath of allegiance to Isolt Wyvern Queen. She—'

'They say she keeps a wyvern that eats out of her hand,' the boy said, interrupting. 'Is it true?'

'It's true.'

'A saltwater wyvern?'

Fyn nodded.

'What's wrong with your hair?' the boy asked. 'Did you have a fever and get it all cut off?'

'No. I was raised to be a warrior monk.'

'Can I see the wyvern?'

'Tomorrow, when your father gives his oath.' As Fyn answered, he noticed Cortovar's mouth twitch. The man thought him weak. He had to remember that these were spar warriors, used to a harsh life.

'Heed me, Cortovar. Your warriors have already paid for Cortigern's folly. Every second man has been executed.' He made it sound as if it had been on his orders. 'Let this be a lesson to you.'

The man cloaked his expression. Once Cortovar was over the Divide he had no reason to honour the agreement.

'You will keep your word,' Fyn told him, 'because I'm taking Cortomir back to Port Mero with me.'

The boy glanced to his father, who had gone very still.

'Do you understand?' Fyn asked.

Cortovar's eyes burned with fury. He understood.

Chapter Nineteen

Piro was up and dressed at first light, surprising the kitchen staff, who insisted she sit out in the conservatory while they made up a breakfast tray for her. By the time the food had arrived so had Feratore, with a nick on his chin from shaving in a hurry. He did not look happy.

'You might as well eat some breakfast.' Piro told him. He didn't answer. 'If you don't, you'll be grumpy. I have brothers. I know these things.'

He grimaced.

'Go on. I'll wait.'

'You'll wait?'

She nodded.

He headed down the hall to the kitchen.

Piro took the opportunity to inspect the plants in the conservatory. They'd been chosen for their beauty and scent, and each was a work of art. When she discovered the aviary, she was reminded of Dovecote and the Old Dove's prize birds. Orrade was Lord Dovecote now, which made her feel like laughing. Skinny, sharp-eyed

Orrie... maybe it was not so ludicrous. Not much would get past him.

Feratore returned, with pastry flakes on his jerkin.

Piro tilted her head. 'Happy now?'

He didn't answer.

Hiding her smile, she went into the passage. House Cinnamome's palace stretched over one entire city block, with many courtyards, buildings and towers. None of the towers were as high as Mage Tower, but because the palace was built on the crest of the island, the tops of the towers were level with it. The buildings were two storeys or three storeys high, and everything was made of white stone, with red tiled roofs.

Sunlight reflected off the white stone and Piro squinted as she entered a courtyard.

Balconies, arched verandas and glass-paned doors opened directly onto courtyard. Byren would not have been impressed. Once you breached the outer wall, the palace was impossible to defend.

Just as she thought this, she spotted an anomaly, a tall wall with no doors and only one row of narrow windows on the second floor. Intrigued, she ducked into the nearest building and made her way down a passage to a solid wooden door. From the size of the hinges, the door was very heavy.

'What lies behind this, Feratore?'

He shrugged. 'Some dusty old hall.'

She lifted the latch and pushed the door open. It was as though she had stepped back over two hundred years, to the days when Ostron Isle had been racked by civil war. Shafts of light lit the hall, descending from the high, narrow windows. Now this was defensible; Byren would approve. She laughed with delight, startling Feratore.

'Don't you see?' Piro spun on her toes, stirring up dust. 'This is where House Cinnamome came from. It's their very first hall.' And she ran across the flagstones to the far corner, where cloths covered what turned out to be nothing more than a pile of sturdy old furniture.

Disappointed, she studied the walls. To each side of the massive fireplace, weapons hung from hooks. Evidence of the days before the original Mage Tsulamyth convinced the great merchant houses to vote for an elector.

Piro eyed the swords on display. Her lessons with the sea-hounds had ended before she could make much headway. She sent Feratore a calculating glance. He looked uneasy.

She found a stool and dragged it over to the wall display.

'Here, what're you doing?' Feratore demanded, sounding more like a man-at-arms than a refined house servant.

She climbed onto the footstool and reached for a sword about the size of the one her mother had used on Cobalt. But when she lifted it off the hook, the weight was so great she overbalanced and had to jump to the floor.

'What do you want with that?' Feratore asked.

Piro swung the blade, putting her shoulders and upper body into the action. It was too heavy to stop, and Feratore stepped in to steady her. Then he tried to take the sword away.

She resisted fiercely. 'They killed my mother.'

'What?'

'They killed her in front of me. I couldn't stop them.' Piro's voice shook with anger and suppressed tears. She would not cry, but she could face the bitter truth. She'd been a coward. 'I didn't even try to help. I hid so they wouldn't kill me.'

'Very wise. Now, give me the sword.'

'I need to learn to protect myself!'

'Little thing like you? Your man'll protect you.'

Why did they always think some man would protect her? Piro glared at him. 'When the Merofynians invaded, my father and oldest brother were killed, my mother was executed and I was taken as a slave. I have to learn to use a sword.'

'Well, it won't be this one. It's too heavy for you.' He gave a grunt of surprise, as she finally let him take the sword from her.

'You're right.' She positioned the footstool under a much smaller sword. 'This one looks about right.'

'That's...'

'That's what? Just right?'

His gaze slid away from hers.

She took the sword, or perhaps it was a long dagger, then jumped down and weighed it in her hand. 'This is much better. It doesn't make my arms ache.' Stepping into a patch of light, she tilted the small sword this way and that. 'There's a symbol on the pommel. A nictocorax.'

The bird that killed in the night. The bird that symbolised Ostron Isle's infamous assassins.

'Put it back,' Feratore urged. 'It's bad luck to—'

'Why does this blade hang in House Cinnamome?'

'Because in each generation, one of our children is dedicated to House Nictocorax,' the old comtissa said as she hobbled into the chamber. 'It is the same with all the other merchant houses.'

'I thought anyone, from noble to baker's apprentice, could pledge their service and become coraxes?'

'Many aspire, but few survive to become fully-fledged assassins.'

Piro wondered who had wielded the blade. House Cinnamome would benefit from having a trained assassin ready to serve them. She looked up. 'But the coraxes pledge their service to House Nictocorax. Wouldn't that create a conflict of interest for assassins from noble houses?'

The comtissa studied her, much as Piro had studied the blade. Before the old woman could respond, a child's voice carried from the courtyard.

'The wyvern has escaped! The wyvern...'

Piro reached the courtyard one step behind Feratore, leaving the old comtissa trailing behind.

'Where is the beast?' Feratore demanded of the boy.

'It's all—' Piro started to reassure them.

But Feratore cut her off. 'Where did it go?'

'I don't know,' the boy confessed. 'I went to feed it, but found the cage door open. They sent me to warn everyone.'

Piro tried to explain again, but the comtissa arrived and issued orders. 'Feratore, collect a dozen men. Arm them and hunt—'

'Comtissa, Comtissa?' A pretty serving girl ran across the courtyard and fell to her knees in front of the old woman. 'The comtes is missing. Kaspian wasn't in his bedchamber.'

The comtissa staggered. Piro steadied her. 'It's all—'

'Abducted,' she whispered. 'Not again, our enemies—'

Piro rolled her eyes. 'If you would just listen!'

A rush of sound and a great whoosh of air hit them, driving them back several steps, and they looked up to see the wyvern descending. The downbeat of its great wings raised small eddies of dust around them as it landed.

The serving girl screamed and threw herself into Feratore's arms. The wyvern's claws scrabbled on the paving as it settled onto its haunches.

Feratore shoved the girl aside, raising the old sword in defence of the comtissa. Piro had to admit he was both brave and loyal.

'It's all right.' Piro darted between him and the wyvern. 'I've been trying to tell you...' She could already feel her Affinity responding to the beast. Power slid down her arms, settling in her hands until they itched and tingled. Approaching the wyvern, she held her hands out and spoke gently. 'Where's Kaspian, Valiant?'

The beast ducked his head, jaws opening, long blue tongue flickering as he explored what Piro offered.

'Watch out,' Feratore warned.

She ignored him. 'Where's Kaspian?'

'I'm here,' the youth called from a ledge on the first floor of the nearest building. He jumped lightly to the ground. He'd removed the bandage from his forearm, and as he strode towards them, it seemed he had also shed his reticence. 'Val wanted to sleep up high. It's natural for wyverns. They like to be able to watch for enemies.' He gestured to the nearest tower. 'We spent the night up there.'

'Grandson, what is the meaning of this?' Comtissa Cinnamome asked.

In answer, Kaspian lifted his hand and the wyvern went to him. Kaspian slid an arm around the beast's neck. They made a stunning pair—the wyvern with its jewel-like scales gleaming and Kaspian bare-chested, long hair loose on his shoulders.

No one spoke. Beast and boy tilted their heads as one. Piro beamed, delighted with her handiwork.

'Kaspian...' The old comtissa blanched and reached for the serving girl.

'It's all right, Comtissa,' Piro said. 'Now that they're bonded, the wyvern won't have to be killed.'

With a gasp, the comtissa clutched her chest and collapsed.

'Grandmother!' Kaspian crossed the courtyard, but the old women shook her head and brushed him away.

'Grandmother...' Confusion and hurt coloured his voice.

Feratore discarded the old sword. Sweeping the old comtissa off her feet, he carried her inside with the serving girl following.

The kitchen boy backed off, then took to his heels.

Left alone with Kaspian and the wyvern, Piro turned to them. 'It was the shock. The comtissa's happy, really.'

Kaspian nodded, though he didn't seem entirely reassured. Then he shrugged as if slipping off a coat and reaching for another. 'I suppose I should get dressed.'

The wyvern made a soft noise in his throat.

'And eat,' Kaspian added.

'You do that, while I go check on the comtissa.'

Before she could find the grand staircase, Piro rounded a corner and collided with Siordun.

He steadied her. 'What's going on? I heard shouting.'

'The comtissa collapsed.' Piro clutched his arm. 'It was awful. Last night at dinner, I saw a skull behind her face. She's going to die, I know it. You have to do something.'

'I've done all I can.' He covered Piro's hand then saw she did not understand. 'The night her niece was murdered, she suffered a seizure that nearly killed her. I've kept her alive since, but...' He shrugged. 'By rights, she should be dead already.'

'That would mean—'

'Kaspian would lead House Cinnamome, but he's not ready. If she dies, Nefysto will have to abandon his sea-hounds. I'd better send for him in any case.' The agent ran his hand through his hair. 'I'm sorry, no lessons for you today, Piro.'

'There's always tomorrow—'

'I have to leave today. That's why I came to see you. I've had word that Lord Dunstany is needed in Merofynia.'

'Word from Fyn? Is he all right? Has Isolt been hurt?'

'They're both well. It's spar trouble. One of the warlords has come over the Divide and attacked an estate. He has to be put in his place before the other warlords get ideas. Lord Dunstany is needed to advise the young queen.'

'Of course you must go.' She nodded, then smiled. 'And I'll go with you. I can be Lord Dunstany's page again.' But he was already shaking his head. 'Why not?'

'It's not appropriate.'

'Why is it not appropriate now?'

He did not answer, backing up a step. 'You'll stay here.'

'But I could help.'

'No, Piro.'

'But...' Something occurred to her. 'If Nefysto is here, how will you—'

'The mage has arrangements with other ships.'

Of course he did. 'I want to come with you. I don't see—'

'Enough, Piro! I must go to the comtissa.' Siordun strode past her and she had to run to keep up with him.

'But you already said you can't help her.'

'That doesn't mean I won't try.'

But when they climbed the steps and rounded the corner, they found the servants weeping outside the comtissa's chamber. Even Feratore sobbed.

Siordun caught Piro's arm, leading her away. A patch of leaf-dappled morning sunlight came through the window at the far end of the corridor. Light danced on the parquetry floor, but they stood in shadow.

'She's gone?' It had to be true, but still Piro found it hard to believe. The comtissa was so sharp, so determined. 'Kaspian will be devastated.'

'He didn't know how serious her condition was. She kept it from him. Only Nefysto knew.' Siordun squeezed her hand. 'Piro?'

She looked up at him.

'You must be very careful. I thought you'd be safe here. House Cinnamome is powerful, and because it provided the last elector, it will not be in contention until the new elector serves out their time. But if the other merchant houses sense a weakness, they'll move on Cinnamome and all its assets. Whether you like it or not, you are a piece in the game of Duelling Kingdoms. You—'

'I'll be fine. But I shouldn't be here when there's been a death in the family.'

'That's true.' His intense, dark eyes fixed on her.

She tried not to look pleased. This was her chance to escape. 'I should go stay with the mage.'

'Yes... but wouldn't you be miserable all alone there?'

'There's always little Ovido and his brother for company.'

Siordun's lips twitched. 'Ovido likes you, but I don't think Cragore approves of you.'

'That's his problem, not mine.'

But he had already moved on. 'I can do no more here. When I get back to Mage Isle, I'll send a carry-chair for you.'

Once Siordun left, Piro ran to her chamber to pack. She had known the old comtissa for less than a day, but she was genuinely sorry to lose her. She didn't think the old comtissa would mind if she took the good red dress. Apart from her sea-hound breeches, she only had one other dress, which had been hers when she had been Isolt's maid. It was as fine as anything a merchant's daughter would wear back home in Rolencia.

That reminded her. She'd meant to tell Siordun about her vision. She would tell him as soon as she reached Mage Isle. Decision made, she slung her bundle over her shoulder.

As she went down the hall, a terrible howl made her heart race. Glancing along the corridor towards the comtissa's chamber, she saw Kaspian and his wyvern. Feratore must have just given him the news. Kaspian looked devastated. The wyvern threw his head back and howled again.

The servants covered their ears.

Tears stung Piro's eyes. She put her head down and slipped away.

When she reached the stable, the carry-chair had not yet arrived, but the news had. The servants gathered in the tack-room, where she could hear them singing a sad dirge. One little lad wept inconsolably. Not wanting to disturb them, Piro went along the stalls.

The inner island was small, but heavily built upon. The great merchant houses kept a few horses for show on special occasions, small ponies or goats were used to pull drays, the poor walked and, most of the time, the wealthy went by carry-chair. The stables contained several ornate chairs suitable for one, two or four people. Each was carved with the House Cinnamome coat of arms, an abeille in a stylised cinnamome tree. Each carry-chair was painted and gilded and each was a work of art.

Piro climbed into one and curled up on the velvet cushion. Recalling her own parents' deaths, she felt a deep sadness. She was nothing, just a piece of flotsam carried on the sea of events. Her brothers were fond of her, but they thought her a nuisance. No one really cared about her except for Lord Dunstany.

And he hadn't been real.

Tears slipped down her cheeks. Her old nurse would have scolded her. How dare she cry for herself when the comtissa was dead? Poor Kaspian... at least he had his wyvern.

She didn't even have her foenix.

Real sobs shook her and she didn't fight them, because there was no one to see. She cried until she had nothing left.

A little later, Nefysto's voice woke her. She rubbed her cheeks and climbed out of the chair to look for the sea-hound captain.

He was with the stable hands. She ran over and hugged him, surprising both him and herself.

'Are you alright, little one?' He searched her face. The swaggering sea-hound was gone, along with the finicky poet. Who was the real Nefysto? 'Tears for the comtissa? Ah, Piro.'

'Kaspian...' She could not go on.

'I know. It will be a shock for my poor little cousin.' He hugged her again, then lifted her chin. 'I hear you are going to stay with the mage. If you need anything, let me know.'

She nodded, but she had no intention of troubling him. Just then, the mage's carry-chair arrived and Piro went back for her bundle. By the time she returned, Nefysto was surrounded by servants. He sent them off one by one with orders, as efficient on land as he was at sea. Kaspian would be in good hands.

Piro climbed into the carry-chair and hugged her bundle to her. Two strong men lifted the chair and she was soon swaying as they walked down the road.

From between the carry-chair curtains, she caught glimpses of buildings and people, flashes of white stone, sunlight on striped awnings, flowering vines spilling from balcony pots and matrons laughing as they met on street corners.

Life went on.

Ostron Isle seemed to have recovered from the street battles after the last elector died. That time she had foreseen the elector's death because it was a...

Nexus point—that's what Siordun had called a moment of change. Pleased, she sat up, tapping her feet with impatience.

A glance through the curtains told her she had come to the long street that led down to Mage Isle. There it stood on a separate island in the Ring Sea, connected to Ostron Isle by a stone bridge. There were chambers on Mage Isle that she hadn't dared to explore back when she had believed the old mage was in residence. Now she had every intention of satisfying her curiosity.

They crossed the bridge, passed under the gate tunnel and came out in the large courtyard where the peppercorn tree grew. It was just like coming home.

She climbed down, thanked the chair-men, then asked the gate keeper where she could find the agent.

'You've missed him. He's already sailed for Merofynia.'

'Already?' Shocked, Piro crossed the courtyard, blinking away angry tears. She had something important to tell Siordun, but he'd made it abundantly clear she wasn't important to him. She didn't give any credence to his excuse for leaving her behind. Looking back, she'd been happy as Lord Dunstany's servant. They'd been a team.

Illogical as it was, she felt jealous of Fyn. He and Isolt would have Lord Dunstany to help them hold Merofynia. Byren had Orrade to help him win back Rolencia.

No one wanted or needed her. She was a spare game piece. All they thought she was good for was being married off to cement alliances.

But she was not that person, and never would be.

Chapter Twenty

GARZIK LEFT TRAFYN complaining that he was hungry. At least the squire was sitting up and clear-headed, which was just as well. They'd be in Port Mero by tomorrow evening.

On the middeck, the bright morning sun made Garzik squint. Half a dozen of the Utlanders left the starboard rail.

'What happened?' Garzik asked Luvrenc.

'Lookout spotted what he thought was a shipwrecked man. Turned out it was only a half-grown dalfino. Rusan got his pipes to see if he could make it sing for us, but...' Luvrenc caught his arm as he headed for the side. 'It's gone now. The mother came and they dived down below.'

Garzik was disappointed. 'Do they really sing?'

Luvrenc nodded. 'That's what I've been told. And they fight off wyverns to rescue men lost at sea.'

Something struck Garzik as odd. 'Why would Utlanders save a shipwrecked sailor, when he might be an enemy?'

'It's the code of the sea. If he's a hot-lander he becomes a slave. If he's an Utlander, he serves his saviours for seven years and then goes home.'

'Like seven-year slaves.' He saw Luvrenc didn't understand. 'In the hot-lands—'

Vesnibor shouldered Garzik as he walked past, knocking him into Luvrenc. Garzik realised it would go hard on the lad when he deserted the ship. 'You shouldn't be seen talking to me,' he said.

Luvrenc snorted and made a rude sign at Vesnibor's back. 'I'm not afraid of him.'

'You should be. He's one of Jost's supporters.' Garzik wanted to say more, but he couldn't reveal his plans, so he went below to the galley.

After collecting a plate of beans for Trafyn, he slung a fresh sack of watered wine over his shoulder. Adjusting his step for the roll of the ship, Garzik headed for the ladder to middeck, but found Jost and his two half-brothers barring his way.

Jost gestured for Garzik to put the food down and come with him.

Garzik heard Olbin's voice on the middeck and looked up to the patch of light above. 'I earned my freedom. I don't have to—'

The blow came so fast he didn't have time to dodge. One moment he was standing with a wine skin over his shoulder and a plate of beans in one hand. The next moment blood was dripping into his eyes, he'd dropped everything and he was on his knees. He gasped as a foot slammed into his ribs and he flew sideways, sprawling on the floor. Before he could suck in a painful breath, Jost took his legs and his supporters took his arms. Between them, they carried him towards an empty cabin.

Garzik twisted and writhed, yelling for the cook. 'I'm a free man. Tell them!'

The cook came out of the galley with an evil grin.

Fury and indignation fired Garzik. Every instinct told him to fight, but there were four of them and he was powerless to stop them.

When it was over, Jost laced up his breeches and sneered

at him. 'Go on. Or do yer want more of the same?'

Shaking with anger, Garzik pulled up his breeches while his four tormentors opened some wine and passed the bottles around.

Wincing with each breath, Garzik left the cabin, making for the ladder to middeck. His lower lip stung where it had split, and he wouldn't be able to sit down for a week. As he stepped over the spilled food, his head wound started bleeding again. Blinking back tears of fury, he wiped the blood from his eyes.

The need for justice consumed Garzik. Climbing out onto middeck, he looked for Olbin and Rusan and spotted them on the high reardeck.

They'd be furious. They'd go right down there to confront Jost. It was stupid of Jost and his supporters to linger in the cabin drinking. They'd get what they deserved. Rusan and Olbin would...

Walk right into a trap. Garzik paused halfway up the steps to the reardeck. This was exactly what the one-eared warrior wanted—a chance to ambush Rusan and Olbin away from their supporters.

Garzik finished climbing the steps deep in thought.

As he walked towards the brothers, the big Utlander glanced his way and saw that Garzik was bleeding. Olbin swore softly.

Rusan frowned. 'What happened to you?'

Garzik held up his hand. 'Promise to listen before you do anything?'

They exchanged looks, then nodded.

'Jost and three others are waiting below deck to ambush the pair of you.'

'They did this to you?' Olbin asked.

Garzik wiped blood from his eyes. 'They did it to make you angry and lure you below.'

'I told you Jost is dangerous.' Olbin turned to Rusan. 'You can't trust him.'

'I don't.' Rusan grimaced in frustration. 'But I can't

confront him until I've won back the confidence of the crew. We lost the oracles—'

'Which wasn't your fault,' Garzik insisted. 'Vultar took them.'

Rusan shrugged. 'We've been too long at sea without a prize, and three men died in the last raid.' He put a hand on Olbin's shoulder. 'After this raid on Port Mero, we'll either be dead or renowned throughout the Utlands. Until then, watch my back?'

Olbin gave a reluctant nod. 'What of Wynn? We can't let the insult go unpunished.'

The captain met Garzik's eyes. 'I promise they'll pay.'

Olbin nodded. 'I'll hold Jost down while you give him a dose of his own medicine.'

Garzik didn't know what to say.

Rusan nudged them both. 'Vesnibor's watching. Give him something to tell Jost.' And he threw back his head, laughing as if Garzik had said something funny.

Olbin followed a heartbeat later.

Garzik found that he could laugh long and loud. Let the one-eared warrior make what he could of it.

FYN KNOCKED ON the door of Isolt's cabin. 'Are you ready?'

She came out, dressed in royal blue as befitted a Merofynian queen. Abbot Murheg and Abbess Celunyd followed one step behind her. They wore rich vestments, inlaid with semi-precious stones that glittered in the mid-morning light. Seeing them, Fyn felt very much the outsider.

Of Sefarra there was no sign. Isolt looked around. 'Where...'

'I had the barge captain set up a dais over there,' Fyn said. 'I'll go fetch the new warlord and his son.'

He went across the deck, past Captain Elrhodoc and his men, dressed in their finest. Fyn caught Rhalwyn's eye and the young Affinity beast-keeper nodded. He'd done what Fyn had asked.

Satisfied with the preparations, Fyn left the royal barge. Ahead of him, the remainder of the spar warriors stood lined up on the shore, where they would have a clear view of events.

Fyn strode towards Warlord Cortovar and his son. The boy looked a little red-eyed, but otherwise seemed determined to do the right thing. Fyn met Cortovar's gaze and the spar warrior nodded. He didn't like it, but knew what was expected of him.

Fyn escorted them both back to the royal barge, to Isolt who was seated on a chair on the hastily rigged dais.

Warlord Cortovar went to drop to one knee.

'Wait.' Fyn beckoned the warlord's son. 'Cortomir, you wanted to see the wyvern? First, take this.' Fyn dipped into the basket Rhalwyn carried and handed the spar boy a sheep's hind leg. Then he clicked his tongue to call the Affinity beasts.

Without warning both Loyalty and Resolute swooped down from the mast to land on the deck between Isolt and the warlord. Confronted by a wyvern and a foenix, Cortomir took a step back.

Fyn put his hand on the lad's shoulder. 'Show no fear. Hold out the meat.'

Cortomir raised it gingerly. With a snap, Loyalty's strong jaws closed on the bone and she went took it to sit at Isolt's feet. The foenix gave voice, indignant at not being fed.

Fyn selected another large bone from the basket and gave it to Cortomir. The foenix's sharp talons flashed out, closing around the bone. The bird took his meat and joined the wyvern in front of Isolt's dais.

Fyn went to stand next to the foenix and gestured Cortomir over. As the lad went to him, Fyn met Warlord Cortovar's eyes, his message clear: *I have your son. His life is in my hands.*

Not that Fyn would hurt an innocent lad of ten, but Cortovar didn't know this.

Fyn nodded to Isolt, who took over proceedings. She'd already had the documents drawn up. Compensation would be paid to the Benetir Estate for the loss of life, and Lord Wytharon's heir would to be recompensed for the loss of his grandfather and aunt. All these documents required the warlord of Centicore spar's signature, or at least his mark.

Fyn had crushed an ambitious spar warlord and replaced him with a more reasonable man. He had proven himself as Queen Isolt's lord protector at last.

BYREN TRIED TO contain his impatience as he lowered the farseer. They'd only just passed the outlying islands of Amfina Spar so they were still at least a day from Rolencia. There was no quick way to sail home from Merofynia. It was either pick your way between the spars' tips and their shattered islands, or swing wide and risk an encounter with Utland raiders.

'Not long now,' the captain said, accepting the farseer. 'We'll be through the passage and into Rolencia Bay by midday tomorrow, and docked by evening.'

Byren nodded. They'd lost a day searching for Orrade, which he did not regret in the slightest, but it meant he would be a day behind the news of his survival reaching Cobalt.

'What will you do?' the captain asked. 'There'll be other men like Talltrees, ready to sell you to the usurper for a bag of gold.'

'But there are more, many more, who are loyal to my father,' Byren said, hoping it was true.

He returned to the cabin, where he found Orrade on his feet, staring out the window. As his friend turned, the midday light revealed features pared back by suffering and Byren was reminded of Orrade's father, the Old Dove. Austere and implacable, nothing would stop the old lord. Orrade might be a lover of men, but he was very much his father's son.

His friend stretched and grimaced. 'I swear I feel a hundred years old.'

'Eat.' Byren gestured to the table, which had been laid with lunch. 'You need to recover your strength.'

'We both do.' Orrade glanced to the table. 'Smells good.'

Byren's stomach rumbled. 'We reach—'

'I thought I was as good as dead. I thought you'd be delivered to Cobalt, trussed like a turkey.' Orrade's voice faltered. 'I thought I'd failed you.'

'Never.' Byren grasped his shoulder. 'I was the one who failed you. I couldn't stop them throwing you overboard.'

'You came back for me.'

'What else would I do?' He poured them both a glass of wine and raised his. 'To friendship.'

'To friendship. May nothing come between us.'

Byren grinned. 'Nothing ever could.'

BACK IN PORT Mero, news of Fyn's success spread fast. The barbarians of Centicore Spar had been taught a lesson. There would be no more raiding parties, not while Lord Protector Merofyn held the new warlord's son hostage. It was very satisfying, but as Fyn approached the queen's chambers, he heard Lady Gennalla trying to soothe Benowyth's sobs and Sefarra's raised, angry voice.

'How could you bring *him* in here?'

Fyn reached the doorway in time to see Sefarra gesture to the fireplace, where both Affinity beasts lifted their heads and whined.

'Don't you like the foenix?' Fyn asked as he strode into the chamber.

Sefarra glared at him. 'I meant the spar brat!'

Fyn hadn't spotted Cortomir, who stood on the far side of the fireplace. Clearly uncomfortable, the lad shifted from foot to foot. With the Centicore emblem on his spar vest, he was an unwelcome reminder of all the indignities

Sefarra had endured at his father's and uncle's hands. Isolt flushed to the roots of her hair. 'I'm sorry. I didn't—'

'Didn't think?' Sefarra cut her off. 'How—'

'She said she was sorry. Now keep your voice down, Sefarra,' Lady Gennalla admonished. 'You're upsetting Benny.'

'Don't cry, little boy,' Cortomir said, looking around for something to distract the three-year-old. He spotted one of Isolt's silk shawls hanging over the back of a day-bed, grabbed it. Throwing it over his own head, he put his hands out and stumbled about the room. 'Where am I? Where did everyone go?'

Benowyth stopped weeping to watch him.

Emboldened, Cortomir fell over the wyvern's tail.

The toddler chuckled.

Cortomir rolled to his feet and waved the shawl around in a flamboyant salute. The end of the shawl flew past Loyalty's face and she snapped at it.

Benowyth laughed.

'Ho! A game...' Cortomir cast the toddler a quick look to make sure he was still watching, then flicked the shawl near Loyalty again. This time both beasts went for it.

With a yell of delight, Cortomir took off running around the chamber, leaping from chair to table, always just out of reach of the beasts. Lady Gennalla was not impressed, but young Benowyth chortled with glee as the Affinity beasts gave chase, clawed feet scrambling on the polished parquet floor.

The spar lad jumped over a table, then ran around the day-bed, past Lady Gennalla and her grandson, who struggled in his grandmother's arms wanting to join in the fun.

Cortomir found himself trapped between the Affinity beasts and the table. It looked like he would have to give up the shawl. But he dived under the table, rolled out the far side and came up, waving the shawl like a trophy.

'Oh, well done!' Isolt clapped as the lad took off again.

Fyn glanced over to Sefarra. A reluctant smile tugged at her lips.

'Watch out!' Isolt cried.

Fyn was in time to see Loyalty take a corner too wide. Her tail toppled an exquisite Ostronite vase, which smashed to pieces.

Cortomir, Loyalty and Resolute all skidded to a halt.

'I'm sorry,' the lad said. 'I didn't mean—'

'Doesn't matter,' Isolt said.

'Doesn't matter?' Lady Gennalla shrieked. Benowyth's bottom lip trembled. 'That was a gift from the Ostronite elector. What's he going to say?'

'Nothing, because I will replace it,' Isolt said quickly.

'Clumsy beast!' Lady Gennalla rounded on the wyvern.

Loyalty whimpered.

'Wasn't her fault,' Cortomir stepped in front of the wyvern. 'I got her overexcited.'

'Stupid boy.'

'Don't pick on him, Mother,' Sefarra said. 'He was only trying to help.'

'You...' Lady Gennalla shook her head. 'A moment ago, you couldn't stand the sight of him. I swear I'll never understand you. I used to wish you'd stop filling your head with useless history. Now, it doesn't matter. You'll never catch a husband—' The noblewoman gasped and covered her mouth. 'I'm sorry.'

Sefarra shrugged. 'I don't want a husband.'

'Then devote yourself to Cyena Abbey.'

'I don't want to waste my life praying.'

'It doesn't matter what you want now. Have you no shame? No sense of family honour?'

Sefarra's face hardened, and Fyn recognised the girl who'd taken her captor's head and balls.

Lady Gennalla must have realised she would get no more from Sefarra, because she rounded on the wyvern. 'Who keeps an Affinity beast this size for a pet? Today it was the vase, what will it be tomorrow? Both you girls need to grow up!' And she stormed out, taking her frightened grandson with her.

Sefarra turned to Isolt. 'I'm sorry. Mother doesn't—'

'No, she's right. Loyalty is too big to be kept indoors. But I can hardly send her to the stables.'

'She might eat the horses,' Cortomir said.

All of them stared at him.

Cortomir shrugged. 'Well, she might.'

Fyn tried not to smile.

'I don't care what anyone says. I'm not locking up Loyalty,' Isolt said. The wyvern sought comfort and Isolt petted her. 'She's smart. It would break her heart if I had to shut her away.'

Sensing something was wrong, the foenix went to Fyn, who rubbed his throat. 'They don't belong in the palace. Resolute should be living high in the mountains. He should be spending his days flying and hunting. Loyalty would be happiest at sea, living in an eyrie.'

'As you suggesting I turn them loose?' Anger burned in Isolt's cheeks.

'No, but we need to find a better place for them. Back in Rolenhold, my grandfather had a courtyard converted into a menagerie.'

'That's it!' Isolt's face lit up. 'The Grotto Garden! It was my favourite place when I first came here. Father couldn't be bothered with me, and Mother faded away after losing three baby boys. I used to sneak away to the grotto.'

Fyn felt for the lonely child that Isolt had been. 'Why don't we go take a look right now?'

Isolt clicked her tongue and both Affinity beasts followed her. Sefarra and Cortomir fell into step behind them. Fyn wished, just once, that he could be alone with Isolt.

The young queen knew the palace better than him. She went down the corridor, through a linking verandah then into the next building.

'It's like a maze,' Cortomir marvelled. 'Are we still in the palace?'

Isolt laughed. 'Every time a new king came to the throne, they set out to leave their mark on the palace. Some built towers, some built whole new wings, others refurbished old buildings or added conservatoriums. But there is only one Grotto Garden.' She slowed and her eyes went very wide. 'Built by the Mad Boy King!'

'Was he angry-mad or crazy-mad?' Cortomir asked.

'Mad-lonely if you ask me,' Fyn said.

Isolt met his eyes over the boy's head and they shared a smile.

'We're going west,' Cortomir announced.

'How do you know? Fyn asked.

'Each time I glimpse the Landlocked Sea, it's on my right.'

'Very clever,' Sefarra said. She seemed to be warming to the lad.

'This way.' Isolt led them down some steps and into an older wing.

The chamber was full of outdated furniture. Ahead, a row of floor to ceiling glass doors opened onto a terrace. In the distance, Fyn could see the Landlocked Sea.

As they stepped out onto the terrace, Fyn saw that they were at one end of a long crescent of three-storey buildings. An ornate staircase led up to the first floor verandah, while wide steps led down from the terrace to a lawn embellished with a fountain, and beyond that was a high hedge. Presumably the grotto garden lay between this and the Landlocked Sea.

With a whoop, Cortomir and the Affinity beasts took off, down the shallow steps and across the formal lawn racing towards the hedge.

Sefarra frowned. 'Should we stop them?'

'Let them have their fun.' Isolt smiled. 'Come and see the grotto.'

Fyn followed Isolt and Sefarra down the steps.

'I like this garden best,' Isolt confided. 'Everywhere else, there are formal terraces stepping down to the sea. Here, beyond the hedge, the gardens have grown wild.'

They followed an overgrown path that wove between blooming bushes and fruit trees, until they came upon a small lake which reflected the grotto like a mirror.

Sefarra gasped. 'It's lovely.'

'It's artificial, even the pond,' Isolt revealed.

The grotto was built of white stone, artfully tumbled and then partially covered with earth and shrubbery so that it appeared to be part of the landscape. Two columns supported the grotto's entrance and water lapped into the opening.

Isolt pointed. 'The Mad Boy King used to lie in his boat and watch the stars here.'

'My mother said that sometimes he slept in the grotto,' Fyn added.

Loyalty frolicked in the water. Resolute stood in the shallows and cleaned his wings. Cortomir rolled up his breeches and paddled.

Sefarra turned in a circle. 'Why have I never seen this before?'

Isolt laughed. 'I'm sure there are chambers I've never seen, and I've lived here for seven years.' Her eyes sparkled. 'Wait till you see inside.'

She led them around the pond to the back of the mound that covered the grotto then dropped to her knees muttering, 'There used to be a secret entrance. Ahh, the wild mint grew over it.' Pushing the mint aside, she revealed an opening just large enough for an adult to crawl through. 'Come on.'

Sefarra followed her, and Fyn came last. His knees and hands crushed the mint, so that he crawled through a dark, sweet smelling tunnel towards the glowing grotto.

'It's beautiful!' Sefarra's voice reached him.

Fyn climbed to his feet. Directly opposite him he could see through the columns, across to the sparkling water to the far bank.

The grotto's white walls and domed ceiling reflected the rippling light from the pond. The water formed a shallow pool, which was just deep enough for a small boat to glide in and moor.

'Where does...' Sefarra held her hand out in a shaft of greenish light. She shaded her eyes and looked up. 'Oh, I see. There's odd-shaped pieces of glass set in the ceiling. What a clever idea.'

'It used to be brighter,' Isolt said. 'But the grass must have grown over in places.'

'I can fix that.' Sefarra crawled out of the tunnel.

'Oh, dear.' Isolt caught Fyn's eye. 'You'd be surprised how hard it is to find the glass panels once you're outside.'

Fyn stretched, his fingers just brushed the ceiling. 'Reminds me of the grotto under Mage Island.'

Isolt smiled. 'We were happy there.'

'Yes.' Back then, there had only been Piro to get in the way.

From the pond, they could hear the splash of the wyvern and Cortomir's cries of encouragement. Fyn was suddenly aware that he was alone with Isolt. His gaze was drawn to her.

An inner radiance filled her eyes, and all sounds seemed to fade. He ached for her. Colour raced up her throat and across her cheeks. Abruptly, a beam of sunlight pierced the gloom, and they both looked up. Through the thick, grainy glass they could just make out Sefarra waving.

'There you are!' Cortomir swam into the grotto through the columns, riding on the wyvern's back. His eyes widened. 'This is amazing. Can I live here with the Affinity beasts? Can I?'

Loyalty climbed out of the pool, opened her wings and sprayed them all as she shook herself dry.

Isolt laughed. 'This is the perfect den for an Affinity beast.'

'Can I be Rhalwyn's apprentice Affinity beast-keeper?'

Fyn thought it the perfect solution. 'Of course you can, if the queen agrees.'

Cortomir turned pleading eyes to Isolt. Just then the foenix gave a mournful cry and Cortomir volunteered to lead her into the grotto.

'An apprentice Affinity beast-keeper, Fyn?' Isolt tilted her head. 'You know Rhalwyn isn't my official Affinity beast-keeper? He was just the cabin boy who fed Loyalty and Resolute while we were on the royal barge.'

'Cortomir's presence in the palace would be an unwelcome reminder of what his uncle did. Here he'll be out of the way and gainfully employed. Besides, you have your duties to attend to, and Loyalty and Resolute need the company. Rhalwyn and Cortomir will have the easiest jobs in the palace.'

'That's true.' Isolt nodded then smiled. 'I guess we'd better tell Rhalwyn he's been promoted.'

A moment later, Cortomir swam into the grotto with the foenix and they told him the good news.

Chapter Twenty-One

MAGE ISLE WAS just as Piro remembered, but without Isolt to keep her company, she was lonely and bored by the following morning. Little Ovido trotted along behind her as they explored the citrus courtyard with its mass of blossoms. Piro sneezed.

'Are the wyvern and foenix coming back?' Ovido asked hopefully.

'No, I had to leave them with Isolt in Merofynia.'

'Is it true you're a kingsdaughter, too?'

'Of course she is,' Cragore said, with all the scorn of an older brother. 'And she doesn't want to be bothered by a silly six-year-old.'

'Ovido can keep me company any time he likes,' Piro said.

'No, he can't. Unlike you, kingsdaughter, he has work to do. Come along, brat.'

'For your information, I *do* have work,' Piro called after Cragore as he marched his little brother off. 'I'm here to be trained by the mage.' Which was all very well, but until Siordun came back, there was no one to teach her.

She glanced up to the tower, wishing Tsulamyth really did sleep in the top chamber. Last time she was here, she'd caught Siordun up there and unmasked his mage disguise. Which reminded her. The mage's war-table was like no other—the pieces moved to reflect real world events. If she could not be with her family and friends, at least she could check on their whereabouts.

Darting inside, she made her way to the war chamber. The balcony looked out over the Ring Sea, but Piro had eyes only for the table.

Fyn and Isolt's pieces were currently in Merofynia. Byren's was on a ship nearing Rolencia, and Siordun's was on a ship sailing for Merofynia. They were safe, or as safe as anyone could be.

She glanced to the little statuette standing on Mage Isle. Back when Siordun had first shown her the war-table, her piece had been without a face. Her stomach clenched and she experienced a moment's disorientation as she picked up her own piece.

It still had no face.

Did this mean she would become the mage's agent and control events from behind the scenes? Or did it mean she would die before she could find her place in the world?

Piro shivered.

Just then a ship passed by on the Ring Sea and she heard a male voice raised in song. Piro went out onto the balcony into the sunshine, and looked down onto the Ring Sea. As the vessel passed, the singer looked up, saw her there and tipped his cap to blow her a kiss. He made her smile. So many brightly painted boats dotted the vivid blue sea it looked like a festival. And across the Ring Sea she could make out white farmhouses dotting the steep slope of the outer island. Across the distance it was too hazy to tell, but she knew the terraces were covered with workers tending vines, orchards and vegetables. Everyone had a job to do. Everyone else's lives had purpose, except hers.

A wave of impatience seized Piro. She felt power gather in her chest and slide down her arms until it settled in her hands. She needed to channel her Affinity but she couldn't use the stone. She needed her foenix.

That reminded her. Last time she was here there had been a pica pair in the mage's chamber at the top of the tower. She glanced up to Mage Tower, so white against the clear blue sky. A black dot swooped in to land on the top balcony.

A bird returning with a message?

Piro took off at run. At the entrance to the staircase, she almost collided with Cragore.

He frowned. 'Where are you going?'

She glanced up the stairwell, and he moved to block her. She ducked past him and took off, glad of the challenge.

Heart thumping, she ran up all five flights of stairs; but when she reached the last door, it was locked. She bent double, gasping. A moment later, Cragore rounded the bend. It pleased her to see he was just as breathless.

She stepped aside so he could unlock the door. As he went to swing it shut, she darted past him.

'These birds are my responsibility,' he protested.

'These birds belong to the mage, and I'm here to study under him.' Ignoring his frown, Piro went over to the perch where the female had landed and was now preening her feathers.

'They don't like strangers.'

No, but they'd like her Affinity. She held out her hands and the bird came to her, rubbing its head and throat on her skin.

Cragore muttered disgustedly under his breath.

Bringing the pica close to her ear, Piro tilted her head to listen to the bird's message. Since the bird sang of Cobalt, she guessed the message came from the mage's Rolencian agent. The bird sang of Cobalt getting married, which confirmed her vision, but...

'*Midsummer, Cobalt Usurper will marry Piro*

Kingsdaughter,' Piro repeated the rhyme. 'But he can't marry me, I'm here!'

'Perhaps he thinks you're still in Merofynia and plans to kidnap you.'

Piro was not convinced.

Cragore shrugged. 'I just pass on the messages.'

He took the bird from her and went into a little room tucked behind the bed. Here she found a wall of caged pica birds, some alone and some in pairs. Each cage was marked with a symbol. On two of the cages Piro saw Lord Dunstany's symbol, the star in the circle. She assumed one was for his estate on the shores of the Landlocked Sea, and the other for his townhouse in port near the palace. Sure enough, on closer inspection one of the cages was marked with the letter P.

Meanwhile, Cragore had returned the bird to its mate and given the pair fresh water and food. As he closed the cage door, Piro noted the symbol—a hat.

Cragore opened a large book in which he wrote down the message, date and time in a column under the initials R and S. Rolencia, Agent S. He tried to block her view, but she'd seen enough to work things out.

'Who is this Agent S? How do you even know he can be trusted?'

'*She*,' he corrected. 'She's one of the mage's best agents because she has access from the highest in the land to the lowest.'

'She's a servant, then?' Piro nodded to herself. 'When I was a slave I heard all sorts of things.'

Cragore did not confirm or deny her guess.

'You don't know who Agent S is.'

'Of course I do.' But he flushed, so she knew he was lying.

He removed a bird from the cage marked with Dunstany's townhouse symbol, then sang a rhyme to the pica.

'You're sending a message to Agent Tyro on the ship?' Piro guessed wrong to test him.

'No.' He sent her a superior smile. 'I'm sending a

message to Lord Dunstany in Port Mero. He'll give it to Agent Tyro.'

This confirmed Piro's guess.

But she still didn't know who Agent S was. Who, apart from a servant, had access to royalty and people on the street? And why did she use a hat symbol?

It had to be Milliner Salvatrix. Back before all this happened, Piro remembered going with her mother to visit the hat shop in Rolenton Square. She'd been bored, because they did not have the glowing hercinia feathers she'd hoped to see. If only she'd known the little silver-haired milliner was the mage's agent.

Piro followed Cragore into the outer room where he set the pica bird free.

Now he had to deliver the message to Tsulamyth, but with Siordun away there was no mage on Mage Isle. It made Piroe wonder how had Siordun had gotten around this. 'Now you tell the mage the message, right?'

'Wrong. I don't bother the mage. No one does. If you could hear him berating Agent Tyro, you'd understand.' Cragore rolled his eyes. 'I put a note in the message slot outside the mage's chamber. If there's a reply, it comes back the same way.'

'I see... And where is his chamber?'

'Two floors below us. You ran right by without even noticing the Affinity coming from it!'

'Really? How careless of me.' Piro hid a smile and left him.

Sure enough, two floors below, she found one of the tower chambers had been divided in half. If her memory served her correctly, the mage's Affinity trophies had been stored here. Now there was a chamber.

Piro stood at the door, opening her senses. Cragore was right. There was Affinity in the room beyond, but not because the mage slept there. She suspected it came from the trophies.

So that was how Siordun maintained his masquerade as the mage...

And that was how Cobalt organised a marriage when Piro wasn't there to take part. He'd hired a minstrel to impersonate her. She burned with indignation.

He wouldn't get away with this. Someone would denounce the impersonator.

But who? Her father's loyal followers had died when they rode out with him under a banner of truce. The servants had either fled or been taken as slaves. It shocked Piro to realise she could count on the fingers of two hands the people who still lived who knew her face. And most of them weren't in Rolencia.

Piro went cold. Cobalt's ploy could well succeed.

This must have been why she'd dreamed about the nexus point. If only Siordun had waited, but no... He'd just sailed off and ignored her.

Cobalt must not be allowed to get away with this. Conviction filled Piro. She would have to stop him, and force Siordun not to ignore her.

She ran down the steps.

BYREN WAS GLAD to be home, but was not happy to find Port Marchand overrun by Merofynian men-at-arms. Brash, foreign braggarts stood on every street corner, ordering Rolencians about and generally making a nuisance of themselves. Surely, they could not all belong to the force Cobalt had been loaned to enforce his rule? Byren suspected most of them now served the greedy lords busily siphoning off Rolencia's grain, wine and cloth before they pulled out.

He saw plenty of women, children and elderly men, but few able-bodied young men. For now, both he and Orrade dressed as sailors. They each carried a blanket-wrapped bundle on their backs, containing weapons borrowed from the Merofynian palace and a change of clothes suitable for nobles.

'Not that way,' Orrade whispered, as Byren made for

the merchant quarter. 'That's where the gold is so it's where the Merofynians will be thickest. This way.'

He led Byren down a narrow side street that ran around the curve of the bay and into the poorest part of port. The overhanging upper storeys made a kind of twilight in the narrow lanes.

Orrade turned a corner and they stepped into a small square that had seen better days. Girls waited in doorways or leant over second storey balconies. Music competed from several taverns and men spilled out into the street. Revellers sang snatches of crude Merofynian songs as they groped serving girls.

'There's Merofynians aplenty here, Orrie,' Byren muttered.

They passed a bare-breasted woman standing in a doorway. She was young and pretty, and she'd tried to hide her bruises with face-paint.

'Come here, lads,' she called in poor Merofynian.

Byren cursed under his breath.

'People have to eat,' Orrade said.

It was true, but Byren didn't have to like it. 'So this is what you were doing last summer. I wondered why you stayed in port when your family came back.'

Orrade said nothing, leading him into an even seedier district. Here, the lanes were barely wide enough for two men to walk side-by-side. Byren felt for his knife, then remembered it was in his bundle. Only Merofynians and Cobalt's supporters were allowed to carry arms these days.

A handsome youth spotted them, pushed away from the wall and tried to block their way. As they approached, Byren prepared to take the youth down with one blow, but he wasn't prepared for the open appreciation or crude suggestion that fell from the fellow's lips.

Orrade brushed past the youth and he stepped aside, but not before groping Byren, who would have turned and thumped him if Orrade hadn't urged him on. Byren flushed as he realised just what Orrade had been up to last summer.

At that moment, a man came out of door and almost collided with them. Byren swore. The man-at-arms wore Merofynian colours, and he was not pleased to see them.

Orrade kept going. They'd just reached the next bend when the man called out. 'Hey, you two!'

'Quick.' Orrade ducked around the corner and took off.

Byren ran after him. A chorus of crude comments and curses followed them as they ran through the narrow lanes of the dilapidated district.

Without warning, Orrade rounded a bend and pulled Byren into a dark doorway with him. They held their breath as their pursuer ran past, hand on his sword hilt.

Byren waited until the footsteps faded. 'What gave us away?'

'You swore in Rolencian and you look like what you are, a warrior. Come on.'

Orrade darted out, going back the way they'd come until they reached a set of rickety stairs.

'Up here. I hope...' Orrade gave him a shove and followed him up the steps to an attic tucked under the roof.

The small landing creaked with their combined weight. Beyond the roof tops, Byren could see the tips of masts out in the bay, like a forest of bare trees against the blue sky.

Orrade rapped on the door. No answer. He knocked again, louder this time.

'Go away,' a muffled voice yelled.

Orrade gave the door handle a practised twist, lifting it as he did, and a catch clicked in response. 'In, *quickly*.'

Byren had to duck his head as he entered. The dwelling stretched the length of the roof, and no lamp burned within. The windows were covered with scraps of cloth. Narrow fingers of light speared through the gaps, barely illuminating the gloom. They revealed a large free-standing brazier, a rich velvet coat thrown over a carved chest and a desk littered with papers and books. The patches of light made the rest of the room seem darker.

The air was thick with a scent Byren associated with religious feast days back home.

'That's...'

'Dreamless-sleep incense,' Orrade said. 'Brings visions.'

'I thought it brought dreamless sleep.'

'If you drink it. The incense brings visions.'

'Orrie?' a hoarse voice called. 'Is that you?'

Byren took an instant dislike to the speaker. For one thing, his accent was Ostronite, for another, he had not earned the right to call Orrade *Orrie*.

'It's me. Are you sick, Palos?'

Byren heard the familiarity in Orrade's voice and noted the use of the alias. Palos was the legendary Rolencian warrior who had almost united the kingdom. He had been a lover of men, and it had been Palos Orrade had spoken of when he confessed his feelings to Byren after returning from port.

A light flared as Orrade lit a lamp, adjusting the wick to reveal the long, steep-ceilinged attic. The dwelling was an exotic piece of Ostron Isle, transplanted to Rolencia. Just inside the door was a shelf with some cups and plates, preserves in jars and several wine bottles. Further down, belongings spilled from carved camphorwood chests. Under a window to the left stood an elegant cedar desk, littered with books. A silk-draped sandalwood screen hid the far right-hand corner of the room. And directly ahead was a large bed, littered with cushions, pillows and eider-down quilts. It was a decadent nest indeed.

By the bed, an incense burner glowed, revealing a dishevelled man with several days' growth on his chin. He lay propped against the pillows.

Orrade cursed and crossed the chamber to pull back the window coverings. The man on the bed winced at the light, which revealed streamers of incense hanging on the air. Orrade opened a window. All the while the man watched him as if torn between amusement and annoyance.

'What have you done to yourself?' Orrade demanded, turning to the man in the bed. 'Don't you know too much dreamless-sleep will rob you of your wits?'

'I know what I'm doing.' His sharp gaze settled on Byren as he levered himself up to lean against the headboard, covers pooled around his naked hips.

Orrade gestured to Byren. 'This is—'

'Oh, I know who it is.' From the tone of the man's tone, he liked Byren about as much as Byren liked him. 'You have me at a disadvantage, Byren Kingsheir. Orrie, see if there's any food. If not, just open a bottle of wine.'

He swung his feet to the floor and walked behind the screen, where he lit a lamp. Byren heard him pouring water.

Meanwhile, Orrade opened a cabinet. He seemed perfectly at home as he tossed some beans and onion in a pan on the brazier. After inspecting the bread for mould, he fried it in butter.

Byren edged closer, whispering. 'We're supposed to be approaching merchants to—'

'I'm not approaching anyone until I know who remains loyal. Palos—'

'Palosino, you mean.' Byren used the Ostronite version of the name. 'How do you know we can trust him?'

'As you guessed, he's an Ostronite. He owes Merofynia no loyalty.'

'And he owes you?'

Orrade did not answer.

'He's loyal to only one thing if he's addicted to dreamless-sleep.'

'He's not an addict. At least, he wasn't when I last knew him.'

Byren was not convinced. He went over to study the books scattered on the desk. Amongst them, he noted Comtes Merulo's treatise on the nature of power and leadership, and another on the nature of the stars, which argued that their world travelled in an elliptical orbit around the sun, explaining the extreme seasons.

Byren had been hoping to identify which of the great merchant houses the man belonged to, but what he'd discovered dismayed him. The Ostronite was better read than he and clearly as smart as Orrade.

'Food's ready.'

Their host came over to the table, which was really only big enough for two. He'd shaved, dressed in velvet and brocade and combed his long hair, which he wore Ostronite style, in waist-length ringlets. Now that Byren could see him clearly, he realised the man could be no more than thirty.

There were only two chairs, and the Ostronite offered them to Byren and Orrade with a flourish. When they were seated, he upended a chest and sat down. 'It's a long time since I entertained.'

Byren didn't like his manner. 'Let me guess, you belong to one of the five great merchant houses of Ostron Isle. You fought a duel with the wrong man and your family had to pack you off. They still send you gold, but you can never go back.'

'Close.' He poured wine for them with effortless elegance. 'But not close enough. I was dedicated to House Nictocorax. I was Lady Death's protégé until I refused to kill a certain man.'

Orrade looked up swiftly and Byren realised this was news to him.

'If you were truly a corax, they would have hunted you down and killed you,' Byren countered. 'When you swear allegiance to House Nictocorax, you're a corax for life.'

'True...' Their host's dark eyes gleamed with sly amusement. 'But you can't kill a dead man.'

Orrade grinned.

Annoyed, Byren gestured to the dwelling. 'Someone sends you money. Someone knows you still live.'

'By the time the gold reaches me, it is untraceable.' The corax gestured to Byren. 'Is he always this rude, Orrie?'

Byren caught the Ostronite's wrist, pulling him off

balance and around the small table so that their faces almost touched. 'I don't trust you.'

Orrade went very still.

'No reason why you should... but I haven't killed you, when I could have.'

Byren felt something dig into his groin and looked down. A wicked blade rested next to his inner thigh. One cut and he'd bleed out within heartbeats.

'Now that you have both proven you have balls for brains,' Orrade said, 'can we eat?'

Byren released the man's wrist.

The corax pulled back with a laugh. 'He does not deserve you, Orrie.'

'But there it is.' Orrade topped up their wine. 'We need your help, Palos. If I know merchants, they'll be paying lip-service to Cobalt and his Merofynian ruffians so they can continue to trade. Do you know which of them are still loyal to Byren?'

One corner of the corax's mouth lifted. 'A merchant's true loyalty is always to gold.'

'You can find out. You have spies.'

The corax feigned hurt. 'So this is not a social visit?'

'You knew that the moment you recognised Byren.' Orrade's voice was sharp. 'Just speaking with us could get you killed.'

'I've missed our little chats, Orrie.'

In the lane below, a belligerent man yelled in Merofynian. The three of them went very still.

'Is there another way out?' Byren asked softly.

'Of course.' The corax nodded to the far screen. 'Through the window and across the roofs, if you've a head for heights and are nimble enough to make the jumps.'

In the lane below there was a thump, several grunts and then running feet, which faded into the distance.

As the corax poured more wine, Byren told himself Orrade had every right to take lovers, and that his dog-with-a-bone attitude towards him was unworthy. But the corax rubbed him the wrong way.

Like now, as the corax eyed them both over his wine glass. 'Why should I set my spies to work for Rolencian royalty? Deposed royalty at that?'

Byren had been wondering the same thing.

Orrade drew breath to answer, but the corax held up his hand. 'Don't tell me Byren is the rightful king. Too much blood has been spilled in the pursuit of power by men who justify their actions because of an accident of birth.'

'If you knew Byren—'

'But I don't. So let him talk for himself.' The corax turned those sharp black eyes on Byren. 'Does it matter which of King Byren the Fourth's grandsons rules Rolencia, as long as we can get on with our lives? Why should I help you defeat your cousin?'

Why indeed? 'Illien of Cobalt married some poor girl from one of Ostron Isle's five great families, then murdered her to win our sympathy by staging a fake Utland raid on his father's keep. This raid removed the wife he didn't want, and the father who stood between him and throne.'

'You're right!' Orrade turned to Byren. 'Why didn't I see it sooner?

'There was a lot happening, but I had plenty of time to think while awaiting execution in Merofynia.' Byren did not take his eyes off the corax. 'The tragic death of Cobalt's bride and father won my mother's sympathy and prompted my father to welcome Illien back into the family. First thing Cobalt did was turn my twin against me. He fed Lence a pack of lies, claimed I wanted the throne and was working behind his back to win supporters.'

The corax looked at him as if he'd said something interesting. 'So you didn't want the throne?'

Once, Byren would have laughed and told him it was too much like hard work. Now he spoke the truth. 'Never knowing if a man was my true friend, never knowing if the woman in my bed wanted me for myself or my crown, having to marry to consolidate the throne—'

'All this is still true,' the corax countered. 'Why do you want that throne now?'

'Cobalt betrayed my father after he welcomed him into our family. He conspired with Palatyne, letting him take Rolencia, and I've no doubt he would have betrayed the Merofynians when they no longer served his purpose. Cobalt will do anything—'

'—for power. Sounds like he'd make an ideal king.' The corax watched Byren closely. 'Ruthless and strong.'

'It is true that a king must be strong enough to suppress threats from ambitious nobles and deter foreign invaders, but a good king serves his people, not himself.'

The corax tilted his wine glass this way and that. 'Was your father a good king, Byren?'

The questions surprised him. He took a moment to consider. 'In some ways.'

'And in some ways not?'

Byren gestured to Orrade. 'He would have banished Orrie twice over.'

Byren expected the corax to ask him why.

But instead he turned to Orrade. 'You have Affinity now, Orrie?'

Orrade's thin cheeks flushed.

'Enough!' Byren cut in. 'I don't need to discuss Merulo's theories on power and leadership. I need to arrange a meeting with the loyal merchants so I can raise an army to oust Cobalt.'

The corax met his eyes. 'That will be hard to do once he marries your sister and legitimises his claim to the throne.'

Byren cursed. 'Piro's in Rolencia?'

'Apparently, Cobalt had her hidden all this time.'

'Captured her, more like,' Byren muttered, glancing to Orrade. They both knew his sister was a law unto herself. 'She must have convinced the ship to drop her in Rolencia.'

'When does Cobalt plan to marry Piro?' Orrade asked.

'It was to be midsummer's day, but now it is the first day of summer.'

Orrade turned to Byren. 'We still have time to raise an army and retake the throne.'

'Aye.' Byren rubbed his jaw. 'And spending some time as Cobalt's captive might teach my headstrong sister to do what she's told for a change!'

Chapter Twenty-Two

Piro packed her old travelling bag. When she'd left Rolencia, she'd been Lord Dunstany's slave, and she hadn't acquired much in the way of personal possessions since then. As she folded the rich fabric of the red dress, she was grateful to the old comtissa. It would not do for Piro Rolen Kingsdaughter to appear in her father's castle dressed in rags, not when she was there to denounce an imposter.

Her bag packed, she was about to run down to the wharf, but she thought better of it. It would be more convincing if she arrived in a carry-chair. Now she waited for the chair to arrive, her heart pounding. Any moment, she expected someone to stop her.

But Siordun wasn't here, which meant she was accountable to no one.

Not questioning her orders, the servants carried her across the short bridge from Mage Isle and around the skirt of Ostron Isle to the wharf where the *Wyvern's Whelp* was docked.

Seeing the ship, her heart lifted. With a good wind she'd be back in Rolencia in seven or eight days.

Feeling more confident already, Piro marched up the gangplank and onto deck. A young sea-hound she didn't recognise hurried over to her. He was about Fyn's age and carried himself as if he was used to ordering people around.

'This is the *Wyvern's Whelp*, sailing under Captain Nefysto's command.'

'I know. I'm not stupid.'

The youth bristled and went to say something.

But the cabin boy bounded over like a happy puppy and cut him off. 'Piro!'

'Runt.' Piro ruffled the lad's hair then turned to the servants. 'Take my things to Agent Tyro's cabin.'

The sea-hound watched sourly. 'We weren't expecting a passenger.'

By his accent he was well educated, probably from a minor branch of Nefysto's family. She looked him up and down. 'You're new. What's your name?'

'Cormorant. And who might you be?'

'This is Piro Rolen Kingsdaughter,' Runt said.

Cormorant blinked then flushed. 'Be that as it may, the captain's not here and—'

'I know he's not here *and* I know why.' She held the sea-hound's eyes for a moment to be sure he understood. 'Where's Bantam?'

'Ashore. He's...' The youth hesitated, colour creeping up his cheeks.

'In that case, send Jaku to me,' she told him, then went down the passage to Siordun's cabin.

She was unpacking her things when Jakulos tapped on the cabin door.

'There you are,' Piro greeted him. 'The mage is sending me to Rolencia.'

Jakulos held out his hand.

She glanced down to his calloused palm, then up to his face.

'Orders,' he said

From the mage, of course. Furious with herself, Piro's mind raced. 'He didn't give me any orders. As soon as he got the pica bird's message, he sent for me. He was in a terrible temper, said I had to sail for Rolencia this very day.'

Jakulos hesitated. He was a big man. Not slow by any means, but not as cunning as Bantam.

'You can send up to Mage Tower for confirmation if you like.' Piro shrugged as if she wouldn't want to be the one delivering that message.

'Cap'n's not here.'

'I know. He'll be held up, sorting things out in House Cinnamome now that the old comtissa is dead.' She saw Jakulos blink and realised that while he might have had his suspicions, he hadn't known the captain's true identity. Good. If she had inside information it made her request appear more legitimate. 'I have to leave today, right now.'

'The tide won't be with us until later. And—'

'That's fine.' Her stomach rumbled, but she focused on what was important. 'Let Bantam know we have to sail.'

'We can't sail until we find a new surgeon's apprentice,' Jakulos said. 'The last one ran off.'

'I'll help the ship's surgeon. I can sew wounds, stop bleeding.'

Jakulos rubbed his jaw then ducked his head into the passage, where Piro caught a glimpse of the cabin boy. 'Fetch Master Wasilade.' Jakulos turned back to her. 'The ship's surgeon can decide if you're up to it.'

Piro relaxed. By tradition, the women of the royal family were skilled in the healing arts. But what if a shade-ray stung one of the men? She knew nothing about the Affinity beast's poison. What if the surgeon found her lacking?

She hadn't had much to do with him on the other voyages. Now she tried to recall everything she knew.

His name was Rolencian, but he spoke Ostronite like a native. He was firm but good-natured.

Wasilade arrived to quiz her. His hair was almost white and his sun-browned skin wrinkled from exposure to the wind and sea. Despite this, he moved with a spring in his step. Piro recognised his type. He had the same kind of wiry strength as Orrade.

'So you think you can saw off a man's leg to save his life?'

'If I have to.' Piro thought about it then added. 'If someone holds him down.'

'We strap him to the table.'

Piro flinched.

'What settles nausea?'

'Peppermint tea.'

'Even a shallow wound can putrefy and kill a man. How do you prevent this?'

'Clean out all dirt, wash the wound in watered wine, make a paste from rosemary and bind it. Change the bandage once a day.'

He nodded to Jakulos. 'If she works as well as she talks, she'll do fine.' He turned back to Piro. 'Hopefully, there will be no injuries and I won't need to call on your skill, kingsdaughter.'

'Piro,' she said. 'And I'm sure there is much I can learn from you, Master Wasilade.' She saw him flinch ever so slightly. Had she offended him? 'I'm sorry, I...'

He shook his head. 'When you say my name the Rolencian way, you remind me of my dear wife, dead these thirty years.' With a curt nod, he left them.

Jakulos closed the door after the surgeon. 'I've never heard him speak of a wife before.'

Runt's stomach rumbled loudly.

Piro laughed. 'Come on, let's go see Cook.'

A little later Bantam arrived in the galley to find her perched on a stool, polishing off a second serving of cold meat and hot beans.

'Do you want some?' Piro offered as the little quartermaster took the stool opposite her. 'It's very good.'

'What's this I hear about the mage wanting us to sail for Rolencia?'

'The pica arrived this morning,' Piro said, glossing over much. 'We're to set sail with the afternoon tide.'

Bantam's eyes narrowed. 'Where Agent Tyro will be waiting for you?'

'Of course not. He's already bound for Merofynia.' Piro took a gamble. 'I'm meeting Agent Salvatrix.' She saw she'd guessed correctly and held out her bowl to the cook. 'More please.'

They sailed with the tide.

GARZIK LIFTED THE farseer to study the four merchant ships and their sea-hound escorts. It was clear now that the ships were holding off some way from the headlands, protecting the passage to Mero Bay.

'What are they waiting for?' Olbin muttered.

'The tide to turn.' Garzik lowered the farseer and returned it to Rusan.

Olbin pointed. 'They're raising sail.'

Rusan nodded, his eyes alight. 'This is it. We follow them in and trust to our disguises.'

They flew the stolen Merofynian flag, and both Rusan and Olbin had allowed Garzik to shave them so that they looked more like hot-landers. With their lower faces revealed, Garzik saw the resemblance between the two half-brothers.

He'd also tamed their waist-length hair by tying each ponytail at the nape of the neck, then winding the tie down the length of the ponytail to form a respectable sailor's queue. They'd both received their share of teasing due to their bare chins, but they'd taken the mockery with good grace.

Since Rusan played the merchant ship's captain, he

wore the fancy velvet coat he'd claimed back when the Utlanders had first taken the vessel. They hadn't been able to find a Merofynian shirt large enough to cover Olbin's broad back, so he wore only breeches and went barefoot, but this was common enough for sailors. Several beardless youths had bound their hair and offered to crew the ship. The rest of the Utlanders hid below deck.

On Olbin's order, the youths raised the sails. Garzik watched the canvases unfold like concertinas. Each sail could be raised or lowered by hauling on a single rope without fear of fouling.

The canvas snapped and bellied out as the sails caught the wind, and Garzik felt the ship respond as if eager for the adventure. Now that his plan was unfolding, he felt nervous. He hoped he'd thought of everything. He didn't want to let Rusan and Olbin down.

What was he thinking? He was going to abandon them before dawn tomorrow.

They sailed past Cyena Abbey on the outer headland. It was built of white stone, glistening like snow in the sunshine. Garzik found it strange to associate a goddess with winter. Everything in Merofynia was back to front. Instead of a benevolent goddess of summer, they worshipped Mulcibar, god of war. And instead of the cruel winter god, Sylion, they worshipped Cyena—pure and perfect, yet able to kill without compunction.

Once the ship entered the passage, the headlands blocked the wind, but even though the sails hung slack, they made good headway, carried by the incoming tide. The quiet of the passage felt strange after the constant sound of the wind and waves.

'We'll need to time our escape so the tide is with us,' Rusan said.

'Let's hope the dawn breeze is good, then,' Olbin muttered. 'Or we won't make it across the bay to the headlands.'

The steep cliffs of the headlands drove them towards the choke point, where a stream of lava oozed down the inner headland's tip—Mulcibar's Gate.

Olbin fingered the hilt of his short sword, and Luvrenc drew closer. He glanced uneasily to Garzik.

Where the molten rock met the sea it sent up great billows of hissing steam. Olbin shook his head. 'I'd heard Merofynians boast of Mulcibar's Gate, but...'

'It's not dangerous,' Garzik said.

Rusan sent him a dry look. 'It's a river of molten rock.'

'A slow-moving river,' Garzik said, but he had to admit, it was impressive. 'They call the steam Mulcibar's Breath.'

'Lower everything but the foresail,' Rusan said. Olbin shouted instructions, and they gave Mulcibar's Gate a wide berth.

Once they'd made it past the inner headland, the broad bay opened before them, with its many inlets and fishing villages. In the distance, Garzik could see the tip of Mount Mero, still coated with snow. Around its base lay the prosperous port.

Once they were beyond the protection of the headlands, the wind picked up. Olbin looked to Rusan.

'Just raise the mainsail,' the captain said. 'We don't want to approach the port before dusk.'

Not far ahead of them, the merchants and their escort of sea-hounds made their way across the bay to port.

'We'll follow them in. They'll know the channels.' Rusan caught Garzik's eye. 'But I still want you in the crow's nest, watching out for sand bars.'

Garzik nodded and ran down to the middeck to climb the mainmast.

As they drew near the port they could see that the wharves were busy. Merchant ships sat at anchor waiting their turn to unload. Scattered amidst them were narrow-hulled sea-hound vessels, built for speed.

With the Merofynian flag flying above, Garzik felt a

savage satisfaction. Last time he'd come here, he'd been a seven-year slave. Now, he was leading a raid to strike a blow for Byren, however small.

Utlanders had not ventured into Mero Bay for a hundred years, and the Merofynians had grown arrogant. An attack on their very doorstep would strike deep. He grinned with grim satisfaction.

Rusan called to Olbin to lower the sail. The ship glided until it lost momentum, and they dropped anchor. By rights they should send a rowboat across to the wharves to report to the harbour-master, but it was late and it would not be unusual for them to wait until tomorrow.

By dawn they'd be gone.

Right now they had to pick their prey. They needed an isolated vessel waiting to unload. Garzik wanted it to be Merofynian, with a cargo of stolen Rolencian goods, but the Utlanders would not care, as long as they could fill their hold.

As the sun bronzed the bay and their vessel swayed on the gentle swells, Garzik studied the nearest ships, settling on a three-masted merchant ship. It flew the Merofynian flag and he'd seen two rowboats make for shore, leaving only a skeleton crew. Decision made, he climbed down to report to Rusan.

At long last, he felt hopeful. By tomorrow morning, he would be ashore with Trafyn, and within a couple of days he would be on his way back to Rolencia with news for Byren.

No longer would he be the barely-tolerated little brother, running along behind Byren and Orrade. He would earn his place at Byren's side. He'd be the king's man.

Florin hated feasts. It would have been good if she could have distracted herself, but Cobalt's manservant never spoke. She had a terrible urge to ask him about coraxes.

How did they train? How many ways could he kill a man? Would he kill on order, or did he refuse to carry out a mission if he did not believe the person deserved death? She'd heard the rumours, and now she wanted to know the truth.

But asking would probably get her killed.

Florin clenched her jaw and stared straight ahead.

Down near the end of the tables, she noticed a servant who looked vaguely familiar and was behaving somewhat oddly.

Rather than attending to the feasters, he was ignoring them as he wove through the tables and columns. Reaching the dais, he slipped around behind it, mounted the three steps and looked towards the royal couple.

Despite the clipped moustache and servant's cap, Florin recognised Winterfall.

Her servant's cap and male tabard only fooled him for a moment. His eyes widened as he realised who she was, then narrowed as one corner of his mouth lifted in contempt.

Florin's first instinct was to protest that she had not changed allegiance, but warning Winterfall about the corax was more important. She tried desperately to catch his eye as he approached the royal couple.

He deliberately ignored her as he came up to stand on Cobalt's right, then leant forward between the usurper and the abbot to pour more wine. With a sleight of hand worthy of a juggler, he pulled a hidden knife and went to drive it through Cobalt's chest.

A savage surge of joy filled Florin.

But the corax was already moving. Amil shoved the would-be assassin face down onto the table amidst the wine, pastries and candles.

Varuska shrieked, tripping in her haste to get out of her chair. Florin steadied her.

Cobalt's chair crashed to the floor as he sprang to his feet. The minstrel ground to a halt and conversation faltered.

The clatter of a pewter plate rolling to a standstill filled the silence as a hush fell over the great hall. Amil stood over Winterfall, pinning him. No one moved.

'Assassin...' the sibilant whisper spread.

'Let me see this assassin before he dies,' Cobalt ordered, his voice hard with anger.

Florin wanted to go to Winterfall's aid, but what could she do? She was unarmed, and the hall was packed with Cobalt's supporters and men-at-arms. Besides, she could not abandon Varuska.

Amil pulled Winterfall to his feet, holding his arms behind his back. 'Winterfall!' Cobalt said.

'Yes, from Byren's honour guard. King Byren lives!' Winterfall's voice gained strength. 'You sent him to Merofynia to be executed, but he killed Palatyne and claimed the Merofynian throne. He's on his way back here to—'

His words ended on a gurgle as Cobalt drove a knife up under his ribs.

But it was too late; everyone had heard and the whispers spread, sounding like rain drumming on the roof, growing steadily stronger.

'Byren lives? Byren lives!'

Florin's head spun. Varuska steadied her.

Blinking, Florin focused in time to see Amil pass the dying Winterfall to the men-at-arms who had reached the dais too late to help their lord.

'Hold him,' Amil ordered, before going through the dead man's pockets. He found nothing. Cobalt's mouth twisted in a grimace of annoyance.

Meanwhile the chatter grew. The leader of the Merofynians came to his feet, with his men at his side.

Cobalt gestured to his men-at-arms. 'Get the assassin out of here. I want his head on a spike over Rolenton's gate.'

Amil stepped closer to Cobalt, speaking Ostronite to hide his meaning from the Rolencian men-at-arms, but Florin had grown up in a tradepost and knew enough of the foreign tongue to get by. 'You could lose everything. You've bought some of the Rolencians' loyalty by recognising their claims to dead relatives' titles, and most of the merchants are with you, but the people will turn on you the moment the Merofynian captains sail home with their men.'

The abbot must have understood as well. He groaned. 'We're doomed...'

'Nonsense, Abbot Firefox,' Cobalt snapped. He gestured to Amil. 'Go, see what you can learn.'

As the Ostronite manservant slipped away, Cobalt turned to the feasters, who fell silent. He gestured to the body being carried away. 'Byren the Usurper is a coward. He sent one of his men to assassinate me at my own table, in my own hall.'

Only Florin seemed to notice the contradiction. This was Byren's hall and Cobalt was the usurper.

'Captain Bevenwal, come here.' Cobalt beckoned to the most senior of the Merofynian captains.

Bevenwal stepped forward with half a dozen men at his back. Cobalt went around the high table to the front of the dais and drew his sword.

According to the castle-keep, Cobalt had been a brilliant swordsman; and since losing his right arm, he'd trained left-handed every day. He raised his blade with practised ease.

'You have proven loyal and brave, Captain Bevenwal,' Cobalt said. 'It is time I rewarded you and your fellow captains. Kneel.'

The feasters whispered in surprise.

Bevenwal sank to one knee before Cobalt.

'I award you Dovecote Estate, confiscated from the treasonous Orrade of Dovecote.' Cobalt touched the sword tip to each shoulder. 'Arise, Lord Bevenwal of Dovecote.'

Bevenwal's men cheered, as well they should. Dovecote Estate was one of the richest in Rolencia, and their newly ennobled leader would reward them well.

Meanwhile, the Rolencian nobles muttered disgustedly.

'Send for your captains, Bevenwal. I have four lesser estates put aside for them,' Cobalt said. 'We'll hold a great feast to celebrate.'

Reluctant admiration stirred in Florin. The Merofynians would never go home, not if they had estates here.

Cobalt sheathed his sword, then gestured to the minstrel. 'Keep playing.'

As he made his way back to his chair, the music resumed and the feasters broke into excited chatter.

The abbot accosted Cobalt. 'What will we do if Byren comes to claim—'

'His mother had Affinity, which annuls her marriage to King Rolen and that makes us both bastards. My claim is better than his as I'm the eldest son of the eldest son. What's more...'—Cobalt's voice grew loaded—'if you check your law books, Firefox, I think you will find that King Rolen issued a decree disinheriting anyone born of an Affinity-afflicted parent.'

The abbot's eyes gleamed. 'I'm sure I'll find that decree.'

'Excellent.' Cobalt turned towards Florin and Varuska. 'I'm sorry you had to see that, Piro. Do not fear, I won't hold your brother's treason against you. Come, sit down and finish your meal.'

Florin was amazed by Cobalt's ability to think on his feet, twisting everything to his benefit, yet a fierce flame of hope burned within her. Byren lived.

Chapter Twenty-Three

GARZIK FINGERED HIS knife hilt, remembering his trepidation the night Byren had sent him to light the warning beacon. He'd been afraid he would flinch when it came to the fighting.

No such fear worried him now.

Since it was his plan, Rusan had given him the honour of leading the boarding party, much to Vesnibor's disgust. The broken-nosed warrior had made it clear he was only coming along because he did not trust Garzik. There were eight of them in the rowboat, all clean-jawed youths dressed as Merofynian sailors, all eager to win fame.

Tonight, patchy cloud partially obscured the stars. The boat glided like a shadow on the sea towards the dark bulk of the merchant ship. A single lantern hung on the reardeck and another on the prow. The windows of the captain's cabin glowed, but that was the only sign of habitation.

The cabin jutted out over the stern and the Utlanders shipped oars as they eased into position. If someone opened one of those windows and looked down, they would see a rowboat full of sailors. They might wonder why the boat was passing so close on its way to shore, but there was no reason for them to be suspicious, not when the merchant ship was moored in its home port.

Garzik came to a crouch and swung the grappling hook. He let it go, heard a soft *thunk*, then pulled on the rope to make sure it was secure. He waited, mouth dry, but no one came to investigate. He scrambled nimbly up the rope.

When he reached the reardeck rail, he peered through the balustrades, looking for the night watch. Seeing no one, he swung his weight over the rail, dropped onto the deck, then signalled to the others.

Of course, Vesnibor was first to reach for the rope. As the Utlander began the climb, Garzik turned to check the deck.

He was just in time to see a man coming his way. Before the Merofynian could yell a warning, Garzik sprang for him. The sailor's cry turned into a grunt as they hit the deck. Garzik lost his knife in the scuffle. Over and over they went. One moment the sailor loomed above Garzik, silhouetted against the lantern on the reardeck mast, the next Garzik was on top.

In desperation, Garzik drove his forehead into the bridge of the sailor's nose.

The Merofynian's grip slackened and Garzik shoved the sailor off. He barely had time retrieve his knife before the sailor tackled him to the deck, pinning his arm, but the knife had been in position and the Merofynian gave a grunt of surprise as the blade slid between his ribs.

Garzik felt him shudder, felt hot blood on his knife hand.

Shoving the sailor aside, he came to his knees to find Vesnibor watching. The Utlander had made no attempt to help.

Garzik retrieved his knife and cleaned it, hoping his hands would stop shaking by the time he stood up. When he turned around, another of the Utlanders had climbed aboard.

Keeping low, Garzik went to the middeck rail. The deck appeared to be deserted. It was dark except for the slight glow coming from the captain's cabin, and the lantern on the fore-mast at the prow.

One of the Utlanders whispered and Garzik signalled for silence as a boy came out of the middeck hatch and headed towards the captain's cabin with a bottle of wine. Garzik waited until the door closed after the lad before turning to face the raiding party.

Young Luvrenc stepped over the dead sailor. 'Was this the only night watch?'

'That I could see,' Garzik said.

'Lazy hot-landers,' Vesnibor muttered. 'They deserve what they get.'

Several of the others smirked and Garzik knew he was already in danger of losing command. 'Quiet. Follow me.'

He led them onto the middeck and down the hatch into the dark, where he could just make out hammocks strung from the rafters. The way the sides of the hammocks closed around the sleeping sailors, they would not stand a chance. Killing a man while he slept made Garzik sick to his stomach, but he knew the pragmatic Utlanders would welcome any advantage.

He gestured to the sleeping sailors. 'Deal with them, then wait while I check the other cabins.'

The cook had finished for the day and the galley was empty. Garzik went through to the surgeon's cabin. Here, he found the air thick with the stench of alcohol and a man snoring heavily. Garzik was reminded of Rishardt, the Merofynian ship's surgeon who had taken him in, and he experienced a pang of loss. Rishardt had been trying to give up the bottle and reclaim his life when the Utlanders had killed him.

Standing there in this Merofynian surgeon's cabin,

Garzik realised he had very little in common with the Garzik who had been Rishardt's apprentice.

Garzik hesitated next to the drunken surgeon's bed. If he couldn't kill a sleeping man, he certainly couldn't kill a drunken man. By the look of him, the surgeon would not be waking any time soon. Garzik slipped out, closing the door behind him.

He checked the other cabins to find they were all being used for cargo before returning to the hatch ladder. Only Luvrenc remained below-deck. He'd lit a lamp and was hanging it on a hook.

Garzik could see blood dripping from the hammocks. 'Where's Vesnibor?'

Luvrenc gestured to the deck above. Garzik cursed and climbed the ladder, heart thumping. He heard a shout, then breaking glass, and caught a glimpse of movement through the open door to the captain's cabin.

Two Utlanders restrained the captain and Garzik arrived just in time to see Vesnibor stab the man before stepping back. The Utlanders tossed the captain's body aside. Three more Merofynians lay sprawled in pools of blood.

Vesnibor wiped his knife and issued Garzik a challenging look. The other four Utlanders waited to see what he would do.

Strength was all they respected.

The broken-nosed warrior smirked and grabbed an open wine bottle. 'I say we—'

Garzik swung his fist, putting all his weight behind the blow. Vesnibor's head snapped back and he collapsed. The wine bottle flew from his hand, hit the floor and rolled. The other Utlanders said nothing. Wine gurgled as it poured from the bottle.

'Go,' Garzik told them. 'Signal Captain Rusan.'

Vesnibor's four supporters hesitated.

Garzik picked up a lamp and gave it to Dizov. 'Go give the signal.'

They shuffled out, leaving Vesnibor to climb to his

feet alone. Blood poured from between his fingers as he clutched his nose, broken for a third time.

Garzik's hand went to his knife hilt.

Vesnibor shuffled out, cursing under his breath.

Feeling slightly nauseous, Garzik bent to get the wine bottle. A pair of frightened eyes watched him from behind the partly open privy door. The cabin boy.

Holding the cabin boy's eyes, Garzik lifted his finger to his lips. He took the lamp and went to walk out, but a stone filled with coruscating reds and golds caught his eye. The captain had been using it as a paper weight. About the size and shape of an egg, it had been polished until it gleamed. The stone reminded him of the fire stones that had sat in his father's great hall. Of course, one fire stone was no use without its mate, but on the off chance he might one day find a fire stone that brought this one to life, he slipped it in his pocket.

Back on deck, he found Rusan's ship drawing close. This was the tricky part. He had seen ships transferring stores while moored, but one of the nearby ship's captains might know the merchant vessel wasn't supposed to make this transfer.

Ropes sailed out across the gap, and the Utlanders caught them and made them fast. Olbin jumped aboard, followed by a dozen raiders.

'Look lively now, and keep it quiet,' Olbin ordered softly. They headed below deck and the big Utlander gave Garzik a nod. 'Well done, Wynn.'

Knowing he would abandon them before dawn, Garzik could not meet Olbin's eyes.

The Utlanders formed a human chain, passing bales, barrels and bundles up from the hold and then across to Rusan's ship, where the stolen goods were stowed away. It was hard, consistent work with barely a moment's pause, done in silence and semi-dark on deck. Below deck they had lanterns, but they were soon sweating in the close quarters.

Towards dawn, Garzik went up on deck to grab a drink and look for Trafyn. They were running out of time. The squire was supposed to be unloading, ready to slip away at a moment's notice, but there was no sign of him. Garzik cursed under his breath.

'Wynn?' Olbin passed him a chest. 'Put this in the captain's cabin for Rus.'

It was the perfect opportunity. Garzik grunted as he took the chest from Olbin. 'What's in it, gold bars?'

Olbin winked. 'Treasure of another kind.'

Intrigued, Garzik flipped open the lid. 'Books?'

Judging by the titles, Olbin had chosen Ostronite books. He'd pretended disinterest in Rusan's lessons, yet clearly he'd been paying attention. It was a shame Garzik wouldn't be around to coach Rusan anymore, but the Utland captain was clever enough to go on alone.

Garzik carried the chest across to the other deck and then into the captain's cabin, where he found the squire sleeping soundly. Furious, he kicked Trafyn's legs, then put the chest down.

The squire woke with a jerk and rubbed his face. 'Fell asleep, waiting for you to call me.'

That wasn't what they'd agreed, but Garzik let it pass.

Trafyn's eyes narrowed. 'What's in the chest?'

'Books, if you must know.'

'What does a savage want with books? It's not as if he can...' Trafyn frowned, then looked shocked. 'You taught him to read?'

'I did. Now come across to the other ship and pitch in. At my signal we go over the side. Got it?'

'It's too far from the shore. I'll never—'

'We can throw a barrel over the side. Come on.' Garzik went down the passage, out onto the deck, and walked through the working Utlanders as though he had no plans to desert them.

Once he and Trafyn were on the other ship, they took their places passing stores across the deck.

Before long, Rusan signalled Garzik. 'Tell Olbin to finish up. The tide's about to turn. We leave with the dawn breeze.'

Garzik nodded, caught Trafyn's eye and went below to find Olbin. Soon the last of the Utlanders carried bales across to the other deck, and Trafyn sat with his back to the ship's mainmast to catch his breath.

'I'll make sure everyone's out,' Olbin called up from the hold.

Garzik nodded. Any moment now, the ships would part and Jost would claim this vessel. He and Trafyn had to be over the side before that happened.

The squire nudged Garzik and gestured to the barrel. 'I don't think I can carry it. I'm exhausted.'

Garzik grabbed the barrel and headed for the far side of the ship. Resting the barrel on the rail, he glanced to the Rusan's deck one last time. Jost's supporters had gathered there.

Time to go.

Then he remembered the cabin boy. Jost would kill him, or worse. He told Trafyn to wait, and ran into the captain's cabin, where he threw open the privy door. The cabin boy gave a squeak of fright. Garzik held out his hand. 'Come with me if you want to live.'

The boy's small hand slipped into his.

'We're going over the side,' Garzik told him. 'Hold onto the barrel and kick for shore.'

'I can swim.'

'Good.' Garzik paused at the door to check the deck was clear. No sign of Jost yet. 'Follow me.'

Trafyn was not waiting where Garzik had left him.

Garzik ran to the ship's side. Sure enough, there he was in the water, holding onto the barrel and kicking for all he was worth.

'Catch up with him,' Garzik told the cabin boy, who gave one quick nod and jumped.

Garzik glanced back to Rusan's ship one last time,

expecting to see Jost and his brothers taking their leave of Rusan. Instead Jost and his two brothers were watching the captain as he stood over the hatch, speaking to someone below.

Jost signalled his brothers. They charged Rusan.

In that moment Garzik knew one ship was not enough for Jost. He wanted both. More than that, he wanted revenge.

As far as Garzik knew, Olbin was still in the captured ship's hold, checking for stragglers. He ran to the hatch. 'Olbin?'

The big Utlander came to the bottom of the ladder. 'What?'

Garzik looked over to the other ship. The brothers had disarmed Rusan and were dragging him across the deck towards Jost, who clearly relished what was to come. 'It's Jost. Rusan's in trouble.'

Drawing his knife, Garzik ran for the other ship, jumping onto the deck.

'Rusan!' Garzik shouted as he threw his knife at one of Jost's brothers and launched himself at Jost.

The nearest brother went down as the knife hit him. The other one was so surprised he released Rusan, who snatched his attacker's blade and turned it on him.

'Rusan!' Olbin bellowed, and others took up the battle cry. Fools, they'd bring the sea-hounds down on them.

Garzik tackled Jost, sending the Utlander's short sword spinning. They wrestled, trying to get the upper hand. Jost pinned Garzik beneath him, fingers closing around his throat. Fighting to suck in a breath, Garzik tried to peel the fingers away. Stars wheeled in his vision. He went for Jost's eyes, couldn't get a grip.

Sounds faded. Fool, he'd missed his chance to help Byren. Now he'd never...

A weight lifted from his chest.

Garzik fought to suck in a desperate breath. It felt like his throat was crushed.

His vision cleared in time to see Olbin toss Jost's body aside. The big Utlander reached down and hauled Garzik to his feet.

'Cut the ropes, raise the sails, take the helm.' Olbin thrust a bloody knife into his hands. 'If we don't make headway, we're dead men!'

Avoiding several Utlanders locked in deadly struggles, Garzik staggered to the ship's side. As he hacked through the ropes that bound them to the other vessel, his head cleared.

They were making enough noise to wake the dead. Worried, he scanned the deck of a nearby ship, where Merofynians were lighting lanterns and calling for arms.

He ran towards the mainmast.

Vesnibor blocked his way, grinning cruelly.

Garzik tried to tell him they had to work together to escape, but it hurt too much to talk. He swallowed, then wished he hadn't.

Vesnibor laughed and lunged to gut him.

It was an attack Garzik had practised many times. His body took over as he side-stepped the strike and drove the hilt of his knife into Vesnibor's temple. Vesnibor dropped and Garzik kept running.

Reaching the mainmast, he hauled on the concertina sail and made it fast. The fighting was slowing as he made for the next mast and did the same.

By the time he'd run up to reardeck and released the sail there, Jost's supporters had been disarmed. Garzik didn't wait to see what would happen as he took the helm.

Lucky for them, the dawn breeze was picking up. But it would also fill their enemies' sails.

He heard shouting as Olbin ordered more sail. The ship responded, gaining headway. They glided past another ship, where the confused crew were still climbing up on deck.

There were other ships scattered out to the west, but

the breeze was coming from the north. Anyone trying to cut them off before they reached the headlands would have to tack across the wind.

Garzik heard the sails creak as the wind picked up and felt the ship gain speed. He turned his head and winced.

One of the sleek sea-hound ships was giving chase. The vessel was a good way off yet, but it was built for speed, unlike their merchant ship. Garzik focused on the bay's headlands.

All they had to do was get past Mulcibar's Gate and the outgoing tide would carry them through the passage. But it would do the same for their pursuers. He didn't see how they could escape. He cursed Jost for a vindictive, short-sighted fool.

Olbin came running up the steps to the reardeck.

Garzik prepared to hand over the helm, but Olbin shook his head, went to the rear rail and studied their pursuers. He strode back to Garzik. 'They'll catch us before we reach Mulcibar's Gate.'

Then, to Garzik's amazement, he laughed.

Rusan came up the steps at a run. 'How many?'

'One... no, two sea-hounds on our tail,' Olbin reported.

Garzik stole another look over his shoulder. A second sleek vessel was making for them, tacking to get the right heading.

'We can't outrun them,' Olbin said.

Rusan judged the distance, the wind and their comparative sails, then strode over to Garzik, who relinquished the helm.

'Arm everyone,' he told Olbin.

'Even Jost's—'

'*Everyone*,' Rusan barked. 'Or we'll all be dead before this day is out.'

Olbin caught Garzik's eye and they made for the steps.

'Wynn?' Rusan called.

He turned.

'You did well.'

Garzik nodded. Apart from the pain in his throat, he was happier than he had a right to be.

Down on deck, he found bloody patches but no bodies. They'd already thrown the dead overboard. Five captured Utlanders lay face down on the deck, their arms tied behind their backs. Vesnibor was one of them.

Garzik cursed. Why had he disarmed Vesnibor instead of killing him? Because his father's master-at-arms had prepared him for life as a Rolencian noble, not as an Utland barbarian.

Olbin released Jost's supporters and the five climbed to their feet. 'Arm yourselves. There's a pack of sea-hounds bearing down on us.'

Garzik tucked his knife in his belt, strapped another to his thigh and buckled the short sword around his waist.

They made good time, and by mid-morning they were approaching Mulcibar's Gate on their starboard side, but the first of the sea-hounds was almost within bowshot. From the look of it they were aiming to board them on the starboard side. And the second sea-hound vessel was rapidly gaining on them.

The Utlanders made obscene gestures, shouting savage challenges at their pursuers.

Garzik studied the ship's position in relation to the inner headland. Surely they were going too wide around Mulcibar's Gate? He climbed the steps to join Rusan at the helm.

The nearest of the two sea-hound vessels was so close he could see their pursuers' faces as they crowded the ship's side.

Garzik was right. Rusan was taking his ship wide.

'Come here.' Rusan took his hands and placed them on the wheel. 'Keep us wide. Feel that?'

Garzik nodded. He could feel the tide sweeping them towards Mulcibar's Gate and into the passage where the water funnelled between the two headlands.

'Keep this bearing for now,' Rusan told him.

'We're too wide,' Garzik croaked.

Rusan smiled grimly. 'Trust me.'

Then he walked to the rail and looked down onto the middeck. Olbin ran up to join him. Rusan issued quick instructions. As Olbin glanced at their pursuers, then Mulcibar's Gate, Garzik wished he could hear what was being said.

Rusan drew his short sword. Lifting it above his head he shouted to his raiders on the middeck. 'We sailed into the hot-landers' jaws, now those jaws are closing on us. But we're going to give them something to remember us by. Are you with me?'

They cheered.

A rush of noise came from behind them as the sea-hounds hurled insults at them. A glance over Garzik's shoulder revealed sea-hounds swinging grappling hooks as their ship approached on the starboard side, between the Utlanders and the inner headland.

He held his position at the helm, held the ship on its course. The sea-hound deck was lower than theirs and he saw the helmsman, gripping the wheel with fierce determination, judging their ships' comparative speeds.

Grappling hooks swung through the air and made fast against the Utlander ship. Almost right away, the two ships shuddered as their timbers met. The moment the ropes were made fast, eager sea-hounds leapt aboard.

Rusan returned to take the wheel. 'Protect me.'

Garzik nodded. There was fighting on the middeck. He glanced behind them. The other sea-hound ship was bearing down. They didn't have long before they were attacked on both sides.

A sea-hound pounded up the steps to the reardeck. Garzik met him with a blow and a kick that send him falling back to the middeck into the melee.

The two ships plunged through the waves, driven by the force of the retreating tide. Garzik checked the second sea-hound ship. It was less than a bowshot behind them, coming up on their port side.

They were approaching the passage now, but Rusan had changed their bearing. He was edging closer to Mulcibar's Gate, to the billowing steam where the sea met the molten rock.

While Garzik was distracted, an old sea-hound had run up the steps. The grizzled warrior aimed a blow at his head. Diverting the strike, Garzik stepped in and drove his short sword into the man's belly, before shoving his attacker over the rail onto the middeck. The sea-hound hadn't expected such swordsmanship from an Utlander.

A second sea-hound approached Garzik. He was no older than Byren, handsome, better dressed than the rest and confident.

They traded blow for blow as Garzik backed up, watching for his chance to slip under the sea-hound's guard. They ended up shoulder to shoulder, swords locked at the hilt.

Garzik caught a glimpse of Rusan turning the wheel sharply and felt the ship respond.

'Be ready to tell Olbin to cut us free, Wynn!' Rusan yelled.

And he understood. Rusan meant to drive the enemy's ship onto the molten rock. In that same instant the sea-hound understood and his eyes widened with horror.

Below the surface, the rocks would tear out the side of the sea-hounds' ship.

Garzik grinned.

The sea-hound sprang back, cast Garzik one last look then leaped over the rail onto the lower deck of his ship. He yelled orders, calling his men off the Utland ship, but they were too intent on the attack. In desperation, the sea-hound captain joined his helmsman and they both tried to turn their ship, but Rusan's merchant ship was the heavier vessel.

'Now, Wynn!' Rusan yelled.

Garzik ran to the rail, shouting for Olbin to cut their ship free, but the big Utlander was in the thick of the fighting and did not hear. Garzik jumped the rail and landed on the deck. He ran to the nearest rope, hacking at it.

He was on the second when Olbin cut the third. Not a moment too soon, as the sea-hound ship struck the rocks. The timbers shrieked and both vessels shuddered.

The impact caused the sea-hound ship's masts to crack with a sound like thunder. Everyone staggered, some fell to their knees.

Two of the masts fell onto the molten rock. Greedy flames consumed the canvas and ropes, racing along the masts and onto the deck. The helmsman struggled to free himself from tangled ropes and sails. Garzik couldn't spot the captain and wondered what had become of him.

All this Garzik saw at a glance as Rusan's ship plunged past the stricken vessel. Funnelled by the headlands, the tidal waters drew their ship along into the passage.

The Utlanders cheered as panicking sea-hounds jumped overboard.

In a matter of heartbeats, the Utland ship was past Mulcibar's Gate and free of attackers, leaving the sea-hound vessel burning fiercely. The second sea-hound ship bore down on the burning vessel, which had been swept off the rocks and now swung sideways across the entrance to the passage. Garzik imagined the second helmsman trying desperately to avoid collision.

A rending of timbers filled the air, as the second sea-hound vessel rammed the first.

A delighted, derisive cheer rose from the Utlanders. Olbin caught Garzik in a hug and kissed him.

Chapter Twenty-Four

BEFORE LUNCH, FYN went to check on Cortomir. Since Rhalwyn was only a little more experienced than Cortomir, it was somewhat a case of the blind leading the blind. But things had gone well so far. Over the last two days, both the boys and the beasts had settled into their new quarters. Isolt seemed to be the one having the most trouble adjusting.

As Fyn stepped out onto the crescent terrace, he spotted the two Affinity beasts at the base of the stairs leading to the first-floor verandah.

'Not, like that, like this,' Cortomir told Rhalwyn. They stood halfway up the stairs on the landing.

He held a large tin platter. 'Throw it high, with spin. Like this, Rhalwyn.'

Flashing in the sun, the dish travelled out across the terrace then over the lawn. Both the wyvern and the foenix ran after it, leaping into the air. Wings beating, they strove to reach the platter. The wyvern shouldered the foenix aside, catching the dish in mid-air. The boys cheered loudly.

Fyn jogged along the terrace and climbed the stairs to the landing, just as the wyvern landed on the balustrade with her prize.

Cortomir accepted the platter and congratulated her. Then Loyalty swooped down to land on the terrace below, where both beasts waited eagerly.

'Can I have a look?' Fyn asked, holding his hand out for the platter.

'It's gotten a bit chewed up,' Rhalwyn admitted. 'But it's an old one so I didn't think anyone would mind.'

Fyn tested the weight of the platter before throwing it in a long, graceful curve.

Both beasts scrambled to catch the dish. This time the foenix used his sharp claws to pluck it from the air before the wyvern could beat him to it.

'Who invented with this game, Cortomir?'

'Da showed me.' The spar lad shrugged. 'Dunno who showed him.'

The foenix returned with the platter, then both beasts waited, ready to play again. This time Rhalwyn threw it and the wyvern and foenix almost collided, jaws snapping, claws flashing. Fyn winced.

Rhalwyn turned to Fyn. 'Will the queen be coming today?'

'Probably. She's having lunch right now.' Fyn headed back into the maze of corridors.

He found Isolt eating lunch on another terrace that looked out over the Landlocked Sea. Sweet smelling flowers spilled from terracotta pots. Lady Gennalla, her daughter Sefarra and grandson Benowyth shared the queen's table, while musicians played softly and half a dozen servants waited discreetly. Fyn would have happily consigned them all to the Utlands for a moment alone with Isolt.

Isolt saw him and smiled. He thought there was a special welcome in her eyes just for him, and he felt his pulse quicken.

One servant set a place at the table, while another offered Fyn a tray of pastries. He listened while Lady Gennalla and Isolt discussed the logistics of their family's return to Benetir Estate. They were concerned for the seven-year slaves who worked in the estate's sorbt mine.

The servants arrived with another course and Lady Gennalla leant close to Fyn, lowering her voice. 'Sefarra's not thinking clearly.'

Fyn glanced to Sefarra, who was staring, stormy-eyed, across the Landlocked Sea.

'First she refused to dedicate herself to Cyena, and now she doesn't want to come home. You must convince her.' Lady Gennalla flushed. 'Isolt has been kind, but there's no reason for Sefarra to stay in the palace. She'll never get a husband now that she's ruined.'

'Then it's lucky I don't want a husband,' Sefarra said, proving she had excellent hearing. 'I keep telling you I don't want to get married. I want to join the queen's guard.'

Fyn winced. Captain Elrhodoc would never accept Sefarra.

Lady Gennalla sent Fyn a silent plea.

'I'm the right age for a squire.' Sefarra turned to Isolt. 'Let me go into training to serve you, my queen.'

Isolt sent Fyn a silent plea.

'Lord Protector?' Sefarra fixed hard eyes on him. He knew what she was capable of. She would never be the girl her mother remembered. Perhaps she had never been that girl.

Even if the nobles had welcomed her back, he doubted she would have been satisfied as the wife of a lord.

'Well?' Lady Gennalla urged Fyn to speak.

Compared with this, defeating a spar warlord was simple. Fyn drew breath.

Just then an altercation caused them all to turn.

'I'll see the queen, thank you very much. And you'd better not try to stop me.'

There was a scuffle. Fyn jumped to his feet as an iron-haired man sent two of the queen's guards flying, then strode across the terrace towards them.

'It's the bay lord,' Isolt whispered to Fyn. Coming to her feet, she raised her voice. 'How nice to see you, Lord Cadmor.'

'They haven't told you, I knew it!' Cadmor cursed roundly.

Despite his grey hair, he'd had no trouble dealing with Captain Elrhodoc's men. Fyn stepped in front of Isolt.

Lord Cadmor looked Fyn up and down, amused. 'So this is King Rolen's pup? Favours his grandmother. Hope for your sake he's as sharp as she was.'

Fyn flushed. He hadn't known his grandmothers. Recollecting his manners, he gave a formal bow. 'Lord Protector Merofyn at your service, Lord Cadmor.'

'*Captain* will do. I come bearing bad news, Queen Isolt.' He glanced to the others at the table and jerked his head towards the edge of the terrace.

As soon as they reached the rail, Cadmor gave his report. 'Utlanders sailed into Mero Bay, bold as brass, and attacked a merchant ship.'

'Utlanders?' Isolt turned worried eyes to Fyn. Just when they thought the kingdom was safe from threat. 'But it must be a hundred years since—'

'Ninety-two, to be precise. My grandfather dealt with them then. This time my grandson gave chase. He managed to lose his ship and half his crew, and get himself burned to boot.'

'That's terrible,' Isolt said. 'Will he be all right?'

A smile broke across the bay lord's face. 'He'll be fine. Bless you for asking. Maybe next time he won't be so hot-headed. The Utland captain was a canny one, he lured—'

'There you are, my queen.' Captain Elrhodoc hurried over to join them, gold braid and silver buttons flashing in the sun. He gave the bay lord the slightest of nods. 'Cadmor.'

'Elrhodoc.' Cadmor looked him up and down. 'I see you take after your father. He never did have any—'

'Over here.' Elrhodoc beckoned Captain Aeran and the harbour-master. As they strode across the terrace, Elrhodoc turned to Isolt. 'Terrible news, my queen, Utlanders—'

'I've already told her,' Cadmor cut him off. He nodded to the captain of the city-watch. 'Aeran.' Then to the harbour-master. 'Still having trouble making your books balance, Fercwyf?'

The harbour-master flushed. 'There's no problem with my books, bay lord. I keep track of all goods in and out of Port Mero.'

'Is that what you call it?'

'I'm guessing Cadmor's told you that Utlanders entered the bay last night,' Aeran said quickly. 'They murdered a merchant ship's captain and stripped his vessel.'

'I've spent all morning dealing with his surviving crew and employer,' the harbour-master said.

Fyn frowned. 'I don't see how an Utland ship could sail into Mero Bay unnoticed.'

The harbour-master turned to Cadmor. 'Well, bay lord?'

'They sailed a captured merchant ship.' Cadmor shrugged. 'No one realised it had an Utland crew. They would have gotten away with it, if trouble hadn't broken out between the Utlanders. As soon as the alarm was given, my grandson gave chase. An Ostronite sea-hound ship followed him. My grandson's ship was destroyed and the Ostronite ship severely damaged.'

'And the Utlanders escaped unpunished. We can't have this. It's bad for trade,' the harbour-master insisted. 'As bay lord, it's your responsibility to protect Port Mero.'

'Let me see...' Cadmor rubbed his jaw. 'It must be over fifty years since the merchants and lords stopped paying their tithe for the bay lord's protection. Reckon that's about right, because I was sent to sea when I was ten and

I'm sixty-five now. Fifty-five years of making ends meet. I reckon my family's owed fifty-five years of tithes for—'

'For what?' the harbour-master sneered. 'For letting the Utlanders escape?'

'For patrolling the bay and deterring Utlanders!'

'And how much of that have you been doing? Half the time your ships are working as common sea-hound escorts.'

'To make ends meet. You've no idea how much it costs to maintain my ships and crews. If the lords and merchants had paid their dues, my other two ships wouldn't have been serving as sea-hounds on route to Rolencia. They would've been patrolling the bay yesterday—'

'But they weren't, and look what happened!'

Cadmor's hands curled into fists. Aeran put a hand on his shoulder.

Elrhodoc turned his back on them. 'We must mount a punitive expedition, my queen. Teach those barbaric Utlanders a lesson. Bring them back and execute them in the town square.'

'But how do we catch them?' Isolt asked. 'Once on the open sea they could go anywhere.'

'It's pointless to go after them.' Fyn spoke from experience. 'By the time we send out ships, the Utlanders will have a day's head-start. Our ships would have to stop and board every Merofynian merchant ship they came across to find the one under Utlander control.'

'It doesn't matter, as long as they capture some Utlanders and bring them back here to be executed,' Elrhodoc said. 'And we can't leave this to the bay lord. He said himself he hasn't any ships to spare. We need the king's ships.'

Fyn's father hadn't maintained a navy. When they needed ships, King Rolen would commandeer merchants' ships. Fyn caught Isolt's eye. 'How many ships in the royal navy?'

'Five in all,' Elrhodoc answered for her. 'We'll—'

'True,' she cut in, 'but when not at war, they serve the crown's interests as merchant ships. I'm not sure how many are in port.'

'I'll find out and bring their captains to the war-table,' Aeran said.

'I'll tell the nobles.' Elrhodoc strode off.

'I'll tell the merchants.' The harbour-master left.

Isolt turned to the bay lord. 'I'm sorry, I had no idea the merchants and lords had stopped paying their tithes.'

'About the same time they stopped offering their daughters to my family. When my father went looking for a wife, every last girl was promised. Or so they claimed.' He shrugged.

Isolt smiled slowly, her eyes lighting up. 'The royal yacht is the best that Wythrontir shipyard has built.'

'I know the royal yacht, she's a beauty.'

'Fit for the open sea?'

'Of a certainty.'

'Then she's yours.'

The bay lord's jaw dropped.

'You lost a ship in Merofynia's service.'

The bay lord dropped to one knee. 'You have my family's loyalty to the end of our days, Queen Isolt.'

Isolt laughed. 'I thank you. But be careful what you swear. Who knows what will happen?'

Cadmor came to his feet and his gaze went past her to where the royal yacht was moored.

'Go look her over,' Isolt said. 'I'll send a message to have her re-stocked. Do you want the crew or your own people?'

'My people, begging your pardon.'

Fyn nodded. 'A captain needs to know he can rely on his crew.'

'Your lord protector has the right of it.' He took his leave, with a spring in his step.

This left Fyn and Isolt virtually alone on the terrace. Lady Gennalla, Sefarra and little Benowyth had slipped away to give them privacy. The servants waited to clear the table.

'You did the right thing,' Fyn said. 'For all his rough edges, I'd trust Cadmor at my back, before I'd trust...' He thought better of criticising the captain of the queen's guards.

'Utlanders in Mero Bay, what next?' Isolt shook her head. 'I know you say we won't catch them, but we have to do *something*.'

'With a spar raid and now an Utland raid, I think you should cancel the royal tour. Your birthday is in midsummer and we're planning a big celebration. Tell the lords to come here, to give their oaths of allegiance.'

'You're right. I can stage a grand ceremony.'

'Have them bring their families, then keep them here.'

'As hostages?'

'As welcome guests,' Fyn said. 'Children who grow up in your court will support you as adults. This is your chance to win the loyalty of the next generation of Merofynian nobles.'

Isolt's eyes widened. 'I must admit, I had not thought that far ahead.'

'I was trained in statecraft.'

'My father made no effort to train me. He thought my mother would give him a son.'

Fyn wanted to reach out and hug her. He folded his arms. 'Do you want to finish your lunch?'

'I don't think I could eat right now. Besides, I had better sign the royal yacht over to Lord Cadmor before he's accused of trying to steal it.'

'THEY'RE LATE.' BYREN adjusted his borrowed Merofynian finery. 'I wish I wasn't meeting Rolencian merchants dressed like one of the enemy.'

'Merofynia is no longer our enemy, now that Queen Isolt is our ally.' Orrade gestured to their clothing. 'And this will serve as a reminder.'

Even empty, the wool warehouse was thick with the smell of lanolin. Byren opened the little window. They were right across from the wharfs and the calls of seagulls carried on the breeze, along with the smell of seaweed.

To one side of where they stood was the shuttered opening where bales were winched up. Light filtered in through the gaps around the shutters.

The corax's voice reached them from the floor below as he welcomed an arrival. 'Markiz Samidor.'

The other merchants greeted the markiz.

'We'll wait for—'

'No point,' someone said. 'The others aren't coming, or they would have been here by now.'

Byren and Orrade exchanged looks.

'Then go right up,' the corax told them. 'I'll keep watch.'

Orrade leant closer to Byren. 'Let me speak first.'

Four well-dressed merchants filed onto the mezzanine floor under the sloping roof. Byren frowned. *Only four?*

Three merchant markizes and one markiza. Byren knew the markiza. Her son, Chandler, had served in his honour guard. The other three he knew by name and reputation, but that was all. He wished now that he had spent more time in trade meetings.

'By now you will have heard the good news,' Orrade said. 'King Merofyn is dead. Byren killed the upstart spar warlord, Palatyne, claimed Isolt for his queen and named his brother lord protector of Merofynia. Now he needs your help.'

They all looked to Byren. He spread his feet and hooked his hands in his belt. 'I'm going to raise an army to remove my bastard cousin from my father's throne.'

'King Rolen's death was a great loss,' the old wool merchant said. He reminded Byren of Orrade's father—tall, thin and austere.

'Thirty years of peace and prosperity King Rolen gave us.' Markiz Samidor shook his head. He was middle-aged and seemed to have a perpetual frown. 'I fear we won't see his like again.'

The others nodded.

'He will be sadly missed.' The plump spice merchant agreed, and Byren recognised his voice. Yarraskem had been the one who said no more merchants were coming. Now the spice merchant gestured, rings glinting as his lace cuff fell away from his hand. 'While we are glad to see King Rolen's son safely returned, having secured the Merofynian queen for his bride, one wonders why he did not bring Merofynian men-at-arms to oust Cobalt.'

Byren was prepared for this. 'Rolencia has suffered at the hands of Merofynia. I'm not marching more Merofynians across Rolencian soil.'

'Besides,' the wool merchant said. 'You could not trust Merofynians to fight their own brothers-at-arms. Cobalt has five captains and their men at his disposal.'

'Forget them,' Orrade said. 'They'll be recalled to Merofynia. In fact they probably won't wait for orders. They'll sail when they hear that Byren is betrothed to their queen.'

'Does this mean you've ordered the Merofynian nobles to relinquish the properties and businesses they laid claim to?' Yarraskem asked.

'Some,' Byren conceded. The Merofynian nobles had not been eager to give up what they'd won. 'They fought a war, lost men and—'

'Stole our stock and confiscated our cargo,' Yarraskem supplied.

'Which is why we need to reclaim Rolencia and make the kingdom strong,' Byren forged on. 'Soon the streets will be clear of strutting Merofynian men-at-arms. Soon our only enemies will be Cobalt's men and those Rolencians who've sold their loyalty to him for land and titles.'

'Civil war...' The markiza shook her head.

'What do you want from us?' Samidor asked, eyes wary. 'Gold?'

'I have the Merofynian treasury.' In theory. But he could not travel with a fortune. Byren had some gold with him and a letter from Queen Isolt. 'I need you to support me. Spread the word that I've returned, so I can gather an army and—'

'An army of cripples?' Yarraskem grimaced. 'Those who weren't killed or captured in the invasion paid with their right hands when they refused to reveal your whereabouts to Cobalt. Who will flock to your banner a second time?'

No one mentioned the Battle of Narrowneck, but Byren knew they were thinking of it. His cheeks burned with shame and frustration. Through no fault of his own, he'd let down his followers, and he hated it.

Orrade gestured to the merchants. 'Each of you keeps hired swordsmen—'

'To protect our property,' Yarraskem said. 'In troubled times, a man needs to protect his family and trade.'

'When Byren is king, he'll re-open trade,' Orrade said.

'Cobalt has already re-opened trade,' Yarraskem said and shrugged. 'And he's lifted King Rolen's ban on Affinity products.'

'Not that it ever stopped you from turning a profit,' Samidor muttered. 'We all know things slip in with your spices.'

Yarraskem bristled. 'What are you saying?'

Byren slammed the flat of his hand on the table. They all jumped and turned to him. 'Fighting amongst ourselves only aids Cobalt.'

Yarraskem and Samidor subsided, radiating affronted dignity.

'I need Rolencian merchants to honour Queen Isolt's treasury letter.' Byren removed the letter from his vest to show them the Merofynian seal and Queen Isolt's signature. 'I need gold to buy food and weapons.'

'We all need gold,' Yarraskem said. 'The Merofynians cleaned me out of stock and burned my warehouse. I've had to negotiate a loan from Ostron Isle to rebuild my business.'

'I'm in much the same position,' the wool merchant said. 'My stock was stolen and I must make five successful voyages before I can repay my debt to the Ostronites.' He shook his head. 'I wish you well, young Byren, but—'

'The Ostronites sat on the fence and profited from this invasion,' Samidor said. 'Take your letter to them.'

Voices reached them from below and the corax ran up the steps. 'A Merofynian patrol has been sighted two blocks over, coming this way.'

The merchants wished Byren well and left. Only the markiza lingered. She placed a drawstring purse on the table.

'Gold,' she said. 'It is all I can manage.'

'I will not forget this,' Byren said, coming around the table. 'One day I will repay you.'

'I want to ask you to make sure my son comes home safe, but...' She gave a sad, proud laugh. 'I know he will be in the thick of the fighting.'

'He's a good lad, Chandler.' Byren kissed her cheek. 'No wonder, when he has you for a mother.'

She left and Byren turned to Orrade, who shook his head. 'How do you know the right thing to say?'

Byren shrugged. 'I spoke the truth, that's all.'

Chapter Twenty-Five

Now that Florin knew Byren lived, she felt her place was at his side, helping him regain the throne. Instead she was stuck here playing the man so Seela could teach Varuska to dance.

'Again,' Seela said.

'I don't see why I have to learn these noble dances,' Varuska muttered. 'I've managed to avoid dancing so far.'

'You'll have to dance at the wedding.'

'Not if we kill him right after the ceremony,' Varuska countered, flashing a cheeky smile. In that moment, she reminded Florin of Piro. Now that Varuska trusted them, she'd grown confident enough to reveal her true nature... when Cobalt was not around.

Seela frowned. 'Don't—'

The door to the women's solarium swung open and Cobalt strode in. He took in their stance and the dolcimela in Seela's hands. 'I see you are practising your dances for the wedding, Piro. Excellent. I've brought our marriage forward. Seven days from now we'll—'

'What?' Seela sprang to her feet. Her actions covered Varuska's cry of dismay. 'But I haven't finished making-over her mother's wedding dress.'

'Set the castle seamstresses to work.' Cobalt dismissed her protest with a wave of his hand. 'I'm tired of waiting.'

He turned and walked out.

As soon as the door closed, Varuska whispered, 'Why—'

'He's afraid of Byren!' Savage delight surged through Florin.

'I should have foreseen this,' Seela muttered.

Varuska would have spoken, but the nurse signalled for silence. 'Florin, go see what you can learn about the wedding plans. We'll need an escape route.'

Florin nodded and slipped into the queen's private chamber. From there, she went down the servant's stairs, then along the corridor and into another stairwell, heading for the castle-keep's study.

Turning a corner, she spotted Cobalt ahead of her and hung back. Then she heard voices and realised the castle-keep had waylaid him on the landing between floors. Florin sank into a crouch, with her ear pressed to the gap between the railings.

'They tell me you've moved the wedding forward. Don't you see it looks bad if you rush things?'

'And it will look even worse if the real Piro turns up.' Cobalt said. 'I've had word from Merofynia. She was there when Byren killed Palatyne. So was Fyn. Byren has named his brother lord protector of Merofynia. Soon all of Rolencia will know. Port Marchand already knows.'

'What will you do?'

'Declare the other Piro to be an imposter and marry the real Piro.' There was laughter in his voice.

The castle-keep digested this in silence.

'Don't worry, Yegora. We'll send out invitations by fast riders. The nobles and merchants will make all haste to join us. They won't want to miss the royal wedding.'

'The castle will need—'

'I don't want the wedding in the castle. I want it held at Narrowneck.'

Florin was as stunned as the castle-keep.

'B-but that's—'

'It's perfect. It juts into Lake Sapphire, bound by cliffs. It's the equivalent of a giant stage. I've already sent men to rebuild the wall across the narrowest point. Only invited guests will be allowed onto Narrowneck, but the ordinary folk can bring boats across the lake and watch the ceremony, which will be held on the point. Narrowneck is defensible, yet open.'

'I don't know, Illien, to wed where so many have died...'

'To wed where Byren was defeated. It sends a message. I'll secure the throne with this marriage, and I'll have an heir before a year is out.'

'The arrangements... So much needs to be done, I don't see how—'

'You have a genius for organisation, Yegora, and you have an army of servants at your disposal. Ah... here comes Amil. Off you go. I know I can trust you.'

Florin heard the castle-keep's footsteps retreating, but she had not heard Amil's approach.

'You sent Lady Death my message?' Cobalt spoke Ostronite.

'Yes. Fyn and Piro will cause you no more trouble.'

'And Byren?'

'As soon as he starts gathering an army, a corax will infiltrate his ranks and kill him.'

'It must look like an accident. We don't want to make a martyr of him. Better they remember him as the fool who lost a battle, won Merofynia, then caught black-spot fever and died.'

'You should have been a corax.'

Both men chuckled.

Florin shivered and crept away, cursing Cobalt.

* * *

Fyn knew the sea. Maybe not as well as the three royal navy captains who gathered around the war-table, but he knew there was almost no chance they'd catch the Utlanders responsible for this morning's outrage.

It was late afternoon and they'd been talking long enough for Fyn to know that the harbour-master wanted to make it clear that he had not been negligent. The merchants wanted assurance Utlanders would not dare to invade Mero Bay again. Lord Cadmor wanted his family name respected. Lord Yorale wanted to advise the queen. Lord Neiron and Captain Elrhodoc wanted their opinions heard even though they knew nothing about the sea.

Isolt looked to Fyn. 'Should we send the royal navy to hunt down Utlanders when we don't know which Utlanders entered Port Mero?'

'All Utlanders are guilty of piracy,' the oldest navy captain said, and the other two agreed.

'We must send a clear message,' Captain Elrhodoc stated.

Neiron nodded. 'He's right. Merofynia cannot be attacked with impunity.'

The merchants and nobles agreed with him.

'For nearly a hundred years, our bay was safe from Utland depredation,' Yorale said. 'Force is all they understand.'

'Send the bay lord,' Neiron suggested. 'Now that he has the fastest yacht ever built, he—'

'He has to defend the bay,' the harbour-master said. 'That's why the queen gave him the royal yacht.'

'I gave him the yacht to replace the ship he lost defending the bay,' Isolt corrected. 'And I wouldn't have had to do that if everyone had paid their tithes.'

There was some muttering.

'I can protect Port Mero best by going to sea,' the bay lord said. 'We have to make sure the Utlanders know if one of their ships ventures into Mero Bay it brings the wrath of Merofynia down on *all* Utlanders.'

'Those are our orders?' The oldest of the royal navy captains asked, but he looked to Lord Yorale, not the queen, for confirmation. 'Sail in convoy, hunt down Utlander ships, capture them and—'

'If you capture one of their ships and kill every last Utlander, how will the others know the missing ship wasn't simply lost at sea?' Fyn asked. 'How will the Utlanders know this was retaliation for attacking Merofynia?'

'Surely you don't suggest we leave some of the crew alive to go home and breed more savages?' the youngest navy captain asked.

'Put them to the sword,' Elrhodoc said. 'The only good Utlander is a dead Utlander.'

'Execute them all?' the oldest navy captain asked Yorale.

At least Yorale had the tact to consult Isolt. 'What are your orders, my queen?'

She looked to Fyn. 'You were a sea-hound.'

'Instead of putting the captured Utlanders to the sword, bring them back.'

'To imprison?'

'No, my queen. Justice must be seen to be done. Word has to spread amongst the Utlanders. They have to know Merofynia has retaliated.'

'And how are you going to ensure they know this?' Elrhodoc asked.

All eyes turned to Fyn, who glanced to Isolt. She was not going to like this. 'We build a gallows on the ocean side of the outer headland, and hang the Utlanders where they can be seen by passing ships.'

'Hang them?' Isolt whispered, shocked.

'They were always going to die. This way, their deaths serve us.' Fyn made his voice hard. He was determined not to lose any of the ground he'd gained with the defeat of Warlord Cortigern. The Merofynian elite had to respect and fear him. 'Leave the Utlanders' bodies to rot, as a warning to any who would attack Merofynian merchant ships either in port *or* on the high seas.'

The others were nodding even before he finished.

'We'll look like barbarians,' Isolt protested.

'*They* are the barbarians,' Elrhodoc said.

'You have a woman's soft heart,' Neiron told Isolt. 'Leave the warring to us.'

'But this will make the Utlanders hate Merofynia,' she protested.

'They already hate us, my dear,' Yorale said.

The bay lord nodded. 'He's right. They kill or enslave the crew of every ship they take, my queen. Sometimes you have to fight fire with fire.'

Isolt flushed and looked down. Yorale gave her shoulder a fatherly squeeze.

'I should lead the fleet,' the oldest navy captain said. 'I have seniority.'

'But I sail the largest ship,' the second captain argued.

The youngest captain turned to Yorale. 'What—'

'You have all served the crown well,' Isolt said. 'But none of you have the fire of revenge in your bellies. I name Cadmor my lord admiral. He's had fifty-five years as a sea-hound.'

There was nothing the three navy captains could say. They left to prepare their ships. As Isolt took her leave, Fyn tried to catch her eye, but she would not look at him.

Meanwhile, the harbour-master, the new lord admiral and Captain Aeran discussed increasing port security with Fyn. Aeran offered to send more patrols to the wharves. Cadmor offered his grandson's service.

'Young Camoric will be up and about in a few days,' Cadmor said. 'He'll be spitting mad to miss the chance to sail on the royal yacht. He can patrol the bay.'

'I thought he lost his ship.'

'That he did, the foolish boy. He'll be captain of a

fishing boat until our other ships return. Teach him to think before he rushes into things.'

By the time Fyn escaped the meeting, Isolt was long gone.

The overcast day brought an early twilight to the palace corridors. Servants were already lighting candles when Fyn went looking for Isolt. She was not in any of her usual places and, according to Rhalwyn and Cortomir, had already visited the Affinity beasts' grotto. Was she hiding from him?

Finally, Fyn learned she was in her chamber, dressing for the evening meal. He asked to see her, but the servants sent him away.

Torn between frustration and remorse, Fyn went to change for dinner. Surely Isolt could see that if the nobles and merchants did not respect him, they would not follow him? And leniency to the Utlanders would only make Merofynia look weak.

A little later, Fyn strode into the palace's dining hall as though he wasn't dreading eating at the royal table. Each evening, Isolt welcomed a different noble and merchant margrave to the seats of honour each side of her. This way, no one could claim she favoured any one above the others.

Every evening, the men set out to charm her, even if they were grandfathers. Usually Fyn smiled at their clumsy compliments, but tonight he was troubled by the distance between himself and the queen. He would ask Isolt to dance, get her alone and... what? Apologise for doing the right thing?

Someone had to make the hard decisions.

Fyn looked up at the royal table as he approached. Behind it, the wall was decorated with a mural depicting stylised wyverns. It was made of many tiny tiles and semi-precious stones. The brilliant blue of the lapis-lazuli glinted in the candlelight.

Isolt did not meet Fyn's eyes as he bowed to her and made his way around the table. Lord Wytharon's grandson, the new lord of Wythrontir Estate, sat on her left. Wythrod was around Byren's age. From his glazed expression it was clear he found the young queen desirable and, finding himself at her side, could not believe his luck.

As Fyn took his seat, he strained to catch their conversation, then realised he was just looking for an excuse to interrupt. He should make be making polite conversation with Travany, who sat on his right, but the middle-aged lord made no effort to include him in his discussion with Lord Rhoderich.

Further down the table, Abbot Murheg caught Fyn's eye. It was a pity they could not continue their debate about the origins of the statues on Ruin Isle.

Neiron, now Lord of Nevantir Estate, ignored his dinner companion to cut into Wythrod's conversation with the queen. Fyn saw Isolt's mouth tighten in annoyance and was glad he had restrained himself.

An altercation over by the main entrance drew Fyn's eye. He could hear a young, hoarse voice protesting. There was a scuffle. One of the ceremonial guards tripped. A filthy youth darted past them and staggered across the floor. He was barefoot and dressed in rags, and his long hair hung in matted clumps. Feverishly, he searched the high table.

'Grab him.' Captain Elrhodoc sprang to his feet. 'Grab the Utlander.'

Men cursed, women shrieked.

'I'm not—' the youth protested.

Before he could finish, several of the ceremonial guards tackled him, pummelling him. Amidst jeers of 'kill the Utlander', they drove him to the ground, then caught him by his arms and lifted him off his feet.

Struggling frantically, he bit the hand that gagged him and managed to shout. 'I'm no Utlander.'

They quickly silenced him. Three restrained him, while a fourth drew his knife and prepared to cut his throat.

'Not here at the dinner table,' Elrhodoc yelled. 'Take him outside.'

'Wait.' Fyn had rounded the table and now approached the captive. 'He spoke Merofynian like a noble.'

'He has filthy Utland eyes,' the guard with the knife announced. 'He's a spy. An assassin!'

Fyn looked into those strange, desperate eyes. Tears of fury and indignation left tracks on the youth's dirty cheeks. 'If he was a spy, he would come amongst us in fine clothes, with a convincing story. Let him speak.'

The guard glanced to Captain Elrhodoc for confirmation, before removing his hand.

'Fa-Father,' the captive youth sobbed, addressing someone at the high table. 'Don't you know me? It's Trafyn!'

'Trafyn?' Lord Travany came to his feet. 'They told me you were lost at sea.'

'Our ship was taken by Utlanders.' Tears of relief poured down his cheeks as the queen's guards stepped back. 'But I escaped.'

'From the Utland ship that raided last night?' Fyn asked.

Trafyn nodded. 'I escaped and swam ashore. I went to Travantir Townhouse, but there was a new guard on the door, and he turned me away. I've been trying to get into the palace to find—'

'Trafyn...' Travany came down the high table, heavy jowls quivering. He swept the youth into an embrace. 'Travrhon, come see. Your brother has returned from the dead.'

Travany's older son approached. 'Trafyn?'

Trafyn swayed on his feet. His father stepped in to support him on one side and his brother took the other.

'Some good has come from the Utland attack after all,' Isolt said. 'Take your son away, feed and clothe him, Lord Travany. Tomorrow he can tell us of his miraculous escape.'

'I killed two Utlanders,' Trafyn claimed. 'Gutted them and jumped overboard.'

His brother cast him a sceptical look, but his father beamed proudly and the diners cheered.

'Thank you, Queen Isolt.' Lord Travany dipped his head. Then he and Travrhon went to back away, with Trafyn between them.

'Wait,' Fyn said. 'You sailed on Lord Travany's ship?'

Trafyn nodded.

'There was a seven-year slave on that ship, a lad about your age, with a slight gap between his front teeth.'

Trafyn nodded.

Fyn swallowed, fearing the worst. Garzik would have fought to the bitter end, but Fyn had to be certain of his death. 'What happened to him?'

'He joined the Utlanders.'

'No!'

'He did,' Trafyn insisted. 'What's more, he advised them to make the attack on our port. He was a vile coward, and if he were here right now, I'd happily cut his throat!'

Others echoed this sentiment.

As Travany left with his sons, Fyn returned to his seat. Why would Garzik lead Utlanders to attack Port Mero, when Byren...

It all fell into place. Garzik didn't know Byren had killed Palatyne and claimed Isolt for his queen. He thought Merofynia was still the enemy.

But why hadn't Garzik escaped with Trafyn?

Later, after Fyn had seen Abbot Murheg off, someone knocked on his door. Half expecting it to be the manservant, Kyral, Fyn answered the door. 'Mitrovan!' He glanced up and down the hall and pulled the scribe inside.

'It wasn't Garzik's fault,' the skinny scribe said as he slipped through the door. 'He thought Byren was still at war—'

'With Merofynia.' Fyn nodded. 'I worked that out. But something about Trafyn's story doesn't ring true. Why didn't Garzik escape with him? What did Trafyn tell his father?'

'He claimed Garzik chose to stay with the Utlanders. But I think he's lying. He told his father the Utlanders spared three lads when they took Travany's ship. One was Garzik, and the other was Lord Istyn's son, who killed himself because he could not live with the shame of...' Mitrovan flushed. 'The Utlanders used the lads like girls, but Trafyn claims he escaped that fate. I ask you, why would they rape two of the lads and not the third?'

Fyn winced for Garzik. Had the horrors of captivity unhinged his mind? To think Garzik had been here in Port Mero last night. If only Fyn had known...

'I should be getting back,' Mitrovan said. 'If they notice I'm missing, they'll beat me.'

'Go. And thank you.'

Mitrovan shrugged. 'I wish I could do more.'

Chapter Twenty-Six

GARZIK RUBBED HIS eyes, then lifted the farseer to search for signs of pursuit. Since escaping Mero Bay, they'd fled east, every sail straining in the wind. With so many dead and the injured to care for, they'd done no more than snatch a moment's rest here and there, and eaten on their feet. But soon someone was going to notice Trafyn was missing, and then they'd want to know how he had escaped. A heavy hand landed on Garzik's shoulder, making him jump.

Olbin laughed. 'Don't worry. We have a day's head start on the sea-hounds, and Rus is going to avoid the shipping lanes.'

'We headed home?' Garzik's voice sounded like boots on gravel as it made its way through his damaged throat.

'Take the stores back and make sure everyone is safe.'

Garzik nodded. Most of the beardless had been killed when Vultar's renegades attacked the settlement. He swallowed and winced.

'That's a fine necklace of bruises,' Olbin said.

Garzik shrugged. 'Others are worse off.'

Olbin scratched his jaw, fingers rasping on the bristles as his beard grew back. 'Why do hot-landers want to look like lads?'

Garzik grinned. 'How long before—'

'Until I look like a man again?' The big Utlander shrugged. 'Dunno. I never shaved before.' He winked at Garzik and jerked his head towards Rusan, who was coming over. 'Bet my beard grows back before his.'

Garzik grinned.

'What?' Rusan asked.

'Nothing.' Olbin looked innocent. 'I was telling Wynn that now that we have supplies, you'll want to build a new ship.'

'With this ship, we were able to slip into port unnoticed,' Garzik said.

'True,' Rusan agreed. 'But this ship couldn't outrun the sea-hounds.'

Olbin grimaced. 'I never want to feel helpless again.'

Garzik could sympathise with them, yet he didn't want to be trapped in the Utlands. 'How long?'

'To build a ship?' Rusan considered. 'Depends on the size and how many men we can spare. Up to a year.'

Garzik's heart sank. If he'd run when he'd had the chance, he'd already be on his way to Byren.

'Don't look so down.' Rusan took Garzik's shoulders in his hands. 'Thanks to you, the hold is filled with stores and the Merofynians will be talking about our raid for years to come.'

'Clever little Wynn!' Olbin caught him in a headlock and knuckled his head.

Garzik laughed. He couldn't help it, but every day he felt himself slipping further into the Utlander ways. Further from Byren and his duty.

'Your plan would have worked perfectly if Jost hadn't betrayed us.' Rusan cursed him.

'He wanted revenge and didn't think beyond himself.' Garzik's voice cracked, reducing him to a whisper. Only two of Jost's supporters had survived. 'What about Vesnibor and Dizov?'

Rusan glanced to Olbin. 'Did they fight bravely when the sea-hounds attacked?'

'They fought to survive.' Olbin was still angry.

'Speaking of cowards, I've searched the ship and I can't find Lazy-Legs.' It was Trafyn's Utland name. Rusan's voice was casual but he watched for Garzik's reaction.

'I'm betting he went over the side when we were in port,' Olbin said. 'And good riddance to him.'

A cry of despair drew them to the middeck rail.

'Crisjon must have died,' Olbin whispered.

Since his wounds had been terrible it was not unexpected. Despite this, his twin howled like an ulfr bereft of its mate and tore his hair.

Rusan looked grim. 'Come with me.'

He led them down the steps to the middeck, where everyone had gathered, drawn by the surviving twin's cries. They had to honour the dead, but Crisdun would let no one help as he stripped his twin.

Unclothed, Crisjon's body bore witness to the life he'd led. Scars old and new puckered his skin—scars earned in the service of his people to ensure their survival. Garzik's throat grew tight and tears burned his eyes.

While Rusan said the words, consigning Crisjon's body to the depths and his soul to a shade-ray, Vesnibor and Dizov hung back. The rest of the crew cast them dark looks.

If the young captain decided on death for the last of Jost's supporters, Rusan would have to kill them himself. If he did this, he crossed a line. It was all very well to challenge a man to a fight and kill him, but to kill one of your crew in cold blood... Garzik did not envy Rusan.

The captain finished the ritual, then put his pipes away. Everyone except Crisdun turned to him. The remaining twin stared out to sea, knuckles white as he gripped the ship's side.

Vesnibor and Dizov exchanged looks. They meant to

put up a fight, and Rusan could not afford to lose any more of his crew.

The moment stretched. There was silence but for the wind in the rigging and the unceasing whisper of the sea.

Luvrenc edged closer to Garzik. 'What's going to happen now?'

He had no idea.

Rusan adjusted his fine velvet coat. 'Twenty-seven of us set sail. Now only twelve are left—'

'And two of those are traitors,' Olbin said.

'You call us traitors? At least we weren't going to jump overboard like him!' Vesnibor pointed to Garzik. 'I saw him with Lazy-Legs. They had a barrel to carry them to shore.'

Luvrenc turned to Garzik, shocked. But Rusan had already nodded to Olbin, who pushed Luvrenc aside and pinned Garzik's arms.

Shame curled in Garzik's belly and the gorge rose in his throat.

'He was going to betray you.' Malice lit Vesnibor's eyes. 'He's been laughing at us all behind our backs!'

'I never!' Outrage made Garzik's ruined voice crack, until it was reduced to an impassioned whisper. 'I wasn't the one who brought the sea-hounds down on us by attacking Rusan after he promised me a ship!'

'Don't listen to him. You can't trust a slave,' Vesnibor sneered. 'He's to blame for the loss of half the crew. He was going to jump ship.'

Rusan stepped up to Garzik. He radiated anger, but under that was pain. 'Were you leaving?'

'Yes,' Garzik admitted. 'And I could have gotten clean away. But when I saw Jost's brothers grab you I came back. I came back for you!'

'He warned me.' Olbin's deep voice rumbled behind Garzik's back. 'He saved your life, Rus. If anyone's to blame for bringing the sea-hounds down on us, it's Jost.'

Rusan glanced from Garzik to Vesnibor and Dizov.

Vesnibor stiffened. 'How can you compare us? Dizov

and I are Utlanders of the Northern Dawn, born and bred.' He pointed to Garzik. 'He's nothing but a two-faced lying slave, fit only for sucking—'

Rusan covered the distance between them in one stride, swung his arm and punched Vesnibor in the jaw with such force he knocked him into Dizov.

Olbin released Garzik, who staggered, knees weak with relief.

'She said you'd do that.' Crisdun shrugged. 'I didn't understand what Tomorrow meant, but now I do.'

'The oracles spoke of this?' Olbin asked. 'Why didn't you tell us? What did they say?'

'That sometimes it is hard to identify the real traitor.'

'Oracles... why can't they say what they mean?' Rusan flexed his fingers and grimaced. 'I know this much. Too many of us have died. It was Jost who betrayed me and Olbin killed him. We have a hold full of stores to take home. It's going to be a challenge with so few crew, but it can be done, if we have good weather.'

Rusan split up the crew, then nodded to Garzik. 'Come with me.'

As Garzik followed him into the captain's cabin, he recalled all the reading lessons they'd shared and felt a sense of loss.

Rusan turned to him. 'Did you set up that whole raid so that you could escape?'

'We both got what we wanted.' Garzik was not going to apologise. 'You filled your ship's hold and would have been rid of Jost, and I almost got to go home.'

'I thought you were Rolencian.'

'I am, but I speak Merofynian.'

'If you went to so much trouble to escape, why come back?'

Garzik shrugged. 'I'm an idiot.'

Rusan gave a bark of laughter. 'I like you, Wynn. I really do. But now... Are you going to jump ship first chance you get?'

Heat raced up Garzik's face. 'Do you want me to speak frankly?'

'Yes. Yes, I do.'

'I didn't ask to join your crew. After that first night I thought about throwing myself overboard, but...' He lifted his hands. 'I'd sworn an oath. I had to go home to make things right.'

Rusan went over to the stern windows, where the setting sun turned him into an enigmatic silhouette.

Garzik watched his shoulders.

Rusan gave an odd laugh. 'Even now, I'd rather have you at my back than Vesnibor.'

A weight lifted from Garzik.

PIRO HAD NEVER been seasick before. She huddled on the bunk and clamped her mouth shut, and she clutched the stupid stone. She refused to throw up, but each time the ship dipped, everything in the cabin swung one way, then the other.

A storm had blown up, driving them off course. All day, the wind and the seas had grown steadily worse. Now Runt poked his head into the cabin, looking wet but annoyingly chirpy. 'Want me to fetch you some dinner?'

She shook her head.

Runt frowned. The ship lurched to the side as if a giant hand had shoved it, and he staggered.

'What was that?' Piro asked. It wasn't the first time this had happened.

'Wind shear. Happens a lot this time of year. We're headed into summer, hot air meets cold.' Runt saw she did not understand. 'Think of it as Halcyon and Sylion fighting to see who has dominance over the sea.'

She nodded, but she must have looked bad. Not long after he left, Bantam turned up. He stood in the cabin doorway, one hand on the wall to steady himself, legs spread, watching her.

She held his eyes, determined not to throw up.

'Bit of a blow,' he finally said.

'If this is a bit of a blow, I'd hate to see a storm.'

He grinned. 'Mulcy girl. I'm taking us further north, to avoid the worst of it.'

'But that'll add days to the voyage.' Piro was dismayed.

'Better to take longer than never get to port.'

'Fair enough.' She frowned. 'But a northerly heading will take us close to the Utlands.'

'In a storm like this, any Utlanders we come across will be too busy to bother us.' He studied her.

She lifted her chin. 'I'm fine.'

'You'd better be. The ship's surgeon took a tumble and dislocated his shoulder.'

Piro's heart sank, but she swung her feet to the floor.

'No need for that. Jaku put it back in, but Wasilade can't do much right now.' Bantam tossed her a small leather satchel.

She caught it automatically. 'What—'

'Basic saw-bones supplies in case someone needs stitching.'

She checked the pouch. It contained a vial of dreamless-sleep, a tincture for cleaning wounds and needles and fine thread for sewing up torn flesh. Her stomach churned at the thought. Hopefully, she would not have to use it.

That night she ate no dinner and could not sleep. Each time the ship reached the top of a wave, she was lifted off the bunk and her heart rose in her mouth. Each time the ship reached the bottom of the valley between the waves, its timbers shuddered and groaned as it fought to ride the slope of the next wave. Piro knew how it felt.

The night seemed interminable, and she was certain the seas were getting worse. Clearly this was not going to be a swift voyage. But she hadn't had another vision, so she figured she was on the right track to stop Cobalt's marriage to the impostor and prove herself to Siordun.

Chapter Twenty-Seven

BYREN CHECKED THE alley, but there was no sign of the corax. He back went inside. 'I don't like it, Orrie. He was only going to be a few moments.'

'Maybe he's setting up another meeting.'

In the last three days, they'd had two meetings, one with the leaders of the craft guilds and another with the lake captains. In both cases, Byren had asked them to spread word that he was alive. The guild-masters had a network of members throughout Rolencia's prosperous towns, and the lake captains sailed the five great lakes, linked by rivers and canals. Any news they picked up in Port Marchand could reach the most distant lake village on the far side of Rolencia within fifteen days.

Byren paced. Thanks to the lake captains, the people of Rolencia would soon know he'd turned the tables on Palatyne and claimed Merofynia.

How Florin would smile... He must not think of her. She was never going to be his, and right now she was on the far side of the divide, safe in Warlord Feid's stronghold, along with the survivors of Narrowneck. Feid would have to be compensated for housing and feeding Byren's men. Before too long, he would need to get word to them. Feid's wife was the mage's agent and had a pair of pica birds. That reminded him. 'Didn't the mage have an agent in Rolenton?'

'The hat maker.' Orrade frowned. 'Salvatrix.' He took a thin volume from the corax's desk. 'I didn't know you'd read Merulo's treatise on power and leadership.'

'I hadn't. I spotted the corax's copy. When he was questioning me I guessed he was quoting Merulo's theories.'

Orrade grinned, thin face creasing. Then the smile left his eyes. 'Much as I hate to admit it, that merchant was right. Thanks to Palatyne, a great many men of fighting age have been killed, crippled or—'

Shouts reached them from the street.

'Probably just some molly-boys fighting over a street corner,' Byren said. All the same, he strapped on his sword and hunting knife.

Orrade did the same.

The commotion began to move away, and Byren gave Orrade a relieved grin.

A heartbeat later, feet pounded up the steps and the corax threw the door open. 'One of my spies betrayed me. Grab your things. Cobalt's knows you're here. He's moved the wedding forward. He marries your sister in four days, on Narrowneck!'

Byren cursed. No time to gather an army, no time to do anything but save his sister. He reached for his cloak.

'Take this.' The corax thrust bread, cheese and a wine skin into a sack and shoved it into Orrade's hands, then ran to a chest, tipping its contents onto the floor. Several bags clinked. 'Here.' He sprang to his feet, tossing a bag each to Orrade and Byren. Then he gestured to the screen at the far end of the attic. 'We'll have to go that way, over the roofs.'

Byren tucked the coins inside his jerkin. 'I'm sorry we exposed you.'

The corax laughed. 'I've missed this.' He grabbed a cloak and his sword, then hesitated at his desk, looking at the books. 'Pity—'

'Come on!' Byren turned towards the attic window.

A thump on the landing made them all freeze. Another softer thump followed.

The door flew open and slammed against the wall. Two lightly clad men stepped inside. One was old, the other young, but both moved with lethal purpose.

Byren's mouth went dry. 'Coraxes...'

'You made it easy, Vilderavn.' The grey-haired man spoke Ostronite. His mouth smiled, but his eyes remained cold.

Their corax took a step back, drew his sword and tossed the sheath aside.

'I told them you weren't dead.' The grey-haired corax drew his weapons. He moved to the right, his companion to the left. 'I told them you were a coward, who ran from—'

'I'm no coward,' Vilderavn said.

The older corax gestured to Byren. 'Why die for a thick-skulled Rolencian royal?'

'At least I choose who I die for. Who do you serve?'

'House Nictocorax,' the younger assassin said with pride. 'Our Lady Death.'

'But who does *she* serve?' Vilderavn countered.

'Don't listen to him, Hraefe,' the grey-haired corax ordered. 'I'll deal with him. Incapacitate the usurper, then kill his lover.'

Vilderavn did not take his eyes off the two coraxes. 'Go now.'

'But—' Orrade began.

'We can take them,' Byren said.

'This man was my mentor,' Vilderavn said, holding the older man's gaze. 'Get out while you still can.'

Before Orrade or Byren could argue, the assassins attacked.

The young corax went for Orrade. Byren darted between them, caught Hraefe's strike on his blade and deflected the blow.

The older corax leapt for Vilderavn. Their blades sang as they sliced the air. Hraefe turned his wrist, trapped Byren's blade, twisted and disarmed him so effectively his hand went numb. Instead of closing in for the kill, the young corax kicked Byren's knee and turned on Orrade.

Byren went down, falling hard. He had to roll aside as Vilderavn and the older corax surged past him, their blades flying in a flurry of blows.

Outside, someone yelled. 'This way. I hear sword fighting!'

Byren could see that Hraefe was every bit as skilled as Orrade, who was the best swordsman of their generation. His friend backed away, defending without counter attacking as he weighed up his opponent. He would not be lured into a strike that left him open.

Byren sprang to his feet, staggering as his left knee gave way. Furious, he drew his knife and threw it. The angle was bad, but it was enough to distract the young corax. Orrade cut him down.

Fight dirty, fight to win, Captain Temor's words came back to him.

Sudden silence made Byren's ears ring. He spun to see Vilderavn near the table. He stood over the older corax, his blade through the man's chest. Byren heard shouting and the thunder of boots on the steps.

Vilderavn withdrew the blade and saluted his old teacher.

The landing filled with Merofynian men-at-arms.

Vilderavn stepped forward to meet them, calling over his shoulder, 'Go!'

With a ragged shout, the men-at-arms charged.

Eyes hard and glittering, Orrade grabbed Byren and pulled him towards the window.

Behind him, Byren heard a cry of pain, smashing

crockery and angry shouts. Ahead of him, Orrade shoved the screen aside and flung the window open.

He took Byren's shoulder and shoved. 'You first.'

With one foot on the sill, Byren levered his weight up and onto the roof. Orrade followed. Byren reached down to help him. Someone made a grab for Orrade, but he kicked the man in the face and the Merofynian retreated, cursing.

The moss covered slates were slippery as a wet mountain slope. They ran across the steep incline, making for the building at the far end. Byren lurched with every second step. Two Merofynians followed.

As the gap to the next roof opened up before them, Byren swore under his breath. They couldn't go back. Orrade did not hesitate.

He jumped, landed lightly and beckoned. 'I'll catch you.'

Byren had no choice. His bad knee went out from under him as he landed.

Orrade steadied him as several slates came loose and skittered off the roof to fall into the alley below.

'Come on.' Orrade took off.

Grimacing with annoyance and pain, Byren scrambled after him, up the slope and over the apex of the roof. Thank Halcyon there was an easy jump to the next roof.

But instead of making the jump, Orrade pulled him sideways along the roof, until they were hidden behind a dormer window.

Byren stretched out on the steep incline, taking the weight off his bad leg. Orrade grabbed a roof slate and threw it at an adjacent rooftop. The clattering sound lured the Merofynians onto the other roof.

As soon as the last pursuer disappeared, Orrade forced open the dormer window and helped Byren into the attic. It was littered with ragged blankets and rubbish, and the wattle and daub walls were exposed in places.

'Can you walk?' Orrade asked.

'I can limp.'

'Then we'll have to dress as beggars to escape.'

Orrade draped them in rags and soon they looked sufficiently disreputable to blend in.

Byren was glad of Orrade's shoulder as they navigated the narrow steps. On the next floor he heard a baby crying listlessly and women arguing. On the ground floor, he caught glimpses of couples in darkened alcoves. No one stopped Byren and Orrade as they passed down the passage and out into the street.

The lane was narrow and fetid, and there seemed to be shouting from every direction as the Merofynians searched for them.

'Lucky for us I know my way around,' Orrade muttered, and they set off.

Byren winced with each step as Orrade led them through back lanes and beer gardens to the nearest square. Seeing the stretch of open ground, Byren hesitated.

'We need to get across to the lakeside docks before the Merofynians can close the wharfs,' Orrade whispered. 'This is the quickest way.'

Byren nodded.

Head down, he leaned on Orrade's shoulder and watched the cobles under their feet. They were halfway across the square when someone shouted at them. 'You two! The crippled beggar and his friend, stop. Stop, I say!'

Orrade reached under his ragged costume.

'Don't even think about fighting,' Byren muttered. 'Leave me.'

Orrade pulled out the corax's bag of coins and tugged the draw-string open with his teeth. 'Pity we have to waste gold, when coppers would've served as well.' He raised his voice. 'King Byren's blessing.' And tossed coins left and right. 'King Byren's blessing on his people!'

Like flies on a corpse, beggars, ragged children, desperate women of the night and eager molly-boys clustered around them. As the port's poor fought over the coins and the Merofynians fought to push through them, Byren and Orrade took off, Byren lurching badly with every second step. Tomorrow, he would not be able to use his leg. But if he didn't push himself now, there would be no tomorrow.

They had to get to the lakeside wharves and find passage on a ship going to Rolenton. And it had to be a fast one, if they wanted to save Piro from her own foolishness.

A little later, Byren hid in an alley out the back of a lakeside tavern, while Orrade went to negotiate passage to Rolenton. Three drunken sailors sprawled in the rubbish nearby, sleeping off a night's overindulgence. From the smell, Byren suspected one of them had been there for several days and would not be waking.

At the far end of the alley, respectable folk walked by with their faces averted. This would never have happened when his father was still king. When he was king, he'd have to make sure—

Half a dozen Merofynian men-at-arms strode past, hands on sword hilts. Byren slunk lower and pretended to snore.

A mangy dog came down the lane, investigated each of the drunks, licked up something which could have been vomit, then sniffed Byren. It went past him and lifted its leg to pee on the dead man before trotting off. Byren was grateful for small mercies. Between the stench of the alley and the ale Orrade had sprinkled on his disguise, he felt ill. It didn't help that his knee throbbed with each beat of his heart.

He tried to flex his left leg, only to discover it had seized up entirely. He was helpless. Equal parts frustration and terror surged through him. If he couldn't run or fight, what use was he?

Orrade darted into the alley, picking his way through the snoring drunks. He carried a bundle of white material and was speaking even before he reached Byren, who struggled to haul himself upright.

'...a lake captain will give us passage. He gave me this.' Orrade unrolled the fabric with a flick of his wrist. 'Get rid of the rags.'

'What—' Byren began, then he realised what it was. 'A fever cloak? Has the blackspot come back?'

'Yes. And, with the over-crowding in port and the filth that's piling up, it'll spread.' Orrade kicked the rags aside, then draped the hooded cloak over Byren's shoulders. 'Now, show me your hands.'

Byren complied, palms up. Orrade turned his hands over, dipped into a jar and dabbed an oily black substance on Byren's skin, producing a scattering of uneven black spots.

Byren lifted his hand to sniff the paint. 'Eh, what is it?'

'An old mummer's trick. Charcoal and oil. Hold still.' Orrade added more spots to his face and neck. He produced another jar. 'Now your hair.'

Orrade rubbed ash through Byren's black hair. 'Now you are my elderly uncle, who's sick with the blackspot fever. No one will stop us.' He pulled the hood up so that it mostly covered Byren's face. 'Don't forget to moan and stagger.'

'Oh, I'll be moaning and staggering all right. I can barely stand.'

Orrade grinned and offered his shoulder. 'Come on, Uncle, not far now.'

Their passage out onto the street and down the steps to the dock was painfully slow. Byren heard Merofynian voices ordering people about, but no one tried to stop them.

He struggled along the wharf and up the gangplank. The moment they stepped onto the deck, the boat cast off. As he and Orrade made their slow way to the cabin, the sailors gave them sharp looks, but did not venture close.

In the cabin, Byren dropped into a chair with relief, stretching his bad leg out in front of him. He gestured to the table, laden with food. 'We're being well looked after.'

'I should think so, Uncle.' Orrade pitched his voice to carry. 'I had to pay double for them to transport a fever patient. I hope you'll remember this next time I gamble away my allowance.'

Orrade closed the door and stood still for a moment, concentrating on the motion of the ship. 'Good, she's making decent headway. The sooner we're out on the lake, the better.'

He dropped to crouch beside Byren. 'Now show me your knee.'

'I don't think anything is broken.' But he couldn't bend his knee to take off his boot. Orrade had to help him.

As he rolled up Byren's trouser leg, Orrade whistled softly and Byren's heart sank.

'I shouldn't have run on it.'

'You had no choice.'

'I was hoping the voyage would give it time to mend, but...'

'I've bribed the captain to take us straight to Rolenton. If the winds are good, it'll only take two days.' Orrade looked up at Byren. 'You'll need the full use of your leg when—'

'I know.' Frustration ate at him.

Orrade rubbed his jaw then seemed to come to a decision. 'You healed me.' He touched his chest, where the scars of the Wyvern attack had faded to pale silver threads. 'You could heal yourself if you drew on my Affinity.'

'I didn't know what I was doing. It was instinct.'

'Then go with your instincts.' Orrade came to his feet. 'What did you do?'

Byren glanced away. They'd been naked, and he'd held Orrade close to warm him.

'The monks told us not to let Power-workers touch our bare skin,' Orrade said. 'You need skin, the more the better, right?'

Byren nodded and watched with growing misgivings as Orrade unlaced his jerkin and hung it over the chair. After tugging off his boots, Orrade pulled his shirt over his head and stepped out of his breeches, which left him wearing nothing but a linen breechcloth.

Byren looked away.

Orrade unrolled a blanket and spread it on the floor, then went to the door and bolted it shut.

Byren still hadn't moved.

'Come on,' Orrade told him. 'If I can do this, so can you.'

He was right. Byren gave an apologetic nod and gestured to his bad knee. 'I'll need a hand.'

Orrade helped him to undress and stretch out on the floor, then joined him.

Byren pulled Orrade's back against his chest. 'Now let down your barriers and summon your Affinity if you can.'

'I'm always repressing it,' he admitted. 'What if I get lost in the visions?'

'Has that happened before?'

'No...' Orrade swallowed. 'But I did some reading in Lord Dunstany's library and...'

Byren hated hearing fear in his voice. Instinctively, he tightened his hold. 'I won't let you go.'

Orrade nodded.

A heartbeat later, Byren felt a teeth-grating sensation as Orrie's power rose. Taking shelter in the seep with the ulfr pack had irrevocably changed him, just as asking the crazy old seer to heal Orrade had changed him. She'd warned Byren his friend would never be the same, and for days afterwards Orrie had been blind. At first, Byren had believed this was what she'd meant, his life in exchange for his sight. But...

'Ready,' Orrade whispered.

'Ready.' Byren slipped into the ulfr breathing pattern. He let each breath take him away and, as if from a great distance, he heard a deep rumble like a great cat purring. A healing warmth built in his body and he focused the power on his injured knee.

Everyone believed he and Orrade were lovers. As he tapped into Orrade's Affinity to heal himself, Byren realised that what they shared went much deeper than that.

Chapter Twenty-Eight

Fyn missed Isolt. She hadn't spoken to him since the war-table meeting two days ago. He'd put the time to good use, researching what was known about bonding with Affinity beasts, but all he could find were myths, and he didn't put much credence in such things.

Isolt ran into the chamber of knowledge. 'Here you are.' She seemed hot and flustered, and unreasonably annoyed with him. 'I've been looking all over for you, and you're reading!'

Heart racing, Fyn marked the place in his book and came to his feet. The urge to grab her and kiss her was very strong.

And completely irrational.

The force of his feelings surprised Fyn. He'd always been the sensible one, yet with Isolt a kind of wonderful madness threatened to overwhelm him.

'The nobles have called a meeting in the war chamber,' she told him. 'Did anyone send for you?'

'No.'

'They didn't let me know, either. I only just heard.' She bristled and held out her hand. 'We need to make it clear that we're in charge. Come on.'

Fyn took her hand, welcoming any excuse to touch her. As they made their way to the war chamber, Fyn spotted Mitrovan. Clearly the scribe had been trying to find him to warn him.

They strode into the chamber, but Isolt dropped Fyn's hand the moment the gathering turned to her. Everyone looked angry and troubled. There were half a dozen merchant margraves, five of the ten lords of Merofynia, and both captains, Aeran and Elrhodoc.

A chorus of voices greeted Isolt.

She signalled for silence. A servant arrived with wine and another with food. Isolt took a glass, before sending the servants around the gathering. 'Now, what is the problem?'

'The spars have attacked my estate!' Neiron announced. 'Amfina and Lincis warlords have come over the Dividing Mountains. My man reports seven hundred spar warriors—'

'Seven hundred...' Dismayed whispers filled the chamber. 'So many...'

'My people had no warning. My estate is already in spar hands. The spar warriors have headed west—'

'West?' Young Wythrod looked horrified 'To my estate?'

'He said west, not southwest,' Yorale said. 'It's my estate that's under threat.'

'They have to take my estate,' Wythrod insisted. His land jutted into the Landlocked Sea. 'They can't leave an enemy behind their lines.'

Fyn was inclined to agree with him.

'This is terrible.' Wythrod turned on Fyn. 'You encouraged my grandfather to save the Benetir Estate, to teach the spar warlords a lesson. He died for nothing!'

'He died to avenge your aunt's murder,' Fyn said. 'If Amfina and Lincis Spars have already taken Nevantir

Estate, that means they planned this attack before Benetir was taken. There hasn't been time for them to hear about the fate of the Centicore warlord.'

'First Centicore, now these two. If three of the spar warlords have dared to come over the Divide, what's stopping the other two?' Travany asked, jowls trembling.

'When they hear I hold the Centicore warlord's son hostage—'

'It'll be too late then!' Travany snapped. 'Spar barbarians are no better than Utlanders. Look what they did to the Benetir girl. Now Neiron's sister is in their clutches. Our wives and daughters are not safe in their own homes!'

Neiron gasped. 'My sister!'

'Don't worry.' Elrhodoc slid an arm around Neiron's shoulders. 'You can't do anything for her. She's ruined.'

Lord Rhoderich ran his hand through his receding hair. 'How dare they—'

'They dare because...' Yorale bowed to Isolt. 'Forgive me, my queen, but I must speak frankly. When the spar warlords look on Merofynia, they see a fifteen-year-old queen, her armies depleted by war. They see a queen who is betrothed to a deposed Rolencian king and they think us weak!'

'Then they're wrong!' Fyn stepped forward. 'They might look over the Divide and see your rich estates and think you soft. They might think to emulate Palatyne. But Cortigern already tried it and we proved him wrong. We executed him, driving his warriors over the Divide with their tails between their legs. And we'll drive these two warlords back to where they came from!'

The margraves voiced their support. War meant the nobles needed armour, weapons and supplies; war meant profit.

Fyn deliberately drew Isolt forward. 'It's time to unite behind Isolt Wyvern Queen.'

'My lord protector's right,' Isolt said. 'It's time to teach the spars a lesson!'

Fyn lifted his glass. 'To another two hundred years free of spar rebellion!'

The lords and merchants raised their glasses, repeating the toast. This time there were no complaints about lack of men.

Fyn gestured to Yorale and Wythrod. 'The spar warriors are marching towards your estates, but Istyntir and Elenstir Estates lie east of the invasion. Where's Lord Istyn?'

'He's in mourning. His only son was killed when Travany's ship was taken, leaving him with five daughters!' Elrhodoc's lips twitched. 'He's already offered me my pick.'

'Five daughters...' Rhoderich shook his head.

Fyn ignored him. 'Neiron, I want you to gather as many fighting men as you can in Port Mero. Elenstir Estate is under threat, so Elrhodoc's brother needs to help you retake Nevantir, Neiron. Once you've reclaimed your estate, march west in pursuit of the warlords' main force. Meanwhile, Wythrod will march his men north towards the mountains and Lord Yorale will march east.' Fyn traced the path of the advancing lords and tapped a point where all three would meet. 'The warlords will be trapped between the mountains and our pincer attack.'

'And you?' Neiron asked. 'What will you be doing while our men take on the spar warriors, Lord Protector Merofyn?' Fyn hesitated. If he stayed here in the palace, they'd call him a coward. If he accompanied the lords, they'd resent his interference. He'd only led the retaking of Benetir Estate because Lady Gennalla's male relatives were all dead or under-age. He drew breath, not sure what to say.

'Lord Protector Merofyn will be with me,' a familiar voice announced, 'coordinating his battle plan.'

'Dunstany...' Isolt whispered. Fyn glanced to her. They both knew Lord Dunstany was really the mage's apprentice; even so, she looked relieved.

Abbot Murheg and the abbess had entered behind the old lord. Dunstany wore the indigo robes of a scholar, and as he made his slow way along the table, leaning heavily on his staff, Murheg slipped around the nobles to stand beside Fyn, and Celunyd joined Isolt. Meanwhile, the lords greeted Dunstany with a deference that barely masked their resentment and fear. He exuded a perceptible aura of power, which Fyn found pleasant but, from their expressions, the other lords found it unnerving.

'They fear him,' the abbot whispered to Fyn. 'And well they should. Dunstany is close to a hundred years old, yet he looks like a spritely fifty. He was already an adult when the oldest of them were born. They cannot forget that the day Palatyne died, lightning struck the tip of Dunstany's staff, leaving him unharmed.'

Dunstany bowed to the queen, then turned to Fyn. He gestured to the windows overlooking the Landlocked Sea. 'You'll need to travel swiftly. Allow me to offer my pleasure yacht. From the *Dunsior* you can coordinate the attack.'

Fyn nodded in thanks.

'You offer your yacht, Dunstany,' Yorale said. 'I trust you'll honour the alliance you made with my grandfather sixty years ago and offer men as well.'

'But of course.' Dunstany gave an apologetic shrug. 'I would lead them myself if it were not for these old bones.'

'I'd offer to help Neiron,' Captain Elrhodoc said. 'But my duty is here in Port Mero, protecting the queen.'

'I won't be here, captain. I'll be on the *Dunsior*,' Isolt announced. 'After all, I cannot remain in the palace while my lords fight for the kingdom's future.' Isolt favoured Dunstany with a sweet smile. 'That is, if there's room for me, my lord?'

'I'd be honoured, my queen.'

'The queen cannot sail unprotected. I'll tell my men to make ready,' Elrhodoc announced.

The abbot nodded. 'This venture will need Mulcibar's blessing.'

'And the queen will need the cool-headed advice of Cyena's representative,' the abbess added.

Fyn hid his disappointment. Once again, Isolt would be surrounded by whispering, fawning courtiers.

'Since Lord Protector Merofyn sails with you, my queen, you'll need someone to coordinate the attack on land,' Neiron said, bowing low. 'Allow me to offer my services as your lord general.'

Isolt glanced to Dunstany.

'Three lords will be leading their men,' Dunstany said. 'Someone must be in charge.'

Neiron cast Fyn a look of triumph.

Fyn caught Isolt's eye and glanced to Yorale.

'You're right, Neiron.' Isolt smiled. 'Lord Yorale?'

The elder statesman sank to one knee before the young queen as she named him her lord general.

It was preferable to Neiron, but it still rankled with Fyn. As lord protector of Merofynia, the nobles should turn to him to lead them.

What more did he have to do to win their respect?

The storm shrouded the ship in perpetual twilight, but Piro guessed it was still afternoon. After two days of battling the weather, she had grown adept at moving on a heaving deck. She'd treated numerous small injuries as well as setting Old Dalf's arm.

She'd been waiting for the storm to ease off a little, before going below to check on her patients, but there seemed to be no end in sight. Slipping off her bunk, she made for the cabin door. The ship shuddered and lurched to one side so violently she fell to her knees.

Cursing the wind shear, she wrapped her cloak around her before plunging out the door and down the passage to the middeck. Ankle-deep water sloshed back and forth in the passage.

She threw open the door to the deck and the sound

of the roaring wind hit her like a physical blow. The ship's nose began to dip into the next wave trough. Even though the ship flew very little sail, the spars creaked and the ropes snapped as the canvas strained above her.

Before Piro could grab for the rope that ran from the hook by the door across the deck to the mast, the ship reached the valley between the waves. Lightning flashed and she saw a wall of water coming towards them.

Her stomach plunged, and her hand went to the stone around her neck.

The ship's nose lifted, trying to climb the wave. Water broke over the prow, forming a knee-high roller. It bore down on her, capped by a crest of foam. She darted back into the passage and slammed the door shut, bracing against it as the water hit.

Judging it safe, she opened the door to middeck to find seawater pouring off the deck through the gaps along the ship's sides. She spotted Bantam making his way down the steps from the reardeck above her. He looked grim. The ship tilted nose-down as it slid into the next wave trough.

Piro stepped onto the deck and stood with her legs braced, holding onto the rope.

Despite his seal-skin coat and cap, Bantam was wet through. He had to shout to be heard above the roaring of the wind, and even then she only caught a few words. 'Shut the bloody door... back... your cabin.'

'I must check on the injured.'

Lightning flashed again, revealing mountainous seas all around them. The ship, which had appeared so sleek and proud in port, now looked small and fragile. Piro's heart quailed. At this moment, Cobalt's duplicitous marriage didn't seem so important, and proving herself to Siordun felt like a petty concern.

Right now she didn't care how long it took to reach Rolencia. She just wanted to be safe on dry land.

'Check them tomorrow.' Bantam gestured for her to go inside.

Before she could move, a wind shear slammed into the ship, and the mainmast snapped with a loud *crack*. Canvas and tangled ropes fell across the deck, trailing in the sea as the deck tilted alarmingly to starboard.

Piro clutched Bantam, horrified.

'Go inside!' he barked, running across the deck.

Other sea-hounds joined him as they tried to cut the damaged sails free. The ship had reached the valley between the waves now, and the nose began to rise, but the drag of the fallen rigging made the ship list badly. Instead of the ship's prow cutting cleanly into the sea as she climbed the wave, a single large wave rolled in from starboard, sweeping sailors off their feet.

An unconscious sailor was carried towards Piro. She just had time to slam the door shut behind her to prevent seawater pouring into the cabins.

Icy cold water swirled around her knees and up to her thighs. Gasping, she clasped the rope and tried to grab the sailor with her free arm. The stunned sailor collided with her just as a flash of lightning revealed his pale face. Cormorant.

In desperation, Piro hooked her legs around him, and the rope sagged with their combined weight. Now she was shoulder-deep in seawater. The wave hit the cabin wall then the water began to wash back as it poured off the deck. This time the water was so high, it went right over the ship's side.

It streamed past her with such force it almost tore her hands from the rope and the sailor from her legs. She prayed he would not drown as water boiled around them. Someone shouted, and she felt the deck rise as the damaged rigging was shoved overboard.

By the time the ship crested the peak of the wave, the last of the water had poured off the deck. She blinked wet hair from her eyes and found herself hanging from the rope with the sailor slumped against her. It was impossible to tell if he was alive or dead.

The ship headed down into another wave trough. She didn't know if she could hold onto him for much longer, but when she tried to call for help her teeth chattered so badly that she couldn't speak. Luckily, Bantam spotted her and came to take Cormorant.

Big arms lifted her, peeling her chilled hands from the rope. She thanked Jakulos and turned to Bantam, who had his ear to the youth's chest. 'Is he—'

'Alive,' Bantam reported. 'Barely.'

Her knees nearly gave way, and she would have fallen but for Jakulos. She felt the ship shudder as it reached the trough between waves and she had to brace herself again.

Bantam passed the unconscious sea-hound to Jakulos, who threw Cormorant over his shoulder and shoved Piro towards the cabin door. Somehow, her frozen fingers managed the door latch, and then she closed it behind them as Jakulos carried the unconscious sailor down the passage to the cabin, where he tipped the youth onto the floor by the brazier.

'Mulcy girl.' Jakulos cupped her cheek, wet calloused palm rasping against her skin. 'See to the lad.'

Now that they were in the heated cabin, Cormorant's head was beginning to bleed. She bound his wound, but before long another injured sailor arrived; and all because she'd tricked Bantam into sailing for Rolencia.

Orrade would have said she hadn't caused the storm, so she wasn't at fault. That didn't stop her feeling responsible for the fate of the ship. If she hadn't tricked Bantam, they would all be sitting safe on Ostron Isle's Ring Sea right now. Instead they battled the storm. Every time the ship's nose struggled to rise, she feared a wave of water would swallow the sea-hound vessel whole.

And still the storm went on.

Chapter Twenty-Nine

FYN SLUNG HIS travelling bag over one shoulder and climbed the gangplank to board Dunstany's yacht. Yorale, Neiron and Wythrod had already sailed across the Landlocked Sea to gather their men.

Once aboard, a servant offered to escort Fyn to his lordship.

'Don't worry, I can find him.' Fyn followed the sound of Dunsany's voice down the passage.

Dunstany looked up as he stepped into the cabin. 'I've told the servants, the abbess can share the queen's cabin and the abbot can share with Captain Elrhodoc. I suppose you'll have to bunk in here with me. But I'm having the bed. These old bones won't give me any rest if I sleep on the floor.' He gestured to a servant, who was putting his clothing in a chest. 'Leave that. See that the bedding is changed in my old cabin. The queen doesn't want to rest her head where an old man has slept.'

The servant nodded and scurried away.

'How do you do it?' Fyn whispered. 'How do you play

Lord Dunstany without slipping?'

'Habit. I've been Dunstany for so long...' Siordun shrugged. 'To tell the truth, I'm more comfortable as him than as the mage's apprentice. He was just an unwanted boy who grew up on Dunistir Estate. You saw how the lords responded to Dunstany. They respect him. They would never acknowledge Dunstany's bastard grandson.'

Fyn had seen the way Elrhodoc treated Captain Aeran. But... 'A man should be valued for his worth, not his birth.'

'So says King Rolen's legitimate son.'

Fyn flushed.

Siordun rose to his feet. 'I'm glad you're here. I've had word from Rolencia. Cobalt is to marry Piro.'

'What? When did Piro return to Rolencia?'

'She didn't. I'm guessing Cobalt has learnt that Byren defeated Palatyne, and he needs a way to legitimise his claim on the throne.'

'So he hired some doxy to play Piro?' Fyn was outraged. 'Surely someone will denounce him?'

'Fear will silence anyone who knew Piro.'

'This is terrible.'

'Not necessarily. I told Orrade to seek out my Rolencian agent. She'll help Byren to rescue the girl.'

'You're not going to tell him that the real Piro is safe?'

'If he thinks he's saving the real Piro, he'll react with genuine surprise and outrage when he discovers Cobalt's deception.' Siordun met Fyn's eyes. 'Byren is a good man, but he's not...'

'Not what?'

'Not devious.'

'That's why he has Orrie.'

Siordun grinned. 'Byren's no actor. It's much better if he reacts with righteous indignation on discovering Cobalt's duplicity. Unmasking the false-Piro will unmask Cobalt for the manipulative liar he is, in front of the most powerful nobles and merchants in Rolencia. The wedding will be Byren's chance to destroy the usurper's credibility.'

'...and win back Rolencia without a costly battle. Excellent. How do you do it?'

'Years of experience, lad.'

Fyn laughed. Siordun was only a few years older than Byren. The iron-haired old man was an illusion. Then he told Siordun about the footpad attack. 'Could they have been coraxes, hired by Cobalt? Could the mage speak to—'

'The mage has a long and troubled relationship with House Nictocorax. Some of its leaders have aided him when it suited them, while others... I wouldn't put it past the current Lady Death to accept a commission from Cobalt. We'll both have to be on our guard. Wait here.' He left the cabin and returned shortly with a walking stick. 'I think it is time Lord Dunstany resorted to a cane.'

'You already have your staff.'

'My enemies know that Dunstany focuses power through his staff. But they will leave an old man his walking stick. I might have to cultivate a feeble walk, but this is no ordinary cane!'

With a grin, Siordun revealed a sword from within the cane, which he flourished. Fyn held out his hand, but there was a knock at the door.

Siordun sheathed the sword cane then leant on it. 'Can't an old man get any rest? Enter.'

A servant opened the door. 'Begging your pardon, my lord. Lord Cadmor's grandson, Captain Camoric, to see you.'

The captain who had let the Utlanders escape walked into Lord Dunstany's cabin. Camoric was no older than Byren, and he moved stiffly as if annoyed.

'My grandfather said I should meet you, Lord Dunstany.' His tone said he didn't see why.

'You should meet Lord Protector Merofyn, too.' Dunstany indicated Fyn.

As Camoric turned stiffly towards Fyn, he saw the reason behind the captain's unusual stance. Livid red blisters covered his lower jaw and neck. From the way he held his right arm, the burns probably covered his shoulder as well.

Fyn had mistaken pain for anger. He gestured to Camoric's injury. 'Your grandfather told us you were burnt, but he said you'd be all right.'

'And so I shall.' Camoric frowned. 'It's worse than it looks.'

'I very much doubt that,' Dunstany said. 'Come here, lad.'

Camoric bristled. 'I'm nearly twenty, and I've been captaining a ship since I was sixteen.'

'When you get to my age, anyone under fifty is a lad.'

Camoric grinned, then winced.

Settling himself on the chest at the end of the bed, Dunstany gestured. 'Kneel down and save an old man's back.'

While the young captain knelt, Dunstany asked Fyn to bring a lamp. Then he turned Camoric towards the light. 'I take it the burns continue under your shirt?'

Camoric nodded. As Dunstany unwound the bandage, Camoric's breathing became laboured. The blisters made Fyn shudder.

'Do you have a salve?' Camoric's voice was strained.

'Yes,' Dunstany said. 'But first I'll help you heal faster. You'll still have scars. I fear complete repair is beyond me.'

'You think I care about scars?'

'You need to relax before I can help. Light the starkiss incense, Fyn.'

He brought the burner over and fanned the incense towards the young captain.

'Inhale deeply,' Dunstany advised.

Camoric did as instructed. After a few moments, the grim lines around his mouth eased and his pupils grew large.

Dunstany gestured for Fyn to extinguish the incense. 'We don't want to become befuddled.'

'Are you trying to confuse me?' Camoric asked, but his voice held only the memory of its former bite.

'No,' Dunstany said. 'I don't want to confuse myself.'

'Speaking of tricking people...' Camoric gestured to Fyn. 'King Cobalt will wish he'd kept his mouth shut.'

'Why?' Fyn asked.

'He burned your body in Rolenton Square,' Camoric said. 'Heard it today in port. Sailors thought it a great joke. Cobalt'll kick himself when he hears you're lord protector now.'

'Cobalt declared me dead?' Fyn was amused by this turn of events.

'Can't have two Fyns,' Camoric said.

'You lay low for so long, Cobalt must have thought it safe to produce a body and declare you dead,' Dunstany said. 'He's tripped himself with his lies. Now put the burner away.'

As Fyn did so, he sensed the surge of Affinity and heard a *thud*. He turned to find that Camoric had slumped forward and went to help, but the bay lord's grandson was already lifting his head.

Camoric moved his arm gingerly, then more fluidly. 'It doesn't hurt anymore.' He glanced over to Fyn. 'By Mulcibar's balls, it hurt like hell before.'

'I'm sure it did.'

Dunstany rubbed his neck. 'I've exhausted myself. There's some salve in my chest, Fyn. Give it to the young captain and see that he gets home safely.'

'Don't bother yourself. I can...' Camoric struggled to his feet, swayed and nearly toppled. 'Mebbe I do need some help.'

Fyn found the salve and slipped it in the captain's pocket. 'Come along.'

As he helped Camoric from Dunstany's yacht, the young captain told him, 'You're not so bad after all.' He frowned. 'Did I say anything stupid?'

'Not at all,' Fyn said. 'Let's get you safely home. We hope to sail by midnight.'

* * *

Byren woke to find the cabin filled with sunshine and no sign of Orrade. For one gut-wrenching moment, he thought he'd failed him, and his friend had become lost in Affinity visions. Then he heard Orrade in the privy. Byren sat up to inspect his knee. The swelling had gone down, leaving the grey-purple of old bruises. He flexed his leg gingerly. It was still tender, but healing well.

Orrade returned. 'How's the leg?'

Byren stood with care. 'So long as I don't try to do too much, I should be alright.'

He slid into the seat across from Orrade, and his stomach rumbled as he took in the preserves, cold meat and watered-wine. Byren reached for a chicken leg. Orrade reached for the bread, his other hand fumbling for the knife.

'You're blind!' Shame and anger filled Byren. 'Why didn't you warn me you risked losing your sight? I would never have—'

'I didn't know.' Orrade cut an uneven slice of bread. 'It's not as bad as the first time and besides, the blind patches never last long.'

'It's happened more than once?'

Orrade nodded, then felt around until he found the cheese.

'Here, give me your plate.' Byren slapped some pickles on the bread and added cheese, placing the food in Orrade's hand. 'I wish you'd told me.'

Orrade shrugged. 'I'll be right by the time we reach Rolenton.'

'Of course you will,' Byren told him. 'Turns out you didn't need to worry about getting lost in your visions...'

Orrade went still for a heartbeat, then kept eating.

'So you did have a vision. What did you see?'

'Fire. Everything burned.'

'A nightmare,' Byren said. 'After the way your father's great house went up in flames, it's no wonder.'

Orrade nodded, but he didn't seem so sure.

Chapter Thirty

Fyn stepped around several servants as they returned Nevantir Estate's crest to its original position above the central hearth in the great hall. He walked past more servants, hauling a new chandelier into position. Everywhere he looked, people were cleaning up or making repairs. They worked feverishly, as if determined to remove all sign that the estate had ever been in spar hands.

The sound of shattering glass made everyone jump, and Fyn turned to see some carpenters removing the shards from one of the floor-to-ceiling windows that opened out onto the terrace.

'Careful there,' Dunstany said, prodding the broken glass with his sword cane.

Through the empty windows, across the grass, partially shielded by a copse of birch trees, Fyn could see the smoking remains of the dead raiders. The barbarian invaders had not been accorded a proper funeral.

Fyn joined Neiron, Elcwyff and Captain Elrhodoc,

who were congratulating themselves on freeing Neiron's estate from spar hands.

'As soon as I let Wythrod know Nevantir Estate has been secured, he'll march his men north,' Fyn said. 'Lead your men west to meet him, Neiron. If you encounter the spar warlords on the way, don't engage. Wait for Yorale to bring his army into position.'

Neiron grimaced. 'I'm not—'

Voices cut him short. Isolt was descending the grand staircase, accompanied by the abbot and abbess. Fyn noticed that Neiron's sister was not with them.

Nerysa had been captive for six days. As soon as he'd reclaimed his great house, Neiron had sent men to find her. When she was delivered to him, he'd announced that her betrothal to Yorale's heir had been annulled and sent the girl to her chamber. Upon learning of this, Isolt had gone upstairs, hoping to convince Nerysa to come down, to no avail. Clearly Neiron's sister was not made of the same stuff as Sefarra.

Leaning on his cane, Dunstany went to meet Isolt. Neiron, Elcwyff and Captain Elrhodoc all hurried over. Fyn hung back to watch.

'I'm sorry, Lord Neiron,' Isolt said. 'Your sister has chosen to dedicate herself to Cyena Abbey.'

'I will see that a suitable donation is made to Cyena,' Neiron told the abbess. He turned to Isolt. 'You must stay. I plan a great feast to celebrate the recapture of my estate.'

'Nerysa does not have much to celebrate,' Isolt observed. 'If *you* were to ask her, she might come down to eat with us.'

'She's better off where she is.' Neiron grimaced. 'Besides, knowing what those barbarians did to her, I can't bring myself to look on her.'

Fyn stiffened and was about to protest when movement out near the smouldering funeral pyre drew his eye. There Isolt's wyvern rose on her hind legs as she tore a strip of meat from a charred forearm. Fyn winced.

Isolt had brought the Affinity beasts ashore because the people of Nevantir Estate expected to see the wyvern at her side. They did not expect to see the beast devouring men, not even dead enemy warriors.

As the foenix landed not far from the wyvern, Loyalty snarled, her tail lashing, wings flexing. Resolute bristled, head crest raised, leg lifted to lash out with his poisonous spur. Fyn's heart raced as the two beats squared off to do battle.

Then, as though an agreement had been reached, the wyvern and foenix lowered their hackles and settled down to feed.

Fyn drew in a ragged breath. This had to be stopped, and quickly. He caught Dunstany's eye and jerked his head towards the funeral pyre.

Dunstany frowned, then strode over to join him. 'Take the Affinity beasts back to the ship. I'll bring Isolt. We'll skip the feast and set sail for Wythrontir Estate. With a good wind, we could be there by evening.'

Leaving Dunstany to extricate the queen, Fyn went through an empty door frame and past the busy carpenters.

Nevantir House was built overlooking a long bay. A few masts poked from the water here and there. Someone had scuttled the estate's fishing boats, rather than let the invaders capture them. Many outbuildings had been burned, but the formal gardens were relatively untouched. Beyond the gardens, the estate's workers were repairing fences and salvaging trampled crops.

Reaching the copse of birch trees, Fyn slipped between their white trunks. Even though a slight breeze was blowing, he found the stench of roasted flesh hard to stomach. He approached the feeding Affinity beasts with caution. How was he to convince them to leave such a feast?

He clicked his tongue and beckoned.

Both beasts lifted their heads, observed him with intelligent but inhuman eyes, then returned to eating.

Fyn shivered. Even Isolt could not have summoned them right now.

Beyond the blackened heap of bodies, he spotted movement. An old man and a boy had finished repairing a fence and were heading his way.

In desperation, Fyn summoned his Affinity, weak though it was. He felt the tingle of awareness move over his skin, as scents and colours became richer; it only made the bonfire smell more putrid.

Holding out his hands, he focused his Affinity. With Piro it came naturally, but with him it took concentrated effort.

Loyalty dropped a thigh bone and came over to investigate what Fyn offered, and the foenix followed.

'Look, Pa, Affinity beasts!'

Fearing the beasts might lash out at strangers, Fyn was careful to maintain the flow of his power. Heart racing, muscles trembling, he let Loyalty and Resolute sniff his hands. The moment they started to lick his skin, he moved off.

They followed him all the way down to the wharf and along to the ship, where he led them below deck, down to the hold. Exhausted, he sank to his knees and let them nuzzle his hands. Now he could feel the beasts actively drawing Affinity from him.

Judging the distance to the hatch ladder, he didn't think he could slip away and secure the hatch without them escaping. Gritting his teeth, he settled in to wait.

A shiver shook him. Who would have thought the day would turn so cold? He huddled down, and still Resolute and Loyalty drew on his Affinity.

Dimly, he heard the queen's party return to the ship, and the farewells from those on the jetty. He was so exhausted he couldn't call out, couldn't stop the beasts feasting on his Affinity, couldn't even lift his head.

* * *

Byren lay on the litter, listening to the sounds of Rolenton Square. Through the muslin curtains, he could see vague shapes passing by, and wondered if that was what it was like when Orrade's vision faded. Luckily, his friend's sight had returned within a day. But even though Byren's knee had healed, he'd had to spend the rest of the voyage confined to the cabin as he was still supposed to be suffering from the blackspot fever.

'Put the litter down here,' Orrade ordered. 'And be careful not to bump my poor uncle. He's not a well man.'

Byren groaned convincingly. Cobalt's men were looking for Byren the Leogryf Slayer, not a sickly fever victim.

Orrade opened the curtain, his eyes gleaming with laughter. 'Hold on, Uncle. I'll be right back.'

As much as he hated lying vulnerable on the litter, Byren figured he was safe from prying eyes. Even so, it was a relief when he heard Orrade's voice. 'Here he is, Milliner Salvatrix.'

The curtain was drawn back and a thin woman with silver hair inspected Byren. Her eyes widened. 'The blackspot fever, and me with a dozen orders to fill before the wedding, but I can't turn away my sister's only son. Bring him in.'

Byren was helped out of the litter and hustled under the sign that proudly displayed the royal seal. He was rushed through the hat maker's shop, past her workroom and into a passage. All the while, the milliner kept up a stream of complaints about the inconvenience of caring for sick relatives.

Salvatrix led them into a storeroom stacked with supplies and indicated the trap door. 'One of you will have to lift it.'

Orrade stepped forward.

'I won't forget your help,' Byren told the milliner. 'And don't worry. We'll go as soon as we rescue m'sister.'

Salvatrix nodded to Orrade. 'Lord Dovecote told me. I haven't had a reply from the mage. We'll just have to improvise. The wedding will be held the day after tomorrow. The royal party are already camped at Narrowneck, and we ordinary folk will head out first thing tomorrow. Your sister didn't order a new hat, so I won't get a chance to warn her. The ceremony will be held on the tip of Narrowneck, where everyone can see. This is your chance to confront Cobalt and—'

'Confront him?' Byren frowned. 'Cobalt'll be surrounded by—'

'Nobles and merchants, who have been cooperating with him for the sake of their wives and children. But I know for a fact many of them are loyal to you, or would be if they had the choice.'

Byren rubbed his jaw.

Orrade swung the trap door open. 'Cobalt's sure to have Narrowneck under guard. How will—'

'Many of the nobles have ordered new hats for the occasion. I'll need delivery boys.' The milliner's eyes twinkled, then she sobered. 'Have you heard about Dovecote Estate, my lord?'

Orrade stiffened. 'What about it?'

'Cobalt declared you a traitor and awarded your estate to the leader of the Merofynian captains. He's rewarded all the captains. They've sworn allegiance to—'

Orrade grimaced. 'When I think of my people forced to serve—'

Someone knocked on the storeroom door, calling for the milliner.

'Go below. I'll send a change of clothes and food,' Salvatrix said and hurried off.

Byren descended the ladder, being careful not to put too much weight on his injured knee. Orrade followed, jumping the last few steps.

A small high window let in just enough light to make out barrels, boxes and bales stacked to the cellar ceiling.

Orrade blew on his hands to warm them. 'We'll slip into Narrowneck and rescue Piro before Cobalt realises.'

'I don't know... According to the milliner, most of the nobles are loyal to me. I want to confront Cobalt and make him—'

'You can't kill him on his wedding day. You'd be branded a dishonourable coward!'

'He's forcing my sister to marry him. When the nobles see—'

'They'll be surrounded by Cobalt's men and the Merofynian captains he's bribed. The nobles aren't going to risk their wives and children. And we haven't made contact with your honour guard yet. No, it's better to get in quick, save Piro and get out.' Orrade clasped Byren's shoulder. 'Don't worry. One day, all of Rolencia will know Cobalt's true nature, and they'll welcome your return as their king.'

'When that day comes, Orrie, the first thing I'll do is help you reclaim your estate.'

LATER—FYN DID not know how much later—he heard Rhalwyn's frightened voice and felt a hand shaking his shoulder.

He drifted off again only to awaken to the abbot's concerned voice, ordering sailors to carry him to the queen. Fyn was vaguely aware as they carried him.

'Put my lord protector here.' Isolt sounded worried, and he wanted to reassure her, but everything took too much effort.

'Rhalwyn found him with the Affinity beasts,' Murheg said. 'No one could rouse him. If only my mystics master was here.'

'Affinity injuries can be life threatening,' the abbess whispered. 'I fear—'

'Leave us.' Dunstany's deeper voice cut through the chatter.

As soon as the door closed, Fyn felt a soft hand on his forehead. 'Fyn, can you hear me?'

He tried to speak, but it was too much effort.

'What's wrong with him?' Isolt asked. 'He was fine back at the estate. Why—'

'The Affinity beasts found the funeral pyre.' Dunstany said. 'They were helping themselves to the spar warriors' remains—'

Isolt gasped and made a strangled sound of disgust in her throat.

'Exactly. I sent Fyn to take the beasts back to the—' Dunstany broke off with a curse. 'I should have realised the only way he could get them to leave the feast was to offer a feast of another kind.'

'Affinity? But Fyn's power is only mild. Is it like blood loss? Can you die of—'

'Move back. Let me try something.'

Fyn felt a strong hand grasp his and a rush of power poured into him. It made his heart race. He gasped and his eyes flew open. The lamp light made him wince.

Isolt knelt on the other side of the day-bed. 'Fyn?'

'I'm sorry—'

'No, *I'm* sorry,' Dunstany said. 'Your Affinity was dangerously low. I didn't think it through.'

'No harm done. I'm fine now.' Better than fine. Feeling invigorated by the transfusion of power, Fyn swung his legs off the bunk. 'And I lured the beasts away from the funeral pyre before anyone saw them eating—'

'They ate human flesh!' Isolt sprang to her feet looking pale and nauseous. 'Now they both have the taste for it. When Loyalty killed Palatyne, it was in my defence. But this...' She wrung her hands, unable to go on.

'This doesn't make them man-eaters.' Fyn took her hands in his. 'Does it, Dunstany?'

'They scavenged the remains of a funeral pyre. It's not as if they hunted a living person,' he muttered, as if thinking aloud. For the first time, Fyn thought he sounded like Siordun, and not Lord Dunstany. 'I'll have to do some research.'

'Ask the mage,' Fyn said. 'He'll know.'

Dunstany nodded and looked away.

'I hope you're right, Fyn.' Tears glittered in Isolt's eyes. 'I don't want to have Loyalty put down.'

He wanted to reassure her, take her in his arms and... He cleared his throat. 'I should let everyone know I'm on my feet again.' Before Elrhodoc decided the young queen was in need of a new lord protector.

'They know you have Affinity now,' Dunstany warned.

'They always knew I was one of Halcyon's monks.'

'But not all monks have Affinity. Now that they know you do, they can use it against you. There are still a dozen Power-workers in the port. King Merofyn asked them to cure him, and they've hung around ever since, peddling their futures and cures to rich merchants and gullible nobles. I wouldn't trust any of them.'

'I'll be all right. The monks taught me how to defend myself.'

'Wait here.' Dunstany slipped out of the queen's cabin.

Isolt looked to Fyn. 'When they brought you in all cold and pale...'

Fyn wanted to hear more. Had her heart turned over? Did she love him even half as much as he loved her?

He took a step closer.

'I want you to have this, Fyn.' Dunstany had returned with a ring. 'It's set with a black gem but it's the same kind of stone as this orb.' He held his staff in both hands and concentrated. 'Watch.'

Fyn felt power gather as the staff's orb flared into life. A bright silvery radiance filled the cabin.

'Beautiful,' Isolt breathed.

'Now you,' Dunstany said, as the light faded.

'My Affinity—'

'Is not strong. I know, but if you can focus, the stone will help concentrate power. Try it.'

Fyn accepted the ring. Right now Affinity coursed through his body. He concentrated and tied to drive it into the ring. The power flowed freely and smoothly, almost as if the Affinity beasts had forged channels when they'd drained him.

The ring's stone flared to life with a silvery glow.

'It's lovely!' Isolt whispered.

'Good.' Dunstany looked relieved. 'One day you may need to produce something showy to make your enemies back down.'

Fyn suspected he'd used borrowed power. 'I'm not—'

There was a knock on the door, and he slipped the ring into his pocket before Dunstany opened the door. A sailor entered to report that they were approaching Wythrontir Estate.

By the time Fyn made it out on deck, the setting sun had turned the Landlocked Sea to molten gold. Ahead of them he could see a forest of masts, and Fyn recalled that the estate was famous for its shipyard and vast sea-wall.

'Why is the wall so high?' Fyn asked Dunstany.

'Storms can stir up huge waves.'

Lord Wythrod was waiting for them on the wharf, with his grandmother by his side. As the sailors threw out ropes, which were made fast to the bollards, Wythrod cupped his hands and called, 'What news?'

'All good,' Captain Elrhodoc shouted. 'Neiron has reclaimed Nevantir.'

There was cheering from the wharf, and then from behind the sea-wall as the news spread. Wythrod went to formally introduce his grandmother to the queen, but the old woman laughed, took Isolt's hands and kissed her cheeks. 'I don't need an introduction to my great-niece. Why, the last time I saw you, you were just a little girl. Now look at you, queen of Merofynia. Welcome to Wythrontir.'

As Lady Isfynia discussed their relatives, the abbess smiled tolerantly and Captain Elrhodoc gave Wythrod the details of the battle for Nevantir.

'We found the spar barbarians sleeping in the great

hall,' Elrhodoc said, voice thick with contempt. 'Killed them as they scrambled for their weapons and built a bonfire of their bodies.'

'And the Lady Nerysa?' Wythrod asked.

Elrhodoc shook his head.

'I'm sorry.' Wythrod gestured to his great house, which stood on top of a terraced hill. The terraces were filled with the tents and campfires. 'My people have also suffered. Hundreds have come down from the north, fleeing the spar invasion. I've armed every man and lad who can hold a weapon. We're ready to—'

'We march tomorrow.' Fyn said. He glanced to Murheg, who had volunteered to accompany the young lord. 'Don't engage the enemy until Neiron and his men meet up with you. By then, Yorale should be in position.' Fyn hesitated. 'From what you've said, the majority of your army is made up of farmers and fishermen.'

Wythrod bristled. 'They are ready to die to protect their families!'

'Better if they live and come home to their families. We...' Fyn was distracted by the sound of raised voices as Isolt tried to convince Lady Isfynia to take shelter on the ship until the spar warriors were defeated.

'Leave Wythrontir?' the old woman cried. 'I've lived here since I arrived as a young bride sixty-five years ago, and a pack of uncouth spar warriors is not going to force me out of my home!'

Wythrod laughed. 'Grandmother ordered a feast when we saw your sails. Come up to the great house.'

As they stepped off the wharf, onto the sea-wall, Fyn told Wythrod, 'My mother used to tell me stories of your estate, how you reclaimed the land from the sea.'

He nodded proudly and pointed to the hill where the great house stood. 'Originally it was a headland, surrounded by marshes. First we built dykes to reclaim the marshes, then we reclaimed land from the sea itself.'

They walked down the slope from the sea-wall, onto

a raised road with embankments on each side. It ran in a straight line to the lowest terrace of the great house.

'We're walking on one of the old dykes. My family's always been ship builders.' Wythrod gestured to the shipyards on their right. Workers swarmed over the vessels. 'Our dry docks are the best in Merofynia. We flood them to launch the ships. Easy, really, since the reclaimed land is below sea level.'

A bell rang and the ship builders downed tools for the day. As Wythrod escorted the royal party along the dyke road to his great house, Fyn noticed that one particular group of workers were nearly naked. Miserable and underfed, they kept their eyes lowered as they passed.

Oblivious to their state, Wythrod waxed enthusiastic describing the new pleasure yacht Neiron had commissioned.

Fyn edged closer to Dunstany and dropped his voice. 'Why doesn't Wythrod take better care of his workers?'

'They're seven-year slaves. And they don't have it as bad as those in Yorale's mines. If they're not crushed in cave-ins, the dust eventually gets into their lungs and kills them.'

Fyn flushed. How could he have forgotten about the Rolencian prisoners of war? As he watched them go past, he wished Byren had been able to negotiate their freedom; but the Merofynian nobles had driven a hard bargain.

Wythrod led his guests up a succession of broad terraces towards the great house. They were soon surrounded by refugees. Children wailed, cows lowed and chickens cackled.

Isolt frowned. 'So many people homeless.'

'I know,' Wythrod said. 'But this is the last of them. The spar warriors are past the turn off to my lands now.' And he continued up the steps discussing the battle plans with Elrhodoc and the abbot.

Meanwhile Isolt paused to survey the old folks, women

and children. 'All the accounts of great battles talked of strategy and bravery. They never mentioned this.'

'That's because the histories are written by the victors, not the dispossessed,' Lady Isfynia said. 'Powerful men don't have to worry about providing meals for hungry children, finding somewhere safe for them to sleep and soothing their nightmares.'

Dunstany struggled on the steps using both his staff and cane. Fyn hid a smile and offered Lady Isfynia his arm.

'Thank you.' She searched his face as she accepted his help. 'You're like your mother. She was a sweet natured child. Always trying to do the right thing.'

Of course, the elderly Merofynian nobles would remember his mother as a small child. He felt her loss all over again.

The old woman paused at the top of the last steps, turning to gesture to the refugees on the terraces below. 'This is why I can't leave. What kind of message would it send to our people?'

'Don't worry.' Fyn squeezed her arm. 'War will not come here.'

Chapter Thirty-One

FLORIN ESCAPED THE bride's tent. If she didn't get away from those chattering females, she would go mad. All day she'd helped Varuska and the girls prepare for the ceremony. Every merchant markiz and nobleman's daughter wanted to be part of the bridal party, and Cobalt had indulged them all.

Now she took the opportunity to look around. Narrowneck had been her home until Byren arrived, fleeing the manticore pride, and turned her world upside down. As far as Florin could tell, the bride's tent had been erected on the site of her family's stables and barn. As she stepped around the Rolencian banner, the gold thread of the foenix's feathers glinted in the sun.

On the other side of what had been the stable yard was the place where her family's trade house had stood for two hundred years. Naturally, Cobalt had pitched his tent on the best spot on Narrowneck, and when he'd raised the royal foenix banner no one had dared protest.

The once densely wooded isthmus was unrecognisable.

Only the biggest trees had survived the fire-storm. Looking down the straight road, she could see the barrier that Cobalt's men had erected across the narrow entrance that gave this place its name. Tents belonging to the nobility and merchant markizes had been pitched to each side of the road. There had been fierce rivalry over whose tent was pitched closest to the two royal tents.

Between the tents, where feet had not beaten paths, knee-high grass grew from the ashes and waist high saplings sprouted, fertilised by the bodies of those who had died in that terrible fire. So many dead... friend and foe alike, the fire had not differentiated.

Florin shuddered and adjusted her cloak. It was mid-afternoon and hot, but she couldn't discard her cloak, which hid the rope she would need later to escape down the cliff.

A cart rolled up, laden with workers and carpets. An officious-looking servant waved her aside. The servant sent several youths to hang fluttering flags from poles, then oversaw others while they unrolled a large square carpet. They laid this over the former stable yard. Next they unrolled a number of long, narrow carpets, leading straight down to where the ceremony would be held.

Time was running out.

As she passed Cobalt's tent, she realised that beneath her feet were the cracked flagstones of the larder and there, behind the tent, were the remains of the taproom's chimney. Many a cold winter's night they had put a whole log on the fire and gathered to listen to traveller's tales. Her, Da and little Leif... Tears stung her eyes and she blinked them away. After this was over, she was going across the Divide to Foenix Spar, to see her family.

Florin made her way down the slope towards the cliffs. They'd run this way when it was clear the battle was lost. Not far from here was the spot where they had leapt into the lake to escape the raging fire.

It presented a very different picture now. On her left

were the cooking fires, where meat had been roasting all morning. On her right, servants were busy setting up trestle tables where the feast would be served. To shade the feasters, muslin had been draped from poles and blackened trunks. The many lanterns would be lit at dusk, when the feast was due to start.

At last she came to the flat ground right on the tip of Narrowneck, where a dais had been erected so that the populace who had sailed or rowed across Lake Sapphire could watch the wedding. Dozens of boats of various sizes, flying banners in every shade of burgundy and red, bobbed on the sparkling water below. She could see people on board already drinking and feasting.

On Florin's right, a dozen musicians tuned their instruments. The castle-keep had outdone herself with the organisation of the wedding. Every detail had been anticipated, right down to the privies.

Florin turned left, following the curve of the cliffs. Here the smell of wood smoke and cooking fires was very strong. At last she came to the only place where the cliffs overlooked a small beach. A platform had stood here, with a winch to bring travellers and supplies up to the tradepost. The platform had burned, leaving stone uprights still buried in the earth.

It was here that Byren had killed a manticore, before the pride's largest male had attacked him, sending them both over the cliff. He'd been lucky. The manticore had hit a rocky projection partway down and cushioned his landing four body-lengths below.

Florin peered down to the beach and then glanced over her shoulder at the rear of the cooks' tents. No one was looking her way, so she slid the rope from under her cloak and tied it around one of the stone uprights, leaving it in a coil on the ground. Varuska could manage the climb, and Seela claimed she was tougher than she looked. She certainly had nerves of steel. It was Varuska who jumped at the slightest noise.

Florin returned to the bride's tent to lend her support. Under canvas it was stifling, as the mid-afternoon sun combined with the lamps.

Looking pale and pretty in a gown of deep red silk, Varuska was surrounded by two dozen excited girls. They wore dresses in their family colours and garlands in their hair. The youngest two were already weepy from overexcitement.

Florin caught Seela's eye and gave the slightest of nods. It was done. Now all they had to do was endure the ceremony and the feast, then kill Cobalt when he retired to his marriage bed.

Seela glanced to the private chamber at the back of the tent, and Florin followed her, weaving through the chattering girls. As Varuska watched them go, she went to call out, then covered her mouth, smudging her painted lips.

Seela parted the muslin curtains to enter the dimly lit private area. There she came to an abrupt stop, and Florin almost bumped into her. Cobalt stood examining the bridal clothes, his back to them.

'My lord!' Seela gasped, recovering quickly. 'Don't you know it's bad luck for the groom to see the bride before the ceremony?'

'I'm delivering the royal jewels for Piro.' He gestured to Amil, who carried a small chest, then nodded to the main chamber. 'Tell the girls there's time to show their families their pretty dresses before the ceremony starts, and tell Piro I'll be with her in a moment.'

As Seela slipped out of the private chamber into the main part of the tent, Florin glanced over her shoulder, wondering how Varuska would cope with the news that Cobalt wanted to see her.

A hand closed over Florin's mouth.

'Scream and I'll kill the old woman,' Cobalt said.

Amil twisted Florin's arm up behind her back so that it felt like her shoulder would pop from its socket. Between them, they dragged her over to the clothes rail and secured her wrists to each post.

Cobalt stepped in close. 'Do you think I'm stupid, tradepost girl? Of course I recognised you. I only saw you that once, when you came to warn King Rolen of the invasion, but I remembered you said your father was visiting his sister in the foothills of the divide, and I deduced it had to be you who helped Byren's army escape over the mountains.'

Florin glanced to Amil. He was taking something out of his pocket. She went with cold with fear.

'I told Amil to watch you,' Cobalt said. 'I knew you were up to something with the old nurse. After this wedding's over, you're going to tell me where Byren is—'

'But I don't know,' Florin blurted.

'I don't believe you. I think he sent you here for a reason.' Cobalt nodded to Amil, who gagged her. Cobalt dismissed him with a wave, and the manservant slipped out through the rear of the tent.

As Cobalt looked Florin up and down, a hungry light came into his eyes. She fought panic, edging back into the folds of rich fabrics.

'I must say the manservant's uniform makes the most of your long legs, but I wonder if there's any woman underneath it...' Taking his ceremonial knife, he slit the front of her thigh-length tabard, revealing the breast band which she wound around her chest each morning. His breath quickened and he cut the material, the tip of his knife perilously close to her flesh.

As the material fell away, he snorted softly. 'Hardly a handful, but...' He pressed the flat of the blade to her right breast. Her nipple reacted to the cold metal and he smiled with satisfaction. 'Responsive all the same.'

She glared at him.

'Oh, yes, I'll have fun with you tonight,' he whispered. Returning the knife to its sheath, his hand continued down to cup her. No man had ever touched her so intimately.

She froze, stunned, and he laughed softly.

Before she could recover from the shock, he removed his hand, his top lip lifting in disgust. 'I can't... no, I simply can't bring myself to fuck you, not when you're more man than woman.'

Heat rushed up her neck, flooding her face.

A deep shout made him turn and look out through the gauze curtain to the main section of the bridal tent, where Seela and Varuska were waiting for him.

Another shout followed. The clash of metal on metal made Florin jump, but it made Cobalt smile.

'I don't believe it,' he whispered. 'Even Byren would not be so stupid.'

Cobalt darted out into the main section of the tent. As he passed Seela and Varuska, he told them, 'Stay here, you'll be safe. I'll see what's going on.'

BYREN WORE A workman's cap and smock, with a leather harness over his shoulders. He stood as if weary, his back bent between the shafts of a small cart. Neither he nor Orrade carried weapons, which was just as well, since the gate guards had been most thorough. After getting past the guards, they'd made their way up the long straight road on the spine of Narrowneck, delivering hats to the tents of the wealthy.

Now impatience gnawed at him as he waited for Milliner Salvatrix and Orrade to return.

Narrowneck was packed. Servants came and went. Carts filled the lanes between the tents, where arguments over right of way broke out as people refused to back up their horses. Everyone moved with purpose except the men-at-arms, who waited outside tents in twos and threes. A few were hard-eyed and serious, but most had already begun to celebrate, surreptitiously passing around wine skins.

As soon as Orrade and the hat maker reached the cart,

Byren bent his shoulders into the harness. The milliner's cart was not heavy, but it was hard to get it moving up the rise. The return journey would be easier, all downhill, with Piro tucked safely in the back under the blanket. To his relief, the gate guards were not checking carts as they left.

They stopped at two more tents before they reached the highest point where the tradepost had once stood. Here the royal tents had been pitched, both flying the Rolencian banner.

Byren backed the cart into the gap between Cobalt's tent and a noble's tent. Salvatrix opened her work basket, while Orrade helped Byren undo the harness.

The hat maker removed her largest pair of scissors, unscrewed them, then gave Byren and Orrade what amounted to a dagger each. 'Here you are. Now, I'll wait here and—'

'Freezing Sylion!' Orrade nudged Byren. 'That's Chandler and Old Man Narrows.'

Dressed as Rolencian men-at-arms, carrying stolen weapons, the pair walked bold as brass up to Cobalt's tent and slipped inside.

Byren swore softly. 'What are they doing here?'

'Getting themselves killed,' Orrade muttered. 'We must—'

'Watch out for Cobalt's manservant,' the hat-maker warned. 'I've heard he's a corax.'

Byren planted a kiss of thanks on her cheek. 'Keep your head down.'

Then he and Orrade made a dash for the corner of Cobalt's tent. Byren gestured to the bridal tent. 'You grab Piro. I'll get Chandler and Old Man Narrows.'

'But—'

A shout, followed by the clash of metal, put an end to debate. Orrade ran for Piro's tent.

Byren used his blade to slit the side of Cobalt's tent. Inside, the hot, still air was heavily scented with

Ostronite incense. By the light of two lamps, he spotted Chandler and Old Man Narrows on the far side of the tent. A manservant faced them, holding a knife with all the confidence of a trained killer. There was no sign of Cobalt.

As Byren crept up behind the corax, Chandler's eyes widened and the corax spun around, slashing at Byren.

Old Man Narrows stepped in with his sword raised, but before he knew what was happening, the corax had diverted his blade and slashed open his belly.

As Florin's father buckled, trying to hold his guts in, the corax lunged for Chandler. The lad threw himself backwards, falling over a chest. Byren pulled him to safety.

The corax backed up as Byren stepped forward. A dozen men-at-arms charged into the tent and stood blinking in the dim, stifling tent.

The corax pointed at Byren. 'It's the usurper. Kill him.'

The men-at-arms spread out warily. Byren snatched a fallen sword and Chandler lifted his blade.

Cobalt arrived at a run. Taller than the rest, he looked over their heads to Byren. His eyes widened with malicious triumph. 'Kill the usurper!'

The men-at-arms charged. Byren threw the sword, spear-like, into the first man's chest. Grabbing the nearest lamp, he flung it on the carpet at their attackers' feet. Flames sprang up between them, and Byren dragged Chandler out through the slit in the side of the tent.

'What of Piro?' Chandler protested.

'There.' Byren pointed. Six paces away, Orrade had bundled Piro into the cart and was covering her with a blanket. Was that his old nurse running back to the bridal tent?

Byren pulled off his cap and smock and shoved them into Chandler's arms, before pushing him towards the shafts of the cart. 'Put on the harness.'

Cobalt's voice carried as he shouted, 'Around the back!'

Orrade caught Byren's arm. 'It's not—'

'Go.' Byren shoved him aside. 'I'll lead them away.'

He darted out from behind Cobalt's tent into full view of the men-at-arms. With a shout, they took off after him and he ran across Narrowneck, his bad knee protesting.

FLORIN TRIED TO pull her hands through the ropes, but they held firm. She tried to work the gag loose, but Amil had known what he was doing.

Through the thin muslin curtain, she saw the flap of the main chamber open as someone beckoned. 'Quick, this way.'

'Orrie?' Seela sounded stunned. 'Where's Byren?'

'Here. Bring... That's not Piro.'

'No time to explain.' Seela grabbed Varuska and yelled over her shoulder. 'Come quick, Florin.'

Florin tried to call out, but all she could manage was a high pitched whine. Outside, she heard shouting and imagined Byren fighting his way to the gate. She should be with him.

She glimpsed someone as they slipped into the tent's main chamber. Only too aware of her vulnerability, Florin went very still, heart hammering.

'Hello?' The girl's voice was vaguely familiar. Had one of the flower girls come back?

The girl strolled into the tent and helped herself to a sip of the sweet wine and a pastry.

In desperation, Florin pulled and jerked on her restraints, throwing her weight against the posts. Half their length had been buried in the ground; even so, she felt them give slightly.

'Why are you tied up?' Varuska's sister stepped into the private chamber of the tent. She put her wine glass aside and tilted her head. 'I saw Ruska run off with an old woman and a thin man. He was dressed as an apprentice, but carried himself like a warrior. What's going on?'

Florin rolled her eyes, unable to speak.

'My sister's run away, hasn't she? Stupid girl.' Anatoley's eyes gleamed with contempt. 'I knew she wasn't cut out for this. Trust her to throw away the chance of a lifetime!'

Florin jerked her head, indicating the ropes that held her.

Anatoley stepped closer and raised her hands, but it was only to stroke a velvet gown. With deft fingers, the girl unlaced her own gown, tossed it aside and slipped the brocade-edged royal gown over her head. She tightened the lacings, then reached into the bodice and adjusted her breasts so that they showed to best advantage.

Florin could only manage a muffled, indignant protest as Anatoley admired herself in the polished silver mirror.

The girl noticed the jewel chest and opened it. With a cry of delight, she placed the pearl and ruby choker around her neck.

'Piro?' Cobalt entered the outer chamber. 'Piro, Seela, are you out the back?'

Anatoley froze and peered through the muslin.

'If she's run off, I'll...' He strode towards the private chamber. But halfway across, he lurched as if to avoid something, cried out and clutched his back.

'You're too late,' Seela said, springing away with a bloody knife. 'The girl's escaped!'

'Why, you scrawny old bitch,' Cobalt snarled. 'I'm going to—'

'I'll tell you what you're going to do,' Seela said, edging away as he tried to circle her. 'You're going to die for killing my little Myrella.'

And Florin remembered Seela had been Queen Myrella's nurse.

As Anatoley drew her knife and slipped through the curtain, joy surged through Florin. Now Cobalt would get what he deserved.

The girl sprang forward, struck and stepped back.

Florin watched in horror as Seela collapsed with a knife in her back.

Cobalt took a step back. 'Who the—'

'I'm Varuska's sister. King Byren the fourth's other great-granddaughter.'

He looked confused.

'Your father wasn't the only bastard,' Anatoley told him. 'Our grandmother—'

'Why did you kill Seela?'

'Because I should have been the one to play Piro, not Varuska.' She adjusted the gown. 'I should be your queen.'

Cobalt swayed, then almost fell. Anatoley caught him and helped him to the day-bed.

'Your wound needs binding. Let's get that shirt off you.' The muffled sound of movement was followed by material tearing. 'What's going on outside?'

'Byren sent men to kill me. That fool doesn't deserve this kingdom. Trying to kill me on my wedding day? He's played into my hands and branded himself a coward.'

'You'll catch him and kill him?' Anatoley asked eagerly.

Florin decided she hated Varuska's sister.

'Of a certainty.' Cobalt gave a soft grunt of pain.

'Sorry.' Anatoley perched on the end of the day-bed beside Cobalt. 'You know, I'm the same height and colouring as Varuska. I could be your Piro. I'd do a much better job of it.' She tilted her head, using the same mannerism as Piro and Varuska. 'Can't you use me, instead of her?'

'Maybe I can,' Cobalt said slowly, coming to his feet. 'You're such a pretty little thing it seems almost a shame to...'

His fist slammed into her face.

Anatoley fell backwards off the day-bed. Blood gushed between her fingers as she pressed her hands to her nose, and stared up at him, eyes wide with shock. 'What did you do that for?'

'You don't look enough like your sister. But with a broken nose, no one will notice.' He offered his hand. 'Come, my dear.'

Anatoley considered for a heartbeat, then took it. Florin cursed. The girl was a faithless opportunist.

They walked out of Florin's line of sight.

A moment later Anatoley staggered backwards, bent over, both hands pressed to her chest.

'Why...' The girl showed Cobalt her bloody hands. A knife hilt protruded from her ribs. She sank slowly to her knees and toppled forward. 'Why...'

'I'm sorry, my dear, but you're more use to me dead than alive. Dead, you'll paint Byren as a kin-slayer.'

Several men-at-arms entered the tent, followed by the abbot.

Cobalt dropped to his knees. 'Piro, my sweet, I failed you.'

'What happened?' Abbot Firefox asked.

'Byren tried to kill me.' Cobalt indicated his wound. 'When I fought him off, he grabbed Piro, said she'd never marry me, and killed her.'

'Byren killed Piro?' the abbot repeated in surprise, then with more conviction. 'Byren killed his sister. The coward!'

'Find him and his rebels.' Cobalt came to his feet, with the dead 'Piro' in his arms. He cut a tragic figure. 'Abbot Firefox, call the nobles and merchants—'

'They've fled. The fire has spread to the other tents and there's no stopping it. We must leave.'

Florin shuddered. Now she recognised the background noise for the roar of a fire.

'I have horses. Hurry,' the abbot urged.

Cobalt glanced towards the private chamber, almost as if he could see through the curtain into the darkness. He knew Florin was still in there.

And he turned away, leaving her to burn.

Florin jerked on the ropes. She tried to scream through

the gag, but only a high whine emerged. Sweat ran down her forehead. Her eyes stung from the smoke, and her panicked breath whistled through her nose.

She was not going to die here. Furious, she threw her weight against the ropes. Her shoulders ached and her wrists burned as the ropes tightened, but she felt the posts give ever so slightly. Heartened, she renewed her struggle.

Chapter Thirty-Two

BYREN RAN UNTIL his bad knee throbbed and the breath burned in his chest. He ran through tents, up lanes, across carts and between horses, doubling back to escape his pursuers. Their shouts became lost in the cries of those trying to put out fires and save loved ones. The smoke was so thick he couldn't see more than a body-length in front of him. He heard the whinny of frightened horses. As they galloped past him, one beast shouldered him aside and he staggered.

Desperate people collided with him as they made for the gate. He could just imagine the bottleneck. The barrier, built to keep people out, would also keep them in. It seemed like a good idea to go in the opposite direction, to the beach on the far side of Narrowneck.

The heat was something fearful, but he made it back to the crest of Narrowneck. As he passed the back of the bridal tent, he remembered seeing Seela. Had she escaped? He slit the canvas and darted into a dim, smoky interior. 'Seela, are you in here?'

In front of him clothing hung from a rail. The gowns heaved and a high whining noise reached him. He stepped around the post and parted the dresses to find Florin tied up. Wisps of her hair had come loose from her plait and clung to her sweat-damp face. Her servant's tabard had been slit from neck to hip, revealing her small, high breasts.

'Who did this to you?' He wanted to strangle her tormentors with his bare hands. Trembling with fury, he sawed through one of her restraints.

She pulled the gag from her mouth. 'Byren!'

'Aye, it's me.' He reached for the other restraint. 'I'm sorry—'

'Byren...' Tears filled her eyes.

'Eh, none of that, I'm here now.' He freed her other hand and she almost fell into his arms. Her wrists had been rubbed raw by the ropes. 'Who—'

'Seela's dead.'

'What?'

She drew him into the main chamber, where flames had begun to eat into the canvas walls. But Florin seemed unaware of this as she knelt and rolled Seela's body onto her back.

Byren sank to his knees beside his old nurse. A roaring filled his head.

Florin looked across at him, tears gleaming on her cheeks. 'She tried to kill Cobalt.'

Behind Florin, the back wall of the tent was alight.

'Come with me.' Byren hauled Florin to her feet and ran for the tent's front entrance. One look outside revealed flying cinders.

Desperate, Byren grabbed an Ostronite wool rug, swinging it over their shoulders. 'Ready? We'll make for the cliffs.'

She nodded.

They ran out into the fiery maelstrom. A mighty wind buffeted them as they staggered. In the maelstrom, Byren got turned around, but Florin seemed to know the way.

The hot air dried out Byren's eyes, and each breath burned his throat. They passed a burning tent, fruit bubbling and blackening on platters.

Through the smoke he glimpsed the lake and they headed that way. Byren's ankles and forearms stung as flying cinders swirled around them. They stumbled on.

Stumbled right off the cliff, plummeting into the lake. The rug was torn from his hands as blessedly cool water closed over them.

And he remembered Florin couldn't swim. Desperate, he reached out, felt Florin's shoulder and pulled her close. Keeping a tight hold on her, he kicked, driving them towards the surface. They came up, gasping for air. The wind howled above them and the sky was full of smoke and cinders.

Florin's cheeks were streaked with soot and her eyes were red-rimmed from the smoke and heat. She clutched him tightly, and he could feel the panic in her body.

He held her eyes. 'I'll keep you safe. Trust me.'

She nodded and he felt the tension go out of her body. Turning her in his arms, he began to swim backwards, looking around for the nearest boat, but the smoke was too thick. So he struck out in what he hoped was the right direction to reach the shore, hoping to feel lake bed under his feet.

Nothing. Maybe he was going in circles.

He was a strong swimmer, but the lake, fed by the run-off from the recent snow melt, was freezing. He could hear Florin's teeth chattering. Just as he was beginning to despair, a small row boat loomed out of the smoke. He called for help.

No one answered. He struck out for it.

When he reached the boat, he guided Florin to the side. 'Hold on, Mountain Girl.'

She clutched the boat, tipping it, and he saw it was empty save for some bundles down near the stern.

'Stay here. I'm going around the far side to get in.'

She stared at him, clearly terrified.

'I won't leave you. I promise.'

She nodded, teeth chattering.

'That's my mountain girl.'

'I'm n-not your girl.'

He laughed and swam around the row boat, where he yelled. 'Hold tight.'

With a kick, he hauled his weight over the side and into the boat. As soon as the rocking stopped, he perched on the bench, leant over the side and hauled Florin into the belly of the boat. She lay there, shivering, trying to catch her breath. Her tabard gaped open to reveal her ribs rising with each breath and her breasts, the nipples tight and dark against her skin.

He turned away and found the bundles in the stern. A quick investigation revealed a blanket and a basket of food.

'Someone planned a picnic,' he said, wondering what had happened to them. Probably panicked and lost the oars, then another boat had taken them in.

He grabbed the blanket just as Florin came to her knees. The boat rocked.

'Take it easy, you'll tip the boat.' He wrapped the blanket around her shoulders. 'There.' Now he could keep his eyes on her face. 'You'll soon warm up.'

'You came back for me.' She shuddered.

If he hadn't come back, she'd have died. He thought better of telling her he'd been looking for Seela. Grief made his throat tight.

'That's t-twice I've jumped off Narrowneck with you,' Florin said, teeth chattering, 'and me unable to swim. Next t-time I'm taking the gate.'

He grinned. 'There's food. We should be alright tonight.' A smoke-shrouded dusk had closed in, but they would need to be off the lake by sunrise tomorrow.

He had to trust that Orrade had led the others out of Narrowneck. Where would they go? Not Rolenton.

Maybe Foenix Spar. No, Byren was certain Orrade wouldn't abandon him.

He'd wait at the old water-wheel. It was where they'd regrouped the night Palatyne had captured Dovecote Estate.

The old mill would be deserted. Orrade's older brother, Dovronzik, had built a more efficient mill-house further down the stream. Poor Dovronzik. He'd died before Orrade was born, executed for his part in the Servants of Palos uprising.

In the thirty years since, the old water-wheel had fallen into disrepair. As children, they'd claimed the old mill-house for their own, bringing blankets and baskets of food. On hot summer afternoons, they used to stretch out on the upper floor and watch the water rush by, dreaming of the brave things they would do when they grew up. Lence would boast to impress Elina, while Piro and Garzik bickered.

Lence, Elina and Garzik... all lost. Pain cramped in Byren's gut. He tried to focus. 'At least Piro's safe.'

'That wasn't Piro. Cobalt was about to marry Varuska.' Florin's voice was rough with tears. 'And it was her sister who killed Seela.'

'Who *are* these girls?'

'The great-granddaughters of King Byren the Fourth. Their grandmother was another of his bastards.' Florin shrugged. 'Varuska looked so much like Piro, it had to be true. Cobalt could have gotten away with marrying her. He had everyone fooled.'

So Chandler and Old Man Narrows had tried to save an imposter. Byren was reminded that Florin's father was dead, and she didn't know. 'I'm so sorry—'

'You've got nothing to be sorry for. You couldn't have saved Seela.'

'It's not...' He looked down at his big, scarred hands. What good was strength if you could not save the people you loved? He hadn't saved his mother or Elina, hadn't been able to save Seela and now... Grief threatened to choke him.

Florin rose to her knees and reached out to cup his cheek. 'Byren, what's wrong?'

He met her eyes. 'Your father's dead. He and Chandler came to save Piro, but they picked the wrong tent and the corax killed him.'

Her face fell. 'Amil killed Da?'

He nodded.

She threw herself into Byren's arms as sobs shook her. He felt her wet hair on his cheek, hot tears on his neck and hot breath on his throat. He wept with her. Wept for Seela, for Old Man Narrows... for everyone he had lost since Cobalt came back. Her tears mingled with his.

Then she took his face in her hands and her sobs turned into kisses of consolation. Clumsy, desperate kisses. Next thing he knew, he had driven her down onto the blanket in the belly of the boat and his bare chest pressed on hers. He kissed her face, her throat, her breasts...

His hands went to his breeches, freeing himself with practised ease. He tugged at her trousers and she lifted her hips. With a tug, he pulled them off, and tossed them away.

Hot skin, smooth and silken—her beauty stole his breath. Her body, so strong and eager, drew him. She tilted her hips to meet him. He felt the heat of her, knew with one thrust he would be home. At the thought, he nearly lost it right then, like an untried lad, but somehow he managed to hold back.

Drawing him down, she welcomed him. He felt resistance and realised she had never known a man.

Realised he was on the verge of repeating the mistakes of King Byren the Fourth, and look what a mess his grandfather had made, scattering his bastards across Rolencia.

There were ways to avoid pregnancy, but the moment he thought his, he realised he didn't want to treat Florin like one of his dalliances. He wanted...

He could never have what he wanted, not when he'd given his word to Isolt. Sanity returned.

With a groan he pulled back.

She came after him, hair wild, lips swollen, lost in passion in a way that made him wish he was free to love her as she deserved.

'Don't.' His hand met her chest. He felt her heart racing, and the rise of her breast. 'I can't...' He shuddered, because there was nothing he wanted more. 'I just can't...'

She whimpered like a wounded animal and seemed to shrink into herself as she hugged her knees, naked in the dimness, waist-length hair dark against her skin. So pale and perfect...

'For god's sake, get dressed.' If she didn't, he wouldn't be able to stop and then he'd hate himself.

She turned away, searching for her clothes. As she bent forward, her wet hair fell over her shoulder, revealing the line of her spine, her waist and the flare of her hips...

He had to put his back to her.

Leaning over the side of the boat, he dipped a hand in the lake and splashed icy water on his face, his chest and his raging erection. The painful cold brought clarity.

He was not the kind of man his grandfather and Lence had been. He might have the same appetites, but he could exercise self-control.

Byren felt for his breeches, tucked himself in and did up the laces. No shirt. It was going to be a cold night. And he dare not cuddle Florin to keep warm.

He glanced over his shoulder. She wore her torn tabard, but her long thighs were bare. 'Why—'

'I can't find my pants.' She sounded aggrieved. 'I think you threw them overboard.'

He slammed his palm to his forehead. He was not taking his breeches off to give to her. That way lay ruin for them both.

'Wrap the blanket around you,' he said, voice raw with desperation.

* * *

FLORIN DID AS he instructed. Byren couldn't bear to look at her. He despised her. She'd thrown herself at him but, just like Cobalt, he found her repulsive. She huddled down in the boat, heart-sick and racked with a bone-deep sadness that went beyond tears.

While she'd been making a fool of herself, they'd drifted across the lake, leaving the smoke behind. She could see by the brilliant stars above that it was going to be a cold night.

'Here.' He offered her a leg of roast chicken, hardly looking in her direction.

She accepted it without a word, and forced herself to eat, curled up at her end of the boat.

'We're drifting west,' he said. 'That's good. We'll take to the woods, find Orrie and—'

'I'm going home.' Even as she said the words, she remembered she had no home. With Narrowneck burned and Da dead, there was only Leif.

'Your brother's safe with Warlord Feid,' Byren said. 'What is Leif now, nine?'

'Ten,' she corrected, noting that Byren did not ask her to stay with him.

Of course not. She was an embarrassment, a woman who was no good at womanly things. Winterfall had warned her that Byren would never look at her. She'd denied her feelings back then, but there was no point lying to herself now.

She'd only ever wanted to be accepted for who she was, and she'd thought Byren accepted her. More than that, she'd thought he respected her. But she'd been fooling herself.

'Here.' He tossed her a water sack. 'You sleep. I'll keep watch.'

'All night? I don't think so. You sleep first. I'm not tired.'

He hesitated. 'You sure?'

'Yes.' She was too heart-sore to sleep.

He took her at her word and huddled down in the stern. Before tonight's disaster, she would have seen this as a sign that he respected her.

Now she couldn't wait to leave.

Chapter Thirty-Three

Byren studied the set of Florin's shoulders as she strode ahead of him. He could tell she was furious and he didn't blame her. Because of him, she'd been forced to wear the blanket as breeches. A strip of cloth did duty as a breast-band. He caught glimpses of it when her damaged tabard gaped. At least she had boots. Just as well he hadn't noticed them last night when he dragged off her breeches or he'd have thrown them overboard, too.

Just the thought of how close he'd come to dishonouring her and himself made the blood rush to his face. Even so, he still yearned for her.

He had it bad. The sooner he was away from her, the better.

'I know how to avoid Cobalt's men and reach the secret pass over the mountains on my own.' She barely glanced over her shoulder, her long legs taking such great strides he had to push himself to keep up.

'Good, you can help Chandler take Varuska to Feid's stronghold. She'll be safe on Foenix Spar.' He owed the girl that much.

Florin shot Byren a dark look. A thrill raced through his body, forcing him to admit that he was keeping her near him because he didn't want to part with her.

'We'll meet up with the others,' he said, 'spend the night in the abandoned mill-house. We can separate tomorrow.'

'Now that Cobalt has blackened your name by saying you murdered your own sister, what's your next step?'

He laughed. 'No one in their right mind is going to believe that.'

What *was* his next step, though? It was a good question, but he couldn't think; not when Florin jumped down from a fallen log in front of him, her strong pale thighs flexing.

GARZIK STOOD ON the reardeck, watching the ospriet far above. With its Affinity-enhanced vision, the bird could spot its prey at a great distance. The ospriet dropped like an arrow, skimmed the water, then rose, huge wings labouring as something writhed in its beak. Garzik raised the farseer and caught a flash of iridescent serpent skin as the ospriet carried off a scytalis.

This time of year, the ospriet probably had a mate waiting on its nest, keeping the eggs warm. That, or it might be trying to win a mate with this offering.

Garzik resumed his scan of the surrounding sea. After Port Mero, the ship had made good time, thanks to a distant storm that had brought strong winds.

'Over the starboard prow,' Olbin said, joining him. 'The Skirling Stones.'

Garzik spotted tall spires of rock surrounded by a mantle of foaming sea. Some of the spires were topped with stunted bushes. The stones reflected the setting sun, as if they were made of black glass. 'I've heard they sing.'

'When the wind is in the right quarter.'

He frowned. 'Are those birds circling them?'

'Winged serpents. We don't venture near the Skirling Stones. Between the rocks and the Affinity beasts, it's too dangerous.'

'You finished with Wynn?' Rusan asked Olbin, joining them. 'We can squeeze in a reading lesson before the night watch.'

Olbin retrieved the farseer. 'Do any of your fancy books mention the Skirling Stones, Wynn?'

Rusan glanced to Garzik.

'No, but there would probably be something on them in the abbey libraries. The abbeys hoard knowledge like treasure.'

Olbin snorted. 'I bet those hot-land books have nothing good to say of us Utlanders.'

Since this was true, Garzik could not deny it. He swore then that when he went home, he would write the truth about the Utlanders.

AS THE SETTING sun illuminated the Landlocked Sea, Fyn stood in the crow's nest searching the foothills of the Dividing Mountains. There was no sign of a messenger on the shore.

His belly churned with frustration. The Merofynian lords had agreed to send news by fast rider, so he'd spent all day searching for a signal. Neiron should have caught up with Wythrod yesterday, or even the day before, and Yorale would have been in position. So why was there no word?

Fyn cursed softly. Too much could go wrong in the heat of battle. If this attack failed, it would make him look incompetent; but he had no control over the Merofynian lords. He had to trust to the abbot's cool head to guide Wythrod.

The wind carried Isolt's voice to him and he spotted her on the prow, throwing treats out over the water for the Affinity beasts. Both the foenix and the wyvern vied for the sea-fruit, getting in each other's way, and the treat dropped into the sea. Loyalty dived, skimmed the waves, then returned to Isolt's side and shook herself, spraying the queen.

Isolt laughed, spotted Fyn and waved to him.

As he joined her, she asked, 'Have they sent a messenger?'

'No, we just have to hope...' Distracted by the way her damp gown clung to her body, he looked past her towards Wythrontir Estate. What he saw made him frown and shade his eyes. 'Does that look like smoke to you?'

Isolt studied the horizon. 'It could just be a forest fire.'

'All the fires we've seen recently have been associated with spar attacks,' Fyn said. 'I should have stayed with the army. Even if we turn back now, we won't reach Wythrontir Estate until tomorrow.' Too late to help them.

TIRED, HUNGRY AND footsore, Byren crept to the treeline to study the water-wheel. Florin joined him. In the branches above them, birds bickered over roosts.

As dusk closed in, a light rain had begun to fall, chilling them both. Despite this, Byren took his time. The old mill-house sat at the top of a small pond fed by a narrow stream.

The mill-house appeared to be deserted, but if the roof hadn't fallen in since last summer, it would be dry.

'There's no one around,' Florin whispered. The night birds gave their hunting cries. 'What are we waiting for?'

'I'm not walking into a trap.'

'The birds are not disturbed. It's safe.'

Even so, Byren waited a little longer before he waved them on.

They crept through the thigh-high ferns through the doorless opening of the mill-house. Inside, the churning of the water-wheel kept up a soft, steady rush of noise. Someone dropped through the hatch from the grain loft, landing lightly. It was gloomy inside the mill-house, but Byren recognised Orrade by the way he moved.

'Orrie!' Taking two steps, Byren embraced him.

'I knew you'd escape.' Orrade's voice was a trifle rough. 'Knew you'd come here.'

Byren grinned and nodded to the floor above. 'Are the others—'

'No. We split up. That milliner is a canny one. She disguised Varuska by packing rags in her cheek then tied a bandage around her face, as if she had a tooth ache. They should be in Rolenton already.'

'If the girl looks so much like Piro, she can't stay—'

'Salvatrix is going to send her to the mage.' Orrade turned away and busied himself with something on a low shelf.

'And Chandler?' Byren heard flint strike, a spark flared bright in the dimness.

'I sent him up to Foenix Pass.' Orrade turned, shielding the flame of a candle stub. 'He should get through before Cobalt can close the pass...'

Orrade ran down as he took in Florin and Byren's state—Byren shirtless, Florin in a torn tabard and blanket instead of breeches. Byren felt his face grow hot. It was obvious what had happened. Only it hadn't, and he had the blue-balls to prove it.

Florin flushed and looked away.

'I...' Orrade's voice faltered, then recovered. 'I see you lost your clothes in the fire. Thank Halcyon you survived. There's a blanket upstairs. I'll go get some horses and supplies.'

He passed the candle to Byren and went to leave.

Byren caught his arm. 'You can't go to the great house. It's—'

'It's necessary. We have nothing, no food, no...' He paused as Byren's stomach rumbled loudly, as if to prove his point. 'They're my people, Byren. Cobalt might have given Dovecote to his Merofynian lackeys to buy the captain's loyalty, but he can't buy the loyalty of Dovecote's people.'

'What if his men see you?'

'I know my way around. No one will see me.'

Byren nodded and let Orrade go.

After a moment, Florin shifted slightly behind him.

'Come here,' Byren said. 'I'll give you a boost up to the attic.'

'I don't need your help.' Striding past him, she peered up at the hatch, sprang onto the stone block, then jumped up to catch her weight on her arms.

Florin's long legs hung right in front of him. She swung one leg, lifting her knee through the hatch. Who would have thought she was so flexible?

Byren's mouth went dry and he had to adjust himself.

'Pass me the light.' She peered down through the opening.

He handed her the candle, then stood on the block and lifted himself up in one easy movement.

She held the candle high, examining the loft. The roof was low and sharply angled, but Byren was pleased to see none of the shingles were missing.

Florin pointed. 'There's Orrie's blanket. You sleep first. I'll keep watch.'

'I'm too hungry to sleep. I'll watch. Better put out the candle.' The flame was guttering in the wax.

She blew out the candle.

Darkness... And her within arm's reach. His heart raced as his body hardened. He knew what would happen if he stayed here alone with her. 'I think it's better if I keep watch outside.'

She didn't argue.

Dropping through the hatch, he went out into the cold, wet night. Clouds obscured the stars. It was a good night for the hunted. He climbed a tree and stretched out on a branch. From here he could observe the path up to the great house.

Half the night had gone before Orrade returned with travelling packs.

Byren lowered himself from the tree. 'Nothing happened with Florin.'

Orrade had been reaching for his knife. Now he put it away. 'That's a good way to get yourself killed.'

'Nothing happened between Florin and me.'

'None of my business.' Orrade tossed a pack to Byren.

They walked on for a bit.

'It was after we escaped. I nearly—'

'I don't want to know.'

Byren glanced to Orrade, but the night was dark and he could barely make out his silhouette on the path. 'Fair enough.'

They walked on.

'I couldn't get any horses. The Merofynian replaced my stable-master.' They were approaching the old mill-house, and Orrade's step slowed. 'So what's the plan?'

'Make sure Florin reaches the secret pass to Foenix Spar, and then...' And then he would be able to think straight.

'Your mountain girl can make her own way back to Feid's stronghold.'

'Cobalt's men are not the only ones on the hunt in the foothills.' The mundane predators were dangerous enough, but there were also Affinity beasts and both would be eager to feed their young.

'Florin will see the sense in that,' Orrade agreed.

And she did. Florin thanked Byren, even though it cost her. He had to bite his tongue to hide a smile.

They dressed warmly, ate a cold breakfast and were on their way before dawn.

Chapter Thirty-Four

'WHAT DO YOU see?' Fyn asked, fearing that Wythrontir's great house would be a blackened ruin.

'There's no sign of fire,' Dunstany said. They leaned against the rail of the *Dunsior*.

Silently, he passed Fyn the farseer. To Fyn's relief, the house on the distant rise stood undamaged in the morning sunshine.

Fyn passed the farseer to Isolt.

'No sign of spar warriors?' Captain Elrhodoc asked. When Isolt didn't deny it, he nodded. 'So there was no need to rush back.'

He'd been saying the same thing since yesterday evening, and Fyn was heartily sick of him.

Isolt lowered the farseer slowly. Abbess Celunyd watched for the queen's reaction. Fyn was heartily sick of her too, but at least she held her tongue.

Not Elrhodoc. 'We should have waited to hear from Lord Yorale, my queen.'

Isolt glanced to Fyn. They'd sailed through the

night, because she trusted him, and now it seemed he'd panicked.

Loyalty nudged Isolt as if to reassure her.

'I'm going to the crow's nest for a better look.' Fyn took the farseer and made for the main mast. As he left the high rear deck, Elrhodoc said something and several of the queen's guards laughed.

Anger burned inside Fyn, and he felt his face grow hot. When he reached the crow's nest, he found Rhalwyn in the lookout.

'Can I?' The lad gestured to the farseer.

'Sure.' Fyn handed it over. Maybe they should let the boy return to the sea. After all, Cortomir had proven such an excellent Affinity beast handler, he'd been disappointed when they'd left him back in Port Mero.

'That's odd...' Rhalwyn said softly.

'What?'

'I don't remember the lake coming right up to the great house.'

Fyn checked. The boy was right. Wythrontir's great house sat on a terraced island. 'There must have been a breach in the sea-wall.' But when he checked, the wall was undamaged.

'I don't understand,' Rhalwyn said. 'If the sea-wall is intact, why did the estate flood?'

As soon as he reached the deck, Fyn asked Dunstany the same question.

'Lady Isfynia must have opened the shipyard floodgates.'

'But that hasn't happened since...' Isolt ran down, looking shocked.

'Since Wythrontir was attacked by Lincis Spar warriors over two hundred years ago,' Dunstany finished for her. 'Back then, it was their last defence. With Wythrod and all the able-bodied men gone, Lady Isfynia would have had no other way to defend her people.'

Frustration churned in Fyn's gut. Wythrontir Estate

shouldn't have been attacked. Abbot Murheg would know what had gone wrong, if he still lived. It surprised Fyn to discover he would miss the historian-turned-abbot.

They studied the estate as the ship drew closer. The water was very still, reflecting the great house like a mirror.

'It's very beautiful, but strange,' Isolt said, then turned to Fyn. 'If the spar warlords were headed west, why did Lady Isfynia have to open the flood gates?'

'There was always a chance they would turn south,' Elrhodoc said.

'But, if that was the case, Wythrod and his men would have been between them and the estate.' Isolt turned to Dunstany. 'I'm right, aren't I?'

The noble scholar shrugged. 'In the confusion of battle, the best laid plans can go awry.'

They fell silent, as the yacht neared the wharf. This time there was no one to greet them. While the sailors made the ropes fast and lowered the gangplank, Fyn lifted the farseer to study the great house again. Two flags flew from the tower. One was the Wythrontir trident and trumpet, symbolising maritime dominion and readiness for war. The other... 'Whose crest is the hammer and hawk?'

'The hammer and hawk symbolise metal forged and determination,' Isolt answered automatically. And Fyn just knew her father had made her memorise all the crests of the noble families. 'That's the Yoraltir symbol. What does this mean?'

'It appears Yorale claims the glory of turning back the spar invasion,' Dunstany said and offered Isolt his arm. 'You must thank your lord general for his service, my queen.'

They made their way from the wharf to the sea-wall and down onto what had been the dyke road. Now it was a causeway, surrounded by water.

Fyn frowned as he surveyed the flood waters. Had the Rolencian war captives drowned in their cells? 'Do they chain the seven-year slaves at night?'

Isolt looked horrified.

'No need,' Dunstany said and Fyn realised that the captives could not escape unless they could speak Merofynian and pass themselves off as locals.

The abbess made a soft noise in her throat and hurried on. Fyn spotted several spar warriors floating face down in the water. To distract Isolt, he pointed to the great house. 'It's lucky the refugees made their camp on the terraces.'

The wyvern gave a cry above them and swooped down to skim across the surface of the water, rising later with a fish in her jaws.

'Did you see that?' Isolt was delighted. 'Here, girl...' She clicked her tongue and the wyvern landed on the causeway in the front of them. With a toss of her head, Loyalty swallowed the fish in one gulp.

'Clever girl.' Isolt patted the wyvern's neck and they continued along the causeway.

The foenix landed next to Fyn, the downdraft from his great wings buffeting them.

'Did you see that, Dunstany?' Fyn pointed. 'Resolute is favouring his left leg.'

As Isolt walked on with her escort, Fyn stroked Resolute's neck and Dunstany knelt to inspect the foenix.

'Can we trust Yorale?' Fyn whispered.

'When Isolt's father seized the throne, Yorale's older brother led an uprising. The Yoraltir claim to the throne was just as good, but Yorale supported King Merofyn rather than his brother. There might be rivalry between Yoraltir and Dunistir Estates, but Yorale has always been loyal to the crown.'

At that moment, Isolt and her entourage reached the first terrace. The refugees surged forward, cheering and waving. Startled, Loyalty reared up and gave a cry. The young queen soothed her with a touch and a word.

'Isolt Wyvern Queen!' someone cried, and others took up the chant. 'Isolt Wyvern Queen!'

'I don't think we need to worry about Isolt's hold on the throne,' Dunstany said.

When the queen's party reached the highest terrace, they found Yorale and Neiron waiting. Dressed in their parade ground finest, the lords and their captains filled the top terrace, their breastplates glinting in the sunlight. Fyn spotted Abbot Murheg and caught his eye, but there was no chance to speak now.

To the people who watched from the terraces below, it must have been an impressive display as the nobles welcomed their queen.

Yorale went down on one knee. 'Your humble lord general welcomes you, Queen Isolt. Wythrontir Estate is safe. The warlords of Lincis and Amfina spars are dead.'

'Thank you for your loyal service. This will not be forgotten,' Isolt said, before looking around at those gathered. 'Where is my great-aunt?'

Yorale pushed himself to his feet with an effort. 'Alas, my queen, the excitement was too much for Lady Isfynia. Her heart gave out.'

Isolt's face fell.

'I don't see Lord Wythrod.' Fyn had been searching the armed men. 'Why isn't he here to greet his queen? Abbot Murheg, you were with him. What happened?'

Neiron glanced to Yorale, and they both stepped to one side as Murheg came forward. 'I'm sorry to be the bearer of bad news. When we came upon the spar camp, I convinced Wythrod to wait in the valley behind it until Lord Neiron arrived. Unfortunately, that night while we slept, spar warriors attacked. Wythrod was struck down as he called for his armour.'

Fyn turned to Neiron. 'Where were you?'

'We arrived the next morning, too late to help.'

'Meanwhile, I was waiting in position to form the pincer attack,' Yorale said. 'By the time I had realised what was going on, the battle was over, Wythrod was dead and his men had been decimated. Trapped between

Neiron and my men, the spar warlords fled south. We gave chase.'

'And we were running ahead of the spar warriors,' Murheg said. 'We reached Wythrontir great house in time to warn Lady Isfynia. Alone and surrounded, she could only watch as they set fire to the shipyards. She waited until night, then ordered the flood gates opened. The water rushed upon them like a great wall, extinguishing the enemy's camp fires and sweeping all before it.'

Yorale nodded. 'We were half a day behind, cleaning up stragglers.'

'So you don't know if the two warlords are dead?' Fyn asked. As far as he could see, it was Lady Isfynia who had defeated the invasion.

'My poor aunt...' Isolt whispered. 'Wythrod was the last of the Wythrontirs.'

'Not quite,' Yorale said. 'My second wife was Wythrod's aunt. My youngest son, Yorwyth, is the next in line.' He gestured to a youth at his side. 'Yoromer, fetch your brother.'

'If we are going to consider the maternal line, Yorale's son is not the only Wythrontir,' Dunstany said. 'Lord Benvenute's heir married Wythrod's aunt. They were both killed in the Centicore Spar raid, but their son Benowyth lives. His claim is just as strong.'

'Not quite. His mother was the younger sister,' Yorale said. 'Besides, Benowyth is the infant heir of Benetir Estate, which is on the far side of the Landlocked Sea. While Yorwyth is...'

'You sent for me, Father?' a youngster asked.

Yorale stepped aside. 'Put the chair here.'

The servant obeyed, and the older brother steadied Yorwyth as he put his crutches aside and lowered himself into the chair. The ten-year-old's right leg was strapped to a board.

'What happened to you, young man?' Isolt asked with ready sympathy.

'I fell—'

'During the Rolencian campaign he served on one of Travany's ships, broke his leg in two places,' Yorale explained. 'But he'll be on his feet by midsummer. In another five years he'll be a man. Until then, I'll leave my most experienced captain to protect the estate.'

'With Utlanders in Port Mero and spar warlords coming over the divide the kingdom needs strong lords, my queen,' Neiron said. 'Lords who are prepared to spill blood in your defence.'

As much as Fyn hated to admit it, he was right.

'Lord General.' Isolt gestured for Yorale to kneel.

'My queen.'

'As a reward for your loyal service, I grant your second son, Yorwyth, Wythrontir Estate. He will be known henceforth as Lord Wythor.' She nodded to the abbot and abbess. 'Draw up a decree to this effect.'

Murheg and Celunyd went off to prepare the papers and Yorale arranged for his youngest son's chair to be carried to the edge of the terrace.

There Yorale lifted his youngest son's arm. 'I give you, Lord Wythor of Wythrontir Estate!'

And the people cheered.

THE VOYAGE HAD taken twice as long as usual and Piro was grateful to be home safe in Port Marchand. The sounds of men shouting as they unloaded and seagulls calling came through the cabin window.

After the storm had eased off, the voyage had been uneventful and they had limped home. Everyone had worked double shifts while she'd nursed the injured under Surgeon Wasilade's watchful eye.

Piro closed her travelling bag and fastened the leather straps. If Bantam or Jakulos heard she was leaving, they'd send Cormorant to escort her to the Rolencian agent, which was quite unnecessary as she knew her way home.

Somehow, she had to stop Cobalt's marriage to the imposter. Back on Ostron Isle, this had all seemed so simple. But now that she was here, she'd decided she needed to go to the mage's agent for advice. Together they would come up with a plan. No more jumping feet first into trouble.

Filled with determination, Piro picked up her bag.

She glanced down the passage to the middeck before heading for the captain's cabin. After scribbling a quick note to Bantam and signing it *Mulcy Girl*, she made for the door.

'This will do,' an old woman announced, her voice carrying down the passage. 'My apprentice and I will share.'

'This one's taken,' Cormorant protested.

Curious, Piro peeped around the door. Cormorant's shoulders hid all but the top of the woman's neat silver bun. They had stopped in front of Piro's old cabin.

The woman opened the door. 'Nonsense, it's empty.' As she ushered her apprentice into the cabin, Piro caught a glimpse of a swollen cheek and a bandage.

'But...' Cormorant followed them into the cabin. Piro could still hear his muffled voice. 'But the ship won't leave until the repairs are completed.'

'That's fine. I could do with a rest. Off you go now, and when the captain returns, send him to me.'

Piro waited until the passage was clear, then left the *Wyvern's Whelp*.

After so long at sea, walking on dry land made her legs feel shaky; or perhaps it was the sight of three Merofynian men-at-arms at the end of the pier. Hands on their sword hilts, they watched everyone with hooded eyes. She kept her head down as she went past. If anyone asked, she was an apprentice going home to nurse her sick mother.

The wharves were packed with ships from Merofynia and Ostron Isle, loading and unloading. Hearing Rolencian accents made Piro realise how much she'd missed her home.

As she climbed to the higher road that circled the docks the smell of hot food made her stomach rumble and she followed her nose to find a young woman serving pies from a goat cart.

Judging by the number of customers the pies were excellent and the pie-girl greeted everyone with a cheery smile.

Piro purchased one of the pastries and sat on a nearby wall to listen to the chatter of the crowd. Behind her, the lower wharf road was busy with rattling carts, barking dogs and busy merchants.

After one bite of the crisp pastry and savoury chicken filling, Piro knew why the pie-girl did such a good trade. A seagull hovered on the breeze overhead, eyeing Piro's food. She broke off a bit of crust and threw it to the bird. In no time, a dozen seagulls had joined the first. Their raucous cries were so loud she despaired of overhearing any news. Then, on some unseen signal, they all took to the air and flew off to bother someone else.

Meanwhile, a stout matron had come over to the girl's cart and struck up a conversation. 'How's your mother, Borodana?'

'Better now we've gotten rid of Ozig and his master.'

'Send them all back to Merofynia, that's what I say. Why, only the other day...' The matron felt silent as three Merofynian men-at-arms approached the pie cart.

The customer who'd just been served hurried off and the matron gestured for the Merofynians to go ahead of her. Two of the men-at-arms ordered quickly, the third glanced at Piro and frowned. His companions nudged him and he turned to give his order.

Piro decided it would look suspicious if she slipped away now. She didn't know the Merofynian. More accurately, she didn't recognise him, but there had been so many guards when she served as Isolt's slave. Fighting the urge to run, Piro took another bite of her pie. Her mouth was so dry she could hardly swallow.

The men-at-arms purchased their pies and moved on, leaving the matron the next in line.

'The usual?' the pie-girl asked.

'Aye. Did you hear about the kingsdaughter?' the matron asked as she accepted her pie. 'Such a shame, and her so young.'

Piro went very still.

'I don't believe it.' Borodana dropped some coins in the change pocket of her apron and served another customer. 'I don't believe Byren Kingsheir would—'

'They're saying he did it to stop the wedding.'

'Cobalt's wedding?' Piro asked.

They both turned to her and nodded.

'But the wedding isn't until—'

'When Cobalt heard Byren was coming back he moved the wedding forward,' Borodana said.

'Much good that did.' The matron clearly relished the tragedy. 'Byren crept into the royal tent and—'

'I don't believe he killed his sister,' the pie girl insisted.

'If Byren didn't, who did? Cobalt? A dead kingsdaughter's no good to him.' The matron adjusted her shawl as if she'd won the argument. 'Besides, they say Cobalt's heartbroken, after saving Piro's life and hiding her all this time.'

'They also say Piro Kingsdaughter is staying in Merofynia with Queen Isolt,' Borodana countered. 'And there can't be two Piros.'

'One's obviously an imposter.'

'Aye, but which one?'

'Who knows?' The matron shrugged. 'This, I do know. Byren Kingsheir is in hiding and Cobalt's turning the kingdom upside down looking for him.'

Mind racing, Piro stared at her scuffed shoes. Byren would never hurt an innocent girl. The false-Piro must have gotten between him and Cobalt while they were fighting. Perhaps the girl fancied herself in love with Cobalt. He could be very persuasive. At any rate, the imposter was dead and Byren was on the run.

'They're coming back,' the matron said. Piro looked up to see the three Merofynian men-at-arms crossing the nearest intersection and the one who'd stared at Piro was looking right at her.

Her mouth went dry with fear. *Sylion's Luck!*

A merchant's fine carriage trundled past, obscuring Piro's line of sight for a moment.

She grabbed her bag and swung her legs over the wall, dropping to the lower wharf road. Her hands and feet stung with the impact, but she was unhurt.

Heart racing, she looked about. In another moment the Merofynians would reach the pie-cart and the wall. She needed...

Laden carts rattled past her, going in both directions. She ran for the nearest, threw her bag onto the back, and clambered up under the canvas, working her way into the midst of a rich family's belongings. There were rolled carpets, chests of all sizes, mirrors, paintings wrapped in calico and blanket shrouded furniture. Piro heard the Merofynians yelling as they searched for her. The cart turned a corner and the wheels rattled over wharf boards.

The men-at-arms ordered all the cart drivers to stop.

Her cart trundled on for a bit, earning abuse from the Merofynians before it came to an abrupt stop.

Meanwhile, Piro scrambled to find a hiding place. Behind a painting, she discovered a blanket-wrapped clavichord. Wriggling through a gap in the blankets, she dragged her bag with her. Underneath the clavichord, she found a shelf filled with clothing.

Heart in her mouth, Piro climbed onto the shelf, adjusted the clothing to cover her and clutched the stone.

'You there, driver, get down.' The Merofynian's voice grew louder as he approached. 'Why didn't you stop the first time I told you to?'

'So much noise on the wharf, I didn't hear ya.'

Piro heard a thwack.

'Eh, thas not fair. I'm a bit deaf. Can't help it.'

'Search his cart.'

'We serve Lord Rhoderich, an' this here's his property bound for Merofynia,' the cart driver insisted.

'Well, we serve King Cobalt, so get out of my man's way.'

'What's he lookin' for?'

'Runaway seven-year slave.'

Piro cursed her bad luck.

The cart dipped as someone climbed up then began moving things about. He was being thorough.

Sick fear made Piro's stomach churn.

Light pierced the gloom under the clavichord as the large painting was moved aside. Piro held her breath and hoped the searcher didn't pull the clothes out and her along with them.

A sword blade shot through the blanket going over Piro's head. It withdrew just as quickly.

Before she realised what was happening, the blade shot through the blanket halfway along, plunging into her stomach. She felt like she'd been punched, had to bite her tongue to stifle a cry.

The blade pulled out and plunged in further along, missing her calves.

'No one here,' the man-at-arms reported.

'I told ya—' There was another thump and a curse from the driver.

'I have a silver coin for anyone who delivers the runaway,' the Merofynian announced. 'And five coppers for information leading to her capture.'

Was that all she was worth? No one volunteered any information and Piro heard boots striding off along the wharf.

'Come on lads, excitement's over,' the cart driver said. 'Back ta work.'

Hot damp spread across Piro's stomach. No pain yet. That would come. She needed to pack the wound, but she felt strangely distant. The cart creaked as it moved on again and stopped shortly after. There was a series of jerks and thumps as the men unloaded.

'Just this bloody clavichord, then we're done, lads,' the cart driver said. 'Lower the ropes.'

Piro heard the men pass ropes under the clavichord and secure them.

'Righto. Take her up.'

With a lurch, Piro felt the instrument lift and swing through the air. She clutched the shelf and her stomach clenched painfully.

After an interminable time spent swaying in mid-air, the men guided the clavichord towards the hatch. Someone called Feovil was in charge and the crew spoke Rolencian. Piro realised the ship was a Rolencian merchant vessel, bound for Merofynia. There was a thump and the instrument settled on the planks. Cold with pain, Piro fought nausea.

'Get this load secured,' Feovil ordered. 'Cap'n wants to cast off with the tide.'

Next thing she knew, several men picked up the clavichord to move it. One of the men dropped his end. Her head clipped the clavichord's leg and she nearly fell off the shelf. Instinctively, she tried to stop her fall. Her hand went through the gap in the blanket, hitting someone's shin. There was a shriek and she pulled her arm back, but it was too late.

'What's the matter?' a gruff voice asked.

'It was a hand,' a lad said, voice breaking. 'A hand tried to grab m'leg!'

'I don't see no—'

'Someone's under the blanket, I tell you.'

'Here, let me see,' a third voice said. 'Bring the lantern over here, Illien.'

Illien? She hoped he was nothing like her bastard cousin.

'Here it is,' the lad said and light glowed through the blanket.

Piro winced as the covering was jerked aside and three men peered in at her. One was the lad, Illien, another was fifty if he was a day, his chin covered in salt and pepper whiskers. The third had a face like a rat, with prominent teeth. They all stared at her in shock.

'Well?' Feovil asked. 'What is it?'

'I think we found what them Merofynians was lookin' for.' The old salt wiped his bristly jaw. 'It's a pretty little ladybird. No wonder they were so hot ta find her.'

'Out of the way.' Feovil knelt and peered in at Piro. His face swam in her vision. 'A stow-away. Bring her out into the light.'

'Wouldn't mind her for my seven-year slave,' rat-face said. He knelt and reached in to grab her. As he dragged Piro onto the floor she gasped in pain. Her skin felt clammy and she fought to stay conscious

'She's bleeding,' Illien said.

'I'm not a seven-year slave. And I'm not a stowaway,' Piro insisted. 'I'm Lord Dunstany's servant and I can pay for my passage. Deliver me to Dunstany in Port Mero.'

As Feovil considered, she tried to focus on his face. If they were not honourable men, they could steal her coins *and* hand her over to the Merofynians for the reward.

Feovil seemed to make up his mind. He sprang to his feet. 'Take her to the ship's surgeon. I'll tell the captain.'

As they lifted her, everything spun past Piro.

The next thing she knew, the ship was at sea and she lay on a narrow bunk in the surgeon's cabin.

'She's awake,' Illien announced. She hadn't noticed him in the shadows. He crept closer.

'So you've come back to us.' The surgeon studied her while she studied him. His red-rimmed eyes and wine-laden breath did not reassure her.

Piro reached for the stone Siordun had given her only to find it gone. Lost, after everything she had been through? Tears stung her eyes.

'Don't worry, you'll be right now.' Illien patted her shoulder then looked up at the surgeon.

He shrugged. 'I've done what I can. If the wound doesn't putrefy...'

Panic seized Piro. She used to think that she was destined for great things, but she'd seen so many people die since winter. Would her life end here? Already her vision was fading, but strangely not her hearing...

'She's asleep again,' Illien announced. 'Is she really Lord Dunstany's servant?'

'Who knows? Let's see what's in her bag.' There was some shuffling. 'Hmmm, either she stole this gown or she's no ordinary servant.' Her coin purse chinked and she heard mumbled counting. 'Take this to the captain to pay for her passage.'

'What about the rest?'

A muffled slap. 'Get moving.'

And Piro knew her luck had well and truly run out.

Chapter Thirty-Five

BYREN CHOSE A spot in a small gully. It was easy to defend, shielded by tall pines on three sides and a rock wall on the fourth. 'We'll camp here tonight, just under that overhang.'

As Florin stepped back and lifted her head to stare at the mountains, silhouetted against the afterglow of the setting sun, Byren just knew she was going to argue with him.

'We should keep going,' she said. 'We're not far from the secret pass.'

'All the more reason to rest now and set off first thing tomorrow.'

Florin tossed her head impatiently, making his heart race. Before she could think of another objection, Byren settled the matter by shrugging his travelling pack off his shoulders and letting it drop with a decided thunk. He took the chance to stretch and heard his joints pop.

As he lowered his arms Florin looked away quickly.

Didn't she understand he was being considerate? She might be as tall as Orrade, but she didn't have his wiry strength. She had to be tired. He'd driven them at a fast march from first light to dusk for three days, avoiding paths and villages, doubling back twice to dodge Merofynian patrols.

'Fine.' Florin shed her pack. 'We can split up first thing tomorrow. I know the way—'

'You might know the way, but these foothills are filled with Affinity beasts.'

'I'm not stupid. I can track—'

'Doesn't matter. Orrade and I have been hunting rogue Affinity beasts since we were fifteen. I've known them to disarm traps and lure hunters into dead-end ravines. I'm not leaving you until—'

'When?' She confronted him, face flushed, eyes furious. 'Until we reach Foenix Spar Stronghold?'

'No...' He took his time answering. He wanted her so angry she'd take a swing at him. He wanted an excuse to grab her.

And that shocked him. Startled, he took a step back.

'If you two are done arguing, I'll cook dinner.' Orrade pulled a rabbit from his pack and laid it on a flat stone, drawing his hunting knife. 'Bring me some firewood.'

'Is it wise to light a fire?' Florin asked.

'We haven't seen a patrol since yesterday morning. As long as we keep the fire small, we're safe,' Byren told her. 'I'll fetch firewood.'

'I'll help.'

Was she trying to drive him crazy? She was like an itch he could not scratch. He had to get out of here.

'Don't bother.' He headed up the path.

'I'm not useless!' she shouted after him.

He did not turn around. Didn't trust himself. Instead, he stared straight ahead as he rounded the bend in the path.

When he had an armful of wood, he returned to camp to find Florin gone and Orrade tending a small fire.

'Where is she?'

'You know, she managed for nineteen years before you came along.'

Orrade was right. Byren rubbed his jaw through three days growth.

Florin stalked into camp and dropped her firewood on the far side of the fire circle. With a disdainful glance in his direction, she walked off.

And he used to think he was good with women.

Orrade sliced up the rabbit meat and tossed it in the pan, where it sizzled. It smelled good but Byren couldn't sit still.

'I'll get more firewood.' He strode off.

FLORIN RETURNED TO camp with another armful of wood. There was no sign of Byren. As she dumped the wood on the pile, she told herself the less she saw of him, the better. But it rankled because he was clearly avoiding her. Every waking moment she was aware of him. She seemed to feel his gaze on her yet, whenever she looked in his direction, his face was turned away. It hurt...

'He doesn't mean it,' Orrade said.

'What?'

'He's like a bear with a sore tooth.'

'He thinks I'm useless.'

'He wants to make sure you reach Feid's stronghold in one piece. After all, now that your father's dead, you're all Leif has.'

She flushed with shame and chewed her bottom lip.

Orrade stirred the sizzling meat with his knife. He'd thrown in some wild onions and it smelled wonderful.

'You're a good person, Orrie. I hope...' She'd seen him frantic with worry for Byren. 'I hope you can be happy.'

Orrade's uncompromising black eyes held hers. 'We both know that's never going to happen.'

'Even so. I wish—'

'What happened the night of the fire?' Orrade gestured with the knife. 'I mean it was always there, this thing between you two, but it's become...'

'Unbearable.' It felt like her heart would break. Every day she spent with Byren, loving him, yet knowing that he could not love her was...

Florin met Orrade's shrewd eyes, swallowed and looked away. She owed him the truth. 'Cobalt left me tied up in the tent. I would have burned to death if Byren hadn't freed me. I guided him to the cliff—'

'You can't swim.'

'Didn't matter as long as Byren was safe. He saved me again in the water, found us a boat.' Now her throat grew so tight it was hard to speak. 'I'd just seen Seela die and I knew how much he loved her. He'd seen my father die. We... we wept in each other's arms and then, somehow, we were kissing. It was like touching flame to tinder.' She shook her head. 'I'd never known anything like it. I would've... But he didn't want me. He pushed me away, told me to cover myself. He made it clear he found me repulsive. I mean, why would he want a raw-boned mountain girl, someone who's more man than woman, when he could have p-perfect, pretty Queen Isolt?'

Furious, she wiped her cheeks and glared across the fire, daring Orrade to feel sorry for her.

He was silent for a moment, then he poked the fire. 'Did Byren say he didn't desire you?'

'He didn't have to. He could hardly look at me. And...' A sob caught her unawares. She fought it, her chest aching with the effort of holding back tears. 'C-Cobalt had already told me. Even with his hands on my b-breasts, he couldn't bring himself to... He found me repulsive.' A storm of tears shook her.

Orrade swore under his breath and came around the fire to hold her. Normally, she would never reveal weakness, but this was Orrie. And besides, the sobs tore from her with such force she couldn't catch her breath, couldn't think.

It was a couple of moments before she began to regain some control, and Orrade seemed to sense the right time to release her.

'Here.' He passed her a watered wine skin, then gestured to the pan. 'Watch this. I'll go tell Byren dinner's ready.'

'Don't—'

'I'll keep him talking. Give you time to...'

She nodded her thanks. 'I don't know why you're so good to me.'

He shook his head. 'Silly mountain girl.'

AS BYREN LIFTED a fallen branch, something moved in the corner of his eye. He caught a glimpse of a thick fur coat, powerful shoulders and the long, loping stride of an ulfr on the prowl. His hand went for his hunting knife.

This was ulfr territory, but that did not mean it was a beast from his pack... *his* pack? He gave himself a mental shake.

A moment later a second, larger ulfr came out of the shadows and stood watching him. Byren recognised the clever pack leader. The Affinity beast's head was level with Byren's waist.

For two heartbeats, the ulfr male stared at Byren, while the smaller beast stood further back in the trees, watching. Then the smaller ulfr made a strange sound in her throat. It was somewhere between a cough and a purr, and it seemed to be an invitation to play. The male trotted over to her and butted his shoulder against hers. She returned the gesture.

Intrigued, Byren crept closer. Now he could see them clearly. The male rested his head across the female's back. Again the male eyed Byren. It was not a threatening look, more an acknowledgement, from one leader to another.

The female made the inviting sound again and trotted off. The male hesitated, looking from Byren to her, before following her. He had only gone two body-lengths when she sprang out from behind a bush and knocked him to the ground. They rolled over and over, growling and nipping like a couple of pups. Byren grinned.

Seeing them together, he thought they were well suited: both powerful, both strong and independent.

The female rose to her feet, then walked away. The male hesitated and Byren approached, crouching low, hand extended. Perhaps he *was* mad, but he wanted to feel that soft, silvery fur again. He wanted to experience the sense of belonging he'd felt when surrounded by the pack in the seep.

The ulfr sniffed Byren's hand, breath hot on his skin. This close, the beast's scent hit him like a physical thing; strangely intoxicating, it was redolent with leaf litter and growing things. The smell took him to somewhere deep and primitive. Byren inhaled and discovered there was an added edge to the ulfr's scent tonight, musky and... The ulfr licked his hand, tongue rasping.

Byren dared to sink his fingers into that fur, rubbing under the beast's jaws. A surge of Affinity enveloped him. The big ulfr came a step closer and Byren brought his other hand up, to cradle the pack leader's head.

Looking into the ulfr's eyes, he saw inhuman intelligence.

The female gave that coughing purr again. It made the pack leader shiver, made Byren shiver. His heart quickened. The ulfr turned and looked over his shoulder towards the female. She stood on the edge of a rise. Lit by starlight, framed by two tall pines, she drew the male with such force that Byren felt the beast's need to go to her.

It was the same need that drove him to taunt Florin. A memory of his mountain girl shimmered in Byren's gaze, and he felt a bone-deep longing.

The pack leader made a huffing noise in his throat and shook his head, dislodging Byren's hands, before padding over to the female. She tossed her head, then went down the other side of the rise. The male followed her.

Byren felt drawn to follow them. As he moved forward, he saw other dark forms approach. Ulfrs of all sizes converged on the hollow. But, like Byren, they stopped at the tree line.

No bracken grew in the clearing and the ground was covered by pine needles. The two ulfrs stood in the centre of the clearing. Even from where he was, Byren could feel the pulsing power of an Affinity seep.

Another new seep. There had been so many since last spring.

The pack leaders frolicked in the pine needles, rolling and luxuriating in the seep's power like cats in sun. Then the female rolled to her feet, gave a little shiver and backed up towards the male, tail hitched to one side.

And Byren finally understood. How could he be so slow? He should have recognised the mating dance. The same restless energy drove him.

This gave him pause. Was he affected by the ulfrs' state? Was this why he was drawn to his mountain girl?

Shocked, he left the Affinity beasts to consummate their alliance, under the protection of their pack.

Stumbling through the starlit forest, he came to a bluff. From here, he could see the surrounding countryside spread out below him. Tree-covered hills stepped down to Lake Sapphire. The water reflected the starlit sky so perfectly that it seemed to be a window to another world.

A sound made him turn.

Orrade waited for a sign that he was welcome on the rocky ledge. Byren gave him a nod.

Orrade hesitated when there was still almost a body-length between them. He inhaled sharply. 'You stink of Affinity beast. The ulfr pack?'

Byren nodded.

'Is it safe to be here?'

He considered. The pack would never hurt him, and Orrade and Florin were *his* pack. If Orrade could scent ulfrs on him, the pack leader would have scented both Orrade and Florin on him. 'You're safe.'

Orrade didn't ask how he knew this. He joined Byren, shoulders touching. 'You didn't come back.'

'I had to think.'

'What's there to think about?' Orrade shrugged. 'The way you look at her... I swear, if I stepped between you two, I'd burn up.'

A laugh escaped Byren, but it was only a short reprieve from the restless frustration. He refused to be led by the needs of his body. He was a man, not a beast. The idea that he'd been influenced by his connection to the ulfrs disturbed him.

'I don't understand,' Orrade said. 'If you want her...'

'She deserves more than a quick roll in the hay.'

Orrade picked up a stone, weighed it in his hand then threw it down into the tree tops below them. 'She thinks you find her repulsive.'

'What? You're joking!'

'She believes you find her too mannish.'

A bitter bark of laughter shook Byren. 'I want her so bad I can't think straight.'

'If you went to her right now and told her—'

'I can't.' Byren rubbed his face. 'I'm betrothed to Isolt. I gave my word.'

'In another life.' Orrade gestured around them. 'You stand at a crossroads. You could slip away with Florin, find a quiet valley, build a cabin and build a life together. You could have her love, Byren, and be richer than any king.'

'If she'd have me...' He stared out at Rolencia, and for one moment he let himself imagine what it would be like. There was nothing he wanted more, but... 'It would mean leaving Cobalt on my father's throne. After all he's done to my family.'

'Yes, you'd have to walk away from that.'

'Could you walk away from Dovecote, knowing a Merofynian sits in your father's great hall and mistreats your people?'

Orrade met his eyes, the planes of his sharp face softened by starlight. 'I don't have a reason to walk away, so I find it easy to do my duty.'

Byren grimaced. 'Whether it's easy or not, I must do my duty.'

'You'll place ambition ahead of love?'

Was that censure in Orrade's voice? Resentment burned Byren. 'I never wanted to be the king's heir.'

'Would you have married Florin if Lence still lived?'

'In a heartbeat.'

'Even if it meant defying your parents?'

'They'd be relieved I wasn't...' He'd been about to say *a lover of men*. 'But Lence is dead and I know my duty.'

'And once you're king, you can set her up as your mistress or marry her off to young Chandler.' Orrade's voice was thin and bitter. 'It's not like he'd say no, if you wanted to bed his wife.'

Byren's first instinct was to grab Orrade by the throat and throttle him, but... he'd been tactless.

Before he could apologise, Orrade shrugged. 'I'm sorry. That was uncalled for. I know you won't be that kind of king.'

Shame held Byren silent.

'Dinner's ready. Are you coming?'

'In a moment.'

'Very well.' Orrade summoned a grin. 'But it'll serve you right if Florin and I eat the lot.'

Byren met his eyes. 'You've been a good friend to me. You deserve to be happy.'

'We don't always get what we deserve.'

'Cobalt will. I'll make sure of that.'

'I hope it's worth it.' Orrade went back the way he'd come.

Chapter Thirty-Six

Florin's stomach rumbled as she stirred the dinner. What was taking them so long? She heard a noise and looked up, expecting to see Orrade and Byren, but the path was empty. Probably just some forest creature.

What if Orrie said something to Byren? She should take her travelling kit and go right now. The secret pass wasn't far from here. She should go while she still had her dignity. Then Byren wouldn't feel obliged to escort her all the way to Foenix Spar. The more she thought about it, the more she liked the idea. No excruciating goodbyes. No more reminders that she was the gauche mountain girl who'd thrown herself at her king.

A pebble clicked behind her; she turned to find two men about to grab her. They tackled her to the ground. Merofynians, by their muffled curses. She writhed and twisted, trying to break free. Uppermost in her mind was the danger to Byren. Just as she drew breath to shout a warning, a hand clamped over her mouth.

Boots appeared in front of her. 'Let's see who this is.'

Her two captors hauled her upright. Panting with fury, she faced a Merofynian veteran. He was shorter than her and missing two of his front teeth.

'That's not Byren's molly-boy.' He spat.

'Yer sure? 'ere, lemme check.' One of her captors reached down between her legs. 'Nah, nothin' but—'

She bucked with such fury her arm slipped his grip and she elbowed him in the face. Before she could free her other arm, a third man grabbed her.

The injured man staggered back, spitting blood. His companions laughed.

Enraged, he lunged for her.

The veteran stepped between them. 'You'll get yer chance, Teg. Tell yer what, yer can have her but only after we've captured Byren. Now shut up an' get into position.'

'Shouldn't we send for the rest of the patrol?' one of them asked.

'Yer wanna split the reward?' Teg snorted.

The others looked to the veteran.

'Teg's right. Split between eleven, we'll be rich. Split between forty, we're drunk and back at work with a hangover tomorrow. Now go.'

They melted into the trees. Florin despaired. How would Byren escape?

'Over there.' The veteran jerked his head, and Florin's captors dragged her up against the rock wall, under the overhang.

There was a scuffle in the bushes along the path and a grunt of pain, followed by a curse and another grunt. Two of the Merofynians dragged Orrade into the light of the camp fire. He shook his head, blinking blood from his eyes.

'It's the molly-boy,' Teg announced.

The other one kicked Orrade's knees out from under him and caught him by the hair as he fell to the ground. Pulling Orrade's head up to reveal his throat, Teg drew his knife and looked to the veteran. 'Kill 'im?'

'Did I tell yer to kill him?' The veteran sounded exasperated. 'He's the kin-slayer's favourite. He's useful.'

'If Byren killed 'is own sister, why would 'e care what happened to 'is molly-boy?'

Florin bit her captor's hand, gulped a deep breath and screamed, 'Run, Byren. Mero—'

A punch to the jaw cut her off. The world swung around her and she didn't know which way was up. The eerie howl of an ulfr cut the night. Even through her confusion, Florin could sense the Merofynians' fear.

The veteran caught Florin's hair, pulling her face close to his. 'If I hadn't promised yer to Teg, I'd cut yer throat for that.' He backed off. 'Bring her down here, the molly-boy too.'

'How're we gonna catch the kin-slayer now?' someone muttered as they all gathered in the centre of the gully, churning up the mulch and leaf litter. 'They say 'e's a giant of man. They say 'e killed a leogryf single-handed. Took down a wyvern with only 'is hunting kni—'

Thwack. The veteran clipped him over the head. 'He's just one man. There's eleven of us, an' we've got his friends. He'll come quietly, if he knows what's good for him.'

They formed a circle around Florin and Orrade. Her jaw throbbed and she tasted blood where her lip had torn on her teeth. She prodded her teeth. None were loose, thank Halcyon. Chill damp seeped up through her boots as their combined weight made them sink into the boggy soil.

'Tie them two together,' the veteran ordered.

Florin was shoved against Orrade's back and Teg bound their arms to their sides, securing them from shoulder to waist. He didn't miss the chance to fondle Florin's breasts. She turned her face away, prompting him to pinch her nipple. The pain made her jerk and Orrade had to adjust his weight. Their boots squelched in the sticky bog, sinking deeper.

Teg chuckled as he finished tying their restraints. Leaning in close to Florin, he ran his hand up between her legs, while rubbing himself on her thigh.

'Feel this. 'ard as a rock, I am. I'm gonna teach yer the difference between...'

The veteran caught him by the ear and dragged him over to stand in the outer circle. The Merofynians had formed a circle facing outward. Florin felt Orrade adjust his feet and had to adjust hers. The thick, sticky bog clung to her boots so firmly she could hardly lift her leg.

'Byren Kin-slayer, we know yer out there!' the veteran yelled. 'Give yerself up before we cut yer molly-boy's throat.'

'Don't do it,' Orrade cried. 'Leave—'

His head snapped back. There was a *clunk* as his skull collided with Florin's. Her teeth clicked down on her lip and blood filled her mouth. She would have staggered, but her feet were stuck in the bog.

One of the Merofynians steadied her, even as he cursed the bog. 'Almost lost me bloody boot.'

'Shut up an' watch the trees,' the veteran snapped. He raised his voice. 'Well, kin-slayer, what'll it be?'

Florin lifted her head. Beyond her captors' shoulders, she saw the camp fire under the overhang. Its glow painted the rock orange. The stone overhang jutted out thick as the eaves of a thatched roof, and above that...

Stood Byren with a huge Affinity beast at his side.

BYREN HAD BEEN about to enter camp when he heard Florin's cry. A gut-deep fear tore at him and he heard an ulfr's haunting howl.

His first instinct was to go to Florin, but he made himself retreat along the path and climb up the far side of the overhang. There he stretched out on the rock and edged forward on his belly until he could look down into the gully.

Eleven Merofynians had captured Orrade and Florin. Fear for them chilled him and the ulfr howled, others joined him, howling in sympathy.

Enraged by his impotence, Byren watched as one of the men bound Orrade and Florin, then groped his mountain girl. Byren wanted to tear his throat out. The urge was so powerful he clenched his teeth until his jaw ached.

One of the Merofynians reached over and hauled the man away from Florin. Just as well. Byren was having trouble thinking clearly.

Something nudged Byren's left thigh and he glanced over his shoulder to find the ulfr pack leader creeping forward, belly pressed to the stone.

As the ulfr joined him, Byren swung his arm over the beast's neck. He could feel power radiating from the ulfr's body. Grateful for the beast's support, he buried his head in the ulfr's neck. Felt the power of the creature and the welcome of the pack.

'Byren Kin-slayer, we know yer out there!' the Merofynian leader yelled. 'Give yerself up before we cut yer molly-boy's throat.'

'Don't do it,' Orrade cried. 'Leave—'

One of them hit him and his head rocked back, slamming into Florin so that she swayed.

A roaring filled Byren's ears and he sprang to his feet with the ulfr at his side. From this vantage point, he saw dark shadows slinking into position in the trees. The Merofynians were surrounded. Byren could see the ulfrs' eyes gleaming from the shadows.

The man who'd pinched Florin's breast pointed and cursed. He panicked and tried to sprint towards the safety of the fire, but his feet seemed trapped. He lurched, falling to his hands and knees. Before his companions could haul him upright, an ulfr dashed into the gully, tore out his throat, then retreated into the trees.

For a heartbeat, the Merofynians stood stunned; then they swore and shouted, waving their weapons at the gleaming eyes watching them from the shadows under the trees.

The Merofynians' leader spotted Byren and pointed. He shouted something, but Byren couldn't hear clearly. Everything seemed too loud, yet strangely distorted.

As soon as the rest of the Merofynians saw Byren, they tried to run. Some lurched forward and fell to their hands and knees, others managed only one step then collapsed. Ulfrs attacked the instant their prey were vulnerable. The beasts dashed into the gully, tore out throats, then retreated before the men could respond. Soon the rich scent of blood filled the air as it soaked into the greedy earth.

The pack leader howled in exultation and Byren shared the beast's savage joy.

While the Merofynians fell around them, Florin cooperated with Orrade, trying to work themselves free, but they'd both sunk calf-deep in the sticky bog. She caught a glimpse of gleaming ulfr eyes in the tree line and felt the instinctive fear of the hunted.

Two paces from her, a man struggled to free his legs but an ulfr took him down, tearing out his throat and spraying them both with blood. Florin shivered.

All around her, as the Merofynians cursed and struggled to escape the bog, silvery, sleek shadows darted in, avoided the trapped men's wild strikes and ripped out throats. She saw two Merofynians die in as many heartbeats.

Her gaze was drawn back to Byren. His hand rested on the head of the big ulfr at his side and the beast had its mouth open, almost as if it was laughing.

Men screamed. The veteran yelled, 'Hold your place, weapons up, present a united front.'

But terror overcame training.

Cursing, the veteran fought the bog and lurched over to Florin, catching her by the front of her jerkin.

She'd almost worked her legs free and fell forward onto her knees. This pulled Orrade over so that he lay on her back struggling against their bonds. His weight pressed her down into the bog and her knees sank deeper. With her arms bound, she fought to keep her face out of the bog.

'Call off your dogs, kin-slayer!' the veteran yelled, and Florin felt Orrie go very still. 'Call them off, or I'll cut his throat.'

Florin didn't dare move.

BYREN CURSED AS the Merofynian leader pulled Florin to her knees, grabbed Orrade by his hair and held a blade to his throat. A roaring filled Byren's head and he leaped off the overhang.

The man tried to bring his knife up, but he was too late. The force of Byren's attack drove the Merofynian backwards, tearing his hand from Orrade's head. Byren felt the man's rib cage collapse as he hit boggy ground.

For a heartbeat the Merofynian lay there looking up, mouth opened in a gasp, head buried cheek-deep in the bog. Then blood poured from his mouth.

Byren struggled to his feet, fighting the sucking action of the bog. At least four men still struggled with the ulfrs. The rest were down and bleeding.

Seeing this, Byren staggered over to Florin and Orrade. They lay on their sides and had sunk deeper into the mud as they struggled to keep their faces above the bog. Byren knelt beside Florin and reached for the rope binding them. Her mouth was bloodied and swollen, eyes wide and frightened.

Seeing something behind him, she sucked in a breath and shouted a warning.

He turned, blocking reflexively. A sword struck his knife, skittered down the blade, sprang off the tip and continued in a stroke which would have ended in his thigh had not an ulfr attacked at that instant.

The beast leapt onto the man's back, driving him past Byren, so that he fell across Florin and Orrade. There was a sickening crack as the ulfr caught the man's neck between its jaws and snapped his spine.

Byren rolled the man off Florin and Orrade, to reveal only upper arms and shoulders protruding from the bog. Grabbing their arms, he hauled with all his strength. The bog resisted.

Desperate, muscles straining, joints popping, Byren pulled them both out. Florin and Orrade sprang free of the mud with such momentum that Byren tumbled backwards, landing on someone's legs.

The legs began to slide out from under him.

He turned, ready to defend himself, but found an ulfr dragging a man's body away. All around him the Affinity beasts were dragging the dead into the trees.

Something shifted and sounds returned to normal. He could hear Orrade and Florin coughing. Blood-soaked mud covered their faces, clung to their hair and slid down their torsos. Fighting the sucking action of the bog, Byren crawled over and cut the rope that bound them.

'Freak!' A Merofynian waved his sword from the tree line. 'You're as much a beast as your namesake, King Byren the Fourth.'

Lurching to his feet, Byren staggered, taking one awkward step, then another. He was almost out of the bog when the man's companion grabbed him and the pair ran off.

Byren surveyed the gully. An ulfr dragged the last body out of sight. The remainder seemed to be only body parts, or bodies so deeply embedded in the mud only an arm or leg remained. And these sank from sight even as he watched.

From the shadows beneath the trees, he heard the crunching of bones. As soon as Orrade and Florin were on their feet, he dropped to his knees, retching. When he could throw up no more, he lifted his head, to find Florin offering him a wine skin.

He swilled a mouthful around, spat it out, then took a big gulp and looked up. She'd heard what those men said. Did she despise him?

But her expression was impossible to interpret through the mud caked on her face 'Are you all right, Byren?'

'Are you?'

'I'm alive.' She grinned, teeth very white.

They both staggered over to the camp. It was good to get firm ground under his feet.

Orrade was already kneeling by the fire, building it up.

'What about you?' Byren asked. 'Are you all right?'

Orrade poked the meat. 'Dinner's burned. Sorry.'

Byren gave a bark of laughter, then sat down abruptly as his knees gave way. 'I couldn't eat anyway.'

'Will the ulfrs deal with the men that got away?' Florin asked.

Byren was amazed that she could be so matter of fact. He considered her question, then shook his head. 'The pack's had more than enough to eat.'

'Then we can't stay here. Those Merofynians were part of a larger patrol.' She gestured to the mountains. 'We should make for the secret pass. Put as much distance between them and us as we can.'

'Burnt dinner and now we have to walk all night.' Orrade gathered his travelling pack. 'I guess that means a hot bath is out of the question.'

Chapter Thirty-Seven

'FYN, DID YOU see Loyalty?' Isolt called from the landing halfway up the stairs. The wyvern swooped in to perch on the balustrade with the glowing platter.

Fyn nodded and waved then turned to Dunstany. 'How did you make the metal glow? Is it an Affinity trick?'

'Why use Affinity when ingenuity will do? I crushed hercinia feathers to make glowing paint,' Dunstany said. They stood on the terrace not far from the stairs. 'Rhalwyn came to me because the warmer weather's been making the Affinity beasts restless. Now they can play at night.'

'Good idea,' Fyn said. He returned to his earlier point. 'Yorale might be loyal, but I don't like to see too much power concentrated in one man.'

'It is unfortunate,' Dunstany agreed. 'For hundreds of years, the rivalry between Dunistir and Yoraltir Estates maintained the balance of power, but my grandfather was cursed by bad luck. His three sons died without heirs and the distant cousin who stands to inherit is a fool.

My masquerade as Lord Dunstany can only last a few more years, before people become suspicious. Duncaer will inherit and ruin the estate with his gambling. When I think of my people being turned out of their homes...' His voice grew thick with emotion. 'And there's nothing I can do to prevent it.'

Fyn empathised, but he had frustrations of his own. 'Why didn't Wythrod make camp further back? The pincer attack would have worked.'

'Young men think they are immortal and feel they have something to prove.'

'Says the old man of ninety-four.'

Dunstany grinned, reminding Fyn that he was really Siordun. If only Siordun was the heir to Dunistir Estate. Isolt could have used his support. A thought occurred to Fyn. 'How do you fool old Lord Dunstany's friends?'

'He didn't have any close friends. All the men of his generation had died off. It's hard to imagine, but my grandfather was nearly forty when Lord Yorale was born. Even the men of Yorale's generation are dying of old age. When a man is as powerful and long lived as Dunstany, he tends to lose friends and gather enemies. Men envy him and plot his downfall. In my Dunstany disguise I haven't let myself get close to anyone for fear of slipping and revealing my secret.'

'Don't you get lonely?'

'The mage took me when I was five.' He shrugged. 'I didn't have time for friends.'

It was a sad. Fyn gestured to Rhalwyn and Cortomir, who were bickering over whose turn it was to throw the platter. 'Speaking of friends, that's an unlikely pairing.'

Admonishing them not to fight, the queen headed down the steps.

'Isolt trusts Yorale,' Fyn said. 'But of all the lords and their heirs, I trust Camoric. Did you hear? Isolt made his grandfather her lord admiral.'

'Winning the favour of a vulnerable young queen can

be more trouble than it's worth. Don't worry, Byren will sort out the nobles.'

Resentment gnawed at Fyn. He'd had to do all the ground work. He told himself it was unworthy of him, and turned to welcome Isolt as she joined them. 'We—'

'Corto, don't!' Rhalwyn cried.

They looked up to see Cortomir astride the wyvern, which was perched on the balustrade landing, silhouetted against the first stars of evening.

'Get down, before you fall down!' Dunstany yelled.

Cortomir whooped and waved. The wyvern leaped out and up, taking to the air. As she fought to gain height, wings labouring, the foenix flew alongside them. 'Corto!' Rhalwyn ran down the steps, trying to catch up with the Affinity beasts.

Fyn, Isolt and Dunstany took to their heels.

Wings battling valiantly, the wyvern clipped the terrace railing balustrade and swooped out over the lawn. One wing tip skimmed the water of the fountain, sending up an arc of spray.

Fyn rounded the fountain in time to see the wyvern land at a run. She lost her footing and tumbled, sending the boy sprawling across the grass.

As Dunstany reached them, Cortomir and the wyvern came to their feet, dusting themselves off. The spar lad laughed. Fyn wanted to throttle him. What would he say to Warlord Cortovar if his son got himself killed?

'Corto!' Rhalwyn hugged the lad, then shook him, then hugged him again. He turned to Fyn and the others, beaming with pride. 'Did you see? I wish I was as small as—'

'We're lucky you're not as big a fool as him.' Dunstany snapped.

'I thought I could do it.' Cortomir turned to Isolt. 'When Loyalty is bigger, she can carry you!'

'Nonsense, people don't ride Affinity Beasts.' Isolt went over to Loyalty.

'Maybe they could. There are myths. I thought them only stories, but...' Fyn glanced to Dunstany.

He leant heavily on his cane and staff, and appeared exhausted; but only a moment before, he had sprinted across the courtyard. If one of Dunstany's enemies had seen him out-race Fyn, the charade would be over. The outraged Merofynian nobles would turn on the mage's agent.

While Rhalwyn and Cortomir chattered, and Isolt assured herself Loyalty was unharmed, Fyn edged closer to Dunstany. 'You forgot your disguise.'

'I know...'

They both glanced up at the three-storey buildings overlooking the terrace. Several chambers glowed. One of the old servants might have been watching.

Dunstany grimaced. 'We can only hope if someone was at one of the windows, they were watching the boy flying the wyvern.'

Fyn nodded and offered his arm, raising his voice. 'Here, let me help you.'

He 'helped' the old noble scholar over to the fountain, lowering him to sit on the rim. Isolt was inspecting Loyalty's wings for damage. Fyn lowered his voice. 'Did you find anything about bonding with Affinity beasts?'

'There was nothing in the palace library. And I haven't been back to Ostron Isle to check the mage's library. I suspect all the stories I've read date from before we had written history. It is as if they were memorised and adapted for different audiences. They're inconsistent and contradictory. For all I know, they are complete fabrications.'

'Well, we just saw Cortomir fly on Loyalty's back. That confirms one of the myths.' Fyn frowned. 'What if Cortomir bonds with Loyalty? He's spending more time with the wyvern than Isolt now. Maybe it wouldn't be such a bad—'

'It would be disastrous. He's a hostage, held as surety of his father's good behaviour, while the wyvern is the Merofynian royal symbol. It would be better to kill Loyalty.'

'It may yet come to that.' Fyn had felt the force of the Affinity beasts' hunger for power. 'Back on your yacht, they nearly drained me. And Isolt has no innate Affinity.'

'Then she's safe.'

'From what?' Isolt asked, joining them.

Fyn did not want to admit they'd been discussing her pet.

The young queen looked from him to Dunstany, then back again. Her eyes darkened and her plucked brows drew together. 'Don't you two start.'

'Start what?' Fyn asked.

'Ignoring me.' Her eyes blazed. 'The lords met behind my back with the merchants and the captain of the city-watch. Even the captain of my own queen's guards presumes to tell me what to do.'

Dunstany stiffened and came to his feet. He frowned at something behind Fyn. 'What's this?'

Fyn glanced over his shoulder to see Captain Elrhodoc and four of the queen's guards striding down the terrace steps towards them. They carried torches, and the leaping flames made the night seem dark.

'Sylion's luck. Someone *was* watching,' Fyn muttered.

'If they arrest me, you two know nothing,' Dunstany said. 'I fooled everyone, you understand?'

'We can't abandon you,' Isolt protested, dismayed.

'You must, or you'll fall with me.'

Fyn's mind raced. 'If the worst happens, I'll go to Dunstany's town house. Gwalt can send a message to the mage.'

'Yes.' Isolt sounded relieved. 'Tsulamyth will find a way to save you, Siordun.'

He glanced to them. His mouth opened as if he was about to say something, then he turned to face his accusers.

GARZIK GRINNED. THE returning raiders had been spotted by the settlement's lookout, and fires burned to guide them up the narrow bay. Every door and shutter stood open, and the whole settlement lined the shore and the jetty, bringing lanterns to lend the scene a festive air. Children danced and shouted, scampering about in excitement.

When he'd first seen the settlement, he'd found it hard to tell the men and women apart. They all wore breeches and thigh-length smocks. Now they looked normal to Garzik. Emotion welled up in him, making his chest tight and his throat ache. Now it felt like home.

Garzik spotted one of the Utland ships at the jetty and wondered who captained it. The settlement had five ships, but the only captain he'd met was Feodan, who'd led the raid when he was enslaved and Rusan was made captain of the captured merchant ship.

'Wynn!' Cheeky-puss jumped up and down on the shore, waving madly until he spotted her.

'Ilonja!' He couldn't help grinning as she ran along the shore, keeping pace with the ship. 'Careful, you'll trip.'

'What?' She dodged some children and ran slap-bang into a group of beardless. They set her on her feet with an admonishment to watch where she was going. She brushed them off and kept running. 'What, Wynn?'

He laughed and shook his head. When next he caught sight of Ilonja, her older sister was telling her off while she danced with impatience. The sisters had both joined the beardless after Vultar's attack. They'd sworn off men, vowing to die in defence of their home. How many women were pregnant because of Vultar's men? Garzik wasn't about to ask. He was glad Ilonja had hidden in the woodheap. Her older sister, Sarijana, had not been so lucky. Ilonja had always meant to become one of the beardless. But Sarijana...

Garzik snuck a look at Rusan and Olbin as they waited for the ropes to be secured to the jetty. After their daring raid on Port Mero, they could have asked the beautiful songstress to be theirs, then gone to the elders for permission to marry, but there was no point now.

As they drew up to the jetty, anxious faces searched the deck of Rusan's ship, looking for loved ones.

'Where's the rest of your crew?' someone yelled.

'They fell in battle when we were escaping from Port Mero!' Rusan yelled.

'Port Mero?' Word spread. People marvelled at their daring, but there were also shocked faces. Some questioned the cost.

Olbin nudged Rusan. 'Ma is not happy with us.'

In the excited crowd, their mother was an island of stillness. Like Olbin, Lauvra was tall and broad-shouldered, but she was a thinker like Rusan.

'Da!' Luvrenc shouted and waved. He nudged Garzik. 'That's my last father. He's a famous ship's captain!'

'Feodan!' Olbin shouted and waved. 'Uncle Feo!'

Garzik recognised Luvrenc's father, feeling the slow burn of anger. Thanks to Feodan, he was here and not in Rolencia with Byren.

The gangplank dropped into place. Luvrenc ran down into his father's arms. Rusan and Olbin went next, with Garzik following.

Captain Feodan laughed and slapped Rusan and Olbin on their shoulders, congratulating them in one breath and teasing them about their near-beardlessness with the next. Then he asked how Luvrenc had done. Garzik understood that Feodan had taken Olbin and Rusan to sea to groom them for command, and when they were ready, he'd given them their first ship. Now they were doing the same for his son.

As Rusan and Olbin made their way through the crowd towards their mother, Garzik tagged along. Their return with a hold full of stores stolen from under the hot-landers' very noses was a cause for celebration, and there was much mock-punching, laughter and good-natured wrestling.

But not everyone was smiling. Less than half their crew had survived. Garzik spotted the surviving twin with a woman. She wept in his arms, while three small children clung to their legs, sobbing.

Rusan and Olbin hugged their mother. Lauvra pinched their bristly chins. 'I send men away to raid and I get boys in return!'

Olbin laughed. Rusan slung an arm around Garzik, drawing him forward. 'Blame Wynn, he shaved us to aid our disguise as hot-landers.'

'Port Mero, Rus?' His mother eyed him. 'Consider the cost. Fourteen of your men lost for the sake of one full hold.'

Rusan looked down. Garzik was about to spring to his defence when Feodan joined them.

'Rus has won more than a full hold, Lauvra. His daring will raise our standing with the other peoples of the Northern Dawn.' He ruffled Rusan's hair as if he was ten, not nearly twenty. Three fingers were missing from Feodan's hand and he was a mass of scars. Garzik wondered how long before he retired from the sea. There were very few old men in the Utland settlement. 'You should be proud of your boys, sister.'

'I am,' she said, but she frowned at Rusan. 'Is reputation more important than the safety of your men, Rus?'

He shook his head. 'It was a calculated gamble. We had Wynn. He knew the port and he knew the language.'

Lauvra did not look convinced. 'I'd rather a full hold taken from safe targets than you seek glory at the cost of—'

'It wasn't Rusan's fault.' Garzik could not remain silent any longer. Glancing over his shoulder, he spotted Vesnibor consoling Jost's mother over the loss of her three sons. 'Rusan would have gotten away unscathed if Jost hadn't put personal vengeance ahead of the crew's safety.'

Lauvra and Feodan exchanged looks.

'Jost always was ambitious,' Feodan muttered. 'You should have—'

'I promised him the other ship.' Rusan's eyes glittered with anger. 'But he chose vengeance!'

'I don't like it.' Lauvra muttered. 'This could tear our people apart.'

Feodan nodded.

Just then, Ilonja threw her arms around Garzik. 'Wynn!'

He laughed and hugged her. 'Are you a fierce beardless now?'

'As fierce and beardless as you!' She tapped his chin, which still showed no signs of whiskers. 'What happened to your voice?'

'Someone tried to choke me.' Garzik glanced to the others. Olbin was organising the unloading of supplies for the feast, Rusan was talking with Feodan, and Lauvra was deep in conversation with the elders. Garzik turned back to Ilonja. 'Has there been any more trouble with Vultar?'

She shook her head. 'When Captain Feo came back, he stayed to be sure we could defend ourselves.'

'Carry this.' Olbin thrust a wheel of cheese into Garzik's arms. 'For the feast!'

Before long, everyone headed up the path from the jetty to the long-house, laden with treats.

Garzik walked several paces behind Lauvra, Feodan and Rusan. He had no trouble with the Utland language now, but the rapidity of their speech—and the way they peppered their conversation with names he did not know—made it hard to follow.

From what he gathered, Rusan was asking Feodan for help building a ship. By the time they reached the patch of level ground in front of the long-hall, it was decided the merchant ship would be kept for short trips between the Utland isles. Meanwhile, Feodan and his men would help Rusan construct the new vessel, which would not be ready until the following spring.

That would be too late for Garzik. Rolencian battles were traditionally fought during summer. Byren would probably win his kingdom before Garzik could return.

The thought made him smile. If that happened, he would rejoice for Byren and his brother. But how would he win a place in King Byren the Fifth's honour guard if the war was over and he was nothing but an ex-slave?

Olbin slung one arm around Garzik's shoulders and the other around Rusan. He turned them to face the long narrow bay. The sky was completely clear, ablaze with stars. The trail of people coming up from the jetty parted around them.

Below, the ships sat silvered by starlight, on the mirror-like bay, as if they floated on a sea of stars.

'Home.' Olbin's voice caught.

'Why you...' Rusan thumped him. 'You're as soft as a hot-lander.'

Olbin tackled him and the pair of them wrestled back and forth. Olbin was bigger, but Rusan knew all his moves. Watching them, it occurred to Garzik that they'd grown up wrestling like this. He envied them. There'd been too many years between him and Orrade. And besides, Orrade had always been closest to Byren. Garzik had only ever been the little brother, trotting along behind.

'Boys?' Lauvra came to the door of the long-hall. 'Come in and take pride of place at the table.'

Chapter Thirty-Eight

FYN FACED THE queen's guards, ready to stand by Dunstany, but Captain Elrhodoc ignored the old lord and marched over to the boys.

He seized Cortomir, shoving the lad towards his men. 'Take the spar brat and hang him from the linden tree—'

'No!' Rhalwyn tried to free his friend.

'What's going on, captain?' Isolt asked, striding towards him with the Affinity beasts at her side. Loyalty's tail lashed back and forth, and Resolute's crest rose in warning.

While his men tried to pry the two lads apart, Elrhodoc gave Isolt an abbreviated bow. 'It's Centicore Spar, my queen. They've attacked Benetir Estate again. Murdered Lady Gennalla and—'

'Da wouldn't!' Cortomir objected. 'He gave his word.'

'The word of a barbarian?' Elrhodoc sneered. 'We know what that's worth!'

One of the queen's guards clipped the lad over the ear. 'Shut up, brat.'

'Stop this,' Isolt ordered. When he did not respond, she plunged into the melee. 'Let the boys go.'

Fyn had to fight the instinct to intervene. The queen's guards had to obey her of their own volition, or they ceased to be her guards.

Either they hadn't heard her or they were too preoccupied with the lads. Rhalwyn bit the guard grabbing him, then shoved the man with all his might. The guard staggered, colliding with Isolt. Fyn darted in to catch her. At the same instant, Loyalty screeched and went for the man, who drew his sword.

Resolute uttered a piercing cry and lashed out with his foreleg. The spur sliced clean through the man's arm and he screamed.

'Stop!' Dunstany slammed his staff on the ground and the orb flashed brilliantly.

Momentarily stunned, everyone hesitated.

The orb of Dunstany's staff settled down to a silvery glow, and Fyn could feel Affinity emanating from it. Naturally the wyvern and foenix were attracted to the power. Dunstany lowered the staff tip a little. Both Affinity beasts rubbed themselves against the orb like cats.

'Consider yourselves lucky I was here,' Dunstany told Elrhodoc and his men. 'Otherwise not one of you would be alive now. Never threaten the queen!'

'We weren't threatening her,' Elrhodoc protested. His four companions shifted uneasily and let the boys go. They went over to the Affinity beasts. 'We were arresting the spar brat.'

'Cortomir is my apprentice Affinity beast-keeper,' Isolt said.

'He's a hostage,' Elrhodoc snapped. 'His life is forfeit.'

'Da would never break his word,' Cortomir insisted. When neither the captain nor the queen acknowledged him, he turned to Fyn. 'Da wouldn't, I swear.'

'Besides,' Isolt said, her voice icy, 'I'm not in the habit of killing children.'

'What good is a hostage if you won't execute him?' Elrhodoc countered.

'They must have killed Da and elected another warlord,' Cortomir announced as if solving a puzzle. 'They wanted a warlord who would lead an attack on Benetir Estate. Da wouldn't so they k—' A sob shook him. 'They killed him!'

Rhalwyn threw his arms around the lad.

'Oh, Corto...' Isolt whispered.

'The boy's right,' Fyn said. 'His father must have lost the leadership of the spar. We can't execute the lad for something he has no control over.'

'We have to execute him, or the spar warlords will think us weak.' Elrhodoc was unmoved.

'They won't care.' Fyn tried to keep the frustration from his voice. 'Think it through. They killed the lad's father. The boy means nothing to them. Killing him is pointless.'

'He's a symbol of spar aggression. We can't appear weak.' Elrhodoc looked Fyn up and down, making no attempt to hide his contempt. 'He has to die.'

Isolt trembled with rage. 'If you think I'm ordering this boy's death, you don't know me.'

'I know this much,' the captain told Isolt. 'Women don't have the stomach for war. They should keep their noses out of what doesn't concern them.'

Fyn glanced to Dunstany. This was a disaster.

'As for you, Lord Protector...' Elrhodoc turned to Fyn. 'If you don't have the stomach to do what's got to be done, I'll—'

'Stop it! You're upsetting Loyalty and Resolute. I don't know how long I can hold them,' Dunstany warned. 'We need to settle the beasts. Come along, boys.'

He walked off with both Affinity beasts and boys. They moved in a silvery sphere created by the glowing orb. As Fyn watched them pass around the hedge, he realised Dunstany would have to satiate the Affinity beasts to calm them, and that would weaken him. Just when they needed him.

Isolt took a step closer to Fyn. She was very, very angry, but also terrified. She'd been reprimanded by the captain of her own guards.

Fyn set out to divert Elrhodoc. 'How do you know that Centicore Spar has broken their word? It could be mere rumour. Who told you about the attack?'

'The Benetir girl escaped with her little brother.'

'Benowyth is her nephew,' Isolt corrected. 'And if Sefarra is here, I must see her. Where is she?'

'In the war chamber.'

Isolt held out her arm. 'Lead me to her, captain.'

Years of training made Elrhodoc take the queen's arm.

Fyn hid a smile. With that command, Isolt had re-asserted her authority. Now he went one step further.

'I know where the war-table is. My queen?' Fyn offered Isolt his arm. She released Elrhodoc and Fyn walked off with her. 'We must interview Lady Sefarra to determine who led the attack.'

Fyn could feel Isolt trembling. To give her time to recover, he said, 'But first we must be sure the Affinity beasts are settled.'

And they headed for the grotto, leaving Elrhodoc stranded. The further they got from the captain, the better Fyn felt.

At last they reached the pond. A soft glow came from the grotto's entrance, reflecting in the water. Pale, silvery beams pierced the dome's glass panels, reaching into the night.

Isolt squeezed Fyn's hand. 'Thank you.'

'Cortomir is safe for now,' Fyn said. 'As long as Dunstany and the Affinity beasts are with him...'

'I hate him!'

Fyn didn't need to ask who she meant. 'We won't go back until—'

'I'm not stupid. I grew up with this. I thought I'd

escaped, but...' Her voice caught on a sob. 'I'll never be free. Not as long as I'm queen.'

Fyn looked for something to cheer her, and noticed a winged creature fluttering in one of the beams of light.

'Would you look at that? If I didn't know better, I'd swear it was a lacewing moth.' He frowned. 'They feed on the pollen of the starkiss flowers. Back at the abbey, Master Sunseed had a theory that the moth and flower formed a relationship, because wherever starkisses were found in the wild, lacewing moths would be nearby.'

The moth hovered over the grotto, weaving in and out of the silvery shaft of light.

'It's very beautiful,' Isolt whispered.

'But odd,' Fyn said. 'In the Rolencian foothills, the lacewings grow only as big as my hand. That moth's wingspan has to be from my finger tips to my elbow. Why would they grow so big?'

'Oh, look.' Isolt pointed. 'Here comes another lacewing, and it's even bigger.'

Sure enough, the wingspan of this moth had to be the length of Fyn's arm. Now five lacewings danced in the silvery beams.

'They're attracted to the light,' Isolt said.

'That and Affinity,' Fyn guessed, as it all fell into place. 'We distil dreamless-sleep from starkiss pollen. It contains a kind of Affinity. Like all Affinity beasts, lacewings are attracted to power. Since last spring, several new seeps have opened up in Rolencia. Has Merofynia—'

'Yes. Back when the Power-workers were trying to heal my father, I overheard them talking about the new Affinity seeps. They said it was an omen.'

'Did the abbot or abbess deal with the untamed power of these new seeps?' Fyn asked.

'Yes. No... I don't know. They should have, but everything's been topsy-turvy since Palatyne declared himself overlord.'

Fyn nodded. 'I think the lacewings have been gorging

themselves on new seeps, accelerating their growth. I wonder...' Fyn held up his ring hand, calling on his limited Affinity. He felt it gather and urged the power to focus in the stone, which glowed pale silver.

'The lacewings are coming over!' Isolt was delighted. 'Can you make the stone glow brighter? I want to see them clearly.'

Could he? He focused and was rewarded with a bright flare, just as the first lacewing fluttered down.

Horns, claws and a questing mouth with a spike-tipped tongue...

Isolt gasped.

Fyn grabbed her hand, turned and ran for the palace.

As they darted around bushes and between fruit trees, Fyn felt something rush by his head.

Fear spurred him on. He dragged Isolt with him. Another lacewing just missed his head. He ducked. They passed the hedge, then the fountain, ran up the steps. When they reached the terrace, it was deserted.

Where were the queen's guard when she needed them?

A lacewing dived, hitting Fyn square between the shoulders. He felt the impact but kept running, intent on getting Isolt to safety. The creature's slight weight bounced as it clung to his shoulders.

Something brushed the back of his neck. He felt a sharp sting and a dreamlike peace descended on him.

Why was he running?

Why was this beautiful girl pulling him towards the palace, away from this starlit night? He planted his feet.

'Fyn, what's wrong?' Her frantic eyes searched his face then widened in horror. 'There are wings behind your shoulders. Cyena help me, there's one on your back!'

Her words made sense, but only if he concentrated, and the moment she stopped speaking he was captivated by her beauty. He wanted her, always had.

She tugged on his arm, opened those luscious lips to speak and...

He pulled her close, caught her face in his hands and kissed her. For a heartbeat, she did not move. Then she bit his lip, hard.

The pain cleared his head. He pulled back, shocked.

She sprang behind him to attack the lacewing. He fell to his knees under the onslaught of her pounding fists.

'It's feeding off you, Fyn. Fight it!' Whimpering with fear and horror, she dropped her shawl over the creature and pulled at it.

Fyn felt the lacewing fighting to hold him, felt claws pierce his skin, then felt a sharp pain as the creature was torn from him.

'Filthy thing!' Isolt flung the creature away and pulled Fyn to his feet.

He felt dizzy. She ran, dragging him with her, until they reached the glass doors that led to the boys' living quarters. She darted inside, slamming the door after them.

Several lacewings batted against the glass doors, trying to get in.

Fyn groaned. He felt shaky and cold.

Isolt knelt beside him. He didn't remember sinking to the floor. 'Are you all right?'

'I...' Fyn tasted blood and his lip stung where she'd bitten him. 'I think I owe you an apology.'

'No need. It was the Affinity creature acting through you.'

But it hadn't been. It had been him, acting without inhibitions. Clearly the kiss had meant nothing to her. She'd had the presence of mind to bite him. What a fool he was.

Isolt glanced to the doors. 'They've gone.' She came to her feet and peered outside. 'I think they've gone back to the grotto. Will Dunstany and the boys be safe?'

'If the moths try to get into the grotto, Dunstany can deal with them.'

Isolt nodded, then gestured somewhat wildly. 'I can't believe the captain of my own queen's guard ignored my orders!'

'You could remove him from his post.'

'That would mean admitting I'd lost control of my own guards.'

'*Almost* lost control.' Fyn smiled but it was short lived. 'Much as I hate to admit it, Elrhodoc has a point. If we don't execute Corto—'

'I'm not killing him.'

'I know. But the lords and margraves will see it as weakness. They'll see it an excuse to make decisions without you, for your own good.'

'What do you suggest?'

'Rhalwyn wanted to go back to sea. The bay lord's grandson could offer to train him.'

'And Cortomir?'

'Him too.'

'But—'

'Who would recognise Cortomir, other than you and me, Dunstany and Rhalwyn?' Fyn's mind raced. 'This is a big city. Boys die all the time. They fall off horses or catch fevers. And their parents take their bodies to Mulcibar's Abbey to be fed to the god.'

She shuddered. 'You're suggesting we ask the abbot to find a boy of similar build who has died within the last day or so? Do you trust Murheg?'

Fyn thought about it, and was surprised to discover he did. 'He wants to ingratiate himself with me. If he does this, he has something to hold over—'

'Oh, Fyn...'

'It means we'll have a body to hang from the linden tree.'

'Dressed in Cortomir's spar vest.'

'Hang him high enough... no one will spot the deception.'

Isolt frowned. 'Elrhodoc might.'

'With Rhalwyn weeping under the tree?'

Admiration lit her eyes. 'Fyn, you are even more cunning than my father!'

'There are times when cunning is better than confrontation.'

'That's true.' She came to her feet. 'And there are times when we can't avoid spilling blood. We need to see Sefarra and find out what happened on Benetir Estate.'

Fyn nodded, but the room spun and he almost fell.

Isolt put her arm around him. 'Are you able to do this?'

'I must.'

Isolt glanced over her shoulder. 'I don't know where Elrhodoc and his men went, or what they're up to. You need to send for Camoric.'

'He's on his way here.' Fyn found he could stand. 'We have a game of Duelling Kingdoms under way. I'll have him sent to the war-table.'

Chapter Thirty-Nine

When Garzik entered the Utlanders' long-hall, he was reminded of the night he'd first come here, as a captive slave. Back then, Affinity beast trophies had decorated the walls, but Vultar had stolen them. At the back of the hall were dark storage chambers. Under the steeply pitched roof, a mezzanine floor held bed chambers. The kitchen was in a separate building nearby. And, by the looks of it, the cooks must have been working since the ship was first sighted, because there was food laid out on the long table.

Lauvra and the women of her generation took pride of place with the elders. The captains and their crews came next, then came the beardless, then the children.

Tonight Garzik took his place at the table, as part of Rusan's crew.

They were served by the slaves, but there were fewer captives than he'd originally thought. Lauvra and the elders dished out punishment to suit the transgressions. If someone was too proud, they had to wash the dishes.

If someone was greedy, they had to give away their most prized possession.

The dinner was supplemented with luxuries from the hot-lands, and everyone spoke at the top of their voices. When the meal was finished, people moved around the table, catching up. Garzik found himself leaning against one stair rail with Ilonja at his side. She offered him a tankard of wine.

He thanked her, then looked her up and down. 'Say, did you get smaller?'

She thumped him hard, making him smile.

One of the beardless yelled, 'Tell us how you sailed into the hot-lander jaws and stole their dinner out of their very mouths!'

'You raiders have all the fun,' Ilonja complained.

'I saw a shade-ray in the starlight,' Garzik whispered. 'Saw it fly through the sea on silvery wings.'

She shivered with awe.

'Tell us, Rusan. Tell us!' the gathering shouted.

'Very well.' He grinned and moved to the centre of the hall, where all could see. Olbin joined him. 'After you hear how we stole into Port Mero, you won't be teasing us about our half-grown beards!'

They acted out how their ship had slipped into the bay and how they'd stolen the stores. Rusan gave Garzik his due for coming up with the idea, and for leading the attack to secure the merchant ship. But he avoided explaining why the sea-hounds had spotted them. The listeners were so caught up in the drama of the ship's race for the headlands, and their miraculous escape through Mulcibar's Gate, that they didn't notice the omission.

Rusan was a natural storyteller. By the time he finished, the hall rang with cheers.

Not Jost's mother. She came to her feet. 'Rusan made his reputation at the cost of my sons' lives. All three of them, dead!' Her voice shook. 'I demand Rusan pay the death price for each of them!'

Everyone was stunned. Everyone but Vesnibor. He looked pleased. Garzik frowned. Didn't Vesnibor realise this would reflect badly on Jost? Perhaps he didn't care. As Byren's old nurse used to say, fling enough mud, some of it will stick.

Garzik expected Rusan to defend himself, or Olbin to defend his captain, but it was Lauvra who came to her feet.

'This was not murder, Pramoza. Your sons gave their lives to bring back supplies. A captain does not need to pay the death price for crew members lost on raids. The price is paid in the bounty that we all share.'

Several of the elders nodded, but some said nothing, watching the mood of the gathering.

'Rusan was careless with his crew.' Jost's mother looked around the long-hall, seeking out certain faces. 'Twenty-seven sailed, fourteen did not return. How many women have lost a husband? How many have lost two? How many children have lost fathers?' She pointed to Rusan. 'All because he craved glory!'

Another woman sprang to her feet. 'Both my husbands are dead. Who will help me feed the children? I demand the death price!'

There was muttering, some in favour, some against, and Garzik glanced to Rusan, willing him to speak up.

'Your family is too proud, Lauvra.' Pramoza's voice took on a malicious edge as it gained in confidence. 'You look too high. I always said so.'

'When my three husbands' ship disappeared, did I come to the elders and demand their death price?' Lauvra asked. 'No, because that is not our way. When my two oldest sons died while raiding, did I demand their death price? No. It is not our way.'

'I know our ways,' Pramoza snapped. 'And it is not our way to sail into Port Mero to win glory. Your sons did not die so that their captain could become the talk of the Northern Dawn peoples. Mine did!'

Garzik glanced to Rusan, and finally he spoke up.

'Did your sons die for glory?' Rusan asked, looking around. 'Yes, they did. But it was not my glory. I promised Jost a ship, but that was not enough for him. He chose death.'

People muttered, turning to each or looking to Rusan for an explanation. Some had already made the leap, and were watching Jost's mother. Garzik glanced to Vesnibor to see if he regretted setting her on this course, but the raider had slipped away.

Jost's mother backed up a step, mouth working even though no sound came from her.

'Pramoza is right about one thing,' Rusan said. 'Too many have died. Let me honour our dead.' He pulled out his pipes.

As he played the Lament for the Dead, Olbin joined him, naming their dead, but he did not have Sarijana's voice, which had soared above all others.

She stood, leaning against one of the poles, arms folded across her chest, mouth stubbornly closed.

Garzik leant close to Ilonja. 'Your sister doesn't sing?'

'Not since...' She did not finish.

It was wrong. Garzik wandered along behind the groups. When he reached Sarijana, he leant his shoulder against the pole beside her. 'So many lost...'

Her mouth hardened. 'Too many.'

'Be angry with Vultar, but don't punish yourself. You love to sing. Don't punish us. We need to hear your voice. If you don't sing, Vultar wins.'

'I can't sing.' She turned angry, tear-filled eyes on him. 'When I try, my throat closes up.'

He winced. 'I'm sorry.' Feeling clumsy, he moved away.

Ilonja joined him. 'You tried.'

'I failed.'

But as he said this, Sarijana stepped away from the pole, lifting her voice in lament. It sounded husky and strained, but even so, an unconscious sigh swept the hall. Some people cheered, others applauded.

Her voice gained in strength; by the time she joined Rusan and Olbin, it soared pure and clear. The power of the song for the dead was such that soon everyone wept, from warriors to small children, from elderly to slaves. Garzik felt tears sting his eyes. He wept for his father, for Piro.

When the song was done, the Utlanders called for another and Sarijana obliged them. Garzik looked around the hall. Only Jost's mother sat alone and hard-eyed.

As Fyn hurried along the corridor with Isolt, he heard a child wailing fretfully and a man berating someone. Fyn recognised Elrhodoc's voice. Before they reached the door to the war-table chamber, he caught Isolt's arm and signalled for silence.

Isolt tugged against his hand. 'That's Benny crying. Sefarra needs—'

'What is said behind our backs is more revealing than what is said to our faces.'

Isolt hesitated.

They both noticed Camoric approaching from the opposite direction. Fyn signalled for him to wait in silence, and they took up position on either side of the door.

Fyn risked a quick glance into the war-table chamber. Little Benowyth sobbed, as Sefarra tried to soothe him and Captain Elrhodoc berated her.

'...should have known the Centicore warlord would break his word. He saw an old woman, a girl and an infant lord sitting in their great house, and he thought you'd be easy pickings. He was right.'

'But it—'

'I'm not done yet.' Elrhodoc raised his voice over the wailing child. 'There's no point calling on Travany and the others to come to your aid. They've already saved Benetir Estate once. They're not going to waste men-at-arms to save it a second time.' He swore viciously. 'I can't think with this noise. Can't you get the boy to shut up?'

'The boy?' Sefarra's voice was icily calm. 'I'll have you know since spring he's seen his mother, father and grandfather killed, and now his grandmother. How brave were you when you were three years old?'

Elrhodoc was silent for a moment, then gestured for her to go. 'Leave the making of war to men and take your brother to the nursery.'

'He's not my brother, he's my nephew. And I was singing him to sleep when spar warriors attacked our home. It wasn't the same warlord who gave his oath to Queen Isolt. It was another warrior, calling himself Warlord Jankigern. And if you kill him, another one will take his place.'

Elrhodoc laughed. 'You're not making any sense. Go put the boy to bed and let me deal with this.'

'I—'

'How can you think with this infernal racket?'

'If it bothers you, don't stay.'

'Fine. I don't know why I try to make you see sense. I can hardly bear to look at you anyway, knowing how those barbarians used you. If you had a shred of decency, you'd have dedicated yourself to Cyena Abbey.'

'Just as well I didn't run away, or Benny would be dead!'

'If you are all he has, he might as well be dead. Your house will fall and your estate will be taken over by one of the lords. And good riddance to you!' He flung this over his shoulder as he strode out.

Camoric confronted Elrhodoc at the door. 'Captain.'

'What're you doing sneaking around, bay-scum?'

'I'm here to see the queen—'

The captain laughed. 'Of course you are. Planning to slip into her bed? You and your house are no better than barbarians yourselves. Now your grandfather's calling himself Lord Admiral Cadmor. Why, there's a dozen men of better birth who should have been given that title.

Trust a girl-queen to make a mess... Don't you smirk at me!'

As he took another step towards the bay lord's grandson, Fyn signalled Isolt to keep silent and drew her into the war-table chamber, out of sight.

Despite Benowyth's cries, they could still hear Elrhodoc.

'Enjoy the girl-queen's patronage while you can, scar-face, because before long she'll have a husband and it won't be some deposed Rolencian kingson. It'll be one of our own lords, and then Merofynia will be ruled by someone who knows what they're doing. Out of my way. I have a hostage to execute!'

A moment later, Camoric stepped into the war-table chamber. No one spoke. Benowyth continued to weep, but his cries were growing weaker as he succumbed to exhaustion.

Isolt trembled with fury.

Fyn went to speak, but Isolt shook her head and moved around the war-table to where Sefarra stood with the lad in her arms. Isolt placed her hand on Benowyth's back.

Making slow circles with her palm, she began to sing. She did not have a strong voice, but it was sweet and true. The song she chose was the same song Fyn's nurse used to sing when he was a baby. He'd forgotten. Hearing it now brought tears to his eyes.

And he knew that one day he wanted Isolt to sing to their children.

Camoric joined Fyn. 'Is that peacock Elrhodoc going to execute Cortomir?' he asked softly.

Fyn nodded.

'And you sent for me to spirit the lad away?'

'Him and Rhalwyn.'

'The Affinity beast-keeper, too? I can...' Camoric frowned. 'We'll be too late. Elrhodoc's gone to get the lad.'

'Both boys are with Lord Dunstany. Elrhodoc won't make a move until Dunstany is out of the way.'

Camoric nodded. 'But Elrhodoc will know you had the lad removed. He'll use it against you.'

'Not if all goes to plan.' Fyn crossed to the sideboard, where he selected paper and a quill. 'I want you to take a message to Abbot Murheg.'

While Fyn wrote, Camoric read over his shoulder. He gave a soft chuckle as he grasped the gist of the plan. Fyn folded the message, then caught Isolt's eye. He raised his hand, indicating his ring finger.

She nodded and came around the war-table to press the royal ring into the wax seal. 'Benny's asleep, poor boy.'

'Can you trust the abbot?' Camoric asked.

Fyn nodded. 'If I fall, he falls.'

Benowyth whimpered and they both glanced over at him. Sefarra had lowered him onto a daybed, and now she soothed him with a word. When it was clear he had settled, she joined them.

'I must speak with Sefarra,' Fyn told Camoric. 'Then I'll take you to Cortomir.'

Isolt's eyes widened. 'Is it safe, Fyn?' She added for Camoric and Sefarra's benefit, 'Wild Affinity creatures caught us out in the open. They went after Fyn because of his Affinity.'

Camoric nodded. 'I wondered. He's as pale as milk, and bleeding.'

Fyn felt the back of his neck. His fingers came away stained with blood.

'Sit down.' Isolt pushed him into a chair. 'Lean forward. I should have noticed, but it was dark.' She pulled his shirt up and pressed the material to the back of his neck. 'It's only shallow. Pressure will stop the bleeding. Filthy things...'

'I can do it.' Fyn didn't want her touching him, not when she didn't want him. He lifted his head.

'We could take torches,' Sefarra said. 'Fire scares off most beasts.'

Camoric glanced to her.

'I'm going to help,' she told him. 'I don't want the boy's death on my conscience. His father didn't break his word.'

'Fair enough.' Camoric studied her.

'What?' Sefarra's eyes narrowed.

'Sefarra, this is Camoric,' Fyn said, wondering if they would rub each other the wrong way. 'He's the bay lord's grandson.'

'The one who lost the Utland raiders,' Camoric explained, jaw clenched, scars gleaming in the candle light. Funny how Fyn didn't notice the burns unless he was reminded.

'Camoric, this is my cousin, Sefarra,' Isolt said.

The girl lifted her chin. 'The one who—'

'Hacked off Warlord Cortigern's head,' Camoric said, and executed a bow that would have pleased Fyn's mother. 'I'm honoured, Lady Sefarra.'

Her mouth dropped. Camoric grinned.

'There's no time to waste,' Fyn said. 'We have to get Cortomir out of the palace and string up another boy's body in his place. But first, we must work out how to win back Benetir Estate.'

'I know how to win back my estate,' Sefarra said.

'How?' Fyn was surprised.

'Our sorbt stone mine is in the foothills, one hard day's march from the great house. There are two hundred Rolencian slaves there, all young, all eager to go home. You remember how we were worried they'd try to escape last time the spar warlord attacked? Well, I'm going to offer them their freedom if they'll fight for me.'

'That'll do it,' Camoric said.

Sefarra met his eyes. 'And I'll offer you my grandfather's yacht if you and your men will fight for me.'

'The *Flying Sarre*? She's a beauty. I accept.'

Sefarra turned to Fyn. 'I don't know what I can offer you, but I want you to lead us. You have the training in strategy and tactics. That's if you can spare him, my queen.' She gave Isolt a small formal bow then spoilt it by adding, 'I don't like the captain of your guards, Izy, you should get rid of him.'

'Izy?' Fyn repeated.

Isolt flushed. 'A childhood name.'

And she hadn't given him permission to use it.

'Sefarra's right,' Camoric said. 'You can't trust Elrhodoc.'

'I've had my eye on him for a while now,' Fyn admitted.

'He's too well connected for me to remove him,' Isolt said. 'And he's not my only problem. Most of the lords would happily see me wedded and producing heirs so they can get on with ruling the kingdom. As long as I have Yorale and Dunstany on my side, they won't move against me.'

But Fyn knew they would not have Dunstany for much longer. Soon Siordun would have to let the old lord die. They had been lucky tonight, however the longer the charade went on, the more chance his disguise would be exposed.

'Don't look so worried, Fyn.' Isolt squeezed his arm. 'For years I lived in a hostile court, with only Yorale and Dunstany for my friends. Now I have all of you. Go save Corto.'

In the predawn dark, Fyn and Camoric neared the grotto. They approached along the shore of the Landlocked Sea. Sefarra had gone to her yacht to prepare it for Camoric, who planned to take Cortomir straight from the grotto to the *Flying Sarre*. Isolt had already slipped into the boy's sleeping chamber to remove Cortomir's leather spar vest. Abbot Murheg had sent word he had a suitable body.

'What if Elrhodoc knows about the secret entrance to the grotto?' Camoric whispered as he and Fyn crept through the overgrown garden.

'Then we deal with the man he left to guard the entrance, and remove his body.'

But no one was watching the back of the grotto. A soft pearly light still spilled from the front, reflecting in the pond and and sending slivers of light into the sky, but Fyn was glad to see there were no more lacewings.

He crawled through the concealed tunnel and into the grotto to find it illuminated with the soft pearly glow from Dunstany's staff, even though Dunstany himself was dozing with his back to the wall.

Fyn stepped over the sleeping boys and beasts to wake him.

But before he could, Dunstany's eyes sprang open. An inner light filled them, or perhaps it was the reflection of his orb.

'Fyn.' He looked relieved and rolled to his feet with more vigour than Fyn had expected, considering that he'd had to share Affinity with the beasts. Dunstany spoke a rushed whisper. 'I was planning to slip out through the tunnel with Corto before dawn. Elrhodoc left two men watching the pond. They...' He broke off as Camoric crawled into the grotto, and when he next spoke it was with the gravity of Lord Dunstany. 'They've been keeping their distance since they saw Loyalty and Resolute hunt down the lacewings.' He gestured to the sleeping beasts. 'They gorged themselves.'

'I see.' After his run-in with the lacewings, Fyn felt no regrets. 'I thought to find you exhausted by the beasts.'

'Turns out the Mad Boy King was not all that mad, but rather very clever.' Laughter lit Dunstany's eyes as he gestured to the grotto's dome. 'Those aren't pieces of glass to let in light. They're clear sorbt stones, the kind that you can use to focus power. As soon as I entered the dome with my staff, they became activated.'

'Fyn? I knew you'd come!' Cortomir woke, then scrambled to his feet. Rhalwyn stirred and shook himself awake.

Fyn grinned and took Cortomir's hand. 'This is Camoric, Corto. He's the bay lord's grandson. He's going to take you on his ship and turn you into a sailor.'

'Lucky old Corto!' Rhalwyn muttered.

Cortomir glanced to the older boy. 'Can't he come, too?'

'He can, but first he has a task to perform to save your life.'

The boys' eyes widened as Fyn laid out the plan.

Chapter Forty

By the time Fyn arrived under the linden tree, the sun was up and a crowd of early market-goers had already gathered. The tree was older than Merofynia itself. According to the legends, it had already been huge when King Merofyn the First had called a council of lords under its branches, planted his family's famous stone under it and climbed onto it to declare himself king.

According to legend, the Merofynity Stone welcomed a true king of the line, and for the first two hundred years of his family's rule, the kings had always stood on the stone to be crowned.

But the stone had another, more sinister function. If someone was accused of treason, the king would stand the accused on the stone under the linden tree to question him. It was said you could not tell a lie while standing on the stone under the linden tree. And it was from the branches of this tree that the guilty were hung.

Today it held sad fruit.

Fyn's only consolation was that the boy had died of natural causes and the real hostage was safely hidden amongst Camoric's people. The dead boy bore enough of a resemblance to Cortomir that once they'd dressed him in the spar vest, breeches and boots, he could be mistaken for the hostage.

From this angle, with the wind blowing his shoulder-length hair over his face, even Fyn could not tell him apart from Cortomir. Dunstany had added some artistic touches—painting his features and packing them to make it seem as if he had died by hanging. Even the unfortunate lad's own family would not have known him.

Dunstany watched from his carriage with Rhalwyn at his side, waiting for Fyn's signal.

'So this is the spar hostage?' someone called as Fyn guided his horse through the crowd and chose a spot under the tree. For now the sweet smell of the linden blossoms covered the smell of death.

'Does this mean the Centicore warlord attacked again?' someone else yelled.

'Didn't you hear?' a busy-body spoke up. 'Hundreds of spar warriors came in the night and murdered the whole of Benetir household in their beds!'

There was a chorus of worried comments. Meanwhile, Fyn dismounted and climbed onto the Merofynity Stone. For a brief moment he felt a superstitious awe and half expected the stone to respond to him in some way. Nothing happened.

As he unrolled the parchment, Fyn saw a gate guard leave his post at a run. The rest of the guards watched, ready to intervene if the gawkers got out of hand. It was market day, and more people poured in from the square as news of the hanging spread.

'I bring Queen Isolt's proclamation,' Fyn announced, and introduced himself by title. Then he read the carefully worded document. Centicore Spar had broken their word. Queen Isolt had exacted vengeance on the hostage. '...so let it be known that all who break their word to the queen will face her justice.'

'Shame on you,' a woman yelled.

But her voice was drowned by the crowd, who delighted in the suffering of others. Fyn looked out over the gathering. Someone had run back to their fruit stall and returned with a basket of rotten fruit. Several youths began hurling them at the body. The crowd jeered.

Sickened, Fyn jumped down. Before he could be showered in rotting fruit, he hung the proclamation on the linden tree. As he climbed onto the Merofynity Stone to mount up, someone bumped him and he fell forward. The pressure of the crowd and the strength of his emotion combined to make Fyn's Affinity surge. The stone on his ring glowed softly, and he felt the stone under his bare palms respond—not because he was of the Merofyn line but because of his Affinity. Under the dust and moss, it was the biggest Affinity stone he had ever seen.

He pulled his hands away before anyone noticed, mounted his horse and guided it to the edge of the crowd.

Just as he'd suspected, Captain Elrhodoc rode this way with a dozen of the queen's guards. Their bright royal blue half-cloaks rippled and their gold braid gleamed. The ordinary folk parted for Elrhodoc, who studied the proclamation then jerked on his reins and walked his horse over to join Fyn.

As he approached, Fyn casually scratched his earlobe. It was the signal for Dunstany to let Rhalwyn out of his carriage. The lad had been carefully coached in his role.

'I didn't think you had it in you. How did you convince the queen?' Elrhodoc asked, eyes sharp with suspicion.

Fyn shrugged. 'Isolt has a soft heart, but she'll see the necessity of this eventually. She is her father's daughter, after all.'

Let Elrhodoc chew on that.

'Out of my way,' Rhalwyn yelled. He darted through the gathering, then came to a complete stop staring up at the body. His howl of anger and horror silenced the crowd momentarily.

Fyn cursed and guided his horse closer. 'Rhalwyn, come away from—'

'You...' The furious lad thrust through the watchers. Tears streaming down his face, he attacked Fyn. 'How could you? He was just a boy!'

Since Fyn was mounted and Rhalwyn was on foot, the best the lad could do was pummel Fyn's thigh, but it made the horse skittish and the gelding sidled away.

As there was only so much entertainment to be had from a swinging corpse, several of the crowd ventured closer to watch. They started yelling advice to Fyn, or backed the lad.

Fyn let his horse collide with Elrhodoc's mount and the rest of the guards' horses began to shift and snort, growing uneasy.

Judging the moment right, Fyn caught Rhalwyn's arm. 'That's it. You're dismissed. I'll find another Affinity beast-keeper. Get out. Better yet, I'll get rid of you myself.'

Fyn hauled the lad over his saddle and urged his mount towards the gate. Camoric's men would be waiting on the corner of Tailor and Sailcloth Lanes. There Rhalwyn would be taken to join Cortomir.

Riding through the gate, Fyn pulled up on the edge of the busy market square. He shoved Rhalwyn off the horse. 'Get out and stay out.'

The lad took to his heels, disappearing into the crowd, just as they'd planned.

Fyn rode back, past Elrhodoc and the half dozen queen's guards, straight past Dunstany's carriage without pausing to speak to him.

Let Elrhodoc make what he would of this. If the captain of the queen's guards believed Fyn was at odds with both Dunstany and Isolt, he might be lured into doing something rash.

There was just time to tell Isolt about the Merofynity Stone before he set sail for Benetir Estate. If it truly was an Affinity stone, then it was beyond price. Should they move it to the treasury? Dunstany would know.

By the time Byren reached the top of the rise and spotted Feid's stronghold, it was mid-afternoon. Between them lay Feidton, swollen with refugees from Rolencia. The steep slope led down to the wharf and Feid Bay, and directly opposite, on a higher rise, stood Feid Stronghold. It seemed to grow out of the cliff in places, the silvery wood of its upper storeys blending in with the dark stone base.

'Not long now,' Byren said.

Florin brushed past him, striding on ahead. Those mud-caked breeches left little to the imagination.

Byren had pushed himself to the limit to get here. Florin had to be exhausted—not that she complained. But there were bruises on her jaw and forehead, and she flinched if her jerkin brushed against her left breast where the Merofynian had pinched her. The thought of that brute laying hands on her infuriated him.

His first instinct was to offer to heal her, but he couldn't attempt it without Orrade's help or access to a seep. And just as well, because he'd be a fool to risk the intimacy. The urge to claim her for his own still rode him.

He was not a weak-willed man like his grandfather. He'd recognised the risk arising from his kinship with Affinity beasts and was on his guard.

Perhaps he'd misjudged King Byren the Fourth. If his grandfather's Affinity had come on him when he was only twelve or thirteen and he'd made a connection with an Affinity beast, then he would never have understood what drove his animalistic nature.

Byren wished his grandfather was still alive, so he could ask his advice. He missed his mother's perceptive advice, and his father's knowledge of men and battles. But they were all gone: his parents, old Lord Dovecote, Captain Temor, Seela and Florin's father.

There she was, striding along, all alone in the world with a boy of ten to raise.

'They've seen us.' Orrade waved to the men on the main gate. He glanced to Byren and caught him watching Florin. 'There's still time to reconsider.'

'I know my duty. I know what I owe all those who believed in me and sacrificed their lives at Narrowneck.'

In silence they strode up the steep switch-back road to the stronghold. As they neared the gate, Florin's brother emerged, stepping into the daylight. He blinked, spotted his sister and made for her. Chandler followed.

'Leif...' Florin dropped to one knee and held out her arms.

The lad ran to her blindly, sobbing. 'Da's dead!'

Byren slowed and came to a stop two paces behind them.

'I know, I know...' Florin sobbed.

Tears stung Byren's eyes. He wanted to wrap Florin and Leif in his arms. He wanted the right to do this.

Orrade stepped forward and embraced them both.

Leif pulled out of the hug and Orrade helped Florin to her feet. She would never have let Byren help her. Byren felt a stab of jealousy, but rejected it as unworthy.

'I told Leif how Old Man Narrows saved my life,' Chandler said, holding Byren's eyes.

He nodded his understanding. 'You can be proud of your father, lad.'

Leif threw his arms around Byren, and he lifted the lad off his feet in a fierce embrace. He felt Leif's skinny frame shake as he sobbed. The boy held on with all his might.

'Eh, lad...' Byren's throat grew tight. He looked up and caught Florin watching. She turned away.

'Why...' Leif pulled back to meet Byren's eyes. He swallowed a sob. 'Why do you smell so bad?'

'We fell in a bog,' Byren said. And for some reason that made them all laugh.

'Byren!' Feid strode down the slope to welcome them. Lady Cinna followed a few steps behind, trying to hurry despite her swollen belly. She was pink cheeked from exertion, and so pregnant she looked ready to give birth any moment.

Byren put Leif down to greet the spar warlord. Feid swept Byren in an embrace, then Cinna hugged him. He felt the hard drum of her belly, and the baby kicked him.

Byren laughed. 'That's a healthy kick. How long?'

'Any day now.' Feid slid an arm around Cinna's shoulders, beaming with pride.

Byren envied him for being able to take the woman he loved for his wife.

Chapter Forty-One

FYN STOOD WITH Sefarra at the prow of the fishing vessel leading their small fleet. The dozen able-bodied youths who'd escaped from Benetir Estate formed her honour guard, and Camoric's sea-hounds packed all three fishing boats. Dunstany and Isolt had remained in port to give substance to the rumours of division between them and Lord Protector Merofyn.

If they were lucky, this would prompt the captain to make a move against Fyn.

'He's clever,' Sefarra said.

'Who, Elrhodoc?'

'No, Camoric.' She gestured to the bay lord's grandson at the tiller. 'If we'd approached the estate in my father's yacht, it would have alerted the warlord, but three fishing boats taking shelter in a cove won't raise concern.'

Fyn nodded as they dropped anchor.

'And you're clever,' Sefarra told Fyn. 'The *Flying Sarre* will keep Jankigern's attention focused in the wrong direction.'

Fyn had told the yacht's captain to approach Benetir Estate at dusk tomorrow evening. By then they should be in position to attack from the inland side of the great house.

If all went to plan.

'Elrhodoc's not.'

'What?' Fyn wondered if it was only him, or if others found Sefarra's manner odd. The more time he spent with her, the more he believed Lady Gennalla had been wilfully blind concerning her daughter's marriage prospects.

'Elrhodoc's not clever. He doesn't see that if you kill a predator, another will move into its territory.' She faced Fyn. 'That's what Palatyne did. According to my father, he fostered jealousy within the spar warlords' own households, brother turned on brother. Then Palatyne stepped in when the spar leaderships were fractured and weak—'

'And defeated them.'

'That's what everyone assumed, but I overheard the Centicore warlord and his brother talking. Palatyne became overlord by promising to divide up Merofynia between the spars.'

'Then they must have been furious when he broke his word and led the invasion of Rolencia.'

'No, he was too canny for that. He told the warlords they'd make their move when the moment was right.'

'And they believed him because they wanted to.'

Sefarra nodded, and Fyn recalled that her father had been the Merofynian ambassador. Clearly she took after him and not her mother.

Her next words confirmed it.

'The nobles have grown complacent in two hundred years of peaceful trade with the spars. But that's two hundred years of them breeding bigger families than the poor spar soil can support. The spars are packed with hungry warriors, eager to win land and riches. They're like ulfr packs, led by the most cunning, strongest males, and there are always younger males ready to take the leaders' places. Jankigern killed Cortomir's father to expand his pack's territory. Until the number of warriors falls below what the spar land can support, we will have war.' She shrugged. 'Executing Cortomir would have achieved nothing, but Elrhodoc could not see this. He's captain of the queen's guard, yet he defied Isolt. She'll have to remove him and make sure another predator doesn't move into her territory by appointing someone she trusts to captain her guards.'

'Your father told you all this?'

'Not specifically. We used to talk and I've read all the histories.' Her chin quivered. 'I wanted to be an ambassador just like him.'

'You never did intend to marry.'

'No.' Her eyes narrowed. 'Not after I saw what happened to my older sister. She was married to Yorale's heir. He beat her when she was pregnant and she lost the baby. Then he beat her *because* she lost the baby. She was scared of him, but she couldn't leave him. Then she met a good man and they fell in love. He challenged her husband to a duel and killed him. Because her husband was the heir to a great estate, the man she loved had to flee. She could have gone with him, but she didn't protest when father sent her to Cyena Abbey. Both their lives were ruined.'

'I'm sorry.'

Sefarra grimaced and her eyes took on that hard look he had come to recognise. 'If I had been married to her husband, the first time he raised his hand to me I would have cut his throat. At the very least I would have defied society and run off with Rishardt!'

'You'd give up everything for love?' Fyn teased.

She took him seriously. 'When you've looked death in the face, you know what's important.'

FLORIN FOLLOWED LADY Cinna as she swept along the corridor, issuing orders. Bedchambers had to be aired, hot water fetched, clothes found and food prepared.

Cinna flung open the door to the stronghold's second-best bedchamber. 'Chandler, Woodend and Wafin have been sharing the bed. I'll have the sheets changed for Byren and send up some blankets. His honour guard can sleep on the floor.'

Florin nodded. With the over-crowding in the stronghold, only the high-ranking visitors would get a bed to themselves. Last time she was here, Florin had slept in the servants' chamber, just off the warlord's bedchamber. It was little more than a cupboard, but the privacy had been a luxury. 'I can sleep in the great-hall on the floor with the rest of the men-at-arms.'

'Nonsense.' Cinna led Florin to what had been her old room and opened the door. 'This will be the nursery, but we don't need it yet, so I ordered a bath prepared.'

'You'll need it any day now. I don't want to get in the way,' Florin protested.

Two sturdy servants arrived with buckets of hot water and upended them into the copper tub, and another two followed.

Florin looked longingly at the hot water. At home she would have bathed crouching over a shallow bowl with a jug of water. 'I don't need—'

'Believe me, you do,' Cinna told her, a twinkle in her eye. She opened a jar and sprinkled rose petals on the bathwater. Their delicate scent filled the air. 'I'll go and find some fresh clothes.'

'Breeches,' Florin warned. No point trying to be something she was not. 'Nothing with frills.'

Cinna rolled her eyes, then left.

Alone at last, Florin stripped and sank into the tub, thinking about the way Feid looked at Cinna...

Tears stung Florin's eyes. She had no illusions. No one would ever look on her like that. She would never have a child of her own.

Furious, she scrubbed herself.

She was just reaching for a jug to rinse her hair, when a Cinna said, 'Let me. Tilt your head back.'

'You're the warlord's lady. You shouldn't be acting as my maid.'

'Before I came here, I slept in the scullery with the other maids. We would do each other's hair and whisper our secrets.' Cinna adjusted Florin's head and poured water over her. 'Now everyone keeps me at a distance because I'm their lord's lady.'

Cinna was the illegitimate daughter of one of Ostron Isle's great families. And she spied for the mage. Was this part of her job? Getting close to Byren's...

'I'm not Byren's lover, if that's what you're thinking,' Florin said. 'I don't know his secrets.' But even as she said this, Florin realised she did. She knew more about Byren than anyone other than Orrade.

Cinna sat back, hands on her hips. 'Have I ever—'

'Don't lie.' Florin pushed wet hair from her face. 'I like you. But if you lie to me...'

As Cinna's eyes glittered with angry tears, Florin realised she had deeply offended the wife of Byren's last remaining ally.

Even so... 'I'll never betray Byren.'

'I know, and I wouldn't ask you to.' Cinna flushed. 'Just as I'd never betray Feid.'

'It's not like that.' Florin wasn't going to explain what it was like. 'Besides, I know you serve the mage.'

'He helped Byren defeat Palatyne and win Merofynia.'

'I thought Lord Dun—'

'Dunstany is the mage's ally. And Mage Tsulamyth's goal is peace.'

Florin blinked. 'How do you know that? Have you met him? And, even if you have, how do you know he speaks the truth?'

'You have to put aside your Rolencian prejudices. Power-workers can be good or bad.' She saw Florin was about to speak and hurried on. 'When I was twelve, and my cousin offered me the chance to serve the mage I asked him much the same thing as you. This is what he said. Tsulamyth is over two hundred years old. He earned the title of mage as the most powerful Affinity worker of our age. Yet he lives on Mage Isle, which is smaller than Feidton. With his Affinity he could rule the known world, but for all these years he's dedicated himself to preserving the balance of power between Rolencia, Merofynia and Ostron Isle. I serve him because he works for peace.' Cinna tilted her head. 'Now will you trust me?'

Florin considered. Cinna had assumed she was ignorant and prejudiced because she'd grown up in Rolencia, but she'd grown up in the tradepost, and knew far more of the world than the average Rolencian. She shrugged. 'I suppose if he wanted to enslave us all, he'd have done it by now.'

Cinna laughed and reached for a cloth. 'Come. Feid will be meeting with Byren. We don't want to miss it.'

That was another thing Florin envied. Feid shared everything with his wife. He might ride off to war with his men, but he'd discuss it with her first. Florin didn't know if other spar warlords were like this, but she suspected they weren't.

One part of her wanted to announce that what Byren did was no concern of hers, and that she was going to collect Leif and go home. Her family had already sacrificed their home, their good name and their father in Byren's cause. Surely he would not ask more of her?

But another part of her was fascinated. She wanted to listen to the war-table discussion. She wanted to see Byren one last time.

Florin dressed hurriedly in borrowed breeches. She bound her breasts, dropped a thigh-length shirt over her shoulders and plaited her still-damp hair. 'Ready.'

'That was quick.'

'That's one of the advantages of being a man.'

'Not in Ostron Isle or Merofynia, where they dress like peacocks.' As they went down the passage, Cinna slid her arm around Florin's waist, speaking softly. 'We've received word that Fyn's been having trouble in Merofynia. There've been spar uprisings and an Utland attack on Port Mero. Byren may want to return to Merofynia. Feid will advise against this. The longer Cobalt sits on the throne, the harder it will be to unseat him. You—'

'Byren doesn't listen to my advice.'

Cinna gave her a shrewd look before opening the door to the stronghold's war-table chamber.

Byren and Orrade stood with Feid on one side of the table, while three foreign-looking men stood on the other side. The tallest of them was no bigger than Cinna, and all wore brightly coloured robes that came to their knees, tight breeches and boots. The robes were decorated with elaborate embroidery. Unusual curved blades hung from the wide belts on their hips.

But this was not strangest thing about them. The strangest thing was their colouring. Rather than the normal blue-black, their hair was a washed-out brown and their eyes ranged from hazel to greeny-blue.

Florin recognised them. 'Snow Bridge people.' She smiled and performed the correct bow of respect, hands folded to each shoulder, bending from the waist. 'Earth-meets-sky, Florin meets...'

'Lord Vlatajor,' their leader supplied and returned the bow. 'Earth-meets-sky, Lord Vlatajor meets Florin. How is it that you know our customs?'

'Some of your people came to my family's tradepost when I was a child. One of them had broken his leg and could not travel, so his companions left him with us while they traded. It was my job to bring him food. He taught me to play spring-seeds—'

'Ah, the spring-seed game,' Vlatajor nodded and glanced to his companions and translated. They nodded in turn.

Florin cast Byren and Orrade a quick, questioning look.

'Lord Vlatajor brings a message from his brother, the king of the Snow Bridge,' Orrade said. 'King Jorgoskev offers trained warriors to help Byren reclaim Rolencia, in exchange for an alliance by marriage with one of his daughters.'

'But...' Florin's mind raced. *Another kingsdaughter, who could offer so much more than her?* Florin hated the girl already, but there was no chance the Snow Bridge kingsdaughter would ever marry Byren, not when... 'But he's already betrothed to Queen Isolt of Merofynia.'

'As I was just explaining,' Byren said.

'And I was inviting King Jorgoskev's brother to feast with us tonight,' Feid said, catching Cinna's eye.

His lady wife excused herself to prepare a suitable chamber and see the cook about the feast. As she left, a servant entered, bearing a tray laden with food and drink. Florin took a glass of wine and approached Vlatajor. 'The Snow Bridge man with the broken leg was called Bozhimir. Do you know him?'

Vlatajor lifted his hands. 'The Snow Bridge is a big place. It is as large as Rolencia. There are six city states, each with as many inhabitants as your largest city. It will not surprise you that I have not heard of this Bozhimir.'

Florin flushed. 'I see.'

One of the Snow Bridge warriors turned to the other, saying something in their language. Florin picked up every third word. 'Judging by his name ... probably a Karpafajite ... always put profit ahead ...'

'You know our language?' Vlatajor asked, his perceptive eyes on her.

'No.' Florin had been surprised she'd understood anything, but now she lied instinctively. 'But the rhythm and cadences sound familiar. They bring back fond memories.'

Vlatajor studied her.

'I do remember this,' Florin offered and deliberately recited a crude rhyme that Bozhimir used to sing when he was drunk.

The Snow Bridge warriors laughed and exchanged glances.

Vlatajor patted her hand. 'Do not sing that in public.'

Florin flushed and apologised.

Orrade tapped the war-table, indicating the Snow Bridge. 'I was taught your land was mostly rocky ridges.'

Vlatajor nodded. 'But between each ridge is a rich valley, and the longest valley stretches the length of the Snow Bridge from north to south.'

'Forgive me, but if your valleys are so large and your cities so prosperous, why do we see so little of your people?'

'Our city states have engaged in endless wars. First one would be in ascendance, then the other. The only thing that united us was our—forgive me—our dislike of flatlanders. But now that my brother has united all the city states, he is opening the Snow Bridge to trade and looks to make an alliance with his neighbours.'

'There is my sister, Pirola Rolen Kingsdaughter,' Byren said. 'She is almost of marriageable age. An alliance through marriage could be negotiated.'

'That is a possibility,' Vlatajor conceded.

Florin wondered what Piro would think of it. Just then, Lady Cinna returned to escort the Snow Bridge ambassador and his men to their chamber.

After they'd left, Feid turned to Byren. 'You'll send for Piro?'

'She's safe in Ostron Isle for now. Let's see what we can negotiate on the strength of her betrothal.'

'Piro won't like it,' Florin said. 'And the king's brother wasn't keen.'

Byren and Feid glanced to her.

'Florin's right,' Orrade said. 'By marrying his daughter to Byren, King Jorgoskev plants one of his grandsons on the Rolencian Throne. By marrying Piro to his son, he gets an alliance with Rolencia, and a grandson on the throne he has already won.'

Byren laughed. 'See, Feid, Orrade can out-think any man I've ever met.'

Orrade turned to Florin. 'You know their customs and understand their language. What did they say when you asked about Bozhimir?'

'Something about him coming from the city of Karpafaje and putting profit ahead of something. I didn't catch it all.'

Byren ginned. 'How is it you speak—'

'It took Bozhimir nearly a year to learn to walk again.'

'You should appoint Florin your ambassador to King Jorgoskev,' Orrade said.

'What?' She shook her head vehemently. 'I'm taking Leif and going home tomorrow.'

'It's not safe for Florin in Rolencia,' Feid said. 'The Merofynians saw her with you and she's so tall, she stands out in a crowd.'

Florin flushed as Byren and Orrade looked her up and down. She was having none of this. 'We'll go to our grandmother.'

'That's the grandmother who gave us shelter?' Byren asked. 'As I recall, we had to climb a mountain path to escape when Cobalt's men turned up. If sheltering you brings his men down on her again, is your grandmother up to that climb?'

'Stay with us, Florin,' Feid urged. 'Cinna misses you and Leif is like a son to me.'

Florin flushed. If she stayed here, every day she would see what Feid and Cinna shared and be reminded that she could never have it with Byren. It would make her hard and bitter before her time. Better she go.

'I know my way around. I can pass unnoticed when I have to,' Florin said. 'We leave tomorrow.'

Chapter Forty-Two

Fyn had to admire Sefarra's determination. They'd walked all afternoon and all through the night, with Camoric's sea-hounds forming a long tail that snaked back down the path.

Now, as the sun rose, they approached the mine. Fyn could smell porridge cooking and his stomach rumbled.

'It's just around that outcrop of rocks,' Sefarra said.

'Come on, I want to get a look first,' Fyn said. 'You never know, the spar warlord might have freed the seven-year slaves.'

Sefarra shrugged. 'He didn't last time.'

'Besides, there's always a demand for sorbt stones,' Camoric said. 'If he had any sense he'd keep the mine running.'

'Come on.' Fyn found a spot where they could stretch out on the dew-damp rocks and get a clear view.

Across from them the mine's entrance was a dark shadow in the cliff wall.

'My family found the cave with the sorbt stones over two hundred years ago,' Sefarra whispered.

Fyn studied the mine, which appeared undisturbed. Under the watchful eye of two guards, four men came out of the mine carrying pots. They went over to an open fire where water was heating and began to scrub the pots. Apart from one building with an overgrown turf roof, the rest of the storerooms and out-houses were made of wood, which had not yet been silvered by time.

'Looks like most of the buildings were erected within the last season,' Camoric said, 'after the fall of King Rolen.'

Fyn flinched to hear his father's death referred to.

'They are all new, except for that one.' Sefarra indicated the building with the turf roof. 'Our workers used to sleep in there. Now it's the guard-house. The seven-year slaves sleep in the cavern just inside the mine's entrance.'

Fyn pointed to the field in front of the mine, where two fences formed an inner and outer arc. They were spaced a stone's throw apart and weren't very sturdy. 'Why didn't they build a palisade? A determined man could easily slip through the first fence and run across the empty field to the second—'

'It's not empty. Come on.' Sefarra returned to the track where the others waited.

All of the sea-hounds had caught up now. They watched as Sefarra beckoned two of her people, telling them to bring something.

She turned to Fyn and Camoric. 'This way. And don't go near the fence, Fyn.'

He saw why when an emaciated lincis crept out of a lair in the cliff at the higher end of the field. Half wolf, half leopard, lincis were generally solitary creatures, but this one was a mother with two young cubs. No wonder she looked half-starved, the cubs were still feeding from her. Fyn didn't like to see creatures suffer.

On seeing the lincis, Sefarra whispered, 'Oh, Father, I would never have...' She glanced over her shoulder to Fyn and Camoric. 'He was so proud of himself. To deter escape, he had the Affinity beast and her cubs captured. They're fed just enough to survive.'

'The mother's thin, but she could still—'

'She won't escape,' Sefarra said softly. 'Go over to the fence, Fyn.'

As he approached, he noticed stones wedged into the posts. And, a heartbeat later, he felt a discomfort that quickly increased until it was painful. 'Absorber stones... But—'

'If enough are placed in close proximity, the effect is multiplied,' Sefarra said. 'So the stones repel the Affinity beasts... ingenious.' Fyn backed away, fighting instinctive anger.

'I understand why the lincis is trapped between the two fences,' Camoric said. 'But how do the guards deliver supplies? Let me guess, they load up the carts with enough stones to deter the beast.' He glanced over to Sefarra. 'Whose idea was it to use the sorbt stones this way?'

She looked uncomfortable. 'I had a theory that it would work. I never... I didn't consider how the lincis would feel.'

As if to echo this, the Affinity beast gave a harsh cry.

Immediately, three men came running from the guard-house and another two came from the mine entrance. They stood on the far side of the inner fence, squinting into the rising sun.

'Don't worry,' Sefarra called. 'No one's hurt.'

'Lady Sefarra?' A grey-haired man turned to the man beside him. 'Your eyes are better than mine, Guto. Who's that with her?'

Sefarra introduced them. 'This is Lord Protector Merofyn and Lord Cadmor's grandson, Camoric. We're coming in.'

'Don't. We haven't fed the lincis. No one's brought us food for a couple of days. The last time this happened—' He broke off as he took in the approaching sea-hounds. 'Don't tell me Centicore Spar attacked again?'

Alarmed, his men called out, asking after their families.

'I don't know what's happened since we escaped,' Sefarra admitted. She beckoned her people and lowered her voice. 'Go up to the high end of the field. Throw half the meat to the lincis. Make sure it falls roughly between the two fences so she can get to it.'

They nodded and moved off.

'How many mine guards?' Fyn asked.

'Twelve.'

'I'm guessing it didn't occur to your father that all the seven-year slaves had to do was kill the guards, feed them to the lincis and walk out?' Fyn asked.

'Walk to where?' Camoric argued. 'They couldn't go over the spar. Spar warriors hate Rolencians as much as they hate Merofynians. If they knew how to sail, two hundred men could have stolen the *Flying Sarre*—'

'You'd never fit two hundred men on my father's yacht,' Sefarra argued.

'They could have used it to attack and steal other vessels,' Camoric said. 'At a pinch, they could have crowded onto three ships and all sailed home.'

'*If* they had enough men who knew how to sail, and only if they had a leader to unite them,' Fyn said. This was what had been worrying him. Two hundred men, armed with picks and shovels, might just turn on his men.

'We're lucky they were farmers and apprentices,' Sefarra said, 'and not warriors.'

A strange coughing bark made them all turn. The lincis was calling her cubs. They trotted up the field to where she stood guard over the meat. She tore off strips of flesh and chewed, not taking her eyes off her human enemies.

'It's safe. We can go in now.' Sefarra indicated the gate down at the lower end of the field. Cart tracks ran through the grass to the inner gate, which opened into the mine-camp.

The gate creaked on its leather hinges as Sefarra opened it. 'The carts carry the stones down to the wharves, where they are taken to the abbeys.'

Fyn hardly heard her. He was concentrating on getting across the field as quickly as possible. Everyone poured across and entered the mine-yard.

'Are you in hiding, Lady Sefarra?' the grey-haired man asked. 'We'll help you, but there's not—'

Sefarra laughed. 'I'm planning to recapture Benetir Estate.'

He blinked. 'With us?'

'With you and with them.' She nodded towards several seven-year slaves, who had been scrubbing the porridge pots.

Fyn edged closer to Sefarra and the captain of the guards. 'Do they know that Byren killed Palatyne?'

'No,' the man said. 'My lord didn't want them getting ideas.'

Fyn caught Camoric's eye. 'Line your men up around the lower end of the field, then come up and join us.' He turned to the grey-haired man. 'Bring out all the seven-year slaves and have them sit down.'

They came willingly. Fyn figured they would; sitting in the sun on a beautiful late spring morning was better than working down a cold, dark mine.

At the high end of the mine-yard, he spotted a woodheap. He was about to climb onto a nearby chopping block when Sefarra caught up with him.

'Fyn? I've been thinking...' She cast the slaves a worried look. 'There's so many of them and they've every reason to hate Merofynians. What if they turn on us?'

'Don't worry,' Fyn said, climbing onto the block. Looking down on the sea of pale faces, he noted that some of captives looked curious, but the majority regarded the Merofynian nobles with resentment. But Fyn wasn't Merofynian.

'Some of you may remember King Rolen's youngest son, who was sent to Halcyon Abbey,' Fyn said, gesturing to his shorn head. 'I am Fyn Rolen Kingson, brother of Byren Kingsheir, and I bring good news.'

Several sprang to their feet, looking hopeful.

Fyn grinned. 'Byren has defeated Palatyne and is betrothed to Queen Isolt. He—'

Their cheering drowned him out.

Fyn gave them a moment to savour the news before gesturing for silence. 'Byren appointed me lord protector to serve Queen Isolt. And I need your help—'

'Anything,' several yelled. 'Name it.'

'Spar warriors murdered the Lady Sefarra's parents and took her home. I need your help recapturing it.'

'Why should we help a Merofynian noble?' someone yelled.

'Yeah, why do we care what happens to them?'

'Byren needs your help to hold onto Merofynia,' Fyn said.

'Last I heard, Cobalt the Turncoat had made a bargain with Palatyne,' someone yelled. 'Last I heard, Byren had no kingdom to go back to.'

Some tried to shout him down, others demanded to know if it was true. Again Fyn signalled for silence. 'When Palatyne attacked, Cobalt did collaborate with the enemy. He became their puppet king...' Fyn had to wait for the outraged seven-year slaves to settle down. 'That's why I'm here, holding Merofynia for Byren. Cobalt still sits on our father's throne. If you help Lady Sefarra reclaim Benetir Estate, she'll declare you free men. Then you can go home to help Byren win back Rolencia.'

They leapt to their feet, cheering.

Fyn was so relieved that when he jumped down his knees nearly gave way, and Camoric had to steady him.

'You did it!' Sefarra said, beaming with pride.

'Well done.' Camoric slung his arm around Fyn's shoulders. 'Now all we have to do is get a small army down the mountain and into position by dusk.'

'Line everyone up, see that they have boots, or some sort of foot covering.' Fyn noticed many of the slaves went barefoot. 'See that they bring something they can use as a weapon, and collect whatever food is left in the guard-house.' He turned to Sefarra. 'After we're gone, I'm going to leave the outer gate open for the lincis and her cubs to escape.'

FLORIN WAS DRESSED and had packed her travelling bag. There was no sign of Leif at the kitchen table or in the dining hall, so she went over to Byren's table, where he was sharing breakfast with the ambassador from the Snow Bridge.

Rather than interrupt their conversation, she slipped around behind the table and leaned over Orrade's shoulder. 'Do you know where my brother is?'

'He's still asleep in our chamber. Wait.' He caught Florin's arm. 'Leif snuck in during the night and climbed into bed with Byren. I heard him weeping, heard Byren singing to him. He didn't stir when we got up. Let him sleep.'

Why hadn't Leif come to her...? Because he would have had to creep past the warlord and his wife. Florin couldn't bear the thought of her little brother crying alone in the dark. 'Would you...' Her throat felt so tight she could hardly speak. 'Would you thank Byren?'

'No need.' Orrade saw her expression. 'All right, I'll thank him. But he's very fond of Leif, we both are. Are you really leaving today?'

'As soon as...' Florin fell silent as she heard the Snow Bridge ambassador's escorts mention her name.

'...the king's half-savage lover,' the tall one said. 'She might as well be a man.'

'From what I heard, that wouldn't bother him!'

'Why do you expect? For all he calls himself a king, he's a barbarian, and he's not king until he reclaims his throne.'

Orrade drew Florin close so he could whisper. 'What are they saying?'

'They think we are savages.'

This stunned Orrade.

She laughed. 'I learnt one thing growing up in a tradepost. Everyone thinks they are more civilised than their neighbours.'

He nodded and released her arm. She slipped away.

When she woke Leif, she found him fretful after a bad night's sleep. As she helped him take off his nightshirt, she realised his skin was too hot, and when she turned him around to help him into his breeches, she found the tell-tale rosettes of summer flower-fever on his belly and chest.

Florin sank into the chair by the empty fireplace. The fever wasn't deadly unless the child was already sickly, but it would delay their departure.

Leif shivered. 'I'm cold. Everything hurts. I want to go back to bed. Why do we have to leave?' Tears trickled down his cheeks. 'Now that Byren's here, I want to stay. Why are you so mean to him?'

'I'm not mean to him.'

'You don't laugh with him anymore.'

It was true. 'He'll be king soon, and we don't even have our tradepost to go home to. When he's king, he won't have anything to do with—'

'He's not like that.' A sob shook Leif. 'He promised to look after me. He promised!'

She hugged him and told him she'd come back with something to make him feel better, then went looking for Cinna. Servants directed her to the scullery, where she found Cinna alone, bent over in pain. Equal parts excitement and dread filled Florin. 'Is the baby coming?'

Cinna laughed. 'No, my back is aching, that's all.' She straightened up. 'Flower-fever has broken out amongst the servants, so I'm going to burn citrus incense to cleanse the air. I'll have to turn the new solarium into an infirmary. I may have to send out for more willow bark and feverfew. I'm glad Nun Anise is still with us.'

Florin nodded. The healer had not been able to go back to the Sylion Abbey since the abbess, bless her, had supported Byren, not Cobalt. 'Leif has come down with flower-fever, too,' Florin revealed. 'And he climbed into Byren's bed last night.'

'Oh, dear...' Cinna looked rueful. 'I hope Byren doesn't get sick. Big strong men make the worst patients.'

Florin grinned. 'I'll find Orrade and warn him. Then I'll bring Leif to the infirmary.'

Chapter Forty-Three

PIRO HAD BEEN right to doubt the ship's surgeon. He was a drunkard who took his first drink on waking and could be found snoring on his bunk by midday.

By the evening of the second day, her skin had burned with fever. Luckily, Illien had come to check on her. She'd asked him to bring her the surgeon's supplies. Unfortunately, they consisted of empty herb pouches and blunt surgical tools.

In desperation, Piro had sent Illien to ask the cook for wine, honey and rosemary. With the lad's help, she'd washed her wound then applied the honey and herbs.

In the days that followed, she'd walked no further than the privy as her fever came and went. At least the nexus point had passed. She'd had no more dreams of Cobalt's wedding, just nonsensical fever-dreams. At times, she thought Dunstany kept her company. She remembered having conversations with *my lord* but, looking back, it must have been Illien who'd cared for her.

Then a few moments ago she'd woken to hear the

familiar cries of Port Mero. Relief made her feel like weeping. Struggling to sit up, she swung her feet to the cabin floor and staggered over to find that the surgeon had already gone ashore. How long had they been docked?

Leaning on the door frame, she looked along the passage for Illien, but there was no sign of him.

She thought she could walk as far as the ladder, but she knew she didn't have the strength to climb it. If she could just get a message to Dunstany's townhouse, he'd send a carriage for her.

'...out of my way!'

Surely that was not Dunstany's voice? She must be delirious again.

'Out of my way! Where is she?'

'I'll take you to her, my lord,' Illien offered.

She saw him scurrying down the ladder. Her heart lifted as Lord Dunstany climbed down after him. She had to remind herself it was Siordun in disguise, but she could see nothing of the mage's annoying apprentice in this man.

Dunstany turned and saw her there. 'Piro!'

As he strode up the passage towards her, she marvelled, wondering if she was hallucinating again. 'Are you really here this time?'

'What have you done to yourself, you silly girl?'

'There was a nexus point. You told me to—'

'Here.' Dunstany thrust his cane and staff into the boy's hands then swept her up in his arms. 'Your skin feels hot. You're feverish.'

'I know, if it hadn't been for Illien...' The cabin spun around her and she fought to hold onto consciousness. 'How did you find me?'

'A drunken ship's surgeon came to my door and refused to lead me to you unless I paid him. The fool!'

She laughed, felt her eyes fill with tears of relief as grey spots ate into her vision, but she knew she was safe. It was good to have Lord Dunstany back. 'I've missed you so much, my lord.'

Dunstany went very still.

'We go home now?' Piro whispered.

'Home,' he agreed.

Fyn's heart sank. He'd crept to the top of a rise with Camoric and Sefarra.

'Looks like the new Centicore warlord learned from what happened last time.' Fyn gestured to the great house and outlying buildings illuminated by the setting sun. 'Not only has he stationed sentries in the outlying buildings, but he's fortified the great house.'

'What do we do?' Sefarra asked.

'A frontal assault will be costly.' And Fyn did not know how well the seven-year slaves would stand up to the spar warrior defences. 'But the freed slaves are ready to attack right now, and if we delay, they might desert. We need to lure the spar warriors out somehow.'

'We could set fire to the house,' Sefarra suggested.

'You'd set fire to your own home?' Camoric asked.

'As a last resort.'

'You won't need to,' Fyn said. 'Spar warriors don't fight as a unit. Each man sets out to win renown for himself. If you send word to the captain of the *Flying Sarre* telling him to mount an attack, as soon as the sentries hear the fighting, they'll leave their posts.'

Sefarra nodded and slipped away.

Camoric shook his head as he watched her go. 'She was ready to burn down her own home.'

Piro woke to find herself in Lord Dunstany's townhouse. She reached for the stone around her neck, only to remember the surgeon had stolen it. She'd slept the afternoon away. Starlight spilled through the window, silvering the bed and the floor under the window.

Gritting her teeth, Piro struggled to sit up. But she

didn't suffer the sharp pain she'd anticipated. Surprised, she checked the wound. Although it was still tender, the healing was much further advanced than...

'I encouraged your flesh to knit,' Siordun said, startling her.

He was dressed as Dunstany, which made her miss the old lord. Yet the Lord Dunstany she had known had always been Siordun.

'I left you safe on Mage Isle.' Without bothering to light candle, he came over to sit on the chest beside the bed. 'Next thing I know, you arrive in Port Mero, barely clinging to life. What possible reason—'

'There was a nexus point. Lord Dunstany told...' She flushed. '*You* told me to tell you if I had a vision. I saw Cobalt at his wedding—'

'Yes, he planned to marry an imposter Piro. I gathered that much when my Rolencian agent sent word of the wedding. I sent Byren to sort it out—'

'Back in Port Marchand, they were saying Byren killed me to prevent the marriage. There was a fire and Narrowneck burned. I don't know if Byren escaped or if he...' A sob shook her. The clenching of her stomach muscles hurt so much, she moaned and doubled over.

'Don't cry.' Siordun urged her to lie down. 'I'll send a message to my agents, see what I can learn. It'll be all right. You're safe now.'

Exhausted, she let him tuck the covers around her.

'You need to rest. I did what I could, but the fever burned away your strength. In fact...' He touched her forehead. 'Yes, just as I feared, you're feverish again, and I can't do anything about it. I need a day to recover.'

'Send the message. Find out if Byren escaped. If he did, warn him about the rumours.'

'I will.' But he remained by the bed. Moonlight silvered his iron-grey hair, while his face remained in shadow.

Piro felt uncomfortable under his scrutiny. 'I lost your stone. I think the surgeon took it.'

'I'll give you another.'

'Don't bother.' She realised she sounded ungrateful and hastened to explain. 'It didn't matter how hard I tried, I couldn't make the stone glow. I'm not fit to be your apprentice.'

'Not everyone can—'

'You said if I can't control my Affinity I'm useless.'

'Don't you be so hard on yourself. Perhaps it was the wrong type of stone. Each stone has different qualities. Each person's Affinity is different. It took me a long time to learn how to focus my power. The mage was a strict teacher. I hated him at first, for taking me away from my family and my home.'

'He had to be strict to help you control your power.'

'I know that now, but try telling that to a child of five.'

'Did you...' She tried to sit up.

But he pressed her back. 'Lie still.'

'Then don't loom over me. Sit there, where I can see your face.' She gestured to the end of the bed. 'Did you start studying right away?'

He settled himself on the end of the bed. 'I didn't begin my formal training until I was ten. I struggled. It was only later that I realised the mage did not expect me to master the exercises right away. He was training me to be persistent, to concentrate and to keep going even when I failed.'

'You loved him.'

Siordun looked away. 'Yes.' His voice caught. 'These last two years, everything has gone wrong. In fact, these last seven years, since King Sefon was murdered and Lord Dunstany died of shock, I've been desperately scrambling to keep up. The mage tried to maintain my lessons, but we seemed to go from one near disaster to another.'

'How old were you when Dunstany died?'

He cast her a dry look. 'If you want to know how old I am, you could just ask.'

'I want to know how much training you had with the mage.'

He grimaced. 'I began formal training when I was ten. I had six years of study, but after King Sefon died, we only managed to snatch moments here and there, like you and I have been doing.'

'We've hardly done anything.'

'This is part of your training. I've told you more about sorbt stones.'

'You're ten years older than me.'

'Nine. You'll be fourteen on midsummer's day.'

Piro closed her eyes. 'I'm very tired. I think you should go now.'

She felt him stand, felt him come closer.

His palm cupped her cheek. 'Did you trust Dunstany, Piro?'

'Yes. And I miss him!'

'I *am* him.'

But she turned her face away.

This time he left and she could not stop the hot tears.

JUST AS FYN had predicted, as soon as the diversionary assault started, the spar sentries left their posts. Dozens of the great house defenders charged down to the shore. Camoric took his men and most of the freed slaves to attack the spar warriors from behind. Meanwhile, Fyn and Sefarra went to clean out the great house.

He led a dozen slaves to check the warren of servants' rooms, while Sefarra led her men up to the second floor of the house.

The freed slaves had soon outstripped Fyn, running ahead, whooping and shouting as they spotted spar warriors. Like crazed beasts, they chased them down and hacked them to pieces. All their pent up anger and resentment had finally found an outlet.

When Fyn entered the great hall with its grand staircase, he found the ex-slaves had battered the last spar warrior to death. Several of the floor-to-ceiling doors had been left open, and when the freed slaves spotted the battle under way down by the shore, they charged down there.

He shuddered and went to survey the rest of the house. Down in the cellars, he found half a dozen of the household servants hiding in the cool darkness.

'Lady Sefarra has routed the invaders,' he said. 'Go to the kitchen and prepare a feast.'

When he returned to the great hall, there was no sign of Sefarra. Had the sight of spar warriors in her home triggered memories of her time as a captive?

Fyn was about to go in search of her, when Camoric returned, triumphant, and reported to him.

'Those ex-slaves showed no mercy. I—'

Cheers interrupted him. The ex-slaves had returned with several crates of wine and were in the process of distributing the bottles amongst themselves.

Camoric glanced to Fyn.

'No point trying to stop them. I ordered the servants to prepare a feast. Have your men remove the bodies and clean up the blood. I don't want Sefarra reminded...'

He fell silent as a hush swept over the great hall. With the feeling this had all happened before, Fyn turned and looked up the grand stair. Sefarra stood at the top, drenched in blood.

'See the fate of Warlord Jankigern!' she cried, lifting the warlord's head by its hair.

'Sefarra! Sefarra!' her men chanted, and the others joined in.

The sound filled the hall, echoing off the high ceiling until Fyn's ears ached. He glanced to Camoric, who looked stunned. At least he now knew Sefarra's true nature.

The household servants arrived with food platters, and Sefarra came down the stairs to organise clearing the table. She seemed unaware of the head hanging from one hand as she gestured with the other.

Camoric nudged Fyn. 'She's going to be mine one day.'

'But...' Fyn was stunned. 'You'd never know what she was going to say or do next.'

'Exactly!'

On second thoughts, perhaps they were well-matched. Fyn preferred Isolt's measured mind. He trusted her to back him up.

'I'll build a pyre for the bodies,' Camoric said.

Fyn joined Sefarra, then reached for the warlord's head. 'Let me get rid of that for you.'

Chapter Forty-Four

Garzik had bunked down with the unmarried men on the floor of the long-hall. After they'd unloaded the ship, Rusan and Olbin had taken Feodan aside and spent a day planning the construction of their new vessel. No drawings were made, but from what Garzik gathered, the ship had already been built in Feodan's head.

According to Lauvra, her brother had been trained by the settlement's old Affinity-touched before he died. The man had been able to commune with trees and, while Feodan didn't have Affinity, he had a knack for finding branches with the right shaped curves for the ship's ribs.

Today Feodan led a party into the high country in search of the right timbers.

Olbin stretched and scratched his belly. 'Where did Rus get to?'

'I'll find him,' Garzik offered, getting to his feet.

He thought he'd seen Rusan slip into one of the store rooms. Sure enough, he spotted a glow right down the back, behind some barrels, but he hesitated when he heard Lauvra's stern voice. He peered between two barrels to see her with Rusan.

'...haven't seen Pramoza since the night you arrived, she's so angry. You owe her nothing, considering what Jost and his brothers did.'

'I know. But I keep thinking...'—Rusan faltered—'about you, the day we got the news that Drav and Stojan were dead.'

'Oh, Rus.' Tough, iron-haired Lauvra took his face in her hands and kissed his forehead. 'You have a good heart. But you can't give Pramoza the basket. She'll take offence. She'll think you're rubbing salt in the wound, or admitting fault.'

'Why would she think that?'

'Because she's petty and vindictive, and she'll assume your motivations are the same as hers. Now say goodbye to Feo and Olbin.'

Before Rusan could catch him eavesdropping, Garzik returned to the long-hall, where those who were going with Feodan were making up travelling packs.

A moment later, Rusan drew Garzik away from the others and handed him a basket packed with hot-land luxuries. 'Take this up to Pramoza's cottage. Knock, then leave it on her doorstep. Don't let her see you.'

Garzik nodded and hid a smile. He slipped out of the long-hall then climbed the hillside. Back when he had first come to the settlement, he'd seen Rusan and Olbin take a selection of treasures to the oracles and their mother, in honour of the service they provided. Now the cottage that had belonged to the Affinity-touched family stood abandoned. Vultar's men had stripped it, murdered the twins' mother and abducted the girls.

Jost's mother lived further up the hillside, in a cottage built into the hillside. No smoke came from the single chimney, and he heard a cow lowing with discomfort in the nearby byre.

Garzik left the basket on the front step, then went

to go, but as he passed the cottage window, something caught his attention.

Through the small pane of rippled glass, he made out a figure standing oddly. A sense of foreboding swept through him. Cupping his hands to the glass, he peered in to see Pramoza hanging from the rafters, bare feet protruding from her nightgown.

He rushed inside, but he was too late. It looked as though she'd been dead for at least a day.

Shocked, Garzik backed out and almost tripped over the basket. Instinctively, he picked it up. As he headed down the path, making for the long-hall, it occurred to him that someone might ask what he was doing with the basket, so he left it on the doorstep of the empty Affinity-toucheds' cottage.

Feodan's party was about to leave, and everyone had gathered on the grassy patch in front of the long-hall to wish them goodbye. As Garzik pushed through the crowd, people commented on his rudeness. At last he found Lauvra bidding Feodan and Olbin good bye.

In his haste Garzik reverted to training and bowed as he would to Queen Myrella. 'Forgive me, but...' He gestured up hill. 'Pramoza has taken her own life.'

Lauvra glanced to Rusan.

'How did you come to find her?' Feodan asked.

Garzik thought quickly. 'When Rusan sent me to pay tribute to the oracles. I heard Pramoza's cow lowing with pain and knew she hadn't been milked.'

Word spread quickly and everyone hurried up the hill, the elders huffing along behind. When they reached Pramoza's cottage, Lauvra went in with two of the elders. After a moment she came out, face solemn. 'It is as Wynn says.'

She stepped aside and the wife of Pramoza's brothers entered the cottage to prepare the body for burial.

As they returned to the long-hall, they passed the Affinity-toucheds' cottage. Crisdun retrieved the basket and thanked Rusan on behalf of his daughters.

Holding the basket as if it was evidence, Crisdun said, 'Rusan has sworn a blood oath to bring the oracles home and kill Vultar.'

The settlement voiced their approval, then continued downhill.

Garzik was close enough to hear Feodan whisper to Lauvra. 'There are some who will blame Rusan and Olbin for this.'

'I know, curse her. She was vindictive even in death!'

'But he's also won many hearts.'

'It is ever the way. The higher we rise, the more we are hated by some and loved by others.'

Rusan caught Garzik's arm, and they stepped aside. The others kept walking, leaving them alone, high on the hill-side looking out over the narrow bay. Mist lay on the water, but the sun would soon burn it off.

'Who were you, back in the hot-lands?' Rusan asked softly.

'What?' Garzik had been expecting Rusan to comment on Pramoza's death, or the way he'd left the basket for the Affinity-touched.

'I saw how you approached my mother, like she was the queen. Are you the missing Rolencian king, the one the usurper offered a reward for?'

A laugh escaped Garzik. The idea that anyone could mistake him for Byren was astounding. 'How do you know about Rolencia's politics?'

'Feo told me. He heard it from an Ostronite captain.'

'Now is not a good time to be laughing, lads,' Feodan said as he made his way back to them. 'What's so funny, anyway?'

Rusan glanced to Garzik, who asked, 'What did the captain tell you about the missing Rolencian king?'

'Just that his people believe he will return and save them from oppression.' Feodan shrugged. 'But that was back at the end of winter. Who knows what the situation is now?'

So Garzik did not learn anything new.

* * *

FLORIN SAT ON the floor beside her brother's bed. He'd woken before dawn, calling for Da, and she'd calmed him with stories of the mountain legends her mother used to tell her. The worst of the fever had passed, but Leif was still weak; even as she watched, he fell asleep.

Nun Anise passed by his bed with a willow-bark tisane for one of the worst-effected fever victims. More were coming down with it all the time. Luckily, Byren hadn't taken sick.

Florin's stomach rumbled. She came to her feet and stretched, joints popping. She'd had very little sleep these last two days, and Cinna had had even less, but she never complained.

As if thinking of Cinna had conjured her, she appeared in the door way, one hand cupping her belly as if she'd been running.

Florin crossed the solarium floor in three long strides. 'What's wrong? Is the baby—'

'No.' Cinna drew her out into the hall and glanced quickly in both directions before whispering, 'I've had a message. There's trouble in Merofynia. Byren is to report to Lord Dunstany.'

'What kind of trouble?'

'Spar uprisings.'

'If Merofynia has to battle its spar warlords just to survive, Byren could lose everything. We must get word to him, but he's off hunting manticores.' Florin cursed. There'd been reports of a pack terrorising travellers over the pass. Feid had asked Byren and Orrade to go hunting and had also invited the Snow Bridge men. The party had left the morning Florin had discovered Leif was sick.

'I've already sent word by fast rider,' Cinna said. 'They'll be back as soon as they can.'

'Byren mustn't appear weak before the Snow Bridge ambassador.'

'I told the messenger only that they were to come straight here. Even so, Vlatajor will know that something's going on.'

'Not if you take to your bed now,' Nun Anise said, surprising them both. 'I'll put it about that you're going to have the baby. When the men turn up, we'll say it was a false alarm.'

'Oh, thank you...' Cinna gave a sigh of relief, then went very pale and swayed. Florin had to steady her.

'Come to think of it, a day or two in bed will do you good, my lady,' Anise said. 'Help her up to her chamber, Florin. I can manage here.'

Hoping to catch a few moments alone with Isolt, Fyn went straight from the yacht to the queen. He found her in the war-table chamber, and she was not alone. Luckily she had Dunstany at her side, for ranged on the other side of the table were Captain Elrhodoc and his brother, Lord Elcwyff, as well as Lords Neiron and Rhoderich.

'...turned the warlord back. Chased him and his men all the way up the Divide to the pass and lowered the fort gate, but it won't hold them,' Elcwyff was saying. 'For the last two hundred years, the fort's been used as a way-house.'

Frown frowned. As he recalled, Elcwyff's estate backed onto Wyvern Spar. Now it seemed the warlord had mounted an attack. Sefarra was right. As soon as they put down one warlord, another replaced him.

'It's the same with the fort pass to Ulfr Spar,' Rhoderich said, his deep voice carrying. 'We're lucky that the warlord hasn't attacked.'

'It's only a matter of time,' Neiron insisted. 'I've rebuilt the fort on the pass to Lincis Spar and made sure it was manned, but somehow a raiding party slipped through.'

'I thought the might of Lincis and Amfina Spars' warriors had been crushed in the Battle of Wythrontir,' Fyn said.

All heads turned towards him. He saw Isolt go to welcome him, but Dunstany took her arm and squeezed, reminding her to sustain the fiction that they'd fallen out.

Seeing him in the doorway, the Merofynian nobles shifted closer together. This left Fyn alone at the end of the war-table, alone and isolated, which was where he needed to be if he was to lure out those who sought to remove him and undermine Byren.

'We did crush the warlords and their men,' Neiron said.

'Yet you say Lincis Spar warriors have been mounting raids?'

Neiron grimaced. 'I don't know how—'

'Secret passes. Byren used one to escape Cobalt's men. Since there are secret passes over the Dividing Mountains in Rolencia—'

'What of the Benetir girl?' Elrhodoc demanded. 'Is she suitably chastened and ready to retreat to Cyena Abbey? We can't mount an attack to save her estate until we've secured our own.'

'You don't need to. Lady Sefarra is reinforcing the defences of her estate and great house even as we speak.'

Elrhodoc frowned. 'But how—'

'Queen Isolt, there's a dozen seven-year slaves requesting an audience with you, and at least a hundred making camp on the terraces,' a frantic servant reported.

Blustering with anger, the Merofynian nobles dashed to the tall windows to peer down onto the terrace.

Neiron turned to Elrhodoc. 'Call out the queen's guards. Round up these escaped slaves. Hang the dozen brazen enough to request an audience with the queen and—'

'They are not escaped slaves,' Fyn said. 'They fought to recapture Benetir Estate in exchange for their freedom. They want the queen to negotiate safe passage to Rolencia. Some have remained on Benetir Estate in Lady Sefarra's employ to help build defences, but the rest—'

'Pay seven-year slaves good Merofynian coin?' Rhoderich muttered. 'What's the girl thinking?'

'They're not escaped slaves,' Fyn repeated. 'They're free men, hiring out their services!'

'How could you free the Benetir seven-year slaves?' Neiron demanded. 'If *our* seven-year slaves hear of it, they'll revolt. Slave revolts on top of Utland raids and spar invasions!' He turned to the others. 'Save me from meddling amateurs.'

'What do you expect?' Elrhodoc's voice was thick with contempt. 'He's Rolencian. He has no love for Merofynia.'

Isolt opened her mouth to protest, but held her tongue.

Fyn needed to appear vulnerable, but not cowed. 'If you offered your seven-year slaves their freedom in exchange for fighting off spar raids—'

'Never! I'm not putting weapons in the hands of our enemy.' Rhoderich's deep voice cut him off. 'My queen, we came to you for help. Is this the best you can offer?'

Isolt lifted her hands. 'Apart from the palace guards and my honour guard, you lords are my captains, and your men-at-arms are my army.'

'You brought this on yourselves,' Fyn said. 'If Merofynia had not sent Palatyne to invade Rolencia, and the lords had not ridden on his coat-tails to rake in the rewards, the nobles' estates would not be ripe and rich, bloated with seven-year slaves. Now you can't defend yourselves because you sent the best of your men-at-arms to die, spilling Merofynian blood on Rolencian soil. And for what? Red wine, grain and velvet cloth!' Fyn's voice shook with anger. 'You sacked Halcyon Abbey. I saw boys and old masters murdered. Potential and knowledge, lost forever. You call Rolencians barbarians, yet thirty years ago, when my father turned back the last Merofynian invasion, he did not sack Cyena and Mulcibar Abbeys. He respected the seats of learning.' Tears of fury stung Fyn's eyes. 'So don't come whining to your queen, not when you let greed guide your decisions.'

'My queen, are you going to put up with this Rolencian upstart criticising Merofynian royalty?' Rhoderich demanded.

As Dunstany caught Fyn's eye, he realised Isolt had to side with the nobles. He'd backed her into a corner.

Fyn bent from the waist. 'Your pardon, my queen. I let the memory of the deaths of my fellow monks and tutors overcome my judgement. I came to report that Benetir Estate is once again in Lady Sefarra's hands and—'

'Hundreds of lawless seven-year slaves have been freed!' Elrhodoc cut in.

'Exactly.' Neiron backed him up. 'Before you know it, they will be roaming the streets, robbing and raping. Call out the city-watch, my queen. Call on your queen's guards. Double the palace guards.'

'The young lord's right,' Dunstany said. 'It would be wise to put Captain Aeran on alert, Queen Isolt.'

'At last someone speaks sense,' Rhoderich muttered.

'Double the palace guards and send word to the captain of the city-watch,' Isolt told Elrhodoc.

He gave the queen a quick bow, before striding out.

'I'm sailing home,' Rhoderich said. 'For it's clear we lords are on our own. Neiron, Elcwyff, are you with me?'

Both lords assured him they were, and all three marched out.

Isolt turned to the servant who had been waiting all this time. 'Give the ex-slaves food and tell them to wait. They are not to be hounded or provoked.'

As soon as he was alone with Isolt and Dunstany, Fyn signalled for silence, checked the hall and shut the doors.

'That certainly set the cat among the pigeons,' Dunstany said.

Fyn flushed. 'I'm sorry, I—'

'Everything Fyn said was true,' Isolt insisted. 'Unwelcome, but true. I wish I could have supported—'

'You played your part well, my dear,' Dunstany told her. 'And Fyn, you were right. The Merofynity Stone is a spectacularly large sorbt stone, the kind that focuses power. Your ancestors must have had Affinity, for the stone to welcome them, but not the knowledge to understand its true potential. It's priceless.'

'Should we lock it up?' Piro asked, intrigued. 'Or is it impossible to move?'

'Not impossible, just difficult,' Dunstany said. 'It's been there for hundreds of years. I don't think anyone is going to run off with it, and people would ask questions of the Merofynity Stone disappeared. In fact...'—he turned to Isolt—'I think you should marry Byren under the linden tree while standing on that stone.'

Fyn didn't want to make plans for Byren to marry Isolt. He changed the topic. 'The lords are right about one thing. Once the rest of the seven-year slaves hear that the Benetir Estate slaves were freed, they'll revolt. We should put them on ships and send them back home as quickly—'

'If you send them home, they'll return to their farms and shops, and Byren will only have to gather them all over again in order to retake the throne,' Dunstany said. 'Much better to keep them here until Byren is ready to move.'

'Keep them camped on the terrace?' Isolt muttered.

Fyn hated to say it, but... 'The queen's guards are loyal to Elrhodoc. You may have need of a hundred and twenty fighting men, Isolt.'

'Rolencians protecting me from my own queen's guards?' Isolt reached for a chair and sat down abruptly.

Fyn felt responsible. How had it all gone so wrong?

'Don't worry, lad.' Dunstany put a hand on his shoulder. 'I've already sent for Byren.'

'Already sent for?' A vicious surge of anger ripped through Fyn. It felt like a slap in the face, after all his hard work.

'Oh, Fyn, that reminds me.' Isolt sprang to her feet and came over to join them. She didn't appear to realise that he had been insulted. 'Piro is here. She's coming to the palace as soon as she's well enough to travel.'

'Piro here? Wait...' Fyn wasn't thinking clearly. 'She's sick?'

Isolt glanced to Dunstany who answered. 'Your sister was wounded, but she's recovering.'

'Good.' But if he stayed, he was going to say something he'd regret. 'If you'll excuse me, I need to clean up.'

And he left them, still burning with anger. Dunstany had sent for Byren without consulting him. He went to his chambers, meaning to gather his thoughts, but he found a servant waiting for him.

'Who are you?' Fyn asked.

'Sebron,' the man said. 'Kyral was sick, so he sent me.'

Since Fyn had managed to convince his former servant that he did not want help, he knew this for a lie. His mind raced. Was this Elrhodoc's answer, a manservant sent to kill him? Just let him try...

'My lord?'

'Hmm?' Mind racing, Fyn rubbed his face as if tired. He wished he was armed, but he'd discarded his sword and knife before going to see the queen. 'Think I'll have a bath.'

He looked down as if to unlace his shirt, deliberately giving the assassin an opening.

Sensing movement, Fyn sidestepped. The manservant stumbled past him, regaining his feet with liquid ease.

The manservant had produced a small, wicked blade. He was all economical movement and total concentration.

Fyn frowned. 'You're a corax.'

A flicker of surprise crossed the assassin's face.

'I don't have any enemies on Ostron Isle...' But that was where Cobalt had spent the last thirteen years. And Cobalt had burnt 'Fyn's' body in Rolenton Square. 'My cousin Cobalt sent you.'

But if he had hoped for confirmation, he was out of luck.

The assassin remained silent as he circled Fyn, trying to pin him between the bed and the wall.

Instead, Fyn backed away, drawing the corax into the bathing chamber.

Heart thundering, Fyn felt his Affinity surge and the stone on his ring gleamed. The corax's gaze flicked down to his hand.

Fyn stepped forward, caught his attacker's knife hand and pivoted, pulling the man off balance in a half-circle, then letting him go.

The assassin skidded on the bathing chamber tiles and fell headfirst into the sunken bath.

With the corax's knife now in his hand, Fyn stood over the tub ready to strike, but the corax lay unmoving. He'd broken his neck when he struck the far end of the bath.

Fyn's legs gave way and he knelt on the tiles. He'd been lucky. But with coraxes after him, from now on he would have to be careful.

Chapter Forty-Five

'Here will do,' Piro said, pointing to a shaded spot under the sweetly-scented lemon tree.

Gwalt nodded to the stable master, who had helped carry the day-bed into the courtyard of Dunstany's townhouse. She hated not being able to do things for herself.

'Thank you.' Piro sank onto the bed with relief.

Gwalt put a glass of lemon and barley water on a small table beside her. 'There we are. Now, you let me know if you need anything else.'

She nodded. He was so different from the ship's surgeon who had terrorised her when she was at death's door. Tears stung her eyes.

'Don't cry.' Gwalt patted her arm. 'What's wrong?'

'Y-you've been so k-kind.'

He smiled indulgently. 'And why wouldn't I be?'

'The cook...' The cook had recognised Piro as Dunstany's ex-slave, and refused to speak to her. Piro wasn't sure if it was because she had been a slave, or because she had travelled with Dunstany dressed as a boy.

'Don't give her a thought.'

'I'm not usually like this,' Piro confessed, brushing away the tears.

'I know. The best thing you can do is rest and get better. That'll please his lordship.'

Piro nodded, although she didn't understand why he thought she'd want to please Siordun.

Gwalt left and Piro lay back to watch the sun gleaming through the foliage. It was mid-afternoon, and her fever had abated for the time being. The servants' chatter as they brought in the laundry was strangely comforting. After facing death, the ordinary concerns of running a home reminded her how precious life was.

She'd almost dozed off when she heard Dunstany's voice.

With an effort, she pulled herself up on one elbow and watched as the carriage with the Dunistir crest—a star within a circle, symbolising purity and fidelity—entered the courtyard. As a stable boy closed the gate, Dunstany climbed down and the carriage continued around the lemon tree into the stables.

'My lord?' Piro called.

He turned and saw her there. 'You're up?' He hobbled over, leaning heavily on the cane. 'I don't think that's wise.'

'I've been shut in a dank, dark cabin for five days with a bad tempered ship's surgeon who smelled of alcohol and despair. If I didn't get out in the sunshine, I'd go mad.'

His lips twitched and his eyes smiled. In the past she'd been delighted every time she'd made Lord Dunstany smile. Now she wasn't sure how she felt.

He sat down as if his bones ached.

'Why do you...' She gestured to the staff and cane.

'Disguise is in the detail. Isolt has invited Piro Rolen Kingsdaughter to stay with her at the palace.'

Piro wrinkled her nose. 'Would I have to be polite and listen to old noblemen tell me things I already know?'

His lips twitched again.

She felt a surge of pleasure, which she ruthlessly suppressed—this was not *her* Lord Dunstany. 'What news of Fyn?'

'Benetir Estate is in Sefarra's hands again. Camoric and his men are staying on to help her make the great house defensible.'

Piro wanted to ask about Byren, but it was too soon for news. 'And Fyn?'

'He returned with over a hundred freed seven-year slaves.'

'Then they can sail for Rolencia.' She saw Dunstany's expression. 'I see. You mean to keep them here until he needs them.' She frowned. 'I wish I knew if Byren—'

'Don't fret.' He cupped her cheek, too briefly for her to object. 'You don't have to go up to the palace until you're ready. My Affinity will be restored by this evening. I'll work on your wound then.'

She nodded and he left her. It was pleasant under the lemon tree, and she let herself drift into a doze. She was still aware of the soft brush of the breeze over her skin, still felt the dappled sunlight like warm kisses on her face and arms, still heard the chatter of the servants in the kitchen, but she drifted free of her body to float above the courtyard.

In this state, she was aware of Siordun's Affinity. She sensed him as if he was a slow burning beacon inside the townhouse. It was almost as if she was using her unseen sight, and she wondered if her Affinity had been restored before her body was fully healed, thanks to Siordun's attempts to heal her.

A delivery cart arrived, and as the cook came out to chat to the carter, Piro wondered if she could use her Affinity to find her foenix, but she was afraid of wandering too far in the unseen world. She might lose herself, and not be able to find her way back to her body.

A bird landed in the lemon tree and began to sip nectar from the sweet flowers. Piro tried to reach out to the creature. Instead, she sensed the Affinity of a half-grown kresillum in the lemon tree, below her. The Affinity creature's back was covered by hard plates. They had an almost mirror-like finish, so that the kresillum seemed to be covered by a shell made of sunlight and leaves.

She wished she had thought to research kresillums after her encounter with the kresatrices on the voyage to Ostron Isle.

Luckily, this creature did not seem aggressive. It scurried down the tree to crouch on the branch directly above her body, possibly attracted by the Affinity she was exerting.

The kresillum twitched as another cart arrived. This cart belonged to a cheese monger; Piro could smell the cheese, even with her awareness hovering above her body.

As the cook made her purchases from the far side of the cart, a muslin flap opened on this of the cart. Intrigued, Piro watched as one long leg slid out, followed by another. A youth climbed down from the cart. The cheese monger's stowaway went barefoot and wore a thigh-length smock over knitted breeches. Their hair was tied back in a long queue, such as sailors wore. The androgynous face and neutral clothes gave no clue as to the stowaway's gender.

Spotting Piro asleep under the lemon tree, the stowaway glanced left and right before drawing a sharp little paring knife.

A corax. Fear froze Piro.

Already the assassin was approaching the day-bed. Piro tried to reach out to Siordun, but he was impervious to her.

The corax's hands neared Piro's throat.

Panic made her Affinity surge. She felt the kresillum jump with fright and emit a high noise.

The kresillum's unearthly song made the corax forget their mission. Face slack, eyes wide and dreamy the entranced assassin swayed in time to the kresillum's melody. But even so the knife remained in their grasp.

As the cheese monger and cook came over to the lemon tree to investigate the sound, Piro felt a wave of relief. They would save her. But by the time they stood under the tree, they were also under the kresillum's spell. A boy came out of the stable and became entranced by the song.

'Here, what're you doin',' the stable master demanded and strode after the lad. 'There's work to... be...'

And he too was lost. This was ridiculous.

Fear churned in Piro, stirring her Affinity. What if the corax grew used to the kresillum's song and managed to throw off its effects? She could end up dead while everyone stood around with silly smiles on their faces.

Here came Dunstany's trusted servant, Gwalt, with young Illien. But they were captured too.

A servant poked her head out the window and gestured to the crowd under the lemon tree. 'What's going on?'

No one answered.

The woman slammed the window shut and a few moments later ran out the back door. Piro wanted to shake her, then realised Dunstany was one step behind her.

The woman lost momentum and purpose by the time she reached the cook, but Dunstany approached as if pushing through thigh-deep snow.

Piro tried to reach out to him but, once again, he was impervious to her Affinity, although the act of reaching out had stripped him of illusion. She now saw Siordun in costume, not Dunstany the elderly scholar.

And despite his own Affinity, Siordun was not impervious to the kresillum's allure. He fought it, raising his cane to prod the creature.

Frustration ate at Piro. The kresillum was not the threat. She wanted to kick Siordun.

The closer the cane came to the Affinity creature, the more intense its song became.

Just before the cane tip struck, the kresillum ended its

song and leaped off the branch, back plates opening up to reveal shimmery gauzy wings that looked too fine to support its weight.

Wings whirring, the Affinity creature swept out over the crowd. Several people fell to their knees, others swayed.

Siordun finally noticed the blade in the corax's hand and rapped the knuckles sharply with his cane.

The corax gave a bark of pain and sprang upright, colliding with the cheese monger. The two of them seemed to shiver. Their slack expressions focused, revealing purpose and training. Both were coraxes.

They made for the gate, leaving the cheese monger's cart behind.

'Coraxes!' Dunstany shouted. 'Stop them.'

But his townhouse servants were still recovering from the kresillum's trance. Only Gwalt tried to tackle the cheese monger, who flipped him over his shoulder, tumbling him to the stones of the courtyard.

'Piro!' Siordun took her shoulders in his hands.

The moment he touched her, she slipped back into her body and regained control with a gasp. Looking up at him, she found he was once again Dunstany.

Behind him, the servants helped Gwalt and tried to make sense of what had just happened. They didn't remember the kresillum.

Illien returned to report, 'We lost them, my lord.'

'Don't worry. We'll be on our guard from now on.' Dunstany dismissed him, and turned to Piro. 'You were under the thrall of a kresillum's song.'

'No, I wasn't. I made it sing to stop the corax from cutting my throat. Everyone else was under the kresillum's spell.' She eyed him. 'Even you had trouble fighting it. Why didn't it affect me when you struggled? What are you not telling me?'

He glanced to the servants. 'This is not the time or place.' He beckoned the stable master to carry Piro inside.

She did not argue.

By the time she was in her bed again, her fever had returned. Dunstany sent the servants away and reached out to her.

She pushed his hand away. 'Why are coraxes after me?'

'Cobalt has told everyone that Byren killed you.' Dunstany went to the door and asked for a tisane to be made up, then returned to sit by the bed. 'It would look odd if there was another Piro in Merofynia.'

'But who knew I was here?'

'The ship's surgeon?'

'I told him I was your servant.'

'Would Lord Dunstany collect his servant in person?'

'You gave me away.'

'The surgeon really annoyed me. The thought of you in his power...' He glowered. 'The coraxes must have been waiting for an opportunity to identify and remove you. A while ago some footpads attacked Fyn, but—'

'Coraxes tried to kill Fyn?' Piro was horrified.

'They were too clumsy for coraxes. '

'Then who tried to kill Fyn?'

Dunstany sighed. 'He advises the young queen. There are many who would like that position.'

'You advise the young queen.'

'Enemies have already killed Dunstany once. One day they will succeed. Before that day, Dunstany will have to die a natural death. If I'm killed, my disguise will be revealed. My fall would bring down Fyn and lose Byren this kingdom.'

Piro found she could not bear the thought of sponging the blood from Siordun's dead body to prepare him for burial.

'I've sent for Byren. Lord Elcwyff has asked for help. The warlord of Wyvern Spar came over the pass and attacked his lands. They were turned back, but I fear...'

'Merofynia is vulnerable.'

'We are all vulnerable.'

She frowned. 'Why was it that I had no trouble controlling the kresillum, but you were almost under its spell? Why can't I make the sorbt stone glow, when you could do it as a ten-year-old?'

'That really rankles, doesn't it?' His mouth twitched, then he sobered. 'What was King Byren the Fourth known for?'

'You mean apart from fathering bastards?'

'Piro!'

'You sound just like my mother.' She could see he didn't like the comparison. 'My grandfather was known for his menagerie... His Affinity was best suited to communing with animals!'

Siordun nodded. 'Specifically Affinity beasts. I'll give you another type of sorbt stone. Maybe it will be easier for you to focus your power in it. As for the coraxes... I think it is time the mage had a talk with Lady Death.'

'But...' That meant he had to sail for Ostron Isle. She had only just found him again.

'Don't worry. I won't leave you unless I have Lady Death's word that she will call off her assassins until after our meeting.' A dark light came into Dunstany's eyes. 'She will regret attempting to kill you.'

Piro shivered.

BYREN TOSSED HIS reins to the stable boy and strode across the stronghold courtyard. Feid broke into a run, outpacing him. The servant had said only that they must make all haste back to the keep, which everyone took to mean that Cinna was having the baby.

'Where's Cinna, is she well?' Feid asked Florin, who stood at the door. 'Is the baby—'

'Cinna's fine, she didn't have the baby. It was a false alarm.' Florin shrugged.

'So we rushed back for nothing?' Vlatajor said, as his two companions caught up. The six Snow Bridge men-at-arms had dismounted. 'I wanted to see how effective the ulfr dung was.'

'Ulfr dung?' Florin glanced to Byren. 'Last time, when we trapped and killed a manticore pride, we used tar and flames to drive them—'

'Aye, but I'm older and wiser now,' Byren said. 'Why use force when guile will do the job?'

Florin looked to Orrade for an explanation.

He grinned. 'Byren found the spoor of an ulfr pack. They're natural enemies, so—'

'—you planted ulfr dung near the upper trail to keep the manticores away,' Florin anticipated, making Byren proud. 'Could work.'

Vlatajor stretched, easing his back. 'If there are no more manticore attacks you'll know it was successful.'

'A bath has been drawn in your chamber, Lord Vlatajor,' Florin said, leading them into the stronghold. 'And Lady Cinna was asking for you, Lord Feid. This way.'

'I know the way to my own bed,' Feid muttered, slipping past her.

'Ah, young love,' Vlatajor said.

Byren would have gone to his own room, but Florin caught his eye and jerked her head towards the warlord's chamber. He and Orrade followed her.

When Florin opened the door to the warlord's private chamber, they found Cinna sitting up in bed while Feid paced. '...Byren has to go.'

'Go where?' Byren asked, as Florin shut the door.

Cinna explained about the spar attacks, finishing with, 'So you could lose Merofynia if you don't make haste.'

Byren cursed. 'I shouldn't have left Fyn in charge. Book learning is all very well, but nothing beats experience.'

'You can borrow my ship,' Feid said.

Byren nodded his thanks. 'I'll take my honour guard, all fifty of them.' After his army had been decimated in the Battle of Narrowneck, the survivors had dispersed, but the most dedicated had trickled over the pass. 'How soon will the ship be ready to sail, Feid?'

'Wait...' Orrade held up a hand. 'Could you repeat the message exactly as the bird said it, please, Cinna?'

She shrugged and obliged. '*Spar warriors threaten the crown, Seek D's seat, lest your lords let you down.*'

Orrade rubbed his jaw. 'Sounds to me like the mage wants you to report straight to Dunstany's estate without stopping in Port Mero. He doesn't want the nobles knowing you've arrived. Sounds like they're the ones letting you down, not Fyn.'

'You're right,' Byren conceded. 'So we sail through the grand canal and across the Landlocked Sea to—'

'Feid is generous to offer his ship, but the arrival of the Foenix Spar warlord's vessel would cause speculation. Everyone knows he's your staunchest ally,' Orrade said. 'On the other hand, Vlatajor wants you to meet the Snow Bridge king. If memory serves me right, the summer journey over the spar takes around fifteen days. We—'

'That's if you take the Rolencian pass,' Feid said. 'If you sail to the southern pass, then take the long valley north, you cut your journey in half.'

'Excellent,' Orrade's said. 'If we enter Merofynia via the Snow Bridge pass that comes out behind Dunstany's estate, we'll have the element of surprise. It will also give you a chance to meet King Jorgoskev and take his measure. No one has united the city states of the Snow Bridge before. Maybe an alliance with him would be a good idea.'

'Piro is not going to be happy if I marry her off,' Byren said. He grinned. 'But I can use the betrothal negotiation as an excuse to meet this new Snow Bridge king who thinks we're savages.'

Orrade nodded. 'You'll need to tell Vlatajor why you're going to Merofynia.'

'If the king's spies are any good, he'll know why,' Byren countered.

'Very likely, but admitting that you're worried about spar invasions is very different from returning to Merofynia to celebrate your betrothal. You need to negotiate the marriage contracts and sit for your formal betrothal portrait.'

'What betrothal portrait?'

'It's an old Merofynian custom. Honestly, Byren, *I* paid more attention to your mother's stories than you did.'

Byren frowned. 'I told Isolt I wouldn't marry her until I had reclaimed my father's throne.'

'This is just the betrothal ceremony. We sailed the day after Palatyne was killed and her father died. It was not the right time to hold a betrothal then.'

'Very true,' Cinna agreed. 'I'll send a message to the mage so that Queen Isolt can make plans.'

'That settles it,' Feid said. 'You leave tomorrow with your honour guard.'

'And Florin,' Orrade said.

'But...' Florin looked horrified.

'Leif will be safe with us,' Feid assured her.

'Besides,' Cinna added, 'he's too weak to travel, and the thin air of the Snow Bridge taxes the strongest of constitutions.'

Byren rubbed his jaw, pretending to consider. 'Florin...'

'She's the only one who speaks the Snow Bridge language,' Orrade said. 'You'd be a fool to give up that advantage.'

Byren turned to Florin. 'I'm not forcing this on you. You can say no.'

'You know very well I can't let you walk into danger,' she told him, quietly furious. 'Not when I can protect you.'

'Then it's decided,' Byren said, secretly delighted.

'Not yet,' Cinna said. 'If Florin goes, she needs an official position in your retinue. She should be—'

'One of your honour guard,' Florin said.

'Done,' Byren said.

She frowned, surprised by his quick capitulation. He grinned and she looked away.

'Stay a moment, Florin.' Cinna patted the bed beside her as the others left.

Florin crossed the chamber and sat down, her back resting against the headboard. She frowned. Knowing Byren could never be hers was one thing, but having to watch him celebrate his betrothal to Queen Isolt was another thing entirely.

'You're angry with me,' Cinna said, taking her hand. 'You love Byren and—'

'No. No, I...' Florin pulled her hand away then flushed, unable to meet Cinna's shrewd eyes.

Cinna patted her arm. 'Where I come from, the Comtes or the Comtissa takes a partner to advance the family. Once the woman produces an heir and a spare, they both take their lovers...' Cinna laughed at Florin's expression. 'You Rolencians are so prudish. Would you rather Byren waste his life in a loveless marriage?'

Florin slipped off the bed. 'Do you plan to take lovers once you've produced an heir and a spare for Lord Feid?'

'Of course not. Ours is a true match. But Byren does not have that luxury. He marries because he must, and he loves where his heart leads.'

Florin shook her head. 'Byren doesn't love me. He doesn't even want me.'

'That's simply not true.'

'Don't.' Heat flooded Florin's cheeks. 'Believe me, I know.'

Chapter Forty-Six

AFTER CLIMBING THROUGH the tunnel into the grotto, Piro had to bend double to catch her breath. Two days had passed since the coraxes had tried to kill her and Fyn. This was the first time she'd managed to escape Dunstany since he'd taken an apartment at the palace next to hers. She had spent much of these last two days watching her brother. She knew Dunstany and Isolt were pretending to be at odds with Fyn, but Fyn seemed genuinely distanced from them.

Piro straightened up and looked around the grotto as Isolt joined her. Beams of sunlight speared through the sorbt stones and reflected off the floor, filling the chamber under the dome with dazzling light. It took Piro's breath away. Everything seemed sharper and clearer, and a strange buzzing filled her ears. 'This...'

'I know.' Isolt beamed. 'It's my favourite place.'

'It reminds me of the grotto on Mage Isle.' And that made Piro feel homesick, except that Mage Isle wasn't truly her home. She didn't have a home anymore.

'What's wrong?'

'Nothing... Is something going on with Fyn?'

'No.' Isolt sounded defensive. 'Why would you say that?'

'He seems to be avoiding us.'

'He's been busy with the ex-slaves. I almost envy them, camped on the lowest terrace overlooking the Landlocked Sea.'

Ripples of light travelled across the grotto ceiling as Loyalty swam in, driving little wavelets across the surface of the pool ahead of her. Resolute followed, although foenixes weren't supposed to enjoy water.

'Resolute!' Piro held out her arms.

Isolt giggled as both Affinity beasts shook themselves, spraying them with water.

'They've grown so big!' Piro couldn't believe her eyes. She ran her fingers through the foenix's fur-like feathers. Her Affinity responded to Resolute, settling naturally in her hands. She rubbed the beasts' throats and they both responded with a growling purr of approval. After a moment, she signalled that this was enough. Loyalty and Resolute begged for more.

'So greedy!' Isolt laughed.

The sound seemed to bounce off the grotto's dome and echo around them. Piro felt weightless, almost dizzy, bathed in Affinity.

Isolt said something, but Piro found it had to think. She glanced to the Affinity beasts. The strange sensation wasn't coming from them. So where...

'I'm worried about Loyalty,' Isolt said. 'She's grown so large she can't get through the tunnel, and... Piro, are you even listening?'

'Hmm?' Letting her vision shift to the unseen world, she made a slow circle of the grotto, holding her hand under each beam of light in turn.

'Piro, your eyes...'

'I can feel Affinity all around me, the air is thick with it. This must be what a seep feels like.' Piro let her sight shift back to normal and pointed to the dome. 'I think the sorbt stones do more than focus power. I think they attract it. What if the Mad Boy King built this place because he had Affinity?'

'No one has ever said he had Affinity.'

'Why did they call him mad? Maybe it was his Affinity that troubled him. Affinity affects people differently, and I'm sure the grotto was built to do something to those with power.'

Isolt frowned. 'If you're right, why did he kill himself not long after he built this place?'

'He killed himself? Mother never said... Of course she wouldn't.'

'No one said it, not in so many words,' Isolt admitted. 'According to the history books, his death was an accident. But why else would he take too much dreamless-sleep?'

Piro almost revealed how Seela had dosed her on dreamless-sleep when she was troubled by visions. 'Oh, I wish...'

'Wish what?'

She wished the mage had not died. There was so much she wanted to learn. Yet, as soon as Lady Death confirmed she had called off her assassins and would meet with him, Siordun was going back to Ostron Isle. Piro had no time to waste. 'I'm tired. I'm going back to the palace.'

'Of course, I'm sorry.' Isolt flushed. 'I'll come with you.'

'No, you stay here with Loyalty and Resolute,' Piro wanted to be alone with Siordun. 'I can find my own way back.'

'You're sure?'

Isolt was so earnest, Piro had to smile. 'I'm sure.'

'You've changed.' Isolt kissed her cheek. 'You've grown up.'

Piro laughed. 'I'm never going to grow up. I never want to be hemmed in by expectations and limited by customs. I'm not so poor-spirited.'

Isolt stiffened. 'Some of us don't have any choice.'

'I'm sorry. I didn't...'

Isolt smiled gently. 'If you weren't stomping on someone's feelings, you wouldn't be Piro. Off you go.'

Piro made her way through the overgrown garden to the fountain. The two queen's guards who were her escort waited on the terrace steps. She'd threatened to set her foenix on them if they followed her down to the grotto.

After what Isolt just said, Piro didn't feel she could face anyone right now. She sat on the rim of the fountain and dipped her fingers in the pool. It was shallow, and the water had been warmed by the sun.

Did she hurt people's feelings? She never meant to. Sometimes she was impatient. Sometimes she said things without thinking, but she never set out to be cruel. Her cheeks burned as she thought of how her mother and Seela used to chastise her. Back then, she had resented their interference. Now that they were no longer here to guide her, she missed them. Tears stung her eyes.

'What's this?' Captain Elrhodoc asked. 'Sitting in the midday sun? Before you know it, you'll get freckles. A beautiful kingsdaughter doesn't want freckles.'

Piro looked away and wiped her cheeks. Clearly, he thought he was being charming. She came to her feet. 'I should go inside.'

But he caught her arm as she went to slip past him. 'Don't run off, my pretty.'

She glanced over her shoulder towards the guards, then realised they weren't the same two who had accompanied her out here. Her stomach lurched.

Elrhodoc's hand tightened on her arm. 'They say you escaped Rolencia, travelling under Dunstany's protection. They say you dressed as a boy. A pretty little thing like you can't be as innocent as you make out. Why, I bet you had the stable lads lining up to lift your ski—'

She slapped him with all her strength, then shoved past him, hand stinging.

But she'd only gone two steps when he caught her. Spinning her around, he pulled her up against his big body and kissed her.

Piro had never kissed anyone. Well, this time last year Garzik had crept up behind her in the mill-house loft and stolen a kiss. It had landed on her ear so it didn't count.

It certainly hadn't been like this, all disgusting tongue and probing hands. What was he doing to her bottom?

Shock turned to fury. She bit down on Elrhodoc's lip and didn't let go until he shoved her so hard she staggered. The back of her legs hit the pool and she lost her balance. Arms pinwheeling, she fell backwards, hitting the water with a smack that stole her breath.

What had made her think the water was warm? Shockingly cold water closed over her face and chest. Gasping for air, she scurried backwards until her shoulders hit the fountain's statue.

'You little bitch!' Elrhodoc fingered his lip then pulled his hand away to find it covered in blood. 'Why, you little wyvern whelp. I'll teach you some manners!'

And he went for her. As she felt for her knife, Bantam's voice returned to her. *Mulcy girl.*

Out of nowhere, Fyn yelled, 'How dare you lay hands on my sister!'

Elrhodoc smiled slowly and Piro had the impression this confrontation was what he really wanted. She had been a means to an end.

She came to her feet and spotted her brother approaching from shore.

Elrhodoc hooked his fingers in his sword belt and rocked back on his heels, arrogance in every line of his body. 'Your sister served Dunstany dressed as his page. Why, she's just a bit of used cunny, fit only for f—'

Without warning, Fyn punched him in the stomach.

The captain doubled over, gasping.

'Stop right there!' the sturdy guard yelled as they both ran down the steps.

Fyn took a step back as the pair of them helped their captain to his feet. Piro studied them, but what she saw did not reassure her. The sturdy one was going to seed, as if the good life as a queen's guard had corrupted him. The second one was younger and looked out of his depth.

Elrhodoc pushed their hands away and confronted Fyn. 'I demand satisfaction. Or are you afraid to meet me?'

Fyn laughed, eyes glittering. 'Nothing would give me greater pleasure.'

'Fyn, no!' Isolt cried, running up, just as Piro lurched to her feet with the same cry on her lips.

'Isolt, help Piro inside and see that she doesn't catch a chill,' Fyn said, not taking his eyes off the captain and his two companions.

'Don't do this, Fyn,' Isolt pleaded. 'Elrhodoc won Mulcibar's sword last midsummer's day.'

'I don't care if he licked Mulcibar's balls last midsummer's day,' Fyn said.

The crudity shocked Piro and silenced Isolt.

'I am going to enjoy teaching you a lesson,' Elrhodoc said. He gestured to his men. 'You saw him strike me. I'm the injured party. I name the time and place. I say here and now, and I say swords.'

Piro gasped. Fyn was just seventeen. Elrhodoc was nearer thirty.

'I don't have a sword,' Fyn said.

The seedy guard unbuckled his sword belt and tossed it to her brother.

'Fyn, please...' Piro pleaded.

He did not look at her. 'Go with the queen, Piro.'

Isolt came over to the fountain pool and reached out to Piro, who waded through the water, teeth chattering from shock.

To Piro's consternation, she saw Elrhodoc had drawn both his sword and knife, as was the Merofynian noble custom. Did Fyn even know his style of swordplay?

Fyn had drawn the borrowed sword and was testing its weight. He hadn't touched his knife.

Isolt steadied Piro as she climbed out of the pool and stood dripping on the grass. 'Are you all right?'

'Yes, but we can't leave Fyn. Stop this.'

'I can't interfere in a matter of honour,' Isolt whispered. 'Challenge has been offered and accepted.' She turned to the men, raising her voice. 'I will be up on the terrace, watching this duel. And if anyone interferes, I will hang him from the linden tree. No... I'll have him strangled like a common criminal and tossed in the sea, forever denied Mulcibar's blessing!'

The young guard glanced to the seedy one. 'Should we—'

'Don't listen to her, Seelon,' Elrhodoc barked. 'She's just a silly little girl who needs to be shown that even queens should shut up and do what their men tell them.'

And, without warning he slashed Fyn's face, ripping open his cheek.

Piro gasped. She glimpsed teeth and bone before Fyn slapped his hand to his face. Blood poured through his fingers and down his shirt.

'Stop the duel,' she cried. The slashing of Fyn's cheek was meant to disable. The wound had to be bound or he would pass out from blood loss. 'That's not f—'

The ringing clash of steel cut her off as Elrhodoc followed up his first strike with a second and third.

Fyn deflected each blow, backing away with one hand pressed to his face.

Piro brushed past Isolt. 'Stop this. You can't—'

'No.' The seedy guard caught her by the arm. 'You can't interfere.'

The guards herded her and Isolt up the steps.

'Stay out of the way, my queen,' the younger guard told Isolt. 'You could be hurt.'

'Don't worry. This won't take long.' The seedy one was clearly enjoying himself. 'If the sight of blood offends you, don't look.'

Piro ran up to the terrace, her sodden clothes and slippers squelching with each step.

The stone balustrade was warm under her hands, but she felt cold to the core, watching Fyn fight for his life. One part of her wanted to run for help, yet she could not tear her eyes off the duellists, not even for a heartbeat.

Fyn backed up until he was pinned against the hedge. He staggered as he took the full force of the captain's blows on his blade.

Isolt moaned.

Piro wished she was big and powerful. Of course... 'Resolute, come to me!'

'Loyalty!' Isolt cried.

Elrhodoc struck repeatedly, driving Fyn down to one knee.

Piro could not breathe.

The captain delivered what looked like a killing blow. Yet somehow, it skittered along Fyn's sword, passing harmlessly to the side. At the same time, Fyn lowered his hand from his cheek, grabbed his knife and drove it up into Elrhodoc's groin.

For a heartbeat no one moved.

Then the captain dropped his weapons, doubled over, staggered sideways and crumpled. As the guards ran across the grass to their captain, Fyn rose somewhat unsteadily. Piro and Isolt ran down the steps. Meanwhile, the guards rolled their captain onto his back.

'He's dead,' the seedy one muttered. 'Bled out like a pig with his throat cut.'

The young guard sprang to his feet. 'Butcher!'

Fyn lifted his sword until the tip hovered at the guard's throat. The point did not waver, but his words were hard to understand due to his injured mouth. 'Did the duel not follow the code?'

'You—'

'Shut up, Seelon,' the seedy one snapped. 'Give me a hand with the captain.' They picked up Elrhodoc's body and carried him away.

Fyn swayed and fell to his knees, just as Resolute and Loyalty arrived. The Affinity beasts gave voice, troubled by the smell of blood.

'Take Resolute and Loyalty back to the grotto,' Isolt told Piro. 'I'll attend to Fyn.'

Piro wanted to help Fyn, but she'd seen the way Isolt looked at him, so she summoned her Affinity and lured the wyvern and foenix back to the grotto.

FYN FELT NOTHING. He knew half his face was hanging off, but he was strangely numb. Isolt leant over him, her plucked brows drawing together in concentration as she cleaned the wound and prepared to stitch it closed.

'I'm going to have to put my fingers in your mouth to hold the cheek in place,' she told him.

He nodded and concentrated on the doorway where a dozen horrified servants stood watching.

'You killed him,' Isolt whispered as she sewed.

He wanted to tell her he would kill Elrhodoc all over again if he had the chance, but all he could do was blink in response.

'Thank you.'

He shook his head and went to reply. She saw he was determined to speak and removed her fingers from his mouth.

'Not enough. Never enough.'

'What do you mean?'

'Dunstany sent for Byren. Nothing I do is good enough.'

'Oh, Fyn. He sent for Byren because—'

'I failed you.'

She held his eyes. 'You have never failed me, Fyn. Never. I—'

'Out of my way, let an old man through,' Dunstany said, hastening into the chamber. He faltered when he saw Fyn. 'They're saying you challenged the captain of the queen's guards to a duel.'

'Fyn fought a duel to protect me,' Piro said, coming into the chamber behind Dunstany. She was wet through, and pale as milk, with bright spots of colour in her cheeks. 'Elrhodoc insulted me. Fyn arrived in time to—'

The servants' shocked comments drowned her out.

'And Captain Elrhodoc?' Dunstany asked, raising his voice.

The servants fell silent to hear Piro's answer.

'Dead,' she said with relish. 'Before the duel started, he slashed Fyn's cheek to get an advantage.'

More muttering from the servants. Soon this version of events would be all over the palace and port, battling with the version Elrhodoc's guards were sure to circulate.

Isolt's busy fingers tugged at Fyn's cheek as she stitched the wound. He winced now that sensation was returning.

'There.' Isolt tied off the thread.

Fyn tried to feel his cheek, but Isolt caught his hand. A line of throbbing fire ran from the side of his top lip, past his nose in an arc along his cheek bone and under his left eye, which wept tears.

'See if you can drink this now.' Isolt gave him some dreamless-sleep.

He tried to take the cup from her, but his hands shook. She held the cup for him. Some liquid dribbled out the side of his mouth. She persevered until the cup was empty.

Then she stepped aside and Dunstany took Fyn's face in his hands, studying the job Isolt had done. 'Very neat. I've overextended myself every day since Piro arrived, but I'll see what I can do. You'll need to give me access to your Affinity, Fyn.'

He fought to concentrate as the room spun. Sefarra had said something important, something about predators... That's right. 'The queen's guard needs a new captain, someone we can trust.'

'I don't trust any of them,' Isolt muttered.

'Make Cam your captain.'

'The bay lord's grandson?' Dunstany thought it over. 'That might just work.'

'It will work,' Isolt said. 'He's loyal, and any men who won't serve under him aren't worthy of being in the queen's guard. I'll send a message to him.'

'Now, let me do what I can for you, Fyn,' Dunstany said.

'What's going on here?' Abbot Murheg demanded, thrusting through the servants. Halfway across the chamber, he saw the extent of Fyn's injury, swayed and reached out for support.

Piro guided the abbot to a chair. 'Lean forward.'

With brusque helpfulness, she pushed his head down between his knees.

PIRO BATHED CAREFULLY. By tomorrow, she would have bruises from Elrhodoc's rough handling. She was lucky she didn't have worse. When she entered her bedchamber, she found Dunstany waiting.

He helped her into bed, pulling up the covers around her. 'You're feverish again. I'm sorry, I've exhausted my Affinity on Fyn.'

'Can't be helped.' She summoned a smile. 'It's an honour to have Lord Dunstany tuck me in.'

But it was Siordun who spoke. 'I've heard from Lady Death, Piro. She has called off her coraxes, but I must return to Ostron Isle to meet with her.'

Dismay filled her. 'You can't leave us now.'

'I have to. Not only is Lady Death expecting to meet the mage, but Milliner Salvatrix has sailed to Ostron Isle to deliver the imposter-Piro and she refuses to leave until she sees the mage.'

'You need someone you trust with your secret on Mage Isle.'

He nodded. 'There were two old servants who helped me when my master first died, but they passed away last winter while I was trying to stop Merofynia from invading Rolencia.' His lips twitched. 'I was hoping you'd fill that position.'

She was thrilled to think he trusted her and frightened by the responsibility. 'I'll do my very best.'

'I know you will. You always do.' He squeezed her shoulder. 'I've booked passage to Ostron Isle. I may have to stay a while. The transition to the new elector was not smooth, and the death of the old Cinnamome comtissa has destabilised the balance of power between the five families. I think this is why Lady Death is testing her limits. I've told Gwalt to bring all pica bird messages to you.'

Piro was honoured. 'Will you be back by the time Byren arrives?'

'I hope to be but if not, I want you to convey the mage's messages to him as well.'

Piro rolled her eyes. 'He won't like being told what to do by his little sister.'

Siordun grinned. 'Byren is coming through the Snow Bridge pass west of Dunstany's estate. I'm expecting him to arrive in another seven to ten days. When I sail, Gwalt will tell the servants Lord Dunstany has been taken ill and he'll send the carriage to Dunistir Estate. In a few days, the Dunistir yacht will arrive at the palace with an invitation for you and Fyn to convalesce on Dunstany's estate. Go there and wait for Byren.'

'What of Isolt?'

'She'll be preparing the contracts and planning the celebrations to announce her betrothal. She's safe here, now that Camoric is captain of her guards.' He hesitated. 'You'll like Dunistir Estate, Piro. I grew up there and often went back when the mage visited my grandfather. These days I hardly ever visit and when I do, it is only as Lord Dunstany. Gwalt's father, Old Gwalt, knows my secret. You can trust him.'

'And your mother, surely she knows your secret?'

His mouth hardened. 'She died.'

'You should forgive her. She wouldn't have been able to care for a child with so much Affinity.'

'She sold me, Piro. How could she do that?'

The pain in his voice made her sit up and reach for him. 'Siordun...'

He pulled away and strode to the door, where he hesitated. 'That's the first time you've used my real name.'

Then he was gone, sailing to confront Lady Death herself. Piro shuddered.

Chapter Forty-Seven

FLORIN TRIED TO focus on something other than her nausea. They'd camped near the cloud-shrouded summit of the Snow Bridge's southern pass, where the sky really did meet the earth. As the sun rose, the mist took on a beautiful pearly glow.

She sucked in a deep breath of thin damp air. It did no good, she still felt breathless. Her head spun and her stomach heaved. She hated feeling this weak.

As soon as she'd set foot on the ship's deck, she'd started throwing up and her stomach hadn't recovered from the sea-sickness when she'd developed sky-sickness. It was no consolation that she was not the only one suffering. The majority of their group were Rolencians. Every third person was struggling with the thin air.

She could hear them speaking softly behind her. They'd eaten breakfast—those who could—and packed up their travelling kits, and now they were waiting for the mist to clear before crossing the pass into the Snow Bridge.

Someone cursed, and made a horrible hacking sound as they threw up.

It was too much for Florin. Her stomach revolted in sympathy and she staggered a few paces out of camp before throwing up.

Somehow, Byren found her and rubbed her back.

'Don't worry. You'll get over it in a couple of days.' He offered her watered wine. 'Try thinking about something else.'

She'd tried that.

'You'll feel better once we're moving.'

She hadn't yesterday.

'It's all in the mind.'

'It's not. It's in my stomach, and I can't get enough air.'

He laughed. Someone called him back to camp and he squeezed her shoulder. 'You'll do, Mountain Girl.'

'If I'm a mountain girl I shouldn't be sky-sick.'

He laughed again. She loved it when he laughed.

Florin flushed. As the mist swallowed Byren, she admitted she wasn't just sky-sick. She was a love-sick fool.

A stone chinked behind her as Orrade stepped out of the mist. He was pale, and his skin shone with sweat.

'*Try thinking of something else. It's all in the mind.* So says someone who has never suffered sea-sickness *or* sky-sickness. Sometimes I could kick him.'

Florin laughed and offered him the watered wine.

He took a careful sip, waited and was able to take another. 'We have to keep drinking. That's what our family healer used to say.'

'Mother said the same thing.' She rubbed her face. 'The mist is clearing.'

'Come on.'

Florin felt sick and shaky. She had to concentrate on keeping her footing on the damp path.

Soon the sun burned away the mist and the air became incredibly clear. They could see far to the north, up the great valley that ran the length of the Snow Bridge.

All day they threaded their way down from the pass, through steep ravines, fording icy-cold streamlets and scrambling across treacherous, rocky slopes.

As they descended, it grew warmer. Tiny wild flowers sprouted in every crevice and covered the patches of grass, where a moment before their arrival shaggy wild goats had been grazing. The goats perched on impossibly steep rocks to watch them pass by.

All through the day, Florin could keep nothing down other than a little watered wine. Her head spun and her thighs ached from the steep slope. She marvelled that Vlatajor could find the path in this maze of ravines.

It felt like the day would never end, but the sun finally slipped towards the western walls of the valley and Florin knew she could rest soon.

Byren set up camp in a small field, which was bordered on two sides by tall rock walls. As he issued orders to make the camp defensible, Florin dropped her pack and walked a little further along the path, until she finally had a clear view up the valley.

The thin air was crystal clear. She could see far into the distance along the valley floor, where lakes were fed by mountain streams. A flock of birds flew in formation, wheeling below her as they made their way to their roosts.

Bozhimir's voice returned to her, singing the praises of the Snow Bridge. As a child, she hadn't understood the longing in his voice. Now that Narrowneck had burned, she experienced the same bone-deep ache for home.

Back then, Bozhimir had taught her a poem about the painted mountains, and now she saw them for herself. As the sun set beyond the western mountains, its last rays painted the eastern peaks a brilliant salmon pink.

Footsteps crunched on the path behind her and she turned, heart lifting, but it was... 'Orrie.'

'You all right?'

'Yes,' she lied. She was grateful for Orrade's company. Only four of their group ever spoke to her. Vlatajor laid elaborate traps to learn more about Byren. Byren treated her with a determined cheerfulness that was incredibly irritating. Chandler seemed to have decided she was one of the lads, to be treated with casual indifference. Of them all, she felt most at home with Orrade.

'You shouldn't go off alone,' he said. 'The Snow Bridge is dangerous. There are Affinity predators...' As if on cue, a deep bellow reached them, followed by a string of huffing barks. The sounds echoed around them so it was impossible to tell where they came from. 'What—'

'Ursodons,' Florin said. 'Horned Affinity bears. In winter, their long fur turns white, but they should have their short golden summer coats by now. They generally live in packs like manticore prides. Yes, I'm aware of the dangers of the Snow Bridge.'

'Sorry.' He offered her a disarming smile. 'If you know all this, why go off on your own?'

'A big group like ours is going to scare away all but the most determined predators. And I wanted to see this.' She gestured to the impossibly beautiful eastern peaks. The colours had deepened as the angle of the sun's rays changed.

'That's...'

Florin grinned. She'd never seen Orrade lost for words. 'They call them the painted mountains. Bozhimir taught me a poem.' Florin tried to translate it. 'The original is better.'

'It's usually that way with poetry,' Orrade said. 'You can't preserve the rhythm and...' He swallowed.

She glanced to him. His skin was pale and clammy. With a word of apology, he made for the nearest large rock and leaned against it to empty his stomach.

Of course that set her off and she stepped off the path to throw up. As the spasms shook her, the ursodons called again. She rolled her eyes. It would be just her luck to be killed while throwing up.

She wiped her mouth and lifted her head, eyes streaming.

Orrade sent her a rueful grin.

'I keep telling myself it'll be over it in a couple of days.' She fished in her pocket for a handful of leaves. 'Try these.'

'What are they? Ginger of some kind?'

'Bozhimir told me about it. It's supposed to help with the sky-sickness.'

'You were eight years old last time you spoke to him. Are you sure this is the right plant?'

'Yes, he made me memorise the plant's description.'

'Why?'

She shrugged. 'He was a scholar and I was curious.'

Orrade grinned. 'You have hidden depths, Florin.'

She shrugged, not sure how to take him. More huffing barks reached them. 'We should get back to camp.'

When they returned, Florin noticed how the men of Byren's honour guard grinned at her and nudged each other. Even the six Snow Bridge men–at-arms smirked. 'What are they grinning about?'

'We went off alone together,' Orrade said.

'So?' But even as she said this, understanding came to her. Heat raced up her cheeks. 'That's... that's...'

'That's just the way their minds work. Ignore them.'

They joined Byren's fire circle in time to see Vlatajor open his pouch and remove his fire stone. It sat neatly in the palm of his hand. With these stones there was no need for fuel, which was lucky, since they had only just reached the treeline.

Small stones had been placed in a circle. A pot sat over them, supported by a metal tripod. Vlatajor placed his fire stone in the circle. 'Hristo.'

A hush fell over those nearby as the older of his two companions removed the other fire stone from his pouch. Florin looked up to see at least two dozen men gathered around to watch.

Hristo held his fire stone on a long metal spoon and leaned forward. When the fire stone was less than a half an arm's length from its counterpart it began to glow. In another heartbeat flames leapt from one stone to the other. By the time he had placed the second stone in the fire circle, a strong fire burned, giving off a fierce heat.

The gathering gave a sigh of wonder and one by one they took burning wood back to their more conventional fires.

'A useful thing for travellers,' Florin said. She had heard of fire stones, but had never seen a pair.

Hristo tossed some leaves into a bubbling pot of water, along with red wine, honey and cardamom.

'My father had a pair of fire stones.' Orrade indicated something the size of a pumpkin. 'This big.'

'A great treasure,' Vlatajor said. 'Your family was very lucky.'

Orrade glanced to Byren, who looked grim.

'We kept them on pedestals, one on each side of the hearth in the great hall,' Orrade said. 'Just far enough apart from them to sense each other. They glowed with an inner radiance.'

'That was...' The ambassador hesitated.

'Dangerous?' Orrade met Vlatajor's eyes across the fire. 'I know.'

'Why?' Florin asked. 'I mean if they're kept apart, they won't burst into flames, surely?'

The roar of a male ursodon reached them, followed by more huffing barks. It seemed to Florin that the pack was closer now.

'Time to check the camp's defences.' Byren nodded to Orrade and they went off together.

Florin watched them go.

'It's true that fire stones flame on contact,' Vlatajor told her. 'But before that there is a point where they respond to each other. Keeping them apart, yet close enough to glow, is asking for trouble. Fire stones have been known to spontaneously flame up in that situation. I heard Lord Dovecote's great house burned to the ground.'

'That's right.' Florin said, bristling at the implied criticism. 'Byren and Orrade burned it to kill their enemies.'

'They have the hearts of warriors,' Vlatajor said.

'It was Orrade's sister who told them to do it.' Florin felt Elina deserved the credit.

He nodded. His Snow Bridge accent reminded her of Bozhimir, but he was a very different kind of man, as his next question confirmed. 'When we were hunting the manticore pride, Byren led us unerringly to ulfr spoor, not once, but several times. How was he able to do this?'

'Ulfr spoor smells pretty bad.'

'Byren smelled the spoor long before the rest of us.'

'Then he must have a better sense of smell.' Florin gave a studiedly casual shrug.

Hristo stirred the bubbling pot. The aroma was wonderful.

A wave of nausea drove Florin to her feet. 'I'll take first watch.'

She picked her way through the camp and eventually found Byren and Orrade on the path leading back up towards the pass.

'What is it?' Florin asked.

'I was just about to send for you,' Byren said. 'Look there.'

She sighted along his arm, seeing nothing but starlit rocks, mottled by dark shadows. Florin ignored the constant nausea and concentrated.

'We saw something glowing and moving amongst the rocks,' Orrade explained. 'There it is again.'

'Bozhimir once told me about a glowing Affinity beast, but...' The name and description eluded Florin for the moment.

As they caught another glimpse of the glow, those huffing barks sounded again. Florin shivered.

'Whatever it is, it's coming closer.' Orrade glanced over his shoulder. 'Our camp fires could be drawing it.'

'I'm not dousing them,' Byren said. 'We'll—'

'Silfron!' The name came back to Florin. 'It means *silver-sniffer*. They have long legs and long necks. When full grown, the bird stands twice as tall as a man. Their wings have a beautiful metallic sheen and their eyes glow in the dark. They live in caves where they feed off silver. If a Power-worker can capture one and bond with it, he can use it to locate seams of silver.'

Byren cursed. 'Looks like the silver-sniffer is leading the ursodon pack right to us.'

'There's too many of us for the ursodons to attack,' Orrade said.

'Normally,' Florin conceded. 'But Affinity beasts consider the flesh of other Affinity beasts a delicacy!'

Orrade cursed.

Florin realised they would certainly consider Orrade a delicacy, and she went cold with fear for him.

Byren jumped down. 'We don't have long. Come on.'

FYN SET UP the board and laid out the Duelling Kingdoms pieces. Any moment now, Camoric would join him. They'd eat dinner, play the game and discuss the state of Merofynia. It was good to have him back.

There was a soft scratching at the door and Fyn reached for his knife. According to Dunstany, the mage had reached an agreement with Lady Death and she had called off her coraxes, but Fyn was taking no chances. He stepped to one side of the door, then opened it.

Mitrovan stepped into the chamber.

Fyn sheathed his knife. 'I thought you were back on Travantir Estate?'

'I was. But...' Mitrovan blinked.

The scribe had just noticed his face. Dunstany had been able to hasten the healing, but the scar would always be there, distorting his face.

'Elrhodoc gave me this to remember him by.' Fyn shrugged. 'I was lucky, I could have lost my eye.'

'They're saying you butchered him like a pig.'

'I had to. I was losing blood too fast for fancy sword work.'

'When Travany heard about Elrhodoc's death, he sent word to the other lords and sailed for the palace. They'll all be here soon.'

Fyn nodded. He had expected as much, although he had thought he'd have more time.

'But that's not all...' Mitrovan broke off as Camoric entered.

'Close the door, Cam,' Fyn said, adding for Mitrovan's benefit, 'He's the new captain of the queen's guard. You can speak freely.'

The scribe glanced to Camoric, then faced Fyn. 'Travany is afraid his seven-year slaves will revolt, so he's cut their food rations and told the supervisors to go hard on them.'

'And he thinks that will win him their loyalty?' Camoric raised an eyebrow.

Fyn grinned.

'There's more. I overheard young Trafyn complaining. He's angry because he won't inherit an estate like Lord Yorale's youngest son. His father told him that Neiron deliberately delayed meeting up with Wythrod, then sent men to stir up the spar warriors and lead them back to Wythrod's camp.' Mitrovan lifted his hands. 'Don't you see? He baited the bear, or in this case the amfina and lincis. He knew the warlords would attack that night. Neiron betrayed Wythrod.'

'It fits with Murheg's description of the attack.' Fyn ran his hand through his short hair. 'I thought it was Wythrod's impatience and the spars' cunning that led to his death. I never thought for a moment that Neiron would betray him. Why? It's not as if he profited from Wythrod's death.'

But Yorale had. His son was heir to Wythrontir Estate through the maternal line. Had Yorale known about

Neiron's betrayal? Could they trust Lord Yorale? Isolt thought so, and Dunstany trusted him, up to a point.

'If the lords are coming here, you can't leave port, Fyn,' Camoric said.

Mitrovan looked to him. 'You were going somewhere?'

'Not anymore. I was going to escort my sister to Lord Dunstany's estate, but it would be a mistake to leave Isolt now.'

There was a knock on the door.

'That will be Kyral with our meal,' Fyn said.

Mitrovan hid, while Fyn accepted the tray and dismissed the servant.

The scribe came out from behind the screen. 'I should go.'

Fyn caught up with him at the door. 'I appreciate the risks you're taking.'

'I promised I'd help Byren's cause.'

Fyn nodded. 'When this is all over, I'll see that you're rewarded.'

The skinny scribe shrugged. 'If anything happens to me and you have to trust one of the Travantir family, trust Travrhon. He was horrified when he learned how Neiron had betrayed Wythrod. Trafyn thought it a clever ploy.'

'Travrhon is the eldest?'

'Yes. I must go.'

There was silence after he closed the door, then Fyn gestured to the Duelling Kingdoms board. 'I never thought I'd be a player.' He took his seat and poured them both a glass of wine. 'Take a seat. We should eat while the food is hot.'

Camoric didn't accept the wine, but instead squared his shoulders. 'Every last one of the queen's guards resigned their commissions today.'

Fyn winced. He knew Camoric's family were looked down on by the other nobles, but he hadn't expected the queen's guard to be so pigheaded. 'I'm sorry.'

'I'd rather have my own men at my back. They're

rough sea-hounds, but loyal.' He winked. 'It's a pity *you* can't replace the nobles with some you trust.'

'If only.' Fyn grinned.

Camoric sat down, saying, 'I hear Dunstany's gone back to his estates. They say he's sick.'

Fyn nodded. He would have liked to tell Camoric the truth about Siordun's masquerade, but it was not his secret to share.

'Merofynia has suffered nothing but setbacks, Fyn. Now Elrhodoc is dead and the lords are coming to the palace. King Byren will lose Merofynia as well as Rolencia at this rate. You need to send for him.'

Fyn stiffened. *Yet another friend who thought he couldn't cope!* 'My brother is already on his way.'

'Good. You need Dunstany. If he's too sick, then at least send for the lords who support him.'

'Your grandfather is still at sea. Lord Istyn suffered a seizure when his son died. That leaves the lords of Benetir and Geraltir Estates, but they're just boys. Sefarra would send help, only she needs to make Benetir Estate defensible. There's Yorale... Dunstany says he's always been loyal to the crown.'

'Then send for him. You need to gather your supporters.'

'There are over a hundred ex-slaves camped in the palace grounds. They bear no love for Merofynian nobility.' Fyn sipped his wine, eyes on the board. 'I don't think Neiron will bring his men-at-arms to port. He can't leave his estate undefended. Besides, if he marched into the palace with a hundred armed men, Isolt could order his arrest.' Fyn shook his head. 'I wish it were that simple.'

The door to Fyn's bedchamber opened and Isolt slipped in. She nodded to Camoric, but addressed Fyn. 'Have you heard? Travany is here and the other lords are on their way. I fear they're going to try to seize power. They've been trying to overrule me ever since Father died.'

'Call a lords' council,' Fyn said. 'That way they are here at your bidding.'

She smiled. 'I'll send for all the lords and those who are underage or absent will have to send someone to represent them.'

Fyn nodded. He would tell Gwalt to send a message to the mage. They needed Lord Dunstany.

Chapter Forty-Eight

Byren sent Orrade to bring the sentries in, grabbed Florin's arm and ran. He began yelling orders the moment they entered camp. 'There's a pack of Affinity beasts headed this way. Pull back to the rock wall!'

Florin moved to pack up their fire circle. Men scattered, reaching for weapons. Some went to stamp out the campfires.

'Leave the fires, but bring any unused wood.' Byren strode towards the rock wall. It was a good defensive position. The cliff was sheer and three storeys high.

Two cooks hissed as they hurried past him, carrying hot pots. Just then, the ravines above them reverberated with the roar of the male ursodon.

'What *are* they?' Chandler turned terrified eyes to Byren.

'It's an ursodon pack,' Vlatajor said. 'Sounds like a male with three or four females. The males have long, wicked horns, but it's the females who do the hunting.'

Chandler grimaced as he dropped his bag against the wall. 'Just what we need, a pack of rabid Affinity beasts!'

'Believe it or not, ursodons can be tamed. As we travel the Snow Bridge you'll see them harnessed to mill-stones, or hauling carts,' Vlatajor said. He turned to Hristo. 'Come get the fire stones.'

The Snow Bridge men-at-arms stood guard while Vlatajor and Hristo retrieved the stones and hurried towards their defensive position.

Byren indicated a spot in front of the semi-circle of defenders. 'Put the fire stones there. It's a pity we don't have a dozen pairs to form a barrier.'

Vlatajor and Hristo placed the fire stones in position, and they flared to life. Byren ordered two more fires made up to form an outer defensive circle, then took up position in the front of their defensive circle. 'Lead by example,' his father had always said.

With the cooking fires still burning across the field, Byren had a clear view of Orrade bringing in the last of the sentries. They made it to safety and everyone waited, weapons drawn, bows strung, arrows ready.

A few moments later, Chandler stumbled to the edge of circle and threw up. That set off others. Then, once again, a hush descended on the camp.

Byren strained to hear the approach of the Affinity beasts above the crackle of the fires. Was that the softest of huffs?

No, it was the steady, rhythmic thump of something heavy running down the path towards them.

'That'll be the Affinity beast they're hunting,' Byren said. 'If it runs past, let it go. If it comes near, kill it.'

The ursodons would drag the carcass away and their problems would be over.

He felt his men tense as they prepared to deal with Snow Bridge Affinity beasts.

No one was prepared for the sight of a long-necked, long-legged bird, with a wizened old man crouched on its back.

The bird skidded in the grass, made a sharp turn and headed for them, eyes glowing like twin lamps. The defenders gaped as the bird barged through their ranks. Despite its powerful legs and razor sharp talons, it sank to cower against the stone wall.

The old man rolled off, staggering to his feet.

Tucking its head under its wing, the bird seemed to shiver, feathers ruffling. To Byren's amazement, the bird's wings, which had been a shimmering pewter colour, became the same mottled grey as the rock wall. A heartbeat later, it was hard to tell where the bird ended and the stone began.

'Well,' Orrade muttered. 'You don't see that every day.'

The old man spotted the Snow Bridge ambassador and executed a brief bow, saying something rapidly in their own language. The ambassador nodded briefly, giving Byren the impression he did not approve of the old man.

'Just as we thought,' Vlatajor told Byren. 'A male ursodon and three females. They'll be here any moment.'

'Light your firebrands!' Byren yelled. He was not going to hand over an old man and his Affinity beast to the ursodons.

The Snow Bridge men-at-arms formed a defensive huddle around the ambassador and his officials. Half a dozen of Byren's honour guard dipped branches in the fires. The ends had been wrapped in oily cloth, which burst into flames. Orrade passed Byren a burning brand.

They'd barely resumed their positions when the first of the ursodons charged down the path. The beast tore up the topsoil in a mad scramble to make the turn. Two more followed.

'Females,' Vlatajor said. 'The male can't be far behind.'

The three powerfully built beasts prowled across the open field, avoiding the fires. At the shoulder they would have been almost chest-high on Byren. Short, sharp horns protruded from their foreheads. Their coats gleamed red-gold in the fire light and one still had tufts of white winter-fur at her throat.

Byren grimaced. They looked like horned bears,

but they moved more like cats, and they were heavily muscled. It would be hard to make a killing blow or shot.

A fourth beast joined them. This one was twice as large, and a pair of huge horns sprouted from his massive head. The ursodon male took in Byren's men, their fires and their blades, then he reared onto his hind legs and roared.

The sound hit the defenders like a thunderclap. Florin ducked. Chandler yelped, then looked around sheepishly.

Raising his sword in one hand and his torch in the other, Byren roared in response. The others took up his battle cry, clashing their weapons to make as much noise as possible. When the male ursodon dropped to all fours, Byren signalled for quiet.

The male made a huffing noise, which drew the three females to him. They put their heads together as if to discuss the situation. Byren did not like it. Bad enough the beasts outclassed them physically, but if the ursodons were also intelligent enough to lay plans...

The wizened old man muttered something that sounded half derogatory, half admiring. Somehow the little Power-worker had ended up at by Byren's side. He held a badly notched hunting knife, but his grip was firm. The old man smelled faintly metallic to Byren, and his skin looked oddly pallid in the firelight.

The Power-worker studied Byren with as much interest as Byren studied him.

'They're moving again,' Orrade warned, voice low and calm.

'Now, why would they do that?'

Byren looked over to see the two of the females trotting off up the track.

The third, with the white throat, resumed her prowling, as if looking for a way past the defenders.

The male made a sound between a bark and a grunt.

The female ignored him.

He repeated the sound.

She tossed her head and trotted over to him. He licked her face. After a moment they both went up the track. The female ursodon reminded Byren of Florin. He looked over and caught her watching him. A frisson of desire hit him. Faced with violent death, he wanted her. Wanted her badly.

'They've gone,' someone said.

Several men swore with relief and many lowered their weapons.

'Don't be fooled,' Byren warned. 'Affinity beasts are smart. I've known ulfrs to—'

A stone clattered above them.

Byren spun around to find a female ursodon standing on the edge of the cliff behind them. It looked as though the beast was searching for a way down.

'Can it make the jump?' Chandler asked.

'No,' Vlatajor said. 'Else we'd be dead already.'

'Front!' Orrade warned.

The white-necked female had slipped back and now crept forward on her belly. She was only two body-lengths from the first rank of defenders. Byren cursed.

Someone let an arrow fly. It skimmed over the ursodon's shoulder. A heartbeat later, a second arrow buried deep in her fur. She flinched, but did not draw back.

'Don't waste your arrows unless you can get a clear shot,' Byren said.

'There's another one up above,' Chandler warned. 'Are you sure they can't jump down?'

Vlatajor did not answer.

Florin ran back to the wall. Byren heard her rummaging around amongst their belongings. A moment later she joined him holding a large Ostronite pottery jar.

'Scented lamp oil,' she said. 'Cinna sent it as a gift for the king. If we smash the jar on the beast, then—'

'—set its fur alight,' Byren and Orrade spoke as one.

Byren glanced back to the white-necked ursodon. A second female had joined her, but did not come as close.

Another two arrows sprouted from the shoulder of the white-necked ursodon. As Byren watched, the female ducked her head under her paw, letting the thick fur absorb another arrow.

'Don't waste your arrows,' he yelled.

Florin adjusted her hold on the jar.

'I'll do it.' Byren took the jar from her before she could protest.

'No, I'll do it.' Chandler snatched the jar from Byren and ran forward.

Byren shouted to distract the ursodons.

Chandler ran five paces then flung the jar with all his might.

The white-necked female shielded her face as the jar smashed on her shoulder and right paw. The second ursodon rushed in from the side to snatch Chandler. Byren darted forward, grabbed Chandler's jerkin and hauled him from the beast's jaws.

The moment he had a clear shot, Orrade released a burning arrow. It hit the white-necked female, and her oil-soaked fur went up in a rush of flames. She screamed.

The other Ursodons barked and roared in fright.

Maddened by pain, the white-necked female ran full tilt across the field and slammed into a boulder. Byren thought she'd knocked herself out, but she staggered to her feet then ran up the path. The second female chased after her.

Byren spun to look up behind them. There was no sign of any beasts atop the cliff.

Relief made him light headed. Florin staggered to the edge of the semi-circle and threw up. This set others off, Orrade among them. Florin shared her watered wine with him. She said something. Orrade grinned. Several men congratulated Chandler, and he laughed.

'Don't let down your guard,' Byren yelled. 'For all we know, the pack will return angrier and hungrier.'

As the outer circle of defenders reformed, the wizened Power-worker bowed to Byren, Orrade, Florin and

Chandler. He said something in his own language, then returned to the wall.

Byren looked to Vlatajor for a translation.

'The silfroneer thanks you,' Vlatajor said. 'And well he should. He brought the ursodon pack down on us.'

'Silfroneer?' Florin asked.

'That's what we call Power-workers who bond with a silfron.' The ambassador lowered his voice and spoke to Byren. 'You are within your rights to exact some kind of payment from him. Make him vow to serve you for a year and a day, then gift him to the king. His service would be a much finer gift than any jar of scented oil.'

'Make a year-and-a-day-slave of him?' Byren repeated, aware of Florin and Orrade listening in. He hated slavery in all forms.

'King Jorgoskev would be most grateful,' Vlatajor urged, eyes bright with cunning.

Byren turned away, and his gaze fell on the wizened man. The silfroneer crooned to his Affinity beast as he stroked his bird's plumage. At his touch, the feathers ruffled then resettled, gradually resuming their darker colour. After a few moments, the bird raised its head; this time its eyes held only a dull glow.

Byren's honour guard muttered uneasily. Someone commented and several of them laughed. He knew the tone of that laughter. They were relieved to find themselves still alive.

'Surely it is too dangerous for one man and a bird to come up into the mountains,' Florin said. 'Even such a long-legged bird.'

'Silfrons can run very fast,' Vlatajor assured her. 'But they couldn't escape a pack on the hunt. Their instinct is to hide, as you just saw.'

'What were the man and his bird doing up here?' Florin asked.

Byren was intrigued. The ambassador wanted the

silfroneer and silver-sniffer for his king. Would he lie to disguise the pair's true worth?

'This is the bird's territory,' Vlatajor said. The ambassador hadn't admitted that the Power-worker used his Affinity beast to hunt for silver, but he hadn't told an outright lie either.

As Florin turned away from Vlatajor, she met Byren's eye. Her expression said, *Now you know where you stand with the ambassador*. She was clever, his mountain girl.

Byren looked around. His men were weary, suffering from sky-sickness and, now that the immediate threat had passed, they looked ready to drop. 'We'll take turns keeping watch.'

He divided the men into three groups, had them build up fires. Florin was taking first watch, Orrade the second and Byren the third, though he would probably wake many times and walk the line this night.

'Is it true?' Byren asked Florin softly. 'Could I ask for a year and a day's service from the silfroneer and his bird?'

Florin glanced to them. The man slept tucked under the bird's wing. 'Yes, but...'

'What do you think I should do with the silfroneer?'

'What the ambassador says make sense,' Orrade said. 'The pair would make an impressive gift for any king.'

'He's a man, not a beast of burden,' Byren said.

'It's only a year and a day.'

'He would not be able to refuse a request.'

'The king would be a fool to risk such a valuable asset.' Orrade shrugged. 'Look, Byren, you need Jorgoskev's help, and all you have to offer him is your younger sister in a marriage of alliance that we both know will never happen.'

'So your advice is to bind the silfroneer in a vow of service, then give him to the Snow Bridge king?'

Orrade's thin face creased into a grin. 'My advice is to weigh up all the factors.'

* * *

Piro snuggled down on the day-bed in Isolt's new chambers. It was just like old times, only now Isolt was queen and she wasn't a slave. Even so, they were still surrounded by powerful enemies.

She was looking forward to leaving the palace, and was ready to sail for Dunstany's estate first thing tomorrow, but she couldn't sleep. There was too much Affinity churning through her. She pulled out the new pendant. Unlike the first one Siordun had given her, the stone was black with a golden sheen.

Piro focused, trying to drive Affinity through the stone.

After several moments of fruitless exertion, she tucked the pendant back into her nightgown. That was when she heard Isolt's soft weeping.

Piro padded into the queen's bedchamber, climbed up onto Isolt's bed and stroked her back. 'I'll stay if you want me to. Or, better yet, come with me. Byren...' Piro hesitated. Fond as she was of Byren, she knew he saw Isolt as a duty.

'I can't leave the palace now that the lords are returning.' Isolt sat up, wiping her cheeks. 'I have to support Fyn, and I have to prepare the betrothal documents.'

Was that the real reason she'd been crying? Was the thought of marrying Byren enough to make her cry herself to sleep?

Isolt had never admitted her feelings for Fyn. Piro suspected Isolt's strong sense of duty would see her married to a man who did not love her. Where would that leave Fyn?

Piro did not want the three people she loved most in the world making the biggest mistake of their lives. 'Why were you crying?'

Isolt looked away, mouth working. After a moment she said, 'I miss Loyalty. Now that she lives in the grotto, I'm afraid she'll grow apart from me and we won't be able to bond.'

'Come on.' Piro slipped off the bed. 'I don't know why I didn't think of it sooner.'

Isolt smiled fondly. 'You're not making sense.'

Piro laughed and pulled her to her feet. 'I can act as a channel to help you bond with Loyalty.'

'You can?'

She nodded. 'I did it for Nefysto's cousin back on Ostron Isle. Come on.'

'Now?'

'Why not? I'm leaving tomorrow.'

They grabbed their slippers, threw shawls around their shoulders and left the bedchamber, running on bare feet through the palace corridors and courtyards.

Piro felt light-hearted. She might not be able to save Isolt from a marriage neither she nor Byren wanted, but she could do this one thing, and if it turned out that this was all her Affinity was good for, then so be it.

Chapter Forty-Nine

PIRO STEPPED OFF the yacht to find four servants lined up on the jetty. Dunistir House stood on a rise behind them. Lights gleamed in a row of first floor windows. Siordun had told her these were Lord Dunstany's private chambers, and this was where the old scholar shut himself away when he was supposedly suffering one of his recurring illnesses.

A richly dressed manservant stepped forward. 'His lordship insisted—'

Piro blinked. 'Soterro?'

He stiffened. 'House-steward Soterro.'

Piro realised she should not have admitted to recognising the Ostronite servant, but the surprise had loosened her tongue. Soterro had been his lordship's head servant during the Merofynian invasion, when she'd served as Dunstany's slave.

The other three servants looked curious, obviously wondering how Piro Rolen Kingsdaughter knew their steward.

'Soterro was kind to me when Lord Dunstany helped

me escape Rolencia,' Piro explained. He had been nothing of the sort. He'd considered her beneath him. 'I recall him with great fondness.'

Soterro had the grace to flush. He bowed low in the Ostronite fashion and gestured to the end of the jetty. 'The carriage will take you up to the great house as soon as Lord Protector Merofyn is ready.'

'My brother remained in the palace. The queen has need of him,' Piro said. She had been about to protest that it was only a short walk to the great house, but the servants looked so eager that she did not have the heart.

As she approached the carriage, the footman opened the door and unfolded the step, then helped her climb in. The vehicle swayed with her weight, then settled. She complimented him on the suspension.

'The best leather straps,' he said proudly, climbing up behind the carriage.

Piro beckoned Soterro to the window. 'Will I see Grysha and Cook?'

He grimaced, obviously remembering how Grysha had grabbed her bottom more than once and Cook had bullied her. 'Grysha ran away to sea, but Cook still rules the kitchen.'

'Please give him my compliments.' Piro was enjoying herself. When Soterro had been in a position of power over her, he had been brusque and high-handed. Now that their positions were reversed, she could be gracious. 'Ride with me, steward.'

'I am honoured.' He climbed into the carriage and sat opposite her. The coachman urged the horses forward. 'Before you say anything, Kingsdaughter, let me apologise. If I had known who you were—'

'You thought I was a slave, and you were not kind.'

'It was not my job to be kind. If Lord Dunstany had thought fit to reveal your true identity, I would have served you as well.' He bristled. 'Never let it be said that I am not loyal.'

They had arrived at the great house's main entrance and he helped her step down from the carriage. A dozen servants waited to greet her. As she was introduced to each one, she memorised their names and positions. Most were elderly, but not as elderly as Lord Dunstany. She guessed they were in their sixties and seventies.

The silver-haired house-keep greeted Piro, eyes bright with tears. 'Welcome to Dunistir House, Kingsdaughter. And if I may say, you're every bit as lovely as your grandmother. She often came here as a young woman, on account of her older brother and Lord Dunstany being such good friends. I remember her well.'

Piro felt a sense of loss and reached out to the house-keep. 'I never met my grandmother. I hope you can find the time to tell me about her.'

The woman beamed. 'Nothing would give me greater pleasure, kingsdaughter. Now, I'll show you to your chamber.'

As Piro was escorted to her room, she had to explain about Fyn all over again. The house-keep was disappointed to hear he would not be coming and bustled off to strip Fyn's bed and put the furniture under dust covers again.

Piro had a message from Gwalt for his father. He was the only person on Dunistir Estate who knew the true state of affairs. 'I'd like to see his lordship now, Soterro.'

'Very well.'

The steward escorted her along the passage to Dunstany's wing of chambers. Light came from under the door, and someone was playing softly on a dolcimela.

The moment Soterro knocked, the music stopped. A tall white-haired man opened the door. The father was the opposite of his son, who was short and stocky. Old Gwalt wore a high ranking servant's tabard. Silver thread had been used to embroider the Dunistir star and circle on the indigo cloth. When he bowed, Piro experienced a strong sense of familiarity.

'His lordship has been looking forward to your visit all day,' Old Gwalt said.

'As have I.' Piro stepped into the chamber. When Old Gwalt closed the door, she saw a flash of jealousy cross Soterro's face. She dropped her voice. 'I think the steward resents you.'

'My family have served Dunistir House for generations.' Old Gwalt made sure anyone listening at the door would overhear. 'The steward is a foreigner.'

Piro hid a smile and looked around. She glimpsed the Landlocked Sea through the curtains. Under the windows was a desk, and nearby were several musical instruments, including an upright clavichord. One wall was completely lined with books. 'What a lovely chamber.'

'His lordship has always loved music and learning.' Old Gwalt tilted his head. They both heard the steward's receding footsteps.

'Fyn did not come because—'

'I know. I keep a pica pair.'

Of course he did, otherwise how could he communicate with Siordun when the agent was in Ostron Isle? She gestured to the private chamber and the room beyond, where she could see the end of a tall bed. 'Is it difficult to maintain the illusion that Lord Dunstany is lying sick in that bed?'

'Only on two occasions has Soterro managed to get into the music room. And both times I was able to divert him by telling him his lordship was in the bath.'

Piro grinned. 'Young Gwalt sent you this.' She handed him a folded message. 'And he sends his love.'

To give the old man some privacy, she went over to the shelves to study the books. To think, Siordun had grown up here. She heard a noise and caught Old Gwalt watching her.

'Does Dunstany's heir suspect?' Piro asked.

'That wastrel?' Old Gwalt's top lip twisted. 'My lord always despised him, and would not have him in the house. Once a year, on his lordship's birthday, Duncaer would bring a gift, only to be turned away at the door. Since Siordun took over, he has kept up the custom. I don't think Duncaer and his lordship have exchanged a word in over twenty years.'

'What about when they're both at the palace?'

'Duncaer is from a minor branch of the family. He might have seen Dunstany across a crowded feast chamber, but that is as close as he'd get.'

'None of the servants suspect Siordun is Dunstany?'

'Not one.' He gave her a wry half-smile.

It made her realise why he was familiar and why he was so loyal to the Dunistir house.

'You're one of Dunstany's by-blows!' Piro said, then blushed furiously and cursed her tongue. 'I'm sorry. I—'

'You're absolutely right. I am related to Dunistir House but I'm not Dunstany's son. We shared the same grandfather.'

'So you're related to Siordun?'

'I look on him as a son.'

FLORIN WAS EXHAUSTED. Byren had driven them in a brutal forced march. Despite the cloudless sky, every fifth man had carried a flaming torch. From the Affinity bird's skittish behaviour, it had been clear the pack kept pace with them. Every now and then, the male ursodon would roar and the females would answer with short, huffing barks.

Florin had breathed a sigh of relief when the path finally left the foot-hills and they left the pack behind, crossing open fields dotted with walled farmhouses.

Now it was almost dusk, but there was still enough light to see the bluish tone of the Silfroneer's skin. At first, she'd thought he travelled without food or blankets because he'd lost them, and that was why he'd slept under the Affinity beast's wing, but after watching him eat nothing all day, she had realised his bond with the beast sustained him, and his bluish colouring was caused by his link with the silver-eating beast.

'I think I'm finally over the sky-sickness.' Orrade fell into step beside Florin. 'I haven't thrown up since this morning. How about you?'

'Lunch time.'

'You're feeling better?'

'Yes,' she lied, determined it would be true by tomorrow.

Orrade sent her a perceptive look. They were the same height and their strides matched perfectly, which made it hard to avoid his eyes.

'There's things the ambassador isn't telling us.' Florin changed the subject. 'I overheard him telling Hristo to organise ursodons for us when we get to the city.'

'Tame beasts.'

'According to Bozhimir, ursodons are never truly tamed. The only way to capture them is to trick them into eating a carcass seeded with sorbt stones. If they eat too many stones, they die. If they don't eat enough, they're still too wild. But—'

'—if they eat just the right number, the stones absorb their Affinity,' Orrade guessed, 'making them malleable. Clever.'

Florin nodded. 'Except for one thing. If they vomit up the stones, they revert to their true nature. You never know if they are going to turn on you.'

'Does this often happen?'

'More often than you'd think. Thieves will feed the beasts purges to take the stones.'

'Why would they want the stones?'

'They're much sought after. While in the beasts' stomachs, the stones soak up Affinity and become beautifully polished. Stones from the male bears are particularly prized. Rich men wear them to enhance their virility. The stones from the females are supposed to make women insatiable.' She blushed.

Orrade laughed. 'I can't imagine Bozhimir telling an eight-year-old that detail.'

'I used to listen at the door when he told my father stories.' It hadn't made much sense at the time, but now... She flushed and hurried on. 'The point is that the beasts can revert to their true nature.'

'If ursodons were too dangerous, the Snow Bridge people wouldn't—'

'I guess the nobles consider the loss of the occasional ursodon handler worth it. After all, the beasts are much bigger and stronger than horses.'

They'd stopped a short distance from the walls of the southern-most city of the Snow Bridge. The walls and buildings of Dezvronofaje were constructed of mottled white-grey stone, with steep-pitched red roofs. Even though the setting sun still painted the distant peaks, the gates were closed and guards watched warily from the towers.

As soon as Byren called a stop, his honour guard sank to sit under the aspen trees by the side of the road, heads bowed.

The silfroneer dismounted and stroked his bird's neck. He kept an eye on the ambassador, who sent the younger of his two companions to the gate, presumably to arrange lodgings for the night.

Two of the men staggered further into the aspen grove to empty their stomachs. Florin was relieved to see she was not the only one still suffering from the sky-sickness. This time she managed not to throw up, but her legs trembled from exertion. She found a fallen tree trunk just off the road and sat down, leaning forward to catch her breath. Orrade kept her company.

Byren strode through the aspens to join them. 'Tired, Mountain Girl? Don't worry, the ambassador tells me he's going to organise transport for tomorrow.'

Before Florin could tell him to beware of the ursodons, the ambassador joined them with Hristo.

Vlatajor gestured discreetly to the silfroneer. 'You should bind this arrogant Power-worker to you before we enter the city. If you don't, he's likely to run away. They—' He broke off as the Silfroneer joined them and switched languages. 'Have you no honour, silver-sucker? This man saved your life and that of your Affinity beast, yet you do not offer service in gratitude?'

'He saved us, this is true, but he is an ignorant foreigner. I owe him nothing.'

'Did Nilsoden not tell you? This is King Byren of Rolencia.'

The silfroneer shrugged. 'What do I care for flat-land kings? From what I hear, there is more than one Rolencian king.'

'This is the one who will make an alliance with my brother, King Jorgoskev.'

The silfroneer glanced around and Florin followed his gaze, wondering what he was looking for. The men were scattered through the aspen grove. 'Tell your brother that Power-workers will never bow to him!' The man gestured and the bird's leg lashed out, its razor sharp talons slashing Vlatajor's torso wide open.

Florin stared in horror.

The silfroneer leapt onto his beast's back and the bird ran off, long legs flashing.

'My lord?' Hristo tried to hold Vlatajor's innards in place as the ambassador crumpled.

Fighting nausea, Florin dropped to her knees and tried to stop the bleeding, but it was a huge wound, from shoulder to hip. Orrade knelt to help her.

'The king will have our heads for this,' Hristo muttered, unaware that Florin could understand him.

Byren leaned over her shoulder, took one look at the wound and cursed. 'We can't move him. It'll kill him. We'll have to camp here.'

Chandler and the Snow Bridge men-at-arms came running, wanting to know what was going on.

Pulling Hristo to his feet, Byren pointed to the city and mimed wrapping bandages. 'Go fetch a healer.'

Hristo shook his head as if there was no hope, but ran off, calling to Nilsoden. The Snow Bridge men-at-arms stood together muttering, pale with shock.

'No healer can save the ambassador,' Florin whispered.

'We'll see.' Byren looked grim. 'Do what you can for him.'

He strung blankets from branches to give them privacy, and hung a lamp directly above them.

Florin met Orrade's eyes across the ambassador. They were both wrist deep in blood, and Vlatajor was white as a sheet. Having done all he could for now, Byren knelt beside her.

'If the king's brother dies, Hristo fears Jorgoskev will execute them,' she whispered. 'But...' There was no hope.

Orrade met Byren's eyes. 'We have to try to save him.'

Byren nodded. 'Are you up to this?'

'What choice do we have?'

Byren came to his feet. Florin could hear him at the entrance to the make-shift tent, telling Chandler to keep everyone away and let them know when Hristo returned with the healer.

When Byren returned Florin looked from his grim face, to Orrade's tight lips. 'What's going on?'

'I have Affinity. Byren can channel my power to heal, but every other time we've done this it's taken all night and the wound has not been so severe.'

Byren grimaced. 'If we don't try, he'll be dead before they return with the healer.'

Orrade unlaced his own shirt, placing Byren's bloody left hand over his heart.

Byren covered Florin's bloodstained hands with his free hand. 'Don't let Hristo catch us like this, Mountain Girl. If the king hates Power-workers...'

She nodded.

Orrade closed his eyes. 'I've stopped fighting it.'

He fought his Affinity? Florin hadn't realised. She felt the gathering of power like the approach of a summer thunderstorm.

Byren closed his eyes and began to hum.

No, not a hum. It sounded more like a cat's purr, deep, rhythmic and soothing, and it came from his broad chest. The deep vibration travelled through his hand, through both of hers and into the injured man.

Florin's mind raced. How long did they have? Hristo would have to send a messenger into the town, locate the healer and wait while they packed their herbs. If healing normally took all night, they didn't have enough time, but if Byren was only trying to keep Vlatajor alive...

Normally, Affinity made Florin uncomfortable, but this rhythmic vibration was strangely soothing. She relaxed, letting herself go with it. For the first time in days, she felt no nausea. Exhaustion swamped her and she drifted into a sort of trance.

It seemed like only heartbeats later that Chandler called her name. Florin fought free of her daze and looked up to find him peering through the entrance of the makeshift tent.

She nudged Byren. 'They're here.'

He blinked and fell silent. As his hand dropped from Orrade's chest, Byren swayed but did not fall.

Florin could hear hurried footsteps.

'This way,' Hristo said.

He threw the blanket back and Florin caught a glimpse of the worried men-at-arms as a little old woman followed him into the makeshift tent, followed by a girl of twelve, carrying a basket.

The old healer's white hair was threaded with many silver beads, which chinked as she moved. The moment she stepped into the shelter, her eyes widened and she hesitated.

Impatient with the delay, Hristo urged her forward.

Florin knew the old healer had sensed Affinity, but she said nothing as she came over and knelt beside the king's brother.

'I need more light,' the healer told Hristo.

'I don't speak flat-lander.'

'The healer will need more light,' Florin said. So far she had not had to reveal that she understood their language, and she hoped to keep it this way. 'Fetch another lamp, Chandler.'

Hristo wrung his hands. 'Are we too late? Is he...'

'The king's brother still lives,' the healer said. She gestured for Byren and Florin to remove their hands.

No one spoke as the healer peeled back the blood-soaked cloth to reveal the extent of the wound. It was no longer bleeding freely, and Vlatajor's organs had settled back into his belly.

The healer swallowed nervously and glanced to Florin.

Chandler returned with another lamp and Nilsoden slipped in with him. The healer beckoned her apprentice.

'Which cleanser, grandmother?' the girl asked.

'The strongest. Then needle and thread.'

The girl passed a jar to the healer. As the small woman cleaned the wound, Florin smelled rosemary and alcohol, and something else.

'Will he survive?' Nilsoden asked.

'I cannot tell,' the healer answered. 'He lost a lot of blood, but the bleeding has stopped.' She cast Florin and Byren a wary look. 'I will sew up the wound.'

Nilsoden pulled Hristo outside but their worried voices reached Florin. 'He had better survive, because—'

'If the king hadn't alienated the Power-workers, we could go to an Affinity healer instead of—'

'Are you saying it was the king's fault now?'

'Of course not,' Hristo replied. 'But if he hadn't executed that Affinity-touched woman from Karpafaje, the silfroneer wouldn't have turned on Vlatajor.'

'You should have stopped him!' Nilsoden said.

'It happened too quickly.'

'I was nowhere near when it happened, and that's what I'll tell the king. I'm not going to be punished for something beyond my control.'

'Do you think Jorgoskev will care? We're in this toge—'

'No. It's your fault!'

'You...'

There was a scuffle, a thump and shouting from the men-at-arms as they pulled Hristo and Nilsoden apart.

'Go see what's going on,' Byren told Orrade, who slipped out of the makeshift tent.

'There, all done.' The healer tied off the last stitch and sat back. Her hands trembled ever so slightly. If Vlatajor died, would the king execute her as well?

'Will he live?' the healer's granddaughter asked.

'It would be a miracle.' The old woman's gaze slid to Byren and Florin. 'But it's a miracle he lived long enough for me to sew him up.'

Orrade returned with Hristo, who was trying to staunch his bleeding nose. He asked after Vlatajor in a thick voice.

'I've done what I can. It is in the lap of the gods now.' The healer sifted through her basket, pulling out several jars. 'This is to bring down the fever. The wound must be cleaned and the dressing changed twice a day. Wash it with this. And this is for pain.'

Hristo nodded. 'How much of the pain killer should I give him?'

'As much as he asks for,' the old healer said. The granddaughter looked up in surprise.

The healer rose, her beaded hair chinking softly. The granddaughter only had one row of silver beads wound through her temple plait. The pair of them packed up and slipped out discreetly.

Byren's stomach rumbled. 'Florin, stay and help Hristo. I'll send in some food.'

At the mention of food, Florin realised her nausea had returned.

Piro moved her Duelling Kingdoms piece. 'You're an excellent player.'

'I used to play with his lordship.' Old Gwalt grinned, reminding her of Dunstany. 'I play with the lad whenever he visits.'

'Siordun?'

Old Gwalt nodded.

Piro looked down. It was odd. Even though she felt like Dunstany was back, she missed Siordun. They sat at the desk in the music chamber, playing the game by lamplight. As far as the rest of the household knew, Piro was entertaining his lordship.

She studied the board. Siordun once told her the original Mage Tsulamyth had designed this game to teach the nobles of the three isles that diplomacy worked better than warfare. But the way her father played it, the game was all about capturing the other king's throne.

Piro turned over her next card. 'Sylion's Luck! The spar warlord has attacked with two hundred warriors.'

'Then you won't be invading Merofynia.' Old Gwalt turned over his own card, holding it at arm's length and frowning as he read. 'A terrible storm has sunk half of my fleet. Looks—'

A knock at the door made them both turn. Old Gwalt slipped through the adjoining rooms to the bathing chamber, while Piro went to answer the door.

Soterro stood there, with a message bearing the royal seal. 'This has arrived for his lordship.'

Piro held out her hand.

'I should give it to him in person.'

'He's in the privy.'

Soterro flushed and Piro plucked the message from his hand before closing the door on him. Suspecting that Soterro was listening at the door, she took the lamp and went through to the bedchamber saying, 'A message with the royal seal for your lordship.'

Old Gwalt came out of the bath chamber. 'Read it, your eyes are better than mine.'

She turned up the lamp. 'Isolt asks Dunstany to attend

a council of lords. She's been forced to call a lords' council, and Siordun had sent word that he can't get back in time.'

'If Lord Dunstany can't attend, he should send someone in his place.' Old Gwalt rubbed his chest absently.

'Are you all right?'

'A touch of indigestion. Normally the lord's heir would go in his place, but Dunstany would never send Duncaer. In fact, he would keep this information from him.'

'Surely Duncaer will hear about the council of lords anyway?'

'Yes, but he'll expect Dunstany to attend.'

'Unless he hears that Dunstany is sick.'

'He's never dared attend such a thing in the past, but he has grown impatient these last two years. I think his gambling debts are catching up with him.'

Piro nodded. 'The nobles fear and respect Dunstany, but they know he cannot live forever. Neiron might seek an alliance with Duncaer to undermine Dunstany. Isolt must delay the council until Byren arrives. I'll write urging her to delay.'

'And if she can't?'

'We'll have to pray for storms on the Landlocked Sea... Isolt can ask the lords she trusts to delay their arrival for as long as possible.'

'She'll have to balance this against the possibility that Neiron and his supporters will hold their own council without her.'

'But that would be treason.'

Old Gwalt nodded grimly.

Chapter Fifty

ORRADE JOINED BYREN as they waited outside the partially completed gates of the king's city. Built on a rise that backed onto a sheer cliff, the city had outgrown its original walls. New fortifications were under construction, enclosing the surrounding high ground.

'Eh, I'll say this for Jorgoskev,' Byren said. 'He knows how to design defences.'

'Jorgofaje...' Orrade said slowly. 'He renamed the city after himself. What does that tell us about the man?'

Byren shrugged. 'Rolencia was named after my ancestor.'

Hristo and Nilsoden had gone to speak with one of the stonemasons working on the new gate tower. A moment later, a boy mounted a shaggy pony and took off at a gallop, up the road towards the old gate.

'Just look at the number of workers.' Orrade gestured. 'All these men are not tilling fields, caring for animals or working their normal crafts. The city must be wealthy indeed. No wonder, when it lies at the centre of the long north-south valley, and at the point where the eastern valley leads east to Merofynia. All trade must pass through here. We were so busy watching Palatyne and Merofynia we did not notice this growing threat, Byren.'

'The six city states of the Snow Bridge have never been united before.'

'Exactly.'

Byren smiled grimly. He felt weary, having spent the last four nights by the ambassador's side, ostensibly so that Hristo could sleep, but really so that he and Orrade could keep the man alive. Orrade had been eating like a horse, yet he was still losing weight. But not as much as Florin, who had not been able to keep a meal down since they set foot on the ship.

She left the wagon, stumbled to the side of the road, leaned against a tree and threw up.

Byren frowned. 'She should be over the sky-sickness by now. Everyone else is.'

'Florin told me of a ballad about a Snow Bridge merchant who fell in love with a flat-land girl, married her and brought her home to live where earth meets sky. She could not adjust to the thin air. Rather than leave the man she loved and her little boy, she killed herself. Very sad.'

'Very silly,' Byren said. 'If he really loved her, he would have moved to the flat-lands.'

'True.' Orrade grinned. 'But Florin might not adjust. Some people don't.'

'Then it is lucky we're not staying. As soon as I've seen the king, I'm taking the pass to Dunstany's estate.'

'What if Vlatajor dies and Jorgoskev has us arrested and thrown in his dungeon?'

Byren shifted his weight and his hand went to the sword at his hip. He had fifty good men. By the look of it, the Snow Bridge king had thousands who could down tools and take up arms at a moment's notice. 'I want you to keep your eyes and ears open.'

'I will, but Florin is the only one who understands their language.'

She stumbled back to the wagon. Her skin had lost its healthy glow, and there were dark circles under her eyes. Byren wanted to send her to stay with Dunstany, but he couldn't, not when he needed her.

He did not like the man he was becoming.

He called to Florin, 'Hopefully, the king's healers will have something for your sky-sickness.'

She nodded and climbed back into the wagon, where the ambassador lay barely clinging to life.

'Do you think Hristo and Nilsoden suspect we've been keeping Vlatajor alive?' Byren asked.

'If they do, they should be grateful,' Orrade said.

'If Jorgoskev fears the power of the Affinity-touched, we don't want him knowing what we can do.'

'Either he is like your father and is not rational about Affinity, or he is a cunning man who wants to control those with power. If it is the first, he may turn on us. If it is the second, you're worth more to him as king of Rolencia... Oh, look, how thoughtful. They're sending us an escort.'

Byren smiled at Orrade's tone.

Two lines of men jogged out of the old main gate. They wore Snow Bridge armour, made of many tiny plates like fish scales, which gleamed in the sun. They kept pouring out of the gate at a steady pace until Byren estimated there had to be about three hundred men. 'We should be honoured.'

By mid-afternoon they had been escorted into the city and up the long straight road to the palace, which was built on the high ground. To get there, they'd had to pass through a series of gates, each representing a growth-ring of the city.

Byren stood in the wagon, gripping the back of the seat behind the ursodon handler, who held the reins. Aware that his life and those of the men who followed him could rest on some small detail, Byren studied everything. When they reached the palace, it was a hive of activity, with old sections being demolished to make way for new, more gracious apartments. Instead of the common white-grey stone, the new sections were built of a glossy white marble with large ground floor windows and doors.

'The king feels confident his enemies will never get this far,' Byren said.

The wagons were directed to one side and around the rear of the palace. As they passed the ursodon stables, they could hear the beasts calling to each other and a strong, musky scent briefly enveloped them.

At last they reached a courtyard full of partially completed corbels. Two dozen workmen stood near a stack of stone blocks, as if they'd been told to put down their tools and get out of the way.

Byren leapt down from the wagon, then turned to help Florin. Orrade jumped down behind her.

About two dozen richly-dressed men strode out of the palace and lined up on a terrace overlooking the courtyard. They wore stiff brocade robes that came to their calves, and wide jewelled belts. None of them spoke or moved.

Florin looked up at the people on the terrace. 'Which one is the king?'

Four men wearing elaborate costumes came, bearing two long horns between them. The horns were so big that the first pair of men wore straps over their shoulders, which supported the ends of the horns at the level of their knees. The second pair walked a body-length behind and wore straps across their chests supporting the mouth-pieces of the horns before their faces.

'Urso-horns,' Florin said. 'They're made from the very largest ursodon males.'

'Those beasts must have been huge,' Orrade whispered.

'Yes, but Bozhimir said they'd only ever found their bones. Cover your—' Florin's warning was drowned by a long, resonating blast from the horns. Like thunder, the sound rolled across to the far side of the valley, hit the mountain wall and reverberated back.

Several of the ursodons reared in their traces, roaring in fright as their handlers fought to control them. It was lucky the ambassador had already been unloaded.

The echo faded and Byren's ears rang with its absence. A grey-haired man walked out and stood between the two horns.

'I think that's the king,' Orrade whispered.

Byren looked down to hide a grin.

By the time he had command of his features, two young men had joined the king. Both bore a strong resemblance to him in manner and looks. Vłatajor had said the king had two sons.

Hristo mounted the steps. Pausing a body-length from the king, he bowed and remained bent over.

Jorgoskev beckoned to a skinny old man and whispered to him. The old man went down to Hristo, who gestured to Byren and his companions. As Hristo stepped aside, the old man came down the stairs, leaning heavily on a staff.

'When you greet the king, stay at least three steps lower than him,' Orrade advised softly.

The old man crossed the courtyard and ducked his head in a short bow. It was probably all his old back would allow. He was so hunched he had trouble tilting his head far enough to see Byren's face.

'Earth-meets-sky. King Jorgoskev meets King Byren and bids him welcome to Jorgofaje, greatest of all cities, jewel in the crown of the Snow Bridge.' He spoke formal Rolencian with a slight hesitation, as if he had not had to use the language in a long time. He gestured to himself. 'Scholar Yosiv meets King Byren. Come this way.'

Byren signalled Chandler to stay with his men before gesturing for Florin and Orrade to follow him. When they reached the steps, Byren noticed how Yosiv struggled. It would have been quicker to pick him up and carry him, but Byren resisted the temptation and instead offered his arm. Yosiv seemed surprised by the courtesy.

Orrade's guess had been good. Even on the third step below the king, Byren's eyes were above Jorgoskev's.

Giving a bow that would have pleased Byren's mother, Orrade addressed the king. 'The people of the flat-lands speak of the beauty of the Snow Bridge. They speak of the great warrior king, Jorgoskev, and the city state that bears his name. But nothing prepared us for the reality.' He paused while the old scholar translated.

The king nodded as if this was his due.

Orrade continued. 'Earth-meets-sky. Byren Kingsheir, son of King Rolen the Implacable, Saviour of Rolencia, Byren Kingsheir the One True King, meets King Jorgoskev, Uniter of the Snow Bridge.'

If Orrade was going to be the courtier, Byren would play the stern warrior. He bowed with his hand across his chest. When he lifted his head Jorgoskev seemed to be weighing him up. Byren held the king's eyes.

'Lord Dovecote, advisor to Byren Kingsheir, meets King Jorgoskev.' Orrade bowed then gestured to Florin. 'Florin of Narrowneck, shield-maiden to Byren Kingsheir, meets King Jorgoskev.'

Jorgoskev looked Florin up and down, then said something to his sons. They exchanged short, contemptuous glances that irritated Byren, but Orrade had already moved on.

'Byren Kingsheir has sat by your brother's side, night after night, since Lord Vlatajor was injured. It is with great relief that we deliver him into your care and trust your healers will soon have him restored to good health.'

Byren hid a smile. This placed the responsibility for Vlatajor's survival neatly on the king. Jorgoskev seemed to consider for a moment, then he nodded. If he felt anything for his brother, he did not show it. Instead, he gestured and the injured ambassador was carried away.

Jorgoskev said something.

Yosiv translated. 'The king appreciates your care for the welfare of his brother and he would have you meet his second son. Chedojor Kingson, soon to be wed to the daughter of Dezvronofaje's greatest family.' A man in his mid-twenties bowed. The scholar indicated the younger man. 'And Dragojor, the king's grandson.'

The lad looked to be no older than fifteen, and he gave Byren the smallest bow of all.

'The king's heir, Jorandrej, is dealing with an uprising in Karpafaje.'

The second son said something, gesturing to Hristo.

The king asked after Nilsoden.

Hristo shaded his eyes to search the crowded courtyard where Chandler and the rest of Byren's honour guard waited, but Nilsoden was nowhere to be seen.

The unfortunate escort apologised.

The king gestured to Byren as he replied and Byren felt Florin tense.

Yosiv turned to him. 'King Jorgoskev asks what you would do with a body guard who fails in his duty.'

Byren rubbed his jaw, playing for time. 'I would not presume to tell a fellow king how to rule his kingdom.'

Yosiv translated. The king exchanged looks with his eldest son.

Jorgoskev seemed to consider, then he spoke to Hristo and Yosiv translated for Byren's benefit. 'I placed my trust in you, Hristo, yet you failed to bring my brother home in good health. Decide your own punishment.'

Hristo swallowed. He glanced to the six men-at-arms who served under him. He could sacrifice one of them to take the blame. Instead, he drew his knife, said something that included the king's name then drove the knife up under his ribs, into his heart.

It was a waste of a good man, and it infuriated Byren, who asked, 'What did Hristo say, scholar?'

'Long live King Jorgoskev.'

Florin made a sound in her throat and stumbled away to throw up. Jorgoskev's grandson laughed.

Byren's men muttered, and he sent Chandler a warning

look. He turned back to Yosiv. 'Please give the king my apologies. My shield-maiden has been sky-sick since we arrived.'

'That is how it is with some people,' the scholar said and translated for the king.

Then they were escorted into the palace, leaving Hristo's body on the steps.

FLORIN'S CHAMBER HAD been completed so recently that she could smell the linseed paint. Since they thought she did not understand them the servants communicated with her by gesture and spoke freely amongst themselves. There were three of them, all youths, all richly dressed and beautiful, if you overlooked their odd colouring. And they were all soft of cheek, even though they appeared full grown.

She brushed away their helping hands to open her travelling bag. Cinna had insisted on packing one pretty gown, but Florin ignored it, laying out clothes befitting a shield-maiden. When Tutor Yosiv had translated this term as *warrior-virgin*, the king had said, 'no wonder the giantess is a virgin.'

One of the youths wrinkled his nose. 'What ugly clothing they all wear!'

'What do you expect of great clumsy giants?' the second muttered. 'Clearly, their souls have no poetry.'

'Yet, they call this one the king's warrior-virgin!'

They all tittered.

'The king is a giant even amongst his own people,' the first whispered. 'He must be hung like an ursodon.'

They giggled and laid bets as to which of them would be the first to glimpse the object of their curiosity.

Florin had to compose her features before she turned around and mimed bathing. They opened a second door to reveal a bathing chamber made of gleaming white stone. Gold-plated taps delivered water to a deep sunken tub. One of the servants sprinkled a mixture of petals in the water. Florin smelled roses and violets. When they tried to undress her, she sent them away.

Disappointed, they backed out.

The bathing chamber was finer than anything in Rolenhold. She suspected it was as grand as those found in the great houses of Ostron Isle or Merofynia. It would have been wonderful, if she hadn't felt so weak. No matter how deeply she breathed, there was never enough air and nausea was her constant companion. Her hands shook, had not stopped shaking since she'd seen Hristo take his own life. What kind of king forced a man to do that?

Florin stripped and stepped into the tub. If she could not be well, at least she could be clean.

The door behind her opened and Byren strode in. Tugging his shirt over his head, he tossed it aside. '...was no need to drive a man to kill himself.'

'We don't know their customs.' Orrade followed. 'He used Hristo's death to make a point, we...' Noticing Florin, he broke off. 'Byren...'

'What?' He turned and saw Florin. 'What are you doing in my bath?'

'This is my bath.' But even as she said it, she realised the servants had assumed *warrior-virgin* was a title, not a description. 'They must think...'

He looked fixedly down at his feet. 'My apologies.'

And he left with Orrade, without a backward glance.

Cheeks flaming, she retreated to her chamber, but not before throwing up again. How was she going to get through the feast tonight?

Chapter Fifty-One

To Byren, the food of the Snow Bridge smelled odd and tasted odder, the conversation was impenetrable and the music irritating. He had expected to meet the king's daughters at the feast, but there was not one local woman at the table, or among the servants. Instead, silk-wearing, soft-cheeked youths served the food. More of them played music and sang and danced while several moved along the tables for no reason other than to flirt with the feasters.

After watching some none-too-subtle fondling, Byren turned to the old scholar who sat between him and King Jorgoskev. 'Why do the boys flirt like girls?'

The old man took his time, apparently searching for the right word. 'They are not boys, but half-men.'

'Half-men?' Byren's balls contracted at the thought.

Orrade nudged him under the table and tried to divert the conversation. 'Have the healers treated Lord Vlatajor?'

'The healers are with him now.'

Since this reminded Byren of Hristo, he moved the

conversation on. 'I thought we would meet the king's daughters over dinner?'

Scholar Yosiv turned to the king and said something.

Byren glanced to Florin, wishing she wasn't on the other side of Orrade. She stared at her plate, looking pale and unhappy. Upon entering the feasting hall, she had been given a robe which, according to Yosiv, made her a man for the evening. It seemed the Snow Bridge people had a rather fluid attitude towards gender.

Jorgoskev said something to Byren.

Scholar Yosiv explained. 'The king has sent for his three daughters. You will have your pick.'

Byren glanced to Orrade.

'We must tell him,' Orrade whispered. 'The longer this goes on, the worse it gets.' He leaned forward, addressing the translator. 'Please convey our apologies to the king. We discussed this with Lord Vlatajor, but due to his injury I fear there has been a misunderstanding. Byren Kingsheir wishes to make an alliance, but he is not free to...' Orrade ran down. An old half-man had returned, leading three cloaked figures, presumably the three kingsdaughters. Two were the same height, but the third appeared to be little more than a child.

With a flourish, the half-man removed the first one's hood to reveal a woman who was not in the first blush of youth. She had the broad cheek bones and pale colouring typical of her people. Her eyes and lips had been painted. By their standards, she would have been pretty, but she stared straight ahead, her mouth set in a thin line of anger.

'Skevlaza.' The king gestured to her.

The half-man undid the clasp at her throat, removing her cloak to reveal...

'She's naked,' Byren muttered. No wonder she was furious. He had to fight the instinct to go over and replace her cloak. Knowing she hated their scrutiny, he could not look at her.

'Skevlaza is thirty-two, but she has already produced

one son, so we know she is fertile,' the tutor said. 'Her mourning period ended long ago, and she is free to marry.'

Byren glanced to Orrade, who was as stunned as him.

The king gestured to his eldest daughter. Small by Byren's standards, she was perfectly made, and graceful as she turned around on bare feet. Byren caught himself watching the sweet curve of her bottom and averted his eyes.

This meant he noticed Florin's expression. If he wasn't careful, she would jump up to her feet and say something that would get them all in trouble.

'Next we have Skevlixa,' the tutor said. 'Even though she is nineteen, she has never known a man. Because of her beauty, many have approached the king with offers, but he has denied them, knowing he could make a great match for her.'

Byren kept his eyes on the girl's face. She was a beauty, even with those strange shallow eyes and odd, red-gold hair. Clearly, she did not mind standing there for all to admire her. She turned on her toes, deliberately alluring. He felt like shaking her. She should be offended by these proceedings, not flattered.

'And next there is Skevlonsa. She is not yet twelve, but you can marry her now and bed her when she turns fifteen.'

This time Byren did not lift his eyes. The thought of Piro being paraded like this infuriated him. He sprang to his feet and gestured somewhat wildly to the three kingsdaughters, who were once again cloaked. 'Your customs are not my customs. I mean no offence, but I cannot do this. Please tell King Jorgoskev I am already betrothed.'

'Betrothed?' Yosiv looked worried.

'Please translate this, scholar.' Orrade came to his feet, gesturing grandly. 'My king is honoured to meet King Jorgoskev's beautiful daughters, each more lovely than the last. But according to our customs, when his brother died, he became betrothed to Queen Isolt.' Orrade gave

Yosiv time to translate, then went on. 'Byren Kingsheir most humbly offers his sister, Piro Rolen Kingsdaughter, as a match for the king's grandson, Dragojor.'

Orrade sent Byren a look of apology. They had to offer the Snow Bridge king something as a sign of good faith.

As Yosiv translated, everyone turned to the youth.

Dragojor looked startled, then grimaced and made a comment that elicited a laugh. Byren wanted to give the smirking youth a good thrashing.

Jorgoskev barked out something that made everyone fall silent. Young Dragojor flushed and came to his feet. He bowed low in Byren's direction and spoke with regret. Jorgoskev echoed him.

Byren looked to the scholar.

'The king apologises for his grandson, and asked you to forgive the rashness of youth.'

'Apology accepted.' Byren bowed stiffly, then had to take his seat again. If he left the table now, they would think he had taken insult.

The king asked a question via the scholar. 'My liege asks if this betrothal to Queen Isolt is not of your making, then surely you do not have to honour it?'

'I gave my word,' Byren said.

When Jorgoskev heard this, he stood and lifted his goblet, making a toast.

'To men of honour,' Yosiv translated.

Relieved, Byren came to his feet. 'To honour.'

Florin slipped into her room. With its pillows and duck-down quilt, the bed looked very inviting but Byren was waiting for her report. She went through to the adjoining bathing chamber, where he was already running the water to cover their conversation.

Byren turned to her. 'What jest did that pup make about Piro?'

'As Orrade said, their customs are different from ours.

You insulted the king. Instead of studying Jorgoskev's daughters and complimenting him on their beauty and child-bearing hips, you could hardly bring yourself to look at them. Then you offered your sister without first presenting her for inspection. All Dragojor said was that he would not buy a horse sight unseen, why should he take a wife without seeing her, and...' Colour raced up Florin's cheeks. 'He added if she looked anything like me, he'd rather have a half-man in his bed.'

'That's it.' Byren flushed. 'We leave tomorrow,'

'We can't leave so soon,' Orrade protested.

Florin covered her mouth and ran to the basin to throw up.

'We'll tell them Florin can't take any more of the thin air and we must leave for her sake.'

'That could work,' Orrade conceded.

Florin rinsed her mouth and turned to him. 'Glad I can be of use, my king.'

Byren grinned and went over to her. 'Go to bed. Play up the sky-sickness. I'll send for Scholar Yosiv.'

So Florin ended up in bed, wishing her part in the proceedings was over. All she wanted to do was sleep, but Yosiv had taken one look at her and sent for the healer. Now he and Byren stood by the bed, while the healer bustled about with his assistant. Both were half-men. One was old and plump, and the other was young and plump.

Byren did not look happy. 'Half-men, Scholar Yosiv?'

'They make the best healers. They cannot be tempted by a man's wife or daughter,' the scholar said. 'I'll turn away and translate. Do you wish to stay while the healer examines your shield-maiden?'

Byren backed out so hastily he bumped into the apprentice.

Florin suffered the indignity of being prodded and poked, and went through the charade of needing the tutor to translate the healer's questions. How often did she throw up? How long since she was able to keep down a meal?

Finally the old healer announced that she was one of those people who might never adjust to the Snow Bridge, and agreed the only cure was for her to leave. He offered to prepare a draught to help her sleep.

When Yosiv went off to tell Byren, Florin lay back on the bed. Over by the fire, the healer and his apprentice ground herbs, adding them to warmed wine, speaking softly.

To think she had been dreading meeting the Snow Bridge kingsdaughter, yet all she felt was pity. She still dreaded meeting Queen Isolt.

The two healers returned to the bed with the draught.

She sipped, hoping it would not upset her stomach.

'Will this help her?' the apprentice asked.

'It won't do her any harm. I put in enough powder to knock out an ursodon. Did you sense Affinity on her?'

'Not in the slightest.'

Florin kept her eyes lowered.

'And you're sure their king had no Affinity?'

'I felt nothing when I touched his skin.'

'Then the advisor must be the one who kept the king's brother alive.'

'Will Lord Vlatajor live?'

'If he's unlucky. Thanks to that silfroneer, he'll be in pain for the rest of his life and no use to the king. That's two brothers and three sons he has lost to win his kingdom. I wonder if he considers it worthwhile.'

Florin finished the drink and thanked them in their own language. She'd deliberately asked Yosiv to teach her a few basic words.

'The giantess shows courtesy,' the apprentice said. 'It seems a shame to reveal the advisor's secret, when he saved the king's brother. What will happen to him?'

'That's up to Jorgoskev, but whatever our king decides, the barbarian king is in no position to argue.'

Her stomach clenching with fear, Florin pretended to fall asleep.

'Do we have to tell our king?'

'Foolish boy. Nilsoden will go to the king. If we don't go with him, it will look like we have sympathy for the Affinity-touched. In the coming days, that will be almost as bad as having Affinity.'

'Why, what will happen to them?'

The old healer leaned close to his apprentice. 'I've seen how Jorgoskev roots out his enemies. He'll offer a reward for any Affinity-touched and pay it out of their confiscated property. Before long, neighbours will be denouncing neighbours.'

The apprentice gasped.

'Get our things. We must return to Nilsoden before he goes to the king without us.'

Their soft talk washed over Florin in waves, and she realised the draught was working. The moment they left, she sprang out of bed, staggered to the bathing chamber and stuck her fingers down her throat. Tears burned her eyes as she emptied her stomach.

Once she'd rinsed her mouth and face, she darted into the adjacent chamber. 'Byren, we... where's Byren?'

Orrade had been unlacing his shirt. 'I don't know. I just got back from telling Chandler we leave tomorrow.'

'Nilsoden's going to betray your Affinity to win favour with the king. We have to stop him.' Florin went to the door and peered out, just in time to see the old healer and his apprentice turn the corner at the end of the passage. 'They're going. Quick.'

'You can't run about the palace in a night gown.'

'Don't lose them, I'll catch up.'

She darted through to her chamber and pulled on her breeches and shirt, sliding a knife into her belt.

She sped down the length of the hall to join Orrade.

'They went into the next passage,' he whispered. 'They were arguing.'

Florin signalled for silence and peered around the corner. The apprentice and the healer were about two body-lengths along the corridor, whispering fiercely.

The old healer took the youth's arm. 'Why do you want to go home now...' His eyes widened. 'Someone in your family has Affinity.'

'Yes, my brother. Please, I must warn them.'

'No. If you're caught with them—'

'Let me go!' He tried to break away from the old healer.

As they wrestled, the old healer tripped and fell backwards, hitting his head on the base of a statue. He lay still.

The apprentice dropped to his knees. 'Master?'

He was so horrified he did not hear Florin come up behind him. She hauled him to his feet. 'Go warn your family, but first, where is Nilsoden?'

He gaped. 'You speak our language.'

'Where is Nilsoden?'

He pointed to the next door, just as Nilsoden opened it and looked out. Seeing Florin and Orrade, Nilsoden took off. Orrade gave chase.

'Go warn your brother.' Florin pushed the apprentice in the other direction.

She caught up with Orrade at the top of a flight of stairs. He stepped away from Nilsoden, who clutched the knife hilt protruding from his chest as he slid down the wall.

Orrade removed his knife to clean it. 'We can either take the body down to the ursodons' stable to be devoured, or leave the body here. There's a good chance the palace guards will assume someone killed him to win favour with the king.'

'Leave it here,' she said, impressed by the way Orrade could think on his feet. 'We don't want to be seen carrying a body around.'

'My thoughts exactly.' Orrade looked at her in approval, and then sobered. 'But where is Byren?'

* * *

As Byren stepped out onto the star-silvered balcony, he looked for the Snow Bridge king. Jorgoskev stood alone, staring out over his city. He nodded in thanks to Scholar Yosiv, then stepped out onto the balcony. The air was cold and sharp, and so clear Byren could see the distant snow-covered peaks on the far side of the valley.

'Wine?' Jorgoskev asked.

'You speak Rolencian...' Byren said as his mind raced. He was reasonably certain they had not revealed Florin's facility with the Snow Bridge language.

'Enough to know you are an honourable man.'

Byren nodded, not sure where this was leading.

'You saved my brother's life.'

'I'm sorry we could not prevent his injury. The silfroneer's attack surprised us all.'

'Power-workers are arrogant. All those with Affinity must swear allegiance to me or die. I can't let my enemies use them against me. You thought it cruel what I did to Hristo.'

'It is not for me to say.'

'This is true.' Jorgoskev studied Byren. 'You are a young man, new to ruling, new to betrayal. I have sacrificed much to forge my kingdom, too much to let it slip through my fingers. I can put a thousand men in the field with a day's notice, but in my experience, one well-placed death can save many lives. Men respect strength.'

Byren nodded. His father had often said the same. 'Sometimes a king must make hard decisions.'

'I knew you'd understand. It is time the Snow Bridge made allies with the flat-lands. So, you have a sister.'

'Yes.' Now was not the time to reveal doubt.

'When you have regained your throne, I will send Dragojor to visit.'

'He will be most welcome,' Byren said, relishing the thought of reversing their positions.

Jorgoskev raised his goblet. 'To our alliance.'

Byren echoed him, raising his own glass.

Chapter Fifty-Two

PIRO PUT DOWN her game piece. It was only mid-afternoon, but the sky was leaden with an oncoming storm so they'd been playing Duelling Kingdoms by the light of a lamp. She tilted her head, listening to distant voices. 'Is that Byren?'

Soterro's protests also reached them.

Old Gwalt frowned. 'I don't—'

'I'll see.' Piro darted out and ran to the end of the hall, where the grand staircase led down to the entry.

'His lordship is not expecting you.' Soterro blocked a portly man in his mid-fifties and a younger, taller man. 'His lordship has left orders you are not to be admitted, Master Duncaer.'

Dunstany's unwelcome heir! Piro froze. Why was he here? Why now? If anything, she would have expected him to be in port, claiming to represent Dunstany at the lords' council.

'I came as soon as I heard my uncle was sick,' Duncaer said. Piro stiffened. He might call Dunstany *uncle*, but she did not sense any genuine concern in his voice. If anything, she sensed a desperate kind of determination. As if, gambler that he was, this was his last throw of the dice. 'I've brought my manservant. He's a healer.'

Piro's sight shifted to the unseen and she recognised the servant for a Power-worker. He radiated Affinity.

Soterro stiffened. 'Lord Dunstany does not need your manservant. He has his own healer, who—'

'Who never gives me a straight answer. Out of my way.' Duncaer shoved past Soterro. 'I will see my uncle!'

Piro ran back to Dunstany's chambers, where she found old Gwalt on his feet by the window.

'That's Duncaer's carriage,' he said. 'I fear—'

'He's here to see Dunstany, and he has a Power-worker with him, one who claims to be a healer.'

'We'll be exposed.' Old Gwalt ran his hands through his receding hair. 'It had to happen one day.'

'But it hasn't happened yet.' She grabbed the Duelling Kingdoms board. 'Come with me.'

She ran through to the bed chamber, where she put the game board on the bed. 'Strip down to your shirt and climb into bed.'

'I can't—'

'You must. You bear a strong resemblance to Siordun and Dunstany.' As she spoke, she ran to the windows and pulled the curtains closed, making the chamber even dimmer. 'You said yourself that Duncaer has not exchanged a word with Dunstany in over twenty years.'

'I look older than Dunstany.'

'He's been sick. Does Duncaer know you?'

'I've seen him, but I doubt if he'd recognise me. Servants are beneath his notice.' Old Gwalt glanced to the bathing chamber, as if considering hiding in there.

'That ruse served in the past, but this time Duncaer's determined not to be turned away.'

'He has a healer with him. I'm not sick. I'll be unmasked!'

'Are you willing to bleed for Dunstany?'

'Of course.'

She pushed him towards the bathroom. 'Go in and make it look like you've had a fall. A bit of blood can distract people.'

The old servant had only just shut the bathing chamber door when the door to the music room opened, and she heard Soterro's raised voice. It was clear to her that he was trying to warn them. Had he suspected their ruse all along?

Piro flipped back the bed covers and rumpled the sheets, setting the Duelling Kingdoms board at an angle so that it looked like they had been playing, then ran through the sitting room to the meet the intruders.

'Soterro? Oh, thank goodness you're here.' She clutched the servant's arm. 'I—'

'Who is this?' Duncaer demanded.

Piro looked him up and down. He had the red nose of a drinker, and the look of a man who would stop at nothing.

'I'm Pirola Rolen Kingsdaughter,' Piro said, adopting her mother's proud bearing. 'Who might you be?'

He took a step back. 'I'm Duncaer.' He lifted his chin. 'Lord Dunstany's heir.'

'His heir? How can you call yourself his heir when you ignore him?' Piro cried. 'He's a sick old man, yet I've never seen you with him!'

Duncaer blinked. 'I—'

'Come quick, Soterro.' Piro ignored Duncaer and took the house-steward's arm, drawing him towards the bed chamber. 'His lordship went into the bathing chamber. I heard him fall, and now he won't answer me.'

She rattled the door knob and thumped on the panelling. 'My lord, are you all right?'

There was no reply.

Soterro knocked on the door. 'My lord?'

No answer.

'See?' Piro wrung her hands.

'My lord, I'm going to kick the door in.'

No answer.

He gestured to Piro. 'Stand back.'

'Be careful.' She clutched Soterro's arm. Duncaer and the Power-worker were watching, so the best she could do was pinch his arm as a warning, and hope Soterro would not give them away when he recognised Old Gwalt. 'What if he's right behind the door?'

He nodded. 'I'll be careful.'

Piro glanced over her shoulder to Duncaer and his Power-worker. They seemed captivated by the drama unfolding before them. Her mother always said she was a born player.

Just then, the house-keep ran in with two stout young footmen. Piro hoped the servants hated Duncaer enough to go along with the lie.

'I'm so glad you're here, House-keep Lynossa,' Piro said. 'Come closer. His lordship has had a fall.'

They all crowded around the door as Soterro put his shoulder to it. On the third try, the lock broke and the door swung open.

'Is he all right?' Piro cried, darting ahead of them into the chamber.

She found Old Gwalt sprawled on the polished boards, wearing his thigh-length shirt under a silk robe. His head lay in a puddle of blood and his white hair was partly soaked.

'Lord Dunstany?' Piro dropped to her knees. 'Oh, why didn't I take better care of you?'

She wept and turned him over. There was a nasty split on his forehead. She covered her mouth, shocked by the old man's willingness to bleed for House Dunistir. Tears spilled down her cheeks and a sob escaped her.

Soterro swore softly.

'There, there, dear.' The house-keep took Piro by the shoulders, helping her to her feet. The old woman did not blink or betray in any way that this was not Dunstany. 'It's a nasty business. Stand back and let the men lift him.'

'Careful, now,' Soterro told the footmen.

Between them, they carried Old Gwalt to the bed.

'Why... he's aged twenty years since I saw him at Palatyne's wedding,' Duncaer muttered, then recovered his wits. 'Out of the way, woman. My manservant is a healer.'

'Oh, good,' Piro said quickly. 'I'll help. My mother trained me in the healing arts.' She took the patient's hand before the Power-worker could get to him. 'Lord Dunstany, can you hear me?' She squeezed the hand and felt him respond, then added over her shoulder. 'He hit his head, so he could be confused when he comes around.'

'Very true, kingsdaughter.' The Power-worker spoke with an Ostronite accent, reminding Piro of the manservant Cobalt had foisted on her father. That Power-worker had nearly killed King Rolen using treatments that gradually sapped his life-force. She feared Duncaer had grown tired of waiting for his inheritance.

This close, she could sense the Power-worker's Affinity as he took Lord Dunstany's head in his hands.

'Hmm, a nasty fall. What did you say was wrong with him?'

'He often complains that his chest hurts.' Piro embroidered on Old Gwalt's recent bout of indigestion, combining it with her observations of the old coachman back in Rolenhold. His illness had been hard to diagnose and equally hard to treat until his heart gave out. 'The pains come and go. He sometimes feels dizzy and cold and clammy.'

The Power-worker rubbed his top lip.

'Maybe Lord Dunstany had a bout in the bathroom. That would explain his fall,' Piro rattled on happily. 'He's been in a lot of pain. Do you have any dreamless-sleep? We ran out.'

'In my bag.' The Power-worker nodded towards a bag on the floor by his feet.

In the spirit of helpfulness, Piro opened the bag and began going through it.

'Do you mind?' The Power-worker took it from her.

'You'll need thread and needle to stitch up that cut,' Piro said, unabashed. 'And you'll need a cleanser to make sure it doesn't fester. Bring more light, so the healer can work.' She was determined to be there every step of the way. She hadn't been able to help her father, but she would make sure this Power-worker did not get his claws into Old Gwalt. 'I think he's coming 'round.'

Taking his cue from her, Old Gwalt moaned softly.

Piro clasped his hand. 'How are you feeling, my lord?'

'Out of the way, girl,' the Power-worker told Piro.

She ignored him. But her subterfuge would only go so far. Once he called on his Affinity, she did not have the training to defeat him.

Old Gwalt blinked, then looked around the bed chamber. 'What's everyone doing here?' He focused on Duncaer. 'You? What are you doing here? And who is this?' He pushed the Power-worker away. Then he noticed his own bloodstained shirt. 'I'm covered in blood. What's going on?'

'You had a fall,' Piro said gently.

He frowned and his gaze went to Duncaer. 'That doesn't explain why he's here. It's not my birthday!'

One of the footmen sniggered.

'Throw him out!' Old Gwalt swung his arm in Duncaer's direction. Piro suspected he was enjoying this. 'And throw this foreign busybody out as well!'

Duncaer drew himself up to his full height. 'I protest, Uncle, I'm your heir and—'

'Don't *uncle* me. You call yourself my heir? It was you who led my youngest boy astray. You were nearly ten years older than him. You took him to the gambling dens. You got him hooked on dreamless-sleep. You corrupted my last surviving son...' Old Gwalt fell back against the pillows, clutching his chest.

Piro saw the pain and panic in his eyes. This time he wasn't acting.

'What's wrong, Uncle?' Duncaer came forward, all eager solicitation.

'His heart's failing,' the Power-worker said. Opening his bag, he removed a jar.

'Let me help.' Piro fumbled as she took out the stopper, dropping the jar. Its contents spilled across the quilt. 'Oh, dear...' She sprang to her feet, knocking the Power-worker's bag off the bed. Jars, bottles, powdered herbs spilled across the floor.

Apologising profusely, Piro scrambled around on her hands and knees. Under the pretext of helping, she managed to spill or smash anything that looked dangerous while pocketing a vial of dreamless-sleep.

'Stupid girl!' The Power-worker swore at her in Ostronite as he tried to save his things. 'Clumsy, stupid girl!'

'Here, there's no call for that,' the house-keep protested. 'She's only trying to help.'

'Yes.' Soterro stepped forward. 'You heard his lordship. He wants you out, so out you go!' He gestured to the young footmen, who moved forward to obey.

'Wait,' Duncaer protested. 'My uncle needs a healer.'

'And he'll have one. But it will be the healer he's trusted these last forty years,' the house-keep said. 'At least we know she won't upset him and give him palpitations!'

The servants united to bundle the protesting heir and his manservant out of the chamber, but Duncaer had scented Dunstany's death and he wasn't giving up so easily.

In desperation, Piro shoved the Power-worker's bag into his arms. 'Get out, both of you. My lord must recover. The queen needs him in the palace for the lords' council, and you're not helping!'

'The queen has called a lords' council?' Duncaer asked.

Piro nodded, knowing that Duncaer would go straight to the palace, where he would add to Fyn and Isolt's troubles. But if it got him and his man out of Dunistir House, so be it. 'Go away, and let us see to Lord Dunstany.'

'Very well.' Duncaer lifted his chin. 'But I will be back with my own servants, and if I learn you lot have failed to provide proper care for my uncle, I'll turn you and your families out with nothing but the clothes on your backs!'

And he would relish doing it, Piro could tell.

The two young footmen escorted Duncaer and his Power-worker out of the chamber, followed by the steward and house-keep.

The moment they were gone, Piro opened the vial of dreamless-sleep and tipped a teaspoon of it onto Old Gwalt's tongue, massaging his throat to help him swallow.

He gasped, pale and sweaty with the pain.

'I'm sorry,' Piro whispered. 'It's not indigestion this time, I fear. All I can do is give you pain relief.'

She sat and held his hand, speaking softly, while she waited for the dreamless-sleep to work. 'You did well. Mentioning Dunstany's youngest son was a stroke of genius.'

'I only repeated the things Dunstany used to say to me,' he whispered. The whiteness had faded around his mouth, and he no longer clutched her hand with such painful force. 'I'm feeling a little better.'

'That's good.' But he wasn't going to get better.

'I've had the chest pains before,' he admitted. 'I rest and I feel better. Don't worry.' He gave a wry smile that reminded her yet again of Dunstany and Siordun. 'We fooled him.'

Tears stung Piro's eyes.

Soterro and the house-keep returned, bickering over who was to blame for letting Duncaer in.

'It doesn't matter,' Piro said, springing to her feet and wiping her cheeks. 'We must be on alert for Duncaer. He brought that Power-worker in here to kill Dunstany, and I can prove it!' She picked up the first jar she'd spilt and ran her finger around the rim. Experimentally, she touched the tip to her tongue, then wrinkled her nose with distaste. 'Monkshead. Already my tongue is tingling. A teaspoon full would have been enough to kill Old Gwalt in his state.'

Piro realised what she'd said and looked over to the steward and house-keep. 'How long have you known Old Gwalt was covering for Dunstany?'

'They didn't know,' Old Gwalt protested.

'I knew the first time I saw Siordun disguised as Dunstany,' the house-keep said. 'Lord Dunstany's power was mild. The lad had much stronger Affinity. It made my teeth ache.'

'And you?' Piro asked the house-steward.

'My father served the mage back on Ostron Isle. Seven years ago he sent me to serve Lord Dunstany. I put it all together.' He bristled. 'But the servants would not trust me.'

Old Gwalt and the house-keep exchanged looks.

'I'm sorry, lad,' Old Gwalt said. 'But—'

'There was so much at stake.' The house-keep shrugged. 'The sad thing is that we didn't even trust each other.'

'You were all wonderful,' Piro said. She felt shaky and reached out to grasp the bed.

'Sit down, lass.' The house-keep guided her to the end of the bed. 'I'll send up a meal for you and his *lordship*.' Her eyes twinkled.

Old Gwalt shook his head. 'You always were a saucy minx, Lynossa.'

Piro smiled.

When the house-keep and steward had gone, Piro leant against the bed base. 'We've bought some time, but how long?'

'There's something I want you to have,' Old Gwalt said. 'Open the big chest at the end of the bed. Look for a small document chest.'

Under lavender scented blankets she found a narrow chest. 'This?'

He nodded. 'Bring it here.'

She turned up the bedside lamp before sitting next to him.

'It is a terrible thing to see your children die before you. When Lord Dunstany's youngest son was killed, his lordship was devastated, especially as he suspected Duncaer had contributed to his son's death. He started preparing documents then to legitimise Siordun.' Old Gwalt unrolled one document. 'This is the forged marriage certificate for his son and Siorra. No one knew she was Dunstany's natural daughter. Here is Siordun's forged birth certificate.'

She studied it. 'It says his name is Dunsior.'

'That's what he would have been called if he'd been legitimate. My lord was going to tell everyone his son had married in secrecy because he feared his father's reaction to him marrying a housemaid. Dunstany was going to say she'd brought the documents to him when she gathered the courage, on Siordun's fifth birthday. But Mage Tsulamyth tested the lad and—'

'Took him away.' Piro studied the aged documents. They certainly looked authentic. 'What do you want me to do with them? It's not like Siordun can claim the title now. He has to...' She'd almost said he had to play the mage. She replaced the documents. 'He has too much Affinity to live a normal life.'

'I know. But one day he may marry and have a son, and that son will be the true heir to Dunistir Estate. I want you to keep these documents safe for him.'

Piro looked at the chest. 'Why don't you just give them to Siordun yourself?'

'The mage made me promise I wouldn't.' Old Gwalt saw her expression. 'No one in their right mind crosses Tsulamyth. When he decided to claim Siordun, even Dunstany had to back down. It was heartbreaking. The boy was only five. He pleaded with Dunstany not to send him away. He called for his mother...' Old Gwalt's chin trembled, and his eyes filled with tears. 'We... we told him his mother had sold him to the mage. If we hadn't, he would never have left. It broke his heart and it killed something in him. But it was a lie. Siorra didn't want to part with him. The mage told her she was being selfish to keep him. He told her Siordun had too much natural Affinity and would not be safe from corrupt Power-workers. They kidnap children with Affinity to keep as slaves.' Old Gwalt shook his head. 'At any rate, the mage convinced Siorra she was doing the right thing to give up her boy, but she took sick and died not long after.' His chin worked as tears rolled down his cheeks.

Piro's heart went out to him, and to little Siordun and his mother. 'I'm sorry.' She wrapped Old Gwalt in a hug, weeping for all the things she could not change.

'There, there.' Old Gwalt stroked her hair. After moment, he cleared his throat. 'Sometimes there are no easy answers. Sometimes, we do our best and people still get hurt. I want to set things to rights before I die. That's why I'm giving you the documents. I'm glad Siordun has you.'

She wiped her cheeks, proud that Old Gwalt had chosen her for this, and that Siordun trusted her to keep his secret. 'I won't let him down.'

Chapter Fifty-Three

FYN STOOD ON the top terrace looking down towards the Landlocked Sea. It was dusk, and servants waited with lanterns on poles as Queen Isolt greeted the last of the nobles.

Lord Yorale was on hand, ready to advise the young queen. Sefarra and the mother of the young lord of Geraltir had sent their captains with twenty men-at-arms. The bay lord was still at sea, hunting Utland raiders, but Camoric spoke for him. The ranks of the new queen's guard were thin and Fyn was grateful for the ex-slaves, who spent their nights camped by the shore and their days preparing for war in Byren's service.

Dunstany remained on his estate, too ill to travel. It was unfortunate that the mage still needed Siordun. Fyn hoped Lady Death would not give him too much trouble. Here, Fyn had enough troubles of his own. Neiron, and the other lords with a vested interest in stripping him of his role as lord protector, dominated the council.

Lord Istyn had answered Isolt's summons, deliberately

delaying as long as he could to give Byren time to arrive, without success.

'Uncle.' Isolt's voice carried to Fyn on the terrace above. Istyn was her mother's older brother, but he looked more like her grandfather, his health shattered by grief. Two burly manservants had delivered him in an Ostronite carry-chair.

'Istyn won't do your cause any good,' Abbot Murheg said softly. 'The lords respect strength and power. Istyn has neither. His body has failed him, and with the death of his son there is no male heir. All he has is five daughters, poor man. He will have to get the queen's permission for his eldest daughter to inherit the title, and her husband will have to change his name.'

'Isolt can do that?'

'She can, but the lords won't like it. You've seen how everyone is related to everyone. Several of them could make a case for inheriting the estate. Younger sons are always on the lookout for ways to rise in the world.'

Isolt and the abbess turned to walk slowly beside the carry-chair as it came up from the terrace.

'I found this. I believe it belongs to your family.' Murheg gave Fyn a small velvet draw-string bag.

'I don't...' Fyn opened the bag and pulled out a lincurium pendant. He checked. Sure enough, the bag also contained the rings. 'Byren had these made as gifts for our parents. The pendant was meant for his twin's betrothed.'

'Palatyne had it amongst his things,' Murheg said softly. 'I must warn you, Fyn. Neiron will cook up a reason to remove you as lord protector, and if Isolt objects, he'll shut her in the queen's apartments just as King Merofyn did to her mother. She'll be a prisoner in her own palace.'

Fyn's hands tightened on the bag.

'There is only one way you can protect the queen. You do want to protect Isolt, don't you?'

'Of course I do.'

'Then marry her.'

Fyn stared at him.

'That's why I gave you the rings. You are King Merofyn's grandson, with more right to the throne than Isolt or any of these lords who whisper behind your back. If you married Isolt, you would have every right to defend her with force, and strip Neiron of his land and title.'

Fyn glanced down to Isolt, who waited patiently as Istyn's manservants negotiated the steps.

'Marry her,' Murheg urged. 'You've already fought to protect the kingdom, which is more than Byren has done. It is time for a bold move. Claim what should be yours.'

Claim what he truly wanted. A rushing noise filled Fyn's head.

Isolt reached the top step. 'And this is Fyn, Uncle, or more correctly, Lord Protector Merofyn.'

Istyn looked pale and tired, but he reached out to Fyn, who slipped the draw-string bag into his pocket and took the old man's hand.

'Isolt speaks highly of you,' Istyn said. 'I'm glad she has an honourable man as her lord protector.'

And that was why Fyn could not claim Isolt, no matter how much he wanted her.

BYREN WAS GLAD to be home again, if you could call Merofynia home. After coming through the pass, he'd hired horses and had made good time on the journey across Dunistir Estate. Now they rode through the orchard, approaching the barns and outbuildings behind the great house. It was late, and Byren was hungry and tired.

'What's troubling you?' Orrade asked, riding at his side.

'I'm tired of being polite to powerful men.' Byren gestured to the great house, visible beyond the smaller buildings. 'Dunstany is a friend of the mage and they've both helped me before, but powerful men always demand a price. That's how they get to be so powerful.'

As they left the orchard, a boy came out of the piggery carrying two buckets. He took one look at Byren and Orrade, yelped, dropped the buckets and ran screaming, '*Spar warriors!*'

'Wait!' Byren yelled in Merofynian, but the lad wasn't taking any chances.

Neither was anyone else. By the time they rounded the stables and entered the courtyard at the back of the great house, a dozen servants stood there with pitchforks, scythes and blades.

The kitchen door was flung wide open as Piro appeared on the back step. 'Byren!' She darted across the courtyard and pushed through the servants. 'It's Byren. I told you he was coming.'

'Yer didn't say he looked like a barbarian warlord,' one of the stable hands muttered.

With a laugh, Byren dismounted and opened his arms.

Smiling with tears on her cheeks, Piro caught him in a hug. Orrade received the same welcome. 'I'm so glad you're here!'

'Obviously.' Orrade grinned.

Piro drew them towards the house. 'It's been awful. Dunstany's heir turned up and... made him so angry he nearly had a heart spasm. Where's Florin?'

'Still sick. The Snow Bridge air was too thin for her.'

'Oh, poor thing.' Piro frowned, then brightened. 'She can stay here with me until she's better.'

Byren rubbed his mouth to hide a smile. Florin would hate the enforced rest, but... 'She needs to regain her strength. Then she can catch up with us.'

They entered the kitchen, where Piro shot off orders in quick succession, arranging food and refreshment for his men. It felt strange, seeing her in charge.

'I'm taking you to his lordship. I'll just make sure he's well enough to see you.' She drew Byren and Orrade into the hall, up the grand staircase and down a passage. Swinging a door open, she gestured to the chamber beyond. 'Wait here.'

As she darted through the music room, Byren strode over to the empty hearth, where two chairs sat. A blanket was draped across one. On the low table between the two chairs was a Duelling Kingdoms board with a game in progress.

On her return, Piro closed the connecting door. 'Lord Dunstany apologises. He isn't well enough for visitors tonight. Perhaps tomorrow.'

Byren's stomach rumbled loudly.

Piro laughed. 'Food's on its way. They'll bring it in here so we can talk. It's so good to see you two.' She treated them both to another hug and held on just a fraction too long.

Byren pulled back. 'Eh, what's wrong, Piro?'

'I've missed you, that's all.'

Byren searched her face. Behind the happiness, he saw sorrow and loss, and he wished he could protect her from the world; but here she was, running Dunstany's great house for him. 'Mother would be proud of you.'

She flushed and turned away, going over to the fireplace. After a moment, she drew a deep breath and gestured to the chairs. 'We need to talk.'

'I'd rather not sit. I've been riding all day.'

She nodded. 'Fyn needs you. I've had Dunstany's pleasure yacht ready to sail for the last two days. You are to set out for the palace tonight. The Merofynian nobles are trying to seize control of the kingdom.'

Byren cursed.

Piro nodded. 'Fyn's had nothing but trouble since you left. There's been an Utland attack in Mero Bay. The spar warlords have made several bids to take various estates. Fyn puts down this raid and kills that warlord, only to find another has risen in his place. The second time Benetir Estate was attacked, he had to free the seven-year slaves to turn back the warlord.

'It made the nobles furious. Now they fear slave uprisings on their own estates. The captain of the queen's guards grabbed me and tried to...' A shadow passed over her face and she hurried on. 'Fyn killed him in a duel. Now the nobles have divided into two camps, one led by Lord Neiron who wants to replace Fyn, and the other led by Dunstany, except...' She gestured to the closed door. 'The old lord is finally failing and I don't know if the men who've supported him over the years will support Fyn, and even if they do, I don't know if they'll be strong enough to stand against Neiron and his supporters.'

Byren met Orrade's eyes. It was worse than he'd anticipated. 'I don't like the idea of sailing into a nest of deceiving nobles, with just fifty men-at-arms.'

Piro went to speak, but someone knocked on the door and entered without waiting. Byren saw the fear cross his sister's face before she mastered her expression.

'Soterro, what's wrong?' she asked. 'Is it Fyn?'

The servant shook his head. 'We've just had word from the men who were patrolling the northern border. The Amfina Spar warlord has come over the pass and marches on Yoraltir great house. We can expect hundreds of Yorale's people to arrive in the next couple of days. Captain Tomos wants to know if he should let them onto Dunistir Estate.'

'Of course he should,' Piro said.

'Better check with his lordship,' Soterro said.

Piro flushed and darted into the adjacent chamber.

After a moment she returned. 'Dunstany says to give shelter to everyone who needs it and to double the border patrols. He thinks the spar warlord must have had someone watching Yorale's estate.' She added, for Byren's benefit, 'The warlord struck after Yorale sailed for the palace. Yorale's defences have been overstretched since he claimed Wythrontir Estate for his youngest son.'

Soterro bowed and withdrew.

As the door closed on him, Piro leaned forward and adjusted a Duelling Kingdoms piece before gesturing to the board. 'Once the warlord takes Yorale's lands, he'll either march on us or march on Wythrontir.' She traced her finger around the circle representing the landlocked Sea. 'If he marches towards us, he is only two estates away from taking the queen.'

Byren cursed. 'Lord Neiron will keep. I haven't come this far and given up...' He censored himself. 'I'm not going to lose Merofynia. I'm sailing for Yorale's estate.'

'With fifty men?' Orrade asked.

'We'll free Yorale's seven-year slaves.'

'Hit the warlord when he's not expecting it.' Orrade nodded. 'I like it. You'll be in a much better position when you confront Neiron, if you've defeated Amfina and you have an army of ex-slaves at your back.'

'That's what I'm thinking.' Byren grinned and headed for the door. 'We'll need someone with local knowledge.'

'What about dinner?' Piro called after him.

'We can eat on the ship. I'm going to tell the lads. We're off to free Rolencians from Merofynian slavery!'

Chapter Fifty-Four

THE WEATHER THE day of the lords' council suited Fyn's mood. The air was hot and steamy, and the sky was heavy and brooding, with the promise of a storm. Knowing Neiron would try to cut his legs out from under him, he'd been on edge all day. It had not started well, with a visit from Gwalt, carrying a message from Piro. Byren had arrived, but had sailed to save Yorale's estate from Amfina Spar, leaving Fyn to maintain control of the lords' council.

Of course, the first thing Fyn had done was to summon Lord Yorale and tell him the news.

'I know your instinct is to set sail for your estate,' Fyn had said. 'But Byren will do everything in his power to turn back the Amfina Spar warlord and we need your support at the lords' council.'

'I would not miss this council for the world,' Yorale said, to Fyn's relief.

'You're very quiet,' Camoric said, adjusting his belt so his sword was within easy reach. He was dressed in fighting garb, his only concession to his new rank the rakish tilt of his feathered hat. 'I have twenty trusted men in the corridor outside the war-table chamber, and another twenty within shouting distance.'

'Good.' Fyn wore simple clothes that could pass for Rolencian. Today he was King Rolen's son, and the lords would do well to remember it. 'I told the captain of the ex-slaves to watch for a signal from the war chamber windows. He's ready to storm the palace at a moment's notice.' And the way Fyn was feeling, he wanted Neiron to give him reason to act.

There was a knock on the door.

'Come in.' Fyn expected it to be Mitrovan with news from Travany, but it was Captain Aeran of the city-watch. 'Captain?'

'Lord Protector Merofyn, Captain Camoric.' Aeran gave them a formal bow. 'If the worst happens, the city-watch will support you.'

'Why?' Fyn tensed. 'What have you heard?'

'The port is abuzz with news of the lords' council. The nobles have moved men-at-arms into their townhouses and there's been brawling in the taverns.'

'What of the merchant margraves? Who will they support?'

The grizzled captain offered him an apologetic look. 'They don't care who the lord protector is, as long as he lives up to his name and they can trade in peace.'

Fyn nodded. 'Come to the lords' council.'

'I'm not a noble,' Aeran answered stiffly.

'You're captain of the city-watch, and I want you at my back. It means if I *do* go down, you'll fall with me. You decide.'

Aeran met Fyn's eyes. 'I'm here, aren't I?'

'Come on, then.' Fyn grinned grimly as they left his chamber and strode down the corridor. Byren had left him here to hold Merofynia, with no support and a pack of ambitious lords ready to stab him in the back.

Now that he had the ex-slaves, Camoric and the queen's guards *and* the city-watch behind him, he felt ready to confront the nobles.

As they turned the corner and approached the door of Isolt's chamber, she stepped into the corridor. Like them, she was soberly dressed. But it did not matter, whatever she did she was still a girl of fifteen and the Merofynian noblemen had made it clear her job was to produce an heir.

As Fyn offered his arm, he realised if he'd taken the abbot's advice they would be walking into the council as king and queen. He wanted Isolt more than anything, and their marriage would have justified using force, but he could not betray his brother's trust.

'You're looking very grim,' Isolt said. 'Hopefully, it won't come to bloodshed.'

'Spilling blood is simple. It's politics that can cut a man's legs out from under him!' He swept her around the last corner, where they expected to see the lords waiting outside the war-table chamber. But...

'They're already inside,' Isolt whispered. 'At least the abbot and abbess are waiting to enter with us.'

Murheg and Celunyd bowed, then stepped to each side of Fyn and Isolt. The war-table stretched before them, bathed in light from the tall windows overlooking the Landlocked Sea. Down the far end, the Merofynian throne had been placed on a dais. From there, Isolt would command the council.

Events had polarised the Merofynian nobility. Neiron and his supporters stood on the left of the table, facing the windows. Dunstany's supporters stood on the right. Today Istyn sat in a normal chair with his two manservants ready to come his aid. The captains from Benetir and Geraltir Estates were not well known to Fyn, but seemed ready to do their part.

Elder statesman that he was, Lord Yorale waited next to the queen's chair.

As Fyn escorted Isolt along the table, he did a mental headcount. With Camoric holding his grandfather's vote, and Dunstany...

'Duncaer,' Isolt said, pausing opposite an over-dressed middle-aged man with a suspiciously red nose. 'Why are you here?'

'You called a lords' council, my queen, so I must represent Dunistir Estate. My uncle's heart is failing. I come from his deathbed.'

Muttering greeted this news, and Isolt glanced to Fyn. There was no Lord Dunstany dying in bed on Dunistir Estate, but they could hardly reveal that.

Isolt stepped onto the dais and took her seat.

She arranged her gown, making them wait, then finally looked along the length of the chamber. 'A ruler needs sound advice from their nobles. As I have newly come to the throne and am only fifteen, I expect you to put aside all rivalry and work for the good of Merofynia. I now declare this lords' council in session. And I introduce the new captain of the queen's guards, Lord Cadmor's grandson, Camoric.'

Neiron and his lords gave barely civil nods.

Fyn waited for them to object to Captain Aeran's presence, but they didn't.

'My queen.' Lord Elcwyff stepped forward. 'I cannot attend a lords' council when my brother's murderer has a place at the table.'

'It was a duel,' Fyn protested. 'Elrhodoc tried to force himself on my sister. When I intervened, he challenged me. He chose the place and weapons, he had two seconds, I had none, *and* he slashed my face before the duel truly began!'

Elcwyff bristled. 'My brother would never—'

'That's what I don't understand,' Yorale said, his voice calm and reasonable. 'Elrhodoc was a champion swordsman. He didn't need to cheat to win.'

'He didn't cheat. And I have witnesses to prove it,'

Elcwyff insisted, gesturing for two men to come forward. 'Here are my brother's seconds, ready to give his side of it.'

One was the seedy guard who had been on the terrace that day, but the other...

'Hold on.' Fyn pointed to the second man. 'He wasn't there.'

'Yes, he was,' the seedy guard said. 'It was me and Grufyd. I can vouch for it.'

'Fyn's right,' Isolt said. 'Grufyd wasn't there. It was a young guard by the name of...' she frowned, then her expression cleared, '...Seelon. I can vouch for Fyn. He's speaking the truth.'

'My queen, you cannot vouch for anyone,' Yorale told her gently. 'When you sit in that chair at a lords' council, you must be impartial. In fact, you may not speak until everyone has said their piece.'

Isolt glanced to the abbess and abbot.

They nodded.

'Tell them, Hywel,' Elcwyff urged.

'We heard shouting and saw the lord-monk'—the seedy guard gestured to Fyn—'having a go at our captain. Of course, we ran over. Before we could do anything, he punched our captain in the gut.'

'He resorted to street brawling?' Neiron sounded shocked, and there was muttering from those around the table.

'Elrhodoc insulted Piro,' Fyn insisted. 'Hywel and Seelon saw him do it, yet they did nothing. I can send for Piro to confirm this.'

Yorale shook his head. 'My queen—'

'You can't call on her,' Neiron sneered. 'She's not a married woman, so she has no husband to vouch for her good sense. And besides, a female cannot give evidence in a man's murder case.'

'So it's murder now?' Fyn asked. Neiron was giving him exactly the motivation he needed to call in Camoric's men.

Neiron hesitated, surprised by his tone.

Elcwyff was too focused to notice. He gestured to the guard. 'Tell them what happed, Hywel.'

'Our captain defended himself. That was how the lord-monk got his face cut up. When he fell to one knee, our captain stepped back to let him get up, but he lunged in like a street fighter and stabbed him in the groin. Bled out like a pig, he did, poor Elrhodoc.'

Elcwyff flinched. He shook with anger as he turned to the other lords. 'See the kind of man you're dealing with?'

'To lose a brother is a terrible thing.' Fyn could tell Elcwyff's grief was genuine. 'But that's not how it happened.'

'The Mulcibar healer who laid out Elrhodoc's body is here,' Neiron said. 'He can confirm the nature of the wound.'

A middle-aged priest stepped from behind the ranks.

Murheg clutched Fyn's arm. 'That's Neiron's second cousin. That's the man I defeated to become abbot.'

'Tell them,' Neiron urged his relation.

'What the guard said is true...'

'I don't deny the nature of the wound,' Fyn had to raise his voice to be heard, as the priest kept talking. 'Elrhodoc had ripped my cheek open to the bone. I was seeing stars. He came in for the killing strike. I had no choice but to strike him down.'

'...strike him down like a common knifeman in a street brawl!' the healer finished.

The sudden silence drummed on Fyn's ears. In a moment of perfect clarity, he saw that Neiron had left him no option. He took a breath to call in the guards.

A young man burst into the chamber, trying to shake off two of the queen's guards. 'Out of the way, I have to see my father!'

Camoric signalled his men. 'Let him in.'

The queen's guards stepped back and the young man stood at the end of the table, battle-worn but defiant.

'Travrhon?' Lord Travany frowned. 'What are you doing here?'

'Ulfr Spar attacked. They over-ran our defences, we—'

'You abandoned our estate? How could you bring shame on the house of Travantir?'

Travrhon flushed. 'I had women and children to think of, Father. We only just made it to the boats. What's more'—his gaze shifted to the queen—'I saw smoke from Benetir Estate. They're under siege.'

The chamber erupted.

Camoric grabbed Fyn's arm. 'We must go to Sefarra's aid.'

The Benetir captain tried to talk tactics, and at the same time, Isolt left her throne and pleaded with Fyn to save her cousin. It seemed all he had done since becoming lord protector was fight to keep the kingdom intact.

With the aid of his servants, Istyn struggled over to join them. He was concerned for his wife and daughters. The only one who wasn't directly threatened was the captain of Geraltir Estate, whose lands backed onto the Snow Bridge. He was sixty if he was a day, and he watched with sympathy as Fyn tried to reassure them all.

Fyn's mind raced. Three out of five spars had come over the Divide within a few days. Did this mean the spar warlords had put aside their rivalry and mounted a concerted attack on Merofynia?

'You said we'd be safe when you executed the warlord's son!' Travany shouted across the table. 'But you brought this on us!'

'Not only is he a murderer, but he's led us into war with the spars!' Neiron gestured to Fyn. 'Call yourself lord protector? I call you—'

'Now is not the time for posturing and politicking.' Fyn cut him off. 'This could be the spar invasion Palatyne planned. All of you must look to your own estates!' He caught Isolt around the waist and lifted her down from the dais. 'There's no time to lose.'

And he swept out with his supporters. At the door to

the war-table chamber he confronted Travrhon. 'Do you want to save your estate?'

'Of course.'

'Will you free your seven-year slaves to do it?'

His mouth dropped. 'I forgot... I hope they're safe. Yes, I'll free them. I heard about the bargain Lady Sefarra struck. It seems fair.'

'Good, come with me.'

Fyn strode down the corridor issuing orders. He sent Lord Istyn back to his estate to see if he could evacuate his non-combatants. Camoric volunteered to find enough boats to transport their men across to Benetir Estate. Hearing this, Travrhon offered the boats he'd used to save his people and the two of them went off together.

Fyn turned to the captain of the city-watch. 'By rights, Camoric should stay here with the queen, but Sefarra's in danger. Can I entrust Isolt's safety to—'

'No Fyn, I'm coming with you,' Isolt protested.

He took her by the shoulders. 'Three out of five spar warlords have attacked. This in an invasion. Stay here.'

'The palace is not defensible,' Captain Aeran objected.

Fyn beckoned Murheg. 'If the worst happens, take shelter in Mulcibar Abbey.'

'I won't be there,' Murheg said. 'I'll be with you. And Neiron's second cousin is the next-highest-ranking—'

'The queen can come with me, back to Cyena Abbey,' the abbess said.

Satisfied Isolt would be safe, Fyn left before she could argue.

FLORIN HAD KNOWN Piro only briefly during the manticore attack on Narrowneck, but they'd faced danger together and that revealed a person's true worth. She liked Piro. Even so, she wasn't happy about remaining behind while Byren sailed off to confront a spar warlord... It made her stomach churn with fear for him.

'Feeling better?' Piro asked.

'Yes,' Florin lied.

They walked along the terrace, in front of the great house, looking east across the Landlocked Sea. The setting sun illuminated a mountain of dark menacing clouds out over the water. Lightning flickered in their depths.

'The storm will stir up the sea. I'm glad Byren sailed last night,' Piro said. 'He's lucky he doesn't get sea-sick. The last time I was caught in the storm, I threw up for days—'

Florin stumbled to a flower pot and emptied her stomach.

'Sorry.' Piro rubbed her back. 'My mother was always telling me to mind my tongue.'

Florin wiped her mouth, disgusted with herself. 'I should be better by now.'

'Maybe it takes a couple of days to adjust to the air at sea level.'

'I never adjusted to the air on the Snow Bridge.'

Piro shrugged. 'You might have caught something while you were there.'

'That must be it.' Florin felt relieved. 'The food was strange. Quite a few of Byren's men developed stomach problems.'

'You'll feel better with some rest,' Piro told her kindly, but Florin noticed how her eyes went to the windows of Lord Dunstany's chambers, and she knew Piro was thinking of the old lord who would not get better.

'You're very fond of Lord Dunstany.'

'Y...yes.'

Florin sympathised. She'd lost her father, but Piro had lost father, brother and mother. Florin slid her arm around the smaller girl's shoulders and turned her to face the Landlocked Sea. 'Where's your foenix?'

'I had to leave Resolute with Isolt's wyvern for company. I miss him terribly.'

Neither of them spoke for a moment.

Florin frowned. The light was fading fast, and it was hard to tell, but she thought she'd spotted a sail heading towards them. It couldn't be Byren, returning so soon. 'Who's that?'

Piro frowned. She ran back to the front door to speak with a servant, then returned to Florin. She stared out to sea. 'If only I had a farseer.'

A dozen servants arrived with makeshift weapons. Florin watched with growing consternation.

'You should go inside, kingsdaughter,' the house-steward urged.

'It's only one boat,' Piro said. 'What if it's a message from Fyn or Byren?'

She went down the steps. Everyone followed, and more armed servants joined them. They crossed the lawns, heading towards the jetty. By the time they reached it, the boat was almost within hailing distance.

'The deck's so crowded. They could be fleeing an attack,' Florin guessed.

'They fly the Istyntir symbol.' Piro cupped her hands. 'What happened?'

A dozen voices answered.

'Istyntir taken and the great house burned...'

'Wythrontir surrounded...'

'Smoke coming from Nevantir...'

'Captain Orwen of the *Sweeping Ospriet*,' the captain identified himself. 'Yours is the first estate we've seen not under attack.'

'What of Yoraltir?' Piro yelled.

'There was smoke. I have my lord's wife and five daughters on board. We claim sanctuary in the name of Cyena.'

'Of course.' Piro turned to the steward, speaking softly. 'Fyn and Byren need to know. Send a message. Tell the house-keep to find suitable chambers for the Istyntir women and their people.'

Soon the jetty was crowded as the old, the injured and women and children disembarked. Lord Istyn's wife seemed lost, as if she had taken a blow to the head. The eldest daughter took charge.

The youngest of the five girls appeared to be about ten and the eldest might have been twenty. They were as alike as peas in a pod.

As Florin helped the injured and the frail into a cart, she felt no surge of triumph. Once she had hated the Merofynians for what they had done to her home. Now she hated war. It was such a waste. No one really won.

FYN STUDIED THE brooding sky. They'd set sail at dusk, hoping to make the crossing before the storm struck. Flashes of lightning lit the clouds from within, reminding him of his mother's tales of boats lost on the Landlocked Sea.

He glanced over his shoulder. The flotilla had spread out. He turned to Camoric. 'Will the storm hold off long enough for us to reach Benetir Estate?'

'We'll be cutting it fine.' Camoric smiled slowly. 'You mean to attack under the cover of the storm!'

Fyn felt an answering smile tug at his lips. Now that he was taking action, a weight had lifted from him. 'The sentries will be huddled in their seal-skins and the drumming rain will cover our approach, but if the storm strikes before we get there the fleet will be scattered.'

'You're taking a gamble.'

'Life is a gamble.' Fyn shrugged. 'We'll shelter in the same bay as last time and go over the hills to Benetir estate. The spar warriors laying siege to the fortified great house will be trapped in the open between us and the house.'

'What if the warlords have made a coordinated attack and they've taken all the other great houses and fortified them?'

'Then we'll lay siege to all the great houses, around the

Landlocked Sea.' He wished he had a pair of pica birds so that he could stay in touch with Byren.

A laugh reached them from the men huddled on the deck. Fyn's ex-slaves and Camoric's men talked softly, or prayed, or slept—or tried to.

Fyn left the rail. 'I'm going to study the map.'

But below deck, he sensed Affinity and went to the forward cabin. Taking a lantern, he opened the door to find Isolt curled up with Loyalty on one side and Resolute on the other. Both Affinity beasts stirred and lifted their heads, eyeing him. Isolt slept on oblivious, making him smile.

Not for one moment did Fyn consider turning back. In fact, he was pleased she had defied him.

He closed the door and let the queen sleep.

Chapter Fifty-Five

GARZIK WAS TIRED. They'd been sailing for two days straight, taking turns at the tiller. Now, as they approached the settlement headlands, a stiff breeze filled the canvas above him. He adjusted the single sail while Luvrenc turned the rudder, watching the sea. The skiff picked up speed like a horse nearing the stables at the end of a long ride.

'I bet we're the first ones back!' Luvrenc crowed.

Five skiffs had set off to circumnavigate the island. The race was a regular event which gave the young lads and beardless a chance to polish their skills while competing for the accolades.

Garzik glanced to Ilonja, who sat in the prow. 'Can you see any of the other skiffs?'

She shaded her eyes. 'Nothing yet.'

'The best three skiff teams will race to Dalfino Island and back,' Luvrenc told Garzik.

'You can reach another island in these boats?' The skiffs were small, barely bigger than rowboats. 'What about Affinity predators, storms? Vultar's renegades?'

'We don't set sail if a storm is coming. We take bows and arrows to fend off Affinity predators. And the Isle of the Dead is in the opposite direction from Dalfino, we'd have to be unlucky to run across renegades.' Luvrenc considered. 'Now that you mention it, the elders mightn't let us go this year. I hope...'

They were through the headlands now, and the long narrow bay opened before them.

'I can't see any other skiffs, but a ship has returned!' Ilonja announced. 'It's Captain Cvetko's.'

Luvrenc grinned. 'He'll be spitting mad when he hears how Rusan sailed into Port Mero!'

But that wasn't why Cvetko was spitting mad. This was the first he'd heard of Vultar's attack, and he was all for sailing to the Isle of the Dead to confront the renegade. Garzik could hear the shouting from the jetty as they anchored the skiff and waded ashore.

'Just our luck,' Luvrenc muttered. 'We're the first skiff back and no one notices because of Cvetko.'

Garzik slipped through the gathering, with Ilonja and Luvrenc on his heels.

'How could you let him sail in here, rape our women, steal our stores and abduct our oracles, Rus?' Cvetko demanded. He was older than Rusan, around thirty, and so angry that spittle flew from his lips. 'What will the other settlements say?'

'We did not shame our people,' Rusan said. 'We burned one of Vultar's ships. He only just escaped.'

'Why didn't you follow him and—'

'We'd lost most of our beardless,' Lauvra told him. 'Only Rusan's ship was here, and half his crew were hunting a manticore pack. The elders decided we would wait until midsummer to mount a counter strike.'

'We'll hold a war council when all the captains return,' Feodan said.

'What of Hedvig and Dragutin?' Cvetko asked. 'What did they say about this?'

'They don't know. When they get back, we'll—'

'How can we even hold the midsummer celebration without the oracles?' He turned on Rusan. 'How could you let this insult pass?'

'We had to protect our people. They're saying Vultar has gathered all the Northern Dawn renegades. He had two ships when he raided here.'

'And you burned one. How many renegades can there be?' Cvetko jumped onto a bale and raised his voice. 'I say we strike a blow for the Wyvern People. I'm not a ballless wonder like the Rolencian king, hiding in the mountains while his cousin steals his kingdom. Vultar will regret taking our oracles!'

Cvetko's men cheered, but the majority of the settlement looked to Rusan. Garzik couldn't hear for the roaring in his head. Even the Utlanders knew of Byren's humiliation. Yet here he was, trapped at the end of the world when he should have been at Byren's side.

Ilonja nudged Garzik. 'Ask her about the race now.'

Lauvra was speaking with her brother and sons. Cvetko had jumped down from the bale, and it looked like one of his men was telling him something important, something to do with Rusan and Olbin, by the way they were glancing in the brothers' direction.

Garzik shook his head. 'It isn't a good time to—'

But Luvrenc had taken matters into his own hands. He approached the settlement's leader, reaching for his aunt's arm. 'Will the race to Dalfino Isle go ahead? Wynn says because of Vultar's threat, the elders will stop it. How can we beat the others, if—'

'Hush, lad.' She turned to her sons and brother. 'Cvetko needs to be diverted. Attacking Vultar now could bring his ire down on us before we're ready. Cvetko always was a hot-head. When he calms down—'

'What's this my man tells me?' The other captain strode over. 'Rusan sailed his ship into the hot-landers' port?'

Rusan shot Lauvra a look before he answered. 'And sailed out again with a full hold.'

'They're saying you destroyed a sea-hound ship, too.'

Rusan nodded. 'Drove it onto Mulcibar's Gate. Last we saw, it was in flames.'

'The goat-boy has come a long way!' But the captain didn't sound pleased. 'Next you'll be declaring yourself king of the Wyvern People!'

Olbin laughed outright. 'We're not hot-landers!'

Cvetko glared at him, then fixed on Garzik. 'So this is the slave who betrayed his people?'

'Wynn is no slave,' Rusan stated. 'He earned his freedom the night Vultar attacked. And he earned it again when we sailed into the hot-landers' jaws.'

'But all that's old news,' Feodan said, slinging an arm around Cvetko's shoulders. 'Tonight we must feast and hear of your raids.'

Cvetko's men agreed. Feodan drew the other captain aside, asking about his adventures, and Rusan followed his lead.

'Goat-boy?' Garzik asked Ilonja.

She glanced to Lauvra who answered. 'When Cvetko made captain, Rusan was only eleven and looked after the goats. Now Rus out-shines him. All the captains strive to outdo each other. Friendly rivalry is good, but I hope Cvetko doesn't feel he has to...' She ran down and hurried off.

THREE MORNINGS LATER, Garzik understood her fears. Ilonja came running into the long-hall just as they were waking.

'Cvetko's gone to teach Vultar a lesson!'

Garzik rolled to his feet and checked the circle of unmarried raiders sleeping around the hearth. Sure enough, none of Cvetko's crew were there.

Everyone ran out of the hall. Dawn mist lay on the bay

but they could plainly see Cvetko's vessel was missing, as was...

'He's taken my ship!' Rusan swore. 'I don't believe it!'

'The thieving nennir!' Olbin reached for his sword, and realised he was unarmed.

'I'll have his balls for this!' Rusan muttered and grabbed Feodan's arm. 'Loan me your ship.'

'Rus...' Lauvra put her hand on his shoulder. 'You would hunt down and murder our own people? Think! It would tear the settlement apart.'

'*He* should have thought of that before he stole my ship, the thieving renegade!'

'Cvetko would never turn renegade. Not when he has three children, with a fourth on the way,' Lauvra said. 'I've sent for his woman. Urzabet will know what Cvetko and his brothers are planning.'

'Lauvra's right,' Feodan said. 'I'd bet my ship he's not going after Vultar. Only yesterday I spoke with him about the dangers of bringing Vultar's raiders down on us before we're ready, and he agreed to wait until midsummer.'

'Then why did he steal my ship?'

'He hasn't stolen your ship, only borrowed it,' Urzabet announced. Cvetko's woman had been escorted by several beardless. She brushed off their hands and smoothed the material over her swollen belly. Her pretty mouth twisted with contempt. 'You think you're so smart, Rus. You think you'll be the one to lead the raid on Vultar. Well, you're wrong. It'll be Cvetko. He's gone to Ostron Isle. He's going to sail into the Ring Sea and bring back *two* shiploads of bounty, and another hot-land ship. Don't worry, you'll get your precious ship back.' Her eyes flashed. 'But you won't get to lead the raid on Vultar, because Cvetko will return triumphant. And he'll return without losing half his crew!'

Garzik glanced around, noting who supported Cvetko's wife. Truly, Byren's mother had been right. The higher you rose, the more enemies you made. He felt the tension build. Was the settlement going to tear itself apart over this?

He glanced to Lauvra, looking for a signal.

'Urza...' The iron-haired woman shook her head sadly. 'We need all the ships and warriors we can muster if we are to defeat Vultar. Cvetko should have consulted with the elders before taking Rusan's ship. Now he's sailed off to use exactly the same ploy Rus used. The hot-landers will be on their guard. You should have advised him against it.' She paused to let this sink in. 'We can only hope he and his men return by midsummer, ready for the raid.'

As Piro guided her horse towards the stableyard gate, she spotted a pica bird circling the old northern tower of the great house.

'We can go riding later,' she told Florin.

'We don't have to.'

'Yes, we do. I need the fresh air and you need to get over your fear of horses.'

'I'm not afraid of horses. I don't like them. That's different.'

Piro smiled as she swung her leg over her mount and dropped to the ground. 'I'll get the message and meet you in Lord Dunstany's chambers.'

Florin opened her mouth to argue, but Piro took off across the stableyard.

There had been no word from Siordun. It was true the ordinary people feared the mage, but Lady Death was no ordinary woman. If the meeting with the leader of House Nictocorax had been straightforward, Siordun would have been back by now.

And now trouble had flared up between the great merchant houses of Ostron Isle. Not so long ago, the streets had run with blood, as the families fought over who would be the next elector. She trusted Siordun to do all he could to keep Nefysto and Kaspian safe, but who was keeping *him* safe?

She ran into Soterro at the base of the tower. 'I saw the pica bird. What news?'

'You have sharp eyes.'

'Was it from Siordun?'

The steward shook his head. 'Fyn.'

'He's back in Port Mero?'

'No. He's retaken Benetir Estate and plans to march to Travantir. He'll send messages to Dunstany's townhouse in Port Mero, and Young Gwalt will send a bird to us.'

Piro nodded. 'If there's anything Byren needs to know, we can send a rider.' It wasn't ideal, but it was the best they could manage. She thanked him, then ran across the courtyard and into the new great house.

Before she reached the passage to Dunstany's chambers, she had to pass the corridor leading to the Istyntir women's rooms. She paused at the corner.

When the family had arrived, the mother had been reeling from her son's death, her husband's collapse and the loss of their home, and she had never really recovered. It had been left up to the eldest daughter to see to the comfort of their people. Piro admired Isfynia's fortitude, but she did not want to be trapped in another discussion about the invasion. Luckily the passage was empty, and she slipped by unseen.

When she reached Dunstany's chambers, she ran through to the bedchamber, where she found Florin with the man she believed to be Lord Dunstany. Piro wished she could tell Florin the truth, but it was not her secret to reveal.

Propped up on pillows, Old Gwalt's colour was a little better today.

'Good news,' Piro announced.

'From Byren?' Florin's face betrayed her.

Piro was so surprised to discover Florin was in love with Byren, she forgot what she'd been about to say.

'Is it from Byren?' Gwalt asked.

'No. As far as we know, Byren is still on Yoraltir's estate.' It had been three days since the Istyntir refugees had sought shelter, and Piro had sent a message to Byren via Captain Tomas the very next day. She climbed onto the bed. 'Fyn has retaken Benetir Estate. He marches for Travantir.'

'Where's that?' Florin asked.

'We need our own war-table.' Piro turned to Old Gwalt. 'Do you have one, my lord?'

'There is a bigger Duelling Kingdoms board. Tell Soterro to put it on the desk in the music chamber.'

Piro ran off to deliver the order. By the time she returned with Soterro and the board, Florin had helped Old Gwalt to the music room. He was pale and shaking from exertion. Piro found him a chair.

'Growing old is a terrible thing,' he said. 'I only hope I can hold on long enough.'

Luckily, Florin did not ask what he meant.

Soterro had set up the game board. It was not to scale and Ostron Isle appeared much closer than in reality.

'This will help us keep track of the spar invasion,' Piro said, unpacking the pieces and putting them in position on the board. 'This one can be Byren.' She put a king piece on Yorale's estate and selected the other king piece. 'And Fyn can go here on Travantir Estate.'

There were five estates between them. She indicated the estates east of Yoraltir. 'Thanks to the Istyntir captain, we know that these three estates have fallen. But we don't know if Elenstir and Rhodontir have been attacked.'

Florin frowned. 'It's been four days with no word from Byren. We should have heard from him by now.'

There was a knock at the door.

Soterro returned to report, 'Captain Tomas sends news. King Byren took Yoraltir great house and rides into the mountains to hunt down the warlord. He'll go to Wythrontir next, to break the siege.'

'Good. Now we know where he is.' Piro moved Byren's piece into the mountains behind Yoraltir's estate.

'How long did it take that message to reach us?' Florin asked.

'Good point.' Piro looked to Old Gwalt.

'Two days, if it came by horse.'

'So he could already be on his way to Wythrontir Estate.' Florin stared at the stylised map of Merofynia, as if it could tell her where Byren was. 'I should be with him.'

'Are you feeling better?' Piro asked.

'Yes.'

But she always said that.

CVETKO'S CONTEMPTUOUS WORDS had been the last straw. If Garzik didn't help Byren win back Rolencia, he would never be respected. He'd just be some poor wretch who'd been enslaved by Utlanders. In fact, if he stayed too long, he feared the change to his eyes would be permanent. Then, when he did get home, they would see an Utlander instead of Lord Dovecote's youngest son.

He knew Luvrenc and Ilonja would be heartbroken, and he hated leaving Olbin and Rusan, but over the last few days he had hidden weapons and supplies in his favourite skiff.

Now, in the dim light of dawn, he would set sail.

Maybe it was madness to cross the Stormy Sea in a three-man skiff, but he could lash the tiller while he adjusted the sails, and he knew how to navigate by the stars. All he needed was a little bit of luck.

And it did seem as if Halcyon was smiling on him, as he slipped down to the shore unnoticed. He passed the cradle that had been built to support Rusan's new ship while it was being constructed. Feodan and Olbin had gone back to the high country looking for more timber. It made Garzik feel as if he was leaving things half-done. But Byren was his first priority.

He waded out to the skiff and leapt aboard, hauled up the anchor, set the sail and took the tiller, all the while praying no one would spot him and sound the alarm.

A slight dawn breeze filled the sail, and his skiff glided soundlessly across the bay. Above him, the rising sun warmed the western bank of the steep-sided fjord. He guided the skiff past the outcropping and turned her nose towards the headlands.

It was thanks to Rusan and Olbin that he dared this. They'd made a seaman of him, and he hadn't even been able to say goodbye. Emotion made Garzik's throat ache. He glanced over his shoulder for one last look at the settlement.

Rusan stood on the outcropping, watching him sail away. Garzik felt sick. He wanted to explain himself, but he dare not return. It had taken everything he had to turn his back on the Wyvern People.

Rusan did not raise the alarm. Instead, he raised his hand in farewell. Garzik returned the gesture and, when he faced the headlands, he could not see for tears.

BYREN CAME DOWN from the mountains with four hundred ex-slaves, every armed man from Yoraltir Estate and the head of the Amfina warlord. He paused where the path forked. If he went right, he returned to Yoraltir Estate, where he'd left Dunstany's yacht. If he went left, he headed for Wythrontir Estate, which according to Piro was still under siege.

Was Florin well enough to join them?

He could sail back to Dunistir Estate, report in person and collect her. He wanted to see her so badly... The more distance he put between them, the better. He had to wean himself off his need for the mountain girl.

'I'm sure Piro and Florin would like to hear from you,' Orrade said.

Byren pointed to the path from Yoraltir Estate. 'Does that look like trouble coming our way?'

'It looks like a dozen men-at-arms led by a lordling.'

'That's what I said.'

Orrade grinned.

Byren stayed right where he was, while the lordling's party came up the winding path. When they were within hailing distance, Byren shouted, 'Who might you be?'

'Yoromer, son of Lord Yorale. You're Byren Kingsheir?'

Byren inclined his head slightly.

Yoromer returned the courtesy. 'My father bids you welcome and asks you to join him at his table so that he may thank you for driving off the spar warriors.'

'Tell you what...' Byren undid his saddle bag and tossed it to the lord's son.

Yoromer caught it and passed it to one of his men.

'Give your father this, with my compliments, and tell him that I thank him for the loan of his men. Tell him I'm off to save his youngest son's hide.'

Yoromer gaped. 'You're riding for Wythrontir?'

'It's under siege. Didn't you know?'

From his expression, he didn't.

His companion opened the saddle bag, froze, and showed it to the lord's son.

Yorale's heir glanced to Byren, gathered the reins and turned his horse for home. The whole party rode off.

'Did you enjoy that?' Orrade asked.

Byren grinned. The Snow Bridge king was right. Sometimes a show of force was what was needed to keep arrogant lords in line.

'What about Florin and Piro?'

'I'll send a message when I take Wythrontir Estate.' And he would keep Florin at a distance.

Chapter Fifty-Six

THE FIRST DAY Garzik had sailed southeast, giving Dalfino Isle a wide berth. On the second day, the wind had shifted and ever since, it had been in the wrong quarter. He'd had to tack to make any headway.

He was exhausted.

The cry of an ospriet sounded far above and he shaded his eyes. The great bird flew over him, heading south-west. Garzik wished he had a farseer.

He turned the tiller and tacked to the west, with the rising sun behind him. Another ospriet flew overhead in the same direction. A flock of the Affinity birds was circling far above. Ospriets were lone hunters so for them to gather like this they must have spotted a feast. He should turn back before he became one of the dishes.

Expecting to see a school of scytalis, Garzik searched the sea. A black speck danced on the sun-speckled waves. He had a bad feeling.

Despite this, he held his course.

As he drew nearer, he made out a small rowboat. It

was hard to tell if anyone was at the oars, but there had to be someone for the ospriets to be gathering.

Even as he thought this, a bird swooped down across the boat and two figures reared up swinging oars. Garzik's heart raced as the defenders drove off the ospriet. Eventually, the ospriets would wear down the boat's passengers and tear them apart with razor sharp beaks and talons. The predators' harsh screeches reached Garzik.

He lashed the tiller in position. Keeping his attention on the beleaguered men, he removed his bow from its oilcloth wrapping, strung it and set the arrows within reach. Then he watched the distant boat, willing the men to hang on.

As Garzik's skiff rose and fell, cutting through the waves, the taller of the rowers spotted his sail. Tearing off his shirt, an old white-haired man waved the garment above his head, shouting for all he was worth. His companion joined in.

The second rower was shorter and also white-haired: an old woman, or a small man.

With Garzik's approach, the ospriets saw their chance of a feast fast escaping and grew more daring, swooping ever lower. All it took was a strike to incapacitate one of the defenders and the other would not be able to hold the birds off.

Garzik readied an arrow, watched the ospriets, then let fly. He thought he'd missed his target until one of the birds faltered. The ospriet laboured, fighting to maintain height. As one wing brushed the crest of a wave, something leapt from the sea, its jaws closing around the bird's leg. The ospriet flapped madly, trying to break free.

At first Garzik thought it was a flying fish that had caught the bird, but then he spotted the distinctive sea-horse head. 'Nennirs!'

The ospriet attacked the nennir with its razor-sharp beak, and other ospriets screeched and came to its rescue. As if this was a signal, more nennirs leaped from the sea.

Shooting straight up, driven by their powerful tails, they snatched birds from the air with ease.

Garzik was fascinated and horrified. Approaching the boat was madness now, unless... He nocked another arrow and took aim at the ospriets. They were closely packed and he loosed three arrows in quick succession, hoping to incapacitate more of the birds and keep the nennirs occupied.

It worked. Freed from attack, the rowers put the oars to work and the boat began to make headway towards Garzik. He swung the tiller, turning to meet them. Between keeping an eye on the Affinity beasts' battle, watching the way the skiff responded to the seas and wind, and gauging the speed of their relative boats, Garzik was fully occupied.

He came alongside the boat, and the smaller oarsman scrambled onto the skiff about a body-length from Garzik. The old man passed him the oars then climbed aboard. The first seaman seemed the spritelier of the two, and joined Garzik at the bow to tie his boat to the skiff. Hand on the tiller, Garzik glanced over his shoulder to see the rowboat bobbing along behind.

'You saved us. Thank you.' It was a boy's voice.

Garzik looked into a young, sunburnt face with strange, ice-blue eyes. 'You're Affinity-touched!'

The lad could be no more than twelve or thirteen. He nodded and went to see to the old man, who lifted his head revealing his own pink-purple eyes. In the Utlands, any deformity usually denoted innate power. No wonder the Affinity predators had been so eager.

Knowing how the Utlanders revered the Affinity-touched, Garzik couldn't think why these two would be out on the open sea.

'Get us into a bay,' the old man urged. 'There's a storm coming.'

Garzik checked the sky. 'Are you sure?'

'Of course he's sure,' the lad snapped. 'He's Inac Storm-warner!'

'I didn't know Affinity-touched could—'

'It's going to be a bad one,' Inac said. 'Take us to the nearest safe anchorage. Your island's closest.'

Garzik nodded. If he went back he might not escape until next spring, but he stopped fighting the wind and turned the prow north. The skiff flew through the sea, as if happy to be going home.

'Will the nennirs come after us, Grandfather?'

'How many ospriets did they get?'

'Three.'

'Then they're probably too busy fighting over the birds.'

'There's food and water. Help yourself.' Garzik gestured to his supplies. By the way the lad fell on the food, he figured they'd been adrift for a couple of days.

'Go slow,' Inac warned. 'Or you'll give yourself a belly ache.'

The lad sniffed the cheese. 'What is this?'

'Hot-land cheese,' Inac said, eyeing Garzik thoughtfully. 'You're one of Wyvern People, right?'

Garzik nodded. 'How did you know?'

The old man gestured to the wyverns embroidered on the cuffs and hem of his red shirt. He'd forgotten.

'Wyvern People are rich.'

Garzik wouldn't have thought so, but then he hadn't seen how other Utland settlements lived, and Rusan's people did have five ships.

The lad took a nibble of the cheese. He wrinkled his nose at the unfamiliar taste.

'There's smoked fish,' Garzik said.

The boy's strange blue eyes studied him. 'You're not one of us.'

'I was a slave. I won my freedom.'

'How—'

'Mind your tongue, Favkir.' The old man sent Garzik an apologetic look.

'If you're Affinity-touched, why were you out on the open sea?' Garzik asked.

'We're Dalfino People.' The old man took a mouthful of watered wine. His voice was weak with exhaustion. 'Your oracles are not the only Affinity-touched Vultar's taken. When our lookout spotted the renegades, our people sent us to hide in another inlet, but the tide turned and we were swept out to sea with only a water sack. Five days we tried to get back, then the ospriets spotted us...' He shuddered.

The lad slid an arm around the old man. 'Lie down, Grandfather.'

He resisted. 'You have not told us your name, or why you were alone in a three-man skiff.'

'Wynn,' Garzik said, mind racing. 'The elders refused to let us race to Dalfino Isle, so I—'

'Took the skiff to make a name for yourself, then discovered you'd bitten off more than you could chew.' Inac eyed him shrewdly. 'You came to our rescue despite the danger.'

Garzik shrugged, his mind on other things. If he turned up after Rusan told the others he'd run off... But he had no choice, if there was a storm coming.

Inac slumped, head in hands. 'I fear for our people. Vultar will be in a temper—'

'Whatever Vultar did to your people, it was done five days ago, and there's nothing we can do about it now.' Garzik realised he was growing hard like an Utlander.

Then he concentrated, fighting weariness, as the wind picked up and the skiff flew across the sea.

IMPATIENCE GNAWED AT Fyn. It was nine days since Byren had arrived in Merofynia. They were both working their way around the Landlocked Sea to drive out the spar invaders: Byren from the west, him from the east.

Yet Fyn was stuck here on Travantir Estate. The last thing he wanted was for Byren to ride in and to save the day. He wanted—*needed*—to meet his brother halfway around the Landlocked Sea, as an equal.

The frustrating thing was that he'd done everything right. Rather than moor the boats in full sight of the great house, he'd dropped anchor in a cove, intending to free the seven-year slaves and attack as they'd done on Benetir Estate. But he'd been spotted by a large party of spar warriors.

By the time he'd returned to the great house, Lord Travany had arrived, moored his boat in full view of the defenders and botched the attack. The spar warriors had fortified the great house. Thanks to Travany, who would not countenance anything that might damage his house or get his men killed, it looked like being a protracted siege. Where possible, Fyn had used the terrain to shield his men, but elsewhere he had ordered them to dig ditches. Of course Travany had objected to having his lawns dug up.

Movement down by the wharf attracted Fyn's gaze.

Sunlight sparkled on the Landlocked Sea as Isolt threw the tin plate out over the water for Loyalty and Resolute to chase. But she was really watching out for Camoric, who had sailed the day before to check on Rhodontir Estate.

The prow of his boat came around the headland. If the western estates of the Landlocked Sea were anything to go by, Rhodontir Estate would also be in spar hands.

They should be moving on, yet they'd been stalled by an incompetent lord. As far as Fyn could tell, Travany's eldest son was the only sensible member of the family. So he strode through the camp in search of Travrhon.

Mitrovan came out of Lord Travany's tent, carrying a bowl of soap suds.

'Travrhon?' Fyn asked.

Mitrovan shook his head and went to speak, but Trafyn's voice reached them.

'I don't see why you don't just send in the seven-year slaves, Father,' the fifteen-year-old said. 'It doesn't matter how many of them die breaking down the barriers.'

'We can't trust them, that's why. They'll loot the house, run off with the silver, and...'

Fyn shook his head and backed away.

Mitrovan gestured. 'Try the tower.'

Travany had ordered a tower built to observe the great house. Fyn didn't know what Travany hoped to achieve. A siege tower on wheels that they could haul up to the house would have been more useful. This tower gave the appearance of doing something while accomplishing nothing.

'Fyn,' Travrhon called, coming down the hill. 'You'll be glad to know the tower's completed. I was going to let Father know.'

Fyn nodded. 'We have enough men to storm the house. Speak to your father, convince him.'

Travrhon looked uncomfortable. 'We don't know how many spar warriors are inside. Father fears what will happen to the women they hold hostage.'

'We know what is happening to them right now, and we know the cellars are packed with wine and stores. The spar warriors can sit in there for a year, if they want to. We have to attack, Trav.'

'You're asking me to ignore my father's orders.' Travrhon met his eyes. 'Would you have done that, Fyn?'

'I wouldn't have had to. My father knew how to lead.'

Travrhon flushed.

'I'm sorry,' Fyn said. 'But the longer we sit here, the longer we have to feed our men. The spar warriors stripped the estate. We're having to range farther and farther afield. We—'

'Fyn?' Isolt called.

He turned to see her coming up the rise with Camoric and both Affinity beasts. The men-at-arms watched her pass by, their expressions ranging from admiration to caution.

Camoric tempered his stride so Isolt could keep up with him.

'Cam,' Fyn greeted him. 'What news? Has Rhodontir—'

'—fallen? Yes. And it looks like we're in for another siege. Lord Rhoderich had the place surrounded.'

Fyn cursed roundly. The last thing he needed was another lord who wanted to reclaim his estate without spilling his men's blood or damaging the crockery.

Isolt sent him a look of sympathy. 'What if you packed up camp and sailed off? The spar warriors might make a run for the pass. Why would they stay and fight when they're outnumbered and there's no hope of rescue?'

'Because it's cowardly to run,' Travany said, joining them.

'Besides, why would we leave?' Trafyn chimed in. 'This is our home.'

'It might draw them out,' Isolt said. Loyalty nudged the queen and she stroked the wyvern, which towered over her now. 'If you offered them safe passage to the spar, would they surrender?'

'We would never accept their surrender. It's a matter of honour.' Travany shook his heavy jowls. 'Not that I expect a woman to understand.'

Isolt bristled. Loyalty lifted her head, wings flexing.

'The tower's completed,' Fyn said quickly. 'Let's go up and see what we can learn.'

It took a while for everyone to climb the ladder. The tower was only two storeys high, but it was positioned on a rise, so that it looked down on the great house and outbuildings.

On reaching the platform, Fyn was disappointed. He'd been hoping archers could pick off the defenders, but they could not see the inner courtyard from here.

The wyvern and foenix circled the tower, their great wings cutting the air.

'You shouldn't spend so much time with the beasts, my queen,' Travany said. 'Bring them out for state occasions, but keep them at a distance. It's not seemly.'

Isolt turned to him, eyes flashing.

'We need to lure them out. Or drive them out,' Fyn said. 'We could set fire to one end of the great house.'

'What?' Travany spluttered. 'I'm not setting fire to my home. It's been in the family for generations.'

'Only a little fire,' Fyn said. 'More smoke than flames. We could use green grass. We need to panic them.'

'Sounds like a good idea to me,' Travrhon said. 'What do you think, Father?'

Everyone watched Travany as he considered this. 'No...' He shook his head. 'The flames could get out of control.'

'Look, some of the spar warriors are coming out.' Isolt pointed to the third floor balcony. 'Maybe they want to negotiate.'

'We don't negotiate with the likes of them,' Travany said.

But the four spar warriors hadn't ventured onto the balcony to surrender. They dropped their breeches and waved their arses at the tower.

Travany flushed and shook his fist at them. 'How dare you?' he shouted. 'This is the queen of Merofynia!'

They laughed and told him what they'd do with the queen if they got the chance, with appropriate hand gestures.

Rage poured through Fyn. He wanted to...

'You shouldn't see this, my queen,' Travrhon said. 'Take her back to the ship, Trafyn.'

'But I want to discuss strategy.'

'Come, my queen.' Fyn offered his arm. Isolt's talk of luring the defenders out had given him an idea, and he tossed a comment over his shoulder as he left. 'Spar warriors don't have the same code of honour as you do, Lord Travany. I wouldn't be surprised if they did try to escape. Spar warriors would rather live to fight another day.'

Fyn climbed down the steps with Isolt. Now that he'd planted the idea, he could circumvent Travany by leading an assault on the pretext that he'd caught the defenders trying to escape and Travany would not be able to prove otherwise.

When they reached the base of the tower, Isolt turned to him. 'Do you need a distraction?'

Fyn blinked. She *was* a distraction.

'Do you need something to distract the defenders so you can get into the house?'

'Yes. A fire would have been perfect.'

She nodded, looking pleased with herself.

He'd seen that look on Piro's face and it never boded well. 'What are you up to?'

Loyalty and Resolute landed.

'Isolt?'

She smiled and walked off with the Affinity beasts in tow.

Chapter Fifty-Seven

Florin strode down the corridor. She hadn't thrown up since the day after they'd arrived, and the nausea had faded until she was hardly aware of it. She was ready to join Byren, but he hadn't sent a message since that first one, and she didn't know where he was. She walked so fast Piro had to take two steps for every one of hers.

Impatience gnawed at Florin's belly. 'If Byren...'

Loud cries of distress reached them from the Istyntir women's chambers.

'Fetch help,' Florin told Piro. Then she drew her knife and took off down the corridor.

Throwing the door open, Florin prepared to defend the women from attackers. Instead she found Lady Travenna and her five daughters all weeping. The eldest girl stood alone in front of the fireplace. The other four clustered around the mother, who had collapsed on the day-bed.

All of them stared at Florin, startled by her sudden appearance with a naked blade.

'I heard cries. I thought we were under attack.'

'So you're Piro's bodyguard,' the mother said, as if she'd been trying to figure out Florin's position in the household.

Florin let this pass. 'What's wrong? I thought someone was being murdered.'

'It's Isfynia.' The youngest girl gestured to the eldest. 'She—' One of her sisters elbowed her.

Piro ran into the chamber with Soterro and three sturdy footmen, all armed.

'False alarm,' Florin said but she caught Piro's eye.

Taking her cue from Florin, Piro dismissed the men and turned to the mother. 'Can I help, Lady Travenna?'

'No.' The mother wept while the four younger daughters tried to console her. 'There's nothing anyone can do. We're ruined.'

'Byren will recapture your estate,' Florin told her. 'Then you can go home.'

The woman glared at Florin. 'What would an ignorant Rolencian girl know? My son's dead and my husband's dying. Even if the Rolencian king retakes Istyntir, it won't be our home for long. There's no male heir. One of the other lords will claim it for his younger son.'

'You could appeal to the queen,' Piro said. 'She could recognise Isfynia's right to inherit, and arrange for her husband to change his name...'

She ran down as Lady Travenna wept inconsolably.

Piro turned to Isfynia for an explanation.

The eldest daughter lifted her hands. 'I—'

'She's gone and gotten herself pregnant,' the sixteen-year-old said. 'She's ruined herself and ruined us, too.'

'Tari is right,' the mother said. 'No man will have her—'

'I was trying to tell you but you wouldn't listen,' Isfynia said. 'Rishardt loves me. He was going to go to Father, but the spar warriors attacked.'

The mother shook her head. 'If he's anything like his uncle, he'll sail off—'

'Rishardt would never desert me.'

'Why should he marry you, when you've already given yourself to him for nothing?' the mother demanded, voice shrill and hard.

'It was only the once, right after Father collapsed.' Isfynia spoke calmly, despite the hectic colour in her cheeks. 'I was weeping in his arms and it just happened.'

Florin flushed, remembering how it had almost 'happened' with Byren.

The mother covered the youngest daughter's ears. 'How can you speak of such things in front of your sisters?'

'Mother...' Isfynia pleaded.

Florin wanted to shake Lady Travenna. She glanced to Piro, who looked to be out of her depth. 'I don't see what the problem is. This Rishardt should be grateful he's getting a wife who can bear children.'

Lady Travenna gave a slightly hysterical laugh. 'She's ruined!'

'All this talk of ruin!' Florin threw up her hands. 'You noble women make life hard for yourselves.'

She walked out. If she didn't get away from weeping women and rejoin Byren, she'd do something violent. At least the eldest daughter had a man who wanted her.

Byren couldn't even bring himself to... Florin refused to think about him.

FYN AND CAMORIC studied the great house. It was dusk and the camp fires were lit, but the sky still held the afterglow of the setting sun.

'See that portico?' Fyn nodded to a door that had been boarded shut. 'I'll climb the trellis onto the portico roof, force the grate, slip inside and open the door. Once I do, I'll signal my men. As soon as you hear us shouting, run to Travany's tent. Tell him the spar warriors are trying to escape. Grab Travrhon and come to my aid.'

'And Travany will be none the wiser.' Camoric grinned. 'If you get any craftier...'

'The queen!'

Fyn sprinted towards the front of the house, where men were gathering, looking up into the sky. Loyalty came into sight, circling above the besieging army. There was something odd...

'Isolt Wyvern Queen!'

Isolt was astride her wyvern.

Fyn cursed. 'What does she think she's doing?'

'Distracting the defenders.' Camoric indicated a third floor balcony where a dozen spar warriors pointed and marvelled. As Fyn watched, another three joined them. But his gaze was drawn to Isolt. She looked so small up there on the wyvern's back.

Camoric signalled a dozen of his men. 'Come on, Fyn. We'll never get a better chance.'

He ran back the way they'd come, the men following. Fyn had no choice but to make for the great house, where Camoric gave him a boost up onto the portico roof. He pushed in the grate, wriggled through and dropped down onto a chest that had been wedged up against the door.

It was dark inside. No lamps had been lit, and the house smelled of wine and stale food.

Heart pounding, Fyn dragged the chest aside, unlocked the door and forced the planks out with several well placed kicks. The sound echoed through the ground floor, but no one came.

Camoric and his men tore off the rest of the planks and poured in.

'Clean out the ground floor,' Fyn said. 'I'm going after the warlord.'

He ran up the stairs, followed by a dozen men. In one of the best bedrooms, he found a huddle of frightened women and sent them to safety.

The upper floor seemed mostly deserted. Isolt's antics had drawn the spar warriors to the top floor balconies at the front of the great house. As yet, the besiegers had not taken advantage of the distraction. Fyn's men poured out onto the first balcony, attacking the spar warriors from behind. They barely had time to draw their weapons.

Fyn's heart nearly stopped when he caught a bowman taking aim at Isolt. With a roar, he shouldered the man aside, tipping him over the balustrade. The bowman's terrified scream was cut short as he hit the terrace. Fyn looked over the balcony in time to see Travrhon lead a charge against the front of the house.

'This way!' Fyn led his men into the dim hall, where they found a dozen spar warriors had rallied. 'To me!'

Shoulder to shoulder, they hacked and slashed in the failing light. As more defenders raced up the hall, they were driven back into a chamber. The spar warriors followed, swords swinging. Furniture splintered, vases smashed and bed curtains collapsed on struggling men, but the tide was turning.

The moment the last defender dropped, Fyn darted out onto the balcony to check on Isolt.

He was in time to see Loyalty swoop down to land. The wyvern stumbled and lost her footing. The queen was thrown forward, turned a somersault in the air and hit the ground hard. She lay still.

He was running before he knew it, running down the corridor, leaping over the bodies of fallen warriors.

Passing Travrhon on the grand staircase, he yelled, 'Check the third floor.'

He didn't wait for a response, but took the steps two at a time, kicked his way through a half-boarded door and ran up the slope towards Isolt, who was surrounded by worried men-at-arms and the two Affinity beasts.

They parted so that the abbot and his four monks could carry Isolt. She looked so pale and small, Fyn's heart twisted with anguish. He caught up with Murheg. 'How is she?'

'Hit her head. No obvious broken bones. I'll take her down to the boat.'

Ahead of them, Trafyn backed out of his father's tent, drawing his sword. 'Hurry up, or we'll miss the fighting.'

Travany stepped out with the scribe, still strapping on his armour. He took in the monks and their burden.

'Fell, did she? I'm not surprised.' Travany turned on Fyn. 'What were you thinking, putting her up to this? Call yourself her lord protector?'

Fyn took two steps towards Travany. He didn't know he was going to punch him until the lord lay flat on his back. Trafyn stared, stunned.

Murheg took Fyn's arm. 'Enough of that! The queen needs you.'

They hurried after the monks.

On the boat, Fyn told the Affinity beasts to wait on deck. Then he paced outside in the passage, as Murheg checked Isolt for injuries.

Finally, the abbot came out of the cabin. 'She must have been born under a lucky star. Apart from a few bruises and a lump on her head, she's fine. You can...'

But Fyn had already brushed past him.

He found Isolt sitting on the bunk, looking pale and dishevelled but pleased with herself.

'Did you recapture the great house, Fyn?'

He caught her by the shoulders. 'You're all right?'

She laughed. 'Of course, I'm—'

'What were you thinking? You could have been killed.'

'I've flown before.' She saw his surprise. 'Back home. I've been practicing since I saw Cortomir fly. Loyalty and I are getting pretty good, although we do need to work on our landings.'

'You never told me.'

'I didn't want to worry you. I'll teach you, if you like. With your Affinity, Loyalty should accept you on her back. That's if you're not scared of heights.'

It was a deliberate ploy to divert him. He wanted to shake her. He wanted to kiss her. He pulled her close and...

Loyalty barrelled into the cabin, knocking the door off its hinges. Resolute followed and the beasts jostled Fyn aside.

Loyalty knelt, placing her head in Isolt's lap. As the

queen stroked the wyvern's beautiful, horned head Fyn understood. 'You've bonded with her.'

'Yes. Piro helped us bond the night before she left.' Isolt smiled as the foenix nudged her, wanting attention. Loyalty snapped at Resolute, but there was no malice in it. After a moment, she allowed Resolute close enough to Isolt to be stroked.

'My queen?'

They turned to find the abbot in the doorway. 'You're both needed up at the great house. Lord Travany has captured the warlord of Ulfr Spar.'

'He'll want you to witness the man's execution,' Fyn told Isolt. 'You don't have to go. I can say you are recovering from your fall.'

'If I don't go, Travany won't respect me.' She stood, then swayed a little.

He steadied her. 'Are you up to this?'

'Of course.'

Admiration filled him. He yearned to claim her, wanted everyone to know that she was his.

'Fyn?' Isolt tilted her head.

'My queen.' He offered his arm.

She took it. 'My lord protector.'

And they went up to the great house together.

FLORIN PUSHED THE board game aside so Piro could climb up onto the bed to read the message. Lord Dunstany nodded his thanks to Florin. She really had grown fond of the old man. Perhaps it was because he didn't look down on her. But she still had every intention of sailing with the captain of the Wythrontir pleasure yacht when he returned to Byren.

'That's odd,' Piro said, tilting the message towards the lamp. 'This is Orrade's writing. I wonder—'

'Has Byren been injured?' Florin fought the urge to snatch the message from her.

Piro eyes darted down the page.

'Read it aloud, child,' Lord Dunstany urged, 'before we die of curiosity.'

'Byren hurt his hand, but Orrade says it's already healing,' Piro said.

Florin suspected Orrade had been cooperating with Byren to speed up his healing.

'They march for Nevantir Estate with the freed slaves. Orrade says... "By the time we reach the palace, Byren will have a loyal army."'

'He's a clever lad, your brother,' Dunstany said. He gestured to the kingdoms' board. 'It looks like they'll meet at either Istyn or Elcwyff's estate.'

'I must tell Fyn.' Piro went over to the desk to write.

Florin retrieved the message and pored over it, looking for her name. Seeing it, her heart skipped: *I trust Florin is feeling better and look forward to seeing you both in port.*

Devastated, she replaced the message. Byren didn't want her to join him.

GARZIK FELT LIKE a failure as he returned to the settlement. He'd failed Byren, and now he'd failed Rusan. Yet he'd only ever tried to do the right thing. He couldn't have turned his back on Favkir and Inac.

He'd hoped to slip in quietly and find Rusan first, but the moment they entered the narrow bay, the storm struck with a vengeance. Rain lashed them, hitting so hard it stung their bare skin. The wind extinguished his lantern, and Garzik had to judge distance and speed by the glimpses revealed by the lightning.

He ran the skiff aground, planted the anchor and helped Favkir with the old man. Now that they were safe, Inac had stiffened up and could hardly move.

A gust of wind knocked the old man off his feet. Garzik lifted Inac across his shoulders. Despite his height, the old man didn't weigh much. Garzik forged uphill in the driving rain and wind, with Favkir stumbling along at his side, trying to help.

Another flash of lightning illuminated the long-hall. Favkir thrust the door open, and Garzik staggered in, followed by a swirl of wind and rain, and a clap of thunder. So much for slipping in quietly.

Everyone turned. Garzik flicked wet hair from his face and eased Inac from his shoulders. Olbin strode over, taking the old man from him. Favkir swayed and shivered.

'Wynn!' Luvrenc greeted him with relief. 'Who—'

Garzik turned to Lauvra. 'They're from Dalfino. This is Inac Storm-warner, he—'

'Everyone has heard of the storm-warner,' Lauvra said.

The crowd gasped and whispered excitedly. Children, raiders, the old and the beardless all gathered around. Lauvra ordered them to bring blankets. Then she drew Favkir and Garzik over to the fireplace, where Olbin had placed Inac in a chair. She saw to the old man's needs first.

Ilonja and Luvrenc pounced on Garzik. Ilonja thumped him on the arm. 'You set sail without us!'

'How could you?' Luvrenc also thumped him, then hugged him. 'Then this storm came up. We thought you lost for sure!'

In a flash, Garzik understood how Rusan had covered his escape. They would have assumed he'd been lost at sea, trying to reach Dalfino Isle.

'Enough.' Feodan shepherded Ilonja and Luvrenc aside, then turned to Garzik. 'You haven't been gone long enough to reach Dalfino Isle, and they would never part with two Affinity-touched. How is it that you brought them back here?'

'They were trying to escape Vultar and his renegades,' Garzik explained, aware of Rusan watching him intently. 'Apparently, Vultar's been kidnapping other Affinity-touched. They were swept out to sea and—'

'And you rescued them!' Olbin shook his head, amazed.

Garzik nodded.

'You've done us proud,' Feodan said. 'They owe us seven years of service.'

'He didn't tell you the whole of it.' Lauvra joined them. 'Inac says Wynn sailed into a battle between nennirs and ospriets, to pluck them from certain death.'

'Clever little Wynn!' Olbin lifted Garzik off his feet, hugging him so tight he saw stars.

Rusan laughed. 'Put him down before you crack a rib.'

Olbin released him, and Garzik staggered.

'He's exhausted. Come here.' Lauvra swung an arm around him. 'Luvrenc, get him something to eat before he drops.' She sat Garzik down next to Inac and wrapped a blanket around him.

Then she sent everyone but the elders away.

Inac struggled to stand. 'By the Utland code, you have our service for seven years and we do not begrudge it. But there are two of us, and our people are now without a Power-worker. Can you send my grandson home?'

Lauvra glanced to the elders. 'We can't do that, Storm-warner. You've seen too many winters. If we sent the lad home, we might lose you within a year. We have a duty to our people.'

Inac nodded as if he'd expected it. As he sank into the chair, Garzik noticed Favkir studying Olbin and Rusan.

'You stare at my sons?' Lauvra said.

'Why are they almost beardless?'

Lauvra and Olbin laughed.

Rusan rubbed his jaw. 'We shaved off our beards to disguise ourselves as hot-landers and ventured into Port Mero—'

'You sailed into the hot-landers' port?' Favkir was astounded.

'And escaped with a full hold,' Olbin said, slinging an arm around Rusan. 'So don't let this lack of beard fool you. We're men, not boys!'

Garzik grinned. It was good to be back, and thanks to Rusan, he hadn't disgraced himself.

Chapter Fifty-Eight

Byren stepped over a bloody patch on the marble. No wonder these elegant Merofynian great houses had fallen like ninepins. All the lords' wealth had gone into display, not defence. His mountain girl would not have been surprised to learn this was the second time since spring that Nevantir Estate had been overrun by spar warriors. Maybe, this time, the lord would learn.

Without Florin's no-nonsense presence at his side, Byren felt like half of him was missing, which only confirmed he'd been right not to send for her.

'Up here,' Orrade called from the balcony.

Byren ran up the grand staircase, flexing his hand. Despite the healing, it ached. Now that the battle was over, he felt all his old wounds.

'Neiron is planning to free Elenstir Estate.' Orrade met him at the top of the stairs.

'Istyntir is closer.'

'They're about the same distance, but Istyntir juts into the Landlocked Sea.' Orrade lowered his voice. 'And I gather Elenstir's lord is a friend of Neiron's, while Lord Istyn supports Dunstany.'

Byren shook his head in disgust. 'If they can't put aside internal politics to face a common enemy, they deserve to lose their kingdom.'

'It's your kingdom they're throwing away. He's in here.' Orrade slowed his steps as they approached a door.

Byren could hear male voices and he recognised the tone of men making plans to kill and claim or, in this case, reclaim.

Orrade caught his arm. 'Don't expect heartfelt thanks. Neiron's furious with you for freeing his seven-year slaves.'

'I freed men whose only crime was to defend their homes,' Byren said, making sure his voice carried. 'I freed them to help reclaim this estate. While his lordship was sitting on his arse, those freed slaves swept over the rise and broke down the barricades.'

He strode into Neiron's war-table chamber to find the Merofynian lord stood behind his desk, illuminated by a single lamp as he studied a large Duelling Kingdoms board.

'I had everything planned,' Neiron said. 'Then you marched in and threw everything out.'

Byren was not about to apologise. With the ex-slaves and Yorale's men, Byren's followers outnumbered Neiron's three to one. And he was sick of wasting his time in Merofynia, while Cobalt still sat on his father's throne.

Byren held Neiron's gaze. 'I'm thinking you need to rephrase that.'

Neiron stiffened, and both his captains reached for their sword hilts.

Orrade took a step closer to Byren.

Chandler arrived to report. 'The outbuildings are all secured and the men are breaking open the food and wine. Should I try to stop them?'

Byren met Neiron's eyes across the desk. 'Men who've fought and bled to free a lord's estate deserve a reward. Wouldn't you agree, Neiron?'

The lord swallowed as if he'd tasted something bitter and gestured to one of his captains. 'Tell Cook to prepare a victory feast. Tonight we celebrate in the great hall.'

The man nodded and ran off.

'Now what's this I hear about marching for Elenstir Estate?' Byren went over to the kingdoms board and indicated Istyntir Point. 'We can't leave the enemy at our backs.'

Neiron rubbed his jaw. Byren waited, ready to marshal more arguments.

But Neiron conceded. 'You're right. Come join me in the great hall. This is a night for celebration.'

As Byren fell into step with Neiron, he caught Orrade's eye. His friend nodded once. The Merofynian noble had capitulated too easily. They'd have to watch their backs.

GARZIK STOOD ON the upper floor of the long-hall, watching for Rusan's signal. For two days, Inac had been bed-ridden, exhausted by his deprivations. But today the old man was well enough to get up, and tonight the settlement planned to formally welcome the two Affinity-blessed and accept their oaths of service.

Through the crowd in the hall below, Garzik saw Lauvra signal Rusan, who sent Garzik the signal he had been waiting for. He returned to the room where Inac and Favkir waited. They looked ill-at-ease in the fine clothes Rusan had given them.

'It's time,' Garzik said.

'Let me see you.' Inac turned his grandson to face him and adjusted the thigh-length velvet tabard.

Rusan had thought he was honouring the two Affinity-touched with these gifts. Garzik did not have the heart tell them the tabards were what high-ranking servants wore in Merofynia. In a way, it was appropriate, since the old man and his grandson were seven-year slaves of the most valued kind.

'You look fine,' Inac said.

Favkir snorted. 'I don't look like myself in these hot-land clothes, and neither do you.'

'A good thing. Now listen, the next seven years will fly by. No... really. You'll be surprised. Smile, try to get on. This could be the worst time of your life, or it could be something to look back on with joy.'

For a heartbeat, Favkir's chin trembled and tears filled his strange ice-blue eyes, then his mouth hardened and he nodded. 'I won't let you down, grandfather.'

'Don't let yourself down.'

Garzik led them out along the balcony then down the steps. Wild cheering greeted them. Garzik's heart raced and his spirits lifted.

The elders sat in a semi-circle at one end of the long-hall. Lauvra stood before them, flanked by her sons and brother.

Inac approached, then stood tall. 'Lauvra of the Wyvern People, your raider saved us from Affinity beasts and the sea. We thank you for giving us back our lives and offer our skills and services for seven years.'

'Welcome, Inac and Favkir of the Dalfino People,' she said. 'You will be our honoured guests. We value your service. When you return to your people, you will go home laden with gifts. While you are here, you will have an honoured place at our table.'

She signalled Ilonja, who led them over to two chairs near the elders. Garzik's stomach rumbled and he glanced to the kitchen door. Judging by the rich aromas coming down the passage, dinner was ready.

Lauvra signalled for silence and nodded to her two sons.

Looking very solemn, Rusan and Olbin came over to Garzik.

As they led him out to stand in front of the elders, and Lauvra and Feodan, Garzik's heart sank. If Rusan had reconsidered and revealed the truth, everyone would know he was a fraud.

He couldn't bear to let them down.

But a grin pulled at Olbin's lips as he put his hand on Garzik's shoulder. 'Thanks to Wynn, we took a gamble and entered Port Mero.'

Rusan's crew cheered and Garzik winced. His motivation had hardly been pure. He'd meant to escape with Trafyn, and Rusan knew it.

Even so, the captain put his hand on Garzik's shoulder. 'Thanks to Wynn, I was alive to lead the escape from Port Mero.'

Rusan's crew cheered again. Garzik noted Vesnibor and Dizov standing in the shadows under the balcony. Had they made a mistake, letting those two live?

Feodan gestured to Garzik. 'Thanks to Wynn, Inac Storm-warner and his grandson Favkir have given us seven years of service.'

Heat raced up Garzik's face.

Olbin and Rusan exchanged a look. Rusan grabbed his right arm and Olbin grabbed his left. As one, they lifted his arms above his head and shouted in unison. 'We name Wynn our brother!'

'Brother!' the hall echoed—feet stamping, tankards clanking.

The brothers turned Garzik one quarter of a circle, raised both his arms again and shouted, '*Brother!*'

The crowd echoed the cry.

They turned him again and he realised they were telling the four quarters of the world so there could be no doubt.

He was so proud, yet at the same time, he wanted to sink through the floor. He had not even given them his real name.

As the last echo faded, they turned him to their mother and Lauvra held her arms open. Garzik had not known his own mother. Queen Myrella had been like a mother to him. When Lauvra swept him into her embrace, he felt the same unconditional love and he knew he was not worthy. Tears of shame filled his eyes.

Lauvra pulled back, saw his tears and kissed each cheek. 'Bless you, Wynn of the Wyvern People. I name you my son.'

Feodan pulled him into a hug. 'I name you my kin.'

A heartbeat later, Luvrenc hugged him, repeating the same phrase. 'I cursed when you went to Dalfino Isle without us, but I never guessed you'd bring back Affinity-touched!'

Garzik did not think it could get any worse.

Rusan and Olbin laughed and called for wine, and Sarijana stepped forward to sing, but Lauvra told them to wait.

She looked to the elders, who gave a single unanimous nod.

Smiling she turned to Rusan, Olbin and Garzik. 'The elders are agreed. You three have earned the right to take a wife.'

Rusan's gaze went to Sarijana. Stricken, she stepped back and went to join the beardless, who closed ranks around her.

Olbin swayed and would have staggered, but Garzik supported him.

After that, they feasted. There was drinking—much drinking—and singing, and there was weeping over the fallen, then more drinking.

Garzik lost track of time. He saw the night in snatches. Singing on a stool. Dancing on the table. Falling off. Captain Feodan and his raiders falling asleep on the floor under the table. Olbin weeping on his shoulder. Rusan waxing philosophical.

Then some more serious drinking.

Towards dawn, head reeling, Garzik went outside to relieve himself. He walked down towards the shore to clear his head. The wood was stacked for Rusan's ship. He leant against the wood to inhale the sweet smell of fresh-cut timber.

Rusan caught him and swung him around, slamming

him up against the wood. 'I covered for you once. I won't do it again. If you abandon us now that we're brothers—'

'If you feel that way, why—'

'It wasn't my idea. Mother an' Feodan...' Rusan shrugged. Despite all the drinking, he barely slurred his words. 'I had no choice. I had to go along with it. To do otherwise would have raised questions you don't want to answer.' He frowned. 'I made you one of my crew. You swore an oath to me, Wynn. How could you—'

'I had no choice. I had to go along with it.' Garzik's voice faltered. 'But I'd already sworn to serve Byren Kingsheir.'

'Back then you were a boy, not yet fifteen.' Rusan released him. 'Your oath wasn't truly binding.'

Garzik was more than a little drunk and he felt his throat grow tight with emotion. 'It was binding to me.'

'Ah, Wynn... To be foresworn is a terrible thing.'

Garzik looked down. For all he knew, Orrade and Byren had already fallen.

'You're a man now and a man can't serve two masters. You have to decide which oath to honour. Are you our brother or are you the king's man?'

'Would you cover for me, if I decided I was the king's man?'

Rusan nodded. 'I'd find some way to hide your desertion. Better they think you dead than disloyal.'

A weight lifted from Garzik. He could go back without dishonouring Rusan and Olbin.

Go back to what?

He'd earned an honoured place here.

'There you are...' Olbin stumbled around the wood heap and collided with them.

They all staggered and ended up sprawled on the grass staring up at the sky. Stretched out between them, Olbin clasped his hands behind his head with a happy sigh. 'I swear those stars are so close I could touch them!'

Garzik looked up. From the position of the wanderer

stars, he judged that it was the darkest time before dawn, but he did not feel despair. He felt part of something greater than himself. He'd brought the Affinity-touched to the settlement.

If he hadn't found Inac and his grandson, they would have died, and he wouldn't have survived the storm... Everything seemed to have led to this night, this moment and this decision that would shape the rest of his life.

Rusan was right. He'd been a boy when he'd sworn to serve Byren. Now...

People depended on him.

Olbin snored loud enough to wake the dead.

Garzik grinned and climbed to his feet. 'Come on, Rus. We can't leave our brother here.'

Byren woke not sure what had disturbed him. The feast had ended late and there had been much drinking, but he had a capacity for wine. Now he swung his legs off the bed. A rooster crowed. It was the dark time before dawn.

Orrade stirred on the blanket by the empty hearth. Chandler snored, as did the other men of his honour guard.

'What's wrong?' Orrade whispered.

Byren padded over to the balcony. The doors had been left open to let in the cool night air. Orrade joined him.

It had been cloudy earlier, but now the stars silvered the night, illuminating the men gathered below. A horse whinnied as Neiron and his captains rode into view.

'I thought he'd capitulated too easily. He's going to save Elenstir Estate,' Orrade whispered. 'What do you want to do?'

'I don't want him at my side when I go into battle. From what I hear, he's nothing but a parade ground leader, more used to brass and gold braid than battle and blood.'

They both watched as Neiron and his men moved out.

'Let him ride off, and good riddance,' Byren muttered. 'If he isn't the leader he thinks he is, I'll be well rid of him.'

Orrade grinned. 'Will you send a message to warn Fyn about him?'

'Tell you what...' Byren rubbed his face, feeling the bristles rasp across his jaw. 'I had no idea what I was dropping Fyn into when I named him lord protector. It's a wonder he's survived.'

Orrade was silent for a moment. 'The Fyn we knew wouldn't have survived. Be prepared, he won't be—'

'You're right.' Byren had always loved Fyn, but he'd often worried that his gentle brother's abbey upbringing had left him unprepared for the real world. 'Hopefully, it's made a man of him.'

Orrade looked as if he might say something, then shook his head.

Chapter Fifty-Nine

Byren had freed Lord Istyn's Estate, but the old lord hadn't survived the battle. Now he rode into Elenstir Estate to find no sign of spar warriors and the great house half burnt. It was midday and a muggy heat hung over everything, promising a storm. Exhausted from the forced march, his men spread across the lawns all the way down to the Landlocked Sea, finding whatever shade they could.

As Byren and Orrade approached what remained of the Elenstir great house, a middle-aged man-at-arms came striding out to meet them with several men at his back.

'Byren Kingsheir and Lord Orrade.' His greeting was polite, but his eyes were wary. 'As you see, my lords Elcwyff and Neiron have routed the spar warriors. Her ladyship has returned and is restoring order.'

'That was quick.'

'Lady Rhoza took shelter on the yacht, along with his lordship's two sons.' The captain gestured to Byren's army. 'The spar barbarians cleaned out our stores. I'm sorry we can't offer—'

'That's understandable. Water would be appreciated.' Byren was already thinking of Rhodontir Estate. He expected to meet with Fyn there. 'We'll be marching after lunch.'

The captain-at-arms nodded.

'One thing,' Orrade said. 'Where are Elcwyff and Neiron?'

'Chasing the warlord over the pass,' the captain said as he walked away.

Orrade sent Byren a look. 'We've been hunting spar warriors since we were fifteen. We know what we're doing.'

Byren shrugged. 'After this, hopefully Neiron and Elcwyff will know what they're doing.'

As they sat to make plans, servants came out with watered wine, distributing it amongst Byren's men.

'Will you send a message to Piro?' Orrade asked.

Before Byren could reply, a woman arrived with a tray of fresh bread, cheese and cold meat. She was followed by a small boy of about six.

'Eh, we weren't expecting this,' Byren said. 'Give your mistress our thanks.'

'I am the mistress,' she said.

Byren and Orrade both came to their feet and bowed.

Lady Rhoza brushed this aside. She wore a grubby work apron over her gown and wisps of dark hair had come loose from her sensible plait.

With a quick glance over her shoulder, she stepped closer and lowered her voice. 'My husband has gone into the Divide with Neiron to hunt down the warlord. Elcwyff took our eldest son to give him some experience.'

Byren and Orrade exchanged a look.

'I suggested to Elcwyff that he free the seven-year slaves to help retake our home. He refused, and our home burned.' Tears of anger glittered in Rhoza's eyes. 'I suggested rather than hunting down the warlord, they let him go and rebuild the pass fort so he can't come back. I'd almost convinced my husband when Neiron marched in and said they had to teach the warlord a lesson. I fear...' She drew her youngest son close. 'Elkrhon is only ten.'

Byren rubbed his jaw. 'I can't interfere with the way a lord raises his son.'

'I'm not asking you to. I'm suggesting you free the Rolencian seven-year slaves. They work the quarry up in the Divide. I'm suggesting you take the freed slaves to make sure the pass fort is secure.'

'That sounds fair enough.' Byren grinned. 'But I'll need someone with local knowledge as a guide.'

'My house-keep's son has already packed.'

So Byren left Chandler in charge of his army and rode out with Orrade, two dozen trusted men and a twelve-year-old boy. That night he freed the seven-year slaves and went to secure the pass.

Midday the next day, they found Merofynian bodies by the side of the trail. The bodies had been left where they fell and plundered.

Byren examined the fire circle and the tracks in the tussocky grass. He rose and wiped his hands on his thighs. 'The spar warriors picked off their sentries, then came down from above.'

Orrade nodded. 'Neiron and Elcwyff are on the run, but they're running the wrong way. Parade ground manoeuvres don't prepare a man for fighting an enemy that comes in fast, strikes hard, and melts back into the mountains.'

Byren adjusted his pack. The path had become too steep to ride. 'Come on.'

They found more bodies, abandoned where they had fallen. The following day, they heard the sounds of battle, echoing from the ravine walls.

'The pass is just up ahead,' the house-keep's son said. Since finding the bodies, he'd kept close to Byren and Orrade.

'Looks like Neiron and Elcwyff are making a stand in the old fort.' Orrade met Byren's eyes. 'There can't be many of them left.'

Byren nodded. If they wanted to save the lad, they had to move fast. 'The spar warriors won't be expecting us to attack them from the rear. Come on.'

The narrow defile was only about five body-lengths wide and a wall had once run from one side to the other. Not much of it was still standing and it had been overrun. About forty spar warriors swarmed the tradepost and stables.

Byren's men swept into the yard. Their sheer numbers overcame the attackers, and drove them out the far side of the fort's old walls. As the spar warriors turned and ran, freed slaves gave chase.

Byren cursed. He didn't want his men being led up dead end ravines and picked off one by one. 'Call them back, Orrie.'

He strode into the tradepost taproom to find Neiron with the last of his men. Of the fifty who had ridden out, less than twenty remained. And all of them were injured, and some could barely stand. Byren cursed again. None of this would have happened if Neiron had waited for him.

'Byren Kingsheir.' Neiron wiped his face with shaking hands. He was unshaven, weary and bloodied, but despite this, he was not happy to find himself saved by one of King Rolen's sons.

Byren had no time for him. 'Where's Elcwyff and the boy?'

'Elcwyff's wounded. We put him in the best chamber.'

Byren ran up the stairs. He found Elcwyff lying bandaged and bloodied in bed. His son stood ready with a knife to defend him.

'Eh, your mother would be proud of you, lad,' Byren said, taking the knife from the boy.

'RACE YOU!' PIRO let her horse have its head.

Before long, they clattered into the stable yard with Piro in the lead and Florin at her heels.

She jumped down laughing. 'You nearly beat me. By the time we get to port, Byren won't know you.'

Florin dismounted and bent to inspect her horse's fetlocks.

Piro was pleased with herself. It had been twenty-five days since Byren left Florin behind. In that time, the mountain girl had learnt to play Duelling Kingdoms and become much more proficient in Merofynian. She'd read to Old Gwalt twice a day, so her reading had improved. She knew how to sit at a lord's table and eat politely. She had a much better grasp of Merofynian history, and she'd picked up the running of the estate without any trouble.

But Florin had refused to cooperate unless Piro taught her to swim. So they'd been swimming every day. If they weren't careful, they'd both end up brown as farm-workers.

Thanks to Piro, Florin was now much better prepared to marry Byren. Not that Piro thought Byren would ever go back on his word to Isolt, but just in case...

Looking rather flushed, Florin handed over the reins to the stable lad. 'Think I'll cool off with a swim. Come with me?'

Piro wanted to join her, but Old Gwalt was all alone.

'I see you've been riding again.' Isfynia sounded wistful as she joined them. 'Mother keeps encouraging me to ride. She hopes I'll have a fall and lose the baby.'

Your mother's a fool. Piro could almost hear Florin's voice in her head. She glanced to the big mountain girl. Florin's mouth was firmly closed, but her face said it all.

Smothering a laugh, Piro changed the subject. 'How are your people?'

'Homesick,' Isfynia said. 'Of course they appreciate Lord Dunstany's generosity—we all do—but...'

She broke off as a boy announced that the yacht had returned with news from Byren.

Piro took to her heels, but Florin's longer legs easily outstripped her.

They met the captain on the terrace, where he handed Piro a message. She broke the seal, reading quickly. 'Oh...'

'What?' Florin and Isfynia asked at once.

Piro lifted her head, meeting Isfynia's eyes. 'Byren says Elenstir and Istyntir Estates are safe, but—'

'Father's dead.' The young woman swallowed audibly.

'I'm so sorry,' Piro said.

Isfynia shook her head. 'It was only a matter of t-time.' She pushed on. 'If we don't want to be turned out of our home, we need to speak with Queen Isolt, so I can inherit and marry Rishardt. Is there news of Rhodontir Estate?'

Piro indicated the message. 'Byren was marching there when he sent this.'

Isfynia nodded, obviously thinking of Lord Rhoderich's third son and the coming battle. 'I should tell Mother.'

'And we should tell Lord Dunstany.' Piro made sure the captain had food and drink, then went to see Old Gwalt.

As soon as they were alone she whispered, 'We haven't heard from Fyn. I hope he's all right.'

'We are not going to die here,' Fyn told his men.

The dozen survivors of the ill-fated Ulfr Spar campaign watched him with hope. They crouched in the ravine not far from Rhodontir Pass, where the fort had been captured by spar warriors, preventing their return to Rhodontir Estate.

They should never have come over the Divide. Fyn had advised against it, but Lord Rhoderich would not listen.

Twelve days ago, he'd arrived to find the lord secure in the great house, while his heir hunted down fleeing spar warriors. Fyn had been ready to set off for Elenstir Estate, until Rhoderich revealed that the warlord of Ulfr Spar had ambushed Rhoderich's second son, killing him and all of his men. He'd claimed the estate's goldmine, along with the seven-year slaves. Rhoderich had sent his third son to lay siege to the mine.

Putting aside the fact that every second spar warrior

was calling himself *warlord*, Fyn was faced with another siege. And this time, the warlord had chosen a highly defensible position.

While riding up to inspect the mine's fortifications, Fyn met Rhoderich's youngest son, Rishardt, riding back with the wounded. Another contingent of spar warriors had come over the pass and attacked them. Seizing the opportunity, the warlord had opened the mine gates and struck from the other side. Rishardt and his men had been lucky to escape.

On hearing this, Lord Rhoderich had declared his youngest son incompetent and ordered him to ride onto the spar to chase down the spar warriors. It was suicide.

Then Rhoderich had compounded this by telling his eldest son to storm the mine. Another suicidal order.

But both Rhoden and Rishardt felt they could not disobey their father. So they set off for the mine. Along the way Fyn won a promise from Rhoden to hold off attacking until he and Rishardt returned. Fyn had a plan to lure the warlord out.

Then he had ridden over the pass with Rishardt and sixty men, leaving twenty men in the fort.

On the spar, they found every cottage deserted. The people had fled into the thickly wooded ravines, taking their animals and food with them. The locals knew every valley and ridge, and used them to their advantage. Spurred on by the determination to defend their homes, they laid ambush after ambush.

After being harried and hunted until his men were reduced to a third of their number, Rishardt had admitted the spar raid was costing more than it achieved and returned to the pass. Only to find that, despite Fyn's precautions, spar warriors had captured the fort.

'We can't stay here, trapped between the fort and the spar,' Fyn said. 'We have to attack.'

Rishardt shook his head. 'Half of us will die before we get over the wall.'

'We're not going over the wall.' Fyn indicated the natural chimney in the cliff. 'We're going to attack from above.'

'You're mad. No one can make that climb!'

'I've climbed sea-hound masts in high seas. Nothing can be harder than that.' Fyn unlaced his boots, took off his sword and tied a rope to his waist.

There was rubble at the base of the chimney; it had formed recently. With his back pressed against one wall and his feet against the other, he edged upwards.

At the top he found a ledge and worked his way along the ravine wall towards the fort. He made a couple of false starts, but eventually found a series of ledges that took him to a point above the fort.

During the two hundred years of peace, the walls had been allowed to fall into disrepair, but the tradepost, stables and storage sheds had been maintained. The defenders had shored up the walls and maintained a vigilant watch.

Fyn made the rope secure only to discover it wasn't quite long enough. He figured they could drop onto the tradepost roof. With the light fading, he needed to get his men in position before dark.

After climbing down the chimney, Fyn's thigh muscles and back protested. 'The rope's in place.'

'Good. But not everyone has a head for heights,' Rishardt said. 'We'd have to leave the injured behind anyway, so some have volunteered to stay and protect them.'

Fyn nodded. 'Be ready when you hear the fighting.'

Then he climbed that chimney again. In the rapidly fading light, they crept along to the ledge directly above the fort. Several of the men looked pale and queasy. The sooner they were on the ground, the better.

'I'll go first,' Fyn said. 'There's a bit of drop to the tradepost roof. I'll guide the next man down. When we're ready, we'll deal with the gate guards and let the others in. If we're quiet, we'll all be inside the fort before the spar warriors know what's going on.'

They nodded.

Fyn climbed down. When he got to the end of the rope, he let go, praying he wouldn't slide on the mossy slates.

He landed well and only slid half his length before catching himself. Heart thundering, he lay still, sprawled on the roof, waiting for someone to sound the alarm.

Nothing.

Looking up, he signalled the next man, who began the climb. Fyn steadied him as he landed.

Still no alarm. A third man made the climb, then a fourth.

As a fifth man dropped, the tradepost roof gave a high-pitched creak and Fyn felt it shift under their feet. Next thing he knew he was falling along with everyone else, amidst broken slates and roof beams.

They landed in a first floor bedchamber. Choking dust filled the air. A great beam pinned Fyn's leg. Someone moaned.

Shouts. Boots running up the stairs.

He shoved the beam with his free leg, felt it roll. Heard a high pitched scream that cut off abruptly and realised he'd made it worse for someone else.

With his bad leg threatening to give way, he pulled himself upright against the wall by the door, and not a moment too soon, as three spar warriors charged into the chamber.

'Another bloody rock fall,' one of the spar warriors said.

In the dusty twilight, Fyn realised his injured men were lost amidst the jumble of ruined roof joists, splintered oak beams and broken slates. Then someone moaned.

One of the men stepped forward. 'What...'

Fyn tripped him, shoving him towards a sharp piece of timber. Catching the second man from behind, Fyn stabbed him in the back. By then the first had rolled over with a splinter of wood through his shoulder.

The third man stared at Fyn as if he was seeing a ghost. Before the man could gather his wits, Fyn stepped in, but his bad leg gave way and he lurched, taking them both down. By luck he fell on top of the man. His knife slid between the spar warrior's ribs. Someone hauled Fyn upright and spun him around.

Fyn tackled the man, driving him back onto the rubble. His hand closed on a slate and he slammed it onto the man's skull. He felt the warrior's body go slack and staggered to his feet.

'Is anyone still alive?' Fyn whispered.

'Over here.'

'And here.'

'I think me ribs are broke.'

There was no response from the fifth man.

Fyn hauled two men out, bleeding and bruised. The fourth man was right, he did have broken ribs. They propped Grufyd against the wall, where he winced with each breath. The fifth wasn't going anywhere.

'Come on,' Fyn said.

'What about them?' One of his men pointed through the shattered roof to the ledge far above, where three men still waited to make the climb.

'They'll have to go back.' Fyn limped through the door into the hall. Light and voices came up the stairs.

'Come on, dinner's ready,' someone yelled. 'We can fix the roof tomorrow.'

Going along the passage, Fyn came to a door. This chamber's windows opened onto the stable roof and he gestured his men over. 'Everyone out.'

While he was crawling across the roof, Fyn spotted someone carrying a couple of bowls towards two guards near the spar-side gate.

Fyn signalled his men and whispered, 'I'm going to lure the gate guards over here. You drop down on them from above, then throw open the gate.'

The others nodded. Hopefully Rishardt would be ready.

Before Fyn could do anything, shouting from the inn told him their arrival had been discovered.

'Poor Grufyd,' one of the men said.

The gate guards ran towards the tradepost.

'Spar warriors,' Fyn muttered. 'No discipline.' He shoved the nearest man. 'Get down and let the others in.'

A few moments later, Fyn met Rishardt at the gate.

'You're covered in dust,' Rishardt said. 'What happened?'

'The roof collapsed under us.'

He gave a bark of laughter.

Then the defenders poured out and it was kill or be killed. Fyn didn't try anything heroic. He took a defensive position at the rear, swiping at any spar warrior foolish enough to come within range.

By full dark, the fort was theirs.

As they were seeing to the dead and injured, a forlorn voice called from the ledge. 'What about us?'

Fyn leant on his make-shift crutch and tilted his head to see three pale faces far above. 'You can climb down tomorrow.'

Tomorrow, they would go to the mine.

BYREN HAD ARRIVED at Rhodontir Estate to find Lord Rhoderich had recaptured his great house, then marched up into the Divide to besiege the spar warlord, who had fortified the gold mine. When Byren learned that Fyn had gone over the pass to hunt down spar warriors he was horrified. 'Why would he do such a foolish thing?'

Rhoderich stiffened. 'They had to be taught a lesson. We cannot risk more warriors coming over the pass.'

'Then rebuild the fort.'

Rhoden glanced to his father, who did not comment. Byren suspected Fyn had made the same suggestion. 'So you sent Rishardt and Fyn over the Divide?'

Rhoderich nodded.

'Fyn recommended we sit tight until he returned,' Rhoden said. 'He had a plan—'

'But I didn't want to waste time,' Rhoderich said. 'So I ordered a frontal assault.'

'And how did that go?' Byren knew the answer.

Rhoderich glanced to his son. 'It was rebuffed.'

Byren was heartily sick of Merofynian lords. 'This is what we will do. A little before midnight, you'll sound the alarm. Your men will run about, yelling that spar warriors have come over the pass and attacked from behind. They will be my men, but the warlord won't be able to tell in the dark. He'll open the gates and send his men out. We wait until they are fully committed, then we overwhelm them. Any questions?'

'Why would the warlord come out?' Rhoderich asked.

'Because he doesn't know I've arrived, and Rhoden here tells me that when he ventured out last time, he routed Rishardt.' Byren rubbed his jaw. 'Orrade?'

'That should do it.'

FYN REACHED THE gold mine to find everyone celebrating. Apparently, his brother had arrived the previous night, saved the mine and returned to the great house. When Fyn heard how Byren had lured the warlord out, he cursed. It was exactly the ploy he had intended to use.

He sent another thirty men to reinforce the fort at the pass, before borrowing two horses and setting off for the great house with Rishardt.

When he arrived, hundreds of seven-year slaves, including the men he had brought with him from Benetir and Travantir Estates, were camped around the house, celebrating in Byren's name. Meanwhile, Fyn limped into the great hall looking like a failure. He spotted Byren at the feasting table, Lord Rhoderich on one side, Queen Isolt on the other.

And in that moment, he hated his brother.

Orrade looked up. 'Fyn?'

'Fyn?' Byren strode over and swept him up in a hug.

And he was *little Fyn* again, safe in the arms of the older brother he trusted more than anyone in the world.

'I'm that glad to see you,' Byren said. He frowned and turned Fyn's face to the light. 'Where did you—'

'The duel with Elrhodoc. He provoked me by abusing Piro.'

'I didn't know. No wonder Piro...' Byren glanced down to the makeshift crutch. 'And the leg?'

Fyn shrugged. 'It's a long story.'

'One I'm looking forward to hearing.' Byren leant closer to Fyn to whisper, 'When I heard that fool lord had sent you over the pass onto the spar, I was ready to throttle him. Why did you agree to go?'

'I had to keep Rishardt alive. He's worth two of his father.'

'Eh, Fyn, you've grown up.' Byren grinned, and called for another chair.

While a place was set for him, Fyn lowered his voice. 'Be on your guard. The Merofynian nobles would rather see one of their own married to the queen.'

'So I gather. You've been having a rough time and it's all my fault. I was so fixed on ousting Cobalt, I didn't think...'

Fyn shook his head. He wasn't fishing for an apology. 'Watch out for Elcwyff, he thinks I murdered his brother. And Neiron—'

'Him?' Byren dismissed the lord with a snort. 'He's all talk. I had to come to his rescue twice, after he botched breaking the siege on his own place and then nearly got him and Elcwyff killed in the pass. He doesn't have the stomach for battle.'

Fyn flushed and held his tongue, as Byren offered him the seat on the other side of Isolt. Pinned between them, she was contained and quiet. It broke Fyn's heart to see her revert to the wary Isolt of old.

Of course Byren was not a bully like her father, but his careful courtesy towards her was almost painful to watch. It was clear to Fyn that Byren did not know what to make of her.

'Chandler will march my army around the coast to port,' Byren said. 'Meanwhile, we'll make the journey by ship. I've already sent word to Piro and Florin. There'll be a big celebration.'

And he'd marry Isolt and that would be the end of it.

A roaring filled Fyn's head. He'd missed his chance. He should have seduced Isolt and run away with her. They would have been happy no matter how poor. As far as he could see, a king's life revolved around defending the throne and dealing with self-important nobles. Why would anyone want a crown?

Chapter Sixty

Piro took her place beside the queen's dais. After meeting with Isfynia and Rishardt, Isolt had consulted with the abbess and called a lords' council in the great hall. The chair beside Isolt was empty, to symbolise that, for the time being, she was a queen without a king.

Isolt had offered Byren the chance to sit beside her, but he had refused, saying that until they were married, he would stand behind the chair. It had been a pretty speech and Piro suspected Orrade had had a hand in crafting it. She wished Siordun was here so they could compare observations. But the mage's agent was currently sailing back from Ostron Isle, which meant Lord Dunstany had not made a miraculous recovery in time for the lords' council. At least there was no sign of Duncaer, for which she was grateful.

Isolt signed the decree naming Isfynia and Rishardt Lord and Lady of Istyntir Estate.

Piro beamed, wishing she could resolve Fyn and Isolt's difficulties with a sweep of a pen.

* * *

BYREN STOOD BEHIND Queen Isolt's chair. If truth be told, he wasn't ready to sit beside her. He did not know what to make of the young Merofynian queen. Unlike Piro, whose every emotion travelled across her face, Isolt was controlled and polite. She didn't laugh at his sallies. In fact, if he didn't know better, he'd think she didn't like him.

His army of ex-slaves would arrive in port soon. Now that he was finally in a position of strength, he wanted to sail home and teach Cobalt a lesson.

He found his gaze going to Florin. She stood near the entrance to the hall with his honour guard and the queen's guards. A hundred times a day during the spar campaign, he'd caught himself thinking of her.

Since arriving in the palace, he'd only spoken with her once, and only in the company of others. Like strangers, he'd asked after her health and she'd called him 'my king'. But her voice hadn't held that familiar teasing lilt. He'd experienced an almost overwhelming urge to pierce her formal façade. He really should avoid Florin, especially here in the palace of his betrothed.

He owed Isolt that much.

But even as he thought his, he caught himself seeking out his mountain girl again. She was an itch he could not scratch.

FYN STOOD ON the left of the queen's dais, careful not to let his gaze stray to Isolt and Byren. Seeing Byren by her side was like prodding a bruise.

The spar invasion had given him the opportunity to win over the heirs of Travany, Rhodontir and Istyn Estates, but their fathers still supported Neiron, and Elcwyff was barely civil to Fyn. As much as Fyn hated to admit it, Byren and his army of freed Rolencians had cowed the Merofynian nobles.

The lords stood on each side of the grand hall, revealing the divide in their alliances. In his capacity as elder statesman, Yorale stood next to the dais on Isolt's right. Ranged along the right side of the hall were Neiron and his supporters.

On the left side of the hall, Sefarra represented Benetir Estate. By her side was the mother of Geraltir Estate's young heir. Isfynia and Rishardt had gone to stand with them. If you included Piro and the abbess, there were more women present than ever before. And this had not gone unnoticed. Fyn had heard Rhoderich and Travany complain that the women would side with the queen.

Orrade stood behind Piro; Fyn found it strange not seeing him at Byren's side.

Byren and Isolt had given their formal betrothal vows, although neither had set a date for the marriage. Even so, the sight of Byren's hand on the back of Isolt's chair was enough to make Fyn bristle. He would not be able to stay here after they were wed.

Duncaer arrived and hurried towards the dais.

'Apologies, my queen.' He dropped to one knee. 'I fear I am the bearer of sad news. Lord Dunstany is dead.'

Isolt glanced to Fyn. Piro had told them of Old Gwalt's part in the subterfuge. Now it had backfired on them.

'How did Lord Dunstany die?' Piro asked, angry tears glittering in her eyes.

'His heart gave out. Ninety-five is a good age.'

'Lord Dunstany will be sorely missed.' Isolt's voice was thick with emotion. 'We'll hold your investiture ceremony tomorrow, Duncaer.'

Florin strode down the corridor, almost blinded by tears. Stupid weak tears...

It was the shock of Lord Dunstany's death. She'd spent the last thirty days reading to him and laughing at the droll things he said.

Seeing Byren up there on the dais with Queen Isolt had forced her to confront the gulf between them. Truly, she had no place in his world. In fact, if Piro hadn't given her a bed, she wouldn't even have had a place to sleep.

'Mountain Girl?'

Florin drew a deep breath and turned to face Byren, giving a formal bow. 'My king?'

He hesitated, as if unsure.

The abbot and abbess passed by with a gaggle of monks and nuns, and Orrade and Fyn arrived in their wake.

'Florin.' Fyn seemed distracted.

'Good to see you're looking better, mountain girl.' Orrade kissed her cheek with genuine affection.

'Orrie.' Her voice broke. She hadn't realised how much she missed him. Tears spilled down her cheeks.

'What's wrong?' Byren reached out, then stopped mid-gesture and folded his arms.

'Dunstany's dead!' A sob escaped her.

'I know...' Fyn had to clear his throat. 'Isolt's heartbroken. He was more of a father to her than her own father.' He slipped away.

Florin took this chance to escape. 'I should go, Piro is waiting for me.'

But when she reached Piro's chamber, it was empty. She sank onto the window seat just as someone knocked on the door. Expecting it to be a servant, Florin remained where she was. 'Yes?'

Isfynia slipped into the chamber. 'No, don't get up.'

'Piro's not here,' Florin said.

The young woman glided over to the window seat and placed a small chest on the cushion between them. 'Would you give her this? It's just a small gift. I cannot say how much she's helped me. What with father's death, losing our home and the constant sickness, I've been bursting into tears at the slightest thing. Everything seemed hopeless. Today is the first day that I feel there is a future for me and my child.' Her hand settled protectively on her belly.

'I'm glad.' Florin thought Isfynia deserved to be happy. She'd worked hard to keep her family together and look after their people.

'And I... I wanted to thank you for what you said, back at Dunistir Estate.'

'Really?' Florin couldn't remember, but she suspected she'd been rude to Isfynia's mother. 'What did I say?'

'You said Rishardt should be glad he's getting a wife he knows can have children. It was so sensible. Thank you.' Isfynia kissed Florin's cheek. 'I hope you can be just as happy. And don't worry, the sickness passes once the first third of the pregnancy is over.'

Florin's mouth dropped open. 'I'm not—'

'Don't worry.' Isfynia squeezed her hand. 'I won't tell.'

She could not be pregnant. That would be too cruel.

A rushing filled Florin's head. Dimly, she heard Isfynia leave.

She could not pregnant. Byren hadn't finished.

He hadn't even started. Had he?

It had all been so intense. Nothing like the jocular slap and tickle she'd overheard men boasting about in the tap room.

She tried to remember when she'd had her last bleed. It had been the day she went to the castle to kill Cobalt. She should have bled twice since then.

But she hadn't.

Isfynia was right. She was pregnant.

What was she going to do?

'I CAN'T BELIEVE Old Gwalt is dead,' Piro whispered. They had retreated to the queen's chamber and dismissed the servants. She frowned.

'What?'

'Duncaer threatened to throw Dunstany's loyal servants out with only the clothes on their backs.'

'They can come here. I'll find work for them.' Isolt wiped her cheeks. 'Dunstany's been dead these last seven years, yet I feel as if I've only just lost him.'

'I know.'

'I'll have to hold the ceremony to recognise Duncaer as the next lord of Dunistir,' Isolt said. 'I can't refuse. Oh, I wish...'

Piro thought of the chest Old Gwalt had given her. But what was the use, when Siordun couldn't inherit?

'Siordun!' She sprang to her feet. He was due back any time now. 'I must warn him.'

'Who? Oh, Agent Tyro.'

'I must go to Dunstany's townhouse. What if Duncaer is already there?' Piro did not want the pica birds to fall into the wrong hands.

'You shouldn't go alone. Take some of my honour guards.'

'I'll take Florin.' She could be trusted to keep her mouth shut.

Piro ran out the door, passing Fyn in the hall.

He caught her arm. 'Where are you off to in such a hurry?'

'Dunstany's townhouse, to warn Siordun,' she whispered.

'Take—'

'I'm taking Florin.'

And she ran to her chamber, where she found Florin sitting in the window seat looking stunned. Poor thing, she'd grown very fond of the man she knew as Lord Dunstany.

'Florin?'

The mountain girl wiped her cheeks. 'Isfynia left this gift, to say thank you.'

'That's kind.' Piro opened the chest to reveal a gold statuette of an amfina. She put it on the mantelpiece. 'But I need you to come with me right now.'

Rather than waste time preparing a carriage, Piro requested two horses. They were soon riding out the main gates, through the market square and down the thoroughfare towards the port.

Florin edged her horse closer to Piro. 'The abbess was talking about one of the women who'd been raped by spar warriors.'

'Lady Nerysa.' Piro recalled the discussion.

'The abbess said she could arrange for her to lose the baby if she was pregnant. I didn't know that was possible.'

Piro guided her horse around a cart, then waited for Florin to catch up. 'Back home, the castle healer knew of such things, but she frowned on them. Said they were dangerous. Besides, she'd sworn to save life, not take it.'

'So any healer would know the right herbs?'

'Healer or Power-worker.' Piro frowned, thinking of the Power-worker in Duncaer's employ. 'And a Power-worker wouldn't be so worried about taking a life...' She ran down as they approached Dunstany's townhouse. To her relief there was no sign of Duncaer. 'This way.'

Piro went around the back to the courtyard, where a stable boy darted out to take the horse's bridle. 'Wait under the lemon tree, Florin.'

Running up the back steps, Piro entered the kitchen. A delicious smell greeted her.

The kitchen maid was standing on a stool to stir the pot of lemon butter. She gave a jump of fight when she saw Piro. 'You scared me outta ten years' growth, miss!' The girl wiped her hands on her smock. 'Shall I fetch Master Gwalt?'

'Don't worry. I know where to find him.'

Piro headed for the study at the front of the house, where she found him working over the accounts. 'There's no time to lose. Duncaer will be here before evening now that Lord Dunstany is dead...' She gasped and covered her mouth. 'I'm so sorry. Old Gwalt was your father. I was thinking about Siordun. Thinking he mustn't turn up at the palace in his Dunstany disguise.'

'Of course not.' Gwalt put his nib aside and came over to her. 'You did the right thing, coming straight here.'

'I'm sorry.' Tears spilled over Piro's cheeks.

'Bless you, child.' Gwalt hugged her, and his voice caught. 'My father was seventy-four.'

Piro nodded and wiped her cheeks. 'There's just so much to think of. You'll have to hide the pica birds. I'm afraid Duncaer might have turned the house-keep and Soterro out of Dunistir Estate.' She gasped. 'What if he found the pica birds?'

'Soterro's smart, he...' Gwalt broke off as a carriage pulled up outside.

Piro peered through the drapes. 'It's Duncaer!'

'Siordun's due in today.'

'I'll stop him before he gets here.'

'Do that. He'll be travelling as Dunstany or himself. Either way, he can't come here.'

They heard Duncaer climb down from the carriage.

'Announce me,' he told the servant. 'You have no idea how much I've been looking forward to turning out this uppity steward!'

'You divert Siordun.' Gwalt pushed Piro down the hall towards the back door.

'Find Soterro and the house-keep and come to me at the palace,' Piro whispered. 'What about your pica birds?'

'Don't worry. Get away before they bring the carriage around.'

She ran out through the kitchen, to the surprise of the kitchen maid. Piro's horse was there, tied to the lemon tree, but there was no sign of Florin. 'Where's—'

'She had somethin' to do,' the stable boy said. 'Told me to tell you she'd see you back at the palace.'

There was no time to worry about Florin. Piro took her horse by the reins and led him out into the lane. She'd just reached the next corner when she heard the carriage turn into Dunstany's townhouse.

Where was Siordun? Sometimes he sent his bags to the townhouse and went straight to the palace. If he turned up there, they'd arrest him for the fraud he was. He'd be unmasked and executed on the spot.

She felt sick at the thought.

Chapter Sixty-One

Florin didn't like the look of the Power-worker or his premises, but she didn't have much choice. She'd gone to a healer first, but on hearing what she needed, the woman had turned nasty.

'If yer were foolish enough to open yer legs, yer can face the consequences,' the woman had said, then looked her up and down. 'What're yer doin', gettin' about dressed like a man, with a sword at yer side? Serves yer right.'

So here she was, on the third floor of a rickety building overlooking the docks, with a grey haired Power-worker who smelled like an Affinity beast. Which was not surprising, since he kept an amfina hatchling for a pet. It lay curled around his neck with a head on each of his shoulders. The dominant head watched while the other slept.

The Power-worker looked her up and down, calculating the cost of her clothing from her boots to her hat, so he could work out what to charge. She used to do much the same thing with customers. But although she wore good leather boots, she was destitute. How was she going to pay for this?

'Well,' the Power-worker prompted, 'what can I do for you?'

'You can tell me if it is worth my mistress's time coming here,' Florin said.

'What would your mistress be wanting?'

Florin felt her cheeks grow hot, but forged on, adapting a story she'd overheard in the tradepost tap room. 'My mistress finds herself in a difficult position. The master has been away since last winter, but she is with child. She needs to be rid of it before he returns.'

'That's not an easy request to fill,' the Power-worker said slowly. 'Your mistress should have taken precautions before the event, rather than after.'

'What can I say?' Florin shrugged.

'How far along is she?' he asked

'Still in the first third. Why?'

'It's less dangerous in the early stages.'

She swallowed.

'What you need is bitter-tears, but I don't have any left.'

'Can you get it?'

'I can. Tell your mistress it will be expensive.'

She'd been afraid of this. 'How much?'

The figure made her gasp.

'That would keep a family for a year!'

'Does she want to keep her husband?'

Florin took a breath to slow her racing heart. 'I'll let her know.' She paused at the door. 'When will you have it?'

'Give me six days.'

She headed down the stairs, wishing she had dressed as a peasant; but then, he would probably have turned her out.

As Florin led her horse up the street she heard Piro's voice and spotted the kingsdaughter jumping down from her mount to stop a tall young man. He smiled, then his face fell as Piro spoke. They both darted into a tavern, leaving Piro's horse with the yard boy.

Intrigued, Florin followed and was just in time to see them slip into a private chamber.

* * *

PIRO SHUT THE door and turned to Siordun. 'I'm sorry. I know you were close to Old Gwalt.'

He went to the empty fireplace, where he leant both hands on the mantelpiece and rested his forehead on them.

'Young Gwalt is going to hide the pica birds,' Piro told him. 'He'll cover for you at Dunstany House. Have you eaten?'

'What? No, I...'

She had never seen him like this. 'We should go back to the palace and have dinner. Byren's there. He and Fyn settled the spar uprising. Byren has an army of freed Rolencians. He wants to set sail for home, to defeat Cobalt. We need—'

'I can't go to the palace, Piro.' He turned to her, dark eyes intense. 'Lord Dunstany could sit at the table with Queen Isolt and her betrothed, and offer advice. But Byren only knows me as Agent Tyro. And the Merofynian nobles regard Tyro with suspicion, since the mage's allegiance is to Ostron Isle.'

Now that Duncaer had inherited Dunistir Estate, Piro realised, Siordun had been stripped of his role in the Merofynian court. 'But if we explained to Byren—'

'He'd feel like he'd been duped. He'd be angry.'

'We should tell him. If we don't and he finds out, he'll be even angrier.'

Siordun rubbed his face. He looked gaunt and exhausted.

'What happened in Ostron Isle? Why did you stay away so long?' She bit her tongue. She'd almost admitted she'd been worried about him.

'It was complicated. I went to negotiate with Lady Death, but ended up stopping an uprising. She tried to use her coraxes to unseat the House Cerastus elector and win the position for her brother. But...' Siordun gave a grim smile. 'She no longer rules House Nictocorax and the coraxes won't be a force to be reckoned with for a long time to come.'

Piro shivered. She didn't really know him at all. 'And Nefysto and Kaspian, are they all right?'

'Yes. But the great houses have paid for her ambition.' He smiled. 'When I arrived, Agent Salvatrix was waiting on Mage Isle. She'd refused to leave until she saw Tsulamyth about Varuska.'

'Who?'

'The girl Cobalt was going to marry in your place.'

Piro stiffened.

'Don't judge her. Cobalt did not give the poor girl a choice. According to my agent, he's cunning and ambitious. In less than half a year he has won over the merchants, installed new nobles, given titles and lands to five Merofynian captains and their men, and blackened Byren's name to such an extent that if Byren were to walk into Rolencia today...' Siordun shook his head. 'There are many who would turn him over to Cobalt for the reward and think good riddance.'

'But that's...' She been about to say *not fair*.

'In the middle of all this, a daring Utland captain sailed into the Ring Sea and tried to make off with a fully loaded merchant ship.'

'What? I thought the Ostronites had a chain they could raise that blocked the entrance to the Ring Sea. How—'

'He had two ships. His Utland vessel waited for him, while he used the same ploy he'd used in Port Mero. He sailed his stolen Merofynian merchant ship into the Ring Sea and we were all so busy fighting amongst ourselves, he nearly got away with it. When we realised what was going on, we reclaimed the stolen vessel and a pack of sea-hounds hunted down his Utland ship. Burned it to the waterline with all on board.'

'The Utlanders are getting daring.'

'Because we fight amongst ourselves. It makes us weak.'

That reminded Piro. 'How can we clear Byren's name and reveal Cobalt for the liar he is?' She frowned as Siordun crept towards the door. 'What...'

He signalled for silence, swung the door open, hauled an eaves-dropper inside and threw him up against the wall.

'Florin?' Piro sprang to her feet.

'You're Florin?' Siordun stepped back. 'Why were you listening at the door?'

The mountain girl flushed and straightened her clothes. 'I heard Byren's name.'

'What else did you hear?'

Florin glanced over to Piro. 'If the old man who just died was not Lord Dunstany, who is the real Dunstany?'

Siordun dropped into a chair by the table. 'The real Dunstany died seven years ago. I masqueraded as him on behalf of the mage. Old Gwalt was covering for me.'

Florin looked stunned. Piro tried to remember if they'd said anything that might reveal Siordun had also played the mage.

Siordun turned to Piro. 'Now that Duncaer has inherited the title, Isolt will be without Lord Dunstany's support. I have no excuse to advise her.'

'They need more queen's guards,' Florin said. 'No one looks at the honour guards, but we go everywhere and hear everything. You could advise her—'

'Can you see me swinging a sword?' Siordun asked. He looked like the scholar he was.

Piro grinned. 'The less imposing you are, the less you'll be noticed.'

That made him smile, but he shook his head. 'Besides, my Affinity is too strong. It has to be part of my disguise.'

'In that case, we need a war-table council,' Piro said. 'And you need to tell Byren and Orrade the truth about Dunstany.'

* * *

Fyn told himself it was only right that Byren should lead Isolt out for the first dance at their first official celebration after defeating the spar invasion.

Between the merchant margraves and their wives, the lords and their ladies, and the servants and musicians, the palace ballroom was packed. Everyone watched as Byren took Isolt's hand and the musicians struck up a Merofynian dance. It was more sedate than the lively dances of King Rolen's court. Just as well their mother had taught them courtly Merofynian manners.

Byren's hands closed on Isolt's small waist and he lifted her high in the air. Her gown flared out, revealing her silk stockinged calves and the back of her knees.

Fyn stiffened. He'd seen more bare skin when Isolt was frolicking in the grotto with Loyalty, but that wasn't the point.

Finally the dance ended and other couples filed out onto the dance floor to form two long lines. Piro appeared at Fyn's elbow and tugged on his arm. 'Come dance with me.'

He couldn't. He was watching to see if Byren would take Isolt back to her seat, and he did.

'Fyn?' Piro pressed.

He left his spot by the wall. 'I'm not dancing.' No, he wanted to sit with Isolt. That would be enough.

'Then I'll ask Orrie.'

In the rush of returning to court, he hadn't had a chance to tell Orrade that his younger brother still lived. But there was the question of Garzik's loyalty, and he did not want Orrade to be ashamed of his brother. Perhaps it was best not to mention Garzik.

Piro darted over to Orrade, who was leaning against a column, chatting to Florin. The mountain girl made no concession to her gender. She wore the same breeches, fine vest and fine calf length coat as Byren, who paused to chat to them. Orrade laughed and Florin smiled stiffly.

When Piro reached them, Orrade turned her down, so she cajoled Byren into partnering her for a dance.

This left Isolt without a partner.

But Neiron reached Isolt before Fyn did and asked her to dance. She glanced around and Fyn tried to catch her eye, but the abbot came between them.

Looking very pleased with himself, Neiron led Isolt out onto the dance floor. Again, Fyn felt the urge to warn Byren, but his brother had been so dismissive of Neiron. Fyn's cheeks burned with the memory.

He leant against the wall and folded his arms.

'I haven't seen a grand ball like this since Isolt's father first came to power,' Murheg said. His hair had been washed and perfumed and lay loose on his shoulders, threaded with onyxes. Yet his appearance was restrained compared with most of the men.

Fyn watched Isolt. The dancers took their positions, moving to the music like a flock of birds wheeling on high.

'I know he's your brother,' Murheg said softly, 'but it's disgusting the way Byren flaunts his lover in front of the queen.'

Fyn had no idea what the abbot was talking about. 'What lover?'

'The mountain girl.' Murheg gestured to Orrade and Florin.

'Florin is Orrade's lover.'

'I heard he was a lover of men.'

Fyn laughed. 'There's nothing to that rumour. If you could have heard my brothers and Orrie boasting about the girls they've bedded... Admittedly that was back when they were sixteen, but I also travelled with Byren's army and it was quite clear that Florin was Orrade's lover.'

Murheg said nothing. The dancers moved in intricate patterns, weaving in and out, taking new partners. Fyn grinned grimly. He liked this dance. Neiron didn't get to put his hands on Isolt's waist. In fact, he hardly got to speak with her as they passed each other yet again and took a new partner. Now it was Yorale's heir, Yoromer, who partnered her.

Murheg leant closer to Fyn. 'It occurs to me that the safest way to hide your lover is in plain sight. After all, if everyone thinks she is your best friend's—'

'Byren's not like that.' Fyn spoke with conviction.

'Perhaps he was not like that once, but power changes people.'

As much as Fyn hated to admit this, it was true.

For the rest of the evening, he watched the three of them. Orrade and Florin were very comfortable with each other. She made him laugh, something that was rare for Orrie. By contrast, Byren and Florin hardly spoke, and when they did, they were distantly polite. In the past they'd been close enough to tease each other. Either they'd had a terrible fight, or they were lovers and were trying to disguise the fact.

Then it occurred to Fyn that Florin was attending the ball as one of Byren's honour guard. Like Chandler, she was probably armed and on watch for threat. This explained her distance from Byren, and her ease with Orrade, who had spoken to all the honour guards.

By the time the ball was over, Fyn had a pounding headache and did not know what to think. He'd barely made it back to his room when there was a knock at the door. Expecting it to be Camoric, he told them to enter.

Piro poked her head around the door, catching him in nothing but his breeches.

He reached for a shirt. 'Piro...'

'I'm your sister.' She rolled her eyes, then beckoned. 'Come with me. I have to show you something.'

'Surely it can wait?' But he reached for his shirt.

Out in the hall, she led him to one of the palace's towers, built nearly six hundred years ago. It was only used for storage now, and several dust-laden chests were piled up against the wall on the ground floor beside the stairs.

'Race you up!' Piro took off as if they were children.

He could not resist. They reached the top of the tower laughing.

Siordun swung the door for them.

Right away, Fyn saw the repercussions of Lord Dunstany's death. 'Are you going to take on a new Merofynian identity?'

'Probably, but not until I find the right one.' Siordun stepped aside, then, to reveal Gwalt.

Fyn greeted the steward warmly. 'Of course, Duncaer took over Dunstany's townhouse. Are the pica birds—'

'Safe? Yes.' Gwalt gestured to an adjacent chamber. 'Like me, they have a new home.'

'Now you don't have to ride to Dunstany's townhouse to send messages to the mage,' Piro told Fyn, very pleased with herself. 'The house-keep from Dunistir Estate is also coming to work in the palace. She'll report to Gwalt and he'll keep you informed.'

Fyn turned to Siordun. 'What about you? We need you more than ever now that Dunstany can't sit on the lord's council and advise the queen.'

'That's why I have to come up with an identity that lets me stay close to the queen, yet spend extended periods away from her. It won't be easy.'

'We'll hold a war-table council tomorrow, just the family,' Piro said. 'We need to tell Byren and Orrade the truth about Siordun and Dunstany.'

'Good. I don't like keeping things from Byren,' Fyn said. But if Murheg was right, Byren was hiding his lover in plain sight. The insult to Isolt made Fyn burn.

AS BYREN JOINED his betrothed and Fyn on the terrace for breakfast, he tried to think of something interesting to say to the queen. He'd left his honour guards and Orrade partaking of a noisy breakfast of ale, cold meat and cheese in the guard hall. One look at the royal table told

Byren he would be sending to the kitchen for something more substantial by mid-morning. Who could live on delicate pastries, slivers of fruit and whipped cream?

Queen Isolt, apparently. He watched as she dipped a hot-house strawberry in cream and nibbled on it.

'I never really had a chance to meet your wyvern,' Byren said. 'What was her name?'

'Loyalty.'

'Good name.'

Isolt nodded and plucked the stem from another strawberry.

'I hear she lives with Piro's foenix in the palace grounds.'

Isolt nodded again. She was paying more attention to the strawberry than him. Was she going to eat it or not?

'Both Affinity beasts sleep in the grotto built by the Mad Boy King,' Fyn supplied.

'The Mad Boy King from mother's stories?' Byren asked, chuckling. 'I always thought she was making him up.'

'Not a bit. In fact...' Fyn began, then seemed to think better of what he'd been going to say.

Byren turned to the queen. 'Will you be visiting your pet today? We could—'

'She's not my pet,' Isolt said primly. 'She's an intelligent creature with free will.' And she left the strawberry on her plate as she came to her feet. 'Please excuse me, I have work to do.'

Byren wondered how he had offended her.

'There you are, Byren,' Piro said, dropping into her seat with more enthusiasm than grace. She took several pastries and even more fruit, piling everything high on her plate. 'I wanted to see you...'

At least with Piro you knew where you stood. She could certainly eat. Before Florin took sick, she used to tuck into her food like this. Where was his mountain girl? Probably with his honour guards. No melon pieces in mint sauce for her. She'd...

'...Byren?' Piro asked, following up with a mock punch. 'You weren't even listening. I said we need to hold a family council in the war-table chamber.'

He nodded. 'I'll let Orrie know.'

When they turned up at the war-table council, Agent Tyro was there and Piro had also brought Florin along. Byren couldn't escape her. A moment later, Fyn walked in with Isolt.

'Good, we're all here.' Piro gestured to the mage's agent. 'Siordun has something to tell you.' Then before he could speak, she plunged on. 'For the last seven years, ever since Lord Dunstany died, Siordun has been impersonating him, so that he could spy for the mage and preserve the peace between Rolencia and Merofynia.'

'And look how well that worked out,' Orrade muttered.

'You knew, Orrie?' Byren asked.

'No.'

'Very few knew, and those who did, protected me,' Siordun said. 'Fyn, Isolt and Piro—'

'And Florin found out yesterday, when I went to warn Siordun not to come to the palace in his Dunstany disguise,' Piro said. 'Please don't be angry, Byren. Siordun has been trying to preserve the peace and help you win back Rolencia.'

HOW MANY KINGDOMS *does one man need?* Fyn thought as he stood across the table from Byren. If his brother reclaimed Rolencia, why should he have Merofynia and Isolt as well?

Fyn was not proud of himself for harbouring these thoughts. But if Florin wasn't Byren's lover, then why was she at their family council? What did the daughter of a tradepost keeper know of strategy and tactics?

Piro's voice pierced Fyn's distraction.

'...I don't see how anyone could believe Byren would kill me, rather than see me married to Cobalt.'

'That's because you would never do such a thing,' Orrade said. 'But there are people who would, so they have no trouble believing it of others.'

'Cobalt would.' Florin shuddered. 'He smiled as he killed Varuska's sister just so he could bury her in Piro's place.'

'That's it!' Piro looked around the table. 'He's buried me twice. If I go back to Rolencia and confront Cobalt—'

'No, Piro,' Fyn protested, and he wasn't the only one.

'Hear me out. On midsummer's day, Goddess Halcyon hands over the kingdom to Sylion, god of winter.'

'We have something similar here,' Isolt said. 'It's a grand ceremony, everyone attends.'

Piro nodded. 'I'll go back to Ostron Isle and collect Varuska to show how Cobalt fooled everyone. We'll confront him on midsummer's day, in front of all the nobles and merchants.'

'How would you get into the ceremony?' Orrade asked.

'The abbess of Sylion Abbey will help us. She hates Cobalt.'

Fyn didn't like it. 'This means sending Piro and the other poor girl into danger.'

'I could go with Piro,' Florin offered. 'Tell how I saw Cobalt—'

'No.' Byren cut her off. 'There's no need for you to go. Piro and Varuska will be enough.'

Fyn glanced to Byren. Was he trying to keep Florin safe?

'Right,' Piro said. 'Siordun can send a message to his agent in Rolencia, so she can get word to the abbess. Maybe after we unmask Cobalt, Byren won't need to lead his army into battle.'

'Eh, you're such a dreamer, Piro,' Byren said fondly. 'Men will fight to hold onto power whether they are in the right or not. And even if every Rolencian turned their back on Cobalt, the five Merofynian captains Cobalt ennobled can never return to their homeland. No, there'll be fighting.' He rubbed his jaw. 'I need to arm my men, find ships to transport them and be in position by midsummer's day.'

'You heard Florin.' Frustration drove Fyn to speak up. 'Cobalt thought nothing of murdering a girl to further his plans. Even with the abbess's support, we can't send Piro into danger.'

'Fyn's right,' Isolt said. 'There must be another way.'

'Piro is safest in plain sight,' Siordun said. 'Cobalt can't lay a finger on her if everyone knows she lives. And she won't be going into danger alone. I'll go with her. Byren, you should take Piro's foenix with you to validate your rule.'

'Then it's settled.' Piro sounded satisfied. 'We sail with the evening tide.'

'We'll leave the *Wyvern's Whelp* for Byren, so the mage can contact him,' Siordun said.

The council ended with Fyn still not sure if Byren was flaunting his lover under his betrothed's roof. One part of him refused to believe it. Another part feared Murheg was right.

Seeing Piro with Florin reminded him that his sister had spent half the summer on Dunstany's estate with the mountain girl. She would know if Florin was Orrade's lover. As everyone left, Fyn caught Piro's eye.

After they'd all gone she turned to him. 'What is it, Fyn?'

He hesitated, afraid he was right and Byren was no longer the man he used to be.

'I'll be all right. I've learnt to be careful.' Piro assured him. 'I'm no longer the silly girl who hid on Ruin Isle to help her brother find Halcyon's Fate.'

'That silly girl was very brave.' Fyn reached out and pulled her close for a hug, then released her. 'Far too brave. I want you to take Florin. She can wear a nun's...'

But Piro was already shaking her head.

'Why not? Will Orrade refuse to be parted from her?'

Piro laughed. 'They're not lovers.'

So the abbot had been right. Fury flashed through Fyn. How could Byren insult Isolt like this?

'Fyn?'

Somehow, he summoned a smile. 'Promise me you won't do anything brave.'

She laughed and hugged him.

Chapter Sixty-Two

FLORIN MISSED PIRO. It was five days since she'd set sail, five days of watching Byren escort Isolt to events, dance with her and sit with her at the feasting table.

To escape this, Florin had volunteered to help Orrade organise fitting out Byren's army. Chandler and the men had reached the far shore of the Grand Canal, and the army was fast becoming a nuisance as the men drank and ate their way through every inn and tavern on the east bank.

When Captain Aeran delivered news of another brawl in the streets, Orrade handed over a bag of coins. 'Recompense shop-keepers and tell Chandler to drill the men until they are so tired they'll have no energy to brawl at night.'

After the captain of the city-watch walked out, Orrade turned to Florin. 'Just as well we're sailing this afternoon.'

She couldn't have agreed more. But before they sailed, she needed to see the Power-worker. He should have the right herb by now. Bitter-tears... even the name held foreboding.

It made Florin uneasy, and the feeling had been growing ever since she'd decided on this course of action.

Orrade bent over the papers on his desk.

'I'm not feeling well.' Florin felt terrible. 'Can I go?'

Orrade put his nib aside. 'You'd tell me if something was wrong, wouldn't you, Mountain Girl?'

'Of course,' she lied.

The look he gave her was far too perceptive, but he waved her off. 'Go on. I guess you might as well rest now, since you'll be throwing up the whole time we're at sea.'

Relieved, she thanked him and slipped away.

Finding enough gold to pay the Power-worker had seemed a huge hurdle but, as it turned out, Piro had forgotten to pack the amfina statuette.

The walk down to the Power-worker's dingy establishment was over far too quickly. Florin ducked into the lane and went up the three flights of stairs. She found the Power-worker grinding something with a mortar and pestle. Today the amfina slept in a basket on the counter next to him, and a boy of eleven stood at the Power-worker's elbow, watching him work.

Florin blinked as her eyes adjusted to the gloom. 'I'm here about—'

'I know why you're here,' he said, and he nudged the boy. 'Go fetch the amfina's food.'

The boy darted through the curtained doorway behind the counter. The Power-worker tipped some fine powder onto the scales and checked the weight before pouring the powder onto a piece of paper, folding it over to form a packet.

'That's the herb for my mistress?' Florin asked.

'It is. You have the gold?'

Florin's hand went to her pocket.

The curtain parted, but the lad did not return. Instead two men-at-arms stepped into the room.

Florin took a step back. One part of her wanted to flee, but she needed the herb. The men-at-arms came around the counter. As she backed up towards the door, two Merofynian lords entered. One was grey-haired and looked like someone's kindly uncle, the other was Neiron.

She turned to run.

'Stop her!' Neiron barked.

The men-at-arms caught her and pinned her arms behind her back.

'This is her?' The softly spoken, grey-haired lord looked Florin up and down.

Neiron's top lip lifted. 'She's not the queen's servant.'

'I still want my gold,' the Power-worker insisted.

The grey-haired lord nodded to his men. One of them drew Florin's arm further up her back until it felt like her shoulder would pop out of its socket. 'Who are you buying bitter-tears for?'

Florin shook her head. The man jerked on her arm, making her gasp.

The kindly-looking lord sighed. 'You're going to tell me, lass, so why not save yourself the pain?'

She turned her face away, only to see Neiron's grin.

The grey-haired lord gestured to him. 'Search her.'

Neiron's hands were far too free. He didn't need to part her shirt to reveal her breast band, didn't need to loosen it and thrust his hands inside to see if she'd hidden anything, not when he'd already taken the golden ornament.

'Just this.' He tossed the amfina statue over.

The grey-haired lord inspected it. 'An expensive little trinket. Not the kind of thing a Rolencian peasant would own. Could you be buying bitter-tears for the queen, after all?' He watched her closely. 'Has she been welcoming the younger brother into her bed, while betrothed to the elder?'

'The little bitch,' Neiron muttered.

As much as she resented the queen, Florin could not let her take the blame.

'It's for me,' she blurted.

'Lies!' Neiron snorted.

She glared at him, torn between outrage and shame.

'How disappointing.' The grey-haired lord stepped back. 'It seems she's telling the truth.' He gestured to the men-at-arms, who let her go.

Neiron turned on his companion. 'You believe her, Yorale?'

'The girl couldn't lie to save herself.' He dropped a small bag of coins on the counter.

'Why are you paying the Power-worker?' Neiron asked. 'His information was useless.'

'This time.'

Florin massaged her shoulder, eyeing Lord Yorale, who still had her ornament.

He noticed the direction of her gaze and tossed the statuette to the Power-worker. 'Give her the bitter-tears.'

'Why?' Neiron demanded. 'If you ask me, any woman who's stupid enough to open her legs deserves what she gets.'

Yorale sighed. 'This sorry excuse for a woman serves on Byren's honour guard. She could be useful, Neiron.'

The Power-worker folded the instructions around the powder packet and gave it to Yorale.

He held it in front of Florin. 'With what I know, I could ruin you, girl. No more honoured place in the king's guard. You'd end up on the street, sucking cock for your supper. But I am not so cruel.' Yorale tucked the herb packet and instructions into Florin's breast band. 'There. Take your bitter-tears and remember what you owe me. Be very sure that one day I will call on this debt. Do you understand?'

She nodded, hating him with all her heart.

Neiron smirked. 'No wonder the baby's father deserted her. He probably woke up, got a good look at her sour puss in the morning light, and cursed himself for a drunken sot.'

The men-at-arms sniggered.

Florin's face burned as they left via the Power-worker's back room.

The baby amfina yawned, stretched then settled itself more comfortably in the basket. The Power-worker sent Florin a contemptuous look.

She hated them all.

Tears of fury stung her eyes as she went down the stairs and picked her way along the alley. Blind with anger, she wasn't prepared when someone grabbed her and swung her up against the wall.

Orrade pressed his forearm to her throat. 'Why, Florin? Why betray us to Neiron?'

'I didn't—'

'Don't deny it. I heard his voice. How could you...'

It was so absurd that she laughed, even as tears poured down her cheeks.

He released her. 'If you didn't betray us, why—'

She shook her head then tried to free herself. Her shirt fell open.

'What's this?' He plucked the herb packet from her breast band.

She tried to retrieve it, but he was too fast. He took in the instructions in a heartbeat.

'You're with child? Whose child?'

She just looked at him.

'But Byren said he didn't—'

'Apparently, he did enough.'

Orrade shook his head.

She held out her hand.

Orrade backed up a step. 'You'd kill Byren's child?'

'What am I supposed to do? I can't provide for my little brother, let alone a baby.'

'You're not using this.' He went to tear open the packet.

She lunged, fighting him for it. They tripped and fell, rolling on the dirty cobblestones. Over and over they went. He was trying not to hurt her. She didn't want to use blinding or crippling blows, so she ended up under him, weeping in frustration, as he sprinkled the powdered herb on the breeze.

'What right do you have to stop me?'

'I'm saving your life. Or didn't the Power-worker tell you this could kill you?'

She flushed. 'Then why do women use it?'

'They're desperate and you're not. If the worst happens, I'll marry you.' He came to his feet and held out his hand.

She ignored it, just as she'd ignored his absurd, insulting claim. Furious, she climbed to her feet. 'You can't tell Byren. Promise me, Orrie.'

He shook his head. 'I'd be lying if I made that promise.'

She glared at him.

With a shrug, he offered his arm.

'I'm pregnant, not an invalid.'

He laughed. 'Byren's a fool. Come on, before the *Wyvern's Whelp* casts off without us.'

FYN WAS GLAD to see the back of Byren and Merofynia was glad to see the back of Byren's army. If Isolt was glad to see the back of Byren she did not admit it.

Together they waved from the docks as the fleet of borrowed merchant ships sailed off across Mero Bay. Then the pair of them climbed into the royal carriage to go back to the palace. Isolt did not speak. She seemed small and sad. Fyn longed to make her smile.

When they reached the stables, he helped her step down from the carriage. 'You're right. I should learn to ride Loyalty.'

This surprised a laugh from her, as he'd hoped it would. She looked up, eyes bright. 'You'd let me teach you.'

He hadn't realised how important it was to her. 'Of course.'

Feeling light of heart, he followed her through the palace courtyards. By the time they reached the crescent of apartments, they were running, and by the time they reached the terrace they were laughing.

Loyalty came flying over the hedge to land on the lawn

beside the fountain. Isolt let go of Fyn's hand and ran down to greet her.

'My poor girl,' Isolt said, reaching up to rub the wyvern's neck. 'You'll miss Resolute.' Isolt turned to Fyn. 'I think the terrace is the best place to start your lessons.'

He gulped.

'You just hunch down low and hold on,' Isolt told him, leading the wyvern up the steps and turning her to face the lawn. 'The trick is to go with Loyalty's movements. Don't fight her.'

'I thought the trick was not to fall off.'

With a laugh, Isolt indicated he was to climb on. As Fyn stepped up to Loyalty, he realised her shoulders were above his head. Isolt spoke soothingly to the Affinity beast while Fyn climbed onto the wyvern's back and wrapped his arms around her neck.

He felt Loyalty's muscles bunch under him, before she leapt upwards with such force he almost lost his grip. Those great, shimmering wings spread out to each side of him and he was flying.

Well, gliding, as Loyalty sailed down from the terrace. Her feet touched down on the lawn and she took several steps before coming to a stop.

A moment later, Isolt caught up with them. 'You did it. And you didn't even fall on landing!'

Because his hands were locked in place. It took a conscious effort to release his grip.

'Doesn't it feel wonderful?' Isolt asked.

And Fyn realised she loved flying.

'There's a headland where I've been practising over the water. That way, if you fall off, you land in the sea. Not that I've fallen,' Isolt told him proudly. 'Come on.'

It was dim and cool under the trees. Birds called above them, crickets chirruped and Fyn immediately felt as if they were in their own little world. He never wanted to go back to the real world. 'Did you bring Byren here?'

'Of course not,' Isolt said. 'Here we are. Loyalty loves

flying from up here. She's better at taking off from a high place.' Isolt steadied the wyvern. 'Up you get, Fyn.'

He glanced down. From the top of the cliff, it was a two-storey drop to the sunlit sparkling sea. He'd never had a problem with heights, but when he climbed, he was in control. While riding the flying wyvern, his life was in the beast's...

'Fyn?'

Despite his churning stomach, he climbed onto the wyvern's back. He did it because he couldn't refuse Isolt.

And because she had not shared this with Byren.

BYREN WAS GLAD to be on his way. They'd made the passage through Mulcibar's Gate on the evening tide, and now they sailed southwest to avoid the dangerous rocks and scattered islands of the spars. He looked behind him at the six merchant ships, packed to the gunnels with men returning home to Rolencia.

'You did a good thing, freeing our people,' Orrade said, joining him.

Byren nodded. 'The merchants weren't too happy about loaning me their ships.'

'They'll make a profit on the return voyage.' Orrade turned to face him. 'Now that you're sailing home with a loyal army, you no longer need Merofynia's support. Frankly, I don't see why you'd want it, not with that pack of nobles looking down their noses at you.'

Byren shrugged. 'I can deal with them. What are you leading up to?'

'Florin.'

Byren's gut clenched, but he summoned a grin. 'When I checked on her, she was already throwing up. She'll never make a sailor.'

'That's not what I'm talking about.'

'I know. I gave my word, Orrie.'

'Queen Isolt's a good woman, but she wouldn't make

you happy. Do you want to wake up next to her for the rest of your life?'

'I can't break my word.'

'Some things are more important.'

'What's more important than honour?'

'You should talk to Florin.'

'In the palace, you advised me to avoid her.'

'I did. But you need to talk to her now.' Orrade's thin face held an intensity Byren could not interpret.

A mixture of concern and curiosity drove Byren to Florin's cabin, where he found her huddled on the bunk, pale and miserable.

She glared. 'Why can't you leave me to die in peace?'

'No one ever died of sea-sickness,' he said, then wondered if that was true.

'More's the pity.'

Byren grinned. He'd missed her. 'Come out on deck. You'll feel better.'

She swung her legs off the bunk and staggered across the cabin.

He took her arm, helping her up to the high reardeck. They stood at the rail, overlooking the middeck. Lanterns illuminated the ship's sails, and behind them, the glowing sails of the merchant ships dotted the sea.

Byren had no idea what to say, so he took a stab in the dark. 'Orrie told me.'

'What?' She was horrified. No, she was mortified, colour raced up her cheeks. 'I specifically asked him not to.'

'He was worried about you.'

'Well, you don't need to worry.' Florin faced Byren, eyes glittering with angry tears. 'I won't make trouble. I'll go away and you'll never see me or the child.'

A roaring filled Byren's head.

'Orrie didn't tell you?' Florin was outraged. She thumped Byren hard enough to hurt. 'How could you trick me like that?'

He caught her wrist before she could hit him again.

'You can't be pregnant. I didn't...' He shuddered, recalling how close he'd come to losing control.

Florin's eyes narrowed. 'Forget I ever told you. Go marry your little queen and be happy playing Duelling Kingdoms. That's not the life for me.'

She walked off, proud and furious. Unfortunately, she had to run to the side to throw up.

Byren shook his head.

Even though he knew she would push him away, he wanted to help her. He waited, but she did not look back as she wiped her mouth and went to her cabin.

He gripped the rail. Florin pregnant. Sylion's Luck. How could she fall pregnant so easily?

'Well?' Orrade prodded.

'She told you rather than me?' Byren was furious.

'I caught her buying bitter-tears to get rid of the baby. I stopped her.'

'You stopped her?'

'It could have killed her. It would have killed your child.' Orrade confronted him. 'If you value our friendship, be careful what you say next.'

'Orrie, you know I can't marry her. I've given my word. What kind of king would I be if I turned my back on my betrothed?'

'What kind of man would you be, if you turned your back on your child?'

Byren felt utterly trapped. He ran his hands through his hair. 'I can't live just for myself. I have responsibilities.'

'So you'll turn your back on Florin?'

'I always meant to rebuild Narrowneck Tradepost for her.' But now...

'So your son will be a tradepost keeper?' Anger made Orrade's voice hard. 'With Florin for his mother, he'll be a big strapping lad. He should do well serving ale.'

With that, Orrade walked off, leaving Byren to wrestle with an impossible choice. If he broke off his betrothal to the queen of Merofynia to marry a destitute mountain girl, Isolt would be a laughing stock. But if he married Isolt, he had no right to Florin or their child. Was there ever a more miserable man?

From the hold below, he heard the foenix's mournful cry. It seemed to echo how he felt.

Chapter Sixty-Three

FYN WAITED FOR Isolt. His whole body ached from the flying lessons of the day before. He'd been tense at first, but by the end he and Isolt had been taking turns with Loyalty. They'd even joked about finding a new wyvern mount for him to ride.

Breakfast was Fyn's favourite time of day, even more so now that everyone else had left and he and Isolt could be alone on the terrace overlooking the Landlocked Sea. Alone, except for the servants.

Fyn watched the lords' yachts moored on the Landlocked Sea, while he waited for Isolt. Some of the nobles had left late yesterday. Others were conducting business and would leave over the next few days.

He glanced up to the queen's private chambers. Her curtains were still drawn. His stomach cramped with fear. It wasn't like Isolt to sleep in. He strode inside, fighting the urge to run.

A servant answered her door. 'The queen still sleeps.'

'Go wake her.'

As the girl hurried off, Fyn told himself he was worrying for nothing. Isolt would join him on the terrace. They would laugh about his fears, then go see Loyalty again.

The maid shrieked. Fyn ran across the greeting chamber and into Isolt's bedchamber.

The maid came out of the bathing chamber. 'She's not here.'

'Look for a note. Maybe she got up early and went for a walk.'

The girl did as she was bid.

But Fyn feared the worst. He went to the window to check on the nobles' yachts. Neiron's yacht had left overnight. Cold fear closed around Fyn's heart.

Neiron had kidnapped Isolt.

It infuriated Fyn to think that the arrogant lord had waited until Byren sailed. Clearly he feared Fyn's brother, but felt only contempt for Fyn.

'There's no note,' the girl reported. 'She's been taken!'

'Quiet, I must think.' Fyn's mind raced. If the merchants and nobles knew the queen had been abducted, there would be chaos. 'We'll say that she needs to rest. Let no one in.'

'But—'

'Everything must appear normal. You understand?'

The maid nodded.

'I'll be looking for her.' And he knew just where to look. Fyn only hoped he was in time. 'Send for the steward and Gwalt.'

As soon as she had gone, Fyn went to Isolt's bed. He stretched out where the queen had lain and pressed his face to the pillow, inhaling her scent. For a heartbeat she was so real to him that he felt as if he could reach out and touch her. Then he had to exhale and, as the air left his chest, a deep sense of loss filled him.

He was Isolt's lord protector. He'd die for her, yet he'd failed her.

By the time the palace steward arrived, Fyn was waiting in the greeting chamber. As Fyn explained that the queen was over-tired and the servants were to let her rest, the steward was visibly relieved. With all the noble guests and festivities, the palace had been in upheaval for days.

Fyn met Gwalt at the door, where a whispered word ensured a message would soon be winging its way to the mage.

But Fyn wasn't going to wait for Siordun's help. He sent a servant to fetch Camoric. The *Flying Sarre* was one of the fastest yachts ever built. When he caught Neiron, there would be blood.

Down on the terrace, he made himself sit at the breakfast table and eat. He speared a piece of honeydew melon on his knife and chewed it mechanically.

All he could think of was Isolt in Neiron's hands.

'Fyn,' Camoric said, dropping into the chair opposite. His eyes narrowed. 'What's wrong?'

'Have something to eat. Don't react to what I'm about to say.' Fyn waited until Camoric had filled his plate. 'The queen was kidnapped last night.'

A mandarin burst in Camoric's hand. 'I failed you. I had men posted outside her chamber, but—'

'I'm not blaming you. Short of sleeping at the foot of her bed, you could not have prevented this. She was taken by someone who knew the palace. Her maid did not hear a thing.'

'Neiron?'

'That's my guess.'

Camoric glanced to the yachts moored just off from the palace. 'He must have sailed in the night. We can beat him back to his estate. When I think of the queen, all alone and frightened—'

'That's it!' Fyn sprang to his feet, relieved. 'Loyalty will be able to find her. They've bonded.'

The captain frowned. 'If the wyvern can sense Isolt, why didn't she come to the queen's rescue?'

'Maybe they drugged Isolt to get her out of the palace.' But now Fyn was worried. 'What if they've killed Loyalty?'

Camoric shook his head. 'The wyvern is always with the foenix. They'd have to kill both beasts.'

'We sent Resolute with Byren, remember.' Fyn sprang to his feet. 'I'm going to the grotto.'

To Fyn's relief they found Loyalty sleeping under the grotto's light-filled dome. The wyvern was glad to see Fyn.

'She doesn't look worried,' Camoric muttered.

'If Isolt is drugged, Loyalty wouldn't sense that she's in trouble.'

'Then how will you tell the wyvern to look for the queen?'

It was a good question.

Fyn reached up to place his palm on Loyalty's throat, then called his Affinity. It flowed easily up his arm, making the stone on his ring glow. Camoric gasped.

In response to the power, Loyalty made a deep purring noise of pleasure. Concentrating, Fyn recalled the moment he'd lain on Isolt's bed and inhaled her scent. The terrible sense of loss returned to him and he felt it mirrored in the beast. Loyalty uttered a heartfelt howl and leapt into the pool, swimming out of the grotto.

'Quick, we'll lose her,' Fyn said.

He emerged in time to see the wyvern spring from the pond, shake herself and flex her wings.

'Loyalty,' he commanded and called his Affinity again. The ring glowed less brightly than before, but the wyvern came to him and let him place his palm on her neck. He visualised the *Flying Sarre* and looked into the beast's eyes. She understood. Even so... 'Better bring some fresh meat from the kitchen, Cam. We don't want her getting hungry.'

Camoric went to see the cook and Fyn made for the jetty, where he found Yorale overseeing the refit of his yacht.

'I hear the queen is not well.' Yorale glanced to Loyalty. Her tail lashed back and forth. 'What's wrong?'

'Neiron has abducted Isolt.'

'What?' Yorale went pale with shock. 'He can't have. That's impossible. Are you sure?'

'The queen is missing and Neiron sailed overnight.' Fyn saw Camoric with two kitchen staff, bringing the raw meat. 'We're going after him now.'

Yorale fell into step with them as they strode up the jetty. 'You think the Affinity beast can find her?'

'They've bonded,' Fyn said.

Yorale was out of breath by the time they reached the gangplank. 'I'd offer to help, but my yacht's undergoing a refit.'

Fyn took his arm. 'Thank you for your support and guidance.'

'Good luck, lad.' Yorale put his hand on Fyn's shoulder. 'When I think of her in Neiron's—'

'Don't worry. I'll bring her home safe,' Fyn said, as he ran up the gangplank.

PIRO STEPPED ONTO the busy Ostron Isle wharf, fanning herself. Soterro stood nearby, waiting for his bags, and from his expression, it was clear he was glad to be home. It was strange, even back when she was Dunstany's slave and Soterro was mean to her, she had never doubted his loyalty.

Piro leant close to Siordun. 'The mage needs someone on Ostron Isle he can trust to cover for him.' Since the day Florin had almost uncovered the truth, they had been referring to the mage as a separate person. 'Soterro—'

'As it turns out, the mage has come to the same conclusion.' Siordun gave her a dry look.

'Won't Soterro be surprised?' She grinned. 'I'll see you at Cinnamome Palace.'

'Don't approach Varuska without me.'

Piro nodded and they parted.

She'd had every intention of keeping her word but, as luck would have it, when she was escorted into a private greeting chamber, she heard singing in the dining chamber next door. She peered in to find her look-alike sitting in a patch of late afternoon sunlight, polishing the silverware.

Piro studied Varuska as she held up a fork to admire her work. The resemblance was uncanny.

'Why do they have you polishing silver?' Piro asked.

Varuska dropped the fork. 'You gave me such a turn...' Her eyes widened as she recognised Piro. 'Kingsdaughter!' She sprang to her feet and bobbed her head, wiping her palms on her apron.

'No need for formalities,' Piro said. 'After all, you were almost married in my place.'

She strolled over to where Varuska stood and studied her frankly. The girl returned her scrutiny, head tilted. The mannerism gave Piro a little jolt of recognition.

Varuska frowned. 'I didn't impersonate you by choice.'

'I know. Florin told me.'

'Is she all right?'

Piro nodded. 'She's sailing for Rolencia with Byren.'

'I'm glad. She kept me safe, and your brother saved my life.' Tears glittered in her eyes. 'I wish there was something I could do to repay him.'

'Actually, there is. I need you to come with me to confront Cobalt.'

'Anything but that.' Varuska backed up a step. 'I can't stand Cobalt. He makes my skin crawl. There's something missing in him.' She pressed one hand to her chest. 'Please don't ask this of me.'

'You'll be perfectly safe. The mage's agent will be with us, and we'll be under the abbess's protection.'

'I can't do it. I still have nightmares!'

Piro caught her hand. 'You have to help.'

With a cry, Varuska twisted free and ran from the room, weeping. She left by one door as Nefysto entered by another.

He cursed. 'What did you do to upset Ruska, Piro?'

'I just asked her to help Byren.'

'By going back to Rolencia and confronting Cobalt?'

She nodded.

He swore, sounding more like Nefysto the sea-hound captain than Natteo the poet. 'She's not strong like you. She needs protecting.' And he strode out muttering, 'As if I haven't got enough on my plate with Kaspian, now this...'

Piro chewed her lip.

A maid peeped in. 'Have you finished the silver, Var—' She gasped and bobbed her head. 'Begging your pardon, kingsdaughter. I was looking for—'

'I know who you were looking for. I'm looking for Kaspian.'

'He lives in the dome tower now, but he won't see you. Since the comtissa died, he keeps to himself.'

'He'll see me,' Piro said. From the sounds of things, Kaspian needed to snap out of his self-pity and help Nefysto. Maybe she could make up for upsetting Varuska.

Piro crossed the courtyard and ran up the tower stairs. She hesitated at the top. A faint breeze came through the gap under the door, bringing with it the scent of an Affinity predator. Her heart raced and her skin prickled with fear. Strange, she was comfortable with Loyalty, why should she be...

The door swung open and Kaspian pulled her into the chamber.

'Who's spying—' He frowned. 'Piro?'

He'd changed. She'd left a beautiful youth of sixteen. Now he was a man, taller, thinner and hard muscled. There were dark circles under his eyes.

'Are you ill?' Piro asked.

'No, I...' He stepped aside and she saw the chamber. There was no bed, only a littered desk over to one side and the wyvern, curled up on a carpet in the centre of the large chamber under the dome.

'Valiant's gotten so big,' Piro marvelled. 'Is he full grown now?'

'He could be.'

She gestured to the balcony. 'How does he get through the doors?'

Kaspian laughed.

'What?'

'Everyone else is terrified of him, but you ask me how he gets through the doors. They fold right back.'

The wyvern stirred and lifted his head. He reared up on his hind legs and extended his wings in display. The tips reached all the way to the underside of the golden dome.

Piro gasped. 'He's beautiful!'

He was, but in the way that a predator is beautiful. When the wyvern dropped to all fours and prowled across to inspect her, Piro couldn't repress a shiver of awe. As the beast drew nearer, she felt her Affinity respond. Siordun was right. Her power was naturally drawn towards Affinity beasts.

The sensation of gathering power was stronger than ever, making her hands and fingers throb. Eagerly, the wyvern rubbed his throat on her.

Kaspian frowned. 'Why—'

'It's my Affinity.' She couldn't be sure, but she thought Kaspian's Affinity was stronger. And now that she was actually touching the wyvern, she understood why she'd found Valiant's scent unnerving. 'He's male. I think he can sense Isolt's wyvern on me. I played with Loyalty before we sailed. Of course, I've bathed since, but an animal's sense of smell is so much stronger than ours.'

'Why are you here, Piro?'

She smiled as she petted the wyvern. 'What? Oh, I'm running an errand for Byren.' This reminded her. 'I should go. I may have put my foot in it. And you should come down to dinner.'

Fyn handed Camoric the farseer. The wyvern had started flying north, but was now veering steadily northeast. 'Neiron's not heading for Nevantir Estate. He's trying to outfox us. From his bearing, which estate do you think he's making for?'

'Could be any estate between Istyntir and Travantir.'

'Elcwyff!' Fyn cursed. 'That lord's been looking for a way to make me pay since his brother died. I bet he's aiding Neiron.'

Camoric lowered the farseer. 'There's another wyvern headed this way. Can't tell if it's freshwater or saltwater.'

'Is it likely to attack Loyalty?'

'They can be very territorial.'

Fyn cursed again. If a fight broke out far above, he could do nothing but watch. He shaded his eyes. 'Is Loyalty coming back?'

Camoric checked. 'Yes. And the wild one's following.'

Fyn made sure there was water and food ready for Loyalty when she landed. The other wyvern circled, coming ever closer. Loyalty lifted her head and eyed it, tail lashing.

'The wild wyvern's making her restless,' Fyn muttered.

'It's a young saltwater male,' Camoric said. 'Might have been blown inland during a storm. Happens sometimes. They see the freshwater wyverns and think they're home.'

'Should we send archers up the masts?'

An unfamiliar cry came from the male wyvern. It made Camoric laugh, and Fyn looked to him in confusion.

'That's their mating cry. The male doesn't want to fight Loyalty. He wants to mate with her.'

Fyn cursed. 'What if he draws her off?'

'We have to hope Loyalty's bond with Isolt is stronger.'

'Than the urge to mate?'

The male called again and Loyalty answered, taking to the air.

Camoric glanced to Fyn.

'We follow Loyalty, for now,' Fyn said. 'If she heads for a wyvern eyrie, we make directly for Elenstir Estate.'

'There's an eyrie not far from Travantir Estate.' Camoric shaded his eyes. 'I think she's flying west towards it. Should we...'

Fyn's stomach churned as he debated. In that moment of communion, he'd felt the force of the beast's bond with Isolt. But what if the mating urge was stronger?

'Fyn?'

'We follow Loyalty.'

Ever since Byren had learned that Florin was carrying his child, he had been trying to decide what he should do. He was reminded of the old seer who had told him that discerning right from wrong was not always easy. Back then he had scoffed. But now, no matter what he decided, he'd do wrong by someone.

It was late afternoon, and he was no closer to finding a solution. Florin should not have to face an uncertain future alone. He could set her up with a farm in the foothills of the mountains, but that meant he would never see his child. And a wealthy woman alone would attract suitors—the kind of men Byren did not want his child having for a father.

But having seen the consequences of war with Merofynia, he could not insult the queen and undo all the work they'd done to establish the peace. It was an impossible dilemma.

If only he could split himself in two... He'd had a twin, but Lence hadn't been the kind of man Byren would entrust his wife and child to. Orrade was more like a brother to him.

Even as Byren thought this, he saw Orrade help Florin out onto the deck. She was pale and shaky but somehow, Orrade made her smile

And Byren had his answer. He went over to the captain of the *Wyvern's Whelp*. 'You can officiate a marriage contract, right?'

'I've never done it,' Bantam admitted. 'But yes, it is something a captain can do.'

Byren caught Orrade's eye and beckoned.

As Orrade settled Florin in a sheltered spot in the sun, Byren marshalled his arguments, striving for eloquence. Yet the moment Orrade approached him, the words tumbled from his lips. 'I can't throw our two kingdoms into chaos. I can't marry Florin. But you can.'

Orrade took a step back.

'Look after her for me, Orrie. Be a father to my child, because I can't.'

'Make your child the heir to Dovecote Estate?'

Byren shrugged. 'You were never going to take a wife.'

'I didn't say that.'

'No, you didn't,' Byren admitted. 'But... Orrie, I'm desperate. I can't—'

'I'll do it.'

'What?'

Orrade laughed, then sobered quickly. 'I said I'd do it.'

'Why?'

'Why do you think?' Orrade met his eyes, angry yet vulnerable.

Byren had to look away. He cleared his throat. 'I've gone about this all wrong. If I lay dying on the battlefield, I'd entrust my wife and child to your care and die happy, knowing they were safe. If our positions were reversed, I'd do the same for you.'

'I know.' Orrade swallowed. 'I won't let you down.'

Byren nodded. 'I know.'

Neither of them spoke.

Then Byren grimaced. 'I should tell Florin.'

'No, you shouldn't. I'll do the asking. She may very well say no. She's proud.'

'She is,' he agreed. 'But she's also desperate.'

'Byren...' Orrade shook his head, ruefully. 'Just as well I'm doing the talking. You'd put her back up for sure.'

Florin didn't like the way the ship shuddered as the prow cut into each wave. The nausea, which had faded on land, had come back as soon as she set foot on the *Wyvern's Whelp*. She'd only ventured out on deck at Orrade's insistence and, when Byren beckoned him, she'd returned to her cabin and climbed onto her bunk.

It seemed like only a moment later there was a knock at her door. She looked up hopefully, but it was Orrade. She hid her disappointment behind a jest. 'I vowed I'd never set foot on a ship again. I should have taken the pass over the Snow Bridge.'

'You would have been just as sick.' Orrade took the chair, turning it back-to-front. He sat astride it, resting his elbows on the backrest, then hesitated.

'Out with it, Orrie. I can take it.'

He grinned briefly. 'How would you like to be the lady of Dovecote Estate?'

Florin laughed until she cried. Then she wiped her eyes. 'So the worst happened?'

Orrade blushed. 'I—'

'Forget it. Look, I normally wouldn't say this, but Byren did manage to burn my home by staging a battle on Narrowneck, twice. If he rebuilds the tradepost, I'll manage fine. Leif will be big enough to do a man's work in a couple of years.'

'You'd be a woman alone with a boy and a baby. A tradepost attracts all manner of men. You owe your child the best possible start in life. Dovecote Estate would provide that.' His lips rose in a half-smile. 'Leif would be ecstatic.'

She laughed. It was true, and that reminded her... 'I could go to Foenix Spar. Lady Cinna would take me in.'

'You could,' Orrade conceded. 'But Byren has many enemies. If his bastard son grew up on a spar, someone like Cobalt could come along and plant ideas in the lad's head about reclaiming his throne from King Byren, who abandoned him and his mother. If the boy grew up on Dovecote Estate, he'd grow up as part of Byren's extended family, and his loyalty would be assured.'

Florin picked at the frayed edge of her blanket. What Orrade said made sense, but it meant she would also be part of Byren's extended family, and have to watch him with his Merofynian wife.

'There's a hundred reasons why this is a good idea, but there's one more,' Orrade said. 'There are rumours about me, and they implicate Byren. I need a wife and heir. You would be protecting us.'

Not only would she protect Byren, but she'd remain in his life. 'I'll do it.'

Orrade rose, put the chair aside and offered his hand.

'Now?'

He pulled her to her feet. 'We're going into battle. If I die, you'll inherit Dovecote.'

'Oh, Orrie.' Tears stung her eyes.

He kissed her forehead. 'My fierce mountain girl.'

She gave him a playful shove. 'Let me get cleaned up.'

She washed her face and considered putting on her one dress, then decided against it. She was who she was.

So, on the deck of a ship heading into battle, she married the wrong man, but she married him for all the right reasons.

Chapter Sixty-Four

PIRO COULDN'T FIGURE out where Varuska fitted into the Cinnamome household. She polished silverware, yet she sat down to dinner with the family, and Nefysto went to great pains to entertain her. In the privacy of his own home, he did not bother to maintain the disguise of Natteo, the finicky poet and arbiter of fashion. In fact, he'd just told a story about Fyn and the Skirling Stones.

Varuska hung on every word. 'Do you miss your life on the *Wyvern's Whelp*?'

'I do. But I'm happy to help Kaspian, if only he'd—' He broke off as the servants entered with the evening meal.

Piro glanced to the empty seat at the head of the table. 'Speaking of Kaspian, aren't we waiting for him?'

Nefysto approved the wine and accepted the first course. 'My cousin takes his meals in his chamber.'

It seemed she'd failed to lure the young man out. She held her tongue until the servants retreated. 'I understand Kaspian is grieving, but Cinnamome House needs a strong leader. Not that you wouldn't lead them well,' she assured Nefysto. 'But if Kaspian isn't seen at public events, people will begin to talk. He needs to do his duty.'

'I've stood at his door and pleaded with him to come out, but...' Nefysto shrugged. 'He hasn't let anyone in since he retreated to the tower. All he ever does is leave messages with his food tray, asking for more manuscripts.'

Piro looked down. Kaspian had let her in. She would go to him again.

FYN WATCHED LOYALTY circle the ship. She was a dark silhouette against the stars, followed by the wild male wyvern.

Camoric pointed to a dark shape on the silver sea. 'If they fly to that island, they're going to the eyrie, if not, Loyalty is leading us to Isolt.'

Fyn gripped the rail, praying that he'd been right to trust the beast.

The male wyvern circled the island, calling to Loyalty. She flew on.

Camoric clasped Fyn's shoulder, and they both grinned with relief.

The male wyvern gave another cry and followed Loyalty.

'He's determined,' Camoric said.

'Not as determined as me,' Fyn muttered.

Camoric glanced to him. 'I didn't expect Travany to betray you.'

'After I broke his nose?' Fyn flexed his hand. His knuckles had been bruised for a week.

'True,' Camoric conceded. We can moor—'

'Once the alarm is raised, Neiron will spirit Isolt away,' Fyn said. 'No, I'm going in with Loyalty.'

'At least take half a dozen men.'

'Loyalty can only carry me.'

Camoric's mouth dropped.

Fyn grinned. 'Loyalty will fly Isolt back to you.'

'And what will you do?'

'Trust to luck.'

'Fyn...'

'You are the captain of the queen's guard. She is your top priority, just as she is mine.'

Fyn lifted his ring hand and called on his Affinity to make the stone glow. Loyalty circled, then landed. As the wild wyvern gave his mating cry, the bonded wyvern shivered and looked up.

Stroking Loyalty's neck, Fyn climbed onto the beast's back. She took a run and leapt over the side of the yacht. They circled the vessel as her broad wings worked to gain height.

Camoric's crew stared up at him.

Fyn waved, but he did not feel as confident as he appeared riding the wyvern. He could only hope Loyalty would listen to him when they approached the house. If she stormed in, she'd get them both killed.

'So if you would just come down from this tower, Kaspian, eat at the dinner table, attend family functions and take charge of the Cinnamome House's business dealings...' Piro ran down. The more she said, the less she could blame Kaspian for avoiding his responsibilities.

She wished he would light a lamp. It was hard to read his expression when the only illumination was starlight. Kaspian stood over by the folding doors, arms folded across his bare chest. Beyond him, she saw the towers and spires of Ostron Isle's princely merchant families. There was no sign of the wyvern, but the beast's Affinity permeated the chamber. It made her own power rise in response. Kaspian shifted, straightening a little. His dark hair was loose on his shoulders, and his feet were bare. He hadn't spoken, yet he had let her in.

So she persevered. 'Where's Valiant?'

Kaspian turned his face to the sky, closed his eyes and inhaled as if he was testing the air. When his eyes opened, the look he sent her was not human. 'Hunting.'

Piro shivered. A breeze stirred the papers on Kaspian's desk. She went over to the manuscripts and adjusted a paperweight. 'What are you working on, anyway?'

'Collating sagas that tell of Affinity beast bondings.'

It was such a sensible answer that Piro felt relieved.

'Why are you here?' Kaspian was right behind her.

Piro repressed a gasp. She turned and found him too close.

'Why are you here with your sweet Affinity?' Kaspian took both her hands in his and lifted them to his face, rubbing them on his throat like an Affinity beast.

Naturally, her Affinity responded. She had to fight to rein it in.

He released her and leant in, placing his hands to each side of her on the desk. Pressing his face to her neck, he whispered, 'Hmm, you smell so sweet.'

She felt the heat of his skin and the flick of his tongue.

'Taste good, too.'

'Kaspian.' Piro made her voice firm. 'People don't go around sniffing and licking other people.' No, but Affinity beasts did. And she'd made sure that Kaspian's bond with Valiant went deep.

A gasp escaped her as Kaspian took her waist in his hands. Lifting her onto the desk, he stepped between her knees.

He caught her hands, pressing them to the bare skin of his chest. 'Do it again.'

She knew what he wanted and her Affinity responded before she could stop it.

A ragged gasp escaped him, and he came in for a kiss. She heard the call of the male wyvern and knew if Valiant reached the balcony, she would not escape.

She scooted backwards across the desk, sending manuscripts and books skidding. A whole sheaf of loose papers fell off the far end of the desk and scattered across the floor towards the balcony. 'Oh, look what you've made me do!'

Kaspian stepped back to survey the mess. The wyvern landed, his eyes glowing with a feral radiance as the down-draft of his wings sent the papers swirling.

'Quick, Kaspian, grab your manuscripts before they blow away.'

The moment he went to retrieve the papers, she slid off the desk and ran for the door. Looking back, she saw the wyvern watching her, the feral shimmer filling Kaspian's eyes.

Heart racing, Piro swung the door shut and ran down the tower steps. She had to tell Siordun.

But what was the point? He couldn't undo what she'd done. She'd been determined to make sure it was a strong, deep bond and she'd done the same for Isolt and Loyalty.

Piro hurried from the tower and stood gasping in the courtyard. What had she done?

The beat of the wyvern's great wings reached her. A moment later Valiant circled the tower and landed on the ridge of the nearest roof. Kaspian sat astride the beast, looking down at Piro over his mount's shoulder, their expressions identical.

Piro remained absolutely still, heart hammering in her throat.

The wyvern swooped down into the courtyard, landing neatly, as his wings folded along his back.

Nefysto stepped out of the shadows, sword drawn. 'Back into the building, Piro.'

He was prepared to kill his cousin to protect her. Her heart went out to him, to them both.

The wyvern lunged.

'Run, Piro!'

She ran. Behind her, she heard the wyvern yelp, then roar. She watched the confrontation from the shadows as Nefysto stared down the wyvern and rider.

A heartbeat later, Kaspian and Valiant took off.

Nefysto shuddered and dropped to his knees. Piro darted out into the courtyard and helped him inside.

'He's become one with the beast.' Nefysto sank into a chair. 'I suspected, but...'

Piro dropped to her knees in front of him. 'It's my fault. I helped them bond. You have to believe me, I was only trying to help. I had no idea.'

Nefysto's expression was bleak. 'Now you know why I can't go back to sea. Kaspian needs me more than ever. House Cinnamome needs me.'

Chastened, she buried her head in his lap. 'I'm sorry. So very sorry.'

'Ahh, Piro.' He stroked her hair. 'I've learnt death is sometimes the kindest way to lose someone.'

FYN HAD BEEN worried the starlight would give him away, but by the time he neared the great house, the clouds had rolled in, blanketing the ground in deepest night. It was just as well he was familiar with Travantir Estate.

He'd half expected to find they'd locked Isolt in Travany's new tower, and had initially planned to land atop it, but Loyalty led him unerringly towards the great house. He was lucky the wyvern hadn't given voice in challenge. Perhaps this was because the male wyvern still circled far above.

As they approached, Fyn wondered where to look for Isolt, but Loyalty landed on a third floor balcony rail. He slid off her back, then went to the doors, only to discover the glass panels had been replaced by wooden ones and the doors were bolted shut. He slid his knife into the gap, working it up and down until he felt an obstruction, trying to lift the catch.

'A moment,' a muffled voice said. The doors opened and Mitrovan greeted him. 'Fyn. Isolt said it would be you and Loyalty. I'm sorry I didn't warn you about the abduction. The first I knew of it was when Neiron turned up on Travany's yacht with the queen.'

Isolt appeared. She wore nothing but a rumpled

nightrobe. With a happy cry, she darted past Mitrovan and threw her arms around Fyn.

He hugged her. It seemed the most natural thing in the world. 'Did Neiron lay a hand on you?'

'No. He drugged me.' She gave an odd laugh. 'It made me throw up. So I pretended to be sick and that put him off.'

'I've been nursing her,' Mitrovan said. 'Every time Neiron checks, I tell him she's still sick.'

Fyn laughed. 'Thank you!' He'd never been more grateful in his life. He drew Isolt towards the balcony rail where the wyvern waited. 'Climb onto Loyalty's back. She'll take you—'

'What about you?'

'Don't worry about me.'

'Fyn...'

He lifted her, still protesting, onto the balcony rail. No sooner was Isolt in position than the wyvern took off, climbing into the sky.

'I'd read of such things in the old sagas,' Mitrovan murmured, 'but never thought...' He shook his head in wonder then turned to Fyn. 'You'll have to hit me.'

'What?'

'Make it look like I've been overpowered. Better yet, stab me where it won't kill me. It has to look real.'

Fyn hesitated.

'Do it,' the scribe urged. 'I'm no use to you if—'

Fyn punched him and the scribe dropped like a sack of grain.

After dragging him inside, Fyn tossed a few things about, and went to tear the bolt off the balcony doors so that it would appear as if someone had forced them from the outside.

'I'm not waiting any longer, Mitrovan,' Neiron announced as he entered. Seeing Fyn, his eyes widened and hatred twisted his features. 'You!'

Before Neiron could alert Travany's men, Fyn reached for his sword.

Having come to rape a maid, not fight a battle, Neiron was armed with only his knife. He launched himself across the chamber, tackling Fyn, and they went down heavily. Fyn felt his sword fly from his hand. Neiron's weight drove the air from his chest.

With the lord pinning him, Fyn couldn't reach his knife. Neiron's hands closed on his throat and he fought to drag in a breath.

'I should have done this the first time I saw you,' Neiron growled. 'Would have saved Elrhodoc's life. Saved so much trouble!'

Neiron's thumbs pressed into Fyn's windpipe, and stars pin-wheeled in his vision.

And Fyn's Halcyon training took over. He grabbed both thumbs, bending them back with such force he dislocated one. Neiron reared up in pain. Fyn bucked, throwing him sideways.

Neiron sprawled on the carpet in front of the hearth. Fyn sprang to his feet, eager to escape, but Neiron kicked his legs out from under him. They rolled over and over, wrestling.

Fyn caught Neiron's arm, bending it backward until he felt the elbow dislocate. Neiron screamed.

Someone grabbed Fyn by his shirt and hauled him upright, twisting his arm up behind his back as they swung around to face Travany and two men-at-arms.

'Are you all right, Neiron?' Travany asked.

'He broke my arm. What do you think?' Neiron snarled and rolled to his feet, nursing his injured limb. 'Mulcibar's balls. I'll geld him for this. Hold him and strip him!'

Panic seized Fyn.

Loyalty screeched as she landed on the balcony.

Everyone jumped. Fyn used his captor's momentary distraction to slip free. He would have run for the wyvern and leapt onto her back, but someone tackled him.

Loyalty uttered a piercing scream and charged into the chamber. The men scattered as Fyn wrestled with his attacker. This time he went for a choke hold and held on until he felt the man's body go loose.

Fyn scrambled to his feet in time to see Travany backing away towards the door behind one of his men-at-arms. The wyvern reared up, wings rising, tail lashing.

Something moved in the corner of Fyn's vision, and he ducked as Neiron tried to decapitate him. Fyn threw himself backwards, fell over the unconscious man and sprawled on his back. Neiron came in for the kill.

Loyalty lashed out with her tail, spun Neiron around and slashed him from shoulder to groin.

He dropped the sword and grabbed his belly. 'Travany...'

His lordship ran. Neiron dropped to his knees and pitched sideways.

Stunned, Fyn stared as the wyvern dipped her head to Neiron's stomach wound. The lord screamed as the Affinity beast tore his organs from him.

Fyn froze in horror and backed away, scrambling to his feet.

In the corner of his vision, he saw the wild male wyvern land on the balcony rail. The beast's call filled the room, pounding on Fyn's ears.

Loyalty lifted her head then made for the balcony. Fyn just had time to leap onto her back as she ran past. A pounding filled his head as Loyalty leaped onto the rail and into the air, climbing into the sky with the male wyvern at her side.

Fyn dared one glance behind him, saw angry men rush onto the balcony. Cursing and waving their swords, they were all bravado now that there was no chance of engaging with the Affinity beasts.

Loyalty and the wild wyvern circled, climbing higher in a great arc before heading out over the bay. Fyn spotted the dull glow of Camoric's shielded lanterns. His vessel lay in a secluded inlet, but Loyalty kept going.

The rush of cold air seared Fyn's face, making his eyes

water. If he fell now, there would be no hope for him. He hunched down low and held on.

Before long, he felt Loyalty spiral down, lower and lower, not that he could see a thing. The wild wyvern uttered his mating cry and this time, Loyalty's response was an answering cry.

Without warning, she tilted her body and gave a shake. Fyn lost his grip, falling into space. He was going to die...

A heartbeat later, he hit grass and rolled down a slope, grunting with the impact. He lay sprawled on his back gasping, with no idea where he was.

'Fyn?' Isolt's questing hand landed on his thigh. 'Fyn, are you hurt?'

'No. Are you?' He sat up, pulling her close.

'Oh, Fyn...' She wept and cried with joy. 'I thought I'd lost you.' She kissed his nose and cheek before she found his lips. It was a desperate, hungry kiss.

An impossible joy coursed through him. Light-headed with relief, he broke the kiss to confess, 'I love you. I've always loved you. When I saw you in the Fate—'

'What fate?'

'Halcyon's Fate. I had a vision of you. But I didn't dare hope you felt—'

She silenced him with another kiss and her body told him what he needed to know. Her determined hands found their way inside his clothes. He'd had no idea skin could be so sensitive.

There was a point when he could have stopped, but she pulled him down to meet her. And then...

He thought he was the luckiest man alive.

Chapter Sixty-Five

Byren braced his legs as the deck dipped and rose. He had not been able to sleep, knowing that Orrade shared Florin's cabin. The fact that she was sea-sick made no difference. It should have been him looking after her.

Lantern light gleamed on the captain's rain-wet cheeks and sealskin vest as he studied the southern sky. Brooding clouds filled the horizon, illuminated from within by bolts of lightning. There would be no true dawn today.

Bantam closed the farseer and raised his voice, yelling over the driving wind and rain. The big boatswain bellowed, the sailors trimmed the sails by half and the ship groaned as the helmsman changed course.

Byren stepped close to the captain, but even so, he had to shout. 'We're turning back?'

'I'm not risking my ship in those seas. I've signalled the other captains. We'll make for Snow Bridge Bay.'

Byren cursed. It was just as well he had left with time to spare. In the face of the coming storm, all he could do was hold on as they made for safe harbour and pray the other captains also made it.

FYN WOKE WITH a shiver. He was covered in dew. From the distant wyvern cries, he guessed they were on same island as the eyrie. The sky had an odd grey tone, as if it was dawn, but heavy cloud prevented the sun from piercing the gloom. Isolt slept naked in his arms. She shivered in her sleep.

He rubbed her back, running his hand along the sweet curve of her hip and thigh, and suddenly he wasn't cold any more. She stirred, opening her eyes. He saw memory return to her and her cheeks coloured.

Fyn kissed both pink cheeks. Their eyes met and he felt the heat of desire flare between them. Pulling her close, he marvelled that he could do this.

Her stomach rumbled and he recalled that she hadn't eaten since the day before yesterday. 'You must be starving.'

He found his shirt and draped it around her shoulders. They had spent the night in a hollow, in a field of tussocky grass. A seagull called and he followed it up the rise to find the land fell away to a small rocky beach. He stepped behind a bush to relieve himself.

A moment later Camoric's yacht come around the headland. Fyn waved. He saw the captain lower his farseer and laugh. Reminded that he was naked, Fyn hurried down the slope into the hollow, where he gathered his clothes. The sight of Isolt standing there in nothing but his shirt, her hair all atumble, robbed him of thought.

She laughed and held out her hand. 'My nightrobe?'

He passed it to her. 'Camoric is here.' As he spoke, he pulled on his breeches, had to tuck himself to one side to get the laces done up. He looked up and caught her watching, fascinated.

They both smiled and he felt the powerful pull of desire. He caught himself wishing Camoric had not found them.

Then Isolt's stomach rumbled again. He buckled his knife belt and tugged on his boots. When he looked up, Isolt was dressed in her thin nightgown. She offered him his shirt.

'You wear it.' He lifted her hair and draped his shirt around her shoulders. Then he just had to kiss the back of her neck. She relaxed against him and his arms slid around her. 'I never want to let you go.'

She went very still. 'Then don't.'

His arms tightened. Voices reached them from the beach and he stepped back. 'Ready?'

She nodded. Taking her hand, he knew what he was about to do would change everything, but he didn't see how it could be any other way.

They reached the crest, to find a rowboat on the beach.

'Over here,' Camoric called.

Fyn helped Isolt down to the beach, then jumped onto the sand beside her.

The captain joined them. 'I thought the plan was to come back to the yacht.'

'The plans have changed,' Fyn said, meeting Isolt's eyes; hers brimmed with laughter. There was no going back. 'As ship's captain you can marry us.'

'I can, but... are you sure?'

Fyn reached out to Isolt.

She took his hand. 'I was never more sure of anything in my life.'

Camoric laughed, then rubbed his scarred jaw. 'What of Byren?'

'Merofynia cannot have an absentee king,' Isolt said. 'I've made my choice.'

'Besides, how many kingdoms does one man need?' Fyn asked, then changed the subject. 'How did you find us?'

'I thought Loyalty and her mate might have come to the wyvern eyrie, and here you are!' Camoric said. 'But we haven't seen Loyalty.'

'I hope she's all right,' Fyn said. 'We...'

Isolt's lips parted in a secretive half smile. 'Loyalty's fine.'

Of course... They shared the bond and both had taken a mate last night. The ramifications should have shocked him, but Fyn found he didn't care. He found Isolt endlessly fascinating.

'You were going to say?' Camoric prodded, with a grin.

'We should get back to the palace.' Fyn had to let the mage know there was no need for Siordun's help. He offered to help Isolt into the rowboat. 'My queen.'

She smiled. 'My king.'

PIRO HID IN the conservatory, waiting for Varuska to come down to breakfast so she could ambush her. Somehow she had to make Varuska see they had to deal with Cobalt. Despite her urgency, Piro fought a yawn and failed. She'd had a nightmare about wyvern riders, and men torn apart and devoured... She shuddered.

Piro heard Siordun approaching and darted through the ferns and exotic blossoms, to return to the breakfast chamber. She was determined to tell him about Kaspian and confess her part in the bonding.

'There you are, Piro.' Siordun looked worried. Had Nefysto already told him? 'Bad news. Isolt has been kidnapped.'

Piro gasped. It was the last thing she'd expected and she said the first thing that popped into her head. 'Poor Fyn.'

Siordun did not ask what she meant.

'Was it Neiron?'

'We think so. I have to leave right now. You'll have to go to Rolencia without me. I'll meet you there are soon as I can. Is Varuska ready to play her part?'

'She's afraid of Cobalt. But she'll come around.'

'Good. Everything is in place. My Rolencian agent says the abbess is eager to help you bring down Cobalt.'

Piro nodded, wondering how she would get on with these two women, both formidable in their own way.

'Piro?'

'Yes?'

'Have you had any visions? With Byren about to reclaim his throne, there has to be a nexus point coming up.'

She gasped, reminded of her nightmare. 'I've done a terrible thing.'

'Oh, Piro.' He laughed, took her shoulders in his hands and kissed her forehead.

'What was that for?' she asked, stunned.

He shook his head. 'You must be very careful. If you do have visions of the nexus point, let me know. I've told Soterro that he is to treat your words as my orders.'

She was honoured and a little overwhelmed. 'I'll do my best.'

'I know you will,' Siordun said, then grew serious. 'You'll be fourteen on midsummer's day, old enough to be betrothed.'

She pulled away. 'I'm your apprentice, I don't have to marry to further my family.'

Siordun opened his mouth, then seemed to think better of what he'd been going to say. 'I should go.'

Piro watched him leave, wondering if he and Byren had cooked up some plan to marry her off. It infuriated her. She'd thought all that nonsense had been laid to rest.

'Was that Agent Tyro's voice I heard?' Nefysto asked.

'Yes. He's returning to Merofynia. I'll be leaving for Rolencia as soon as Varuska is ready.'

'She's not going,' Nefysto said. 'She's already faced death because of the Rolencian royal family.'

'If I could just talk to her—'

'She doesn't want to talk to you. She wants a quiet life.'

'I promise she won't have to speak to Cobalt. All she needs to do is stand next to me. We'll be under the protection of the abbess.'

'No, Piro. Haven't you done enough damage?'

She flushed and tears stung her eyes. 'I told you I was sorry.'

'Kaspian did not come back last night.'

She felt terrible.

'I'll book passage for you.'

Piro flushed. Clearly Nefysto was keen to get rid of her.

The following day, before she sailed, Piro knocked on the door of Varuska's chamber. 'I must speak with you.'

'I know what you're going to say and I don't care who rules Rolencia. I wish I'd never heard of our family connection!'

'But we are family. We need you.' There was silence, and Piro grew hopeful.

'Anatoley was my family. My sister grew hungry for a crown and look what happened to her!' Varuska bit back a sob.

'I'm sorry about your sister.'

'I'm sorry, too. The price you pay to play Duelling Kingdoms is too high.'

Piro leant her forehead on the door. She'd lost her brother, mother and father. Tears stung her eyes. 'You're right. Stay here. I'll let the mage know.'

Siordun and his Rolencian agent would have to tweak their plan. Piro set off for Mage Isle to send the pica birds. She took Old Gwalt's chest, containing the documents establishing Siordun's right to Dunistir Estate, and placed it in the library with all the other document cases. Then she went to the top of the tower, where she found Cragore tending to the pica birds. He eyed her resentfully.

'Good, you're here,' Piro said. 'I need you to send a message to both Rolencia and Merofynia.'

'I can send it to the *Wyvern's Whelp*, too,' Cragore boasted.

'Really?' She'd known that, but she managed to look impressed.

He indicated a cage. 'It takes a deeply bonded pica pair. Lady is so smart she can find her mate on a ship anywhere on the Stormy Sea.'

'Lady?'

He flushed.

Piro stroked the bird. 'She suits her name.'

Mollified, Cragore tended to the picas. While he taught the birds to memorise the message about Varuska, Piro headed down the steps.

A moment later, Cragore called after her. 'There's news from Merofynia. Fyn has married Queen Isolt.'

'What?'

He nodded. Full of importance, he announced, 'I must tell the mage.' And he ran down the stairs.

She let him go, secure in the knowledge that Soterro would cover for Siordun. Meanwhile, she ran back up the steps.

Byren needed to know he was free to marry Florin. Piro made up a simple rhyme and sang this to Lady before releasing the pica bird. Now Byren would be happy, too.

Feeling pleased with herself, Piro boarded the ship bound for Rolencia.

BYREN PACED HIS ship's deck. Dawn revealed Snow Bridge Bay, but no more ships had arrived overnight. For two days a fierce storm had raged. Even here in the protected waters behind the headlands, the ships had been tossed about like corks. Of the six vessels that had followed the *Wyvern's Whelp* through Mulcibar's Gate, only three had made it into the bay.

'I don't like the way that ship's sitting.' Orrade pointed to one of the merchant vessels. 'She's too low.'

'She must be taking water,' Bantam said. 'We'll make a sailor of you yet.'

Byren shook his head. 'Three ships missing. All those lives lost...'

'There's a chance one or two of them may limp into port somewhere along the spars,' Bantam said.

Byren met his eyes.

'But it's more likely they were battered to pieces on the rocks,' the captain admitted.

'So our army consists of the men on these four ships,' Orrade muttered. 'That's cutting it awfully fine.'

But Bantam was shaking his head. He gestured to the ship sitting low in the water. 'If the captain's lucky, he'll make it back to Port Mero. But he'll have to lighten his ship by unloading your men.'

'Sylion's Luck!' Byren muttered. Was there ever a man more cursed with bad fortune? 'They'll have to travel over Cockatrice Spar. Tell Chandler I want him.'

Orrade nodded and left. Bantam called for his boatswain and they went off to check the ship for damage before taking her out onto the open sea.

A few moments later Orrade returned with Chandler. When Byren explained that he would be entrusted to take the men over the spar to Rolencia, Chandler was not happy.

'I should be with you when you defeat Cobalt.'

'If you move quickly and the Cockatrice Spar warlord lets you travel through his lands without trouble, you can be over the spar and down into the Rolencian valley in time for midsummer's day. Now pack your things and go. I'm relying on you to get these men home safe.'

Chandler gave him a Rolencian salute and went below deck. A moment later Florin came out onto the middeck. Byren took in the way she moved. Everything was an effort. His poor mountain girl... she'd hate being so weak.

'I'll send Florin with Chandler, so she won't have to endure sea-sickness all the way home,' Byren said, and called her.

Orrade caught his arm. 'I don't like it. What if the new warlord of Cockatrice Spar gives Chandler trouble?'

'I'm sending Chandler over the spar with a hundred and fifty men. She'll be safe.'

'Not if the warlord thinks Chandler is invading.'

'Chandler will tell the warlord—'

'What if he's an arrogant prick who takes insult because you didn't negotiate for your men to pass through his territory yourself?'

'Since when did you get to be so cautious?'

'Since I had a wife and child to consider. It's safer to go by sea.'

'What if there's another storm?'

Orrade bit back his reply as Florin joined them on the reardeck.

She pointed. 'Is that a pica bird?'

Byren and Orrade exchanged a look. The mage would only contact them if something had gone wrong. Byren's stomach knotted. If anything had happened to Piro...

Orrade lifted his arm, and Byren sensed his Affinity rise. Attracted by the power, the bird went to Orrade. As he bent his head to listen to the message, Byren watched his face closely.

When Orrade's gaze flew to Byren and his expression closed down, Byren expected the worst. 'Out with it. Tell me.'

'Fyn has married Queen Isolt.'

'What? No.' Byren took a step back, shaking his head. 'There must be some mistake. Fyn would never betray me.'

'I listened to the message twice.'

A rushing sound filled Byren's ears. Fyn *had* betrayed him. He'd lost Merofynia. He'd lost his army and—he raised his head to meet Florin's shocked eyes—he'd lost his mountain girl.

FOR ONE STUPID, exhilarating moment Florin thought Byren would say that this changed everything and they could be together, but she was forgetting that he didn't want her. He only looked so shocked because Fyn had betrayed him. And besides, she'd put her name to the wedding contract before the whole ship. She could not dishonour Orrade.

Byren was ashen.

Orrade's hand settled on Byren's shoulder. 'You're free of a betrothal you never wanted.'

But Byren had less than half the men he'd set sail with, and he'd lost Merofynia. No wonder he shook his head as if he was having trouble thinking.

Shrugging off Orrade's hand, he walked to the stern of the ship, where he gripped the rail. Florin could see the tension in his shoulders and neck.

Orrade joined Florin. 'Go to him.'

'And do what?' All she could offer was comfort, and Byren needed an army. Only one person could give him an army. As much as she hated to say it... 'The Snow Bridge king offered you an alliance.'

Byren exhaled and for an instant his shoulders seemed to sag, then he turned around, speaking decisively. 'Orrie, I need you to go to King Jorgoskev.'

Orrade took a step back.

'He claimed he could send a thousand men into battle at a day's notice. Tell him I'll marry his daughter, if he gives me six hundred men. You'll need to force-march them down into the Rolencian valley in time to help me defeat Cobalt.'

Orrade lifted his hands. 'But Byren—'

'I must strike a decisive blow. If I don't cut Cobalt down now, I might as well...'—he gestured to the ship—'sign on as a sea-hound!'

'What of Florin?' Orrade asked.

Byren didn't so much as look at her. 'She goes with you to make sure they don't cheat us.'

Orrade opened his mouth, then closed it. Finally, he nodded. 'If that is what you want, but the thin air will make her sky-sick again.'

'I go where Byren needs me,' Florin stated.

'It's settled.' Byren joined them. 'I'll give you half a dozen men and enough gold to hire mounts and move fast. Don't fail me in this, Orrie. If you arrive too late, you'll have to bury me.'

Orrade stiffened. 'You know only death would prevent me from meeting you.'

Florin asked the question no one had asked. 'Which daughter?'

Byren shrugged. 'The second eldest. She seemed happiest with the arrangement.'

Florin hated the girl with every fibre of her being.

'I'll draw up the papers.' Orrade frowned. 'What was her name?'

Byren shrugged. 'Skev... Skev something.'

'They were all Skev something,' Orrade muttered. 'I was too astounded seeing the poor girls naked to take in their names.'

'Me too,' Byren admitted.

'The youngest was Skevlonsa.' Florin remembered that much.

'Skevlaxa?' Byren muttered. 'That was it. Tell him I'll marry Skevlaxa in return for six hundred men. Let's hope we all meet on the battlefield, with Cobalt's body at my feet.'

FYN'S HEART ROSE as Isolt returned to their private chamber. Even if Byren never forgave him, he had no regrets. Not that he thought Byren would hold a grudge. 'What did she say?'

'Nerysa fears the nobles will reject her.'

'You pointed out that Sefarra—'

'She said Sefarra is an eccentric who doesn't care what people think.'

Fyn grinned. With Neiron's death, they needed a new lord of Nevantir Estate, and it had to be someone they trusted. 'Will she leave the abbey?'

'Honestly? I don't know.' Isolt came over to stand behind him. She slid her arms around his shoulders, pressing a kiss to his cheek. 'We have until the nobles arrive for the midsummer festival to convince her. I hope Byren—'

'Byren has his army. He has Orrade and the mountain girl, Piro and the abbess.'

'You're still angry with him.'

'He insulted you.'

'I don't want to come between you and your brother.'

Fyn didn't want to upset her. 'While you were busy with Nerysa and the abbess, I was busy with the Merofynity Stone. I've had it cleaned of moss and dust, and on midsummer's day, we'll be crowned...' He broke off as a servant arrived with a tray laden with wine and cheese.

Isolt frowned. 'We didn't order...'

'Siordun.' Fyn recognised the mage's agent, despite his servant disguise. They really needed to create a new identity for him so he could visit them without subterfuge. 'Did Gwalt provide the costume—'

'What were you thinking?' Siordun demanded. 'How could you betray Byren?'

The intensity of his anger surprised Fyn. He came to his feet, stepping in front of Isolt.

She moved around him. 'Please understand. We love each other.'

'Love? Royalty doesn't have the luxury of love! Didn't your mothers teach you that?'

'My mother hated my father so much she took her own life!' Isolt was pale as a sheet.

Even from across the chamber, Fyn could feel Siordun's Affinity. He slid his arm around Isolt's shoulder. 'This—'

'This marriage has undone thirty years of work to bring peace between Rolencia and Merofynia.'

'There is still peace between our kingdoms. Rolencia is still my home. Byren is still my brother.' Anger flashed through Fyn. 'Tell him, even though he brought his lover into the palace and flaunted her in front of Isolt, we bear him no ill will.'

'What?' Isolt turned to Fyn, shocked. 'Who?'

Siordun echoed her. 'Who—'

'Florin the mountain girl. She travels as part of his honour guard and pretends to be Orrade's lover.'

'I would never have thought it of him...' Siordun ran his hands through his hair then turned to Isolt. 'I'm sorry he insulted you this way, but it doesn't change things. Fyn, Byren left you to protect—'

'Byren left me in an impossible situation. Between the spar warlords and traitorous Merofynian nobles, we needed Lord Dunstany, yet he repeatedly deserted us.'

'The mage needed me back on Ostron Isle. Two of the great merchant houses believed they'd been overlooked for the electorship. House Nictocorax became involved. There were duels, assassinations and poisonings.'

'Couldn't the mage have dealt with this?' Fyn asked.

Siordun's mouth opened and closed.

'What's done is done.' Isolt went to the table and poured wine for them.

Fyn joined her and raised his glass. 'Be happy for us, Siordun.'

'I am happy for you, but now I'll have to take the fastest ship I can find and hope to reach Piro by midsummer's day.'

'You'll smooth things over with Byren?' Isolt asked.

Siordun nodded. 'I'll try.'

'Tell him we bear him no ill will, despite the insult. We want only peace between our two kingdoms.' Fyn raised his glass. 'To peace!'

Chapter Sixty-Six

PIRO ARRIVED IN Rolencia with two days to spare. The ship dropped her at the wharf below Sylion Abbey, which was built high on the eastern headland, overlooking the bay. If her father had lived, she would have been forced to serve the cold god of winter. Back then she'd seen her Affinity as an affliction, but now she knew better.

Piro clutched her bag, which contained her best gown and jewellery suitable for a kingsdaughter to wear when denouncing a usurper. She climbed the seven flights of stairs. At the top, she saw why Cobalt had not attempted to pry the abbess out of Sylion Abbey. A sheer white wall greeted her.

The only entrance was a narrow tunnel, closed off at each end by a barred gate. Curious, Piro peered down the tunnel. Beyond the second gate, she saw afternoon sunlight on white flagstones and heard sweet singing. She rang the bell.

After a moment, the outer gate rose. Piro had the impression she'd been inspected and deemed safe.

Even so, the inner gate did not open.

A novice nun, wearing a pale blue robe the colour of thin ice, stepped in front of the gate to study Piro. She was joined by an incredibly old woman who wore the white of pure snow.

'I've come to serve.' Following instructions, Piro presented herself as an aspiring novice.

The old woman told the girl to open the gate and take Piro to the abbess. The novice led her across the courtyard, through a maze of corridors and buildings. They went past other courtyards, where Piro saw novices tending vegetables, and yet other courtyards where they were spinning and weaving.

She remembered her mother saying Halcyon and Sylion Abbeys were wealthier than all but the king. They owned land and businesses and had tithes coming in from all over Rolencia. Cobalt's confiscation of Sylion Abbey's properties must have hit the abbess hard. They were lucky she had remained loyal.

The novice let Piro into a greeting chamber. She'd heard the earthly palace of the winter god was furnished with every possible luxury. Piro walked on white marble floors, and two statues embedded with semi-precious stones stood to each side of the great double doors. The doors were covered in silver and embossed with Lord Sylion in all his guises: the lizard that could extinguish flames with his breath, the man-lizard, and the man with the pure white skin and eyes like winter skies. Along one wall was a tapestry so brilliantly coloured it seemed about to come to life.

'Fifty nuns laboured for twenty years to produce that tapestry,' the abbess said.

Piro jumped. 'Abbess Afanazia.'

'Pirola Rolen Kingsdaughter.' The abbess was a short, plump woman who Piro had always thought should have been making pastries rather than running the winter god's abbey. But the last half-year had not been kind to Afanazia. She'd lost weight. Her face was lined with worry and there were white streaks at her temples. The abbess gestured to the tapestry. 'The stitches are so fine several of the nuns went blind.'

'How...' Piro had been about to say *how awful*, but restrained herself. 'How sad for them.'

'They should be honoured to serve Lord Sylion.' A second woman joined them. She was half a head taller than Piro, with wide cheekbones and a pointed chin like a cat. She should have been beautiful, but her mouth was thin and hard.

Surely Piro would have remembered a face like that. 'I don't think we've met.'

'This is the new mystics mistress, Zoraya,' the abbess said.

'Mystics mistress.' Piro dipped her head. The last mystics mistress had been very old.

'Come, through here.' The abbess led Piro into her private chamber. It was even more richly appointed. The only touch of colour was the torc made of red carnelian stones that the abbess wore around her neck to signify her status.

There was no sign of the mage's Rolencian agent. Not wanting to give the woman away, Piro did not ask after her.

The abbess settled herself in a chair that was almost a throne. Piro noticed how she paused to catch her breath. Without warning, Piro's sight shifted to the unseen and she saw a skull beneath the abbess's face.

The mystics mistress made a soft noise of surprise and Piro's gaze was drawn to her. She radiated cold power, like a finely honed blade. It made Piro wonder how the mystics mistress saw her.

With an effort, Piro reined in her Affinity.

'You have Affinity,' Zoraya accused.

'A little.'

'Don't lie to me. Why didn't King Rolen dedicate you to Sylion?'

'It only came on me recently.'

The mystics mistress did not look pleased.

'Well, she's here now, Zoraya, so no harm's done.' The abbess gestured to the mistress, who removed a neatly folded blue robe from a cabinet. 'You will wear the blue.'

Piro nodded. 'A novice's costume.'

'It is not a costume.' Zoraya stroked the material reverently. 'It is a sacred robe.'

'My apologies.' Piro did not miss the abbess's slight grimace of annoyance.

'We sail tomorrow,' the abbess said. 'That way we'll be rested for the ceremony, the day after.'

Piro had seen plenty of midsummer ceremonies. No woman could set foot in Halcyon Abbey. They got around this by holding the ceremony in the huge courtyard. Her family used to stay in the apartments on one side of the courtyard, but she had never thought to ask... 'Where do Sylion's nuns stay?'

'There are bedchambers in the wall above the gate.' The abbess's lips twitched. 'Strictly speaking, that is not within Halcyon Abbey.'

Piro smiled, surprised to discover she liked the abbess.

The mystics mistress made a soft noise of censure.

There was a tap at the door.

'That'll be the novices mistress. She will show you to your room. As far as she is concerned, you are here to become a novice.' The abbess raised her voice. 'Enter, Lizavet.'

The novices mistress was tall and broad-shouldered, and looked like a farmer's wife.

Piro had hoped to have more time with the abbess to go over their plans for midsummer's day. She nodded to the novices mistress and clutched her bag.

'Leave that,' Mistress Lizavet said. 'You can collect it in a year and a day, if you decide not to give your vows.'

'Yes, mistress.'

'Come along, girl.'

Again Piro was led through a maze of corridors and buildings, while the novices mistress told her all the things she could and could not do, interspersed with complaints about the journey tomorrow and the poor quality of the lodgings for the mistresses at Halcyon Abbey.

'...at least at Rolenton Castle, Queen Myrella knew how to look after us.'

Remembering her mother preparing the bedchambers for the influx of guests each feast day, Piro felt tears sting her eyes.

They'd arrived at a narrow novice's cell, consisting of a low bunk and a thin blanket and not much else.

'Don't sniffle, girl. That's not the way to start your service to Sylion,' the novices mistress snapped. The evening bells rang out. 'Time for prayers, then the evening meal. Novices help in the kitchen. As this is your first day, you can make yourself useful by washing dishes. Hurry up.'

Piro did as she was told. Stripping off her gown, she dropped the novice's robe over her head. Her waist-length hair was already in a long plait, so the mistress took her to the kitchen.

For the rest of the evening, Piro washed dishes. It seemed an unnecessary length to go to for her disguise, but she kept her mouth shut and was doubly thankful that she hadn't ended up dedicated to Sylion Abbey working as a drudge.

As THE SUN rose on the day before midsummer's day, Florin rode to the top of the hill with Orrade at her side. Long shafts of dawn light shot over Florin's shoulders, illuminating the lakes, fields and woodlands of Rolencia. On mornings like this, she used to go to the tip of Narrowneck to watch the dawn sun burn the mist off Lake Sapphire. Back then, her heart would lift with joy, but she would never be that girl again.

'Merofynia, with its Landlocked Sea, never felt right to me,' she said. 'It's good to be home.'

Orrade pointed to Lake Viridian, glimpsed through the tree tops. 'We still have to cross the lake or travel around it to reach Halcyon Abbey. In some ways, travelling in midwinter is easier. At least then we can skate across the lakes.'

A horse whinnied behind them and they both turned to look down to the valley floor, to where Jorgoskev's warriors were breaking camp.

'Do you think it will matter that the Snow Bridge king could only spare four hundred warriors?' Florin asked.

Orrade shrugged. Not one of the warriors was taller than Florin's shoulder. Orrade had pushed them mercilessly across the Snow Bridge, over the pass and through Rolencia, but they never complained.

'Their endurance is amazing,' Orrade said. 'It must be because they're used to the thin air. Even so—'

'We aren't going to reach Byren in time, are we?' Thanks to the kingsdaughter, they were running late. She travelled veiled inside a closed carriage, the body of which had been manhandled over the pass with her in it. As soon as there was a decent path, her retinue had reassembled the carriage. Orrade had hired four horses, great big things with shaggy hooves, but the carriage had been built for ursodons, and the farmhorses laboured to pull it.

'Tomorrow is midsummer's day,' Orrade said. 'I can't fail Byren.'

'Leave me with the kingsdaughter. We'll meet you at Halcyon Abbey, when all the fighting is done and Byren is victorious.'

There was no alternative to victory. If Byren lost this battle, they would be hunted down and executed. It struck Florin that King Jorgoskev had a great deal of faith in Byren, or his warriors—or both—to put his daughter in such a precarious position.

'You don't mind me leaving you behind?' Orrade asked.

'I would not suggest it if I did not mean it.'

He grinned.

'What?'

He shook his head. 'Come on.'

They went down the slope towards the camp. When they were about halfway down and still illuminated by the rising sun, Orrade reined in his horse and stood in the stirrups. He lifted his fingers to his lips and whistled. It was hardly the equivalent of an ursodon horn, but it worked. Everyone looked towards them.

'We leave the kingsdaughter with thirty warriors to protect her, under the leadership of my sweet lady-wife.' He caught Florin's hand and kissed it, a wicked grin lighting his eyes.

She couldn't help but smile.

'We take only our weapons and the food we can carry,' Orrade announced. 'We make for Halcyon Abbey and battle!'

The men cheered.

MIDAFTERNOON ON MIDSUMMER'S eve, Byren stood on the high rear deck as his men disembarked from the *Wyvern's Whelp*. There were two ports in Rolencia Bay. Port Marchand had the larger docks, and most of the wealthy merchants lived there. But Port Cobalt lay closer to the abbey, and belonged to Cobalt Estate. It amused Byren to make use of it.

'Won't the people of Cobalt's estate resist you?' Bantam asked.

'Cobalt's been back half a year. Before that, he spent the last thirteen years in Ostron Isle. Why, he even dresses like an Ostronite. I'm returning with Rolencia's freed men-at-arms. Who do you think the people are going to cheer for?' Byren asked, hoping he was right.

'Someone may ride ahead to warn Cobalt.'

'I certainly hope so. I want everyone to know Byren Kingsheir marches to reclaim his father's throne. That way, when Piro appears on the dais and unmasks Cobalt for the liar he is, all the nobles and merchants will know it's time to decide who they support, Cobalt the Usurper or Byren the True King.'

Bantam grinned. 'I wish you luck.'

Byren clasped his arm, wrist to elbow. 'I thank you.'

He was going to need luck. Talk of justice might sway the old nobles, and the fact that his father had given them thirty years of peace and profits might convince the merchants, but there were five companies of Merofynian men-at-arms, and the newly made nobles who would support Cobalt out of self-interest.

'Looks like Wafin's found a mount for you.' Bantam gestured to the wharf, where the youngest of Byren's honour guard led a sturdy, shaggy hoofed beast.

With his size, there were not many horses Byren could ride.

'What'll you do now?' Byren asked Bantam. 'Go back to Ostron Isle?'

'No. Agent Tyro told me to stay here, in case we were needed. Here's your Affinity beastie.'

A sailor arrived with the foenix.

'We're home, Resolute.' Byren reached out and stroked the bird under the jaw.

As he walked down the gangplank, the foenix took to the air, circling overhead, and the people of Port Cobalt pointed and whispered.

'The one true king has returned,' young Wafin cried. 'Byren the True King has returned!'

The people took up the cry.

And Byren had come home.

Chapter Sixty-Seven

PIRO HELPED THE abbess to climb the steps of Halcyon Abbey's gatehouse. The other mistresses had remained below at the dinner table, but the abbess was exhausted. This was Piro's first chance to be alone with her.

Now she opened the door to a simple chamber overlooking the large courtyard. Directly opposite, Halcyon Abbey was built into the mountain. Three rows of arched windows gleamed in the night. Somewhere in there, Abbot Firefox was preparing for tomorrow's ceremony.

In the centre of the courtyard was the fountain, with its pond that never froze, even in winter, as a sign of Halcyon's blessing. Piro smiled, remembering how she'd laughed when Fyn explained the water never froze because it was pumped up from the hot pools below.

To the left were the stables and store rooms, and to the right were the apartments where Cobalt, and the nobles and merchants, had taken up residence, ready for the ceremony tomorrow.

As Piro watched, a rider came through the gate below,

and galloped across the courtyard towards the stables. A moment later, he left the stables and ran towards the apartments on her right.

'A messenger has just arrived,' Piro said softly. 'I bet he carries the news that Byren is marching for the abbey.'

She closed the shutters and turned to find the abbess slumped on her bunk, lips blue.

With a cry of dismay, Piro ran to her. She helped her settle more comfortably on her bed and adjusted the pillows. 'There, that's better.' But Piro had foreseen the abbess's death, and any healer would have recognised the signs. The woman's heart was failing. 'Can I get you anything?'

'Dora... Dorafay.'

Ducking her head through the door, Piro spotted a novice and told her to fetch the healing mistress. Then she returned and took the abbess's hand.

'So cold.' Piro rubbed her skin, trying to warm her.

'I'm sorry. I wanted to see you confound Cobalt.' The abbess's colour was a little better. 'You're a good girl, like your mother. The old mystics mistress and I knew she had Affinity, but she did so much good that we made sure no one realised.' The abbess smiled at Piro's surprise. 'When I die, Zoraya will take over from me. I fear she'll be much stricter than I ever was...' The abbess paused to catch her breath. 'Should Cobalt turn on you, Zoraya will whisk you away, and the mage's agent will see to it that you're safe. But we're hoping your presence will reveal Cobalt for the liar he is, and only a few supporters will remain with him when he marches out the gate to confront Byren.'

Footsteps approached the chamber.

'They're here. You'll feel better soon.' Piro squeezed the abbess's hand and came to her feet.

Cobalt opened the door.

Unable to believe her eyes, Piro took a step back and felt the wall behind her.

The healing mistress swept in after him, followed by the novices mistress.

'Dorafay? Lizavet?' the abbess whispered. 'What have you done?'

'We're making sure Sylion Abbey is not destroyed by your lack of judgement,' the novices mistress told her, as the healer opened her bag and sorted through it.

'Where's Zoraya?' the abbess asked.

'Snoring on her bunk,' the healer said. 'I gave her enough dreamless-sleep to knock out a horse.'

The abbess tried to get up, but didn't have the strength.

'You told me she'd be dead by now, Dorafay,' the novices mistress complained.

'How was I to know her heart would hold out so long? I'll just mix up some more—'

'You should have doubled the dose.'

'Oh, cease this bickering!' Cobalt took two strides across the chamber, pulled the pillow from behind the abbess's head and held it over her face. Even with one arm, he had no trouble smothering the frail woman.

Horrified, Piro tried to pull Cobalt away.

But the novices mistress grabbed Piro by her plait and swung her around, slapping her so hard she flew across the room and hit the wall. The back of her head struck the stone with such force her teeth seem to rattle in her head. The room swung around Piro as her knees gave way and she sank to the floor.

'If there's one thing I can't stand it is a stuck up little kingsdaughter!' the novices mistress said, standing over her.

A buzzing filled Piro's head. It was so unfair. 'But I did a mountain of dishes.'

'What's she saying?' Cobalt asked.

'No idea,' the novice mistress said.

Reaching down, Cobalt took Piro's arm and pulled her to her feet. For some reason, her legs wouldn't work. She had to clutch him for support. He searched Piro's face. She couldn't focus on him.

Cobalt frowned. 'You didn't have to strike her so hard.'

'She hit her head on the wall.'

'You're certain only you four know about the plan?' Cobalt asked.

'Three, now,' the novices mistress said. 'And Zoraya will keep quiet if she knows what's good for her.'

'Check the passage.'

As the healer did so, the novices mistress said, 'I don't know why you don't just send the kingsdaughter back to Sylion Abbey. I'd make sure she never gave you trouble ever again.'

The thought horrified Piro. Imprisoned in Sylion Abbey for life...

'I'm going to make her pay for all the trouble her family's caused me,' Cobalt said.

Piro thought she heard a noise outside and tried to call for help.

Cobalt swore. 'Give me some dreamless-sleep.'

'I'll do it,' the healer said. 'Hold her mouth open.'

Piro fought wildly as Cobalt held her up against the wall. The novice mistress covered her nose, until she had to open her mouth to breathe. The healer tipped the liquid down her throat and she had to swallow.

'Will that be enough?' Cobalt asked.

'She's only a little thing. It'll knock her out.'

Piro let her head fall forward onto Cobalt's chest. They did not know she'd built up a tolerance to dreamless-sleep when she'd tried to dull her Affinity visions.

'That's the kingsdaughter dealt with. Now for Byren,' Cobalt said, filling Piro with dismay.

'I hear he's marching with an army,' the healer said.

'Don't worry about Byren. He won't live long enough to disrupt tomorrow's ceremony. My men are ready to ambush him in the woods.'

There was a knock at the door, and something was wheeled into the chamber. Piro caught a glimpse of two monks with a large wicker laundry cart.

'Help me lift her,' Cobalt said.

The novices mistress bundled Piro unceremoniously into the cart. Head spinning, she looked up through her messy hair only to see the lid close.

Piro had to warn Byren. The movement of the laundry basket made her dizzy. She fought to stay conscious.

The next thing she knew was Cobalt discussing her with someone.

'...don't want her where one of Byren's sympathisers can find her, Firefox. Put her somewhere safe. When all this is over, she's going to regret ever crossing me.'

'I have just the place,' the abbot said.

Piro's heart sank. How would she warn Byren?

Even though she tried to stay awake, the gentle rocking of the laundry basket lulled her to sleep. The next time she woke, she found herself lying on the ground. She could smell Cobalt's Ostronite perfume nearby. The golden glow of a lamp came through her closed lids. She felt nauseous with exhaustion, and sounds around her echoed strangely.

'Should we leave her a candle?' the abbot asked.

'No,' Cobalt said. 'A day or two in the dark with nothing but water will make her more cooperative.'

She would never cooperate. She'd tear his throat out with her teeth.

As they left, the abbot said something, and they both laughed. Piro's stomach knotted with fury and fear.

She forced her eyes open. The world spun but she glimpsed the glow of the lamp as Cobalt and the abbot entered a passage. The glow dimmed as their footsteps faded, along with all thought.

FLORIN WALKED THE camp. She passed the four men-at-arms who took care of the two huge ursodon horns. They sat by the fire oiling and polishing their cumbersome instruments with loving care.

The old scholar hobbled over to Florin. Surely they could have found someone younger to translate for the kingsdaughter? Sending him on a long journey in his condition seemed cruel.

'We will reach the abbey tomorrow?' Yosiv asked.

'Late tomorrow,' Florin said. By then, the battle would be over, while she was stuck minding Byren's bride-to-be.

The kingsdaughter had six servants. They finished preparing her meal and placed it on a silver tray. The old scholar bid Florin good night and went to join the kingsdaughter for dinner. She always ate inside her carriage, although it had to be hot and stuffy.

Anger burned Florin. The kingsdaughter had never had to do a day's hard work in her life and never would. Florin had worked from before dawn until she fell into bed exhausted.

Florin wanted to march over and open the carriage door, throw back the veil and confront the pretty kingsdaughter. The memory of the way Skevlaxa had preened for the men of her father's court still infuriated her. Stupid girl. She thought her beauty gave her power over men. Didn't she realise they saw her as a prize, not as a person?

She wanted to ask Skevlaxa how it felt to know her father had purchased a husband for her. The girl had to know Byren was only marrying her for her father's army. Maybe she didn't care. After all, Byren would still be coming to her bed each night.

Florin gasped and bent double.

She felt like she'd been punched. Why should this woman, who did not care for Byren, have what Florin could not? Byren had only chosen her because one sister was too old and the other too young.

And she was beautiful...

Florin had to turn and walk away before she did something terrible.

* * *

Byren remembered travelling around the foothills of Mount Halcyon, back when he'd been escaping the Merofynian invaders. At the time, he'd been injured and desperate. Now he was returning with an army to confront Cobalt.

As they ate a cold meal and bedded down on blankets on the forested slopes, he went from group to group, talking of his plans for Rolencia.

Later he returned to his bedroll and found young Wafin waiting up for him.

'No need to act as my squire,' Byren told the lad. 'Where's the foenix?'

'He took off a little while ago. I thought he'd gone to find you.'

Byren stretched and felt his joints pop. Resolute flew overhead, giving voice. The foenix's piercing cry echoed through the forest. 'Eh, he'll give us away, calling like that.'

The foenix cried again, urgently.

'It's a warning!' Byren said and sure enough, he heard shouting and the clash of metal on metal.

'It's coming from up there,' Wafin pointed. 'Now it's coming from over there. We're surrounded!'

'We've been betrayed.' Bitterness closed around Byren's heart. At least Orrade and Florin were safe.

'Who would do that?'

'Doesn't matter. Come.' Byren snatched his blade and ran towards the nearest sounds of fighting with Wafin at his heels.

There was no time for strategy, only hacking and brutal killing on the dappled, starlit forest floor. The first man he killed had run ahead of the others and paid for it. The second put up more of a fight, and the third met him blow for blow. Even as he fought, Byren realised all three men had worn a strip of white cloth around their heads. Deflecting a strike, Byren's blade skipped over his attacker's defences and slid into his chest.

Putting his boot on the man, he pulled his sword free.

'I heard him curse in Merofynian,' Wafin said.

'Cobalt trusts the turncoats to do his dirty-work.'

Byren ran on, calling to his men, trying to rally those nearest him, and they succeeded for a time, but were gradually driven back amidst the screams of the dying and the cries of the wounded.

Byren found himself in a hollow where the leaf mulch was knee-deep. Somehow, Wafin was still at his side. In the confusion, Byren tripped over a body and went down on one knee. Wafin blocked a blow and lost his weapon. Shoving the lad out of harm's way, Byren swept his blade around and took the man's legs out from under him.

They had to get out of this hollow. He sprang to his feet, hauled Wafin upright and forged up the rise. Taking heart, the men followed him. They broke through the fighters and ran through the trunks, cutting down those who gave chase until the fighting was left far behind them.

Byren called a halt. Seventeen men, two of them wounded. No sign of Wafin. When had he lost him?

'Take the white bandanas from the dead,' Byren told them. 'Tie them around your heads and come back with me.'

His men had just escaped with their lives, but their companions were being butchered and they did not falter. They came up behind the fighting and attacked their enemies' backs.

The white bandannas confused the Merofynians. Byren and his men fought their way through to a knot of defenders. As his supporters dealt with the last of the attackers, Byren diverted a desperate blow from one of his own men. 'It's me. Put on a bandanna and come with us.'

The second time Byren used this ploy, he had more followers and they overcame the attackers quickly. The third, fourth and fifth time, they were just as successful.

The sixth time they had to go further to find the fighting. This time, they were too late to reach their men. Not one man was left alive.

In the dawn light, a Merofynian captain rode by and ordered them to fall in behind him with the rest of his men. As the captain joined a much larger group of men from different companies, Byren warned his companions to keep their heads down and follow his lead. He hoped they would find more of his men and be able to set them free before turning on the enemy. He hoped to find Wafin. The lad had come so far and survived so much, it would be too cruel if he'd died on the slopes of Mount Halcyon.

Before long, they met up with two other Merofynian captains and their men. As the captains shouted news to each other, Byren realised his men were the only survivors of the attack. Bloodied and muddied, they hid in the dishevelled ranks of the Merofynians.

In the dim light of dawn, they reached the shores of Lake Viridian, where Cobalt waited astride a horse.

'Did you find Byren?' he asked.

'He's dead. We left no one alive!'

'That's what my captains always tell me, and next thing I know Byren is back causing trouble.' As Cobalt stood in the stirrups to survey his men, Byren kept his head down. 'Go back into the forest. There's a pouch of gold for the man who brings Byren's head to the abbey!'

They cheered.

So Byren turned back with his followers, close to eighty of them now, to search for himself. The captain sent men out and Byren led his men up the slope, higher and higher, until they lost sight of the others. Now they moved through the sparse pines and rocky outcroppings.

Something stirred above them and Byren called up the gully, 'I see you up there.'

'Byren?' Wafin rose from behind a rock, and five more men came out of hiding.

'Come down here.' Byren hugged Wafin.

'I lost Resolute,' Wafin confessed. 'I don't know where he went.'

'Don't worry. He will have gone back to the ship.'

By midmorning, they had found more survivors and were high enough to look down on the abbey from above and see the crowd gathering in the courtyard.

Wafin lay on a rock next to Byren, surveying the scene. 'What will you do?'

'We stay hidden. There's over a hundred of us now. Enough to cause trouble. Sometime today, Orrade will arrive with Snow Bridge warriors and Chandler will come in from the spar.' Byren's mind raced. They'd been betrayed, but... 'Cobalt doesn't know about Orrade and Chandler. When he sets off for the castle tomorrow, he'll ride right into our ambush.'

Chapter Sixty-Eight

FYN STOOD BESIDE Isolt's chair on the royal dais at the lords' council. Later today, they would hold the coronation and accept loyalty oaths from the nobles and the conquered spar warlords. But right now, they were about to decide the fate of Nevantir Estate. There were several contenders eager to advance their families.

Fyn looked out over the gathering. The abbess and abbot stood to each side of the dais, with several nuns and monks. The nobles lined up on each side of the chamber. Travany had not attended, as he was under house arrest. By rights, they could have confiscated Travantir Estate, but they both felt they'd rather Travrhon inherited the title and supported them. Just as they would rather the new lord of Nevantir supported them.

Isolt caught Fyn's eye and he announced, 'Lord Yorale will speak to the fate of Nevantir Estate.'

The elder statesman stepped forward. 'Three noble houses have legitimate claim to Nevantir Estate. Elcwyff and Travrhon's mothers were both daughters of Nevantir, and so was Rhoderich's second wife. Each noble house has younger sons.'

'If all three lords have equal and legitimate claims, we don't want to stir up resentment,' Fyn said, looking to Isolt.

'As it turns out, we don't need to go back a generation to find an heir,' Isolt said. The rich tone of her voice told Fyn that she was enjoying herself, and so she should. She'd argued long and hard to convince Nerysa to leave Cyena Abbey. 'Not when Neiron's sister lives. Come forward, Lady Nerysa.'

Wearing the pale blue robe of a novice, Nerysa stepped from the ranks of the nuns. She pushed back her hood and knelt before the queen. There was much whispering from Rhoderich and Elcwyff's supporters, and Fyn caught the word 'ruined'.

Nerysa flushed, but kept her eyes on Isolt.

'This woman spent five days in the hands of the spar warlord,' Rhoderich protested. 'How do we know she does not carry a spar bastard?'

'Lady Nerysa is not with child,' the abbess said.

'Since I have granted Lady Isfynia special dispensation to inherit her family's title, I can hardly refuse Lady Nerysa the same consideration,' Isolt said. 'Rise, Lady Nerysa of Nevantir Estate. Any child of your marriage will be a Nevantir.'

'What nonsense is this?' Rhoderich sneered. 'She'll never marry.'

Nerysa's cheeks flamed and she looked to the queen.

'Really, my lord?' Isolt bristled. Fyn hid a smile. 'Why would that be?'

'No honourable man would take a spar warlord's discard for his wife.'

Sefarra's angry muttering reached Fyn, and he half expected her to come to Nerysa's defence.

But it was Camoric who stepped forward. 'If a man let this consideration prevent him from offering for Lady Nerysa, or any other woman who has been unfortunate enough to suffer at the hands of spar warriors, I would consider *him* dishonoured!'

'Well said!' Isolt applauded. The nuns, Isfynia and Rishardt, and the mother of the young Geraltir lord all joined her.

Sefarra took Nerysa's arm and drew her into their ranks.

Elcwyff had been about to speak, but he stepped back, leaving Rhoderich to shake his head. 'I don't know what this kingdom is coming to. Our forefathers must be turning in their graves.'

Isolt glanced to Fyn.

'Let's find out, shall we?' Fyn said. 'We will stand on the Merofynity Stone under the linden tree just as our forefathers did, and you will see for yourselves if it welcomes us.'

A buzz of excitement travelled through the hall.

A little later, they approached the linden tree, dressed in simple white robes. Fifty common folk, drawn by lot, watched from the front ranks of the crowd. The nobles and merchants watched from horseback, and from the comfort of their carriages.

Barefoot to symbolise their connection to the land, Fyn took Isolt's hand and they stepped onto the Merofynity Stone.

Abbess Celunyd and Abbot Murheg blessed them and Fyn and Isolt bent forward to be crowned. As they lifted their heads, Fyn summoned his Affinity. He felt the rush of power slide down his legs and pool in his feet, before flowing into the stone. It glowed under them, enveloping them in a beam of light which rose up through the linden tree and high into the sky.

The crowd gasped. Fyn turned to Isolt, took her face in his hands and kissed her, for all the world to see.

The crowd broke into a deafening cheer.

* * *

Byren watched from a vantage point high above the abbey, where the events in the courtyard seemed to be played out on a distant stage. At midday, amid pomp and ceremony, the abbot formally handed over custodianship of the kingdom to the abbess. They stood on a dais by the central pool. Byren had held out hope, but there was no sign of his sister or Siordun. Cobalt mounted the dais to receive the gods' blessing. What had they done with Piro? How had they overcome Siordun?

Wafin came scrambling up the steep slope behind him, then crawled across the stone to stretch out beside Byren. 'A message from the western lookout. They spotted a large force coming around the lake shore.'

'Orrade?'

'They think so.'

There were still some bands of Merofynians searching the slopes of Mount Halcyon. Byren didn't want them stumbling across Orrade and the Snow Bridge warriors and racing back to Cobalt with the news.

'Stay here and watch Cobalt,' Byren told Wafin. 'Report to me if he leaves the abbey.'

Returning to the gully, Byren gathered his men. When he reached the western lookout, they pointed to where Orrade had been spotted. Byren led his men down the slope, hoping to meet up with Orrade, but a band of Merofynians had found him first.

Dividing his men, Byren sent half of them to make sure none of the Merofynians escaped to warn Cobalt, the rest he led down to support Orrade. By the time they arrived, Orrade's men had dispatched a group of around thirty Merofynians.

Byren drew Orrade aside to explain what had happened.

'Betrayed?' Orrade asked. 'What of Piro and Siordun?'

'There was no sign of them. The ceremony went ahead as usual. I didn't recognise the abbess. Wasn't she a little, plump woman?'

'She was.' Orrade nodded grimly. 'Father used to say ambition and loyalty made poor bedfellows.'

'Eh, I could do with the Old Dove's advice right now. Seems every decision I make turns out to be wrong.'

'You've had Sylion's Luck since Merofynia invaded.'

By now Byren could see the majority of the Snow Bridge warriors in the clearing and scattered throughout the trees. 'Where's...' He'd been about to ask after Florin. 'Where's King Jorgoskev's daughter?'

'Florin's bringing her. The carriage slowed us down.'

'Carriage?'

'According to their customs, you've already looked her over.' Orrade shrugged. 'You won't see her now until the wedding day.'

Byren didn't want to think about the wedding day. He changed the subject. 'Will Cobalt go home by boat or horse?'

'If he takes a boat, he abandons his men and tradition. If Cobalt believes you dead, or at least reduced to leading a few survivors, he won't change his plans. He doesn't know you have four hundred Snow Bridge warriors at your command.'

'Four hundred? Jorgoskev boasted he could put a thousand in the field on a day's notice.'

'Remember the trouble he had with the Affinity-touched? There was an uprising, and—'

'Four hundred will have to be enough. I have around a hundred, but a third of them are injured.'

'Your father used to break the journey back to Rolenhold at Steadford Castle. I hear the new lord of Steadford Estate owes his title to Cobalt. We need to ambush him before he can take sanctuary in the castle.'

Byren nodded. 'We'll march—'

'You march,' Orrade said. 'You can't leave an enemy at your back. Abbot Firefox serves Cobalt, and from the sounds of it, there's been a coup in Sylion Abbey. I'll remain behind with a hundred men. As soon as

Cobalt marches out with his supporters, I'll go to the abbey and install a new abbot and abbess, people loyal to you. Meanwhile, I'd better set a watch on the road around the lake's shore. We don't want Florin riding into the abbey and into Cobalt's arms with the Snow Bridge kingsdaughter!'

'Of course. Why didn't I think of that?'

Orrade grinned. 'That's why you have me.'

But Byren knew why he hadn't thought of Jorgoskev's daughter. He didn't want to think about the price he had to pay for these Snow Bridge warriors. With the abbess's betrayal, it was just as well he had them. 'I want to know what Cobalt did with Piro and Siordun. If they've hurt—'

'I'll hold the abbot and abbess personally responsible,' Orrade promised. 'You ambush Cobalt before he reaches the Steadford Castle. We don't want a protracted siege. This has to be a decisive victory.'

A TERRIBLE THIRST woke Piro, combined with a pounding headache. At first she had no idea where she was. Then it all came back to her... the betrayal, and Byren walking into an ambush. When would Cobalt return?

Down here in the dark, she couldn't tell how much time had passed. Except that she now realised that it wasn't completely dark. Something shone through the pale blue material of her robe. She pulled out her pendant to reveal her glowing sorbt stone. She couldn't focus her Affinity in the stone; if it was glowing, she had to be in the presence of a powerful seep.

They must have imprisoned her in Halcyon's Sacred Heart, where the bodies of the most pious monks were interred to become one with their goddess. Fyn had told her how he'd led the lads down here to escape the Merofynian invasion. He'd found a secret passage through the heart of the mountain to the far side.

If she could just remember the details...

Ignoring the headache and nausea, Piro held the sorbt stone. It was only a small stone, and it cast a correspondingly small glow. She found a water-skin, and after drinking and washing her face, she felt a little better. Working on the assumption that she would find her way out, she slung the water-skin over her shoulder.

Something shimmered ahead of her.

By the stone's silvery glow, she discovered a statue of an old man kneeling on a knee-high stone with his hands palm up in his lap. Of course, this was no statue. It was an honoured monk. His organs had been removed and his body had been preserved and placed on a plinth under one of the long fingers of stone that extended from the ceiling, growing drip by drip. According to Fyn, eventually the stone would meet the monk, encasing him in a translucent column.

As she studied the preserved monk, she heard footsteps on stone.

'Piro?' Cobalt called softly.

Startled, she darted around the kneeling monk. The deeper she went, the more completely the bodies were encased in stone, until they formed columns with the monks entombed inside.

The glow from Cobalt's lantern reached into the huge underground cavern, helping her to see a little further ahead.

'There's nowhere for you to run, Piro.'

She froze amidst the columns, with their half-hidden profiles encased in stone. Heart hammering, she lifted her hand to cover her glowing sorbt stone.

'I know you can hear me,' Cobalt said. 'I will find you.'

She crouched behind a monk and peered through the forest of columns.

'My men routed Byren's army in the forest. They brought me Byren's head as a gift. I'm taking it back to Rolenhold to set on the spike over the gate.'

Bile rose in Piro's throat. She'd failed her brother. Worse, her plan had led him into a trap.

'I'm coming for you, Piro. Down here, no one will hear your cries for help.'

His unhurried steps approached. She crept further into the cavern.

'King Cobalt?' the abbot called.

'I told you not to disturb me.'

'This is important.'

Whispers, then... 'Very well, hide, little Piro, but know this, there is no escape from Halcyon's Sacred Heart. I *will* be back.'

Piro remained still as the light and footsteps faded. How dare they shut her away in Halcyon's Sacred Heart? The only female who was allowed in here was the abbess...

That reminded her of how Fyn had found his way out.

Closing her eyes, Piro counted to ten, before uncovering her stone.

If she could find the sylion symbol on the far wall, she could escape.

When she reached the far wall, Piro made her way along, searching the carvings for... The sylion. The lizard had been portrayed dancing on a bed of flames.

Somehow Fyn had tripped the secret door. Determined to spring the catch, Piro set about prodding, poking and pressing the carving until it gave way and a panel slid open.

Now all she had to do was follow the lizards carved into the passage floor until she came out on the far side of Mount Halcyon. But there had been no such escape for Byren.

With a broken heart and tears streaming down her cheeks, she set off.

BYREN PAUSED TO get his bearings as they rode ahead of the army through the pine forest. 'We can split up here...' He frowned as he spotted Wafin running down through the pines.

He rode up the slope to meet the lad. 'What is it?'

'Thank Halcyon I found you!' Wafin gasped, bending over to catch his breath. He lifted his head, cheeks pink. 'Cobalt rode out of Halcyon Abbey when the bells rang for afternoon prayers. He rode at the head of around seven hundred men.'

'No man sets off on a journey this time of day unless he's forced to,' Orrade muttered. 'Cobalt must know about the Snow Bridge warriors.'

Byren cursed. 'We've still got to cover the ground between here and the abbey.'

'I'll go straight to the abbey. All is not lost. If you're lucky, you'll trap Cobalt between your army and Chandler coming down from the spar.'

'Chandler would have been here already, if he hadn't run into trouble crossing the spar.' Byren grimaced. 'His mother was one of the few merchants who supported me. I wish I could have delivered him safely to her.'

'You may yet.'

'Not if my luck stays true to form.'

Orrade drove his mount closer to Byren's so that their thighs touched. 'I believe we make our own luck. I'll be doing everything in my power to ensure you defeat Cobalt!'

'Orrie...' Byren grinned.

They parted, with Orrade making for Halcyon Abbey and Byren driving his army in a brutal forced march.

They ate as they walked, and they walked by starlight. Before long, they passed wounded Merofynians, who had fallen by the wayside. Their companions had tried to hide them in hollows and under fallen branches. Byren's men wanted to pause to deal with the wounded Merofynians, but Byren did not have the time to spare. If they were too weak to walk, the men were no longer the enemy.

* * *

By the time Florin arrived at Halcyon Abbey, it was dark. She found around seventy Snow Bridge warriors camped near the courtyard's central fountain; it appeared the rest of the Snow Bridge warriors had ridden on with Byren.

As the carriage trundled in behind her, Florin turned to the scholar. 'Rest here, Yosiv. I'll go find Orrade.'

Directly opposite the gate, the abbey was built into the side of Mount Halcyon. Women weren't allowed within the abbey, so she turned to her right, to the wing forming this wall of the courtyard.

A dozen Snow Bridge warriors stood guard at the central apartment. Once inside, Florin found another four Snow Bridge warriors on each side of the entrance to a large, crowded chamber. As she paused to look for Orrade, the low hum of worried voices greeted her. There was a high table on a dais directly in front of the door, and two long tables ran the length of the room.

At the nearest long table sat around a hundred and fifty monks. Halcyon's fighting monks had been decimated by the invasion. As she recalled, Fyn had led the young boys to safety, and what she saw before her confirmed it. The monks ranged from the old to the very young, but half the table had to be under the age of twelve. At the far end, the youngest boys dozed with their heads on the table, reminding her of Leif, though it was a while since he'd been that small.

Directly in front of her was the high table, where about a dozen nuns and novices sat. Most had their backs to Florin. Orrade was not with them, but his travelling bag had been slung over the largest chair, so Florin made for that.

A tall woman wearing the white of Sylion Abbey, and the red stone torc of the abbess, sat at the closest end of the table. Her companions clustered around her, speaking softly.

'He should have been back by now. We should go,' a little old woman was saying to the abbess as Florin came up behind them. 'We don't want to be trapped here. What if the abbot—'

'What's this about the abbot?' Florin asked.

All the women turned to look at her. Travel-stained and weary, dressed as a man with weapons strapped to her hips, she could not be more different from them in their pale blue and white robes. They were so stunned no one spoke.

'You're the abbess?' Florin asked.

'Yes, Abbess Zoraya.' The woman rose. She was tall, but she still had to look up to Florin. 'Who are you?'

'I'm looking for Orrade.' Florin saw she did not understand. 'Lord Dovecote.'

'Abbot Firefox went with him to release Pirola Kingsdaughter.'

'But he hasn't come out,' the old woman told Florin. 'He should have returned with the kingsdaughter by now.'

Fear cramped Florin's belly. 'Where's the mage's agent?'

'He didn't come,' the abbess told her. 'Piro said he was delayed.'

This just got worse and worse. Florin shook her head. She gestured to the long table. 'What happened here?'

'Lord Dovecote's warriors turned everyone out of the abbey. He had the abbess arrested and the mistresses chose me to replace her,' Zoraya said. 'Lord Dovecote was about to arrest the abbot when Firefox said that he was the only one who knew where the kingsdaughter was. He said if anything happened to him, she would starve to death alone in the dark. So Lord Dovecote took six men and the abbot, and went to save her.'

Florin understood why Orrade had gone, but she didn't like it. 'Come with me.'

Halfway across the courtyard, she spoke with Scholar Yosiv. 'I need thirty armed men. I fear the abbot has led Orrade into a trap.'

The scholar selected an escort for Florin.

She strode through the ground floor archways into Halcyon Abbey, half expecting the abbess to protest. Before them, a wide staircase led to the floor above.

There were so many doors and passages Florin's heart sank. How would she find Orrade?

Turning to the men, she selected four to stay with her and sent the rest to look for him. Then she turned to the abbess. 'What's your best guess?'

She shrugged. 'I've never...'

The clash of weapons cut her off. Florin took to her heels. As she ran along the corridor, the pounding of boots told her that the Snow Bridge warriors were right behind her.

Around a corner, through a chamber, the sounds grew closer. If she was too late...

Throwing open a door, she found Orrade, back to the wall, head bloodied, arm hanging useless, trying to hold off three attackers, while a monk, presumably the abbot, looked on.

Orrade's escort lay dead on the floor amidst the bodies of other monks, who must have hidden when the abbey was emptied.

Florin didn't remember drawing her sword. She didn't remember crossing the chamber. The first thing she knew, she was pulling her sword from a dead monk's back.

Snow Bridge warriors dealt with the rest of the attackers.

She stepped over the body, going to Orrade.

He was pale but pleased to see her. 'My sweet lady-wife, come to save me with her sword dripping blood.'

Florin's hands shook as she cleaned her sword. 'What did you think you were doing, going off alone like this?'

'The abbot was the only one who knew where...' Orrade's eyes widened. 'No, don't!'

She spun around to see one of the Snow Bridge warriors run the abbot through.

Orrade went ashen. 'Poor little Piro...' He swayed and nearly fell.

Florin caught him, calling for help.

'Here, let me.' The abbess pressed a cloth to the gash on Orrade's head and guided him to a chair. 'We need to stop the bleeding and get that arm set. You should send for the healing master.'

'Can we trust him?' Florin asked.

The abbess nodded. 'He was out of favour with Firefox.'

Orrade grinned. 'I think that's a good recommendation.' He sobered and turned to Florin. 'I want every chamber searched. Send in as many Snow Bridge warriors as it takes. I don't care if they have to open Halcyon's Sacred Heart itself, I want Piro found.'

'I'll see that it's done.'

Later that night Florin returned to Orrade to find him with his arm in a sling and his head bandaged, forging a new agreement with the abbot and abbess in Byren's name.

'We didn't find Piro,' Florin reported, heavy of heart.

'Did you search everywhere?'

Florin nodded. 'Even Halcyon's Sacred Heart. There was no sign of her anywhere. If Piro was here, they've moved her.'

Orrade looked relieved. 'You're right. They could have hidden her in Cobalt's supply wagons. First thing tomorrow, we ride. See how many mounts you can muster, Florin. If we're to be any help to Byren, we must reach him before he catches up with Cobalt.'

Chapter Sixty-Nine

PIRO STUMBLED OUT of the cavern onto the side of Mount Halcyon early the next morning. Even though the sky was filled with sullen clouds, the light made her flinch and her eyes ached. Dimly, she realised she was still suffering from the blow to her head, but she was too weary, hungry and thirsty to think straight.

Power prickled through her body like a restless wind, making her skin itch and tingle.

Her hand went to the sorbt stone. Although it no longer glowed, she could still feel the residual power within it. No wonder her Affinity was giving her trouble. The stored power in the stone had been flowing into her. She should try and drive the Affinity back into the stone, but she already knew it was useless to try. Her power was like her grandfather's, linked to Affinity beasts. It was all very well for Siordun...

Tears stung her eyes. She missed him. If he'd been here...

The new abbess would have probably colluded with Abbot Firefox to have him killed. She was glad Siordun hadn't been with her.

Sinking onto the grass, she hugged her knees and stared out across the bay. Directly across from her, on the distant headland, stood Sylion Abbey. They'd betrayed her and she'd led Byren into a trap, when all she'd ever tried to do was help him. Now, with no one to see and judge her, she gave in to a fierce storm of tears.

Through her sobs, Piro thought she heard the cry of a foenix. She looked up to see it circling far above her. Resolute was with... her heart sank. If Byren was dead, then so was her foenix. Resolute had trusted her since the day he'd hatched and she'd sent him to his death. More sobs shook her.

When the storm of tears had passed, she looked up, but there was no sign of the wild foenix.

Sitting here was pointless, but where would she go?

Cobalt still ruled Rolencia and there was no way for her to get back to Merofynia or Ostron Isle.

She shivered despite the muggy heat, fighting the excess Affinity that coursed through her. Could you get sick from too much Affinity? She would have to ask the Affinity warder, but Springdawn had never liked her... What was she thinking? Her father's castle had fallen and Springdawn was dead.

Piro pressed her hand to her forehead. She was delirious with Affinity fever.

A great down-rush of wind hit her as the wild male foenix landed less than a body-length from her. He folded his huge wings. The scales of his chest glistened like rubies in the sun. His crest rose and he turned his head side-on to observe her, just like...

'Resolute?' Piro came to her knees. Her pent-up Affinity surged through her body, sliding up her arms, making her skin tingle. Tears of relief poured down her cheeks as she opened her arms.

The foenix came to her, sank to his knees and swept his wings around her. His chest scales were wondrously smooth, like warm satin on her cheek. Sunlight glowed through the red feathers of his enveloping wings. She felt safe, as if she'd come home. Sinking her fingers into the fine downy feathers under his wings, she felt a rush of power roll from her into the Affinity beast, then return infused with the predator's own power.

She'd bonded with her foenix. A soft crooning sound came from deep within Resolute's chest. She'd never heard it before, yet it felt familiar.

Weariness swamped her. Resolute would protect her if she slept. She curled up under her foenix's wings with his heartbeat against her ear and his Affinity enveloping her.

BYREN REACHED THE crest of the hill at midday. For some time, he had been thinking of calling a rest so his men could eat but he feared Cobalt's army would make it across the bridge onto Steadford Estate before them. The new lord supported Cobalt, and Byren wanted to engage Cobalt before he could reach the lord's castle.

As he'd hoped, from the crest he could see the broad river bordering Steadford Estate. The little township that made its living by offering accommodation to those who used the toll bridge appeared undisturbed. There was no sign of Cobalt's army on the road that ran out of Tolton and across the rolling farmland before disappearing into the forest. Surely Cobalt could not have already crossed the bridge and made it into the woods?

Byren shaded his eyes. Starting from the bridge, he searched the road on this this side of the river, following it through rolling fields dotted with small farms. Again, no sign of Cobalt's army until...

There, at the base of the steep hillside far below, he spotted Cobalt's men.

'We've nearly caught them,' Wafin said, joining Byren. His face fell. 'What if they cross the bridge? A small band of men could hold the bridge while Cobalt escapes!'

'That's why we have to hurry. We'll trap them at the

bridge. With their backs to the river they'll have nowhere to run!' Byren turned his horse. 'You take the lead, urge them on.'

As Wafin rode on ahead, Byren rode back along the rows of marching Snow Bridge warriors until he spotted the military translator and told him the situation. Then he turned his horse and made for the head of the column.

At the crest, he saw the outriders and the leaders of Cobalt's army following the winding road towards the bridge, which was still a good distance from them. If Cobalt was smart, he'd set up a rear-guard to delay Byren while his men crossed.

Driving his horse on, Byren began the descent. Halfway down, rounding a steep bend, he found Wafin watching from a lookout and rode up to join him while his men poured past.

The lad shaded his eyes. Menacing clouds gathered to the south, promising a storm, but the valley was still in sunlight for the moment. 'The first of them have reached the bridge, but they're not crossing, for some reason.'

'Give me your reins. Climb that tree and see if someone has closed the tollgate.'

Wafin scurried up the tree, hooked a leg over a branch and shaded his eyes.

'A band of men have closed the toll gate and are holding the bridge,' Wafin yelled. 'I bet it's Chandler!'

'I could kiss him,' Byren laughed.

Wafin climbed down and mounted up again.

'Stay here,' Byren told him. 'Give the Snow Bridge translator the news. I'll ride ahead. We have them now!'

If Chandler could hold out.

Byren had no idea how many of Chandler's men remained. But he put that thought from his mind as he rode down, shouting the news, urging the men on. This was his first piece of good luck since Merofynia had invaded—no, since his cousin Cobalt had returned to Rolencia.

On the valley floor, he caught up with his men and rode ahead, over rolling hills, past a worried farmer in his field, to the last rise before the bridge.

Here Byren sat in the saddle and watched as Cobalt's stragglers ran up the road towards the bridge, where his cousin's men had congregated, unable to cross.

The river was broad and swift and was inclined to flood the valley floor. No wooden bridge had withstood the regular floods for more than a few years.

Twenty years ago, Byren's father had ordered the Royal Ingeniator to design a bridge. He had chosen two small hills roughly opposite each other, and built a bridge that not only spanned the broad river, but linked the hills as well. It had taken eleven years to build, and to cover the cost, a toll had been imposed on all those who used it.

On the far side of the river was Tolton. Built on the gentle slopes of the hill, it had serviced the army of men who built the bridge, and then it had serviced those who passed over the bridge. This side of the river, the hill had been quarried to build the bridge and the bank dropped away sharply.

Cobalt had used the sloping approach to his advantage, overturning the provision carts to create a barrier in a semicircle, and fanning his men out behind it. He held the high ground.

From here, Byren could see Chandler's small band on the stone tower that housed the tollgate. Cobalt had overturned another cart just beyond the highest point of the bridge, and his men were attacking the tollgate from this position.

Byren hoped Chandler had enough men to hold the gate. What if the townspeople turned on them? What if Cobalt sent men to swim across the river upstream, and enter Tolton from the other side to attack Chandler from behind?

Byren took Wafin aside. 'Find thirty men who can swim. Go back the way we came and make your way upstream around the bend in the river. Cross over and reinforce Chandler.'

As more of Byren's men arrived, he divided them into three columns, sending some to the south and north of Cobalt's men, retaining the third column for a central attack. With luck, he would be able to surround Cobalt's army and crush them, though there was the concern that with Byren's men spread so thinly, Cobalt's Merofynians might be able to break through and make their escape.

Dark, brooding clouds blanketed the sky now, and the air was still with the promise of a storm. Despite the heat, Cobalt's men worked feverishly to build up their defences. They cheered as they overturned another cart, strengthening the barrier across the road.

Byren could see Cobalt now at the bridge's entrance. Secure in the knowledge that he was beyond bowshot, Cobalt climbed onto the stone balustrade and stood directing his men.

As Byren surveyed the scene, he was astonished to see half a dozen riders come over the rise from the west. They weren't his scouts. Cobalt must have sent them to look for a merchant boat, or anything to ferry his men across the river.

Cobalt's scouts charged the western arm of Byren's forces, who stood no chance against mounted men riding downhill at a full gallop. The first rank of his men dived out of the way. Where his men were more thickly packed, the horses ploughed through them. Mistaking the screams, shouting and clank of metal for the signal to attack, Byren's men on the eastern side charged Cobalt's position. With no choice, Byren led his force up the road towards the overturned carts.

FLORIN RODE AHEAD of the column with Orrade. He had asked her to come with him, but they had been riding in silence for a while now. She was hot and tired, and wished the storm would break.

'You saved my life last night,' Orrade said at last.

She shrugged.

'You could have let me die and been a rich widow.'

She stared at him, shocked.

He laughed, then winced, his hand going to his bandaged head.

'Are you sure you're up to riding further? We could make camp.'

'We go on,' he said. With one arm in a sling and the bandage at a rakish angle on his head, he made her smile. 'What?'

She shook her head. 'It's a pity that Byren's not here to help heal you.'

'The abbey's healing master did what he could. But he would never have risen to become a master if the invaders hadn't murdered most of the monks.'

'To think of all that knowledge lost...' Florin shook her head. She noticed Orrade's expression. 'What?'

'You didn't say "to think of all those lives lost."'

She flushed. 'Well, of course, I meant that as well. But I thought I didn't need to state the obvious with you.'

'My prickly mountain girl, you...' He broke off and stood in the stirrups. 'I knew it!'

They'd reached the crest, revealing the valley below, and the winding river which formed the border of Steadford Estate. From here they could see the two armies.

'They've already engaged,' Orrade cursed.

Fear for Byren made Florin's heart race.

'I'll ride ahead with the Snow Bridge warriors,' Orrade said. 'You camp in the hollow behind us. When we've won, I'll send a messenger. Bring the kingsdaughter, along with the abbot and abbess. They can declare Byren king and officiate the marriage.'

As Orrade turned his mount, she caught his arm. 'I won't be able to come to your rescue tonight.'

He gave her a wolfish grin. 'Don't worry about me, I still have to ride into Dovecote Estate, wipe out that nest of Merofynians, free my people and reclaim my home.'

He rode back along the column, shouting orders.

A few moments later, the Snow Bridge warriors marched past. Leading them were the four ursodon hornsmen.

'You're taking the ursodon horns?' Florin was flabbergasted.

'We've lugged them all this way. I might as well use them. Besides'—Orrade gave her a knowing look—'why shed blood when intimidation will do the job!'

She shook her head as he rode off to go to Byren's aid. What would Byren do without him?

What would she have done without Orrade?

'PIRO?'

The foenix's soft crooning almost drowned the words. For a moment, she didn't know where she was or how much time had passed.

'Piro?'

Resolute lifted his wings and nudged her. She rolled over to see Siordun kneeling about a body-length away from her on the grass, in a patch of afternoon sunlight. 'Piro?'

She blinked. 'How did you get here?'

Siordun gestured to the foenix, who had risen to his feet and was grooming himself. 'Resolute came to the ship when he first spotted you.'

'I thought you were in Merofynia.'

'I was. I set sail hoping to get here for the midsummer's ceremony, but missed it by a day. I spotted the *Wyvern's Whelp* in Port Cobalt and...' He gestured down the slope to Jakulos and several of the crew. 'I wasn't sure if it was safe to approach.'

'Of course it's safe.' Piro rolled to her feet. Patches of grey floated in her vision. She swayed.

Siordun caught her. 'You're burning up.'

'They shut me in Halcyon's Sacred Heart. Can you get sick from too much Affinity?'

'It appears you can. Why did they shut—'

'Oh, Siordun, Byren's dead...' Sobs overtook her.

He let her cry. When she lifted her head he asked, 'Who told you this?'

'Cobalt.'

'Did you see Byren's body?'

'No... You mean he lied?'

A smile tugged at Siordun's lips.

'Of *course* he lied!' She felt like such a fool. 'But the nuns really did betray us.'

'Tell me from the start.'

When she'd finished, Siordun shook his head. 'I should never have left you.'

'I'm glad you did. Cobalt would have ordered you killed. Me, he...' She shuddered.

'Did he—'

'He didn't get the chance.' A fierce anger rushed through her. Resolute lifted his head and raised his wings, giving voice. The cry echoed off the mountain behind them. Siordun glanced from her to the bird and his eyes widened. 'Piro...'

'Don't you start.' The fever swamped her, her vision swam and she swayed. 'I just want to go home.'

'Of course.' He steadied her. 'With any luck Byren will be sitting on your father's throne by the time we reach Rolenhold Castle.'

But Piro had been thinking of going home to Mage Isle. The realisation stunned her. She grasped Siordun's arm. 'If Byren's king, he'll try to marry me off. I won't—'

'Don't worry.' Siordun's dark eyes grew intense. 'You won't end up be a game piece.'

BYREN HAD BEEN leading skirmishes since mid-afternoon, and now they fought by the light of the burning carts. The coming storm had brought an early twilight. Occasional flashes of lightning appeared in the underbelly of the low clouds. If the storm hit before he broke through Cobalt's defences, they would be bleeding and dying in the mud.

Twice now, Cobalt's men had broken through Byren's encircling army and twice they had been beaten back. Byren was pretty sure some had escaped, but he did not have the men to spare to go after them.

At one point he'd seen flames in Tolton, but Chandler and Wafin's men held the tollgate, just as Cobalt's men held this side of the bridge.

Between the exhaustion and the leaping light of the burning carts, it was hard to tell who was an enemy and who was a friend, especially as there were Rolencians on both sides.

Byren would not put it past Cobalt to desert his army and flee, and that was why he had to make an end of this soon, before the storm broke. Having recalled his men to prepare for another assault, Byren mounted up and rode to address the enemy.

'I know there are Rolencians in Cobalt's ranks, and it grieves me to kill my own people,' Byren shouted. 'If you put down your weapons now and step beyond the barricades, I give my word you won't be harmed. Think it over. Rolencians don't kill Rolencians!'

'You can talk,' Cobalt shouted back. He'd hoisted himself onto the balustrade of the bridge and stood there in the torch light. 'How can you lead heathen Snow Bridge warriors against good, honest Rolencians?'

'King Jorgoskev is no heathen,' Byren said. 'He's the first man to unite the city states of the Snow Bridge. He can put a thousand men on the battlefield at a day's notice, and I'll marry his daughter when I sit on my father's throne!'

'That's right. You always wanted to steal your twin's crown!'

The way Cobalt twisted everything infuriated Byren. He drew breath to refute it...

At that moment, a horse galloped up beside Byren's. He'd been so focused on Cobalt that he'd barely registered the pounding hooves. Orrade's mount pivoted and reared as he held the reins with one hand. The other was in a sling, and a bandage had begun to slip over one eye.

'Byren is the one true king!' Orrade shouted. 'He killed Palatyne and freed the Rolencian seven-year slaves. Now he's going to kill Cobalt and free Rolencia!'

Byren's men cheered. And even though they'd no idea what was being said, the Snow Bridge warriors cheered too.

Orrade winked at Byren. 'You make the mistake of trying to argue sensibly with a liar. Keep it simple.'

'I was offering the Rolencians who serve Cobalt the chance to walk away with their lives.'

'Good. Men who have no hope will fight to the death. It was Comtes Merulo who said the battle is won or lost in the hearts and minds of men.' Orrade stood in the stirrups to shout. 'I bring six hundred fresh Snow Bridge warriors to support Byren. They'll be here in a few moments. You have until they arrive to lay down your arms and surrender!'

A muttering swept through the defenders. They'd fought all afternoon. They were tired, hungry and thirsty. They'd seen the men beside them cut down, but they'd held on. Now they faced a fresh enemy.

'Will it work?' Byren whispered.

'We'll see...'

A glow came over the rise as the first ranks of Orrade's Snow Bridge warriors approached, bearing flaming torches. They marched four abreast, and out front four men carried huge horns, supported on straps across their shoulders.

At Orrade's signal, the Snow Bridge army stopped marching. The ursodon hornsmen stepped out in front. Then a blast of sound rolled down the hill towards them. It felt like a wall of thunder. The ground seemed to vibrate under their feet as if the earth itself roared.

Byren's Snow Bridge warriors cheered wildly.

'Those bloody great horns!' Byren turned to Orrade, laughing as Orrade's Snow Bridge warriors kept marching over the rise. How long before it was clear there were less than a hundred of them?

The horns sounded again and men kept pouring over the rise.

A shout went up from the enemy, as Cobalt's supporters fought to escape the defensive position. As soon as one man turned and ran, panic spread. Seeing Cobalt's men desert, the defenders on the tollgate cheered.

Byren rode along his army, shouting. 'Let them through. Let them pass.'

Chandler opened the tollgate and his men streamed out to attack Cobalt's men on the bridge, as Byren led one last assault.

This time, even the Merofynians were disheartened. They threw down their arms and offered their services as seven-year slaves. It was a sweet turn-about for the men Byren had freed. A pity so few of them had lived to see it.

He rode up the rise and onto the bridge itself, searching for Cobalt. His cousin had been here only moments before, twisting everything Byren said.

'Can you see him?' Orrade shouted. He was having trouble controlling his horse with one arm in a sling.

'No, can you?'

They dismounted and made a systematic search of the dead, in case he was hiding amongst them. Then they searched the captives but they could not find Cobalt.

Byren cursed fluently.

Orrade put a hand on his shoulder. 'You've beaten him. Send scouts out to check the town and fields. He can't have gotten far. I'll go back and fetch your bride. You can be married on the battlefield!'

And he rode off.

Chapter Seventy

FLORIN HEARD THE horns from a great distance, echoing across the valley. The sound was both eerie and threatening. Even from this distance, she could see the defenders break.

Scholar Yosiv turned to her, his features illuminated by her torch. 'He's a clever man, your husband.'

Florin found it hard to think of Orrade that way. In her mind, you weren't really married if you didn't share a bed. The old scholar returned to camp and Florin returned to studying the distant battlefield. Byren must not fall now, not when victory was within reach.

A shout made her turn around. Men ran into the camp, their silhouettes dark against the two camp fires. Believing the enemy to be contained, Orrade had taken all but six of their escort. And the royal carriage was clearly laden with riches. Florin cursed and ran down the slope towards their fire circle.

The abbot called his monks, who snatched up their weapons. The abbess called her nuns to her and somehow the five of them were lost in the commotion.

Florin saw the Snow Bridge servants snatch up pots and flaming branches, but they were cut down. The attack had come on them so quickly there could be no concerted defence. She ran through the chaos, slammed her torch into an attacker's face, then pulled a stunned acolyte to his feet.

Around the far side of the carriage, Florin was in time to see the old scholar help the veiled kingsdaughter climb down. Just then a man arrived, swinging a bloody sword.

Yosiv stepped between him and the kingsdaughter, and was cut down with one blow. The kingsdaughter cried his name and fell to her knees. The man grabbed her by her head-dress.

Florin could have left the kingsdaughter to her fate. No one would have known. But she couldn't leave a woman at the mercy of a man like this.

Tossing the torch aside, Florin caught the man around the neck and ran him through. Even as he fell, Florin grabbed Skevlaxa's arm and darted into the trees with her. The trunks were lit by the dancing flames of the burning carriage. Someone gave chase. Before he caught up with them, someone else came in from the side, tackling the kingsdaughter and driving her to the ground.

As he sat astride her, gloating, Florin swung her sword, taking his head off with one blow. Momentum carried her around to face the second attacker.

Seeing what she'd done to his friend, he backed off, then ran for the clearing. Through the trees, she could make out men putting out the flames so they could loot the carriage.

Good. That would keep them busy, and give her a chance to get away with the kingsdaughter.

Covered in blood and shaking, Skevlaxa struggled to push the dead man's body off her. With a kick, Florin sent the headless body sprawling. She hauled the girl to her feet. The head-dress and veil had already worked loose, and now fell away, revealing...

The wrong kingsdaughter. Shocked, Florin stared at the oldest sister.

'I knew it,' the kingsdaughter whispered, unaware that Florin could understand her.

There was no time. Any moment, more men might come after them. Florin grabbed the woman's arm, but she twisted free, bending to retrieve her head-dress and veil.

Florin drew her into the woods until the shouting faded. They had to pick their way in the dark; the woods were lit only by the occasional flash of lightning. Florin stumbled across a shallow brook and led the kingsdaughter upstream to cover their tracks. Finally, they both climbed out, drenched from the knees down, shivering and shaking.

Florin found a spot under the trunk of a huge fallen tree. She settled the kingsdaughter, then sat with her back to the woman.

What was Byren going to say?

Nothing. He was an honourable man.

He'd accepted King Jorgoskev's warriors, which meant he had to marry this woman even though she was eleven or twelve years older than him. 'Oh, Byren...'

'The shield-maiden hates me,' the kingsdaughter muttered. 'He'll hate me. How could you do this to me, Father?'

'I can see *how* he did it,' Florin said, turning around. 'I just don't see why.'

'You can speak our language? You're a spy!'

'You're in no position to accuse me of double-dealing, not after what your father's done, Skevlaxa.'

'I'm Skevlaza, my sister is Skevlixa... Oh, I see. It was the names... King Byren wanted my sister. All the men want her.' She spoke in a rush. 'That's why Father used King Byren's mistake against him. He doesn't want to part with Lixie. As long as the lords aspire to marry her, he can play the city states off each other. Whereas I'm...' Burying her face in her hands, she wept bitter tears.

As Florin listened to those wretched sobs, she was moved to reluctant sympathy. She reached out and patted the woman's back. 'It's not your fault.'

'No, but I'll be made to pay. King Byren will be furious. I told Father there had to be some mistake. A handsome young man like King Byren wouldn't ask for a middle-aged widow like me. But it all happened so quickly... No wonder Father made me promise to uphold the old customs and remain sequestered on the journey. I'll tell Byren he doesn't have to marry me. He can send me away.'

'He can't insult King Jorgoskev.'

Skevlaza was silent for a heartbeat as she thought it through. 'You're right. That's what Father was counting on.'

'Why didn't you object?'

'No one argues with King Jorgoskev, least of all the king's eldest, unwanted daughter. Besides, I had to think of my son's future.'

Florin heard the Merofynians' shouts echoing through the forest. 'They're looking for us. Hush.'

They remained huddled in the dark.

A little later, Florin woke to a familiar voice calling her name. 'That's Orrade.' She cupped her hands to shout. 'Over here, Orrie. I'm with the kingsdaughter. We're alright.'

'Stay there. I'm coming.'

Skevlaza caught her arm. 'You saved my life, for which I thank you. But please don't tell Lord Dovecote the truth. I want to speak with King Byren and explain myself.'

'Very well.'

'Florin?' Orrade climbed onto the fallen trunk, just as the kingsdaughter replaced her head-dress and veil. He held a flaming torch high. 'You're both covered in blood!'

'None of it ours,' Florin said.

He laughed, jumped down to hug her. 'And you told *me* to be careful.' He gestured to the kingsdaughter. 'You saved her life. Byren will be grateful.'

Florin was not so sure. 'Who attacked us?'

'Cowardly Cobalt deserters.'

'Cobalt's dead?'

'He lost the battle. When I left, Byren was searching for his body. Come on.'

Back in the clearing, they found a dozen men waiting with horses. The abbess was there with all her nuns. Only two of the monks had survived. Both the abbot and the acolyte had been injured.

Orrade took Florin's hand, leading her into the clearing. 'Thanks to my sweet lady-wife, the kingsdaughter lives.'

The men all looked at her askance. With her hair askew and covered in blood, she was a sight. Yet in Orrade's eyes she saw only pride and admiration.

While he made arrangements for the dead and found mounts for the living, Skevlaza leant close to Florin. 'You are lucky your husband loves you.'

But Florin knew that Orrade had lived a lie for so long, he was a consummate actor. She wished...

She wished none of them had to live a lie.

THIS SHOULD HAVE been Byren's moment of triumph, but frustration ate at him. Cobalt had escaped, and the bride he did not want was arriving any moment.

Of course, he'd done his duty. He'd seen to the wounded, secured the captives and assured the mayor of Tolton that his people would be recompensed for damages and food consumed.

Now he went to the stone balustrade where Cobalt had stood only moments before they'd routed his men. How had his cousin escaped?

Byren took two burning brands and dropped them over the side of the bridge. They fell away into the darkness, landing on the rocks below in a shower of sparks. By their light, Byren studied the quarry wall. There was no sign of anyone clinging to a ledge. The skirt of rock where the first arch stood was empty of hiding places, and then there was the swiftly moving river. No boat had come by since the battle began. Cobalt was not among the dead, wounded or prisoners. Where...

'Byren.'

He turned to see Orrade leading his bride's party. Florin carried a torch. Blood smeared her face, and her clothes were black with blood. His bride rode at her side, her gown stained with mud and blood, face hidden under a veil. The abbot slumped in his saddle, obviously injured. 'What—'

'Deserters attacked them, stole your bride's wedding chests and made off with everything. The abbot is only just holding on.'

Jorgoskev's daughter whispered something to Florin.

'My king,' Florin said. 'Your bride wishes to speak with you.'

If she wanted to complain, he didn't want to hear it; and if she wanted him to sweet-talk her, she was out of luck. 'We can talk tomorrow. I've set aside rooms in the best tavern. It's been a long day, and—'

The storm which had been holding off all day chose that moment to strike. There was a flash of lightning and a crack of thunder so loud the horses shied and everyone ducked instinctively. Lightning flashed through the low clouds and sheets of rain fell as the skies opened.

Within two heartbeats, their torches flickered and died. Now Byren could only see by the flashes of lightning and it was impossible to talk. He was glad—frustrated and exhausted, he was liable to say something he'd regret.

As the kingsdaughter fought to control her frightened mount, he stepped in, caught the reins and led the horse across the bridge and up the main street of Tolton.

At the tavern, he sent Florin and the kingsdaughter upstairs to bathe and rest, then drew Orrade into the private dining chamber. 'Cobalt's sure to find a way to cause me trouble. First thing tomorrow, I'm going to ride out after him. Which way do you think he went? Straight to Steadford Castle, or towards Rolenhold?'

'You want my advice?'

'That's why I'm asking.'

'I think it's already tomorrow. And I think you should marry Jorgoskev's daughter on the bridge where you crushed Cobalt's army.'

'I might have crushed his army, but I haven't killed Cobalt. I'll marry her in my father's great hall.'

'The Snow Bridge warriors have bled and many have died for you. They need to see you honour their king's daughter. You need to marry her in front of them and smile while you do it.'

Byren strode to the window. Rain still fell, drumming on the shingles, pouring off the roof and hitting the cobble stones. 'At least the rain quenched the last of the fires.'

'Byren?'

Now he knew why Lence was always in a foul mood. But he was not his twin and he was not going to take it out on those who served him. 'I know my duty. Organise the ceremony.'

FLORIN FOUND A warm bath waiting for the kingsdaughter. The chamber was richly appointed, with a fine four-poster bed and velvet curtains. Florin put the lamp on the chest at the end of the bed, unbuckled her sword and knife and left them there.

Then she tore off her jacket, glad to be rid of the bloody thing. Skevlaza pulled off her head-dress and veil. They both shivered. The rain had been icy and coming on top of everything else... 'You'll feel better when you're clean, kingsdaughter.'

Skevlaza nodded numbly, tired fingers fumbling with the belt at her waist.

Florin moved to help her. 'Here, let me help.'

She peeled off Skevlaza's belt and then her sodden brocade coat. Next she went to undo the under-shirt.

'Sweet as this is, that's enough,' Cobalt said.

Florin stared in shock as he stepped out from behind the curtains.

'Who's that?' Skevlaza whispered.

'Cobalt.' Florin backed up, the kingsdaughter behind her. She glanced over her shoulder to the door, but one of Cobalt's men stood there. 'Scream!'

Skevlaza made a muffled sound.

Florin spun around to find another of Cobalt's men had grabbed the kingsdaughter from behind, lifting her off her feet with ease.

Sucking a breath, Florin went to shout for Byren, but the man by the door grabbed her. She twisted, elbowing him in the ribs, and he grunted in pain.

'Bitch!' He belted her so hard she lost her balance, staggered and fell across the bed.

In a heartbeat, he was on her, shoving his hands up under her wet shirt.

'None of that,' Cobalt warned. 'We're not barbarians.'

'Surely we can have a bit of fun with them before we kill them?' the man protested. 'It's not like this one matters.'

'On the contrary.' Cobalt stood over Florin. 'This one matters more than you think. Stand her up.'

The man hauled Florin off the bed and turned her around to face Cobalt. She could feel her captor's body pressing against her back. He pinned her arms with one of his, and covered her mouth with the other hand. The more she struggled the more it aroused him, so she went very still.

Cobalt studied her. 'There's only one person who could have saved you from Narrowneck. But why would Byren bother?'

Florin had no intention of answering him, even if she could have.

'Bring them both,' Cobalt said.

'I thought you were going to kill—'

'I've had a better idea.' Cobalt went to the curtains and pulled them aside to reveal a balcony. The rain was easing.

He signalled someone below. They lowered the kingsdaughter over the balcony into waiting arms.

Florin did not fight as they lowered her over the balcony. She had to pick her moment if she was going to save Skevlaza. Cobalt followed, swinging by one arm and landing lightly.

'This way,' Cobalt said. 'I'll make Byren regret he ever captured that bridge.'

The window to the private dining chamber was open, and Florin could see Byren inside. If they could just alert him...

She tossed her head back, smashing her captor's nose, and shouldered him aside, lunging for Skevlaza. 'By—'

A fist slammed into her head.

Chapter Seventy-One

BYREN LOOKED UP as Orrade ran into the chamber.

'Cobalt's taken her!' Orrade snatched Byren's sword from the back of a chair and threw it to him. 'Come on.'

Byren collided with Wafin and Chandler in the passage outside. 'Sound the alarm, then follow me.'

One step ahead of him, Orrade ran out onto the street, paused, looked both ways, then took off downhill. Byren ran after him, as Wafin followed and Chandler roused the men.

The rain had stopped and the streets were wet and slick, gleaming in the starlight. Down near the tollgate, Byren saw several men. One was dragging a small woman, and another carrying a bigger woman over his shoulder. Florin.

The figures disappeared in the shadow of the tollgate tower.

'I'll kill him...' Byren muttered. He'd strangle Cobalt with his bare hands. He put on a spurt of speed.

Once he was through the tollgate, Byren found Cobalt standing on the centre of the bridge with three men. One of them held the kingsdaughter. From this distance all Byren could see was the white of her undershirt and a pale, frightened face. Her captor forced her head up, holding a knife at her throat. The other two were supporting Florin, who swayed as if stunned. What had they done to her?

Byren strode across the bridge with Orrade at his side, a dozen men at his back and more arriving every moment. He could hear the shouts of outraged Snow Bridge warriors behind him.

The warriors' translator pushed through the crowd to join him. 'What's going on?'

'That's close enough,' Cobalt yelled. 'I'm glad you could join me, Byren. As a wedding gift, I was going to leave the body of your bride in your bed. Then I thought it would be so much more satisfying for the Snow Bridge warriors to find the daughter of their king strangled and mutilated on the very bridge they'd captured for you. But now...'—Cobalt glanced from the kingsdaughter to Florin—'now I think I will kill your ally's daughter while the Snow Bridge warriors watch. Then I'll take the mountain girl as my hostage, because we both know she's the one you really want!'

'What's he talking about?' the translator demanded.

'Don't listen to him. He's trying to destroy the alliance,' Orrade said.

Byren cursed, furious with Cobalt. Furious with himself, because he did not see how he could save Florin or the Snow Bridge kingsdaughter.

'What was that, cousin, feeling impotent?' Cobalt was enjoying himself. 'Once your allies see how powerless you are, they'll abandon you. I'm going to take everything from you, just as your father took everything from me—my father's love, the woman I loved and the kingdom that should have been mine. King Rolen was a brute and boor, and you're not much better. But what can you expect of the product of rape?'

'Don't listen to him!' Orrade caught Byren's arm. 'Do you hear me? Your parents loved each other.'

Byren kept his eyes on Cobalt. 'I need our best archers, Wafin.'

But even as the lad ran off, Byren realised they wouldn't arrive in time. He needed a distraction.

A rider arrived on the far side of the bridge, leading four mounts.

Hearing the horses whinny, Cobalt glanced over his shoulder. Florin fainted.

No. She'd ducked, and now punched her captor in the balls, before springing to her feet.

Byren was already running. His brave mountain girl did not stand a chance against four armed men, and the poor kingsdaughter would be dead in another heartbeat. The rider galloped up the bridge, his horse's shod hooves rattling on the stone.

Cobalt signalled to the man holding the kingsdaughter, who went to kill her.

But before he could, Florin tackled him, and they fell on the bridge's slick stones. The man remained down as Florin scrambled to her feet.

Still three body-lengths away, Byren knew he was not going to be in time.

Cobalt drew his sword on Florin.

She backed away, the kingsdaughter behind her.

Trapped between Cobalt and the rider, Florin backed up until she was pressed against the balustrade. Both of Cobalt's men had now recovered and were getting to their feet, angry and eager for revenge. Byren shouted.

Cobalt's men lunged in for the kill.

Florin swung her arm around the kingsdaughter and rolled them both over the balustrade and off the bridge.

Everything went silent. Time slowed as Byren charged. He ran one man through, freed his sword, elbowed another in the throat and faced Cobalt. He was vaguely aware of Orrade matching the fourth man blow for blow.

Cobalt lifted his sword tip and circled Byren. Swords were second nature to Byren. He had grown up practising with Lence, who had strength, and Orrade, who had speed and skill.

Orrade killed his man.

Cobalt struck. Within two heartbeats it was clear he was fast and he was skilled.

But for once, he wasn't working poison with words.

Starlight flashed on their blades. Everything came down to this moment, to the slippery wet stones under Byren's feet and the singing steel.

Twice, Cobalt offered Byren a target, and both times he didn't take it. Cobalt was too good a swordsman to make those mistakes. Byren saw the ploys for what they were.

Then Byren let his guard drop, and Cobalt made the fatal mistake of underestimating him. Byren diverted Cobalt's strike, turned his blade, and followed through, bringing his sword around in an arc that took Cobalt's head clean off.

Cobalt had always been vain about his long dark hair; now it flew behind his head like a banner, but Byren didn't bother to collect his trophy.

Dropping his sword, he ran to side of the bridge.

This was where Florin and the kingsdaughter had fallen, mid-stream where the current was strongest. Starlight silvered the river. He searched, but he could not see a pair of dark heads. Florin couldn't swim.

'Can you see her?' Orrade asked.

The last of Cobalt's men made a break for it. As Wafin and Chandler cut him down, the mounted man galloped off, hooves clattering on stone.

The translator joined Byren. 'Can you see her?'

'No. Can the kingsdaughter swim?'

'No.'

Byren shook his head. 'Then there's no hope.'

'You mean the bodyguard couldn't swim?' The man clutched Byren's arm. 'Why did she take the kingsdaughter over the bridge with her?'

Byren found he could not speak.

'To give Byren a chance to kill Cobalt,' Orrade said, eyes glittering with tears. 'And to shift the guilt of their deaths from Byren's shoulders.'

'There's still a chance,' Byren said. There had to be. He refused to give up. A quick look around told him the four remaining horses had trotted a little way off. 'Grab the horses, Orrie. Search the right bank, I'll take the left.'

No one told him it was pointless.

Wafin and Chandler volunteered to help, taking a horse each. Orrade returned to the Tolton bank with Chandler, while Byren and Wafin took the far bank.

Byren rode down the road where so many had died the previous afternoon. He looked back to see silent warriors lining the bridge.

It was the darkest time of night before the dawn, but because the wind had swept the sky clean of clouds, the stars shone brightly enough to cast shadows. He and Wafin made their way off the road, past the quarry, down the slope and along the river bank.

Byren rode, watching for bobbing heads or bodies clinging to rocks in the bends.

He rode until the sun came up, and even then, he was reluctant to admit that their search was pointless.

Wafin did not speak.

After three days with almost no sleep, Byren's head buzzed from exhaustion. Dawn's long rays shot across the valley. Byren shaded his eyes as he looked to the far bank. There was no sign of Orrade, and no reason to think he'd found the two women.

No Florin to contradict him in her abrupt forthright way. No more Florin... He couldn't bear the thought. How could he go on without her?

And Jorgoskev's daughter. He'd failed the poor girl. To think her last moments had been filled with terror.

Byren's tired horse came to a standstill and began cropping grass.

'Byren!' Orrade yelled from the far bank as he rode out of a copse of trees. 'Behind you, back around the bend. Two bodies.'

Byren turned his horse and urged it to a gallop. Where the river rounded a bluff, he dismounted and climbed down the bank. He found a small patch of pebbly bank where the two bodies had washed up. Florin's legs were still in the river, which tugged at her as if trying to reclaim her. The kingsdaughter was about a body-length away, draped over a rock. At least he would be able to take their bodies home.

Florin's arm moved. She lived? 'Florin!'

FLORIN WAS COLD. Something tugged at her legs and the ground shifted under her. It was really important that she wake up, but she couldn't seem to hold her eyes open. When she breathed, it hurt like a knife sliding between her ribs.

She heard Byren call her name and tried to lift her head.

A moment later, she felt his warm, strong hands pulling her out of the river and into his arms. His rough jaw rubbed her cold cheek as he kissed her. She felt his hot tears on her skin.

'You're alive. I thought I'd lost you.'

'Careful.' She winced. 'Think my rib's broken.'

He laughed and kissed her again. 'Must have broken when you hit the water.' He pressed his lips to her forehead. 'You can't swim. I thought—'

'I can swim. Piro taught me.' She forced her weary eyes open. 'Did you think I'd fling myself and the kingsdaughter into the river if I couldn't swim?'

'Orrie said... But that's him, all stiff-necked honour.' Byren shook his head. 'You're my practical mountain girl. I shoulda known you wouldn't throw away both your lives—'

'The kingsdaughter?'

He shifted a little to reveal Skevlaza hanging over a

rock behind him. Her face was hidden behind her tangled hair. What if she was awake? Shame filled Florin and she pushed Byren away. 'See to your betrothed.'

'I will.' But first he helped Florin to her feet and waved to the far bank, where Orrade stood shading his eyes and watching.

While Byren moved the poor kingsdaughter onto the shore, Wafin offered Florin his coat. He was a head shorter than her so she kept it for the kingsdaughter.

Byren pressed his ear to Skevlaza's chest. 'She breathes.' He raised his head. 'You saved her life, Florin. I couldn't save you, couldn't save either of you. I never felt so useless in my life.'

'Cobalt's dead?' she asked.

He nodded.

'Good.' She spread the coat over the kingsdaughter and pushed Skevlaza's hair back from her face. 'Her skin's so cold.'

Byren frowned. 'This is not...'

'Not the right kingsdaughter. I know,' Florin admitted. 'Jorgoskev didn't want to give up Skevlixa so he sent his older daughter. He sent her knowing that you are a man of your word and you'd marry her anyway.'

Anger tightened Byren's face. 'The lying, deceitful...'

Florin reached across Skevlaza to Byren. 'Don't blame her. She had to obey her father for the sake of her son.'

Ashen faced, Byren stared at her. 'How long have you known?'

'Only since last night. That's why she wanted to speak with you.' Florin shrugged. 'I'm sorry.'

Byren shook his head. 'You have no idea how sorry I am, Mountain Girl.'

Skevlaza whimpered.

Byren rubbed his face, fingers rasping over his jaw. 'Ask her if she's all right, Florin. Tell her I'm sorry that Cobalt captured her and she had to go through... Tell her...' He could not go on.

Florin translated the sentiment, finishing with, 'Skevlaza, can you hear me?'

Her odd blue-green eyes opened, awash with tears. She nodded and blinked.

'How do I say I'm sorry in her language?' Byren asked.

Florin told him and he repeated the words. For some reason this made the kingsdaughter sob.

Byren slid his arms under the kingsdaughter, lifted her and climbed to his feet.

While Wafin helped Byren up the bank with the kingsdaughter, Florin stumbled along behind.

When they reached the path by the river, Wafin offered her his horse. Florin glanced across to the far bank and saw Orrade keeping pace with them, accompanied by Chandler.

By the time they reached the bridge to Tolton, Byren's army and the townspeople were all lined up to see them return. Byren rode with the kingsdaughter in his arms. The crowd cheered from every balcony and window, waving red scarves and shirts. The true king of Rolencia had returned.

Once they'd crossed the bridge and entered the town, Orrade fell in beside Florin, but with all the shouting and cheering it was impossible to talk.

Florin felt numb. There'd been one small part of her that had hoped that when Byren discovered the deceit, he would reject King Jorgoskev's daughter.

At the same time, Florin was not in the least surprised to see that he treated Skevlaza with grave courtesy as he carried her up to the best bedchamber.

Florin had to admit to a certain satisfaction when Byren called for a healer rather than offering himself and Orrade to heal the kingsdaughter.

BYREN WAITED FOR the healer to arrive. The moment he'd shown the old woman into Skevlaza's chamber, he shut the door on them and pulled Orrade into an empty chamber. 'Did you know about the switch?'

'Of course not.'

Byren cursed, then realised he was looking for someone to blame. Blame was pointless. 'I've already had the use of Jorgoskev's army, and I can't dishonour the poor woman by turning her away, especially after this. I'll have to marry her.'

Orrade said nothing.

Byren paced. 'Jorgoskev played me for a fool.'

'I suspect he plays everyone.' Orrade shrugged. 'Cobalt's dead and you've won the people over. They're already composing songs about the battle of Tolton Bridge and your fight with Cobalt.'

'Florin was the true hero...' Byren shook his head. 'Piro taught her to swim, but she risked her life to save Skevlaza and give me a chance to kill Cobalt.'

'I won't argue with that.' Orrade folded his arms and leant against the door.

Byren glanced to him. For a heartbeat he wondered if Orrade was angry with him. 'I've won Rolencia but I've made a terrible mistake, Orrie. It's Florin I love.'

'You had your chance. When we were in the mountains, you could have slipped away and made a life for the pair of you, but you chose Rolencia.'

'I had no choice. I had to do my duty.'

Orrade shrugged. 'I guess it all depends on what's important to you.'

'I had to do the right thing. You know that.' Byren glanced at him. 'And now I'm saddled with a queen who's more than a decade older than me. How will I get an heir from her?'

'The usual way, I guess.'

'You *are* angry with me. I don't see why. I've only ever tried to do the right—'

Orrade caught him by the shirt and swung him around, slamming him up against the door. 'Then keep your hands off Florin.'

Anger flashed through Byren. Why should Orrie care? It wasn't like he wanted Florin. But Byren held back the words. He was not proud of himself for even thinking them. 'I'm not Lence. I won't dishonour our friendship. I'll marry a woman I don't love for the sake of the kingdom.'

'Your mother didn't love your father when she married him to keep the peace. They grew to love each other. You—'

'King Byren?' The healer's voice reached them from the passage.

Byren looked to Orrade, who let him go with a gesture that made it clear all was not forgiven. 'Orrie, I—'

'You're needed.'

'My king?' the healer raised her voice.

Byren straightened his shirt and went out into the passage.

'I gave the kingsdaughter something to help her sleep,' the healer said. 'Considering what she's been through, she's doing well. All she needs is a few days of rest.'

Byren nodded. 'Thank you. Now I need you to see to—'

'My wife,' Orrade said. 'Come this way.' And he led the healer to Florin's chamber.

Byren considered going in to see the kingsdaughter, but he was tired and angry, and didn't trust himself to say the right thing.

FLORIN CURSED SILENTLY as the healer strapped her ribs, gave her something to drink and propped pillows behind her. After the healer left, Orrade returned.

'Byren tells me Piro taught you to swim. Still, you took a risk going over the bridge.'

She shrugged, then regretted it. 'I wasn't going to give Cobalt the satisfaction of killing Skevlaza and ruining Byren's alliance with King Jorgoskev.'

'You could have been killed. You could still lose the baby.'

Florin flushed, reminded that his concern for her sprang from his concern for Byren's child. The baby did not feel real to her. She didn't know what to say, so she said nothing.

Orrade walked to the window. He seemed to be troubled, but when he spoke his words were dispassionate. 'The abbot died overnight. A new abbot will have to be elected. We should delay the marriage until all the nobles and merchants can come to Rolenhold and swear allegiance to their king and his queen.' He turned to Florin. 'You knew she was not the right kingsdaughter, yet you saved her life. You could have let go of her, let her drown.'

'You must have a very strange idea of me if you think I could do that. Besides, none of this is her fault. Sometimes you have to do the right thing, no matter the cost. You, of all people, know that, Orrie.'

'I saw him kiss you. Did he tell you he loves you?'

And she understood. No one loved him and the one person he loved had rejected him. 'Orrie...' She sat forward, wincing. 'Come here.' She took his hand and held his eyes. 'I will never dishonour you. You are the best person I know. In fact... I suspect you are a better person than Byren.'

He laughed. 'Yet you still love him.'

'As do you.'

He lifted her hand and kissed it. 'I fear we are both fools, but I think we can be happy together.'

And strangely enough, she thought he was right.

Chapter Seventy-Two

BYREN FOLLOWED ORRADE up the steps to Eagle Tower. It was his wedding day, and he'd never felt less like getting married.

In the six days since Byren had returned to his father's castle, it seemed everyone in Rolencia had tried to speak with him—some wanted to complain, some wanted justice and others wanted to convince him that they had remained loyal even though they had accepted lands and titles from Cobalt.

He was heartily sick of it all.

And very relieved to have Orrade back. Not that he'd been able to snatch a moment with him in private. After reclaiming his estate, the new Lord Dovecote had returned late last night. As far as Byren knew, Orrade was still angry with him. He needed to make things right between them.

'We could have met in the war-table chamber and saved the climb,' Byren said.

'I remember the days you'd race Lence...' Orrade hesitated. They'd reached the ladder to the tower top. 'I asked about him and Elina but the fire stones burned so fiercely their bodies were never recovered. I've ordered the stone-mason to carve a statue of Elina with a fire stone in each hand to commemorate her bravery.'

His voice broke and Byren wanted to hug him, but he stood helplessly by while Orrade regained control.

'We were so young...' Byren shook his head. 'If I could go back and—'

'We don't get to go back,' Orrade said, voice brittle. 'We make the best decisions we can with the knowledge we have to hand. I want you to remember this, when...' He glanced up.

Byren frowned. 'Who's waiting for me?'

'Siordun, representing Fyn.'

The mage's agent had arrived with Piro two days ago, but Byren had put off a private meeting, because he knew what Siordun wanted and he was just too angry with Fyn to be polite. For once, his sister had showed remarkable restraint and had not broached the subject. In fact, if he didn't know better, he'd think Piro was avoiding him.

With a grimace, Byren climbed the ladder to find the tall, thin agent waiting. 'If you're here on behalf of my lying, conniving brother—'

'Hear me out,' Siordun said. 'If Fyn hadn't rescued Queen Isolt, she would have been forced to marry Neiron and you would have lost Merofynia. The storm would have still decimated your fleet and stripped you of two-thirds of your army, and you would have been forced to ally yourself with the Snow Bridge king anyway.'

'You've been talking to Orrie.'

Siordun nodded. 'On the other hand, if Fyn had rescued Isolt and returned her to the palace, the storm would have happened anyway and you would have been forced to either break your word to Isolt to ally yourself with King Jorgoskev, or you would have lost to Cobalt, because the abbess betrayed your plans and you needed the Snow Bridge warriors.'

Much as he would have liked to argue, Byren could not fault the logic.

Siordun squared his shoulders. 'Queen Isolt and King Fyn asked—'

'King Fyn!' Byren muttered. 'That should be King Merofyn the Seventh.'

'He's still your brother,' Siordun said.

Byren hardened his heart. 'Whatever you say, the fact remains that I left Fyn to take care of my betrothed and her kingdom, and he married her behind my back. Don't try and make out that he did me a favour.'

'I won't,' the agent said. 'Fyn is well aware that he has wronged you. He asked me to tell you that he loves Isolt with all his heart—'

Byren laughed bitterly. 'Kings don't get to marry for love.'

Siordun ignored this. 'And Fyn hopes that, given time, you can forgive him. Both he and the queen want peace between Merofynia and Rolencia. He sent this as a token of his true regard.'

Byren accepted the velvet draw-string bag with a certain amount of contempt. No matter how much these trinkets were worth, they meant nothing to him. He loosened the drawstring and tipped the bag's contents into his hand. The lincurium rings and pendant sat on his palm like three drops of frozen fire.

Orrade gasped.

'I thought them lost,' Byren whispered, as he was transported back to last winter, to the day they found the stones. 'Do you remember, Orrie? '

'How could I forget? You saved my life,' Orrade said, emotion making his voice waver. 'You had the rings made for your parents, and you had the pendant made for Lence to give to his queen.'

Byren stared into the fiery depths of the lincurium stones. So much had happened since that day.

'Can I tell Fyn he is forgiven?' Siordun asked.

Byren tipped the stones and rings into the bag. 'You can tell him I want peace.'

PIRO LOOKED UP as Byren strode into their mother's solarium—only the chamber now belonged to the Snow Bridge kingsdaughter. Surprised by Byren's arrival, Skevlaza said something that sounded like a protest.

Byren glanced to Florin, who translated, 'The kingsdaughter says according to Snow Bridge customs it is bad luck for the groom to see the bride before the wedding.'

Byren went down on one knee. 'Tell my wife-to-be that it is our custom for the groom to give the bride a wedding gift.' He removed a small pouch from his vest and offered it to the kingsdaughter.

Since arriving in Rolenhold, Piro had tried to be friendly to the Snow Bridge woman, but without a common language it was hard. And even after Florin arrived, Skevlaza did not have much to say. Piro was burning to ask Florin how she'd ended up Lady Dovecote, when it was clear she loved Byren and he loved her. But Piro was no longer the headstrong child who blurted out her every thought.

'Open it, Skevlaza,' Piro urged.

The woman loosened the drawstring and tipped a large lincurium pendant into her hand. It sat on her palm, exquisite and rare, yet she did not react. Piro did not understand.

'Let me...' Byren took the pendant from Skevlaza and hung it around her neck. On his knees he was almost as tall as her. He glanced to Florin. 'Please tell her, this is a rare Affinity beast stone.'

Florin began to translate, but Skevlaza cut her off.

'She thanks you and asks who it was made for.'

'Tell her I found the stone myself and had it made for my twin on his betrothal.'

As Florin translated, Skevlaza flushed and said something.

'She apologises. She does not have a gift for you,' Florin said.

'Tell her it does not matter.'

It was all very proper, yet all strangely hollow. Piro felt sad, for there was no joy in Skevlaza or Byren.

He came to his feet and turned to Piro. 'A word with you, sister.'

BYREN LED PIRO out of the solarium and down the corridor to what had been her old bedchamber. When they entered, he saw her travelling chest sat open by the bed. 'You haven't unpacked.'

'I'm not staying.'

'This is your home. You—'

'I don't want to be a kingsdaughter. I—'

'Don't be childish. Piro. We're royalty, we don't get to choose who we marry.' Unless you were Fyn and were willing to ignore your duty. Anger made Byren's voice hard. 'Now, I've had an offer of alliance from House Merullus of Ostron Isle. The comtes is—'

'I'm not marrying him. I'm not marrying anyone!'

'Of course you'll marry,' Byren snapped, exasperated.

'I can't. I have Affinity. If I stayed in Rolencia I'd have to serve Sylion Abbey.'

'I'm going to repeal Father's laws. It was unfair and—'

'I won't—'

'I suppose you consider yourself in love with someone unsuitable.' A spasm of anger rocked Byren. 'Get over it. You're a kingsdaughter and you'll—'

'Why are you being so hateful?' Piro backed away, tears spilling down her cheeks.

Remorse made Byren reach out to her. 'Piro...'

'No.' She darted past him and flung the door open to reveal Siordun about to knock. 'You knew about this? How could you?'

She ducked around the mage's agent and Byren heard her footsteps as she ran down the passage.

Siordun sent Byren a questioning look.

'I've had an offer of marriage from House Merullus.'

Siordun came in and shut the door. 'Piro can't marry. She's bonded with her foenix.'

'So? He always was her pet, and now that I've defeated Cobalt, I don't need the foenix by my side. From what I hear Ostron Isle's merchant families cultivate eccentricity,' Byren said, but Siordun's expression was serious. 'What aren't you telling me?'

'This kind of bond is not like the bond a man has with his hunting dog. It's much deeper. Piro's Affinity is still growing in strength. I suspect she takes after your namesake, King Byren the Fourth. He...' Siordun ran down.

'I've heard the rumours. He could commune with Affinity beasts.' Byren was not about to reveal that he could commune with the ulfr pack. 'They called him Mad King Byren.'

'Then you realise she can never live a normal life.'

He hadn't. 'Poor little Piro.' No wonder she'd been distraught. Anger stirred in him. 'The mage should have warned us.'

'The mage...' Siordun shook his head. '...has been busy trying to avert war on two fronts. I've only put the clues together since spring. I'll take her back to Mage Isle with me. The foenix will come with us.'

'Of course.' Byren felt bereft. His parents were dead. Lence was dead. Fyn had turned on him and now he'd lost little Piro.

Siordun put a hand on his shoulder. 'I promise I will do the very best I can for Piro.'

Unable to speak, Byren nodded and left.

On returning to his chamber, Byren found his wedding clothes laid out on the bed. He couldn't bear to look at them. Instead he went out onto the balcony to clear his head. From up here he could see the preparations for the wedding ceremony, far below in Rolenton Square. His parents had been married there, just over twenty-one years ago. His father's peaceful, prosperous reign was remembered with nostalgia.

Byren tipped the lincurium rings onto his palm. The matching rings had originally been a gift for his parents on their wedding anniversary, to symbolise enduring love and loyalty. Now... when he put the ring on the Snow Bridge woman's finger, it would symbolise his servitude to a crown he'd never wanted.

He'd never wanted to be king, particularly a king with a wife foisted on him by his enemy, a king with no family left that he could trust to place his kingdom's needs ahead of their own.

He heard the door open and Orrade came to the balcony door. 'It's time.'

'I know.'

'Your mother was only fifteen when she—'

'Married my father. Yet they grew to love each other. I know my duty, Orrie. I will stand by Skevlaza.'

'Then what is it?'

Byren hated feeling estranged from his one true friend. Lence had turned on him, Fyn had betrayed him. Piro would soon leave him. Florin... He had done wrong by his mountain girl, despite the best of intentions. If Orrie hadn't come to her rescue...

Orrade had remained true, even after everything that had happened. Byren reached into his pocket. 'Come here and hold out your hand.'

'Why?' Orrade did not move.

'Just do it. We're not ten and I don't have a toad in my pocket.'

'Very well.' A half smile lifted Orrade's lips. He stepped out onto the balcony. 'But I'm not closing my eyes.'

Byren dropped the smaller of the lincurium rings onto Orrade's palm. 'You may have to get it resized.'

'Byren, no. This—'

'You were with me when I found the stones. You were

with me every step of the way since. If it were not for you, I would not have defeated Cobalt and reclaimed my father's throne. You are my one true friend.'

Orrade held the ring up to the light. The stone glinted like captured fire. 'I should refuse.'

'But you won't.' Byren slid the other ring onto his finger. 'You'll wear it with honour.'

'What if someone asks why we—'

'Tell them...' Byren bared his teeth in a grin. 'Tell them to ask me, if they dare.'

Orrade laughed, and Byren felt ready to face the future.

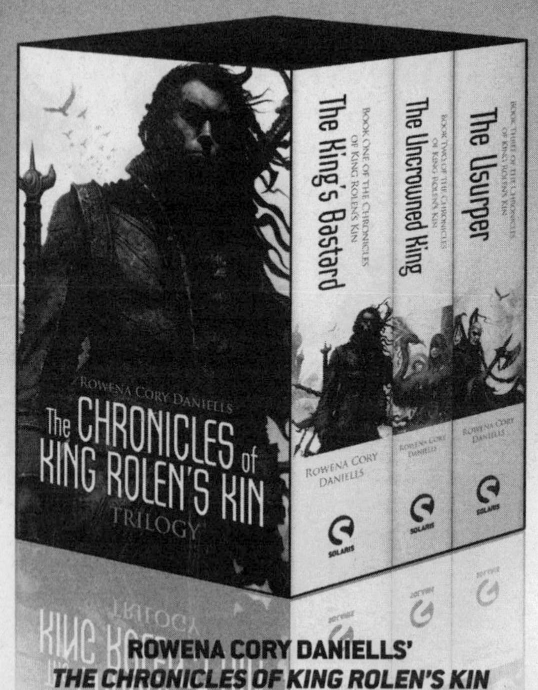

ROWENA CORY DANIELLS'
THE CHRONICLES OF KING ROLEN'S KIN

The King's Bastard • ISBN: (UK) 978 1 907519 00 0 (US) 978 1 907519 01 7 • £7.99/$7.99
The Uncrowned King • ISBN: (UK) 978 1 907519 04 8 (US) 978 1 907519 05 5 • £7.99/$7.99
The Usurper • ISBN: (UK) 978 1 907519 06 2 (US) 978 1 907519 07 9 • £7.99/$7.99

Only seven minutes younger than Rolencia's heir, Byren has never hungered for the throne; he laughs when a seer predicts that he will kill his twin. But the royal heir resents Byren's growing popularity. Across the land the untamed magic of the gods wells up out of the earth's heart, sending exotic creatures to stalk the wintry nights and twisting men's minds, granting them terrible visions. Those so touched are sent to the Abbey, to learn to control their gift, or die.

At King Rolen's court, enemies plot to take his throne, even as secrets within his own household threaten to tear his family apart.

Political intrigue and magic combine in this explosive new fantasy trilogy.

"Pacy and full of action and intrigue."

– Trudi Canavan, author of *The Black Magician* trilogy.

 **WWW.SOLARISBOOKS.COM**

Follow us on Twitter! www.twitter.com/solarisbooks

ROWENA CORY DANIELLS

BESIEGED

BOOK ONE OF THE OUTCAST CHRONICLES

UK ISBN: 978 1 78108 010 8 • US ISBN: 978 1 78108 011 5 • £7.99/$7.99

Sorne, the estranged son of a King on the verge of madness, is being raised as a weapon to wield against the mystical Wyrds. Half a continent away, his father is planning to lay siege to the Celestial City, the home of the T'En, whose wyrd blood the mundane population have come to despise. Within the City, Imoshen, the only mystic to be raised by men, is desperately trying to hold her people together. A generations long feud between the men of the Brotherhoods and the women of the sacred Sisterhoods is about to come to a head.

With war without and war within, can an entire race survive the hatred of a nation?

Rowena Cory Daniells, the creator of the bestselling *Chronicles of King Rolen's Kin*, brings you a stunning new fantasy epic, steeped in magic and forged in war.

WWW.SOLARISBOOKS.COM

Follow us on Twitter! www.twitter.com/solarisbooks

ROWENA CORY DANIELLS

EXILE

BOOK TWO OF THE OUTCAST CHRONICLES

UK ISBN: 978 1 78108 012 2 • US ISBN: 978 1 78108 013 9 • £7.99/$7.99

Slowly losing himself to madness, King Charald has passed his verdict on the mystic Wyrds: banishment, by the first day of winter. Their leader, Imoshen, believes she has found a new home for her people, but many are still stranded, amidst the violence and turmoil gripping Chalcedonia. A reward is offered for their safe return, and greedy men turn to abduction.

Tobazim arrives in port, to ready the way for his people, and finds their ships have been stolen. Sorne, the king's halfblood advisor, needs to find his sister and bring her to safety. Ronnyn and his family, living peacefully in the wilderness, are kidnapped by raiders eager for the reward.

Whether the ships are ready or not, the Wyrds must leave soon; those who remain behind will be hunted down and executed. Time is running out for all of them.

WWW.SOLARISBOOKS.COM

Follow us on Twitter! www.twitter.com/solarisbooks

JULIET E. McKENNA'S
CHRONICLES OF THE LESCARI REVOLUTION

BOOK ONE

IRONS IN THE FIRE

ISBN: (UK) 978 1 906735 82 1 • £7.99
ISBN: (US) 978 1 84416 601 5 • US $8.99/CAN $10.99

The country of Lescar was born out of civil war. Carved out of the collapse of the Old Tormalin Empire, the land has long been laid waste by its rival dukes, while bordering nations look on with indifference or exploit its misery. But a mismatched band of exiles and rebels is agreed that the time has come for change, and they begin to put a scheme together for revolution. Full of rich characters and high adventure, this novel marks the beginning of a thrilling new series.

"Magically convincing and convincingly magical."
– Dan Abnett

BOOK TWO

BLOOD IN THE WATER

ISBN: (UK) 978 1 84416 840 8 • £12.99 (Large Format)
ISBN: (US) 978 1 84416 841 5 • US $7.99/CAN $9.99

Those exiles and rebels determined to bring peace to Lescar discover the true cost of war. Courage and friendships are tested to breaking point. Who will pay such heartbreaking penalties for their boldness? Who will pay the ultimate price?

The dukes of Lescar aren't about to give up their wealth and power without a fight. Nor will they pass up some chance to advance their own interests, if one of their rivals suffers in all this upheaval. The duchesses have their own part to play, more subtle but no less deadly.

"If you're not reading Juliet McKenna, you should be."
– Kate Elliott

BOOK THREE

BANNERS IN THE WIND

ISBN: (UK) 978 1 906735 74 6 • £12.99 (Large Format)
ISBN: (US) 978 1 906735 75 3 • US $7.99/CAN $9.99

A few stones falling in the right place can set a landslide in motion. That's what Lescari exiles told themselves in Vanam as they plotted to overthrow the warring dukes. But who can predict the chaos that follows such a cataclysm? Some will survive against all the odds; friends and foes alike. Hope and alliances will be shattered beyond repair. Unforeseen consequences bring undeserved grief as well as unexpected rewards. Necessity forces uneasy compromise as well as perilous defiance. Wreaking havoc is swift and easy. Building a lasting peace may yet prove an insuperable challenge!

"Shows McKenna at her best."
– Paul Cornell

WWW.SOLARISBOOKS.COM

Follow us on Twitter! www.twitter.com/solarisbooks

GAIL Z. MARTIN'S
THE CHRONICLES OF THE NECROMANCER

BOOK ONE

THE SUMMONER

ISBN: 978 1 84416 468 4 • £7.99/$7.99

The world of Prince Martris Drayke is thrown into sudden chaos when his brother murders their father and seizes the throne. Forced to flee, with only a handful of loyal friends to support him, Martris must seek retribution and restore his father's honour. But if the living are arrayed against him, Martris must learn to harness his burgeoning magical powers to call on different sets of allies: the ranks of the dead.

The Summoner is an epic, engrossing tale of loss and revenge, of life and afterlife – and the thin line between them.

"Attractive characters and an imaginative setting."

– David Drake, author of *The Lord of the Isles*

BOOK TWO

THE BLOOD KING

ISBN: 978 1 84416 531 5 • £7.99/$7.99

Having narrowly escaped being murdered by his evil brother, Jared, Prince Martris Drayke must take control of his magical abilities to summon the dead, and gather an army big enough to claim back the throne of his dead father.

But it isn't merely Jared that Tris must combat. The dark mage, Foor Arontala, has schemes to cause an inbalance in the currents of magic and raise the Obsidian King...

"A fantasy adventure with whole-hearted passion."

– Sandy Auden, *SFX*

WWW.SOLARISBOOKS.COM

Follow us on Twitter! www.twitter.com/solarisbooks

PAUL KEARNEY'S
THE MONARCHIES OF GOD

a
the
ern
rom

ree
the
hold
tion,

two
will

VOLUME TWO

CENTURY OF THE SOLD

ISBN: (UK) 978 1 907519 08 6 • £8.
ISBN: (US) 978 1 907519 09 3 • $9.99

Hebrion's young King Abeleyn lies in a coma, his capital in ruins and his former lover conniving for the throne. Corfe Cear-Inaf is given a ragtag command of savages and sent on a mission he cannot hope to succeed. Richard Hawkwood finally returns to the Monarchies of God, bearing news of a wild new continent.

In the West the Himerian Church is extending its reach, while in the East the fortress of Ormann Dyke stands ready to fall to the Merduk horde. These are terrible times, and call for extraordinary people...

"Simply the best fantasy series I've read in years and years."

– Steven Erikson, author of the *Malazan Book of the Fallen*

WWW.SOLARISBOOKS.COM

Follow us on Twitter! www.twitter.com/solarisbooks